The Barforth Women

BRENDA JAGGER

The Barforth Women

DOUBLEDAY & COMPANY, INC.
GARDEN CITY, NEW YORK
1982

ISBN: 0-385-17623-6
Library of Congress Catalog Card Number 81–43054

Fiction
Jag

The Barforth Women

Chapter One

MY MOTHER had been a lighthearted seventeen on her wedding day, my father a stern, fastidious forty-nine; and although no part of their marriage contract required her to be brokenhearted at his death, some twenty years later, it was generally assumed that, without him, she would not know which way to turn.

Possibly she had not loved him. In view of his age, his gloom, and his autocratic disposition many people would have been surprised if she had. But she had certainly depended upon him. He had been much more to her than a husband. He had been her teacher, on whose judgement of matters ranging from the care of her immortal soul to the choice of a parasol, she had unquestioningly relied. He had been her guardian, taking care never to expose her to the dangers of going out alone, and keeping a supply of sensible, solid women on hand to accompany her about the town when he could not. He had been, beyond all doubt, her master; his decisions had been considered absolute.

"Poor Elinor," they said, when his illness first struck. "She will not have the slightest notion of how to face the world on her own."

"I fear he has gone, madam," the doctor told her, positioning himself to support her should she crumble and fade away then and there at his feet.

"Oh, dear," she said. "Oh, dear. How terrible. I think I had better be alone."

And going downstairs, as gentle and unassertive as a captive dove, she stood for a moment in the centre of the darkened drawing room, and there, fancying herself alone, began to spin out her skirts in a billowing, carefree dance. She was my father's pampered, submissive little wife no longer, but a girl who had once been poor enough to marry an old, austere man for his money, and to live to regret it.

She had been Miss Elinor Barforth of Low Cross Mill, daughter of a careless father who, at a time when the cloth trade was thriving and other men making their fortunes, had committed the sin of extravagance, which had inevitably led him to the far greater sin of poverty. Instead of harvesting his profits and ploughing them back into his weaving sheds, Grandfather Barforth had spent them on fancy waistcoats and fancy women and at the time of her marriage my mother had had little to recommend her but her slight, dainty figure, the pale blond ringlets framing her porcelain complexion, the unusual blue-green colour of her eyes—qualities not much valued in a wife by the hard-headed Yorkshiremen of our industrial, industrious Law Valley. And in our town of Cullingford, where a man's worth was measured by his standing in the Piece Hall and at the Cullingford Commercial Bank, she must have been astonished and intensely grateful when my father, Mr. Morgan Aycliffe, had offered to take her as his second wife without a dowry.

My father had been well-to-do all his life. The son of a master builder, he had inherited a business so well established that his own hands had never been obliged to trouble themselves with bricks and mortar. He had been, not brilliant, perhaps, but shrewd, a man who knew the value of being in the right place at the right time and how to get there, so that at a moment when the steam engine, the spinning frame, the power loom had brought vast industrial expansion to the north—and a vast influx of humanity with it—my father had been on hand to fill the bare West Riding landscape with the six-storey mills, the towering chimney stacks, the warehouses, the unkempt sprawl of workers' cottages, which had transformed the pleasant townships of Bradford, Halifax, Cullingford, and Huddersfield into grim-visaged factory cities.

There had been two textile mills in Cullingford when my father built himself a house in the then almost rural tranquillity of Cullingford's Blenheim Lane. Twenty-five years later, when he had buried his first richly dowered wife and engaged himself to

marry my mother, there were fifty, most of them constructed, to
his designs, by gangs of Irish navvies he had imported for the
purpose. Blenheim Lane itself, at its lower end, being malodorous with factory smoke, raucous with factory operatives,
emerging only as it climbed the hill out of town as a fit place for
a gentleman to reside. And having inherited one fortune and
made another—having married a first wife for profit and a second for pleasure—he had turned, in his later years, to the fresh
delights of power.

Cullingford, in the year I was born, had no politicians, since
politics had been designed for gentlemen, for those who owned
the land rather than those who scratched a living from its soil or
defaced it with their foul-belching commercial enterprises. Government—always—had been aristocratic, an affair very largely
of the southern, agricultural counties where one solitary, but
noble, gentleman might control the votes of half a dozen constit-
uencies. And while the north remained a bleak, forgotten upland
where hill farmers precariously raised their sheep and cottagers
wove the fleeces into cloth, taking a week, perhaps, to produce
one coarse, laborious piece, there had been no one to complain.
But the steam engine and the power loom put an end to that,
my father being one of the first to join the campaign for Parliamentary Reform, demanding that our newborn industrial towns,
crammed with so many newborn millionaires, should no longer
be forced to accept the rule of country squires, that Parliament
should cease to be a meeting place for landed gentlemen and listen to the voice of the belligerent, possibly vulgar, but increasingly prosperous north.

"Cullingford must have the vote," my father had insisted,
finding no lack of millmasters and ironmasters, worsted spinners
and brewers to support him. And when the vote had been obtained, he had secured election himself and served Cullingford's
interests most faithfully until the day he died.

Yet for all his gifts of public oratory my father was an almost
completely silent man in his private life, his one pleasure being
the refined but solitary pursuit of rare china and porcelain, items
of Sèvres and Meissen which he displayed in the glass-fronted
cabinets of his drawing room, promising unmentionable doom
to any child depraved enough to touch. But the temptation, in
fact, seldom came our way, for my father, who was not fond of

children in any case, could rarely bring himself to admit us to his drawing room, preferring, when absolutely necessary, to meet us on our own ground, upstairs in the nursery wing devoted to our care.

There had been a son of his first marriage, a most unsatisfactory young man who, having objected to a step-mother younger than himself, had been banished from hearth and home, his name erased from the family Bible, from the last will and testament, and from our memories. And I cannot think that, at his time of life, my father had welcomed other children. Yet we existed, not even boys who could have been groomed to help him in his business or succeed him at Westminster, but girls who would be very likely to cause him trouble, and would certainly cost him money. Daughters: and since the only profit a man can expect to make from a daughter is the acquisition of a useful son-in-law, we were, from our earliest days, moulded deliberately for that very purpose, not by our mother, whose sole task in life was to entertain her husband, but by such nannies and governesses as were considered best qualified.

The guidelines of our education were very clearly set down. Respect for authority first of all, since a girl who learns to obey her teachers and her father will extend the same wide-eyed, unquestioning docility to her husband. Punctuality next—since gentlemen do not wish to be kept waiting—every morning of my childhood finding me up and dressed by six o'clock to begin a day irrevocably divided into tidy, busy hours, controlled by the nursery clock, which could tell me far more precisely than any governess exactly when I must put my sketchbook away and take up my embroidery frame, the very moment when I must cease to play my scales and begin the daily chanting of French verbs and English prayers, without listening to either.

We were taught to sing and to smile, to speak without really saying a word, enough mathematics to appreciate the value of our dowries, enough religion to make us understand that God, having created us weak and female, had also designed us for the convenience of man, an arrangement it would be sinful even to question. We were taught to be innocent by the simple procedure of removing from our sight, our grasp, our hearing, anything which might arouse our curiosity. We were taught to be industrious in private—mending our own stockings and petticoats—but to be idle in public, displaying a piece of cob-web–fine embroidery in languid hands, since a woman who has no work to do herself offers proof of her husband's ability to pay servants' wages. We were taught to dress for the occasion, to be appalled by a crumpled glove or a shower of rain, to go into maidenly raptures at the sight of newborn kittens (without daring to ask how it was they had appeared so suddenly in their basket, since no one is quite so innocent as all that and we knew the question would be termed "improper"). We were the perfectly mannered daughters of Morgan Aycliffe, as bereft of individuality as our mother, who would go to our bridal beds, in due season, as quietly as we had gone to our piano practice—obedient, punctual, innocent, accomplished, and very bored.

No difficulty was ever anticipated with my younger sister Celia, who was tense and timid and most anxious to be married. Nor with my elder sister Prudence, although her keen, disciplined intelligence often caused my father to regret she had not been born a boy.

Celia was fashionably small, fashionably demure, far more concerned, at fifteen, as to when she could reasonably expect her flowery wedding veil, her hour of bridal glory, than with the identity of the bridegroom himself.

My sister Prudence was taller, less amenable, her eyes a shade too watchful, her wits too sharp to find favour in a world which did not encourage cleverness in women. But there was a certain air of efficiency about her which, my father believed, might attract the eye of someone with a large household to manage, a certain elegance which, if properly nurtured, would make her the kind of hostess much sought after by the socially ambitious male.

Celia, it was hinted, would go to an industrialist, a newly rich man of the Law Valley who could give my father solid support at election time. Prudence would make a political marriage, a promising newcomer to the Whig party, perhaps, who might well attain the cabinet appointments my father had missed. But I was somehow more difficult to place in my father's mind, and he was inclined to be ill at ease with me.

Coming between my sisters in age I resembled my mother closely in some ways and, quite sadly, in others was her direct opposite. I had inherited her pale blond hair, except that mine, unlike her silken curls, was straight and heavy, difficult to manage, its weight defeating the bonds of pins and ribbons so that there was usually a ringlet tumbling down, stray coils escaping from underneath my hat, loose tendrils taking flight at the very moment it was essential to be neat. My eyes were blue enough, I suppose, to please anyone, except that they were shortsighted, often clouded over with the boredom that caused me to be inattentive to my teachers, neglectful of my studies, retreating from the straitjacket of my father's reality into a far more pleasant world of my own. And worse than that perhaps since it could not be corrected, from the age of fourteen I had started to grow, outstripping Prudence, who was herself quite tall enough, winning no favour with my father, who in the last months of his life had been seriously displeased to find my eyes on a level with his own.

Naturally he would succeed in finding me a husband for, like my sisters, I would have my dowry of 20,000 pounds and my share of his estate, half of which was to be held in trust for us during our mother's lifetime. But clearly I worried him, causing him to conduct long discussions with our governess, Miss Mayfield, as to the nature of my crimes, the list—as he grew weaker and I grew stronger—appearing more alarming every day. I had left my sketchbook on the hall table and when accused of untidiness had answered carelessly, "Oh, heavens, Miss Mayfield, I suppose so." I had sat all morning, my needlework in my hands, without taking a single stitch, so deep in my forbidden daydreams—and of what was I dreaming? of whom?—that I had answered her reprimand with a shrug, an unmannerly, "Gracious me, Miss Mayfield, I doubt it will cause the sky to fall." But on the afternoon I spent ten sinful minutes gazing at myself in a mirror deciding that my pale eyebrows were insipid, and was caught, later, trying to darken them with a solution of Chinese ink and rosewater, my father, nearing the end of himself, shuddered quite visibly and informed my mother, "I had best speak to Joel about that girl, for you will never manage her, Elinor."

And that same day he sent for my mother's brother, Mr. Joel Barforth of Tarn Edge, appointed by the terms of Father's will to watch over us; and warned him, one supposed, that although

Celia would always be obedient and Prudence reasonable, he could only speak with regret of his troublesome daughter Faith.

"She is perhaps just a trifle scatterbrained," my mother had suggested, her voice dove-gentle as always, her eyes downcast, not wishing to question his judgement, merely to soften it.

"She is insolent," he had said, "and disorderly. And worse than that, she is vain."

And those were the last words I ever heard him speak.

His funeral service in the parish church high above the town was extremely well attended, for my father had not only served the political interests of Cullingford's manufacturers for more than a dozen years, but had possessed a hardheaded grasp of commercial affairs which had made him a valued, if not a popular man.

As Morgan Aycliffe master builder he had been responsible for the erection of Cullingford's magnificent Assembly Rooms, for every factory of size in the district, and for the grandiose villas of the men who owned them. He had built square-shouldered, no-nonsense chapels for Dissenters, gracefully spired churches for those who kept the established worship of the English realm, a college for Roman Catholics, another for Quakers, had commenced construction of a station and a station hotel in readiness for the day, surely not long distant, when Cullingford would be joined at last by branch line to Leeds.

Nor had he neglected the lower sections of our society, for it had often been pointed out to us as an example of his shrewdness that every one of the mean, narrow streets cobwebbing from one set of factory gates to another, tight-packed with their low, two-roomed workers' cottages, had been designed by him. And I had heard him declare with pride that he knew how to squeeze in more families per acre than anyone else in the county of Yorkshire.

As Morgan Aycliffe, member of Parliament, he had spoken warmly in support of Free Trade, had denounced the Corn Laws, which, by forbidding the import of cheap corn and keeping the price of home-grown grain high, had worked to the advantage of the landowners and against the industrial interest he had been elected to serve. He had opposed, unsuccessfully, the introduction of factory inspectors and the passing of laws to control the number of hours our local industrialists—most of them our relatives and friends—could oblige women and children to work in their weaving sheds. He had laboured hard to prevent the introduction of the bill forbidding the employment of children under the age of nine, arguing that tiny bodies were essential to the spinning trade, since only they could crawl under the machines to mend the broken threads, and that the parents of such child operatives were in dire need of their wages. And on his last appearance in the House he had spoken out bitterly against the proposed introduction of a ten-hour working day, an unpardonable intrusion, he had declared, into the business affairs of his constituents, and no help at all to the labouring classes, who would be thus obliged to exist on ten hours' pay.

And so, as we drove at the head of his funeral procession on that chill, January morning, up the steep cobbled streets that would take him to his final rest, the churchyard was surrounded by closed carriages, the church itself most flatteringly over-crowded with substantial, silk-hatted gentlemen and their ladies, come to pay him their parting respects.

The worsted manufacturer, Mr. Hobhouse of Nethercoats, was there with his wife and the eldest of their fourteen children; the banker Mr. Rawnsley, with whom my father's credit had always been high; the worsted spinner Mr. Oldroyd of Fieldhead, a widower himself, who had already called at our house to offer his private sympathies to my mother; the foreign-born, exceedingly prosperous Mr. George Mandelbaum, whose wife, her emotions nurtured in a warmer climate than ours, actually shed a tear. There were manufacturers and professional men from Leeds and Bradford, the members of Parliament of both those cities, a scattering of our local gentry who, although they had disapproved of my father's politics, were finding it expedient, these days, to cultivate the newly rich. And, as a final honour, there was a carriage bearing the coat of arms of Sir Giles Flood, lord of the manor of Cullingford, although that noble and decidedly disreputable gentleman did not come himself.

"What a sad loss," they said. "Poor fatherless children. Poor Elinor. No one could be surprised to see her follow him by the month end. Good heavens—only think of it—we must all of us come to this. How terrible." They lowered his coffin into the hard ground.

"He was not a *young* man," they said. "Older than I, at any rate."

It was done, and I went home with Prudence and Celia to serve glasses of port and sherry to my father's mourners, who had their own ideas as to what he had been worth and—if they happened to be the parents of sons—couldn't help wondering how much of it, besides that 20,000 pounds apiece, he had left to us. He was gone, there was no doubt of it. I had seen him go. But throughout the whole dreary afternoon I failed to rid myself of the sensation of his eyes still upon me, that he would suddenly appear, his cold face pinched with disapproval, and demand to know what these people were doing here, cluttering up his drawing room, setting down their glasses on his immaculately polished tables, their careless hands and wide skirts a danger to his porcelain; his presence so very real that I wondered if my mother, sitting so very still, looking so very frail, was aware of him too.

But the Hobhouses and the Oldroyds, the Mandelbaums and the Rawnsleys, the gentlemen from Bradford and Leeds and Halifax, having done their duty, were not disposed to linger and, approaching my mother one by one to mutter their self-conscious sympathy, were soon heading either for home or the Old Swan in Market Square to drink hot punch and transact a little business so that the entire day should not be wasted. And soon there remained in my father's drawing room only my mother's family, the Barforths, who had once been poor and now were very rich, my father having no one of his own beside ourselves and the son of his first marriage, whose name I had never once heard on my father's lips.

I had been acquainted with wealthy and powerful men all my life—indeed my father had allowed us to be acquainted with no other—but it was generally acknowledged that my mother's brother, Mr. Joel Barforth of Tarn Edge, of Lawcroft Fold, of Low Cross—the three largest textile mills in the Law Valley—was of a far higher order than any of these. For, rising above the legacy of debt and disgrace his father had bequeathed him, he had been the first man in Cullingford—perhaps the first man in the world—to see the advantages of the new, power-driven machines, and to possess the courage to exploit them.

Following the slump in trade after our wars with Napoleon,

when most manufacturers had been shaking their heads and keeping a tight hold on their purses—muttering that the "old ways" were best—Joel Barforth, then a young and reputedly reckless man, had filled his weaving sheds with the new machinery, turning a careless back on the handloom weavers who came to complain that he was taking their living away, shrugging a careless shoulder when they threatened his devilish innovations with hammers and his property with fire. He had spent money which the Hobhouses and other well-established residents of the Law Valley had considered criminal folly on a new breed of men called engineers and designers, purchasing their inventive and creative skills to make Barforth cloth not the cheapest, certainly, but the most efficiently produced, the very highest quality available, not merely in Cullingford but in the world. And because he had seen no reason to be modest about his achievements, because he had strolled into the Piece Hall in Cullingford as if he owned that too, and had greeted with no more than the tilt of a sardonic eyebrow the news that his competitors—with their faith in the "old ways"—were not all doing well, he had not been popular and many had wished to see him fail.

But now, with scarcely a handloom weaver left in the valley, Uncle Joel had passed far beyond the possibility of failure, his factory at Tarn Edge alone, I'd heard, capable of producing five thousand miles of excellent worsted cloth every year, his order books permanently full, his authority in the town of Cullingford very nearly complete.

Yet, as I watched him that day sitting at ease beside his serenely elegant wife, too large a man for my father's fragile brocade-covered chairs, I somehow feared his influence less than that of his sister—who was my mother's sister too—our aunt Hannah.

Uncle Joel was too splendid, I thought, too remote to concern himself in any great detail with the comings and goings of his orphan nieces, or, if he did, would do it with style, with the same breadth of vision he extended to all his enterprises. But Aunt Hannah had always been a source of authority in our lives, a woman of immense determination on whose judgement my mother frequently relied, a woman, we were given to understand, who deserved our respect and consideration because her life, unlike my mother's, had always been hard.

She had kept house for Uncle Joel during his early struggles, had sacrificed her youth to his convenience, and then, when neither he nor my mother needed her, had married late and somewhat unsuitably, reaping no advantage from her brother's subsequently acquired millions. Yet her husband, Mr. Ira Agbrigg, who had been a widower with a half-grown son and daughter at the time of their marriage, was now the manager of Lawcroft Fold, perhaps the most important of the Barforth factories, a man whose quiet authority was well acknowledged in the textile trade, and it was the long-held opinion of Mrs. Hobhouse and Mrs. Rawnsley that if Aunt Hannah could learn to content herself with a manager's salary she would do well enough indeed.

But it was not in her nature to take second place to a Mrs. Morgan Aycliffe, her own sister, nor to a Mrs. Joel Barforth, her own brother's wife, both these ladies younger and, in her view, considerably less able than herself. And although she was ready enough to borrow our carriage horses and to help herself to the surplus products of the Barforth kitchens—unable, she said, to tolerate waste—I had always recognised her as a great power.

Uncle Joel, no doubt, would wind up my father's business affairs, or keep them ticking over as he thought fit, but unless my mother, who, so far as I knew, had never made a decision in her life, chose now to stir herself, it occurred to me that the minutiae of our daily lives—of far greater importance to us than building land and railway shares—would be left to Aunt Hannah.

Uncle Joel, apparently disinclined for conversation, planted himself on the hearthrug, dominating the fire, and reaching for his cigar case—although I did not think that even he would dare to smoke here, in my father's drawing room—he allowed his gaze to rest speculatively on my father's glass-fronted cabinets and his intricately inlaid, expertly polished tables, each one bearing the treasures of Sèvres and Meissen, Minton and Derby my father had cherished far more than his children.

I saw Aunt Hannah's husband look down uncomfortably at his feet, his sense of propriety telling him it was time to leave, his sense of reality reminding him he would need his wife's permission to do so. I saw my uncle Joel's wife, kind Aunt Verity, smile with tolerant, tranquil understanding at her husband, well aware, I thought, of his urge to light that forbidden cigar, and of the commercial instincts which were now leading him, from force of habit, to assess the value of my father's porcelain.

And for a while there was no sound but the busy crackling of the fire, the ticking of the ormolu and enamel clock standing, as it had always done, at the very centre of the mantelpiece, a black basalt urn perfectly placed at either side. But Aunt Hannah was not given to prolonged meditation and, fixing my mother with an irritable eye, announced: "Well then, Elinor—it's a bad business."

"Yes, dear. So it is."

"Indeed. And he'll be sadly missed, for heaven knows how we'll find another member of Parliament to serve us so well. I suppose the by-election must be quite soon . . . ?"

"Yes, dear. I suppose it must."

"And I wonder if you have given any thought to a suitable memorial?"

"Oh—my word. Should I do that, do you think, Hannah?"

"I think it will be expected of you, Elinor. A headstone will hardly suffice, you know, for so distinguished a man. No—no—something altogether out of the ordinary . . . And it strikes me that if the worthies of this town could be prevailed upon to subscribe towards the building of a concert hall, then there would be every reason in the world to name it after your husband. Now what do you think to that?"

"That would be splendid, Hannah."

"Well then—if you agree, of course—a committee could easily be formed for the purpose, and in view of Mr. Aycliffe's services to the community I can anticipate no difficulty. Really—it would be most appropriate."

And as my mother continued to smile, a placid little woman who had no objection to monuments or concert halls or anything else so long as she was not required to stir from her own warm corner, my uncle Joel, that most awe-inspiring of gentlemen, grinned suddenly, as mischievously as a schoolboy, and said, "Aye—most appropriate. And if the firm of Morgan Aycliffe should undertake the construction work then I'd think it more than appropriate. I'd think it shrewd."

And with an air of enormous unconcern—master in his own home, and master, now, it seemed, in ours—he selected a cigar, lit it, and inhaled deeply, bringing home to me by that one simple, almost contemptuous gesture that my father, who had not permitted tobacco in his house much less his drawing room, was dead indeed.

"Joel," Aunt Hannah said, quite horrified. "Good heavens— what are you thinking of? Not in here."

But, standing in the centre of the room, his bulk overshadowing the memory of the narrow, silent man whose ghost he had so easily laid to rest, he did no more than shrug his powerful, expensively covered shoulders.

"If Elinor doesn't like it I reckon she can tell me so."

"Elinor?" Aunt Hannah cried out, the hint of nervous tears in her voice causing me to wonder if she had indeed cared for my father as sincerely as she pretended. "Elinor has nothing to say to it. This is Morgan Aycliffe's house, as you very well know, and when did Elinor ever have any sense of what's right, or any sense at all? It's not decent, Joel. The poor man is scarcely in his grave—and it's the porcelain . . . You know the care he took of his porcelain and how he feared the tobacco would stain it."

"Ah yes," my mother murmured, perfectly serene in the face of this tirade. "The porcelain—the famous, beautiful porcelain— there is a word to say, Joel, is there not, about the porcelain?"

And rousing herself suddenly she smiled at me, and at Prudence, and at Celia, and sent us off to bed.

We had rooms of our own now below the nursery floor, identical toilet tables swathed in white muslin, narrow, white-quilted beds, nothing to distinguish one from the other except that Prudence and Celia maintained their possessions in immaculate order while I, alas, did not. And as Celia bade us a sedate good night, hurrying off to dream, with total fifteen-year-old contentment, of the 20,000 pounds which would secure her the wedding, the christening, the smart new villa of her heart's desire, I joined Prudence for a moment at her fireside, neither of us ready to be alone.

We had not loved our father. He had not required it and it had occurred to neither of us to do so. Unlike Celia, who had felt secure beneath the wing of his authority, we had been oppressed by it, yet now there could be no sense of relief, no real hope of broadening our narrow spirits, our restricted horizons.

Possibly—without my father to run to—our governess, Miss

Mayfield, might prove a trifle less invincible. We may, with some contriving, be at last empowered to pay calls and receive them without her eagle-eyed supervision, to write letters without submitting them for her inspection, to hold conversations out of her hearing. We might, indeed, be allowed to choose our own gowns—within reason—to make the momentous decision between lace or ribbons, a bonnet crowned with feathers or with a satin rose. And it was the measure of my father's defeat that only one of his three daughters could content herself with that. Celia would do well because she wanted only what it was right and proper for her to have. Prudence would find life hard since she wanted to make up her own female mind as to its direction. I had no idea what I wanted—except that I had not met it yet, except that it was not to be found in Blenheim Lane.

"What of the porcelain then?" I enquired carefully. "Is it to go to our brother, do you imagine?" And having lived in fear of those frail treasures all my life—for if someone's skirt had ever dislodged one of them it would certainly have been mine—I added, "Well, and I shouldn't mind."

"Nor I," she answered, continuing to stare into the fire, her face, in its tight concentration, more like my father's than ever. "Indeed, it is only right that he should have something, especially when one considers that if he had not quarrelled with Father he might have had it all. But he is a man. One supposes he is able to take care of himself. I would like to worry about him but I have other things on my mind. I am far too busy wondering whether it will be a Hobhouse or a Rawnsley they will purchase for me with my 20,000 pounds."

"Perhaps Mother will still give you a London season, as Father planned."

But Prudence, her mouth hard and sarcastic, although she had not wanted to go to the London marriage market in any case, shook her head. "Oh no. Mother will do exactly as she is told. You know how she is with her 'Yes, dear—no, dear'—except that now she will be nodding and smiling to Uncle Joel instead of Father. And although I am sure Uncle Joel means us no harm and would add to our money rather than cheat us of a single penny—and believe me, there are uncles who *would* cheat us— well, he won't take the trouble to send us to London. He knows he has to get us married, and he'll do it, but he won't be as careful as Father. He'll accept anyone who offers, so long as he's respectable—anyone Aunt Hannah draws to his attention—just to get the job done. And all Mother will say is, 'Yes, dear. How very splendid.' What a poor, silly creature she is, Faith. Was she always like that, do you suppose, or was it Father—twenty years of Father—that turned her into a porcelain doll? I have a nightmare sometimes that I could be the same."

I kissed her lightly, knowing she did not really like to be touched, knowing there was no lasting comfort I could give, and crossing the landing to my own room, I wondered about that porcelain doll, that dainty puppet who had waltzed so blissfully the night her puppet-master died. And so I became, once more, an unseen, unwilling witness.

Below me, in the darkened hall, Uncle Joel and his wife were taking their leave and, as Aunt Verity stooped to kiss my mother's cheek and then moved away, my uncle paused a moment, cigar in hand, its unaccustomed, male fragrance shocking and attracting me, so that I paused too, looked down, and then, afraid of discovery, was obliged to remain.

"There's a lot of money, Elinor," I heard him say. "Not bad, eh, for twenty years' work, however tedious. And you're still young enough, like I said you'd be. The world's wide and you can afford to enjoy it now, if you'll bide your time. All I ask of you is to wear your widow's weeds like a good girl, as long as it's decent, before you start spreading your wings."

And smiling up at him, neither docile nor helpless but radiating an enchanting, altogether wicked sparkle, my mother threw both arms around his neck and, standing on excited tiptoe, hugged him tight.

"Yes, Joel, a twelvemonth of black veils, isn't it, for a husband, then lilac and grey for a year after that. I'll do it, don't fret yourself, for I've no objection to black. But it strikes me no one could really blame me if I went off to wear it in a sunnier climate. The northern winter, you know, and my tendency to take cold—in fact my doctor may positively insist upon it."

"Aye, I reckon he might."

"Italy, I thought, or southern France—for a while, Joel—I've earned myself that, surely? Hannah can see to the girls—and Verity—for the whole world knows me as a woman who couldn't be trusted to arrange a tea party, much less a wedding."

"So they do. Just promise me you'll arrange no weddings of your own—in Italy and France."

"Oh, Joel," she said, hugging him again, her face, glimpsed behind his shoulder, vivid and alive. "I think you can be sure of that. No weddings for me, darling, not until I'm old, at any rate. And I'm not old—oh no—*that* I'm not."

And standing in the doorway she waved her hand, a free-flowing, graceful movement of her whole body, stretching herself in the crisp night air—without a shawl, without a chaperone—until his carriage was out of sight.

Chapter Two

MY MOTHER took to her bed the very next day, suffering, they said at first, from the effects of fatigue and sorrow, which, combined with the biting January wind—the prospect of a raw February, a howling March to follow—could well settle on her lungs. And so it was left to Uncle Joel to inform us that my father had bequeathed his entire collection of porcelain to Prudence, thus causing much distress to Celia, who did not care about the porcelain but, being the youngest, the smallest, the only one who had really believed in Father's teaching, would dearly have loved to be singled out.

"It's worth thousands," Aunt Hannah declared accusingly, as if Prudence had been a scheming parlourmaid. "Thousands and thousands—and to a girl not yet nineteen. Good heavens, I can hardly think it wise. Naturally there can be no question of removing any part of it, Prudence—in fact you would do well to think of yourself merely as a guardian, until such time as you are married and your husband can take proper charge of it."

But an hour later, having thought the matter out, I noticed she was kinder to Prudence than usual, for this legacy would make her the most marriageable of us all, and we had no need to be reminded that Aunt Hannah's stepson, Jonas Agbrigg, was in need of a rich wife.

Nor was I surprised, some three weeks later, to find myself accompanying my mother to Leeds, the first stage of her journey to London and abroad, in search of the softer climate she had convinced our family doctor she required, and then returning with Prudence to Aunt Hannah's house, where Celia—who also suffered from the cold—was waiting.

There had been some suggestion, hotly contested by Aunt Hannah, that Prudence should accompany my mother, a further suggestion that we should all three remain in our own home, under the combined supervision of our housekeeper, Mrs. Naylor, and Miss Mayfield, our governess, whose duties, now that our education appeared to be over, were becoming vague. But although our house had been kept open and a somewhat tearful Miss Mayfield assured that there would always be a place for her therein, Aunt Hannah had insisted that, for a week or so at least, we were to be her guests. And as I sipped her weak tea and ate her scanty slices of bread and butter on that first afternoon, I felt it was by no means all she would insist upon.

My aunt's house at Lawcroft Fold was old and plain, a square, smoke-blackened box hugging the hillside above Lawcroft Mills —owned by her brother, managed by her husband—her windows, although she managed to ignore it, offering a view of the factory buildings crouching in the valley, the high, iron-spiked factory wall, the huddle of workers' cottages around it; her morning rest disturbed by the hideous five o'clock screeching of the factory hooter, the clanging shut, a precise half-hour later, of the massive gates.

Yet the house itself was decently proportioned, a solid oak door at the centre, two high, square rooms on either side, a sufficiency of bedrooms, the front parlour—for the benefit of Aunt Hannah's guests—offering a brave show of plum-coloured velvet upholstery, a busily patterned carpet that would not show the years, a jungle of bright green foliage in ornamental pots, a great deal of fancy needlework, embroidered fire screens, cushion covers, table runners, tapestry pictures in heavy frames, done with immense skill by Aunt Hannah herself to conceal the lack of the Meissen and Sèvres and the antique silver to be found in such abundance in Blenheim Lane.

But, in complete contrast, her back parlour was achingly clean, exceedingly bare, and for that interminable week or so, I was obliged to spend my mornings in that cheerless apartment, assisting with the household's plain sewing, submitting myself to the tyranny of hemstitch and blanket stitch, the bewilderment of buttonholes, at which I did not excel; and my afternoons at the front of the house, my chair well away from the fire, listening, speaking when spoken to, as Aunt Hannah issued tea and instructions to the ladies she had involved in her works of charity —colleagues in their opinion, assistants in hers—and who, because of her desire to spare her own, elderly carriage horses, were obliged to come to her. And it was a constant proof of her natural authority that these ladies, the wives of owners, not managers, although they disliked and resented her and frequently threatened, among themselves, to rebel and ignore her, could be reduced, after ten minutes of her company, to obedience.

She had, as always, a dozen schemes afoot. There was her plan to educate orphan girls for domestic service and then to "place" them in the houses of her friends; her long-standing efforts to provide blankets and good advice for such poor families as she deemed worthy, her determination that our local manufacturers should open their hearts and their bank accounts to Cullingford's need for a concert hall—since Bradford had one —and that it should be named after my father. But, most of all that winter, her mind was occupied by the proposal that Parliament should be petitioned to grant Cullingford its Charter of Incorporation with the right to elect our own mayor and town council; not, one felt, because she was really troubled by the inefficiency of our present parochial system of local government, which had failed to pave the streets or provide an adequate water supply—in some cases no water supply at all—to the poorer sections of the town, but because she intended her husband, Mr. Ira Agbrigg, to be our first lord mayor, she his mayoress.

Mr. Agbrigg could not bring her riches, but he could—at her prompting—offer her prestige, and since there were others who felt they had a greater claim to civic honour, it suited her, when Mrs. Hobhouse of Nethercoats Mill and Mrs. Rawnsley, the banker's wife, came to call, to remind them that her nieces were the daughters of the late Morgan Aycliffe, M.P., her brother Mr. Joel Barforth himself.

"Naturally my brother is most anxious for the charter to be granted," she would throw casually into the pool of conversation, her keen eyes assessing the ripples she had created. "He feels local government to be altogether essential—since who bet-

ter to ascertain our needs than ourselves—although he was telling me the other day that the office of mayor will really be most
arduous." And here she would smile directly at Mrs. Hobhouse,
whose husband was not noted for his energy.

"And of course the mayoress will have her duties to perform—"
she would murmur, glancing sidelong at Mrs. Mandelbaum,
the wool merchant's wife, who was of a retiring disposition,
hated crowds, and when she was nervous, did not speak good
English.

"But will your brother not wish to take office himself?" Mrs.
Rawnsley, the banker's wife, once asked her.

"Ah no," Aunt Hannah replied. "His time is too fully occupied,
but he will certainly put forward his nominee."

And since Mr. Rawnsley's bank would have been hard-pressed
to support the withdrawal of Barforth favour, his wife had no
more to say than, "Oh yes—quite so. Assuredly Mr. Barforth's
views will be listened to."

"Naturally," Aunt Hannah told her kindly, enjoying her mo-
ent of power as hugely as if she had already instructed Uncle
Joel to transfer his funds, as if she really believed he would obey
her. "I could not say, at this stage, just who that nominee may
be. But I think we can all agree on the soundness of my
brother's judgement, and his desire to serve the best interests of
the community. Now then, ladies, if we could turn our attention
to this little matter of a concert hall . . ."

And having reminded them—humble manager's wife that she
was—of her grand connections, the intricate financial web which
bound most of them to her brother, the extreme eligibility of her
sister's daughters, which was a matter of some importance to
those with marriageable sons, she would, without once mentioning her husband's name, pass on to other things.

We had not, of course, expected to be pampered in Aunt Hannah's house, for although her husband's salary was known to be
ample—my uncle Joel being generous to those who gave him
value for money—her charitable and social activities, her insistence on living, at least on the surface, as a Barforth rather than
an Agbrigg proved an evident financial strain.

The future mayoress of Cullingford could not refuse to contribute substantially to the charitable foundations she had herself brought into being, could not, in fact, give less than the

women she had bullied into giving anything at all. She could not refuse invitations to dine from ladies of substance whose husbands she intended to cajole into supporting Mr. Agbrigg's candidacy; and having accepted, she was obliged to invite them in return. And when she did her table must have its share of crystal and silver, and no one must be allowed to suspect that she had herself prepared the sauces and deserts which were far beyond the skills of the aging kitchenmaid she called her cook.

But, in the more private areas of her home, she could keep a watchful eye on coals and candles, could employ her own half-trained charity children as maids, reserving just one presentable parlourmaid for the serving of drawing room tea. "Ah—what have we here, I wonder?" she would ask at the appearance of her tea tray, her smile half-amused, half-sarcastic as she served, with immense composure, the gingerbread and chocolate cake, the apple curd tarts and cheese muffins she had baked herself only a few hours before.

Yet, from the start of our visit, although Celia and I were obliged, as usual, to do our own mending and keep our own rooms in order, thus freeing her servants for the downstairs dusting and polishing that would "*show*," she extended such leniency to Prudence that Celia, who was easily offended, soon began to complain.

"She wants you to marry Jonas," she said, her face sharpening as it always did when there was a marriage in the offing. "Well, that's what comes of being Father's favourite and getting all the porcelain. But I suppose it's only right you should get married first, you being the eldest—and they say Jonas is very clever."

And when Prudence, seriously annoyed, declared that marriage was not greatly on her mind, Celia, who feared nothing in the world so much as being left on the shelf, calmly replied, "That's nonsense, Prudence. Of course you're thinking about marriage. It's the one thing everybody thinks about—and you should be quick about it, so Faith and I can have our chances."

I had been acquainted with Jonas Agbrigg all my life, or for as much of it as I could remember, yet all I really knew about him was the much vaunted fact of his academic brilliance. He had, it seemed, shown from the very first a flair for learning far in advance of his years and his relatively humble station. At the grammar school, long before Aunt Hannah's marriage to his father had given him a degree of social standing, he had easily outdistanced the sons of our local "millocracy"—on whose generosity the school depended—and had been something of an embarrassment even to certain schoolmasters who had found themselves hard-pressed to keep up with him. He had shown himself, indeed, to be so universally gifted that Aunt Hannah, whose pride in him was boundless, had been unable to decide just where those gifts could be best employed. She had, to begin with, planned to make a churchman of him, dreaming, perhaps, of bishoprics, archbishoprics—of herself installed as hostess in some ecclesiastical palace—until a certain tartness in his manner, a decided lack of saintliness, had inclined her to consider the law. And now, having returned from the University of Cambridge, an opportunity had been purchased for him, with the help of Uncle Joel, in the legal practice of Mr. Corey-Manning, a neighbour of ours in Blenheim Lane, who was—according to Aunt Hannah—exceedingly fortunate and immensely grateful to have obtained the services of Jonas.

He was a young man of twenty-four, pale and expressionless, a taller, better-nourished version of his father, although he had not inherited Mr. Agbrigg's stooping shoulders and big-knuckled, work-scarred hands. Jonas' hands, on the contrary, were long and lean and perfectly smooth, with never so much as an inkstain on his carefully, by Cullingford standards almost effeminately manicured fingers. And although he dressed plainly, he was, at all times, immaculate and far too conscious of it for my comfort.

I could, if I put my mind to it, understand that we had not always been kind to Jonas. During our early childhood, when the boys and girls of the family had been allowed to play together, my uncle Joel's sons, Blaize and Nicholas Barforth, had mocked him quite mercilessly for the care he took of his clothes, being completely careless of the damage they inflicted on their own. Their sister, my cousin Caroline, possessing from birth a fine appreciation of the social order in which a mill manager's son had no more importance than a groom, had often snubbed him and encouraged us to do the same.

"Oh, it's only the Agbrigg boy," Caroline would announce. "He won't want to play." And Jonas, his long, up-tilted eyes scowling, would walk off, making us somehow aware that, in his view, our games were infantile and each one of us a bore.

And even now, although he was always scrupulously polite, he was not a comfortable young man, his return home each evening bringing a certain tension which stemmed, in part, from the surprising coolness between him and his father, a circumstance of which Aunt Hannah herself seemed unaware.

"Good evening, sir," Jonas would say.

"Evening, lad," he would receive in reply, and, brought up on Aunt Hannah's extravagant hopes for her stepson's future, it astonished me that his own father should have no more to say to him than that. Yet Mr. Agbrigg, his thin face quite haggard in the lamplight, a faint odour of raw wool often discernible about his clothing, would eat his supper in silence every evening, his shrewd, narrow eyes registering nothing as Aunt Hannah requested Jonas to give us his opinion of the day's news, expressing no opinions of his own, and then, folding his napkin with those big, work-hard hands, would say simply, "I'll be off back to the mill, then, to see the night shift come on."

My aunt's ambitions for Jonas, of course, were of a far higher order than those she entertained for his father. Mr. Agbrigg, self-educated but unpolished, his speech still retaining the broadness of the West Riding, could be pushed just so far and no farther. He was, without doubt, exceedingly well respected in Cullingford's Piece Hall, where men were more concerned with cash than with culture, and would be a popular mayor with our town's largely unlettered population. But Jonas, with his academic distinction, his neutral accent, his chilly determination to succeed, could do Aunt Hannah credit not only in the eyes of Cullingford, but in the world.

She knew exactly what she wanted for him. To begin with, when his childless employer, Mr. Corey-Manning, decided to retire, Jonas must be in a position to take over the business, and then, with a well-established legal practice behind him, a year or two's experience as a town councillor, a member of this committee and that, the way to Westminster, my father's old seat on the Whig back-benches, a cabinet appointment—Whig or Tory mattered little to Aunt Hannah—would be open.

But even Jonas' talent, even his genius, could not hope to succeed without the cash in hand to buy Mr. Corey-Manning out when the time came, without a sufficient income not only to fight a decent election campaign but to maintain himself in office when he succeeded. And since Aunt Hannah had no money to give him and Uncle Joel could not be relied on for-ever, the only course open to him was to marry someone who could.

Naturally he would leave the choice of a wife to his mother, and she had selected Prudence for a number of reasons, largely, of course, for the dowry and the porcelain, but also because Pru-dence herself was exactly the kind of efficient, energetic girl who would help a man to go forward, rather than hold him back. And also her alternatives were, in fact, limited to the three of us. Jonas, she well knew, would never be permitted to approach a Miss Mandelbaum or a Miss Rawnsley, whose fathers—like ours —required something a little more solid in a son-in-law than am-bition, self-confidence, a university degree, which, in their expe-rience, had never been an essential ingredient in the making of fortunes. But my father was dead and, having only my mother, her own younger sister, to contend with—in Aunt Hannah's view no contest at all—she began her campaign with vigour and a lack of scruple which enabled her to drop the most transparent hints to Mrs. Hobhouse of Nethercoats Mill, who had ten sons of her own, that Prudence was spoken for.

But Mrs. Hobhouse, who had clearly informed herself how much my father's porcelain would be likely to fetch at auction, was as fond a mother as my aunt, and the next time we called at Nethercoats, Prudence found herself burdened with another suitor in the hearty, heavy shape of Freddy Hobhouse, the eldest of the ten equally heavy Hobhouse sons.

"Prudence is such a dear girl," Mrs. Hobhouse enthused, beaming as she saw how obediently Freddy was plying my sister with tea and muffins; while Aunt Hannah, knowing that Freddy, who should have been at the mill at this hour, had been specifically summoned to his mother's drawing room for the pur-poses of seduction, sat straight-backed, her mouth very hard.

"Yes," she said. "As you know, she is a great favourite of mine. A parent must be impartial, but I think an aunt is entitled to her preferences . . ." And later, as we drove home, Freddy, a warmer man than Jonas, having spent longer than necessary in arranging my sister's portion of the carriage rug, Aunt Hannah enquired tartly if, in view of her recent bereavement, Prudence thought it proper to pass her time in flirting. To which my sister, with a cold fury equal to her father's, her fastidious nostril quivering in exact imitation of his, replied that she did not understand Aunt Hannah's meaning; and that if she had understood it, she felt certain it would have given her much offence.

"The Hobhouses," Aunt Hannah announced at dinner that evening, speaking directly to her husband, "are in a sorry state indeed. It saddens me, every time I go over there, to see the worsening of their affairs—for they are worsening, Mr. Agbrigg, are they not? My word, when I think of Nethercoats as it used to be, in old Mr. Hobhouse's day . . . And when Bradley Hobhouse took it over from his father it seemed as solid as a rock. Certainly Emma-Jane Rawnsley, as she was then, thought so, or she would hardly have married him. But Bradley has never been a man of affairs, too easy, too apt to leave it all to others. I have heard my brother say so many a time, and although Emma-Jane is a good soul, she is not a strong character either. Well, as to how Nethercoats may provide a living for those ten boys, and dowries for those four girls, I haven't a notion. And neither has Emma-Jane. They have made room for Freddy and Adolphus, but the younger boys will be forced to take employment elsewhere, which is a great pity, don't you agree, Mr. Agbrigg? Really—one can only tremble for their future."

But Freddy Hobhouse, completely untroubled by that future, attended the parish church the following Sunday, an act almost amounting to a declaration since the whole world knew the Hobhouses to be Methodists; and afterwards, in the churchyard, he gave Prudence his arm as she picked her way over the frozen ground, having first elbowed the physically and socially inferior Jonas aside.

"Can't have you coming a cropper, Miss Aycliffe," he announced with all the breezy self-assurance of a man who has always known where his four square meals a day are coming from. And, following them, I couldn't fail to observe the taut yet perfectly controlled anger in the arm Jonas offered to me, nor the pouting outrage of my sister Celia, left to pick her way across the ice without any man's arm to lean on.

And it was perhaps just as well that Uncle Joel's wife, Aunt Verity, took note of the situation and rescued us.

"They must come to me now," she said at the end of the second week, and although Aunt Hannah was not pleased, Aunt Verity, after all, was Mrs. Joel Barforth of Tarn Edge, and Aunt Hannah was obliged to agree.

"Very well, Verity. But I must ask you to remember that they are still in full mourning and should not be taken out a great deal. In fact they should not really go out at all—their father was most precise in such matters."

But Aunt Verity's beautiful, silk-upholstered, silver-mounted carriage was at the door, her fur rugs swiftly wrapped around our knees, and within the hour we were installed before a happily crackling fire, our feet on velvet stools, while this younger, kinder aunt asked nothing of us except that we should be at ease.

Uncle Joel's house at Tarn Edge was scarcely a dozen years old, and although it was but a mile or two distant from the largest of his mills, the windows of its principal rooms were turned away from the scowling city skyline, with its fringe of chimney stacks, to offer a view of old trees, thinning as they climbed the hillside, and to sharp-scented, sharp-tufted moorland.

The house itself, a Gothic structure of spires and ornamental towers, had always been something more than a mere dwelling place. For, unlike most Law Valley men who preferred to confine their surplus cash in bank vaults or invest it in objects large and solid enough to announce their own value, Uncle Joel saw no shame in self-indulgence. And so, as a tribute to his own unflagging energy, he had built himself a palace, its treasures displayed not with the glass-fronted, locked-away care of my father, but with a nonchalance that some called arrogant, others magnificent.

The vast hallway was medieval in feeling, a life-size bronze stag guarding the foot of the stairs, a gigantic stained-glass window at their head, casting its ruby and emerald light on a wealth of intricately carved panelling, dappling the limbs of a white marble goddess and attendant nymphs standing in splendid, some said shocking, nudity, on the wide landing. But, these sombre glories apart, the rest of the house was as light and pastel-tinted as a summer garden, blue velvet or honey-coloured velvet underfoot, blue silk walls rising to ceilings that were moulded in blue and white and gold and set with the brilliance of crystal chandeliers. While in the ballroom, recently added for my cousin Caroline's convenience, a dozen windows opened directly on to a broad, paved terrace, a landscaped acre of roses, a trellised walk, a lily pool.

No one at Tarn Edge House ever gave a thought to the household's plain sewing except an elderly woman employed for the purpose, while, at all hours of the day, one could encounter a cheerfully starched maid running upstairs with hot water or a deliciously laden tray. At Tarn Edge, certainly, no one counted coals or candles, nor cared how many times the horses were got out, and had I found my uncle's presence less overwhelming, I would have been well content.

He was, undoubtedly, a handsome man, massive of build, exceedingly dark of hair and commanding of eye, but, accustomed to my father's narrow, stooping shape, Uncle Joel's very maleness, the rich odours of wine and tobacco hovering about him, his luxury and freedom of speech, all, in their various ways, alarmed me. My father's authority had been a chilling but restrained whisper, Uncle Joel's a mighty bellowing at the foot of the stairs whenever his sons, as often happened, were delaying his departure for the mill. For my uncle, in the fiftieth year of his age, still chose to be at his factory gates most mornings at half-past five o'clock, watch in hand, to check the punctuality of his employees, the stamina, perhaps, of his managers and his children; and the greatest source of discord at Tarn Edge was that my cousins, Blaize and Nicholas, were rarely of like mind.

"Get yourselves down here, damn you!" I grew accustomed to hearing him shout. "We've a business to run, and God help it when it gets into your idle hands. But so long as it's mine—so long as I'm paying your bills—you'll jump when I tell you—damn you!"

And my cousin Nicholas would run scowling down the stairs, as big and dark and angry as his father, his waistcoat undone, hastily shrugging on his jacket. My cousin Blaize, on the other hand, would come sauntering behind at his leisure, his own brocade waistcoat correctly fastened, his curly-brimmed beaver hat and light-coloured kid gloves nonchalantly in his hand. From my room at the front of the house I would hear the crunch of wheels on the gravel, the growled commands of my uncle as he mounted his carriage, and would watch, sometimes, from my window, as my cousins, on their thoroughbred bays, raced each other for the lodge gates, Nicholas, hatless more often than not, bound for Lawcroft Fold to be instructed by Mr. Ira Agbrigg into the intricacies of textile machinery, Blaize, his hat tipped at a rakish angle, heading for the smart new suite of offices at Tarn Edge, to be initiated into the religion of profit, the mortal sin of loss. My uncle was known throughout the West Riding, with some justice, as a man who had everything. No business enterprise of his had ever failed, but, in addition to that, at a time and in a place where men took wives for convenience, he had married a woman who was not only graceful, sweet-natured, and most pleasing to look at, but who actually loved him, was loved by him, displaying an open delight in his company which I, moulded by the long silence that had been my parents' marriage, found intriguing, something, I suspected, to be envied. And it followed, perhaps quite naturally, that this handsome, affectionate couple should have fine children. Caroline and Nicholas, the younger son, were as dark and immediately striking as their father; Blaize, the elegant, careless first-born, was a shade or two lighter and finer, his mother's child, who would, one felt, float effortlessly through life protected from misfortune by the power of his unique, altogether disarming smile.

On countless occasions during our childhood I had seen that smile flash out, melting the hearts of any irate adult from maid-servant or gardener to Aunt Hannah herself, so that, knowing Blaize to be the real culprit and the one who invented mischief for others to perform, they were nevertheless conquered by that impish charm. And, somehow or other, they ended by meting out their punishments to the well-meaning but stubborn Nicholas. Although Blaize was decidedly less handsome than his brother, his light grey eyes in no way to be compared with Nicholas' eyes, which were almost black, his straight, chocolate-coloured hair nothing to Nicholas' ebony curls, his face quite unremarkable until it was illuminated by his smile, he had been born, it seemed, with so much easy assurance, a total conviction that everyone must notice him first and like him best, that so, indeed, it was.

"Yes, of course I'll do as you ask—why not?" Blaize had declared almost daily throughout our childhood. And then, with everyone off their guard, he had always done exactly as he pleased.

"That's nonsense," Nicholas would always declare. "I won't do it," proceeding to stand his ground, black eyes scowling, as he took his own punishment and, quite often, Blaize's punishment as well.

It was Nicholas, straightforward, obstinate, who, on every occasion, growled out, "I don't see why I should apologise when I'm not sorry." Blaize who, gracefully shrugging his shoulders, declared himself quite ready to be as apologetic as anyone pleased, after which he would do whatever it was he had apologised for all over again. It was Nicholas who, disliking any kind of failure, had worked hard at school and had managed, somehow, to win a reputation as a difficult, argumentative boy, prone to use his fists. Blaize, who barely worked at all, was remembered as a likeable, witty young rascal who could have done wonders had he condescended to try.

And all my life I had been dazzled by Blaize, who was never defeated, never dismayed, for whom life seemed a carefree, cloudless summer day, and—being often in disgrace myself—I had felt an immense sympathy for Nicholas. Yet both these cousins, having strutted through my early years like young lords of Creation, were separated from me now by the unseen barrier surrounding all marriageable girls, and it was their sister Caroline, who, finding Prudence too serious and Celia too young, dominated my time.

"I know Faith is in mourning," she explained to her mother, who was not, in any case, too severe about such things, "but no one could possibly criticise her for going around with me." And, quite soon, I became not only Caroline's best friend, but her property.

"We are to drive to town this morning," she would announce, walking into my room long before breakfast. "And then, when I've done my shopping, we are to call on the Mandelbaums, which is a great bore, since the Mandelbaum boy wants to marry me. But you can chat to him, Faith, because it would be much more sensible of him to want to marry you. Manufacturers again and their wives at dinner tonight, I'm afraid—really, you'd think Father would see enough of them elsewhere—but we can escape to the landing sofa afterwards, and I shall rely on you to protect me from the Battershaw boy, who wants to marry me too, according to his mother. Battershaw's Brewery, Faith—of course you know them—they make thousands and thousands a year with their light ales, Mrs. Battershaw was telling me, which I thought very vulgar of her. So what do you think I should wear this morning? Come on, Faith, you're quite good with clothes— the blue velvet pelisse with the swan's-down trim and the bonnet with the white feather? Yes, I thought about that too, except that my dear friend Arabella Rawnsley has had one made just like it—or as near as she could manage—and I really can't drive down Millergate looking like a Rawnsley. Hurry up, Faith, and we'll go to the Swan and see if the mail coach is in, for I'd like to know just where my parcels from London have got to. Really —you'd think they could deliver on time, since they must know there's absolutely nothing fit to buy in Cullingford."

A young queen—my cousin Caroline—who required a lady-in-waiting, and I suppose I had always known that however rich I might one day become Caroline would be richer, whatever marriage I might make Caroline's would be grander. And I was happy enough to drive with her, at least twice daily, from Tarn Edge down the leafy slope of Blenheim Lane, the steep, cobbled track called Millergate that took us via the even steeper, stonier Sheepgate, directly to Market Square, flanked at one side by the Old Swan, where the London coach still clattered in each afternoon, and, at the other side, by the ancient Piece Hall, a relic almost of a bygone age, when the handweavers had come down, every Thursday, from their moorland cottages, to offer their heavy worsteds for sale. The old market buildings had been removed now, at my father's instigation: the fishmongers and the butchers, the butter and cheese sellers concealed, in these prosperous times, behind an elaborate stone façade, an Italianate structure which had won my father much praise. His Assembly Rooms—his greatest architectural triumph—were visible too from Market Square, a smoke grey building in the classical style, Doric columns and graceful proportions contrasting and partly concealing the weed garden of warehouses crumbling on the canal bank behind it, their cellars foul with floodwater, their floorboards sodden and dangerous with half a century's rain.

And if nothing in our main shopping area of Millergate was worthy of purchase, that did not prevent us from looking, touching, did not prevent me—since I was, as Caroline had said, quite good with clothes—from combining two lengths of silk, a little ribbon and lace into a confection which, more often than not, would find its way into our carriage.

"Miss Aycliffe has taste," they said of me in Millergate, implying, I suspected, that since I lacked the striking dark eyes and black curls of Miss Barforth, I had need of something to see me through. Yet, although I was myself condemned to wear black at least until the month of June, I enjoyed not only the colour and texture of these rich fabrics, but the advantage this instinctive sense of dress gave me over Caroline, who had the advantage of me in every other way.

"What about this, Faith?" she would say, throwing a length of purple velvet across her shoulder.

"Oh no, Caroline—at least, not until you are a duchess."

And while she tried on something else, pouting, shrugging, but doing as I told her just the same, I took advantage of those large, dressmakers' mirrors to discover that even a mourning dress might be improved by a high, ruffled collar, which could make a long neck seem longer, that a black frill so near the face made a pale complexion paler, fair hair a shade or two fairer, that a strategically placed lamp, or a branch of candles, could even turn that heavy, unruly hair to silver.

"What are you doing, Faith?"

"Thinking about myself, Caroline. When you're not beautiful —when you're tall and fair, and small, dark women are all the rage—it takes thought."

Of all the Barforths, Caroline was the one who most resembled Uncle Joel, possessed of the same energy and endurance that had made him his not altogether unblemished fortune. Like him, Caroline would always head directly towards her goal, demolishing rather than climbing any obstacle foolish enough to block her way, and her problem lay not so much in deciding what to do with her life—since she believed she could do anything—but in what she would like to do best.

Marriage, of course, would be her eventual destiny, as it was the destiny of all female creatures who got the chance, but Caroline's marriage, like her London gowns and her French

gloves and parasols, would need to be of a quality and a rarity
not easily found in Cullingford. No "Battershaw boy," no "Mandelbaum boy" would suffice for Caroline Barforth, and it was a
contradiction of her nature that although she was fiercely proud
of her father and more than ready to enjoy his colossal fortune,
she preferred never to refer to the means by which that fortune
had been made.

Money, to the Barforths and the Hobhouses, to the Oldroyds
and the Mandelbaums, was equally desirable from whatever
source it came, but Caroline, with all the money she could ever
require so readily to hand, had turned her mind to finer things,
having learned, quite early, that to the few landed gentlemen
who had so far come her way, the only wealth they really valued
was tied up in ancestral acres, ancient names and traditions,
which Barforth looms could not provide.

Her father was certainly a great power in Cullingford, his
influence could make itself felt in the commercial circles of
Bradford and Leeds, and even in London. But to the sporting
squires who came north to hunt foxes, course hares, shoot grouse
and pheasant—to the disreputable, almost penniless Sir Giles
Flood, lord of the manor of Cullingford—Mr. Joel Barforth was
no more, and no less, than a tradesman, a man to whom one
might nod in passing, but would not expect to receive through
one's front door. And, being a true Barforth, wanting whatever
was difficult, whatever the world told her she could not have, I
believed that Caroline had set her obstinate heart not only on
entering those noble front doors, but on being well received inside, on becoming, as her brothers had always called her, not
Mrs. Battershaw, or Mandelbaum, or anything at all, but Lady
Caroline.

"I suppose your sister Prudence will settle for Freddy Hobhouse," she told me one wet afternoon as we sat on the landing
sofa. "Because, after all, even if Nethercoats is going down, he
can always build it up again, and she could hardly consider the
Agbrigg boy. She'll have a nice little house and a nice little mill,
and I can't think that Freddy will be hard to handle. And you
and Celia will get just the same. Yes, it's all quite simple for you.
I envy you, Faith, really I do—because I can't see myself in a
millhouse at all. And they are millhouses, aren't they, whatever

one does to them, full of millmasters and brewmasters, talking wool and light ale. Good heavens—I couldn't bear that."

And, responding to her shudder with a smile, wondering what her father would say should he hear her refer to Tarn Edge as a millhouse, I failed to notice Blaize until he flung himself lightly down beside us and drawled, "Don't fret, Caroline. If a manufacturer is beneath you we can always get you a lord. We could even try for Sir Giles Flood, for they say he has an eye for little girls since he turned eighty."

"And that," Caroline said, squaring up to him, "is enough of that."

"Oh—I don't know."

"Well, I know. And furthermore, brother dear, shouldn't you be at the mill?"

"Of course. I'm just a manufacturer after all—where else should I be?"

And, stung by the mischief in his subtle, smiling face, the composure she knew to be her best defence faltered, and she snapped, "Yes, a manufacturer. And not even a good one, Father says . . ."

"Ah well, if Father says . . ."

"Yes, he does. And there's no need to look so smug. He says you're a fly-by-night, whatever that may mean . . ."

"Oh, you know," he said, very much amused. "You know very well what it means. And so I am. But you can rest easy. I'll settle down—eventually—and work, not so hard as Nicholas, I grant you, but hard enough, so that when you marry your lord we'll have the money to pay off his mortgage and his gambling debts—"

"You'll do no such thing."

"Well, and if we don't, love, you'll have a poor time of it, for why else would a lord marry a tradesman's daughter?"

"My father," she said, quite viciously, her jaw clenching with the effort to hold back her temper, "is not a tradesman. And I'd like to hear you call him so, Blaize Barforth, to his face. Not that you ever would, for with all your airs and graces, you're still afraid of him, and so is Nicholas. You can grumble, the pair of you—Nicholas thinking he knows more about cloth manufacture than Father, and you pretending you don't care—but you'll always do as he tells you, just the same. And so you should, when you consider his position and everything he's done for you."

"Quite so," Blaize murmured, less mischievous now although a slight smile still touched the corners of his lips. "He's done a great deal for me. He's made a manufacturer of me, which is very splendid, provided that's what I like to be."

"Like it," she snorted, the duchess giving way now to the child I remembered who had never scrupled to use her fists—fierce and determined Caroline, with her belief, apparently by no means dead, that the Barforths were the greatest people in the world. "Like it? And what has liking to do with it? You'd better like it, for if you let him down I'll never forgive you. He's spent his whole life building Tarn Edge and Lawcroft Fold and Low Cross, and he's entitled, Blaize—he's entitled—"

"Entitled to what? My gratitude?"

"Yes, so he is. Your gratitude, and your labour."

And suddenly I saw a new Caroline emerge, or perhaps simply the old one—the real one—stripped of her genteel pretensions, a girl who, had she been born of an earlier generation, would have laboured alongside her men, a hardheaded, tough-fibred girl of the West Riding who would have brewed nettles for food when times were bad, who would have endured and overcome as those older Barforths had done, and who surely, in her heart, must secretly despise the airs and graces of that class above her own to which she now aspired.

"My word," she muttered, "if he could pass the mill on to me I'd take care of it for him. I'd be down there every morning, just like he is, to see the hands arrive on time and make sure the managers don't rob me—I'd—"

And as she paused breathlessly, painfully aware of her self-betrayal, Blaize smiled.

"Dear Caroline—good heavens—you'd be a manufacturer yourself, if you did that. Can you mean it?"

"Damnation," she said, a word I had never heard on female lips before, and clenching her fists in a gesture of total fury she jumped to her feet and swept away as regally as she could contrive.

"That was not kind of you, Blaize," I said serenely, no stranger to Barforth tantrums.

"No—but then, she'll forgive me, you know, since I am, after all, her favourite brother."

"Are you?"

"Oh yes—I do believe so. And it does her good to remember how proud she is of Father. Poor Father, I suppose he wishes she had been born a boy, for he declares I am not much use to him, and he cannot get on with Nicholas."

"Is it true that you don't like to be a manufacturer?"

"Gracious me," he said, laughing. "You look as shocked as if I had declared myself a Roman Catholic or a socialist. Do you know, I am not really sure whether I like it or not—and certainly I like the money it brings. And my brother Nicholas likes it well enough. You wouldn't catch him coming home in the middle of the day to change his clothes and slip over to Leeds, as I mean to do."

But here, it seemed, he was wrong, for as he lingered a moment on the sofa—asking me if there was anyone I had in mind to marry, asking how Prudence would manage to dispose of Jonas without being disposed of herself, most painfully, by Aunt Hannah—there was a step on the stair, and Nicholas came into view, a man decidedly in a hurry, his neckcloth a little awry, by no means disposed to linger. Seeing us, he stopped, stared, his eyes narrowing as if it surprised him, did not altogether please him, to find his brother sitting there in such merry, easy tête-à-tête with me. But, in the moment before I allowed myself to be flattered, I remembered that all their lives these two had wanted, instantly, anything which seemed to attract the other, had fought each other murderously for trifles, from the simple habit, bred in them by Uncle Joel, of competition, of proving, each one to himself, that he was first and best.

"Do I believe my eyes?" Blaize asked. "Brother Nicholas deserting his sheds in the middle of the day—?"

"Aye, you can believe it, since I was there all night. And even I feel the need of a clean shirt after sixteen hours."

And as Blaize got to his feet and sauntered away, looking as if the mere thought of a sixteen-hour stretch at the mill fatigued him, or bored him to death, Nicholas sat down in the exact spot his brother had vacated, at my side.

"Blaize hasn't been teasing you, has he?"

"Oh no. He's been teasing Caroline. He overheard her saying she didn't care for manufacturers and then trapped her into admitting she'd be the best one in the valley—if she'd been a boy."

He smiled, with no sudden, luminous brilliance like Blaize, but a slow, almost unwilling release of mirth that tilted his wide mouth into a smile, soon over, as if smiles, like time and money, were valuable and should not be squandered.

"Maybe she would. Better than Blaize, at any rate."

"Is he so bad?"

"Bad enough. He could manage all right if he wanted to. He knows how to go on. He just doesn't care."

"But you care? You like being a manufacturer, don't you, Nicholas?"

"Ah well," he said, leaning back against the red velvet upholstery. "I haven't got my brother's imagination. I've never thought about being anything else. It's there—a good business ready and waiting—and only a fool is going to turn away from that and go into something else just for the sake of making changes. Blaize is no different, when it comes down to it. He may not want to be a manufacturer but there's nothing else he wants to be either, and since he's nobody's fool, I reckon he'll take his share of the business when it comes to us. I'll just have to make sure he does his share of the work."

And he smiled at me again, by no means a man flirting, but a man who was willing to confide in me his shrewd assessment of his brother's character, his belief in his own good sense and ability, which would be enough, when it came to it, to bring Blaize into line.

"You're all right are you, Faith—I mean, here, with us?"

"Yes. I'm very well."

"I'm glad to hear it."

No more than that. He got up, offering only a half smile now, his mind already returning to whatever problem had detained him so long in the sheds, leaving me alone on the landing sofa. The house was very still, Aunt Verity out visiting somewhere, a hushed, lamplit tranquillity settling almost visibly around me as the early winter dark came peering through velvet-shrouded windows, the distant crackling of a dozen log fires keeping the cold at bay. Nothing had happened. Nicholas Barforth had sat down beside me, had spoken a few unremarkable words, given me his slow, quite beautiful smile, not once but twice, his hair very black against the red velvet sofa cushions, the handsome, sullen boy changed into a handsome, hardheaded man. His voice was still, somehow or other, in my ears. Nothing had happened at all. Yet I couldn't rid myself of the belief that at last—without my father to frown at it, without Miss Mayfield to spy on it—my life was about to begin.

Chapter Three

I WAS IN NO HURRY to return to our tall, cool house in Blenheim Lane and the chaperonage of our now considerably diminished Miss Mayfield. But Celia, feeling herself slighted by Caroline's attentions to me as she had felt slighted at Lawcroft Fold by Aunt Hannah's attentions to Prudence, soon began to fancy herself unwell, and although I suspected that had Caroline offered to drive her to town, or Blaize spent a minute or two with her on that red velvet sofa, she would have made a most rapid recovery, my cousins did not oblige, and there was nothing for it but to take her home.

Miss Mayfield, ready to do anything that would justify her continued employment, put her to bed, consoled her with herb-scented pillows and raspberry-leaf tea, dabbed at her forehead with aromatic vinegars, murmuring to her, no doubt, that she would soon have a husband to protect her from neglectful cousins, spiteful sisters, from the world's ills with which Miss Mayfield herself, a spinster lady of no fortune and some forty-five summers, was obliged to cope alone.

And although, just occasionally, I was aware of my father, stooping beside one of his cabinets, moving a fragile Meissen shepherdess a fraction nearer to her shepherd, an ivory-limbed nymph nearer to the light, his face pinching with its sudden ill-temper at the sight of a pair of Minton potpourri vases set a hairsbreadth askew, I found that if I stared at him hard enough his shadow would fade, that if I drew back the curtains to let in the sun he would go away, leaving me to enjoy this incredible luxury of having no one to please but myself.

Mrs. Naylor, our housekeeper, had her own work to attend to. Miss Mayfield, that fire-breathing schoolroom dragon who was sadly reduced now to a scampering little mouse without the prop of my father's authority, was too afraid of losing her place to make any real attempt to control us. Until Mother came home we were, quite incredibly, free, Celia having nothing to distract her from the imaginary music of her wedding bells, Prudence, no longer held in bondage by her embroidery frame, beginning gradually to assume command, ordering tea to suit her own convenience, not Mrs. Naylor's, making free use of the carriage in all weathers, at all hours, whether the coachman liked it or not, crisply ordering Miss Mayfield to "Tell Mr. Jonas Agbrigg I am not at home," whenever he happened to call.

"Oh, dear—dear me, Miss Prudence, this is the second time you have refused to receive him, and I could tell he was quite peeved about it. And what will Mrs. Agbrigg say, for you are to dine at Lawcroft tomorrow and cannot avoid seeing Mr. Jonas there."

"Well then, my dear," Prudence told her, clearly disinclined to listen to her nonsense, "you must write a note to Lawcroft explaining that I am not well enough to dine."

"Poor Miss Mayfield," I said as she hurried away, flustered and tearful. "She lives in terror that Aunt Hannah will accuse her of incompetence when Mother comes home. Poor soul. I hardly think Mother will turn her away, but how dreadful—at her age and with those nerves she is always complaining of—to be obliged to find another situation."

But Prudence's fine-boned, fastidious face held little sympathy.

"Then she should have taken care, long ago, to avoid such a position."

"She has no money, Prudence. She is forced to depend on someone."

"Exactly," she said, biting off the word like a loose embroidery thread. "I am glad you call it depending on someone rather than earning a living, for that perfectly describes her situation here."

"Father thought well of her."

"Yes, for she suited his requirements. She is a gentlewoman, you see, possibly a shade better-bred than we are since her father was a clergyman and her mother an attorney's daughter.

She was educated to be an ornament, and when her family fortunes declined and she could find no one to marry her, there was nothing else to do but hire herself out as a governess, so she could pass on her ornamental knowledge to others. She knows nothing, Faith. And neither do I. And I think that is why I am so hard on her. She has crammed me with embroidery stitches until they have turned my stomach. She has tittle-tattled about flowers and ferns until I can no longer bear the sight of either. She has marked my arithmetic correct when I have deliberately done it wrong to catch her out. And it strikes me that her notions of grammar change with the waxing and waning of the moon. She is ignorant, Faith, and so are we, which is just as it should be. Girls are meant to be ignorant, you know that, so they hire ignorant women to make sure of it, to stop us from asking awkward questions later, when we are married. Doesn't it worry you, Faith, that you know so little?"

"I try not to let it show."

"Well," she said flatly, "it does show. And when Jonas Agbrigg looks down his long nose at me and reduces his conversation to the simple words he thinks I can understand—well—I can't blame him, can I, however much it maddens me. And when Freddy Hobhouse offers me his arm and his protection I could laugh and cry at the same time, because he may be a man but, oh, dear, he's so simple. Believe me, the idea of spending a lifetime honouring and obeying a muttonhead like Freddy has a comic side to it."

"You mean to refuse them both, then?"

"I don't know what I mean to do. And I am in no hurry to decide. I have nothing against marriage—really, in some cases, one can see that it could be quite delightful. But to marry now, when I have seen nothing, when I know nothing—oh no. Why on earth should I end all my opportunities in that fashion? Celia may be ready to shut herself up in some man's drawing room and never come out again—and really, I think it would be the best place for her—but it wouldn't do for me. Not yet, at any rate. It strikes me that I could have rather a pleasant life, here, for a year or two, as a 'daughter-at-home' for I think I can find the way to manage Mother when she comes back again. Yes, indeed. At the end of a year or two I might have made something more interesting of myself than a china doll."

"You don't think of—falling in love?"

"Why?" she said. "Do you?"

And because there was no doubt of it and because it was as yet too precious, too uncertain to be held up to the light of day, I smiled, shrugged, pretended to hear carriage wheels suddenly, steps on the drive, and hurried to investigate.

The spring of that year saw the opening of Cullingford's branch line to Leeds, an event occasioning much excitement and rejoicing, among the manufacturing classes who most urgently required this new, rapid method of moving their goods, and among those of us who, with the price of a railway ticket at our disposal, were now provided with easy access to Liverpool and London and even the heady temptations of "abroad."

For twenty years and more the rutted, bone-shaking turnpike road from Cullingford to Leeds had been slowly sinking beneath the weight of carts heavy-laden with finished pieces, a slow, perilous, inadequate beginning of their journey to the markets of the world. For almost as long the canal, an even more leisurely process, had been a stinking, festering disgrace, unable to accommodate the requirements of a trading community which, in forty years, had eight times doubled its size.

Industrial machinery, the steam engine, the spinning frames, the power looms, had changed Cullingford from a nondescript market town of cottage industries and peaceful pleasures into an unco-ordinated, explosive sprawl where men like my uncle Joel had first devised and operated the factory system, herding the sudden influx of work-hungry field labourers and bread-hungry Irish to work together under one roof, arriving at an hour convenient not to them, but to him, taking their departure only when the specified daily quota was done. And every new invention, while bringing prosperity to some, had been the destruction of others. The spinning frames had forced Law Valley women to abandon their domestic wheels and take employment with men like the great worsted spinner Mr. Oldroyd, of Fieldhead, who expected long, hard labour for his wages. The power loom, which required only the hand of a woman or a child to operate, had forced Law Valley men to chop up their handlooms for firewood during the hungry winters when there was no work, leading them eventually—if they could get it—to take employment, submitting not always willingly to the tyranny of the mill and the millmaster, the stringent discipline of my uncle Joel's factory clock.

Cullingford, I knew, was a snarling, perilous place whenever trade was bad and resentment high, its streets uneasy with ill-fed men who, having spent their childhood working at the loom, had been discharged, more often than not, as soon as they grew old enough to ponder such matters as social justice or an increase in their wages, their employment taken by women who were concerned only that their children should be fed. And if our town was graced by the elegance of Blenheim Lane, mill-masters' palaces and the bright new villas of their managers, I could not be unaware that in the Irish quarter of Simon Street and Saint Street, whole families were living without light or water, without heat or hope, without anything I would be likely to recognise as food.

But even they, it seemed—the unemployable, the malcontents, the desperate, the weak, Irish and English, Catholic or of any other denomination—would benefit from the introduction of the railway, since this efficient means of transport, capable of carrying great numbers of people at a time, could be used to persuade them to emigrate, a fund for this purpose having already been started, to which Uncle Joel had contributed 1,000 pounds, although he had not stated, in my hearing, just where he wished to send them, nor what he proposed they should do there.

Uncle Joel, like my father, had always believed in the railway, although there had been great opposition to it from the very start. Those with a financial interest in the canals or the turnpike roads had declared it, from its conception, to be a great evil. Landowners, appalled at this desecration of the countryside, had soon convinced themselves and each other that the foul belching of trains would abort their cattle, fire their corn, distract their labourers from their proper duties. A few political notables, the Duke of Wellington and our own manorial lord, Sir Giles Flood, among them, had issued dire warnings that the railway would assist the working classes to congregate and air their grievances, or to receive visits from radical hot-heads who could explain to them what their grievances were.

Yet, as inevitably as the power looms, the railways had come snaking up and down the country, joining city to city, market to market, until Cullingford men could no longer tolerate that

bone-shaking turnpike to Leeds, and Parliament had been petitioned for the granting of a Cullingford and Leeds Railway Bill,
presenting engineers and investors alike with so many setbacks,
such a quantity of digging and tunnelling through the sharp-
sided, stony hills with which Cullingford was surrounded, so severe a plague of navvies, making their camps on the wasteland
beyond Simon Street, brawling and drinking their wages, that
our more sober citizens had found themselves in agreement with
the Iron Duke, while others had feared the project would never
end.

In April of the year my father died—too late for him to realise
his profits from the station and the station hotel—the Cullingford line was officially opened, the first train setting out at ten
o'clock of an uncertain, misty morning, ladened with cigars and
champagne and over a hundred of our town's most substantial
gentlemen, on its long-awaited journey to Leeds, that flatter,
smoother town, whose main lines to London and Liverpool
would set Cullingford free.

I had written a careful letter to my mother, still sojourning
abroad, suggesting she might care to witness the great event,
hoping, in fact, that she could be persuaded, on her return, to
put an end to our period of mourning. But, without exactly saying she would or would not come, she did not appear and I was
obliged to content myself with my eternal high-necked black
dress, and to subdue, as best I might, my envy of Caroline's
dashing blue and gold stripes, which I had chosen for her, and
the graceful, coffee-coloured flounces of Aunt Verity's lace.

I drove to the station in the Barforth landau, our own carriage
following behind with my sisters and Aunt Hannah who, as always, was anxious to save the legs of her own carriage horses
and unwilling to risk them in a crowd. But we arrived almost at
the same time, picking our way together through the elated,
flag-strewn station yard, a good half of its surface invisible beneath the marquee, erected overnight, to house the massive
luncheon of duck and turkey and thirty prime Yorkshire lambs
provided to refresh the travellers on their return; every other
available inch of space being crammed with carriages and carts,
with tall silk hats and plumed bonnets, with clogs and cloth caps
and shawls, with "good" children clinging sedately to parental
coattails, and "bad" children swarming everywhere, unsuper-

vised and dangerous, unsettling the horses and the tempers of the coachmen, a sticky-fingered, mud-spattering menace to frock coats and skirts alike.

The platform, to which we were admitted by invitation only, was a jubilation, more flags festooning the track on either side, two brass bands playing martial music in strident competition, the engine itself a brand-new marvel, boldly striped in red and black and gold, already quivering with its own terrifying capacity for speed, its iron-clad ability to endure as no carriage horses could ever do. And although I had made the coach journey to Leeds on several occasions in my father's austere company and boarded the London train, I knew that this engine was different and felt as thrilled—briefly—as the mill urchins who, slipping unbidden on to the platform, were being almost good-humouredly cuffed away.

We had no lord mayor as yet to shake the driver by the hand, but Uncle Joel, whose dress goods would dominate the freight trains and who had a great many railway shares in any case, was well equipped to perform the office, quite ready, should all run smooth, to remember the man's name and offer some suitable recompense. And, as the early veils of mist lifted, leaving only the pall of smoke which hung continually over our city—smoke to which we were well accustomed, of which we were even fond, since it was a visible announcement that our mills were working to capacity, that we were prosperous—the pale spring sun broke through, glinting on trumpets and drums, on gold watch chains and busily waving Union Jacks, catching the sparkle of Aunt Verity's diamonds, the lustre of Hobhouse and Mandelbaum pearls, the well-nourished smiles on those several hundred faces, as if the elements too wished to share our self-content.

And, without doubt, we had ample reason for contentment, for we, but a generation or two away from the weavers cottages, a life of toil and trouble with never a penny to spare, had invented, developed, operated the machines which had altered the fabric of our society. We, some of us rough-spoken still and hard-handed, all of us hardheaded, had built the factories at which the landed gentry shuddered, had made the fortunes at which they were amazed, since no commoners, before us had been able to compete with their affluence, had dared to demand a share of their privilege. And now this railway track, this engine, was ours, not theirs, made necessary and possible by the yarn we spun, the cloth we wove, by the industry and enterprise, the thrift, the stamina, the self-discipline of which we were so justly proud.

Everyone, of course, among that favoured platform party had desired to ride on Cullingford's first train, many had been disappointed, and we had talked of little else for weeks past. My uncle Joel's place had never been in question, nor that of Messrs. Hobhouse, Mandelbaum, Rawnsley, and Oldroyd, whose claims were almost as well substantiated. Sir Giles Flood of Cullingford Manor had been approached and had disdainfully refused, but his cousin, Sir Charles Winterton, who had property in Cullingford and debts in just about every other city in the West Riding, and whose son, "the Winterton boy," had now placed himself among the multitude of those who wished to marry Caroline, had been less disdainful. Mr. Corey-Manning, the lawyer, had eagerly accepted the invitation, despite his age and Aunt Hannah's loud-voiced opinion that he would do better to stand down in favour of Jonas; although, with Uncle Joel's help, she had secured a seat for Mr. Agbrigg, a triumph, she felt, which would assist immeasurably in his mayoral campaign.

The landlord of the Old Swan, our most important coaching inn, was to make the journey, a gesture, one felt, of recompense for the loss of business he would be bound to suffer when those fourteen coaches, which set off every day from his inn yard, became passengerless, obsolete. But competition for the remaining seats had been so murderous that when Uncle Joel had proposed taking his two sons, Mr. Mandelbaum his five, and Mr. Hobhouse had countered by proposing all ten of his, each gentleman had been limited to one son apiece—the eldest—and, in order to avoid a blood feud, all had eventually agreed.

Freddy Hobhouse, then, was to go and Jacob Mandelbaum, young Jack Rawnsley, and Benjamin Battershaw of Battershaw's light ales, and, to represent the next generation of Barforths, my cousin Blaize, a decision which had given rise to sharp words between Uncle Joel and Nicholas, who was exceedingly interested in trains, and between Nicholas and Blaize, who, while openly avowing his total indifference, seemed determined to make the trip if only to annoy his brother.

"Such a fuss," Caroline told me, wrinkling a fastidious nostril at the first whiff of engine smoke. "They agreed eldest sons, so eldest sons it must be, and one can hardly blame Blaize for being born first. It's not a question of whether one wants to go, it's a question of privilege. If one gets a good offer one takes it, it's as simple as that. I wouldn't have stepped down—if I'd been invited—for anybody."

But Nicholas, standing at the footplate with his father, seemed to be bearing his disappointment well enough, holding an animated, probably very technical conversation with a group of railway employees, his dark eyes keen and interested, the first sight of him causing my stomach to lurch in a most shocking fashion so that the whole of that raucous crowd was instantly reduced in my mind to a set of nondescript, wooden images; and Nicholas Barforth. And, for the life in me, I could not have said why.

The moment of departure, it seemed, was very near, drawing —as the favoured few began to climb aboard—an ear-splitting, cheek-bulging crescendo from the bands, a great whistling and steaming from the train, a tremor of anticipation that interrupted even Aunt Hannah's conversation with the wife of our new member of Parliament, whose good offices she was clearly seek n on her husband's behalf. There was a flutter of applause from correctly gloved, ladylike hands, a certain feeling of relief since the spring weather was unreliable, the sky clouding over again, and we had been standing rather a long time. A few flags began to wave, Mrs. Hobhouse took out a sentimental handkerchief and, for reasons unknown, dabbed at her eyes. My sister Prudence, anxious to avoid an invitation from Aunt Hannah to go back to Lawcroft with her—and Jonas—was already whispering a request that I should give up my place to her in the Barforth carriage, when Uncle Joel, instead of boarding the train, came striding towards us, cigar in hand. The crowd, who knew a man in a rage when it saw one, parted before him as he made directly for his wife.

"Where's Blaize?" he demanded, and Aunt Verity, the only person in the world, I think, who could have met his onslaught with so serene a smile, replied, "Darling—I couldn't say."

"He told me he was coming in the landau with you."

"Why no, dear. I was to call for Faith and had no room to spare."

"And he knew that? Yes, of course he did. So where is he then?"

"Joel," she said softly, very urgently. "Does it really matter?" And responding, it seemed, to her appeal, his jaw clenched suddenly, his whole powerful body stiffening with the effort to hold back his temper, not out of any consideration for the onlookers, the gossip, the fear of spoiling this great day, but for his wife's sake.

"I try, Verity," he said. "Believe me, I try not to let them provoke me—the pair of them—but, by God, sometimes, they go too far."

"I know, darling. They seem determined to prove just how far they *can* go. Don't worry about it now."

"We'll wait, then," he snapped, and striding back to the engine, exchanged a few words with Mr. Hobhouse, who had put his head enquiringly out of a window, and then paced, for a moment or two, along the platform, glancing first at his watch and then at the brand-new, impudently ticking station clock.

"We'll wait," I saw his mouth say to the startled railway officials who were now running after him, much concerned with their own watches, pausing apologetically at the windows, every one of which was filled by an important, impatient Law Valley head. While on the platform, although the bands continued to play, flags were lowered uncertainly, enquiries made. Had the engine broken down, then, before it had started, which would suit the landlord of the Old Swan if no one else? Had a tunnel caved in somewhere along the line, as a certain wisewoman of Simon Street had predicted it would? And even if it hadn't, Mrs. Hobhouse suddenly discovered she would be easier in her mind if Freddy—obediently installed beside his father—did not go after all. Or was it just Mr. Barforth, as usual, insisting on having everything his own way?

"Oh, dear," Aunt Verity murmured, a certain rueful amusement in her voice.

"What ails the man now?" Aunt Hannah demanded loudly, taking the opportunity to prove that however powerful her brother may be, she, at any rate, was not afraid of him.

"Nicholas," Caroline called out imperiously, beckoning him to her side. "I expect this is something you've cooked up together—you and Blaize—so if you know where he is you'd better say so."

"I don't know anything about it," he said flatly, and meeting his angry eyes, I felt a quick upsurge of satisfaction, not only at his closeness, but because if Blaize could not be found, then surely Nicholas would be allowed to go instead.

It would last, I thought, but a moment longer, for even Mr. Joel Barforth in full fury could not be oblivious of that engine steaming and straining at its leash, of the smiles slipping from even the most amiable faces, could not compel a hundred of Cullingford's most prosperous citizens to postpone their journey while he sent to fetch his eldest son, could not neglect the hundred others, waiting, on what now threatened to be a rainy day, on the platform in Leeds. And clenching his watch in a hand that shook with frustration—the unpalatable, amazing truth that he, of whom the whole of Cullingford stood in terror, could not always control his sons—he strode back to Aunt Verity, glaring first at her and then at Nicholas.

"Good God, Verity, this is intolerable."

"I know. You must go without him, Joel. And there may be a good reason."

"Aye—he may have taken a fall from that thoroughbred mare I bought him and broken his neck. But it's not likely."

"I do hope not."

"No—and he'll not be at the mill either, so engrossed in his work that everything else has slipped his mind. I can guarantee you that."

And turning to Nicholas, he said curtly, his voice amounting to a snap of the fingers, "All right, lad, you've got what you wanted. Get on board in his place."

That, of course, should have been the end of it. Had Nicholas been less a Barforth he would have jumped immediately on board, chuckling at his own good fortune and the retribution which must surely be in store for his brother. Had Uncle Joel been less a Barforth he would have issued the invitation a shade more graciously, since, in his heart, he was probably just as willing to take Nicholas as Blaize, and had, indeed, tried his best to take them both. But—unlike Blaize and Aunt Verity, who would always bend, most gracefully, with the wind—they were true Barforths, hard and unyielding, who would take the wind by brute force, if they could, to suit their own purposes, or die in the attempt. And as Uncle Joel began to turn away, considering the matter closed, Nicholas said very quietly, "I don't think I can do that, sir."

"Don't you, by God!" his father answered him, his lips barely moving. And as those nearest to us began to press closer, eager to witness the stag-antlered combat of the Barforth males, which was becoming a legend in the valley, Aunt Verity put a hand on her husband's arm, her whole body flowing towards him in urgent, loving intervention.

"Not here, Joel. Please, darling—"

But, realising that he could see nothing now beyond his conflict with his sons, with Nicholas, a man like himself, too stubborn in his pride to care for retribution, I cannot believe she hoped to prevail.

And for a very long time, or so it seemed, with curious, envious, malicious Cullingford buzzing and bustling all around them, they stood and measured one another, a raw contest of wills that tightened the air.

"You'll get on that train, Nicholas."

"Hardly, sir."

"Nicholas—you'll do it."

"I don't see how I can, sir. Eldest sons—that's what you decided. No exceptions, no matter what the circumstances, that's what you told me when I asked. And I'm needed at the mill because it won't run itself. You told me that too."

And knowing of old that he would have to haul Nicholas by the scruff of his neck into that train—and wondering, perhaps, if, at fifty years of age, he could still manage it—my uncle snarled something very low, doubtless very obscene, and with a gesture that struck terror certainly into my heart, strode away.

No one spoke to Nicholas as the flags began to wave again, the train to draw slowly out of the station, Mr. Hobhouse beaming jovially from his window, Mr. Mandelbaum from his. No one spoke to him as he shouldered a way for us through the crowded station yard to our carriages, although we all spoke heartily, quite falsely, to one another.

"I am so glad the rain has kept off," Aunt Verity said.

"Yes, I knew it would," Aunt Hannah replied. "I had quite made up my mind to it."

"It would have ruined the marquee otherwise," I offered, trying to play my part.

"I think I have taken cold," Celia whimpered.

"Nonsense," Prudence told her. "It is only that you like to think so."

Caroline, taking off her gloves and putting them on again with great deliberation, no doubt to stop her hands from fastening around her brother's throat, said not a word. But when we were settled in the carriage and Nicholas, for whom no place could be found, stood alone at the step, raising his hat to us, I was unable —whether he had been right or wrong—to do other than call out, "Good-bye, Nicholas," earning myself a smile from Aunt Verity and a glare of pure contempt from Caroline.

We were to dine at Tarn Edge that evening, three little blackbirds in our mourning dresses among the peacock splendours of Aunt Verity's guests, arriving to find her as serene as ever, Nicholas and Blaize showing no obvious scars, even Caroline smiling again at everyone but the Winterton boy on her right, and the Mandelbaum boy attached just as firmly to her left.

Dinner at Tarn Edge was always a formal occasion. We were met in the hallway by an array of servants, who removed our cloaks as reverently as if they were of the finest sable, escorted to the drawing room door by a butler as suave and benign as any bishop, who, having known us all our lives, invariably announced us as if we had been the most opulent of strangers.

"Miss Aycliffe. Miss Faith Aycliffe. Miss Celia Aycliffe." And we would advance straight-backed, mindful of our lessons in deportment, across what had often seemed to me an acre of blue and gold carpet to shake hands with our host and hostess. There would be a hushed half-hour then, a quick appraisal of gowns and jewels, while Aunt Verity made soft-voiced introductions and my uncle, majestically circulating, informed each gentleman which lady he must take in to dine.

He led the way that evening with Lady Winterton, who, as a representative of the landed gentry, must be considered the most distinguished lady present and probably thought herself the only real lady there at all. Blaize took Miss Rebecca Mandelbaum,

Nicholas Miss Amy Battershaw of Battershaw light ales, a circumstance which did not please me, even though Amy Battershaw—a close friend of Celia's—was sallow and silly, and one
did not expect the son of the house to be wasted on a cousin.
Prudence went in with Jonas. I accompanied Freddy Hobhouse,
whose mother, despairing perhaps of Prudence, had decided
that my 20,000 pounds, without the porcelain, would suffice,
while Celia, who had first declared herself too ill to come at all
and then wept copiously because we had not begged her to
change her mind, was left to a younger Hobhouse boy, an arrangement not at all to her taste—since Adolphus Hobhouse
could entertain no thoughts of marriage until Freddy should be
settled—and which would cause her to grumble all the way
home that, once again, she had been slighted.

Caroline accompanied the Winterton boy, Aunt Verity his father, Sir Charles, a distinction perfectly understood by all, for although the Wintertons were known to be losing their money, the
rest of us to be making ours, they were the possessors of that
one commodity beyond our reach, the privilege not of hard cash
but of pedigree.

Winterton land, no matter how sadly mortgaged, had been
handed down to them through generations when Barforths and
Hobhouses alike had been no more than common weavers.
There had been a Winterton at Waterloo commanding a regi-
ment when Uncle Joel's father had been struggling, at the then
almost bankrupt Low Cross Mills, to keep himself above the
precarious level of the ordinary workingman. No Winterton had
ever soiled his hands with trade, had ever bought or sold anything but acreage, bloodstock, the occasional work of art,
whereas my uncle Joel, even now, would not hesitate to roll up
his fine cambric shirt sleeves and dirty his own hands whenever
the need arose, nor to buy and sell anything, provided he could
do so to his own advantage. And although the present Sir
Charles, while privately considering my uncle to have no more
social standing than a village blacksmith, was ready to dine at
the Barforth table, ready, even, to permit the common, trading
blood of the Barforth daughter to mingle with his own, if the
price was right, he was, nevertheless, a landed gentleman, to
whom our grandfathers would have instinctively doffed their
caps, and we were still, I believe, a little in awe of him.

Uncle Joel's dining room, like everything about him, was on
the very grandest scale, panelled from floor to ceiling in wood
that had the sheen and colour of ebony, its sombre expanse broken by gilt-framed, oval portraits of Aunt Verity and Caroline,
and by a row of long windows draped ornately in white muslin
and velvet of the richest, darkest red. The table, set between two
ebony-coloured sideboards, was a masterpiece, a foamy white
lace cloth garlanded with ferns and mosses, trails of ivy from
candelabra to candelabra, primrose-tinted candles gleaming on
silver and crystal, pyramids of spring flowers, daffodils and pale
narcissi, the delicacy of violets, the bold, brave stripings of the
tulip. And, for the space of two hours, while Freddy Hobhouse,
forgetting that the principal duty of a dinner party is conversation, crunched his way through salmon and whitebait, beef ol-
ives, quails and plovers, creams and sponge cakes and tarts, I sat
and thought, mainly, of Nicholas.

Sitting beside Amy Battershaw—how was it that I had once
thought her a pleasant enough girl?—he was assisting her, quite
correctly, in the arduous task of dining. He had made sure she
was comfortably seated, had himself retrieved her gloves when
she had somewhat wildly abandoned them, had indicated her
menu card, hiding, in its silver-filigree holder, among the forest
of crystal bordering her plate, and then, knowing her to be
shortsighted, had read it aloud to her, suggesting—as a son of
the house who knew the specialties of his mother's cook—which
dishes she might like to attempt. But Miss Amy Battershaw,
whose governess, like ours, had taught her that a lady's appetite
must be no bigger than a sparrow's, had most likely taken the
precaution of stuffing herself with muffins and gingerbread before leaving home, and, in the approved fashion, could manage
nothing but a morsel of this, a spoonful of that, a simpering, fluttering sip of champagne.

Odious girl, I thought, allowing my own champagne glass to
be refilled to the brim, glancing from Miss Battershaw to
Rebecca Mandelbaum, who was playing the same charade with
Blaize, and only a look of pure horror from my sister Celia,
whose appetite was indeed very small, stopped me from accepting a second helping of chocolate cream.

Odious girls, all of them, dressed-up little dolls—and badly
dressed at that—too much beribboned and curled, too sugar-

plum sweet, too good to be true, and, surprised at my own
savagery when only last week I had been perfectly happy to
take a carriage drive with Amy and had thought Rebecca's performance at the piano most skilful, I realised, quite abruptly,
that just as the male population had become divided between
Nicholas and those who were not Nicholas, so had the world's
females grouped themselves into those who might, and those
who might not take him from me.

Not that I, in any way, considered him mine. Not that I had
so far considered anything but the odd sensation his presence
brought me. Certainly I had not yet paused to ask myself why I
had chosen to care for Nicholas, who was, without doubt, every
bit as stubborn and quick-tempered as everyone said, instead of
for Blaize, who was charm personified, or for any other man. I
had not asked myself if, perhaps, it could be nothing more than
an extension of my childhood sympathy for the younger brother
who had always had to work harder, play harder, than his dazzling senior to obtain the same degree of praise. I had asked myself no questions at all. But how many of us, at seventeen, care
overmuch for reasons?

The meal ended, leaving no more than a vague impression of
excellence on my tongue and, rising in obedience to Aunt
Verity's signal, I returned to the drawing room where coffee was
already waiting, accompanied by baskets of cakes for those of us
—like Miss Amy Battershaw—who had not wished to eat too
heartily in the presence of gentlemen. But Caroline, quickly
bored by any gathering of women, soon made a signal of her
own which took us both upstairs to our cosy, confidential sofa.

"That's better," she said, "for I cannot bear to hear the old
hens tittle-tattling. I expect you saw Lady Winterton keeping a
place for me beside her?—well, and so she might, for her
Francis is becoming very persistent, and, for all her title and her
breeding, she is pushing him at me just as eagerly as Mrs. Battershaw with her Benjamin. Well—as to Francis Winterton—
maybe I shall and maybe I shan't. But what is certain is that it
won't be until I've convinced Father to give me a proper London
season and a trip to Paris. And it won't be difficult, especially
now that I'm altogether his favourite child."

"There was bloodshed then—when your father got back from
Leeds?"

"As you might expect."

"And they are both in disgrace?"

"Oh yes, except that Nicholas caught it the most, as he always does, and I can perfectly understand why. Really, Faith, there's no reason for you to look so surprised, since it was Nicholas, after all, who shamed Father in public. My word, it seems Mr. Hobhouse spent the entire journey giving Father advice on how to bring up sons, and you can't expect Father to forgive Nicky for that. And, of course, the whole point of the exercise was that Blaize never intended to go in the first place. He doesn't care about trains, but if he'd said as much and offered to give up his place to Nicholas, Father would just have gone on muttering about eldest sons only and refused to allow it. So Blaize played their game, like he always does, and then, when the time came, he just wasn't there. He knew Nicholas would be at the station and that Father would offer to take him. It was his way of making Nicholas a present. And Nicholas knew it well—oh yes—and so did Father, because Blaize is always doing that kind of thing. It's his style exactly. All Nicholas had to do was jump on board and by the time they got home Father would have forgotten all about it. But Nicholas, of course, had to stand there growling back at Father just to prove to himself that he dared, going too far as always and then too stubborn to back down. Hasn't that always been his way? And you've always felt so sorry for him, Faith. I can't think why, since he's perfectly able to fend for himself."

We came downstairs together, Caroline walking a step or two ahead in her determination to be first at the drawing room doors, since she could not be certain I would stand aside to let her pass. But, as she made her entrance, I felt an all too familiar movement at the back of my head, the dread sensation of hairpins coming loose, and, judging my plight too urgent for the upstairs journey to Caroline's bedroom, took refuge in the back parlour, situated at the end of the passage behind the stairs.

There was a mirror there, high above the mantelpiece, a degree of privacy, since only a habitué of the house would be likely to use this room. Standing on the fender, my skirts swinging perilously towards the grate and the small fire appropriate to a spring evening, I had shaken my hair loose, combing through it with hurried, unkind fingers, when the door opened, snapped shut again, and Nicholas stood there, scowling at my back, the set of his jaw and the irritable, down-drooping line of his mouth saying to me very clearly, "Good God, is there no peace in this house?"

"Faith, what on earth are you doing here?"

And, from an excess of wanting to be warm and encouraging, my answer came out cold, clipped, and distant.

"As you see, my hair is coming down—which is a great nuisance."

"I do see that. And unless you get down from that fender you are bound to set your skirts on fire, which would be an even greater nuisance."

"Really—do you think so?"

"I am sure of it."

"Well then, I will just have to take my chance and prove you wrong, since I need the looking glass."

"Evidently," he said, as curt and sarcastic as he always was in the face of mild annoyance, of foolish young girls who intruded on his desire for a moment's peace and quiet and disregarded his good advice. But nothing, now, would induce me to leave my precarious perch until my task was done, no matter how right he was, no matter how anxious I had now become about the small but vigorously burning fire. And having good reason to recognise stubbornness when he saw it, he said quickly, "Look here, Faith, do get down. There have been disasters enough today. You could spare me another, for if you roast they will surely manage to blame me for it."

"Oh, if it is yourself you are thinking of I will get down at once. I should not wish to cause you a moment's unease."

"That is very good of you."

"So it is. And I have finished now in any case, without so much as a scorched hem, so I will say good night to you, Nicholas."

"Yes. Good night."

But, as I got down from the fender and faced him, knowing, behind the protective shield of my hostility and my cool Aycliffe manner, that in ten minutes' time, back in the drawing room, I would be grief-stricken and furious at this lost opportunity, something penetrated the fog of his ill-humour, drawing through it his unwilling, rueful smile.

"Oh, dear, poor Faith. Will you never learn to manage your hair? I have seen you like this many a time when we were children, spilling hairpins—and do you know, I believe we once sat behind you in church, Blaize and I—do you remember?—at somebody's wedding?—and undid your hair ribbons . . . ?"

"Yes, I remember. I'm not likely to forget it, nor the scolding it earned me afterwards."

"Well, I'm sorry for that. You could have said it was our fault, you know. I reckon that's what we expected you to do. I thought only boys were brought up not to tell tales, and that girls were allowed to tittle-tattle as much as they pleased. Caroline always does."

"Perhaps she has a lot to tell tales about."

"Aye," he said, his gloom shredding clean away, to be replaced by a most decided, most unexpected grin. "I reckon she might."

And it was unfortunate that we were still smiling at each other when the door was thrust open again and Uncle Joel, wreathed in cigar smoke and bad temper, stood there, seeing not a pair of cousins alone together by chance, reminiscing about a shared childhood, but a young man, his earlier misdemeanours by no means forgiven, who had now committed the further crime of neglecting his mother's guests in the company of a marriageable and apparently flirtatious young lady. And until I saw it in his face I had truly forgotten the enormous damage that a few moments alone with any young man could inflict upon my reputation.

He came into the room, shutting the door behind him, sealing it with his powerful, impenetrable presence, and stood for a moment in silence, his hard face so furious and yet so satisfied that I knew he wanted to think ill of us, and would not listen to reason.

"Father—" Nicholas said, his own face hard too, yet the fact he had spoken at all betrayed his alarm, and I knew, through my own, dry-mouthed panic, that whatever we were to be accused of, he would be made to suffer for it the most.

"It occurred to me," my uncle said, "that you had been a long time away. And I ask myself why I am surprised to find you in these circumstances."

"I think you mistake the circumstances, sir."

"I think I do not."

"I insist that you do."

"You are in a position to insist, are you?"

"Possibly not. But just the same, I must ask you to hear my explanations."

"I do not choose—" Uncle Joel began, but seeing the black, snarling anger in his face, which did not mean to be cheated of its outlet, and the answering snarl in Nicholas, more than ready to offer the combat his father clearly required, I took a hasty step forward, knowing full well that this, being an extension of what had occurred earlier at the station, had very little to do with me, but compelled, nevertheless, to intervene.

"Uncle Joel—please—my hair was coming down, which happens to me often enough. I came to use the looking glass—"

"And my son followed you."

"He certainly did not. He was not even pleased to see me—"

But it had not been a question, merely a statement of what he intended to believe, and I was appalled when Nicholas, raising his shoulders in a careless shrug, announced suddenly, "Of course you are quite right, sir, as always. I did follow her here, with the most questionable of motives, which, unfortunately for me, she did not share. So I am entirely to blame and I think you may allow Faith to return—unscathed—to her sisters."

"Oh, Nicholas," I said, "Nicholas," and for a moment there was nothing to do but watch, fascinated and terrified, as they stood quite still, jaws clenched, mouths down-drawn with their fierce, knife-edged anger, a clashing of identical wills, my own will flickering feebly between them, pale and insignificant, perhaps, but persistent, since I was half a Barforth too.

"Back down, Nicholas," my will pleaded. "Please—back down, as Blaize would do. There's no shame. He wouldn't think ill of you. In fact I believe he'd like to back down himself and can't. Do it for him, because he's older, and it would be easier for you." And when I saw that he would stand his ground, not yielding an inch, totally regardless of consequences—as his father would have done at his age—I murmured, "Uncle Joel—" striving to remind him that he couldn't really thrash his son in the hearing of his wife's guests, and that if he did many of them would be only too pleased about it.

"Quite so," he said, apparently reading my mind, an iron lid almost visibly descending over his temper, clamping it down. "Well then, for the present, my lad, you had best go back and show your face in the drawing room. And you'd best look pleasant while you're about it, for I'll not have your mother upset again. And as for you, young lady, your father had a word to say to me on your account before he died. I well remember it, and it strikes me I may have a word of my own for your mother—should she ever decide to come home."

And turning abruptly, letting the door slam shut behind him, he was gone.

I was, for a dreadful moment, consumed entirely by embarrassment, hot and sticky with it, painfully aware that this could in no way endear me to Nicholas, who would be very likely to save himself from further awkwardness by ignoring me entirely.

"Don't worry," he said quietly, not looking at me, staring instead at the square of carpet his father had just vacated. "He will say nothing to your mother, nor to anyone else. By the time he reaches the end of the passage he will have realised how trivial his behaviour has been, and he may well make himself very pleasant when he sees you again. He may even buy you a present to make amends, for that is how I got my chestnut mare, and Blaize his bay. You are quite safe."

"Oh, heavens—I don't care about that."

"But I care about it. I don't wish to upset you, Faith. And, as it happens, neither does he—not really. You were just there, at a time when he needed an excuse to be angry, and he has a great talent for making the most of whatever he finds to hand."

"I'm not upset. I'm just sorry—and Nicholas, do tell me, you really wanted to take that train today, didn't you?"

"Oh that," he said, dismissing it. "That precious train. Yes, of course I wanted to take it. Didn't everybody?"

"Blaize didn't."

"Only because Blaize likes to be different. And I refused to take his place because I am the jealous younger son who doesn't care to pick up his brother's leavings—and because I wished to annoy my father. Isn't that what Cullingford is saying?"

"Yes, and I wonder that you should have given them the opportunity, especially if you wanted to go . . ."

"Yes," he said, very low. "Why should I deny myself the very thing I wanted? That is what Blaize thought. He meant to give up his place to me from the start. I realise that. He'd gone to a lot of trouble for me, even fixed himself up with an alibi at the mill—some tale of his being needed in the sheds, which takes a lot of believing— But there you are; I was offended, or perhaps I didn't want to be manoeuvred—or I was just pigheaded. And I reckon I'll behave just as badly the next time—we all will. You should go back now, Faith, or Aunt Hannah may be the next one to find us—and she'd really believe what Father only pretended to believe."

"Yes, I'll go back. And you? He said you were to come too."

"Yes. But we can hardly go back together. Tell him 'presently' if he asks, which he won't. Good night, Faith. You'd better run."

And for the rest of the evening, while Prudence made her cool replies to Jonas, and Celia tried hard to find someone to care that her head was aching, I sat in silence, contemplating that, whether it had been for good or ill, something real, something that far exceeded the expectations of my milk and water girlhood, had entered my life. As I had hoped, and prayed, life was beginning, expanding, unrolling itself before me like some vast fabric woven with hope and opportunity, with a hundred brightly shaded threads of possibility, with Nicholas: and I was more than ready.

Chapter Four

THE SUMMER, that year, presented us with two events worthy of mention, the eighteenth birthday of Miss Caroline Barforth, and the repeal of the Corn Laws, those hated measures invented by the gentry to be a scourge and an abomination to all commercial men.

Introduced at the end of Napoleon's wars to keep out the cheap foreign corn and protect the landowners, who had been charging as much as they pleased for their own crops while the French blockade lasted, this legislation had caused enormous hardship in the industrial cities during all the years since Waterloo. For when the price of corn rose, the price of bread rose with it, and when the cost of a loaf was high and incomes low, the only results could be hunger, resentment, violence sometimes in places like Simon Street, when Uncle Joel and others like him refused to pay higher wages, and put money, indirectly, into the pockets of the squires.

Nor had the farmers themselves—or, at least, the smaller ones—benefited greatly, since men reduced to beggary could not pay their price, forcing them, in their turn, to sell out to the big landowners, and to join the ranks of the landless poor, many of whom found their way, annually, to Cullingford. And, in the year my father died, thousands of men, women, and children in the richest, most rapidly expanding country in the world, were being kept alive—only just—by the haphazard, not always gentle hand of charity.

I had grown accustomed to tales of agricultural workers, the very ones who harvested the protected grain, dying of starvation in their cottages, of handloom weavers who, in this machine age, could not earn the coppers necessary to keep body and soul together, expiring at their looms of the same dread disease. I knew that whenever the winter was harsh, the spring late and inclement, the summer cool and soon over, producing a poor harvest, or no harvest at all, that corpses would be discovered under the hedgerows, or picked up in our own, littered back alleys, the pathetic remains of men who had gone on the tramp to look for work, and had failed.

Free Trade, clearly, was the only answer. My father had fought for it all his political life, had promised it, at the hustings, in every electoral address. Free Trade, cheap bread, an end to the Corn Laws, were the only answers, but our current political masters, Sir Robert Peel—who had not endeared himself to us by reintroducing income tax at the terrible rate of seven pence in the pound—and his closest associate, the ancient, aristocratic Duke of Wellington, who believed that industrialists, like all other upstarts, should learn to know their place and mend their manners, had proved impossible to convince.

Elected by a party of country squires to serve the interests of country squires—to ensure that Englishmen ate English corn or no corn at all—they had, for years, resisted all pressures from the industrial towns, and we had needed Ireland, where more than a quarter of the population were entirely destitute and the rest not too much better off, to present a situation where the choice could only be cheap food, or the most bloody revolution.

The Irish had long been with us in Cullingford, coming in boatloads and cartloads, barefoot and desperate and alarmingly prone to multiply, escaping from famine in 'Derry and Kildare to famine in Simon Street, since even our weaving sheds—where mainly women and children were required in any case—could not accommodate them all. But, in the year before my father died, the potato crop quite inexplicably began to rot in the fields, bringing hardship to poor men in England, who relied heavily on potatoes for food, bringing panic and chaos to poor men in Ireland, who had no other food on which to rely.

And, as Ireland began its death agony, and unrest at home began to simmer—yet again—into a revolutionary brew, the radical leaders making full use of the railways, as the Duke of Wellington had always said they would, to muster their forces

together, it became clear—apparently even to Sir Robert Peel—
that if the people were to be fed and pacified, then the foreign
corn must be allowed to flow.

"Peel cannot do it," his startled, landowning friends said of
him in London.

"He will not do it," we had declared scornfully in Cullingford,
for, having risen to power as a staunch protectionist, we knew
that his own party would not support him, that his own career
was at stake, the flamboyant, fast-rising Mr. Disraeli having already dubbed him a turncoat and a traitor, even the Duke of
Wellington, who disliked reform of any kind and thought the
Corn Laws rather a good thing, holding himself aloof.

Even then, had the next year's potato crop shown a healthy
face, perhaps Sir Robert would have hesitated, modified, compromised, saved his face and his prospects, as, indeed, we all expected him to do. But the new season's potatoes were as black as
their predecessors. The remnants of the Irish people—those who
had neither starved nor emigrated to Cullingford—were living
on weeds and nettles and a murderous hatred of certain English
landlords who, apparently unaware of the famine, went on
insisting that their rents should be paid, and issuing eviction notices when it wasn't. And so, Sir Robert Peel, well aware that his
own career would probably be demanded as a sacrifice, forced
his Bill for Repeal of the Corn Laws through a hostile House of
Commons, persuaded the Duke of Wellington, who still did not
believe in it, to put it before a well-nigh hysterical House of
Lords.

"God damn the traitor Robert Peel," they said of him in the
agricultural shires, the manor houses, the green and pleasant
corners of our land.

"So he's seen sense at last," they said in the Old Swan, the
Piece Hall, the factory yard. "And not before time, either."

And although Peel himself was forced, predictably, to resign
his premiership soon after, the ports at last were open, bread
would be cheap again, cheapening the cost of labour with it,
and Cullingford cloth—Barforth cloth—could be acknowledged
as the marvel it was in every corner of the world.

"We should do something for Sir Robert Peel," Aunt Hannah
announced at the Repeal Dinner—one of many—which she had
organised in celebration. "We asked the poor man for Free

Trade, and now that he has given it to us and ruined himself in the process, it would seem appropriate to put aside our grievances about the income tax and write him a word of thanks. It would be a graceful gesture on our part and may do him a world of good—for he can't quite like being out of office. I know I shouldn't like it."

And, since Aunt Hannah had a draft letter, in Jonas' elegant copperplate, most conveniently to hand, it was considered, agreed, signed Barforth, Hobhouse, Oldroyd, Mandelbaum—not Winterton, of course, and certainly not Flood, since both these gentlemen would be fully occupied now in trying to sell their corn as best they could on a free market—and despatched.

"The dear man has sent a most cordial reply," Aunt Hannah told us a few weeks later, "although I hardly know what may be done with it, since we have no town hall, no official building of any kind in which to display it," and it was no surprise to us that when Sir Robert's correct, somewhat stilted letter had been passed from hand to hand, it made its final appearance, neatly framed and pressed, neither at Nethercoats nor Tarn Edge, but in Aunt Hannah's own drawing room at Lawcroft Fold.

My mother returned home for Caroline's birthday dance, descending upon us unlooked-for one afternoon, delighted with our surprise, although I did not miss the faint wrinkling of her nose as she entered the drawing room, the gesture of one who, having grown accustomed to sunshine and sea breezes, did not at all relish the taste of stale air again.

"How dark it is," she said. "Will the curtains really not open any wider? No, I suppose not, but then, it is so light abroad—France all sparkle, and Italy so pink and gold, that I had forgotten how grey— Ah well, that was yesterday and now I am quite recovered from my ills and come home to introduce myself to my daughters—for, really, girls, we have been sadly little acquainted. See, I have brought you all a present, lots of presents . . ."

And suddenly her magpie hands were full of froth and glitter, pink silk and blue silk, bracelets and earrings of coral and enamel and tiny seed pearls, feather fans and lace fans, and extravagant lengths of embroidered, foreign-looking brocade.

"I thought you would want something to wear—I always did so at your age—and, unless you particularly desire to continue it, it strikes me you may leave off your weeds now. Six months, is it not? My word, six months. Well, I must stay in black for another year and more, and then run through all the shades of grey and lavender, but you are not widows, after all, but young ladies who are allowed to be vain. Goodness, Faith, these blue bows and sashes and little rosebuds will do admirably for Celia, but you are so—so grown, I suppose. Dear girl, no one in Venice would ever believe you to be my daughter. A sister, perhaps, for you have my eye and hair colour—which is something very much out of the ordinary in Venice, I do assure you. And yes—in other ways too, dear—I believe you are turning out to resemble me."

"Hardly, Mamma. I am inches taller, and my nose is much too big."

"Yes, but such details, you know, do not really signify. A clever woman learns how to create an illusion—"

"Father said I was the one most like you," Celia cut in, tossing her head to set her ringlets dancing, determined, for once in her life, to win her fair share of attention.

"Yes, dear," my mother said absently, not even glancing at her. "You are a positive enchantment. And, Prudence—good heavens —you remind me of someone I have not seen for ages—a relative of your father's."

"She means you remind her of our brother," Celia said later, imparting the information because, our brother having been sent away in disgrace, she could not believe it to be a compliment. But my mother, whose understanding was sharper than one at first supposed, soon made amends to Celia by smothering her in all the lace and ribbons she could desire, and to Prudence by paying her the compliment of leaving her alone, while she and I soon formed a relationship which hung tenuously but pleasantly on our shared enthusiasm for fashion.

"One must develop a style," she told me. "One chooses not to copy, but to be copied—a dear friend in Paris told me that, although I had always suspected it and behaved accordingly. You are tall and so, since you cannot shrink, you must make yourself look taller—simple, classical lines, bold colours, or plain white, and no fuss, and a bonnet, I think, when you are a little older, with a positively towering feather. What fun. I was never allowed to dress you up when you were small. There was always a

Miss Mayfield to do that. And as for your nose, dear, and the fact that your mouth is rather wide, you must cultivate an air of feeling so sorry for all these poor girls who are cursed with rose-bud lips and button noses and dimples. If you appear to like what you have, dear, even if they don't quite like it themselves, at the very least, it will make them wonder."

For Caroline's birthday dance my sister Celia had a dress of palest pink gauze, its flounced skirt strewn with knots of silver ribbon and sprays of pink and white flowers; Prudence a more restrained outfit of pale blue which, with its touches of cream-coloured lace and her tall, straight figure, gave her a quiet, but most decided elegance. My dress was white, a swan, I'd thought dreamily, as our seamstress had pinned the vast skirt into place —"Too plain," Celia had told me—a white flower at the waist, another at the shoulder—"White is for brunettes," Celia had said, "Everybody knows that"—my hair dressed low on the nape of my neck in one massive coil with a single white rose at its centre, a chignon devised by my mother to look so heavy that anyone who noticed it would be aware that my neck was long and slender and might miss the fact that my nose and mouth were of a corresponding size. I had pearl droplets in my ears, a broad velvet ribbon embroidered with pearl clusters around my throat, a pair of wide-spaced, worried, shortsighted blue eyes above it, since I was by no means so confident of this unusual outfit as I pretended, feeling, in fact, as the time of our departure grew imminent, that although these classical lines and colours might be all the rage in Venice, Cullingford was far too accustomed to seeing its young ladies in sugar-pink gauzes and ribbons—like Celia—to be anything other than puzzled.

My mother, who should not have attended a dance at all until her mourning period was over, or, if she managed to justify it on the grounds of family commitment and chaperonage, should have been excessively discreet about it, appeared in a black gown of the most stunning extravagance, cut as low as she dared, its flounced skirt encrusted with jet beads, her blond head crowned by black plumes and swathes of spotted black net de-signed, undoubtedly, to supply Cullingford with gossip for many a long day.

"Aunt Hannah will not approve of that," Prudence told her as we were about to set off, her light eyes very much amused, but my mother merely patted the black rose placed strategically and most enticingly at her bosom, and smiled.

"Ah well, dear, Aunt Hannah finds so very much of which to disapprove that one may suspect she enjoys it. And if I cannot win her favour then there is always Aunt Verity, who is the most elegant of women, and who will not have forgotten the value of a wisp of perfumed chiffon. Yes, girls, you may stare, but I remember your aunt Verity, in the days before she fell into such a trance of love for Uncle Joel, wearing a gown—my goodness, such a gown, this one of mine would look staid beside it. Yes, a wisp of perfumed chiffon, no more, I do assure you, with gold sandals on her feet and a gold ribbon through her hair. Lord— how everyone stared, and with good reason, for when a woman uncovers her shoulders and paints her toe nails one may be sure she intends it to be noticed. And I may have been the only person in the Assembly Rooms that night who understood her reasons; certainly her husband did not for I well remember how he scowled at her, as black as thunder. Yes, you may find it hard to realise that your aunts—and your mother—have had their share of heart-searchings, in their younger days. Ah well, it is long ago now. Everything has been settled on that old score. And I imagine Aunt Hannah may be too preoccupied with your appearance this evening, Prudence, to give much thought to mine. Oh, dear, have I said something amiss, for if I did not know you to be incapable of such bad manners, I would almost think you were glaring at me."

"Naturally not, Mamma," Prudence said, her face sharpening. "May I take it that you have heard something concerning me and Jonas Agbrigg? If so, then I must tell you—"

"Oh no, dear, please tell me nothing. I have every confidence in you, Prudence, and whether you mean to take him or not to take him—well—I am sure you are quite right either way—"

But Prudence, who had grown so brisk and businesslike of late, so very conscious of her rights and so very determined to preserve her new, hitherto undreamed-of liberty, slowly shook her head, detaining my mother with a gesture of authority unthinkable in my father's lifetime.

"No, Mamma, that is hardly enough. You must offer me a little more guidance, or show me a little more involvement than that.

Am I to understand that Mr. Jonas Agbrigg meets with your approval?"

"My dear, he is stepson to my own sister, and I can do no more than share her golden opinions. Of course he has no money, but he has the air of a man determined to succeed—I can only tell you that your father believed he would succeed—I forget at what—politics, I believe, of which your father was very fond. Power, you know, is very attractive to some men—and to some women also. And should you care to be the wife of a powerful man Jonas may be a reasonable choice. Freddy Hobhouse will never be powerful, my dear, and he would spend your money far more recklessly than Jonas. He has nine brothers to settle in life, after all, and four sisters to marry, and your dowry, divided among them, would not seem so splendid. But I am sure you know that, dear, and that whatever you decide will be for the best."

And telling us not to delay since the carriage was already at the door, she patted her tulle rose once again, and tripped away.

"You wanted your liberty, Prudence," I told her, and she smiled, half-amused, half-angry.

"So I did. But I believe she could have helped me a little more than that. Clearly Aunt Hannah has let her know that Jonas intends to propose, and she has already given her consent. Well, so much the better, since I don't think he cares for it any more than I do—except that he needs the money—and the sooner it's over and done with the faster he can start angling for you, Faith. Who knows, he may even come after you, Celia."

"Well, and if he does, I shall not treat him as you have done," Celia told her in the high-spirited fashion only the subject of matrimony aroused in her. "I know I am the youngest and that you and Faith think me stupid, but you cannot deny you have blown hot and cold with Jonas—and with Freddy Hobhouse too, for that matter. And that is the surest way to lose them both, and end up on the shelf."

"Really—?"

"Yes—really. And I will tell you something else. You may not have noticed it, Prudence, but both Freddy Hobhouse and Jonas have been making themselves very pleasant to me—oh yes, I know you are 'not at home' when they call, and that Faith is always gadding about somewhere with Caroline, so that I am the only one here to receive them. But that does not explain why they have lingered so long, paying me the most marked attentions—to tell you the truth, Prudence, if they were not both halfway committed to you, I believe I could be Mrs. Hobhouse or Mrs. Agbrigg any time I liked."

"Indeed?"

"Yes—indeed. You should make your intentions clear, Prudence. I believe people are of the opinion that until you are settled it would not be right to look at us. Aunt Hannah has said as much. And if Faith doesn't seem to mind, I can't quite like it—seeing heaven knows how many chances go by, just because you are so hard to please."

"My word," Prudence said, once again half-angry, half-amused. "Never fear, Celia. I will take whichever one of them should ask me first and endeavour to be married at the month end, just to oblige you. But it is Cousin Caroline they are putting up on offer tonight, you know, so you'll just have to stand in line like the rest of us, Celia Aycliffe, and wait your turn."

The whole of Tarn Edge was illuminated that night, a jewel casket in the distance, spilling a diamond brightness over the acre of roses, the driveway fringed with wide-spreading chestnut trees, the sloping lawns; Aunt Verity waiting to receive her guests in a hallway that had been transformed into a flower garden, a profusion of pink and white blossoms apparently growing from the marble at her feet, vast hothouse arrangements on every step of the stairs, exotic plants of an intense crimson, a barbaric orange, jungle flowers and desert flowers raising their expensive, exceedingly rare heads among masses of polished foliage.

Everything was to be done that evening in accordance with Caroline's wishes—the proceedings to be conducted, in fact, in the manner of high London society, whose fringes she had, once or twice, encountered, and whose inner circle she was determined, one day, to penetrate—and she had really desired to take her stand at the head of the stairs, like some Mayfair duchess, an arrangement which, her mother's ballroom being on the ground floor, would have forced us all to climb up the staircase and then down again, a manoeuvre deemed most unnecessary in

Cullingford, where most of us were still suspicious of London ways.

But, this apart, everything was to be the essence of good taste and high fashion, an obedient procession waiting to shake their host and hostess by the hand, and to murmur a word of congratulation to Caroline herself, her smooth shoulders rising, strong-boned, amber-tinted, from a tight bodice of white, embroidered silk brocade, no demurely shrinking young miss but a hostess full-fledged, a triple strand of birthday pearls wound proudly around her throat, diamond and pearl drops in her ears, each ebony ringlet secured with a knot of silver ribbon and a pearl-headed pin.

It was, of course, too much. The pearls were too fine and too numerous, the diamonds inappropriate in a girl of eighteen. The silk brocade with its cobwebbing of silver thread was certainly extravagant, or so it would seem to Lady Winterton, whose pearls had been eaten up long ago by the mortgage on her land, whose capable, horsewoman's hands bore nothing, now, but a single antique ring; and to Lady Annabel Flood—the guest of honour, a social triumph for the Barforths—her own jewels and her dowry having fallen early victim to the extravagance of her father-in-law, that old Regency buck, our manorial lord, who even now could not deny himself the purchase of a thoroughbred horse or an enticing woman.

Yet both these ladies arrived most flatteringly early, Lady Winterton—for Lady Annabel's benefit—making a great show of friendship to that tradesman's wife, Aunt Verity, Lady Annabel who, apart from her connection with the Floods, was herself an earl's daughter, a person of consequence in her own right, greeting my aunt very warmly, forgetting, it seemed, that she had never before condescended to accept anything from the Barforths but an occasional invitation to take tea.

But now—sacrificing themselves in this vulgar company as English gentlewomen have always sacrificed themselves in the interests of their class and their clan—both these ladies were affability itself, having clearly decided, after much heart-searching, to hazard their sons in the marriage stakes, Francis Winterton being placid, disinterested, biddable; Julian Flood already possessed, at twenty-two, of his grandfather's rake-hellish quality, which would make him unpredictable and expensive.

And, behind them, came the Mandelbaums with their musical, dark-eyed Jacob, Mrs. Battershaw with her hopeful Benjamin, Mrs. Hobhouse of ailing Nethercoats Mill with her Freddy and Adolphus and James, her eyes so dazzled by Caroline's diamonds that my 20,000 pounds, without the porcelain, grew very pale.

"Good evening," Caroline said to everyone. "How do you do?" her smile never wavering, its degree of brightness identical for Mandelbaums and Wintertons alike, extending to Lady Annabel Flood, whose ancestors had arrived with William the Conqueror, no more and no less warmth than to Mrs. Hobhouse, who had no ancestors worth speaking of at all.

"Good evening," to each Hobhouse boy in turn, with nothing in her career hostess's manner to indicate she had ever met them before, much less boxed the ears of all three, soundly and more than once, in childhood.

"Good evening," too to Julian Flood, who was indeed almost a stranger, glimpsed only occasionally in church or as he drove his grandfather's curricle at breakneck, arrogant speed through what he still considered to be his grandfather's town, her very refusal to single him out telling me that she was really very flattered—very excited—indeed.

"Good evening," she said to me, too intent on her own appearance to notice mine. "I shall pass my partners on to you, Faith, and if they have anything to say about me you can let me know."

The orchestra, brought over from Manchester at the recommendation of the Mandelbaums, was already playing in preparation for the dance, installed on a raised platform at the end of the long, white and gold ballroom where, not too many years ago, Caroline and I had run races, our skirts clutched high around our knees. Refreshments, of course, were instantly on hand, and would be served throughout the evening, claret and champagne and a tantalising—possibly unnecessary—variety of cakes being set out in the small dining room, accompanied by sorbets and ices, an endless flow of tea and coffee, to refresh the dancers and sustain the chaperones until supper time.

But my mother, unlike the Ladies Winterton and Flood, who had evidently forgotten to eat their dinner, would take nothing but a glass of wine, satisfying her own appetite, I suspected, on the shocked, even hostile stares of Cullingford's matrons, and the stares of quite another order drawn from the widower, Mr. Oldroyd of Fieldhead, and a series of other—in my eyes quite elderly—gentlemen as she passed them by.

"By God, can that be Elinor Barforth?" I heard Mr. Hobhouse demand of his comfortable wife, forgetting she had been Mrs. Aycliffe these twenty years. And his astonishment could not surprise me for although she had always been a pretty woman, Cullingford had grown accustomed to seeing her following demurely in my father's shadow, a tender dove eating passively from his hand, with no hint of the flaunting, diamond sparkle she was exhibiting tonight. And if that sparkle was indecent in a woman just six months a widow, few could deny its allure.

"We will not go into the ballroom until the dancing begins," she told us, "for although no one may dance with me—poor little widow-woman that I am—I have no mind to sit among the wallflowers. We will wander around a little first, and see what we can see, never mind the crowd. And if you are feeling faint already, Celia, then Caroline's nanny will be pleased to take care of you, for I am sure I cannot. I have your sisters to chaperone, after all, and I must not fail in my duty. So run along upstairs, dear, if you feel you must."

But even Celia, clearly disliking my mother's boldness, believing, as she did, that no lady should ever put herself forward, and should shrink from attention rather than set out to attract it, would not be confined to the nursery on such a night and soon swallowed her complaints.

"Good evening," my mother said to all and sundry in quite a different tone from Caroline's, her twinkling, dimpling smile, her nodding plumage, her artfully exposed bosom telling anyone who cared to look, "Yes, here I am, Elinor Aycliffe, whom you thought to see crushed and helpless without her husband. Yes, here I am, bubbling to the surface of myself, and loving it—oh yes, loving it."

And watching her, understanding each gesture, each nuance of her face from the part of myself which was, indeed, like her, I came near to loving her too.

The ball was opened by Caroline, my uncle Joel taking her a turn or two around the floor, his eyes very well satisfied, but straying from time to time to Aunt Verity, who danced first with

Sir Charles Winterton, as the senior representative of the landed gentry, and then with Mr. Mandelbaum, reputedly the most prosperous of our merchants. Uncle Joel, abandoning Caroline to the multitude of her admirers, then danced with Lady Annabel Flood and, while these formalities were being observed, my heart quickened, as surely the heart of every other girl must have quickened, sitting on those long rows of gilt-legged, velvet-covered chairs, as even Prudence's heart must have skipped a beat at the possibility before us all of disaster, or success.

Yet this was not the first dance I had attended and I knew, by the unwritten laws governing such occasions, that even without my white rose and my vast, swanlike dress, without my audacious white velvet ribbon and the air of pity I was trying so hard to cultivate for such females who had failed to grow at least five inches taller than the fashion, I would not lack for partners. Girls who had neither beauty nor expectations might be condemned to spend the evening on that terrible row of chairs, counting the candles and the petals on the flowers, the lace flounces on the skirts of other girls as they danced by, hoping Aunt Verity would notice their plight and conjure up a man—any man—to relieve it. But a Miss Aycliffe, with 20,000 pounds cash down and the firm promise of more to come, need have no such fears.

Naturally every man present must first offer his attentions to his hostess and her daughter. Naturally Blaize and Nicholas would have been provided with a long list of females—which would not include cousins—to whom courtesy was due. Uncle Joel, his duty dances done, would have time for no one but his wife. But there would be partners to spare, a great many of them, and, as I sat between Celia, who was eager to dance with anyone, and Prudence, who was eager to dance with anyone but Jonas, I was forced to admit that the deeper layers of my mind, the ones I could not really control, were entirely occupied with Nicholas.

And my preoccupation was not a happy one. I had gorged myself, for a day or two after the incident of the train, on thoughts of him, indulged myself by building and rebuilding in my mind the dark, determined lines of his face, the slight cleft in his chin, the unexpected humour of his smile when it managed to chase his ill-temper away. And, indulging myself still further,

I had relived the whole of our encounter, repeated our conversation over and over again, added to it, including the things I had wanted to say, or had only thought of much later, as if they had actually been spoken. Yet, in the end, I had been forced, quite abruptly, to leave the comforting realm of fantasy and to consider, more precisely than ever before, my exact situation and what, if anything, I could reasonably, logically, hope to achieve.

Not even my father's scrupulously contrived efforts to raise his daughters in total innocence had concealed from me that there were various categories of womankind, for which men had many and equally varied uses.

There was the category "lady," to which I belonged, whose duty it was to be pure of heart and delicate of constitution, designed to arouse the protective, possessive instinct in man, to be kept in luxurious idleness in exchange for the devotion and self-sacrifice with which she would hazard herself—sometimes annually—in the perilous task of childbirth.

There was the category "maidservant," so much stronger and more enduring than the lady that it was difficult to class them as members of the same species, a tireless variety of woman intended for the scrubbing of floors, the laying of grates, the carrying of water, and the mangling of linen, her reproductive functions being so little encouraged that she would be dismissed the moment it was suspected they had been put to use.

There was the category "mill hand," even hardier, capable of fourteen hours a day hard labour in the agonising heat and noise of a weaving shed, and then another five with wash tub and scrubbing board at home. And, as gentlemen turned to these tough plants for the practical, daily needs their little, orchid house wives could not supply, so too there was the category "mistress," a wild, jungle weed, coarse-fibred enough to glory in the rough handling no orchid could be expected to endure.

And I knew, quite simply, that none of this concerned me. No one would ever be likely to ask me to lay a grate or tend a fire, or expose me to the heat and promiscuity of the sheds. I was, most definitely, a lady, created not to be loved but to be married, and even if, by some miracle, Nicholas could be induced into thoughts of matrimony, his family—which was partly my own family too—would not approve of me.

I might be considered a good match for a Hobhouse or a Mandelbaum, a brilliant one for Jonas Agbrigg, but the Barforths would require some stupendous alliance for all three of their children, and had I been a little older than seventeen, possessed of a greater share of Prudence's common sense, I would perhaps have smiled more convincingly at Jacob Mandelbaum, who liked me, at jovial Freddy Hobhouse, who seemed willing to like anyone, and shut my thoughts of Nicholas away.

"Enjoy yourselves," my mother commanded, smiling as Jonas Agbrigg bowed stiffly to Prudence, the Battershaw boy first to me and then to Celia, since Freddy Hobhouse had claimed me first. "Enjoy yourselves, while Aunt Hannah and I sit and tell each other how much better things were in our day." And although my appetite for enjoyment was less acute, now that its fulfilment depended so largely on Nicholas, I made up my mind to obey.

I was not certain what I hoped for, since I could not hope for Nicholas, except that it was not Freddy Hobhouse, hot-handed, heavy-footed, hugging me in a cheerful polka, nor even Jacob Mandelbaum, serious and supple, who would rather have been playing the violins than dancing. Certainly it was not Francis Winterton, holding me a yard away, talking languidly about Caroline, nor Julian Flood, who, having come here to marry one young lady was reckless and arrogant enough to make himself gallant to another, escorting me to the refreshment room where his mother, whose financial commitments my 20,000 pounds could hardly satisfy, put herself instantly between us, walking back with us to the ballroom to make sure we went there, and that I was duly returned to my relations.

It was a dance, the most thrilling of all events permitted to young ladies, fraught with great hopes and great agonies, the making or missing of marriages and reputations, no different from the dozen or so others I had attended, except that it was more splendid. And for the first hour or so everything was just as it should have been. The three immense chandeliers suspended from the high, gold-painted ceiling shimmered and sparkled, the dozen long windows open to the terrace offered a breath of garden-spiced air as one danced by. The violins played their polkas and quadrilles and country dances, their waltzes, every bit as tunefully as had been promised. The young ladies danced, or most of them did, at least once, provided with partners by Aunt Verity, who, gracefully, tirelessly, circled the room making her introductions. "Miss Smith, allow me to present Mr. Brown, who is quite an expert at the polka. Why, Miss White, do not say you are too exhausted to dance, for here is Mr. Jones, who would be delighted . . ."

The older men, having seen their wives and daughters suitably catered for, retired to refreshment room and smoking room; the chaperones drew their chairs closer together, sharp-eyed and anxious, some of them, others heavy-lidded with fatigue and the boredom of so eternally discussing the splendid prospects of my cousin Caroline. Aunt Hannah had placed herself firmly beside Mr. Fielding, our new member of Parliament, who was certainly unaware that she intended, eventually, to obtain his office for Jonas. And, while keeping up a steady flow of question and answer, demanding to know the progress of Cullingford's Charter of Incorporation, and when she could expect her husband to be elected mayor, her restless eyes never ceased to check the progress of her adored, adopted son, noting who danced with him and who did not, noting who dared to trespass on his preserves by dancing with Prudence. And her chaperonage, it seemed, extended also to my mother, so that when she returned, not for the first time, from the refreshment room where the widower, Mr. Oldroyd of Fieldhead Mills, had been plying her with champagne, Aunt Hannah leaned forward and snapped, in the exact tone she had used often enough to me and Celia, "Elinor—*do* behave."

Enjoyment was not lacking, but no greater than I had experienced before, nothing I would spend tomorrow in silence remembering. Neither Nicholas nor Blaize would have time to dance with me—although Blaize did smile at me once or twice behind his partner's head, letting me know, by a sweeping, admiring glance, that my dress and my hair had won his approval —and gradually the evening began to settle down, to acquire the same bland flavour of every day, to be entirely predictable, until, having taken a second glass of lemonade with Jacob Mandelbaum and returning to the ballroom, Jacob a step or two behind me, I found myself entangled, just inside the doorway, with Nicholas and Caroline, drawing back as I heard her hiss at him, "Nicholas, for heaven's sake, you have not yet danced with Amy Battershaw, and she most particularly wishes for it—"

"I daresay. But I have danced with all your other tedious friends, and I think you may allow me a moment—"

"Nicholas," she said, her voice rising in a way that proved her composure to be less than it seemed. "Please oblige me in this, for you know quite well Amy Battershaw and I are to travel to Paris together, and if she should take the huff and decide not to go, then I shall be saddled with some dreary paid companion."

"Or Father will forbid you to go at all."

"No, he will not. And it is quite odious of you to provoke me tonight when you know quite well how important— Oh, Nicky, for once please do as I ask, for she is sitting there, the silly goose, waiting, and I do believe she has turned someone else away—"

But Aunt Verity, as usual, was at hand and flowing between her warring children like cool water, drawing me with her for support, or distraction, she murmured, "Faith dear, how well you look tonight. That dress becomes you perfectly—don't you think so, Caroline? And, Nicky darling, do go and dance with Miss Battershaw—a bore, I admit, but only five minutes of your time—not worth the fuss."

And he would have gone at once, I think, the corners of his mouth already tilting with a wry, affectionate smile, had not Uncle Joel abruptly intervened.

"What's all this?" he demanded, and instantly Caroline—his favourite child, the apple of his powerful, vengeful eye—spun round to him, certain of his support.

"It is Nicholas turning stubborn again, and saying he will not dance with Amy Battershaw."

"Oh, but he will," my uncle said, the familiar snap of temper in his eyes. "He will—and before he's ten minutes older."

"Dearest," Aunt Verity murmured, her endearment addressed, I think, to them both, and, not wishing to endure again the backlash of my uncle's anger, I began to move away when Nicholas, unable, as always, to back down, but willing, perhaps, to offer his mother a compromise, said crisply, "Of course I'll dance with Miss Battershaw—there was never any doubt about it—but you'll have to extend your ten minutes, I'm afraid, since I am promised to dance first with Faith."

And instantly—or so it seemed to me—a row of Barforth eyes were riveted to my face, my uncle's hard and suspicious, the thought behind them, "Ah yes, so it's the Aycliffe girl again, turning out as flighty as her mother"; Caroline's warning me she did not expect her friends to turn traitor and would make short work of any who did; Aunt Verity alone prepared to retain a sense of proportion, to understand that I could only aggravate the matter by a refusal.

"Ah well," she said lightly. "I doubt if Miss Battershaw will die of the suspense," and there was nothing for me to do but give him my hand and wait for the music to begin.

I had longed for this dance, and now—as often happens with the things one longs for in life—it was an embarrassment, an ordeal, a bitter disappointment. I had thought of him so often, not only with the excitement of budding emotion, but with anxiety too, had defended him when Caroline, and Celia, accused him of moodiness and malice, had worried about his stormy relations with his father, remembering all the times I had seen him take his punishment with a stubborn pride that made my uncle's tongue harsher, his hand heavier. Yet now I hoped, with unashamed ferocity, that Uncle Joel would thrash him and batter him at the end of every disagreement, wished, in fact, that he had broken his back and his spirit long ago.

"You are looking very well, Faith."

"Thank you."

And then, as I continued to stare over his shoulder, making it clear that there was nothing more I wished to say, he added quickly, "Faith—I am sorry."

"Why? Have you done something amiss?"

"Ah well—as to that—but I did not ask you to dance with me merely to escape Amy Battershaw."

"My goodness—whatever gave you the notion I could think you had?"

They were playing a waltz, and because I had waltzed with him in my daydreams since the day Aunt Verity's invitation had been delivered to our door, because I should have been happy—because Celia, if she noticed me, would think me happy—I had never been so miserable in my life, this new, acute sensation of distress, the first real pain I had ever suffered, acting like a hot stone flung into the quiet pool which had so far been my life, sizzling and hurting in its contact with hitherto unruffled waters. And I would have been proud of my composure had I not required every ounce of concentration I possessed to maintain it.

"You are quite right to be angry, Faith."

"Angry? Heavens, what an idea. I am enjoying myself immensely, Nicholas. It is a splendid party. Everyone says so."

And sighing, he made no further attempt to talk to me, while I became so stiff and cold that he may have been as glad as I when the music stopped and he could return me to my mother, going off at once to present himself to a much-beribboned Amy Battershaw.

"Well, we are having so much fun," my mother told me, her eyes extremely bright with mischief and champagne. "Prudence has danced twice with Jonas and managed to avoid him twice more, largely with the aid of your so very accomplished cousin Blaize. Yes, he knows exactly what is going on around him, dear Blaize—I have always thought so—and I have passed a pleasant half-hour wondering just why he came so artfully to her rescue. I mean, what amused him most? Was it the look on Aunt Hannah's face? Or was it Jonas, who has no look on his face at all? Or did he merely wish to make Prudence admire him, since she refuses to admire anyone else? I am inclined to think that must be it, for he is a little heartless—Blaize—clever men often are, I find, which makes them no less attractive. However, it makes no difference, since Aunt Hannah has got her safely back again—look, there she is, sitting between Hannah and Mr. Fielding, with Jonas standing guard behind her chair. And Celia has been doing remarkably well—she has danced with Jonas and Freddy and Adolphus, and has abandoned all her notions of having a headache."

But my mother's chatter irritated me, since I cared, at that moment, neither for Celia's triumphs nor Prudence's captivity, and excusing myself, murmuring something about a hairpin, a handkerchief, I hurried away to Caroline's bedroom, the old, comfortable nanny sitting by the fire surrounded by her stock-in-trade of needle and thread, hairpins and smelling bottles, ready to mend a torn frill or a broken heart without too much interest in either.

"You look pale, dear," she said. "Drink this," and I drank something bland and neutral that had an echo of my childhood about it, turning cold and hot and then very cold again as, ravaged by the strength of my raw, seventeen-year-old emotion, I faced the unpalatable truth, the depth of the pit into which I had so willingly fallen.

I was in love with a man who was not in love with me, which was, in itself, quite bad enough, but my feeling for him was so unconnected with marriage, depended so little on marriage, that for a moment I was almost as shocked by it as my father would have been. But perhaps my father had not always been so wise —so dry; perhaps he too, when he had made his unlikely second marriage to my mother, had been driven by needs he chose later to deny.

I did not completely understand the sexual act. For a married woman—according to Miss Mayfield's hints and evasions—it was a duty, for an unmarried woman so unthinkable that it could only be the result of brutal rape, which, even then, should she be indelicate enough as to survive, would effectively ostracise her from decent company. And I had witnessed but one remotely sexual contact between my parents, a faint, uneasy thing, my father's hand hovering, not quite touching, my mother's shoulder, his pinched lips saying, "Elinor, it is time for bed," my mother's head turning briefly away, nostrils wrinkling, eyelids lowering to hide the protest she had been unable to suppress; and then, turning back to him, offering her meek, empty smile, nothing warmer than her submission. "Why yes, dear." And my feelings for Nicholas had nothing to do with any of that.

But, still gazing into the fire, I began to remember other things, young couples strolling tight-clasped together on quiet evenings, common people, we had been told, who should have been at home preparing themselves for tomorrow's labours instead of "asking for trouble" in this unseemly fashion. "Look away, girls." But I understood that, in this case, we had been instructed to avert our eyes not from depravity but from pleasure, the simple joy—forbidden to us—that two young bodies, two loving, sympathetic minds, could find in each other, a joy that had nothing at all to do with dowries and marriage contracts, the propagation of a man's name and his money.

"Look away, girls." But no one had forbidden me to notice the softening of my uncle Joel's face whenever he looked at his wife, the way her hand, very often, would seek his, a certain glow of memory and anticipation between them which, I realised, had sometimes embarrassed my father and Aunt Hannah, and had caused my mother and Mr. Agbrigg, Aunt Hannah's plain-spoken husband, to lower their eyes, as if they not only understood very well what that glow meant, but had something in their own lives to remember.

Clasping my hands tight together, giving my whole mind to the task, I understood that everything I desired in life was contained in that warm glance between my aunt and uncle. I was not concerned with social success, like Caroline, nor with social ideals like Prudence. I had small interest in domesticity, like Celia. I simply wanted Nicholas to smile at me through the lamplight one evening, as his father—who was gentle with no one else—smiled at Aunt Verity, to reach out his hand in a gesture of perfect confidence and understanding, knowing that mine would be there to meet it. And although I was not even acquainted with the word "sensuality," much less its meaning, I think my body understood it, dimly perhaps, but joyfully, and loved him too.

"And what do you think to my Caroline tonight," the old servant enquired, not interested in my opinion, but feeling I had been silent long enough. "A real beauty she's turned out to be—aye, and they're all after her. But she'll take the one she fancies when she's ready, mark my words. Not that she's ready—not by a long chalk—for she's had a taste of London now, and she's pestering to go to Paris, which means she'll surely be going, for I've never known her father refuse her anything. Aye, she'll have what she wants, Miss Caroline. She always was that way, just like her father. And when she gets it, whatever it is, it won't turn out to be good enough. She'll have to alter it, and better it, just like him. Now then, Miss Faith, you'll be going downstairs now, I reckon, so nanny can get on with her knitting. Just a dab of cologne—that's better, eh?"

"Yes, nanny. Thank you."

But the old woman's evident desire to return to her knitting needles was frustrated yet again by the abrupt arrival of my eldest sister who, ignoring nanny's comfortable, "And what can I do for you, Miss Prudence?" said quickly, "Faith, I am absolutely mortified—indeed I have never been more so in my life—"

"With Jonas?"

"Oh—naturally with Jonas—but mainly with myself. I have amazed myself. I did not know I could be so—oh, I don't know what to call it, weak I suppose."

"Good heavens, Pru! You have not accepted him, have you, because you couldn't bring yourself to say no?"

"Indeed I have not—but what I have done is almost as feeble. I was to dance the waltz with him that is just starting, and seeing him coming towards me I felt quite certain that instead of dancing he was going to suggest something quite stupid like a walk in the moonlight, and propose. And instead of facing up to it—for, good Lord, it is only Jonas and I am not in the least afraid of him—I suddenly found myself bolting up the stairs like a scared rabbit—exactly the kind of silly, schoolgirl antic I would expect from Celia. Faith, how could I do such a thing?"

"I don't know," I told her, meaning it, since I had admired her courage all my life, relied heavily on her cool, disciplined powers of reason on the many occasions when my own had failed me. "Perhaps you thought the place ill-chosen, or that Aunt Hannah would make a scene when you refused him."

"Did I? And, of course, she would. But I am not sure it was that. No—he has been so strange all evening—well, he is always strange, but tonight—oh, dear, I don't know. And the whole thing suddenly seemed to be so distasteful—so sordid. But that is no excuse. I should have been able to stand my ground. And what on earth am I to do now? He will be waiting in the hall, and will expect some explanation. Goodness—how sickening."

"Then I will go and explain for you."

"Faith, I can't ask you—"

"You have not asked me. And I am not so fastidious as you are, Prudence. I will simply tell him you are indisposed at the moment, and whether he believes it or not he can hardly say so. And when you come downstairs again you should behave as if you had not been indisposed at all—which is no more than the truth—and that will put him off from bothering you again to-night. That is the way these things are done, you know. I'll see to it."

And delighted at this opportunity to protect her, when all our lives she had looked after me, I went downstairs.

Chapter Five

HE WAS, INDEED, waiting in the hall, positioned at the foot of the stairs where no one could escape him, his eyes no colder than I was accustomed to see them, his thin mouth no more disdainful. The Agbrigg boy of my childhood, wearing his dress suit and ruffled shirt a shade too correctly, too much the gentleman, as if he found it hard to forget that his birth did not entitle him to be a gentleman at all. Just Jonas, who, well aware that we had always despised him, might be hurt and angry but hardly surprised to find himself rejected again.

"I am come with Prudence's apologies," I told him lightly, expecting no difficulty. "She finds herself somewhat indisposed and asks me to say she cannot dance."

"Really?" he said, not believing me but not, it seemed, much caring. "Nothing of a serious nature, I hope and trust."

"Oh no. She will be down presently, I imagine."

And that should have been the end of it; he should have bowed, smiled, offered to escort me back to my mother, I should have accepted his arm, made some slight remark about the splendours of the evening, the excellence of the music and the champagne, and we should have gone our separate ways. But instead, without in any way altering his expression of cool indifference, he murmured, so low that I had to step closer to hear him, "And do you also imagine that her recovery would be more rapid if I were to make my excuses to Mrs. Barforth and take my leave?"

"Good heavens," I said, laughing, hoping it was indeed a joke although I knew quite well it wasn't, "I don't know why you should think that, Jonas."

"Do you know anything very much at all, Faith?" he replied so tonelessly, so calmly, that it took me a second to understand his rudeness. But when I did, I knew it authorised me to stop playing the young lady and to answer him back just as rudely as I pleased.

"I shall not ask you to apologise for that, Jonas, since you are probably not sorry. But, as it happens, I am not stupid, and if Prudence is avoiding you then she must have her reasons—and that is not my fault."

"Did I say so?" he enquired, a lawyer lecturing me, examining me from a lofty, intellectual height, although his pale, slanting eyes were on an exact level with mine, his shoulders not much broader. "And she has no reason to avoid me that I know of. Why should you think otherwise?"

"Well—I did, that's all."

"Because you thought I meant to propose?"

"Yes," I said, considerably startled, yet determined to defend my sister whatever the cost. "So I did. And it would be most ungentlemanly of you to try to deny it."

"Really? Why is that?"

"You know quite well why—and will you please stop talking to me like a lawyer."

"But I am a lawyer, Faith—a very good one, as a matter of fact."

"I am glad to hear it. And in that case you must know that having paid attentions to a lady—well, a lady may put an end to such things, a gentleman, once he is committed, may not— Of course you meant to propose."

"Indeed," he said, his thin lips sketching a smile that was entirely without humour. "Naturally you must be right—since a lady can never be wrong—and it is no secret that my mother would like to see me married, preferably to Prudence. But what my mother would like, and what Prudence would like—what I would like myself—cannot always be the same. I think we should let the matter rest there. You may tell your sister so."

"Yes, I will, and I am glad, at any rate, to see you are not brokenhearted."

"Are you?"

"I beg your pardon?"

"I said, are you glad to see that I am *not* brokenhearted?"

And, for an instant, his hooded eyes shot wide open, colourless almost, unaccustomed to the light, but leaving me in no doubt that he was deeply offended and had perhaps been so all his life, his habitually neutral expression chilling me now with the kind of anger I had seen, often enough, in my father, the twisted emotion of a man who, feeling he cannot afford emotion, denies it, conceals it, comes eventually to despise it, and is seriously displeased with himself and anyone else who happens to be nearby on the rare occasions when it breaks free.

Yet Jonas, I felt quite certain, was not in love with Prudence, had, in fact, presented himself to her in a businesslike fashion which even she had found too cool, too obviously motivated by Aunt Hannah's advice and his own good sense. And I was so intrigued by this show of feeling in a man I had believed entirely passionless, that when he took my arm and obliged me to walk a step or two with him down the passageway behind the stairs, I did not resist.

There were few people in that part of the house, just a servant or two, hurrying soft-footed about their duties with no great interest in a young couple who, by the look of it, wished to be alone. And wondering why on earth he had brought me here— since no matter how pressing his financial needs it was a little too soon, surely, to propose to me in my sister's place?—I said primly, "I would like to go back to my mother."

"Of course."

But he was still taut and painful with his anger, its intensity both amazing me and giving me cause for concern, since later, when he returned to his habitual composure, he would not remember me kindly for having witnessed it.

"Tell me something," he said, his voice clipped and sarcastic, a lawyer again demolishing the evidence of a witness who was, in any case, somewhat beneath his notice. "Obviously my attentions—such as they were—have not found favour with your sister. And since I perfectly agree with my mother that I should marry, and that it should be sooner rather than later, perhaps you will let me know how I have most displeased her. I realise, for one thing, that I have committed the crime of poverty—"

"That has nothing to do with it."

"Has it not? Do you know, Faith, in your case I am ready to believe you. There is no need for you to think about money, is there, since you have never been without it. Unfortunately, some of us are less happily situated. I spend a great deal of my time thinking about money. I am obliged to do so, since ambition is expensive and I am very ambitious; I admit it freely. It may seem strange to you that a man of ability and energy cannot progress in this world even half so far as a muttonhead who has a few thousand a year behind him—it has often seemed strange to me—but so it is. I have learned to accept it and accommodate it, since I intend to make more of my life than I suppose a man of my origins has any right to expect."

"I know nothing of your origins, Jonas."

"Nonsense," he snapped. "You know quite well that my father was a weaver once in your uncle's sheds, and that he first married a weaver, if, indeed he troubled to marry her at all. It costs money, you see, to get married. A man can't go to church in clogs and a cloth cap. The parsons don't like it, and there's a little matter of putting something in the collection plate afterwards. So mostly, among the labouring classes, they save their money and don't bother. They just wait until their first child is on the way and then move into the same back-to-back hovel and set about having more. Marriage, after all, is about property, and if a man has no property what difference can it make to him if his sons are legitimate, or even if they're his sons at all? Nobody in Simon Street—which is where my father came from, where I was born—gives a thought for such things. But naturally, it must make a difference to a Miss Aycliffe."

"Jonas," I said, shocked, fascinated, beginning now to pity him, wishing I could find the courage to make him stop hurting himself in this way. "You should not speak to me like this. For one thing, I am not supposed to understand such matters—but since in fact I do know what you mean, I will tell you that it makes no difference to me at all. And you should not be ashamed of it either."

"Ashamed?" He flung the word at me, every line of his overstrung body a snarl. "Did I say I was ashamed? What have *I* to be ashamed about? I don't remember Simon Street. I don't remember the day my mother took me into the mill, when I was seven years old, and set me to work. I don't remember going

home every night stinking like a pig and getting into bed with
God knows how many brothers and sisters who stank worse than
I did, because they were older and bigger and had more muck
on them. I don't even remember those brothers and sisters, since
they died, every one of them except me because they didn't have
the energy to stay alive—or couldn't see the point to it. I don't
remember, because, by the time I was ten my father had
wormed his way into your uncle Joel's good graces and could
afford to take me out of the sheds and send me to school. Your
uncle made him manager of Low Cross Mill and gave us the
millhouse to live in, which was no palace. They use it now for
storage, but after a 'one up and one down' in Simon Street it
was all too grand for my mother. She couldn't make herself into
a manager's wife, you see, and so she lost her wits over it.
Started wandering in the end, going back to Simon Street to find
her old workmates, who didn't want her any more, and worrying
herself sick that she was holding my father back—which she was
—and holding me back, since I was at the grammar school by
then with all the Barforths and the Hobhouses—little gentlemen
all together, except that I was cleverer, a damn sight cleverer—
and I couldn't be expected to like it when she turned up at
school one day with a shawl on her head and clogs on her feet.
Of course I don't remember that either. I don't even remember
the way the Hobhouses sniggered, or your cousin Nicholas
looked away—most of all I don't remember how your cousin
Blaize raised his hat to her and said, 'Good day to you, madam.'
It's completely gone out of my mind. She died when I was about
thirteen, and my father had some very hard words to say to me
that day—you may have noticed that we don't get on too well
together even now. He suggested I'd be relieved to be rid of her,
glad that I wouldn't have to feel ashamed of her any longer in
front of my friends, although I can't think just who he meant by
that. He was quite broken up about losing her, my father, although he recovered soon enough. He married Miss Hannah
Barforth no less, the very minute he was out of mourning—for
my sake, he said, since she liked the idea of having a clever son
and was ready to do great things for me. And if my father, with
his accent and the calluses still on his hands, could marry a
Barforth—well—I really don't think a Miss Aycliffe should be
beyond my reach, do you?"

But, understanding what it meant to him to expose himself in this painful fashion—what it would have meant to my father—I was appalled and fearful and could find nothing to offer him in reply but a whispered "Jonas—please—do not—"

"I am extremely sorry," he said, the whole of him coming to an abrupt halt, his very breathing suspended for a moment as if he needed his entire, doubtless formidable powers of concentration to retrieve the rogue part of his nature which had so disastrously escaped its bondage.

Surely nothing more could now be said? Surely he would take me, in silence, back to the ballroom and would, from then on, avoid me as much as he could? But after that moment of total stillness, he turned and stood directly in front of me, closer than I had anticipated, so that, retreating, I found my back against the wall.

"Faith," he said very quietly, his eyes completely hooded again, something just beneath the surface of him so tense, so watchful, that it caused me to hold my breath. "I have not proposed to Prudence, mainly because I was unwilling to risk a refusal, for there is no doubt she would have made me an excellent wife. There is a saying that every man encounters three kinds of women in his lifetime, the woman he knows would be good for him, the woman he would like to have, and the woman he can get. Certainly Prudence would have been good for me. My mother made an excellent choice in drawing her to my attention."

"I will tell her—"

"There is no need. We did not, in any way, commit ourselves. In fact we were both very careful not to do so. The matter is entirely closed. You need tell her no more than is required to set her mind at rest. My mother considers you a great scatterbrain, Faith."

"Well—she is right again—for so I am."

"I know."

And, my back pressed against the wall, the air in that narrow, dimly lit passageway so taut now that it hurt me to breathe, I understood—without in the least knowing how I had reached so shattering a conclusion—that this bloodless man had actually brought me here not to complain of my sister, but because, incredibly and considerably against his own better judgement, he had wanted to be alone with me; wanted now, although his eyes were still hooded, his jaw set, to kiss me. And, pitying him, yet knowing he could not tolerate pity, fearful of wounding his bruised self-esteem once again, astonished and just a little curious, for I had never even suspected I held any appeal for him, I understood that I must stop him at all costs. For a kiss was far more personal and important than a proposal of marriage, even if the proposal was almost certain to follow after. The rejection of an offer of marriage could be construed simply as the rejection of a man's prospects, a business arrangement which, for a hundred acceptable reasons, did not suit. But to turn my head away from his kiss would be a terrible thing, something he would find hard to forgive, while to accept it would be dangerous, foolish, unkind. I did not wish to encourage him, certainly, but I did not wish to hurt him either. Nor did I wish to hurt myself, for I had never been kissed before, and although I was quite ready for the experience, I didn't want that first, special kiss to come from Jonas.

"I am indeed sorry for the things I said to you just now, Faith —although oddly enough it doesn't disturb me that you should know them."

"Why should it? I shall not tell anyone else, you can be sure of that. And, after all, we are cousins."

"Not really. There is no blood relationship between us. Faith —you really are scatterbrained, aren't you, and extravagant too, I suppose, like your mother?"

"Oh yes. Very like my mother. I am not at all a favourite with Aunt Hannah."

"I know that. But aunts, and mothers, tend to look mainly for accomplishments in a young lady. There are other attributes."

And there it was, Jonas, who was beyond folly—who could not afford it in any case—committing folly for my sake, bending his narrow head towards me, his thin mouth smiling with a slight, rueful amusement, directed, I supposed, at himself, although I could see no cause for amusement. I was struggling instead against a panic certainty that when he finally made up his mind to deliver his kiss I would push him away, or, far worse than that, would wound us both by a fit of hysterical laughter. I even closed my eyes, steeling myself to endure, praying for the sophistication that would enable me to wave it gracefully away, to make light of it without awkwardness, to suggest, somehow, that while not taking it seriously I had not found it unpleasant. But such compassionate artifice was not within my capabilities in those days, and when, after a moment, he did not touch me after all, I opened my eyes again to find him staring at me, understanding my dilemma too well it seemed, no softness, no rueful amusement in him any more.

"I believe you wished to return to your mother, Faith."

"Yes. So I did."

And, escorting me in silence to the ballroom door, abandoning me there quite abruptly, I was not certain, from the closed, cold lines of his face, if I had acquired a lover or an enemy.

I should, of course, have gone at once to Prudence, was about to turn round and make my way upstairs again, when Celia appeared as if from nowhere, struggling pink-cheeked and breathless towards me through the ballroom crowd.

"Heavens, Faith, what are you thinking of—you have been gone for ages—you and Prudence—leaving me to manage alone. Well, you are to come at once, for Mother has taken it into her head to dance! Yes, and with Mr. Oldroyd, who must have lost his wits, or is in his cups, for he can only laugh and encourage her. The next waltz, she is saying, and you must come and stop her, Faith, for I could not bear it—only six months a widow, and his wife not dead a year yet. Nobody has ever heard of such a thing. She should not really be here at all, and if she disgraces herself by dancing, then we are all disgraced too. Her reputation could never recover from it, and our reputations would be ruined too—like mother like daughter they will say, and who can blame them, for I believe I would say the same myself. Faith— do something—for I have been so enjoying myself and she has no right to spoil it. She's had her life, Faith—it's simply not fair."

I discovered my mother, a moment later, leaning back against her chair, bubbling with a soft, altogether wicked laughter, Aunt Hannah sitting, tight-lipped beside her, delivering a most stringent, most indignant warning.

"You are not in Venice now, Elinor."

"No, no, dearest—that is all too apparent. But such a fuss, Hannah. Matthew Oldroyd has asked me to dance, which I thought very kind of him, and unmannerly of me to refuse—"

"He did not at all expect to be taken seriously, Elinor, as you well know. He was merely being gallant—or trying to be—in his clumsy fashion, and I never saw a man more startled in my life when you agreed. And where is he now, I should like to know? Gone to find his hat and order his horses, if he has the sense he was born with. Really, Elinor, such things may be permitted in Venice, but they would not be understood here. You should give some thought to your responsibilities, and your age."

"Ah—as to that—" my mother began, ready, I thought, to put forward some startling theory of her own as to the nature of responsibility. But, happily, all further discussion was cut short by a sudden hush, a tailing off of violins in mid-polka, a standing on tiptoe and craning of necks which could only mean some momentous event was about to take place. And, as the double doors from the drawing room were thrown open, and Aunt Verity appeared, there was a moment of incredulity, a collective intake of breath, as the tall, military-looking old man walking beside her was recognised as Sir Giles Flood, our manorial lord.

He was not quite eighty, as Blaize had once told me, but perhaps not too far away from it, a heavy-featured, autocratic countenance, the total self-assurance that is bred through generations of authority, managing, even in the black evening clothes then in fashion, to have something of the old-style Regency buck about him. He who had once, in rainbow-coloured silks and satins, played whist in high company at Carlton House, and to whom the sinful splendours of Brighton, in the prince regent's day, had not been unknown.

"What a triumph for Verity," my mother murmured, all other mischief forgotten. "What an absolute triumph—" For Sir Giles, whose family had held the manor of Cullingford for three hundred years, and who had himself inherited his title at a time when every cap in the Law Valley would be instantly doffed as he passed by—and at a time when there had been the lord in his castle, the parson at his altar, the peasants in the fields, and the weaver in his two-room shack, when every man had been aware of the place to which God had called him and had been ready to keep it—had vowed publicly, and very loudly, that nothing would induce him to set foot in the house of any upstart manufacturer.

One could be civil to the breed, he declared, if one happened to meet it, as a gentleman was in honour bound to be civil to his groom or his grocer. But he saw no reason to encourage it, and had delivered many a dire warning to his peers—Sir Charles Winterton among them—against these jumped-up millmasters who, with their dirty machines and their dirty money, seemed possessed of the amazing and impertinent notion that they were as good as anybody else.

No one had campaigned more vigorously than Sir Giles to keep his manufacturing neighbours well away from public affairs. Government, as everyone knew, or ought to know, was the business of gentlemen. He had refused to sit, as a Justice of the Peace, on the same bench as any man who was tainted personally or paternally by trade. He had raised a considerable outcry when the Reform Bill of 1832 had first allowed the local industrialists to elect their own member of Parliament—my father—and even now was preparing most viciously to attack Cullingford's Charter of Incorporation, which, by sweeping away the ancient, manorial offices of local government, would subject the town he still thought of as his personal property to the interference of some low-born manufacturing mayor.

Yet here he was, his hand resting with no apparent distaste on Aunt Verity's arm, and as he led her into the centre of the empty floor and swung her, with amazing vigour, into a waltz, the assembled, manufacturing company broke, quite spontaneously, into a round of applause, as if it had been the Duke of Wellington, or Prince Albert himself, dancing there.

"So it's to be Julian Flood is it—for Caroline?" Aunt Hannah muttered, her head very close to my mother's in perfect harmony. And my mother, unable to take her eyes from that disreputable but lordly figure, breathed, "Yes, indeed—Joel must be even richer than we thought, or the Floods poorer. Just think of it, Hannah—Caroline at Cullingford Manor. My word, I think Lady Winterton is having a fit, and Lady Annabel Flood is like a cat in a cream pot."

Caroline herself took the floor now with Julian Flood, Celia with Freddy Hobhouse, Jonas with some young lady who looked as if she might be worth a few thousand a year, and, making my way once again to rescue Prudence, still hiding upstairs, I found myself face to face with Nicholas, whose request for a second dance with me drove Prudence, and all else, entirely from my mind.

He took me very firmly by the hand, very firmly by the waist, and said, his voice equally determined, "I have to apologise properly to you, Faith. You were in too much of a huff to listen earlier, and I have been waiting my opportunity ever since."

And I felt such a winging, soaring delight that I could have wished him to do something really dreadful, so that I could forgive him even more.

"There's no need, Nicholas."

"Of course there is. And you have been looking so distracted—"

"Oh well—that has nothing to do with it. My mother has had a set-to with Aunt Hannah, and, to tell the truth, I am not certain, but I think Jonas Agbrigg may have asked me to marry him."

"Good Lord, Faith," he said, quite horrified. "Either he has asked you or he hasn't. I hope you are certain as to whether or not you have refused him."

"Oh yes, there is no doubt about that. But I believe I have done it awkwardly, and hurt his feelings."

"Jonas? Nonsense. He has no feelings to hurt. He's the coldest fish I ever did see. Don't worry about him. It's his pocket, not his feelings, that he worries about, and it's no secret that he's hard-pressed for cash right now, since old Mr. Corey-Manning has decided to retire. The old man has bought himself a house in Bridlington, and can't wait to get there, didn't you know? Jonas will have to get the money from somewhere to buy him out, stands to reason, or he could find himself with a new senior partner who may not be to his liking. All it needs is for some energetic fellow to come along, with sons of his own to find places for, and Jonas will soon find himself squeezed out."

"Won't your father help him?"

"I reckon he might. But he'll expect Jonas to have something of his own behind him. There's more to it than just the money for the partnership, after all. If Jonas wants to step into Corey-Manning's shoes he'll have Corey-Manning's social position to keep up—which can't be cheap. More than Aunt Hannah can manage, since she'll need every penny she can scrape together to stake herself as mayoress. They can't expect my father to stand it all. He'll listen to a business proposition, I don't doubt, but he's not a charity. He might help, but Jonas will have to do something to help himself, first."

And having made our peace, we danced for a while in a comfortable silence, until the music suddenly tailed off again, a mark of respect for the exit of Sir Giles and Aunt Verity, and a signal that it was supper time.

"Thank goodness for that," Nicholas said. "I thought the old man would never come—and I reckon he didn't really want to, if the truth be known—and since we couldn't start supper without him, and then we had to make sure everyone saw he was here— Well, I'm starving. Come on, Faith—you'll have supper with me?"

Instant, incredible joy. "Oh yes, Nicholas." And then, remembering my place and his, and that Uncle Joel expected him to earn his keep, "But won't your father have arranged—? Shouldn't you be taking Miss Battershaw, or someone?"

"Not a bit of it. He's so pleased now, with Sir Giles, that the Battershaws can all go hang. Come on—before the Hobhouses and the Wintertons clear the board—"

Lady Winterton, indeed, was there before us, circling eagle-eyed around the table, making a most thorough inspection of the cold beef, already sliced and tied back into shape again with satin ribbon, prodding an inquisitive fork into the salmon as if she thought—or hoped—it might have been taken illegally from her river, accepting liberal portions of every dish she passed and wondering out loud if it was really necessary to provide so many.

Sir Giles, with Aunt Verity and Uncle Joel, was installed at a table set apart, screened from the common view by the deft hoverings of butler and head parlourmaid, a dish of oyster patties and a well-iced magnum of champagne to hand, his eldest daughter-in-law, Lady Annabel, offering her erstwhile friend Lady Winterton a slight, immensely superior smile as she came to join him.

"Where is Julian?" snapped Lady Winterton, who always knew the whereabouts of her Francis.

"Oh, somewhere with Miss Barforth," Lady Annabel was quick to reply—already basking in the possibility that her father-in-law's bills might now be paid.

"I don't fancy eating in this crowd," Nicholas announced suddenly, apparently displeased by Lady Annabel's self-assurance as much as by the assembly now jostling and snatching around the supper table. "Let's make for the back stairs." And whispering to a harassed parlourmaid his instructions for a supper tray, he shouldered a way to the door and hurried me along the same passage where I had walked, an hour ago, with Jonas.

I had sat on these back stairs a dozen times before with Blaize and Nicholas and Caroline, all of us huddled together, children long past our bedtime, watching the dinner-party dishes as they came out of the kitchen, scuffling like puppies for the leftover chocolate creams and ices the maids handed up to us, Prudence and I round-eyed with admiration when Blaize and Nicholas once downed the contents of a forgotten claret jug, Celia tearful with fatigue and the fear of discovery.

Yet it was different now, settling my wide, silk skirts—my lovely swan dress—on the shallow steps, Nicholas lounging on the step below. Quite different, in the half-dark, eating our supper from a tray laden with cakes and champagne, both of us knowing full well that our being there was not entirely innocent, since the conventions which ruled our lives quite clearly forbade us to be alone together at all. Discovery might mean no more than a tolerant reprimand. "Young lady, you had best go back to your mamma, and we will say no more about it." But it could also mean accusations of improper behaviour, loss of reputation, and he would not have brought me here unless he was prepared to defend me if the need arose, unless he really found pleasure in my company.

"You are so changed," he had said to me in my daydreams. But now, in fact, he said, "We are friends again?" It sufficed.

"Yes—although you have twice embroiled me with your father, who terrifies me. Doesn't he terrify you?"

"He does not. I daresay he would like to, or perhaps he merely thinks that he should. But he does not."

"Then you are very brave."

"Oh yes—a lion. I wonder how Julian Flood will fare at his hands. My father likes a decent return on his investments, so I reckon young Julian had best watch out."

"You're not pleased, are you, that Caroline should want to marry him."

He shrugged, his face in concentration and in shadow quite dark.

"I've nothing against him—so far as the gentry goes he's right enough, and a sight better than that sickly Winterton. But he *is* gentry and she's not, and yes, I have my doubts."

"But she'd be so good at the manor, Nicholas."

"I'm not denying it. She wants the manor all right, and the title, but I'm not sure she understands all that goes with it. Blaize now, he could marry a duchess and manage all right, but he's not like the rest of us. Caroline looks like a duchess, but she's a Barforth. She likes money, but she understands how it's made and the men who make it, and I'm not sure she'll ever understand the Floods."

"They like money too."

"Aye, or they'd not be here tonight. But they want it for different reasons. Look—I reckon you know how my father has spent his life building up Lawcroft Mills and Tarn Edge and Low Cross? But he'd sell them tomorrow and go into something else—and so would I—if it was to his advantage. The Floods can't bring themselves to part with one useless acre, just because it's been in the family for three hundred years. I'm not saying it's right or wrong. I'm saying it's different. And Caroline's not like that. She'd try to run that manor like my father runs the mills, and even if she made the Floods a profit I reckon they wouldn't approve of her methods."

"They'd take the money, though."

"So they would."

We laughed open-heartedly, two people who understood each other, a hardheaded Law Valley man, shrewd and straightforward, who would not always be easy on his woman, rarely romantic, his well-shod feet at all times firmly rooted to the ground; a Law Valley woman, tougher than she seemed, who understood the demands and hazards of his trade, who wanted the things he wanted and appreciated the skill by which they were obtained.

We were alike. We matched, and as I got slowly to my feet, shaking out my skirts and smoothing my hair with hands that trembled and needed to be occupied, I saw in his face the same, narrow-eyed intensity I had seen in Jonas, that spark of awakening and instantly controlled desire that I suppose any man may feel for any presentable woman in a lonely place, but which, far from repelling me as it had done in Jonas, caused my whole body to sway forward, as if it had dissolved in the air between us and was being wafted irrevocably, magically, towards him. And only the fear that is bred into all females who are required to remain virgin—marketable—forced me to pretend that I had stumbled.

"I should go back now, Nicholas."

"Yes," he said, for although his own virginity was a long-past memory, offered, one supposed, in approved Law Valley fashion, to the ladies of the Theatre Royal, he knew he would have to be very careful, very sure of his ultimate intentions before making the very tiniest assault on mine.

"I'll take you back. They'll not have missed you, in all the confusion of supper and Sir Giles."

Yet we had lingered too long, it seemed, for suddenly there was the rustle of a skirt at the far end of the passage, perhaps only the maid come back to fetch her tray, perhaps a stranger who would look askance and go away, perhaps not. I shrank back against the wall, appalled now, when it was too late, by the possibility of discovery and misunderstanding, realising, as so often before, that I should have thought of this sooner.

"Don't worry," Nicholas said, but I think we were both relieved when a voice enquired, "So—and just what is going on here?" for it was only Caroline, her white and silver skirts blocking the passageway, her face—when I was calm enough to look at it—no longer aglow with triumph but creased with ill-temper and the need, perhaps, of finding someone to blame.

"Oh, it's you," Nicholas said. "Thank God for that."

But clearly something was very much amiss, for instead of laughing and coming to join us on those familiar, friendly back stairs, she continued to stand, hard-faced and glaring—as her father had once done—looking for trouble and almost grateful to find it.

"I asked you a question," she said. "What are you doing here, Nicholas?"

"Minding my own business, as you should be minding yours."

"It is my business," she snapped. "This is my party, and I am responsible for the way it is conducted."

And even then he was not really concerned, for it was just Caroline, on her high-horse, as we had seen her many a time, and she would soon climb down again.

"Come on, Faith," he said. "Let's find Aunt Elinor."

But Caroline, suddenly, was a barrier planted before us, refusing even to draw her skirts aside.

"You'll go nowhere, until I've got to the bottom of this."

"Caroline—why the devil must you always interfere?"

"Don't use foul language to me, Nicholas Barforth."

"You've heard worse than that—and from your precious father, too."

"You'll leave my father out of this. He's had more than enough to bear from you. And as for you, Faith Aycliffe—"

"That's enough, Caroline," Nicholas told her, meaning it. And placing myself between them—having enough experience of their tempers to know that some form of distraction was required—said sharply, "What about me, Caroline?"

"Yes, indeed—what about you? I thought I knew you, Faith, but this is the second time you have been caught alone with my brother—well, the first time I was ready enough to believe your story, but I'm not sure what to think now—"

And swiftly, before Nicholas could answer for me—knowing that once battle commenced between them I would be unable to make myself heard—I said coolly, "Well then, Caroline, you may think exactly what you please, for if you can do no better than draw these foolish conclusions then you are as great a goose as my sister Celia—"

"How dare you speak to me like that?" she asked, quite stunned, really wanting to know, and since it was important to me that Nicholas should realise I could defend myself, that I was no simpering, schoolroom miss only too happy to be compromised, I was ready enough to explain.

"There's no daring about it, Caroline. You are being quite stupid, and I see no reason why I shouldn't tell you so."

"Then I'll give you a reason. You are a guest in my father's house, where certain standards are always maintained, and you have behaved shockingly."

"I have done no such thing, and you know very well I have not. Most likely it is Julian Flood who has done something shocking, by the look of you, for why else are you here, dashing up the back stairs—which happens to be the quickest way to your bedroom. And I won't be the scapegoat for it, Caroline, so you'd best go to nanny and have a good cry."

There was, of course, the possibility that she would hit me, that Nicholas would roughly intervene, that nanny herself would appear and go running for Uncle Joel, who would then thrash Nicholas, a scene I had witnessed more than once while we were growing up. But realising, even in her outrage, that the repercussions would be different now—that she was, in fact, quite fond of me and knew I was fond of her—she unclenched her reckless Barforth fist and contented herself with the lesser violence of hissing at me, "I never thought this of you, Faith. I never thought you'd turn on me. Well, it's envy, I suppose—just envy—and I should be accustomed to that."

"My word," Nicholas said, when she had pushed me aside and mounted the stairs, one imperious step at a time, hoping I had not noticed the tears in her eyes. "Who's the lion now?"

"Yes—but I suppose I had better go after her and say I am sorry—which indeed I am—since I think she is very sorry herself. What on earth can Julian Flood have done to her?"

"Nothing much. Tried to kiss her, I expect, and if she doesn't like it then she should stop thinking about the manor, since one thing goes with the other. Leave her to it. She'll come looking for you tomorrow to apologise and tell you all about it. But come, Faith—quickly now—for we have been away long enough."

And taking my hand he hustled me to the end of the passageway and out, through a little side door I had forgotten about, not into the deep midnight I had expected but a clear, rose-tinted daybreak.

"Oh, Nicholas—look. I have never stayed up all night before."

"No, I suppose you have not. Listen, we cannot go in together now. You must go round the side of the house and through the garden door to the back parlour, and then through into the hall. Do you remember the way?"

"Oh yes. But what a pity to go in at all."

"Faith," he said. "Don't you know the fix you could be in?"

But he was laughing, anxious and amused at the same time, a Barforth who did not wish to compromise me because he did not wish to be compromised himself, but who, with his share of inherited recklessness, of lusty Barforth appetite, was unwilling to miss an opportunity, so that naturally and easily he bent his head and brushed his mouth lightly against the corner of mine; a half-kiss which would have been acceptable, between cousins, under the mistletoe at Christmastime, no more than that now, perhaps, to him, but the most important thing, I believed, and so far the most thrilling—in my life.

"Run," he said, and I ran, giddy and glowing, through the garden door, not caring if even Aunt Hannah should be there, since Nicholas had kissed me. But the back parlour was empty, the crowd thinning in the hall, music still playing, servants still hurrying to and fro, an air of impending departure, of cloaks and carriages, of battles already won or lost. Surely I had been missed? Surely there would be the ugliness of questions and recriminations, a dreadful poking and prying into the crystal-clear enchantment I was still feeling, that I believed I would feel forever? But, reaching the ballroom door in a state of considerable alarm, I saw, as often proves the case, that everyone had found his own affairs more interesting than mine, my mother still lounging in her chair murmuring wicked replies to whatever Mr. Oldroyd, on the chair behind, was whispering over her shoulder, my forgotten, abandoned sister Prudence sitting patiently beside Aunt Hannah, while, a chair or two away from them, Jonas—desperate, hard-pressed, offended Jonas—was most surprisingly, most deeply in conversation with Celia.

Chapter Six

AUNT HANNAH, it seemed, was not so entirely in her stepson's confidence as she imagined, for when he proposed to my sister Celia the following week, during the course of an Assembly Rooms charity ball, she was quite taken aback and, to begin with, not greatly pleased.

"Jonas—what *do* you mean?" she said to him when he and Celia approached her hand in hand at the close of the dance. And since she could not believe Jonas capable of impropriety, she turned her formidable Barforth eye on Celia—recognising a scheming young hussy when she saw one—and ordered, "You had best go to your mother, young lady, and inform her that I shall have a word to say on your account."

We took Celia home in a state, almost, of collapse, weeping in a corner of the carriage and complaining most bitterly that the whole world was against her, that neither Prudence nor Faith would have been treated in this fashion, that she had done nothing wrong.

But the next morning, when Jonas had made it clear that Prudence would not have him, and stressed, no doubt, what Mr. Corey-Manning's retirement could mean to them both, my aunt appeared very early in Blenheim Lane to announce herself highly delighted, and to set Celia's mind at ease.

She was prepared, within the privacy of the family circle, to admit—although not in Celia's hearing—that Jonas' attentions to one sister and his subsequent proposal to another may be thought rather bold, but then, it was well known that young people were impulsive, apt to be carried away by their tender feelings, and so far as the outside world was concerned Jonas—clever, crafty Jonas—had not committed himself to Prudence, and there could be no question that she had been jilted, or that Celia was second-best.

It had, of course, been somewhat headstrong of Jonas to approach Celia directly, without first requesting the opinion of her guardians, but, once again, the natural ardours of youth must be held to blame and, before calling on us, she had gone first to Tarn Edge and spoken to Uncle Joel—whose consent, by the terms of my father's will, would be necessary—and had made all smooth with him. His niece could be married, he had declared, whenever she pleased, and there seemed little doubt that in his desire to see her well settled, his assistance to Jonas in a certain matter of business would not be denied.

Aunt Hannah, in fact, was happy, for now, with the solid capital of Celia's dowry behind him, Jonas had set his foot on the first, golden rung of the ladder she had long ago designed on his behalf. Mr. Corey-Manning's business would soon be his. He would be a householder, a man of substance and authority, while she, relieved of the anxiety of his expenses, could devote herself entirely to her civic campaign. Jonas himself, one supposed, and for the same reasons, was happy too. Celia, having received her first and presumably her last proposal at the tender age of fifteen—before either of her elder, more highly regarded sisters—could hardly contain her bliss. But when Aunt Hannah had gone to announce her news elsewhere, and Celia, exhausted by rapture, had retired upstairs with Miss Mayfield to discuss her trousseau, Prudence, who had been ominously silent all morning, planted herself firmly in front of my mother, and said, "You cannot permit this, Mamma."

"My dear, what an odd notion. Why on earth should I wish to prevent it?"

"You know very well why, Mamma, for they are totally unsuited. She is not yet sixteen and she is not clever. She has no idea of the consequences—"

My mother smiled. "Oh—cleverer than you think, my dear—surely—since she knows exactly what she wants in life, as you do not. And as for the consequences, if one gave too much thought to consequences I doubt if one would do anything at all."

I saw Prudence flex her hands slightly, a movement as nervous yet as fastidious as a cat's, expressing her utter dislike of artifice, her rejection of all those—my mother among them—who lived by it.

"Quite so, Mamma. But in fact she is being manipulated to suit the interests of others, who are not greatly concerned as to what Celia's own interests might be. And if you do not choose to understand that, then— Really, Mamma, I shall have no alternative but to go and see Uncle Joel."

"My word," my mother said, her face dimpling and twinkling with smiles, "how brave you are. Would you really go to my brother and demand his attention? Why yes, I believe you would for, truly, you are so much like your half brother, of whom we were never allowed to speak. Dear Crispin, so prickly and difficult, and such a great romantic, just as you are, dear— he had such wide, shining ideals. I daresay I am not the only woman in Cullingford who sometimes wonders what has become of him. But never mind that— You would go to your uncle, would you, Prudence? And what would you tell him? That Jonas Agbrigg wishes to marry your sister for her money? He is perfectly well aware of that, dearest. Money is a perfectly acceptable reason for a young man to marry. In fact, when Jonas approached your uncle some weeks ago about this business of Mr. Corey-Manning, your uncle himself suggested that the quickest way out of the dilemma would be to find a suitable wife. My brother's generosity is realistic rather than philanthropic, and although he has great faith in Jonas' ability, he was unwilling to elevate him to a position he could not maintain. His marriage to Celia will provide him with the means to maintain it, and will provide her with the wedding ring which, you cannot deny, is the one thing she desires. My dear, I am not forcing her to the altar. You may think me insensitive, but I can assure you I would never do such a thing. She wants to marry him. You tell me I cannot permit it, but even if you could prevail upon me, and Uncle Joel, and Aunt Hannah, to cancel, then Celia herself would thwart you. I believe you will find, when you are calm enough to talk to her, that she has fallen in love. Oh yes, my dear, and why not? In a few months' time she will be the mistress of her own home, with her own servants to do her bidding and her own horses to be got out whenever it pleases her to drive into town, while you and Faith remain here with me. She will have her own calling cards to deliver, with her own name writ large for everyone to see, while you and Faith will have to make do with your names printed, very small, under mine. And she can do no less than fall in love with the man who has made such wonders possible."

"I *will* talk to her, Mother," Prudence said, her chin at a mutinous angle. "I *will* point out to her the sheer folly of it all, the incompatibility of their natures and what it could lead to—and then at least one of us will have made an attempt to do right by her."

"As you wish, dear," my mother murmured very sweetly. "But I cannot advise it. It will merely convince her you wanted Jonas for yourself, which is something she will be well pleased to believe—and since he did not actually propose to you—did not, in fact, give you the opportunity of refusing him—she may feel quite justified in saying so."

We went upstairs together, Prudence and I, hesitating at Celia's door.

"It's my fault, of course," Prudence said, straight of back, straight of soul. "If I had done as I ought and allowed him to propose to me, instead of scuttling upstairs in a panic, then he could hardly have gone from me to her a week later. There would have been at least a decent interval, time for her to think. Well, I have never shirked anything before, and I promise you I will never do so again."

"It was not like you to run away, Pru."

"No. And if I had seen any possibility of an honest exchange of views between us I would not have done so. If he could have brought himself to say to me, 'I need your money, Prudence. And in exchange for it I will make you independent of your mother, who irritates you, and of my mother, whose interference you cannot tolerate. Marry me, and I will be rich and you will be free to lead the life of an adult female, not a grown-up child at home.' If he had said that, then I would still have refused him, since there is much in his nature I cannot like, but I would have respected him. I would have given an honest answer to an honest question. But no—I knew he would feel obliged to offend my intelligence by talking of his tender feelings, as he has clearly done to Celia, and I would have been forced to play out the sickly charade by murmuring something about being honoured by his attentions. I could not do it. And Mother, for once, is quite right. Anything I might say to Celia would be instantly misconstrued as jealousy."

"Mother is often right, Prudence, if one listens carefully. Say nothing. We always knew Celia would take the first man who asked her, and Jonas is not so—so very much worse than anyone else—is he?"

"Worse? No, I do not think of him as bad. In fact if Aunt Hannah had not got her hands on him so early and filled him so full of her social climbing nonsense, then he might have been a great deal better. He is very clever, and perhaps he is rather cold by nature, but I think it is Aunt Hannah who has made him so resentful. Whereas Celia—oh, heavens, Faith—Celia is such a goose."

There was, in fact, very little amiss with my sister Celia that a few more years of residence in the world would not have mended. She was, quite simply, too young, for which the cure was obvious, too apt to feel herself slighted and to draw attention to herself by falling unwell, quite natural, perhaps, in a younger child too often excluded from the pastimes and confidences of her sisters. But when I went in to see her that morning, as my mother had said, she had already passed from the smug contemplation of herself as a bride—the very first of her generation to marry—to a state of blissful, if self-manufactured love which was undoubtedly giving her immense satisfaction.

"I know he paid attention to Pru," she told me, with genuine concern, since, in the overflow of her own heart she had no desire to wound others. "But he explained all that to me. He considers Pru to be an admirable girl, which indeed she is, and when Aunt Hannah suggested she would make him an excellent wife, he was bound to agree. But gradually, during his visits, he found himself drawn quite against his will to me, not realising the implications until it was too late—and I will confess, Faith, that I had begun to suspect it, for I told you, on the night of Caroline's dance, which way I thought the wind was blowing. Well, I found myself thinking about him too, far more than I should have done, and he was in a positive quandary, in case he had committed himself too far with Prudence. Only think of it, he was worrying about upsetting Prudence all the time I was worrying about Prudence upsetting him, which seems so foolish and so sweet now, the way things have turned out. Of course he didn't mean to propose to me last night. He'd made up his mind that he was honour bound to withdraw a little—cool off, you know, with Prudence, before he could decently approach me. And naturally he thought I was too young and would take fright and he felt he should be very careful so as not to risk losing me. My word—how sweet. But then, last night, we danced and talked—you know how it is—and it just happened. He was so correct and polite, and then, when I had accepted him, so masterful. I was to leave everything to him—Aunt Hannah and Uncle Joel and everything. Prudence will have chances to spare, you know she will. There is Freddy Hobhouse, who thinks the world of her—and I have seen Jacob Mandelbaum looking at you."

Clever Jonas, I thought, cold, clever Jonas. There is the woman a man knows would be good for him, he had told me, the woman he would like to have, and the woman he can get. But, his needs being too pressing to risk a refusal from the first, he had thought better of the second, and had settled, cold-bloodedly, for Celia, who, in her race to reach the altar, would have accepted very nearly anyone. Yet, had I really been the one he would have liked? And if so, if I had managed, without even noticing it, to captivate this man who had certainly not wished to be captivated, whose satisfactions, I believed, came from the manipulation of legal documents and the amassing, in any way he could contrive, of money, then could I not do the same with Nicholas? But in the bright light of Celia's betrothal morning, I concluded that no more than a fleeting physical impulse, such, I well knew, as a man might feel for a pert housemaid, had inclined Jonas to me, an impulse he had at once stifled and forgotten, returning, with relief, to his natural habitat of self-interest and ambition, where Celia would suit his purposes just as well.

"I hope you will be very happy," I told her.

"Oh—assuredly," she replied, and for the rest of the summer we had nothing to do—were allowed nothing to do—but busy ourselves with Celia's trousseau, Celia's linen and china, Celia's carpets and curtains, and her wedding guests: an occupation frequently tedious but useful, sometimes, when I needed to stop

myself from wondering why, these past weeks, I had seen so little of Nicholas. "I shall ask Cousin Caroline to be a bridesmaid,
of course," Celia announced grandly, "and I can hardly avoid
Cousin Lydia from Sheffield, who used to be my best friend.
And then there are the four Hobhouse girls, and my own two
sisters, which makes eight in all—and since I would not like
Arabella Rawnsley and Rebecca Mandelbaum to feel left out I
had best ask them too. And I have always been quite fond of
Amy Battershaw. What do you think? Although it means asking
someone else to make up a pair. I could have Rebecca's sister
Rachel, who is rather small, or Lydia Rawnsley—although, since
she must be fast approaching twenty-three, perhaps it would not
be kind." And pausing, the marvellous processions forming in
her mind's eye, all these pretty, well-dowered young ladies, the
great Caroline Barforth among them, preceding little Celia
Aycliffe down the aisle, she laughed out loud, flushed and almost
vivacious in her delight.

"They never expected me to be the first," she said. "None of
you did. But there it is. Oh, do be careful how you cut out that
muslin, Faith, for I shall want at least two dozen petticoats from
it, and I have seen a wine-red velvet at Miss Constantine's in
Millergate—no, Faith, not for an evening gown, can you think of
nothing but dress?—for curtains. And with cushion covers and a
mantel valance to match I think it would be an improvement in
any drawing room. Please do not look so astonished at me,
Faith. You may continue to amuse yourself with ribbons and
frills and lace shawls for a while yet, but I am now obliged to
turn my mind to more serious issues."

"Oh yes," Prudence replied tartly, "serious issues indeed . . .
is it to be wax flowers or stuffed birds under glass on the hall
table? My word, how are you ever to decide?"

But Celia, having so easily achieved the summit of her
dreams, was good nature itself, treating us already with the toler-
ance of an adult towards a pair of quarrelsome children, an attitude she felt quite entitled to adopt, since her marriage to Jonas,
arranged for October when she would be just sixteen, would
make her socially older than Prudence and myself, a woman
who "knew," while we remained girls who merely thought we
did.

"I cannot bear it," Prudence told me more than once. "If she speaks to me in that superior manner just once again I shall box her ears. She is living in a dream. Can you make no attempt to being her back to reality?"

And, of course, I could not, for Celia, beyond all warnings, continued to float through her betrothal days on a blissful cloud, composed mainly, it seemed, of carpet samples and heavy, flock wallpapers, mahogany sideboards and red plush armchairs, Jonas—fully occupied by his negotiations with Mr. Corey-Manning—appearing content to leave all such arrangements to her.

"After all, she is paying for them," Prudence snorted as we sat together at our eternal sewing.

"Yes, but she is having such a good time, Pru—surely you can see that. And they may not do too badly together. He will have his business and she will have her furniture. It may suffice."

"He will have his business, certainly, and he will have ours as well, if he sees half a chance of it."

"Prudence, whatever do you mean?"

"Only this," she said, plunging her needle with apparently lethal intent into a fold of fragile, spotted gauze. "He is a man and we are four women alone. At the moment he is no more to us than the stepson of our aunt, whose opinions or demands may count for little. But when he marries Celia he becomes our brother. And if you have not thought of that, then I am quite sure he has thought of it, and Aunt Hannah too. Yes, at the moment there is Uncle Joel, but he will not live forever, and supposing I do not marry, or you do not, or that we are widowed? What happens to spinsters and widows, Faith? They remain at home, or they return there, under the guidance of their closest male relative. And in return for the protection of that male relative they devote themselves and their incomes to his best interests—or a way is found to compel them to do so. Women need a man to speak for them in legal matters and in all other matters of greater importance than a tea party—I am well aware of that—and if I remain single I cannot imagine Jonas allowing me to take my money and live alone, not without a fight. He is a lawyer, remember, and he will know best how to maintain his authority. After all, why should he be content with one dowry, if there is the slightest chance of helping himself to two, or three? And the only way I can avoid it is to get married myself."

Caroline, having completely disregarded our quarrel, was still a regular visitor in Blenheim Lane, still, it appeared, on negotiating terms with Julian Flood, although no announcement had yet been made.

"My word, Celia," she declared, "what a regular beehive—I never realised it took such a quantity of muslin and taffeta to be married. And by the way, if it is to be October, my love, then I fear you can't count on me, for I shall be in Paris by then—which is rather a pity—but you'll not miss one bridesmaid, surely, from among so many. The Battershaws are taking me, and I understand the Floods are to be there for part of the time, which will be very pleasant, except that, really, one can see the Floods at home, any day of the week, and one may feel inclined—in a strange place—to make the acquaintance of a few strangers. One hardly takes the trouble to go abroad for a family party. Well, Celia, I do wish you every happiness. When I get back from France you'll be Mrs. Jonas Agbrigg of—where is it you're going to live?—Albert Place? My Goodness—Mrs. Agbrigg of Albert Place—it doesn't sound a bit like you."

"The date could be put back until Miss Caroline comes home," suggested Jonas' father, the taciturn, hard-working Mr. Ira Agbrigg, who, having made a marriage of convenience himself, was apparently not too pleased to see his only son do likewise. "The lass is young enough, and I reckon my lad can bide his time."

But Mr. Corey-Manning, anxious to hand over his offices in Croppers Court and his good will in Cullingford as a whole, and remove himself to the healthier, quieter air of Bridlington, was in a most decided hurry, quick to insinuate that he had had other offers which he could always reconsider. Aunt Hannah, with other schemes afoot, saw no reason for delay. The very house Celia declared she had always dreamed of was miraculously offered for sale. And when my mother announced that she too would prefer "sooner" rather than "later," October it was certainly to be.

"The house is in excellent condition," my mother insisted. "All they need do is select their furnishings and have them carried inside, and as for the linen and the trousseau, it need not be done entirely at home. It is altogether permissible and fashionable, nowadays, to *purchase* such things ready-made, and we have these marvellous trains, do we not, to fetch them to us?" Having no more taste for wedding fever, it seemed, than Prudence, my mother at once obtained the services of upholsterer, cabinetmaker, plasterer—trades I had not realised she knew existed—went herself to Leeds and Bradford and over the Pennines to Manchester for the items our local shopkeepers could not supply, despatched a team of scrubbing women to the newly acquired, four-square house in Albert Place, engaged a cook, a parlourmaid, a pair of Aunt Hannah's charity girls to do the "rough," an outside man, who was at once kept busy fetching Celia's parcels from every train. And I knew my mother well enough to realise that all this was being done to suit neither Celia, Jonas, nor Aunt Hannah, but herself.

"You did not know I possessed such energy, did you?" she told me, coming into my room a fortnight or so before the wedding. "But since Celia so greatly desires to be married, I may as well give her a little push in her chosen direction. And I will confess to you, Faith, that when I came back for Caroline's party I did not intend to stay even this long. No—no—I required merely to sort out my affairs with Uncle Joel—matters of finance which I make no effort to understand since my brother is so good as to understand them for me, and will not cheat me in any case. And now, my dear, with this wedding almost out of the way, I really do not feel up to another Cullingford winter."

"So you will go abroad again, Mamma?"

"Yes, dear, as I would have gone three months ago, had it not been for Celia—although, as it turns out, this marriage relieves me of the obligation to have her suitably cared for while I am away. I have only Prudence and yourself to think of, and Prudence is well content to stay here with Miss Mayfield, who is quite terrified of her and will allow her to do just as she pleases. She will have a married sister, after all, and a most efficient brother-in-law who may be applied to in case of need, so there is no impropriety in leaving her behind. You, dear Faith, are to come with me. Now—what do you think of that?"

I sat down carefully on the corner of my bed, thinking, quite simply, of Nicholas—Nicholas—unable to tell her that I could not bear to remove myself from the place where I might see him—although lately I had seen him so seldom—and go to a place where there was no hope of seeing him at all.

"It would be very—pleasant—Mamma—except that, perhaps —I think I should stay with Prudence—"

"Now why should you think that?" she said, her smile twinkling across the room to me. "I am sure Prudence has no particular need of you. Whereas I, my dear, have encountered certain annoyances in travelling alone. I have arranged for us to set off at once after the wedding—you see how masterful I can be when I set my mind to it—for if I stay to see them back from honeymoon I may be obliged to delay even longer for the birth of my first grandchild. And, in any case, dearest, apart from the fact that travel broadens the mind—and, heaven knows, a mind raised in Cullingford could not escape being narrow—it would be as well for you to be away from Nicholas Barforth."

I felt not only the colour flooding my cheeks and then leaving them—leaving me very cold—but far more than that, a sense, I think, of enormous protest, followed first by the fear of loss, a desperate urge to prevent it, and then the certainty that he was lost already, a terrible feeling, so that I could only mutter, "Mamma—if you imagine—"

"Oh," she said, still smiling, "I do not imagine. I do much more than that. I may not be clever, Faith, like your father and Prudence, nor am I a domestic mouse like Celia, but what I have always been able to do, quite unerringly, is to see exactly what is going on between a man and a woman. It is my one talent. Dearest, I am not being unkind, you know, just sensible. I would be delighted to see you married to Nicholas Barforth. It would be altogether splendid. But there is so much against it, not least the sorry fact that you are ready for marriage, and he is not. My dear, only poor men and old men have need of wives. Young men who happen also to be rich can afford to marry late, or indiscreetly, or not at all, but usually they wait and enjoy their freedom, until middle age inclines them to sobriety. When they become forty, or fifty, they may begin to think of the advisability of having sons to assist them in their businesses and to inherit their money—and they require young girls for that. When Nicholas has sown his oats—of which, my dear, he has an ample store, for he is my brother's son, and Joel was not always so steady—it would be too late, my love, for you. I am sorry to put it to you so bluntly, but it is the way of the world, my poor Faith, and I cannot alter it. Blaize is the same, and Jonas even would be like them if he could, for why should a man rush to limit himself in marriage when its pleasures are so readily available to him without responsibility—without encumbrance? A spinster is a sorry sight, my dear, but a bachelor who has his youth and looks and money to spend—that is another story. You need marriage, Faith. It is the one career open to you, and if you do not succeed in that, then your whole life will be accounted a failure. If Nicholas stays single all his days, he may still be acknowledged a dashing fellow. And, in any case, I have good reason to believe he is not ready, and that he knows he is not ready to settle down. The world is wide for him, it is very narrow for you, and you may console yourself, when you are weeping for him tonight, that he would not voluntarily have kept his distance these last few months had he not felt a certain measure of attraction. Had he seen you merely as a pleasant, friendly girl —well—he would have continued to see you, would he not, and to dance with you, and take you in to supper, and neither Aunt Verity nor I would have troubled to notice it. But we have noticed it, and he, my love, has chosen—for once in his life—to be sensible. So must you."

"Yes, Mamma."

"Excellent. And you need not be so cast down, for you will find much in France and Italy to distract you. We do not know each other very well, Faith dear, for I will confess that your father had but a poor opinion of me, and obliged me to keep my distance from his children—fearing I would muddle your heads with my foolish notions. But I am really quite agreeable, you know, and will try to be a good companion. It is settled then? Of course it is. My goodness—will that confounded wedding day never come."

The Barforths gave Celia a magnificent Coalport dinner service, my mother gave furniture and carpets, Aunt Hannah, who could not be outdone on these occasions, gave the drawing room sofa and chairs. Mr. Fielding, the occupant of my father's seat at Westminster, gave a silver salver for the placing of calling cards, everyone else presented whatever seemed suitable. And as Celia entered the parish church that brisk October morning on Uncle Joel's arm, I would not have believed she could ever look so beautiful.

She had always been a pretty girl but also somehow, quite unremarkable, a face that did not linger in the memory, often ailing, often, in her own opinion, overlooked. But as she drifted down the aisle to her cool, pale Jonas, pure radiance transformed her, its aura lending her so delicate a loveliness that I could well understand why weddings were occasions for tears. Celia, in fact, was in a state of complete fulfilment, that rare feeling of total self-content where she believed everything she could ever want in life was to be hers. Jonas seemed well satisfied. My mother wept most gracefully throughout the service and later, at the reception, became so misty with tears that it took several pairs of manly—if elderly—arms to console her. The bridesmaids were much admired, although, in the blue organdie of Celia's choosing, I did not feel my best and was not sorry that Nicholas, having been despatched to London on his father's business, could not attend.

There was champagne and cake and cordiality, white horses to drive the bridal pair to the station, Celia still radiant—still beautiful—in her going-away dress of powder blue.

"Well—God bless you, then," Prudence said, more moved than she'd expected.

"Kiss your new brother, girls," Aunt Hannah bid us, and when it was done and we had waved them away, my mother could not return fast enough to Blenheim Lane to pack her own boxes and mine, her eyes every bit as bright and excited as Celia's.

"You are going to have so much fun, Faith darling," she told me, and since I was Morgan Aycliffe's daughter, trained to believe that even when one's heart was aching and one's hopes in ashes, one should have the good manners not to embarrass others by letting it show, I answered, "Yes, Mamma."

And so, the next morning, we were separated for the first time, the Aycliffe girls who had spent their quiet lives identically together, going now their different ways, Celia most incredibly to Scarborough with Jonas, Prudence to Blenheim Lane and the chaperonage of Miss Mayfield, which was no chaperonage at all, myself, quite simply, away from Nicholas.

"Write to me, Prudence."

"Yes, at least once a week. To promise more would be foolish. Please remember to reply."

"I don't want to go."

"No. But when the time comes, I expect you won't want to come back either."

I had made up my mind to be miserable, but I was still only seventeen, and even the train to London, which I wished to find uncomfortable and tedious, became less wearisome after a mile or so, the novelty of a hotel bedchamber, a restaurant, my mother's light chatter, no longer mother to daughter but woman to woman, first diverting, then almost exciting.

"We need clothes, dear," she said, "in Paris." And so we had clothes, purchased from a tiny, irritable creature with the face of a beribboned terrier who caused us to wait his good pleasure, no humble seamstress this, but a man of authority who gave to the designing of women's clothes the same dedication and self-importance with which other men built bridges.

"He will not dress you unless he likes you," my mother murmured, surprisingly nervous. "And you may not say what you would like. He will tell you what you must have. Be careful, my dear, for when I was last here I saw him turn away the wife of an ambassador, and also a countess."

A far cry, then, from the dressmakers of Cullingford who would come scurrying to attend us in our own homes, only too eager to dress anybody in anything they had in mind. But when M. Albertini had prowled around me for a tense moment, wreathing me in the smoke from his continual cigar, the entire salon —where even his assistants had the hauteur of great ladies— hushed with the anticipation of his verdict, he came to an abrupt halt, clapped his hands together, and declaring my green crepe de chine to be an abomination—"London? Of course— what else could one expect?"—announced that if I came back in a day or two, and if his inspiration had matured by then, he would create a toilette for which I would shed tears of gratitude.

Yet, the one thing I did find—and fairly soon—was that this prancing little ballerina was, in fact, as shrewd a man of business as any I had met in Cullingford, his taste—and his tyranny —veering always to the expensive, the rare, the unattainable, which he—by his genius, his magic—would obtain for "madame" at a price. And until he explained them to me, I had not fully understood the variety of my needs.

There were his peignoirs, delicate, foamy creations designed for the sipping of early morning tea, the opening of letters and invitations, to be worn in the luxurious, languid hours before one put on one's stays. There was his pelisse—on another plane entirely from the pelisses I had known, and which he advised me to consign to the fire—still a morning dress, but a little more substantial, more elaborate, in which one could receive one's callers. There was his elegant, superbly cut redingote for the afternoon, should madame decide to drive or stroll in the park, the lavishly flounced and embroidered round-dress, should she decide to remain, just as splendidly, at home. There was, most decidedly, his evening dress, its bodice cut low, moulded to bosom and waist, a rich satin which, he assured me, was the exact pale blond colour of my hair. And then there were the "little things," as he called them, lace-edged shawls from Cashmere, flowing soft-tinted and supple from shoulder to ankle, fans and reticules and pairs of gloves in the dozens, feather bonnets and frilled bonnets, a dashing military cap with gold tassels and bold plumage, ivory combs to put up my hair by night, tortoise shell inlaid with mother-of-pearl by day.

"You will think me extravagant—and somewhat frivolous," my mother said, surveying our purchases, her own far exceeding mine. "And so I am. But this is *my* time, Faith—the only time in my life when I have been allowed to do as I pleased, to think what I like rather than what is expected of me, and it may not last for long. Something will force me back to Blenheim Lane, sooner or later—Jonas will set up a caterwauling that I am running through my money and there will be none left for Celia, and Joel will curb my spending. Something will happen to restrain me, and restore me to respectability, and even if it should not, then eventually I shall grow old. So you will be a good-hearted girl, dear, and will not grudge me my special time."

We remained in France until mid-December, moving south as the winter sharpened to a villa on the outskirts of Rome, marble floors leading one to the other in swirling patterns of blue and purple, walls bright-painted with scenes of a voluptuous grape harvest, crumbling stone steps descending to a formal garden of clipped box hedges, stone basins, and water-bearing cupids, where a gentleman who had called to renew his acquaintance with my mother, kissed the palm of my hand and my wrist and was never seen by me again. We went to Naples to greet the springtime, then on to Monaco and back to Rome where another gentleman, more appreciative of my mother's maturity, was waiting.

"Do I shock you?" she asked me. "I suppose I do. I believe I shocked myself to begin with. But it is quite amazing how quickly one grows accustomed to one's own frivolity. I do not think I am *entirely* frivolous. It is just that I cannot nourish myself with ambition like Aunt Hannah, and did not have the great good fortune to fall quite blissfully in love with my husband a dozen years after I had married him, like Aunt Verity. So I must do the best I can, dear, for as long as I can—surely . . . ?"

There were sudden departures in perilous coaches, the caprice of every butterfly moment, strange inns by the wayside—malarial, Aunt Hannah would have named them—beautiful houses placed freely—one supposed—at our disposal by my mother's last year's acquaintances. There were flowery hillsides at noon, mounted on donkeys, red wine and garlic-flavoured cheeses eaten carelessly on the sparse grass in view of a gold-speckled slumbering sea. Perfumed rooms in the evening, candle-lit frivolity, a rose-petal world where men with dark, supple faces—reminding me far more of Blaize than of Nicholas—whispered entertaining nonsense to my mother, and, quite often, to me.

"It is a very small place, Cullingford, is it not?" she often asked me, and I don't know how it was that I knew—or exactly when I knew—that the suave, eternally good-humoured Signor Marchetti, who had so willingly lent us his Roman villa, was her lover, except that, without witnessing the slightest physical contact between them, I knew it, the realisation coming so gradually that when the truth finally dawned it did not even surprise me.

"Paris again," she announced one morning and, at her restless, magical command, there was an apartment built with its feet in the Seine, the soaring façade of Notre Dame filling our windows, morning promenades shaded by frilled parasols and chestnut trees, a certain Monsieur Fauret escorting us most courteously to the opera, the ballet, to Versailles, offering us his carriage for our drives in the Bois de Boulogne, waiting most patiently as we made our purchases from the couturier, Monsieur Albertini, or from my mother's favourite perfumerie in the rue St-Honoré. He was a slightly built, middle-aged man, this M. Fauret, scrupulously correct at all times in my presence, making his formal bow over my mother's hand.

"Will you do me the honour of dining, madame—and mademoiselle?" But there were occasions when my mother, in her extravagant, spangled black gauzes, would set out alone, returning late and oddly languorous, smiling and sighing over the flowers which would arrive the following day. And although she never spoke of love, or passion, or whatever name she had for it, I knew: and, forgetting such weighty matters as sin and the certain retribution I had been taught must follow, it intrigued me that a relationship between a man and a woman could be so light yet so obviously satisfying to them both.

Naturally, the rules she had chosen to live by—while her special time endured—could not apply to me. My own virtue must remain not merely intact but utterly beyond reproach. Yet my fast-growing knowledge of life as a reality rather than a nursery tale designed to frighten me into obedience caused me to examine each one of my girlhood prohibitions, to sort out, as best I could, the sense from the nonsense, the necessary from the purely repressive, so that I became older, at seventeen, and then at eighteen, than I might otherwise have been. I acquired, with a deliberate effort, a little poise—more than would be thought proper in Cullingford. I applied myself to the art of conversation, the art of listening, the art of making the best of what nature had given me. I applied myself to the art of forgetting Nicholas Barforth, of reducing him to the provincial young man who had charmed me in the days when I had been a provincial young lady. And I pretended to succeed.

I heard news, erratically, from Caroline, to whom Paris, with the Battershaws, had been something of a disappointment. And although she referred often enough to the Floods, either Julian had made no definite proposal or she, somewhat inexplicably, was managing to keep him at bay. She had spent Christmas Eve at Cullingford Manor, she told me—a sure indication of intent—but then, instead of the announcement I had been expecting, her letter had altered course, recounting that Blaize, as reluctant as ever to spend his time in the weaving sheds, had decided—and was attempting to convince his father—that his talents would be best employed in selling Barforth cloth abroad.

"He means to wine and dine his way all over the world," she wrote me, "with snippets of cloth in his luggage, doing his selling in fancy hotels and restaurants instead of the Piece Hall and the Wool Exchange, like everybody else. Very pleasant for *him,* Nicholas says, although I believe Father may be agreeable, for it is true that unless we know what weight and what design of cloth will suit the tastes and climate of various parts of the world, we can hardly supply it. And Blaize, who can be very pleasant when he likes, will give a good impression of us abroad, which is something to be considered now that so many new-comers are pushing into the textile trade, as fast as they can get themselves fixed up with looms."

Strange preoccupations, I thought, in a future baronet's lady, and although she told me that Nicholas, accepting Blaize's challenge, had declared himself ready and able to handle any shipping orders his brother sent home, she omitted to mention if he had danced with Amy Battershaw or Rebecca Mandelbaum at the Assembly Rooms Ball, or if—a dread possibility with which I sometimes scourged myself—he had encountered someone new, whose mysterious allure might tempt him from his cherished bachelorhood.

From my sister Celia I received a fortnightly catalogue of domestic trivia—the devastating effect of sunlight on her dining room curtains, the inefficiency of Mr. Corey-Manning, whose affairs in Croppers Court had been left in such disorder that Jonas was obliged to spend most of his time putting them straight. Prudence wrote to me dutifully, weekly, as she had promised, her elegant copperplate revealing not only her preoccupation with literature, liberty, and mathematics—her determination to acquire some real knowledge—but a concern my mother found amusing, amazing, for the foul condition of Cullingford's streets and the inadequacy of its water supply. She had made new acquaintances, she told me, without describing their faces, giving me the impression that they were serious—I presumed elderly—people, who organised lecturers at the Mechanics Institute on subjects designed to improve the minds and the prospects of the more responsible section of the working class; who raised money to re-equip Cullingford's inadequate infirmary, and spent their leisure hours discussing the desirability of cleaning up the Cullingford Canal, the four vapours of which had been known to blacken silver, or of relieving the squalid overcrowding in Simon Street. And when Cullingford was at last granted its charter, during my balmy Neapolitan springtime, with authority to elect a mayor, fourteen aldermen, and forty councillors—gentlemen who must be possessed of property valued at a minimum of 1,000 pounds, or rated at no less than 30 pounds per annum—Prudence filled many pages with her expectations.

Results, she felt, would be less than perfect, since election in many cases had been sought for prestige rather than a desire to be of service, and it seemed unfair to her that from a population of over seventy thousand only some five thousand persons had a property qualification high enough to enable them to vote at all. But the town council would do more, surely, than the old Lighting and Watching Commissioners had ever done—would have to do more, since the councillors had made such a fuss about getting the charter in the first place—and she could think of no one better, she assured me, than Mayor Agbrigg, to lead them.

"We have always seen him as a quiet man," she wrote, "the least regarded of all that family, where it was always Jonas' brilliance and Aunt Hannah's determination we were taught to admire. A gloomy man, with just cause to be gloomy, perhaps, since I am now sufficiently in his confidence to have been informed of the hardships and sorrows of his past. But a sound man, who has not taken office for his own glory, nor because his wife wishes her share of it, but because he intends to be useful. I like him."

And, in the manner of Caroline, she forgot, or did not think it worth a mention, that Freddy Hobhouse had proposed to her and offered to wait indefinitely for a reply.

"Dear Hannah," my mother had murmured that same morning, sentimental with chianti and sunshine, "what a great day for her—we shall have our concert hall now, with your father's name upon it, you may be very sure. I must write to her at once, and have something delivered—something quite splendid as a token of our congratulations—for she will need our help now, poor Hannah. I doubt if she can extract much more from Joel, and she will spend every penny her husband possesses to make sure his term of office is remembered, and to pave the way for Jonas to come after him. Goodness—if she knew what this lilac taffeta has just cost me."

And it surprised us both, I think, for a moment or two, that Ira Agbrigg's first act as mayor was not the drumming-up of subscriptions for that famous concert hall, but an attempt to purchase, with public money, the privately owned and disastrously mismanaged Cullingford Waterworks Company, so that Simon Street—that putrid district where Prudence, it seemed, in the company of her serious-minded friends, had actually set foot —would no longer be forced to rely on a single standpipe, turned on half an hour a day, or the erratic services of a water cart.

"Good heavens," my mother said, wrinkling her nose, "I do not think Hannah will take very kindly to a Waterworks as a memorial. Could it be that Mr. Agbrigg is not really so tame as we supposed? Ah well, we will go to Switzerland next, Faith—next week, in fact—for they have an abundance of water there. And you may tell dear Prudence that I cannot approve of her visits to Simon Street, nor in the least understand what she can find to do there. In fact I am quite shocked, and not altogether comfortable about yesterday's news that I am to be a grandmamma. No, I realise you were not aware of it, for Celia wrote to me in great secret, considering it improper for young ladies like yourself and Prudence to be informed. However—she describes herself as being in an 'interesting condition,' which I assume to mean 'with child.' And that, my dear, is bound to take us home again—in six months or so—since both Celia and our lady mayoress will expect me to be in attendance at the great event. Ah well, Monsieur Fauret is going to Martinique in any case. Switzerland, then, and Paris to follow. And I think we had best start saying to ourselves, over and over, how pleasant it will be to see Cullingford again."

Chapter Seven

WE WERE AWAY just over a year, journeying north again through a raw November, a pall of thick, yellow fog obscuring the platform at Leeds where we changed trains for Cullingford, so that my mother murmured, again and again, "Heavens, how dark it is. One forgets, every time—how dark—how very meagre . . ."

And since she had come home merely to await the birth of her grandchild and to review her finances with Uncle Joel, it was as well she could not know that events in Europe would soon prevent her from setting off again.

We were standing, all unawares, on the threshold of a revolutionary year, when the people of France would rise up once again and replace their aging king, Louis Philippe, with a new republic, releasing a spark of disobedience which would consume, with stunning rapidity, the autocratic governments of Italy, Germany, Bavaria, Hungary, a vast earthquake of revolt against poverty and oppression, against the yoke of the Hapsburg Empire, the yoke of the landlord and the proprietor, against the old tyranny of the aristocrat and the new tyranny of the industrialist. It was a year in which hundreds of that desperate class we called the "labouring poor" were to sacrifice themselves in the street-fighting in Milan, in Berlin, in Vienna when the Hapsburgs marched in to take it back again; hundreds more who tore up the paving stones of my mother's beloved Paris, and were slaughtered at their barricades, searching, one supposed, for the liberty and equality which all previous revolutions had promised and then managed somehow to deny.

It was the year when our own revolutionaries, the Chartists, would attempt to march on Westminster, bearing a petition of five million signatures, and as many men as they could muster, demanding a vote for every adult male in Britain, and that old revolutionary dream, a secret ballot, to shield him from the persuasion of landlord and millmaster.

Yet we knew nothing of that, standing chilled and travel weary in the swirling fog of a Leeds November—luckily, perhaps, since my mother, who had grown quieter, sadder with every Northern mile, may well have turned tail and rushed back at once, while the ports were still open, and risked herself at the barricades.

"How dark," she said again, as Cullingford loomed into sight. "Midnight at four o'clock in the afternoon. Have I really spent my life here?"

And even I—for whom this was a true homecoming, the rest already little more than a summer dream—was briefly saddened by the rain-soaked, wind-raked hills, the chimney stacks belching their malodorous welcome on the sky line, by the soot-blackened mass of Cullingford itself as we stepped out of the station, a town not planned for beauty, not planned at all, but thrown down anyhow to suit the convenience of millmasters, a factory here, a nettle bed of workers' cottages there, even the parish church—which no longer seemed so noble to my travelled eyes —obscured now by the hastily constructed demands of industry.

"The people—" my mother moaned. "How sad they are . . ." And so they seemed, bowed heads shawl-wrapped and cowering against the cold, perpetually hurrying since nothing in these cobbled, narrow streets offered an inducement to linger; closed carriages looming mud-spattered out of the fog, a sudden cough, muffled by thick air and distance, and then another, a grey drizzle, a factory hooter somewhere mournfully marking time.

"I had forgotten how they cough," my mother said, shivering. "I suppose it is the smoke, and those unsanitary dwelling houses your sister speaks of."

And pressing her handkerchief to her face, she walked quickly across the station yard to where our coachman was waiting.

"Well then, Thompson. We're home again."

"Aye," he replied. "Dratted train was late."

And we set off for Blenheim Lane.

Prudence was in the hallway to greet us, crisp and neat in a gown that had all her usual quiet elegance, her hair a shade or two darker than I remembered, parted in the middle, drawn smoothly over her ears into a low chignon that gave her narrow face a becoming air of maturity. And although I loved her and had longed to see her again, there was a moment almost of shyness when I knew we had not really missed each other.

For the past year, apart from the ineffectual flutterings of Miss Mayfield, she had been her own mistress, had made her own arrangements, her own acquaintances, expressed her own opinions regardless of effect or consequences, come and gone to suit no one but herself, certainly not her whimsical, capricious mother. But now we must both be "young ladies at home," and as the house I still thought of as my father's reached out to claim me—so dim and cool, so very still—I could not tell how long it would be before we found each other again.

"My word, you are very smart," she said, coming to assist with the unpacking of my boxes. But my tales of Monsieur Albertini, the couturier, of Roman gardens and flirtations under Parisian chestnut trees did not interest her, while her references to Mayor Agbrigg's plans for drainage and sewage were an astonishment to me.

"And what has become of Aunt Hannah's concert hall, then?"

"Oh, she will have it, I suppose. But Mayor Agbrigg will not be remembered for that. He has sense enough to know that if Aunt Hannah is allowed to busy herself about the concert hall she will not interfere with his own projects. And his projects are admirable, Faith—truly. He will have a great fight on his hands to buy the Waterworks, for the owners do not at all wish to relinquish it. But he will succeed. It is useless, you know, to preach about 'cleanliness being next to godliness,' to people who are without sufficient water for drinking and cooking, let alone washing. If you live in a street where the standpipe is only turned on once a day and you have but one bucket capable of holding water—and you have a family of eight or ten children in your two-roomed cottage—you do not use that water for scrubbing your floors. You boil your potatoes in it, no matter how discoloured it may be, or what nameless particles of filth you find floating in it, and then you drink the potato water. Presumably you make tea with any drops that are left, and then wait—

all eight or ten of you thoroughly unwashed—until tomorrow, when the tap is turned on again. It is water they need, Faith, not a sermon—and not a concert hall either. And I am convinced Mayor Agbrigg can provide it."

"Goodness, such fervour. I do hope so. And what of Celia, and our dear brother, Jonas?"

She made a slight movement of her shoulders, a half shrug of impatience and a little pity. "I rarely see them. He works. She polishes her silver teapot. I have been too occupied to spend much time with her."

"Occupied with what, Prudence?"

"Well, I have made an acquaintance or two, you know. I have not been dull. In fact I have been quite daring, for I have even had some correspondence with Mr. Crispin Aycliffe, our brother."

"Prudence, you have not! My word, how very interesting . . ." And much impressed, since this was a name we had been forbidden to mention, I sat down on my bed, the contents of my boxes scattered everywhere, the distance between us melting away.

"Yes—I discovered that an acquaintance of mine is acquainted with him too—a most odd coincidence—and so I obtained his address and wrote him a line or two about father's death and the arrangements which had been made—since I suppose no one else had troubled to inform him . . ."

"You mean you offered him a share of your porcelain?"

"Well," she said, flushing slightly. "So I did. And I would have made sure he got it, too, whatever the Barforths and the Agbriggs may have had to say—since it is simply sitting there, behind those glass cases, doing nothing. And he may have been in need. However, he replied most courteously, thanking me but declining, and I have exchanged half a dozen letters with him since then. He has been living abroad but is now in London, married, respectable I suppose, except that he is a Chartist."

"Oh, surely, Pru," I said, fascinated, quite pleasantly horrified, "he cannot be that? Chartists are revolutionaries—and criminals, are they not?"

"Are they? They are demanding one man one vote, which may seem criminal to those who have the vote already. Hardly to those who do not."

"Well, I have never thought much about that. But who is this new acquaintance then? Is he a Chartist too?"

"Possibly. It is a Dr. Ashburn, who comes originally from Cheshire, although he has travelled a great deal and has not been long in Cullingford. He gave a most memorable series of lectures last winter, to which Mayor Agbrigg escorted me, mainly on social issues—starvation and alcoholism and infant mortality, that sort of thing, of which he has ample experience, since he has a great many patients in Simon Street."

"Good heavens. I thought no one in Simon Street could afford a doctor."

"They cannot—or very few—and so it is fortunate for Giles that he has private means."

"Oh yes—Giles, is it? I see."

"I think you do not."

"Do I not? Well then, Pru, what is he like, this Giles? Is he seventy-two, and bald, and fat as a bacon pig?"

She smiled, a trifle unwillingly to begin with, but then with a decided glint of amusement in her eyes. "No. I think he may be thirty, or not much above it, and he is lean rather than fat. And yes, Faith—since you are clearly wondering—I do see him fairly often. But then, I see Freddy Hobhouse even more, and like him better than I used to, since he has stopped trying so hard to marry me. And I see a number of other gentlemen quite regularly besides—none of whom are seventy-two and bald—including Blaize Barforth, which may surprise you." And, in my relief that she had not been seeing Nicholas, I said, without meaning to be unkind, "So it does. I cannot imagine what Blaize may find to amuse him in public health—and sewage."

But my composed, apparently very contented sister was not in the least offended.

"Oh, he does not care a scrap about such things. I believe it merely amuses him to observe a young lady who does—since we are quite a rarity. And, when he chooses, Blaize can be very useful. He will work wonders when it suits him—as he did about the new equipment Giles wanted for the infirmary—although he tends to disappear the moment something else comes along to distract him. Well, one must accept him as he is, and get the best out of him when one can. He and Giles Ashburn are great friends—which may surprise you too."

We went, the next morning, to Albert Place where Celia, much altered by her condition, greeted us as if we had never been away, or, at least, as if she had not really noticed it. And as she drew my mother aside for a whispered consultation about the forthcoming event, of which Prudence and myself were supposed to be unaware, I saw that she, too, had but little interest in our travels.

Everything in Celia's square, immaculate house was just as it should be, her red plush curtains exactly matching her red plush easy chairs, her tasselled footstools, her painstakingly embroidered sofa cushions, the fringed valance hanging from her mantel shelf. Her walls were most fashionably covered with a dark, heavy paper, her floors by a busily patterned carpet of serviceable browns and reds and golds. Her silver teapot was an exact, if smaller, replica of my mother's, the ormolu and enamel clock directly at the centre of her mantelpiece chosen, quite clearly, with my father in mind. The ornamental plates and jugs and china figurines on the shelves above the fireplace were most meticulously arranged, everything, from her profusely carved mahogany sideboard to the leaves of her potted plants, exhibiting a most luxurious polish. But even so, in the midst of the well-ordered, well-sheltered comfort her nature craved, she had her share of complaints.

"Yes—as I told you in my letter, I was obliged to get rid of that kitchenmaid. Aunt Hannah may not have liked it, since she recommended her to me, but her tabletop was a disgrace, and her boots—treading dirt into my house—and leaving her pans to soak overnight to save herself the trouble of scouring them. I have seen five girls already and am not entirely satisfied with one. Well, Jonas leaves it all to me, since he has not a moment to call his own. He is always at that dreadful office, slaving away—clearing up Mr. Corey-Manning's mistakes. My word, you are very smart, Faith, but you will not wear a light-coloured gown like that more than twice in Cullingford, before the dirt will begin to show. I confess I have lost my taste for fashion since I was married. If I may be tidy and presentable it is all I ask—and all one should ask, I think, since a married woman has so many other matters on her mind, and should not, in any case, make herself conspicuous. You may give my regards to Caroline when you see her tonight, for she never comes near me these days—and I could not, at the moment, risk myself outdoors." .

We drove next to Lawcroft Fold, to pay our respects to our lady mayoress, finding her far too occupied by personal affairs and civic affairs—the two being apparently quite interchangeable—to have more than a brief moment for our travellers' tales.

Yes, she believed Paris to be a most interesting city, but were we aware of the scandalous refusal of the Cullingford Waterworks Company to co-operate with her husband? Yes, she had heard that the climate and architecture of Italy were very fine, a land of immense achievement in art and music, but we must surely have heard from Celia how very well Jonas was doing, how, in these days of expanding trade, of contracts and disputes and newfangled regulations, even such substantial businessmen as Oldroyd and Hobhouse, Mandelbaum and Barforth, were showing themselves grateful for his advice.

Mr. Corey-Manning, we must certainly remember, had given much of his time to the defending of felons—being a man of a dramatic disposition, more suited, she felt, to the odd calling of an actor than the dignified practice of the law—but Jonas, finding nothing to amuse or challenge him in such petty crimes as were to be found in Cullingford, had chosen, very shrewdly, to concentrate on civil matters, which would bring him to the attention of those who could pay.

"The dear boy—" my mother said vaguely.

"Yes, Elinor, and you will be settling yourself down at last, now that you are to be a grandmamma?"

"Oh—as to that—"

But, happily perhaps, my mother's declaration of intent was interrupted by the arrival of Mayor Agbrigg himself, no less haggard and hollow-chested for all his civic dignity, bringing another gentleman with him who, very clearly, did not find favour with my aunt.

And, as always, in a mixed, unexpected gathering, there were shades of greeting.

"I'm right pleased to see you," Mayor Agbrigg said to my mother, wishing her well when he remembered to think of her at all, which was probably not often.

"Well—and you're looking grand, miss," to me, his stock attention to any young lady to whom attention was due.

But: "Now then, lass, and how are you today?" to Prudence, really wanting to know, his craggy face warming, something in him suggesting his readiness to take action should she be less than "very well indeed."

"And how are you?" she enquired with equally genuine concern. "You seemed so tired on Wednesday evening at the institute."

"Aye—but it was only from listening to old Dr. Blackstone droning on. If your aunt Hannah hadn't kept on nudging me I'd have fair disgraced myself and nodded off."

"Ah well," Aunt Hannah said, clearly displeased. "We can't all be so fluent as Dr. Ashburn—"

And, with the air of a woman acting very much against her will, at the dictates, merely, of Christian conscience and common politeness, she waved her hand vaguely in the direction of her husband's companion, and said coolly, "Elinor—this is Dr. Ashburn. Dr. Ashburn—my sister, Mrs. Aycliffe, and her other daughter, Miss Faith Aycliffe. Prudence you already know."

And it was very apparent that, if she had had her way, he would be acquainted with none of us.

I found myself looking at a man of medium height, medium colouring, brown hair, brown eyes—although I could not afterwards remember their exact shade—no sinister revolutionary as his Chartist sympathies might have led me to believe, but slightly and quite finely built, a face that was almost delicate, a great air of quietness about him, a man—certainly a gentleman —who observed life, perhaps, more readily than he participated.

"I am delighted to meet you at last," he told me, his accent quite neutral, giving no indication of his place of birth, his voice rather low so that one had to listen in order to hear him, but not hesitant, perfectly in keeping with that first impression of inner quietness.

"Dr. Ashburn is becoming very famous among us," Aunt Hannah cut in, her voice, following immediately after his, sounding very shrill. "He has set himself to teach us the error of our ways. He believes we neglect our workpeople and that your husband, Elinor, provided them with shocking, even dangerously constructed houses. He makes us all feel quite ashamed."

"Now then—now then—" Mayor Agbrigg said easily, obviously well accustomed to this.

"And so we should," Prudence muttered.

"Should we?" my mother asked lightly. "Well, I have never examined my husband's houses very minutely, but I do not think I would care to live in one of them. Do you live in an Aycliffe cottage dwelling, Dr. Ashburn?"

"No," he told her, smiling, completely untroubled by my aunt's hostility, "I am in Millergate, madam."

"Oh good—so near to us. You must call—in fact, you must dine, since I believe you call already. Would next Tuesday evening suit you?"

And as he replied that it would suit him very well I glanced at Prudence, finding her surprisingly calm, far calmer than I would have been in the presence of Nicholas.

"You will have come today to patch up our rioters, Doctor," Aunt Hannah said, her sarcasm deepening, her eyes sliding to my mother, who rose, predictably, to her bait.

"Rioters, Hannah? Whatever can you mean?"

"Only that you have chosen an unfortunate time for calling, Elinor, since our local Chartists are coming today—have already arrived, if I am not mistaken—to present their petition to our workers in the mill yard. Yes—you can see them from the window—they have overturned a barrel to serve as a table and are collecting signatures, or are trying to, since I doubt if there are many who can write their names. Well, they went to Nethercoats a month ago, and when Bradley Hobhouse discharged all those who signed there was a scuffle and a few broken heads. So my husband has taken the precaution of inviting his doctor, I presume."

"I hope I may not be needed, Mrs. Agbrigg."

"I daresay. But if you are, it will not be the first time. It may interest you to know—you and my niece Miss Prudence Aycliffe, who interests herself in these matters—that my brother's wife—your aunt Verity, Prudence—saw her father murdered down there, in this same mill yard, when she was no more than sixteen, and the night after was at her brother's side when he was done to death—horribly done to death—by felons who called themselves Luddites in those days—Chartists today. I do not forget it—even if others do."

"Hannah—my dear Hannah," my mother murmured, her hand going out in a gesture of comfort and affection to her sister, my invincible, immovable aunt Hannah, who seemed most amazingly close to tears. But the weight of memory between them was clearly burdensome to Mr. Agbrigg, who, his face for a moment more drawn than I had ever seen it, blinked hard, needing, I thought, to clear his vision, to shut something away.

"There'll be no bloodshed today," he said gruffly. "I'll go down and see to it."

"I'll come with you," she said.

"There's no need."

"I did not say there was need. I said I will come with you, as far as the bottom gate. And Dr. Ashburn will remain here. The presence of a doctor is an announcement that we expect violence, and so may invite it. He can be sent for."

She picked up her shawl, wrapped it firmly around her shoulders, and went out of the room, leaving us without a word, her face set and stony. And we gathered instinctively at the window where, positioned as we were so high on the terraced hillside, we could see right over the factory wall to the yard, which appeared, I thought, very much as usual. There were the carts I was accustomed to see in that place, piled high with wool sacks on entering, with bales of dress goods on leaving, shire horses standing massive and patient between the shafts, the usual comings and goings of equally patient women, heads bowed, submissive, slow-moving as herd animals transferring from one place of labour to the other. Nothing in any way disturbing except a knot of men in a far corner, indistinguishable by their stooping shoulders, their narrow backs, from Mr. Agbrigg himself, indistinguishable from the villainous, riotous Chartists who were every bit as hollow-cheeked and meagrely put-together as they.

I saw Aunt Hannah come to a halt at her garden gate, the final vantage point, shielding her eyes from the uncertain winter sun as her husband walked on through the herd of weaving-women who, without raising their eyes, made way for him, until, reaching the barrel, he lifted his narrow shoulders in a shrug that said "All right then, get on with it," and remained standing there, only his good suit and the glint of his gold watch chain setting him apart.

"Poor Hannah," my mother said. "She would have had a better view had she remained here, at the window, but she is making a pilgrimage. She was to have married Aunt Verity's brother,

Edwin Barforth, who was murdered down there so long ago.
How sad, for I can barely remember him—only that he would
have inherited the mill, had he lived, and would have made
Hannah so very rich. Mr. Agbrigg was here too, that day, when
Edwin died—it comes back to me now—and then afterwards the
mill was left to Verity, who married my brother Joel, and made
him rich instead of Hannah. I see that she has not forgotten it,
for she has gone down to the gate so that we cannot see her
tears, you may be sure—which cannot be altogether comfortable
for her husband.

"My goodness, how strangely things turn out—how terrifying
it all is—for if that young Luddite had not stabbed Edwin Barforth to death then I do believe, girls, that none of you—and I
include your cousins Blaize and Nicholas and Caroline—would
ever have been born. With Edwin alive the older generation
would have had no need of Joel to run the mill and would not
have obliged Verity to marry him. She would have married—
good heavens, yes—she would have married your half brother,
Crispin Aycliffe, except that he would not have been your
brother since your father, in those circumstances, would never
have married me. One young bride in Blenheim Lane was more
than enough for him. He would not have burdened himself with
two. I might have found a clergyman to take me, or a schoolmaster, and lived out my days in genteel poverty, borrowing
Hannah's carriage and begging her cast-off bonnets instead of
giving her mine. And Verity—well—she would have had her
grand dowry, just the same, and her moment of romance, but I
cannot think your brother Crispin would have made a comfortable husband. And all this because of one starving lad down
there in the mill yard with a carving knife. I wish you would
stop me from running on so, Prudence, or I shall give myself
nightmares . . ."

My mother returned to her chair, somewhat tearful herself,
leaving me at the window with Prudence and Dr. Ashburn. Both
their faces were intent, concentrating hard on that upturned barrel where the Chartist petition was laid out, on the men who
were standing around it, some of them making the earnest gestures of persuasion, others listening, walking a step or two away
and shuffling back again, glancing sidelong at Mayor Agbrigg,
who, with that eternally patient ebb and flow of working women

around him—whose signatures were of no interest to anyone—
made no attempt to intervene.

"I don't understand," I said. "I feel that I should, but I don't
know . . ."

"Hush," Prudence muttered. "Be still. It's important."

But Dr. Ashburn, who had perhaps witnessed these scenes
often enough to be fairly certain of the outcome, turned to me
swiftly and with great courtesy.

"They hope to present their charter—they call it the People's
Charter—to Parliament in the spring, and since one of its
demands is that the right to vote should be extended to every
man in the country, they feel that as many workingmen as possible—being the class not yet empowered to vote at all—should
sign the petition which is to accompany it."

"Yes, I see that. But why come to the mill, disrupting working
hours? They could sign it later, couldn't they, somewhere else,
with no fear of Mr. Agbrigg taking their names—or whatever it
is they are afraid of?"

"My word," Prudence snapped, as sarcastic as Aunt Hannah.
"That was spoken like a true Barforth, sister. If our cousin Nicholas were here today I imagine he would turn every one of them
off for the crime of time-wasting, as Mr. Hobhouse did. Fortunately, I suspect Mr. Agbrigg arranged for Nicholas to be busy
elsewhere this afternoon, which, while it may lessen our entertainment, will at least prevent violence."

"I do beg your pardon," I told her, half-laughing, but quite
ready to defend myself until, once again, Dr. Ashburn came
quickly, and with great good humour, to my rescue.

"Yes, and I think some of them were expecting to meet Mr.
Nicholas Barforth, and may even be disappointed."

"Giles, how can you say that, especially since I know you believe their cause to be just?"

"Indeed I do. But there are some among them who do not object to violence, who will provoke it and use it quite coolly for
their own purposes—and who will manage themselves not to be
hurt by it. They will tell you it is necessary because the majority
of their colleagues are unreliable. And so they are, both unreliable and afraid, since they have known hunger before—as you
and I have not—and are so terrified of being hungry again that
they will be slow to make a united stand. And even when they

can be stirred to protest, the moment things improve even a little they will all go quietly home again. That is why reform is so long in coming."

"I am sure you are right," I told him.

"Oh, Faith, you know nothing about it," my sister replied. "You are agreeing with Giles now, but when you have listened to Uncle Joel and Nicholas tonight at Tarn Edge, you will be saying the same to them. Giles believes that every man, regardless of rank or bank balance, should have the right to decide how he wishes to be governed. The Barforths will tell you it is wrong to extend the franchise to the men in the mill yard because there are more millhands than Barforths, and if they all had a vote the millhands would win."

"Thank you, Prudence, for putting it in such simple terms for me."

"There is a little more to it than that, of course," Giles Ashburn said, quietly smiling. "They are asking for a secret ballot so that they may cast their votes without fear of losing their employment, and without fear of intimidation. They are also demanding the abolition of property qualifications for members of Parliament, and that such members should no longer be obliged to support themselves in office, but should be paid salaries like other professionals. All of which is very revolutionary, and quite frightening to many people. Understandably so, in fact, since it could involve a considerable transfer of power . . ."

"He means," Prudence said, her eyes still on the mill yard, "that if the charter should be granted, anybody—anybody at all —even one of those millhands down there, could stand for office. All it would take would be brains, and eloquence, and determination, not money and having friends in high places."

"And being a man, of course," I said quite wickedly, finding, somewhat to my embarrassment, that as Mr. Agbrigg turned and walked back towards the house, having avoided trouble by banishing Nicholas, and by his own shrewd, rough-spoken skill, and as Aunt Hannah came back into the room, still sharp and stony but resolutely dry of eye, Dr. Ashburn seemed quite intent on watching me.

"You have made a conquest," Prudence said calmly as we drove off, leaving him on the drive, his hat in his hand.

"No, I have not. He was pleasant to me because I am your sister, that's all."

"Nonsense. I know him well, and he is not usually so pleasant to young ladies. He does not have the time to spare. Well, if it amuses him to stare at you in that moon-struck fashion I am sure I do not mind a bit. I merely mention it in case it should worry you."

"Prudence, I am sure you are mistaken."

"I am sure I am not. And there is no reason to look so guilty. We are friends, Giles and I—yes, fancy that—friendship between an eligible gentleman and a marriageable young lady. Impossible, you might think, since marriageable young ladies rarely have friendship on their minds. But in this case, I do assure you, it is the exact truth. And I would be considerably startled if he began to gaze at me like that. Mother will say the same—won't you, Mother?"

"Yes, dear," my mother said. "So she will. In fact your mother is merely surprised, Faith dear, that you did not notice it yourself. If something should be obscuring your vision—well—ask yourself, my love, does anything in Cullingford seem changed?"

I knew, well enough, that there was no way of telling what meeting Nicholas again could mean to me. I had not pined continuously for him this past twelvemonths, had, in fact, met several other young men who had charmed me briefly, one image fading under the impact of the next. Yet, as I dressed for dinner that night, more than half convinced—or so I believed—that all I really wanted was to impress him, and Blaize too, with my Continental airs and graces, I became increasingly tremulous on the inside, clumsy and irritable on the outside, so that my hair would not take its usual smooth coil, my lovely blond satin gown, of which I had such high hopes, seemed at once too much and too little, my nose most certainly too long.

"Good heavens," Prudence said, slipping unaided into her light green silk, her hair going up without effort, "it's only Tarn Edge. You're not going to a ball. I expect you want Caroline to turn green, and Blaize, of course, always knows about one's clothes. I wouldn't expect Nicholas to notice—if that's what you do expect—because he'll know by now why Mr. Agbrigg sent him to Leeds this afternoon, and will be thoroughly displeased about it."

I would be cool, I decided, as I crossed the hallway at Tarn Edge, glancing with affection at the bronze stag which still guarded the stairs, the vast, stained-glass window still casting its patterns of ruby and emerald and gold on the landing sofa I had once shared with Nicholas. I would be a traveller returned from exotic places, hinting, most discreetly, most skilfully, at my store of new wisdom and experience, giving only a little of myself—as I'd seen those Parisiennes, those Roman ladies do—leaving no one in doubt that there was so very much more.

But I was, in fact, in a state of totally unsophisticated turmoil, dry-mouthed and breathless, and alarmingly, comically disappointed to find that Nicholas was not there.

"Faith—how lovely," Aunt Verity said.

"Aye—I'll not quarrel with that," said Uncle Joel.

And while I kissed my aunt, and my uncle bent his head to kiss me—bathing me in his remembered odours of brandy and tobacco, his dark face so very much like Nicholas'—my ears, my nerves, were straining for the sound of his arrival, so that when the door clicked open, and it was Blaize who stood there, my eyes, for an instant, did not see clearly, and I turned to him with all the slow, careful nonchalance I had rehearsed for Nicholas.

"Faith?" he said, his voice containing a slight question.

"Yes, Blaize—how do you do?"

"Extremely well before—better now."

But such mysterious allure as I had managed to acquire, which had been in some measure appreciated by Blaize and Dr. Ashburn, and which had not gone unnoticed by my uncle, was not at all apparent to Caroline, who, coming in behind her brother, announced that dinner would be ages yet and that she and I had ample time for a chat—very evidently about herself—upstairs.

"Well, you have travelled even farther than I, and I must say it suits you," she said, "although I am not sure I would like to go abroad again. Mrs. Battershaw was sick on the crossing and Amy was such a bore. I was glad to be home again, where everybody knows me. And I am glad to see you back too, Faith, for there is no one—really—to whom one can *talk*. I have quite broken off with Amy Battershaw, and Prudence can think of nothing but drains and bandages, which will do very well for a doctor's wife, since I imagine she will take the Ashburn man, don't you, whatever she may say to the contrary? Well, we have plenty of time to talk now, especially if we are to wait for Nicholas, who has been over to Leeds and then gone straight from the station to the mill. There is a lot of extra work at Lawcroft, you see, since Mr. Agbrigg became mayor, and has his civic duties to attend to."

"Blaize seems to have finished on time."

"Yes—Blaize always does, if indeed, he has been to the mill at all. He will have found some excuse, I expect, to spend the afternoon drinking somebody's whisky, which seems a peculiar way of going about selling cloth, although, oddly enough, he *does* sell it. But Nicholas will be in the sheds all right, grinding away. Aunt Hannah is as pleased as punch, as you might expect, never thinking of the inconvenience it is causing to us, especially since Father relied on Mr. Agbrigg to keep an eye on Nicholas at Lawcroft. And now that he is so busy with his water carts Nicholas may have extra work to do, but can do it as he pleases."

"And what about you, Caroline? We have been expecting to hear your wedding bells for months . . ."

"Ah," she said. "Yes—I suppose I may be married whenever I make up my mind to it."

"And you have not made up your mind?"

"Very likely I have. It is just that everyone expects it of me, and sometimes I wonder if it is too soon."

"The Flood boy will not wait forever."

And, drawing herself up like the empress we had always known her to be, she said, "That is entirely his affair."

"Yes, indeed—and if that is how you feel about it, Caroline, then, although it would be a great feather in your cap to marry a Flood, it would be an even greater one to turn him down."

"You are very bold," she said, annoyed at hearing her own thought spoken. "I think we had best go downstairs, for even Mother cannot keep dinner waiting forever for Nicholas."

And then, already halfway to her feet, she said most unwillingly, "You are not by any chance acquainted with Matthew Chard? No, I hardly see how you could be, for he has only recently moved north. He is Sir Matthew Chard, in fact, since he has just succeeded his great-uncle at Listonby Park. Yes, the real heir—the grandson—was killed last year out hunting, and old Sir Richard Chard was obliged to send for Matthew, who had never lived much in Yorkshire before. And now he has inherited the loveliest house I think I have ever seen. I went there with the Floods in September—Julian and Matthew hunt together. He is a Leicestershire man."

"And you like him, this Sir Matthew Chard?"

"Heavens—I have no reason to dislike him. He is perfectly agreeable. Is that the dinner gong at last, Faith? I suppose they have decided not to wait for Nicholas, as we are only a family party and need not go in in pairs. We had best hurry, for Father is sure to be hungry."

But Nicholas was in the hall as I came downstairs, offering me the perfect opportunity to reveal my new self to him at its best advantage, my blond satin dress rustling on each shallow step as I descended, my fair hair as silver pale in the lamplight—I hoped—as my mother's, so that, had all gone according to plan, he should have looked up and seen a captivating stranger walking slowly towards him, smiling a cool, mysterious stranger's smile, until, quite suddenly, she became a girl he had once known and—if Fortune should favour me—would be anxious to rediscover. But Fortune, it seemed, was entirely absent. I saw him fling his hat and gloves irritably on to the hall table, heard his father's sardonic question, "What kept you? I suppose we may eat now, Verity, since your son has arrived?" and Nicholas' curt reply, "Good Lord, I can't come to the table like this— straight from the sheds. Go in and I'll join you when I'm ready."

And because I was overwhelmed, quite shattered by the sensation leaping inside me, I said, not coolly but coldly, "Good evening, Nicholas."

"Good evening!"

"Are you well?"

"Passably. And you?"

"Oh yes—very well."

And knowing that my tone had implied, "What a pest you are, Nicholas, to keep us waiting," and his had answered, "Idiotic girl —I am already late, so why must you delay me?" I went in and took my place at table, my artistry all gone, nothing any longer in my head but the one impassioned plea, "Look at me, Nicholas. Look at me!"

Chapter Eight

JULIAN FLOOD proposed for the second time to Caroline a few days later and was refused in a manner allowing no possibility of a third, thus causing enormous offence to his family, who declared, with some justice, that Caroline had led Julian on.

"Dreary manufacturing bitch," he referred to her one evening, after a brandy or two at the Old Swan, unaware of Nicholas, in the far corner, until my cousin got quietly to his feet, picked the young lord up by his coat collar, and knocked him down again, giving offence this time to Caroline, who, perhaps on account of Matthew Chard, was unwilling to be the subject of a tavern brawl.

"I do not at all wish my affairs to be the talk of the town," she told me, more agitated than I had ever seen her before, a sentiment quite easily understood since, in refusing one offer—and a brilliant one at that—for nothing more definite than the hope of another, she had taken an immense gamble at which not all of her acquaintances would be sorry to see her fail.

"She is angling after Matthew Chard," my mother told me unnecessarily, "and he will not be easily caught." For Sir Matthew, it seemed, although not a wealthy man by Tarn Edge standards, was not desperately in need of money, could manage—or just about—on his own income and what his grandfather had left him to maintain his three thousand acres of moor and pasture and woodland in reasonable condition. And since he appeared to be a reasonable young man whose tastes were not unduly extravagant, having no racing stable like the Floods but contenting himself with hacks and hunters, his kennels containing retrievers and terriers rather than the Floods' ruinously expensive pack of foxhounds, we concluded that Caroline would have her work cut out.

"I can't think what has possessed her," was my sister Celia's opinion when I called to take tea in Albert Place. "One family is just as noble as the other. Cullingford Manor is just as big as Listonby Park, and just as difficult to keep clean, I shouldn't wonder. And frankly these squires all look the same to me—long noses and loud voices. I am surprised at Caroline."

And perhaps Caroline, who had never expected so foolish and painful an accident as this to befall her, was surprised at herself.

Caroline, in truth and quite simply, was in love; concerned no longer with lands and titles but with such idiotic considerations as the light auburn tint of Matthew Chard's hair, the quite unremarkable, but, in her eyes, miraculous hazel of his eyes, a certain quality—real or imagined was of no importance—which set him apart from all the other young men she had ever seen. He was taller, a shade wilder than Francis Winterton, considerably less wild and not nearly so handsome as Julian Flood. He entirely lacked the easy charm of her own brother Blaize, the intellectual finesse of Jacob Mandelbaum, even the cold dignity of Jonas Agbrigg. He was, in fact, a perfectly ordinary young squire, a fresh-air man of healthy appetites who asked from life nothing more complex than the pleasure of shooting flying game and running game in season, of riding to hounds four or five days a week while the weather and the foxes lasted. He was a little arrogant, perhaps, since no one had ever questioned his right to privilege, a little self-centred since the situation to which he had been born suited his nature exactly, causing him to believe that if he wanted something then everyone around him must surely want him to have it too. But Caroline loved him, and being in love myself, I was well able to sympathise.

"She has no access to him," my mother explained. "She met him through the Floods and they will be unlikely to take her over to Listonby now."

But Caroline, too inwardly desperate for pride, too truly a Barforth even to acknowledge the possibility of defeat, would have driven unannounced to Listonby herself and taken it by storm, had not Aunt Verity smoothly intervened, inviting the young baronet so regularly to Tarn Edge that his continued presence there became such a commitment in itself that it was understood that if he had not proposed by Christmastime then Uncle Joel would feel entitled to demand the reason why.

"It will not be necessary," my mother said. "Verity will see to it. If it is upsetting Caroline, then it must certainly be upsetting Joel, and Verity will not allow that. We shall have the wedding, you may be sure of it, if Verity has made up her mind."

And although I wished Caroline well, and felt sure of her success, I believed that this year in which we stood, and the one to follow, would not be her special time, but mine.

Nicholas called at Blenheim Lane a few days after our return, to deliver some message from his mother to mine, and despite our bad beginning, lingered an hour in the drawing room, questioning me about my travels—the first of all our acquaintance to do so—a circumstance made more delightful because I knew full well that he had no real interest in exotic places beyond their profitability as markets for Barforth cloth, which was information I could not supply.

He sat behind me at the Assembly Rooms, a week later, listening with unconcealed irritation as our two best-established and most expensive physicians, Dr. Blackstone and Dr. Overdale, explained that we should regard our town as an object of pride, while Prudence's friend, Dr. Ashburn, congratulated us, most courteously, on the fact that even in London and Glasgow he had seen few slums to compare with ours.

And afterwards, having escorted us home, he remained in the drawing room so late that when Prudence had retired to bed and my mother was herself feeling drowsy, she felt obliged to tell him, "Nicholas, my dear boy, although your company is quite delightful, I would not have your mother accuse me of making a night-rake out of you."

"Oh, Lord," he said, getting easily to his feet. "Is it really so late? You're such a charmer, Aunt Elinor, you see. You'd make any man forget the hour."

"You can be quite charming yourself, Nicholas, when you want to be," she told him, looking very tiny, very fair, beside him as she gave him her hand, knowing perfectly well that he was smiling at me over her head, saying to her and asking me, "I'll be off then—you'll be at the Assembly Rooms dance on Wednesday, I reckon, won't you?"

"Faith dear," she told me when he had gone, "I would not wish you to be encouraged. He is by no means so enraptured by you as Dr. Ashburn is—who was quite nervous about his lecture tonight because you were there—but yes, assuredly, the fact that Nicholas attended the lecture at all and stayed here so long afterwards— Yes, there is something there. But he is a hardheaded young man, Nicholas Barforth, and by the time he reaches home —or the Old Swan, which is somewhat more likely—he will have remembered that, in fact, he is still reluctant to settle down. It will take a great deal to shake him from that resolve, my dear, and if he should now begin to avoid you, then you may feel flattered, for it can only indicate that he is tempted . . . Flattered, Faith, but not too hopeful, dear. You may be sure I am right."

And so she was, for the Assembly Rooms dance that following Wednesday proved no more than a miserable ordeal of waiting for Nicholas, who, arriving very late and very clearly from the direction of the Old Swan, lounged in the refreshment room for half an hour, spoke two words to me, and went away again. But the next afternoon when we called at Lawcroft to see Aunt Hannah, he came up from the mill, the coolness we may both have intended to show thawing instantly because, quite simply, we were pleased to see each other.

I had not dazzled him. Beneath my Paris gowns and my high-piled, elaborate hair-dressing, which had impressed some others, my body was still too familiar to him to arouse the kind of physical desire which would demand a swift conclusion. It must, I knew, be a much more gradual process than that. But he was pleased—always—to see me, looked for me in any room that he entered and was satisfied when he found me, began to add, at the end of any discussion, "Oh, Faith will know what I mean." And so I did.

He called often to see us—as did Blaize and Dr. Ashburn and some others—tearing up and down Blenheim Lane in the kind of sporting phaeton his father, who had driven an equipage every bit as lethal in his day, considered no more than a young man's fancy, but which caused great alarm to the more sedate of our neighbours.

"Old Miss Corey-Manning thought I meant to run her down."

"Yes. I saw from the window. You've done her a kindness.

She'll have something to talk about now, for the next six months or more."

"Aye—Blaize is off to America by the look of it, in the summer."

"Do you mind?"

"If you mean do I want to go with him, or instead of him—no, not a bit of it. I'm all right where I am. If he'd take Father, I wouldn't complain. I get on well enough with old Agbrigg, but Father—well—he should make up his mind. Either he wants me to run the mills, or he wants to go on running them himself. He's got to decide. He tells me to use my judgement, tells me he's done his share and its time he was taking things easy, and then, when I do just that there he is, like a bolt from the blue, telling me I'm going behind his back. You'd think he'd be glad, wouldn't you, to have somebody willing to take over?"

"He is glad, Nicholas. It's just that he's been in control so long, and it's hard for him to let go. And perhaps he doesn't like to admit how much he relies on you. I think you'd be the same."

He grinned suddenly, a flash of rueful self-knowledge, of pleasure, perhaps, of being able to share it with me.

"Maybe I would. He's not a bad sort—in fact he can be downright splendid at times. If he'd just listen to reason about the combing machines. People are making fortunes in Bradford, Faith, out of the combing machines. It's the last section of the industry to get mechanised, and I don't know what he's waiting for. It's been on the cards for years that somebody was going to come up with a combing machine that would work—it stands to reason—the wool has to be combed before they can spin it, and they have to spin it before we can weave it, and nobody could expect the hand-combers to keep pace with us. My father went in for power looms when everybody said he was a madman, and made his millions, and now, when I put it to him about the combing machines, he gives me the same answers they were giving him twenty years ago. Wait and see. Let them get rid of the teething troubles. I know it means throwing the hand-combers out of work, but that never bothered him before. By God, if I had the capital, I'd set myself up as a wool comber right now—there's plenty of factory property going begging, and I'd still be able to manage Lawcroft, and Tarn Edge as well, if he'd let me. He could come in with me, it wouldn't hurt him. I'd be glad of his advice, and his money to begin with, but I wouldn't want him to do any work. I'd pay him back and make him a profit, and it would be *mine*, Faith. You understand that, don't you?"

"Yes, of course I do. And so does he. I suppose he's cautious now because he's older, and he's done what he wanted to do. But he's bound to appreciate how you feel. If you persist—show him you really mean it—then I'm sure you'll convince him."

"Yes," he said, leaning towards me, almost taking my hand. "It's not enough, Faith, just to take over another man's achievement and keep it going. I'll do that—of course I will—and double it if I can. But I want something that I started, something with my mark on it. I want my father to know—and I want the Piece Hall to know—that I can make it on my own."

"And so you can."

"Faith, why do I always feel better when I've talked to you?"

He had not said he loved me, had in no way committed himself. But there was something between us. And if it was left alone to grow—if I remained patient and careful, so very careful, never forgetting its fragility—then it would grow, surely, into the one thing in the world I desired? For if Nicholas wanted me, no one could really prevent it. My circumstances had not changed. I was not the great match he could make, but I was good enough—as Jonas had been good enough for Celia—and even if his father objected to the point of casting him out, which seemed most unlikely, my money and his own commercial acumen would suffice. Yet I spun no dreams of elopements and love in a cottage, for Nicholas would have no part in such things. I looked now to reality, to a shrewd, ambitious man who would claim his share of the Barforth mills and have his combing company besides, who would live comfortably, self-indulgently even, as he grew older, and who might—who must—live with me. I knew, without any shame whatsoever, that my body desired his. I knew that our minds matched, that our senses were in harmony. I knew I could make him happy. And I would wait, motionless, in the place where he could always find me, until he acknowledged it too.

Dr. Ashburn was also with us a great deal in Blenheim Lane, so quiet, so unobtrusive, that it took a while to recognise his charm, and although I knew I had impressed him to begin with, he was so very much the gentleman, so courteous to everyone, that—my vision clouded perhaps by Nicholas—I managed to convince myself, if not my mother, that his partiality for me did not go deep. Yet Aunt Hannah, retaining a proprietorial interest in our dowries, clearly saw Dr. Ashburn as a threat to Jonas' position as head of our family, and since, in addition, he greatly encouraged her husband's preoccupation with standpipes and drainage channels, he could do no right in her eyes.

His visits to Simon Street she saw not as an act of charity—although she was a genuinely charitable woman herself—but a deliberate encouragement of the lower classes to idleness. They would make no effort to pay for medicine or anything else, she declared, once they saw it could be obtained free of charge, while Dr. Ashburn's attendance, as a physician, at certain very private establishments in the same area, she considered to be no fit subject for her own ears, let alone ours. Nor could she approve of his work at the infirmary, although she had herself raised a great deal of money for the old hospital building in Sheepgate to be repaired. But raising money was one thing, personal involvement quite another, and we all knew that hospitals were not for decent people, who would be properly cared for at home, but for vagrants, drunkards, disreputables, who should be moved on, as soon as they were sufficiently recovered, to be a burden on somebody else's rates. We all knew that hospital nurses were foulmouthed, gin-soaked, the dregs of the human barrel, quite ready to supplement their incomes by offering services which were not of a medical nature, that hospital doctors were very young men, at the start of their careers, or very old ones whose careers should have long been ended. And since Dr. Ashburn was highly qualified and highly acclaimed, having other patients who could afford to pay and were not slow to praise, Aunt Hannah declared him to be sanctimonious.

"Was that St. Ashburn I saw just now?" she would enquire, "driving his shabby gig up the lane as if he hadn't a feather to fly with?"

"But it would be foolish to leave a smart new curricle in Simon Street," Prudence would reply, demure but no less dangerous for all that.

"Indeed, for they would pick it clean and have the horse to market before he had set foot across the first threshold—which is all the thanks he is ever likely to get. Well, every time he sits down at my table—since Mr. Agbrigg persists in inviting him—I shudder at the thought of what may be lurking on his coat or underneath his shoes. I wonder, Elinor, that you do not feel the same. Yes, it may all seem very grand to you, girls—these ideal-istic notions. But your mother and I, having lived longer in the world, have seen it all before and know where it leads to. And, whatever my husband may say, there is something not quite right about that man."

Yet he was undoubtedly a person of impeccable background, the son of a fashionable London parson and a lady of landed connections in Cheshire where, following his parents' early death, he had been brought up. His breeding, in fact, was better than ours, his education infinitely superior, his experience of life wider, since he had worked in many of our major cities and travelled extensively abroad. A gentle, not unattractive man, his quietness spiced with intellectual curiosity, with radical ideals that must appeal strongly to Prudence. And I watched him care-fully when, spending time he perhaps could not spare, he would turn to my sister, not eagerly but with a warm attention, as she offered him some article of a medical or social nature, some list of facts and figures she had copied out herself.

"This will interest you, Giles."

"So it does." And rapidly scanning every line, he would give no indication that he had—I suspected—seen many of these doc-uments before.

"They would do so very well together," I told my mother, and because I wanted it to happen, wanted to believe it, it all began to fall neatly, happily into place, a patchwork of glowing colours with each one of us in the very square we desired. Caroline would be Lady Chard, mistress of Listonby Park. Giles and Pru-dence would surely find each other. Celia already had her flock wallpaper and her papier-mâché chairs, Jonas his office in Croppers Court, his growing importance in the community. Blaize had his freedom, had already discovered the way to be a manufacturer in a congenial fashion. I would have Nicholas—perhaps?—surely?—if I held my breath and continued to treat the growing feeling between us with the same care I had seen my father lavish on his porcelain, handling it so gently that it could not break, so firmly that it could not slip away. Surely? And there was so much emotion inside me that I was translucent with it, its radiance spilling out through my skin and my eyes, a joyous overflow of feeling which I could offer most lovingly to everyone. "Prudence, how cleverly you have done that." "Celia, your house is a dream—absolute perfection." "Mamma, you look not a minute older than nineteen." "Of course he cares for you, Caroline—who would not?"

Matthew Chard declined to eat his Christmas dinner at Tarn Edge that year, his responsibilities as squire anchoring him, he explained, to Listonby. Nor could he risk engaging himself for the day after, since Chards and Floods and Wintertons rode traditionally to hounds on Boxing Day, an occupation which did not allow the making of firm promises. But, depending on the vagaries of the hunt, if they did not draw for an afternoon fox, he might ride over at some unspecified hour to take a glass of wine, possibly with a party of friends.

"Very handsome of him," Uncle Joel said dangerously, "and he'd best ride in to make his intentions clear, or he'll ride out again in no doubt at all as to mine."

And so Caroline spent Christmas Day in a sulk, finding no consolation in her overladen present table when she could have been making herself gracious to Sir Matthew's tenants in the Great Hall at Listonby. While on the morning after she was on such tenterhooks that her very presence was painful.

Uncle Joel's mills, of course, were back at work by then, his engines having shuddered to a halt at ten o'clock on Christmas Eve, to start up again at five o'clock on Boxing Day morning, a circumstance which would take Nicholas and Blaize, if not my uncle himself, to the sheds. But Aunt Verity had secured their early release, unwilling, perhaps, to remain too long alone with the tormented Caroline, and Blaize was already in the drawing room when we arrived, looking as if he had never seen the inside of a weaving shed, Nicholas coming soon after, galloping hatless up the drive, his neckcloth askew, calling out from the hall, "I'll only be a minute," intending the words, I knew, for me.

"Must you make such a racket?" Caroline called after him. "And you'll need more than a minute to make yourself decent. Not that green jacket again, Nicholas—Blaize, do tell him, for in the distance it looks like nothing but a workman's corduroy. Goodness—who is arriving now?"

But it was only Aunt Hannah, delayed by her husband—

since Mayor Agbrigg too had been required at the mill today—but well pleased with herself just the same, having finally prevailed upon him to call a public meeting to invite subscriptions for the concert hall.

"I have already seen Mr. Outhwaite," she told Uncle Joel, mentioning the name of a local architect once closely associated with my father, "and we have fixed on a minimum of fifteen thousand pounds, to be raised in ten-pound shares. What do you think, Joel? He has promised to let me have his thoughts on design by next Wednesday at the latest."

"Twenty thousand," my uncle said, luxuriously at ease by his fireside, the inevitable cigar in his hand. "You could do it for less, but if you're going to do it at all, Hannah, then do it right."

She settled down beside him to discuss her views on the site most likely to be chosen, the suitability of Corinthian pillars, who should be invited to lay the foundation stone; her husband, having given my mother the latest information regarding Celia, who had not cared to venture out, began to talk quietly to Prudence, and I went with Caroline to the sofa on the first-floor landing, to await the good pleasure of Sir Matthew Chard and to endure the almost visible agony of her nerves.

He would not, of course, put in an appearance. She had quite made up her mind to it and could offer a dozen excuses. The hunt would be unlikely to pass this way. Having started out in the crisp air of that Boxing Day morning, a white haze on the horizon, frost pitting the ground, he would have found himself miles away by noon, too dishevelled and weary to call on a lady, even though that lady would be more than willing to send him home in her carriage, and stable his horse most lovingly until he required it. It would be unreasonable to expect him, foolish to regard his absence in any way significant, since, having inherited his great-uncle's position as master, he had been obliged—absolutely in honour bound—to attend the hunt.

"He may even have broken his neck," Blaize told her, coming to sit beside us. "Have you thought of that? He may be lying in a ditch somewhere, gasping out a dying message to his groom. 'Go tell my lady that, regrettably, I shall not be dining—' Now that, dear sister, has a certain style to it, you must admit."

But Caroline's mind was too full, too busy straining for the sounds of hooves and doorbells, for real anger.

"Nonsense, he is too good a horseman for that—isn't he? For he has been riding all his life."

"So have we all."

"Oh, not like you," she said, magnificent even in this absent-minded disdain. "Not like you and Nicholas on your showy hacks that can take you to the mill yard and back, or to the train. I mean real riding—days in the open country jumping fences—steeplechasing. And when did you and Nicky ever go hunting?"

"Never," Blaize said with an exaggerated shudder. "Too hearty for me, I'm afraid—"

"You mean you haven't the courage."

"No, he doesn't," Nicholas said, appearing suddenly behind us in the green jacket Caroline had affected to despise, although there was nothing about his gray brocade waistcoat or the neat, white folds of his cravat about which she could complain. "He doesn't mean that at all. He means hunting pink doesn't suit him, and even if it did, he'd see no profit in risking his neck, or riding down some poor devil's crops, to catch—what? A fox. There's no money in foxes that I ever heard of."

And he sat down beside me, not touching me, but his long hard body making contact, somehow, with mine, a most comfortable home-coming, a sense of naturalness, rightness, that we should be sitting here together.

"You know nothing about it," Caroline said loftily, rising with ease to their combined bait. "And why should you? How can one expect it? Blaize will not go hunting because he never does anything at which he knows he cannot excel. But you wish you could, Blaize, even if you won't admit it. Oh yes, you do—you'd love to be the dashing hero, leaping those hedges and lording it afterwards—hunt balls and steeplechases by moonlight—yes, you would, if you thought you'd be any good at it. Whereas you, Nicky—you're just not made for such things."

"No," he said bluntly, "I'm not, and I'll tell you why. I can't afford the luxury of a broken leg. I've got a living to earn, as your father would be the first to tell you, and a man who needs to be in his mill yard at five o'clock every morning can't work up much enthusiasm for steeplechasing at midnight. Now, if there was a profit in foxes I'd chase 'em all right—in a pink coat if that was the best way to do it—and I'd catch 'em too. Except that I'd find an easier way to go about it—or get somebody to invent a machine to do it for me."

"If you've nothing more intelligent to say than that," Caroline informed him, "then I'll thank you to hold your tongue when Matthew comes—he wouldn't understand."

"If he comes."

"Oh, he'll come," Blaize said, smiling an altogether false reassurance. "And don't worry about anything Nicky may say to him, for he'll only think it quaint. And he'll be too busy, in any case, telling you where they found and when they killed, and how many hounds it took to tear the poor beast apart."

"Foxes," Caroline said, getting up, "are vermin. They kill chickens and—and—other things— If you were a countryman, a gentleman, you'd know. And you, Blaize Barforth, if they paid you, you'd tear one apart with your bare hands, unless you happened to have your best jacket on. And you, Nicholas, you'd do it in your evening clothes if the price was right. Not that I care —oh, why must you provoke me—it's not fair—it's simply not fair—"

"I don't think she much cares for hunting either," Blaize said quietly as, gathering her skirts together, she swept away from us to find her father, doubtless aware that he too would be unlikely to hazard his horses, certainly not his person, for pleasure.

"Then she'd best accustom herself," Nicholas replied, "for what else is there to Matthew Chard? He hand-rears his game birds and his foxes for half the year and then slaughters them the other half. And when he's not doing that, he plays whist and faro, which is something else she doesn't much care for."

"He's not a bad fellow, Nick."

"I never said so. He's not our kind, that's all. Put Lawcroft or Tarn Edge in his hands and we'd be in queer street at the end of the month, whereas Caroline—she may look like a duchess—but she'd keep those looms turning, one way or another."

"So she would," Blaize said, affection warming his perpetually quizzical smile. "And she'd wear her coronet too, while she was about it. Dear Caroline, she'll find good reason for not following the hunt, and if Matthew Chard lives with her for fifty years he'll never know it's because she can't ride. Believe me, once she's Lady Chard, she'll know more about horses, from the ground, than the rest of them put together. And there'll be no better stirrup-cups served anywhere in the county than at Listonby."

We went downstairs then, companionably smiling, pausing before the huge, Germanic pine tree that dominated the hall, its open arms bravely bearing their load of tinsel and candles, a new innovation this, spreading north from London, inspired by our Queen's serious-minded, much-loved Teutonic husband. "Can it really be comfortable indoors?" I wondered, remembering it, aloof and stately, in the garden a week ago.

"The roots are still there," Nicholas said, smiling, but Blaize, taking my arm, murmured, "Let's ask it. A little nearer, Faith— that's right—just there, under the mistletoe." And, one cool hand tilting my chin, he took the traditional Christmas liberty, his lips, as cool as his fingers, curving into a smile as they kissed me, a fresh, sharp scent about him, a man, as Caroline had said, who performed only those acts in which he knew he could excel; and, in their performance, was truly most excellent.

"Merry Christmas," he whispered, his cheek brushing mine. "Or should it be Happy New Year? That's better, I think, since it lasts longer. Don't move. We've not done with you yet."

And, his teasing eyes moving behind me, he said, "Your turn, brother. It's the only time we can do it and get away with it— supposing one wishes to get away."

"Blaize," Caroline called from the drawing room. "They're serving tea."

"I'm coming," he said, and their voices were very far away, heard through forest trees and water, the other side of a meadow, as Nicholas touched me, not at all as Blaize had done, although perhaps no casual observer would have seen the difference.

It was only a piece of nonsense, after all, this Christmas kissing, a breach in the walls of etiquette and propriety, acceptable between young people at this season, something to be whispered about afterwards. "I turned quite dizzy—my word, I declare if it had lasted a moment longer, I would have swooned." Or: "Odious boy, for it is the second time this Christmas Day, and if he comes after me again I shall tell Mamma."

But now there was no swooning, no recoil, a smile, simply, of welcome, as he leaned towards me, a feeling of space condensing around us, his mouth polite at first, as Blaize's had been, and then opening slightly, his hands not touching me since he must have known I would not back away.

"Happy New Year," he said, and kissed me again, holding me now in case the alien sensation of his tongue parting my lips should startle me, unaware, perhaps, in his effort to seem not too urgent, of the giddy overflow of my senses, a joyful movement of my whole mind, my whole body towards fulfilment.

"Good heavens, Nicholas," Caroline called again, still at the drawing room door, seeing only his back screened by the branches of the tree, a fold of my skirt, too intent on her own heart-searchings to notice ours. "We must get tea over and done with, don't you see that? Aunt Hannah is wanting to be off, for Celia is not well and has only Jonas to sit with her. Nicky—what are you doing out there?"

"He's kissing Faith," Blaize said, appearing beside her. "What else should a sensible man be doing out there?"

And we went in to take tea together.

The afternoon was drawing in, the early winter dark settling, fog-tinted, behind the windows, a sudden tapping on the glass, half rain, half snow, warning us that no horsemen, surely, would venture to Tarn Edge today.

"Come then, Mr. Agbrigg," Aunt Hannah said, worried as always about her horses' legs on the wet cobbles, especially now, since, with a donation towards the concert hall to find, they could not be easily replaced. "We'll be on our way then since I like to take my time going down the hill. I'll see you at Lawcroft tomorrow, Elinor. And the young ladies? Well, Faith at least, since Prudence finds so much else to occupy her these days. Jonas, of course, will look in although I cannot be sure of Celia. I have told her repeatedly how mistaken she is to shut herself away so much—what she is suffering from is hardly a disease. But she has grown quite morbid, Elinor, and you should really have a word with her. You are welcome to come too, Verity— yes, yes, I know how you are situated at present, but if there are to be storm clouds ahead you may appreciate a change of scene. I leave it up to you. Tomorrow then, at tea time." And it was as her carriage was moving carefully away and my mother, survey- ing the remains of plum cake and pepper cake and hot mince pies somewhat ruefully, her stomach still queasy, perhaps, from yesterday's champagne—was about to suggest we should be leaving too, that the drive erupted with hoofbeats again, not the patient plodding of Aunt Hannah's aging nags, but a wild-riding, hell-raking sound that brought Caroline to her feet, and held her in an appalling, quite helpless rigidity.

"Here they are," Blaize said. "Young lords at play."

And, quite abruptly, the hall seemed full of them, their size and their noise, their superb self-command diminishing the towering pine tree, overpowering the bronze stag, a pink-coated army, mud-spattered, and most viciously spurred, an invasion as alarming as if they had ridden their foaming mounts directly up the stairs.

"Boots," Uncle Joel said ominously, his eyes on the carpet, but young gentlemen such as these, accustomed to their stone-flagged ancestral halls, where such carpets as they possessed hung mouldering on the walls, did not share my uncle's precise awareness of the cost per yard—and mill price at that—of these brand-new, deep-pile floor coverings; would have shown no interest had they been told. And it was a measure of his affection for Caroline that he did not tell them, allowing Aunt Verity to move forward with her smooth, "How very nice of you to call," separating them into individuals so that we realised, with surprise, they were but four in number, Matthew Chard, Francis Winterton, another man, and a girl.

She was not, I thought, at that first glance, a person about whom Caroline need be concerned, a thin, breathless figure, laughing and swaggering among the men, every bit as hearty and arrogant, and as dirty, as they. She was nineteen or twenty, auburn hair escaping from her tall hat, the lamplight picking out a hint of red, a dusting of freckles across her nose, a pointed face, wide at the cheekbones, tapering to a kitten's chin, a wide mouth talking, talking, half-sentences unfinished, ending in sudden laughter.

She had a riding habit which had seen better days, a long, flat patch of mud on the skirt, a rust-coloured stain on her cheek, fox blood, one assumed, proclaiming her the first lady to reach the kill—laughing, I had no doubt, as they had daubed her face with the dismembered tail.

"Glorious day," she told Aunt Verity, in a high, clear voice, the long vowel sounds of privilege. "Is that a Christmas tree? I never saw one before. The rage in London, now, they tell me, but I hate the city—and my grandfather is too old-fashioned for Christmas trees. You know my grandfather? Surely? Matthew—do come and explain me."

And stretching out her hand to Aunt Verity, an abrupt movement followed by a wide, disarmingly frank smile, she said, "I am Georgiana Clevedon, and very pleased to make your acquaintance. I am by way of being a cousin to Matthew, or something very like it. My grandfather is Mr. Gervase Clevedon, and we have the abbey—Galton Abbey, although I never remember to call it so, since I cannot really believe there is another like it. There, I have explained myself, haven't I? And you must be Caroline."

"Indeed," Caroline said, considerably displeased by this unsolicited use of her Christian name, a liberty to be taken, in our experience, only with parlourmaids. "I am delighted to meet you, Miss Clevedon."

But Miss Clevedon, unabashed, held out her grubby hand again. "Heavens—Miss Barforth—please do excuse me, for I am sadly lacking in manners. And when I have been all day in the saddle I lose them altogether. Matthew, do come and aid me, for I have blundered. And, Perry, do come over here and be presented to Miss Barforth. Miss Barforth, this is my brother, Peregrine—who has no manners either. Although one day he will have the abbey, so we are glad to excuse him."

I stood in the drawing room doorway, near enough to observe, too far away to be noticed or overheard, Blaize and Nicholas standing a step ahead of me, close together; and I was still excited and happy, still very far from the notion that these boisterous, brash young men, this strange young woman, could have anything to do with me.

"Now that," Blaize said, his eyes narrow with careful appraisal, "is a very rare bird of the wild wood, brother—very rare indeed."

"Difficult," Nicholas replied, his own eyes just as calculating, the hint of coarseness in them both comforting me, I think, since I believed this was the way men looked at actresses and adventuresses, the kind of women, in fact, men did not marry, and who could be no threat to Caroline—no threat to me.

"Difficult, Blaize—damn difficult to tame—"

"Couldn't tame it," Blaize said, clearly forgetting my presence. "Wouldn't want to. I told you, it's straight out of the wild wood, and there'd be no point any more if you managed to get it to eat out of your hand. But I wouldn't mind a scratch or two making the attempt."

And then, suddenly, as they both at the same moment became aware of me, there was a sharp, "Blaize—that'll do," from Nicholas, and from the unrepentant Blaize, a laughing, "I do beg your pardon, Faith. May I hope this is the one time you don't know what we mean?"

But Caroline was now walking stiffly towards us, leaving the much-longed for Matthew in the hall, every bit as offended by his boots as her father, and not greatly pleased with Miss Clevedon, uneasy, I thought, at the state of her riding habit, and altogether shocked—although she would not have admitted it—by the blood on her cheek.

"This," she said, with no more than common politeness "is my cousin, Miss Aycliffe. And my brother, Mr. Nicholas Barforth."

And I felt a great, nameless relief when he nodded, quite curtly, and merely said, "Miss Clevedon—" staring with a sarcasm that veered on rudeness at her soiled skirt, the emblem of savagery flaking now against her fair skin.

"And this is my elder brother—Mr. Blaize Barforth. Blaize—Miss Clevedon."

"Yes," he said, his face alive with the very same collector's excitement I had seen in my father whenever he had brought home some rare piece of porcelain, some totally unexpected find: except that with Blaize it was warmer, would be more quickly over. "Miss Clevedon—so it is—and you are quite wet through. I suppose there is no likelihood that you may catch a chill?"

"I shouldn't think so," she told him, her abrupt hand stretching out again, her own expression registering a certain surprise, as if she had not expected a member of the manufacturing classes to possess such charm.

"No—I didn't for a moment imagine it. But do come over to the fire, just the same, Miss Clevedon. I am sure you are above such trifles as the weather, but you must allow the rest of us to be concerned—"

"Blaize," Caroline said, the flash of her eyes warning, "Boots—carpets."

But ignoring her, Blaize took Miss Clevedon's shabby elbow in a careful hand and led her away, glancing at Nicholas in a manner which plainly said, "I told you. This is a rare one. We'll see, shall we—"

"What an odd creature," Caroline muttered.

"Yes," Nicholas said, not listening to her, staring at Blaize, watching too intently, neither condemning nor excusing, saying too much by saying nothing at all, so that I—as taut as Caroline —nervously enquired, "What do you think?"

"About what?"

"About Miss Clevedon?"

"Oh—not a great deal."

And although he smiled at me then, stayed beside me, walked with me to the carriage, waited, bareheaded in the rain, to see me drive away and promised he would come and rescue me from Aunt Hannah the following afternoon—and indeed came— I knew, not that night but soon after, that the special time I had marked out for myself, and which had only started with my return home in November, was already over.

Chapter Nine

THE BARFORTHS were invited to Listonby Park for New Year's Day, a meagre enough occasion, Aunt Verity afterwards told my mother, nothing but plain roast meats on the table, indifferent service, a housekeeper, she felt, who would have been more inclined to receive them at the tradesman's entrance and, in Uncle Joel's opinion, would not have paid their bills too promptly at that. A beautiful house, indeed, the original medieval Great Hall stone-flagged, oak-ceilinged, a long gallery lined with an impressive array of ancestral portraits and not much else, an early eighteenth-century wing so mellowed, the plasterwork and paintwork so obviously nearing its century that it had reminded Aunt Verity of the musky beauty of rose petals approaching decay.

Uncle Joel and Sir Matthew went outside together when the meal was over, to smoke their cigars, strolling along the avenue of wych-elms a distant Chard had planted in the park, admiring the sycamores, the gnarled and knotted oaks from an even earlier generation, my uncle taking this opportunity to discover, as he had no doubt expected, that although there was money enough for essentials, Sir Matthew's pleasures, albeit of a less dissipated nature than Julian Flood's, were nevertheless not cheap.

The maintaining of even a provincial hunt like the Lawdale—the feeding of fifty couple of hounds, the salaries of huntsman, whippers-in, earth stoppers, the upkeep of coverts—would be likely to exceed 3,000 pounds per annum, of which his own subscription could not be less than 1,500. His personal stable expenses, without much effort, could cost him 2,000 pounds and rising, every year, his private kennels a further 500. There was, in addition, the expense of preserving game birds on his land, their careful hand-rearing and safekeeping from poachers and predators, so that they could be shot in due season, and by invitation only. And it became clear to them both that in Sir Matthew's costly and time-consuming pursuit of sport, a wealthy and efficient wife would not come amiss.

He proposed to Caroline the following morning, riding over to Tarn Edge immaculately turned out this time, his boots well polished and clean, his manner ardent enough to please anyone, being a healthy man more than ready to take a healthy mate. And almost at once, having longed for him, despaired of him, she was no longer sure of herself, riding down, in her turn, to Blenheim Lane to bring me her news, her triumph, and her heart-searchings.

"I'm to be Lady Chard."

"Oh, darling—I never doubted it."

But she had not quite forgiven him for his unruliness of Boxing Day, his inbred arrogance, which had seen nothing amiss in trampling mud on her father's floor, the oft-repeated hunting tales which bored her, making her too aware of the very real gulf between them. Yet—apart from the fact that his presence still caused her heart to miss a beat, the fact that, without having the words to describe it or the courage to admit it, his sharp-edged, patrician profile, his lounging body, had aroused her sensuality—she had already won herself a reputation as a jilt by refusing Julian Flood, and could not do the same again. And, when all was said and done—and she said it many times, over and over again—although he was not rich, at least he had no gambling debts, no creditors waiting, on their wedding day, to be paid off at the church door, and there was no reason why handsome, energetic Caroline should not be loved for herself.

"He was quite charming," she told me, "almost emotional—said he had known at once, seeing me at Listonby, that I belonged there. And, indeed, it is a lovely house. I could do so much with it, Faith. There is a staircase leading out of the Great Hall, carved oak with painted panels on the walls, leading to an enormous room, the size of the hall itself, not used for anything at all—quite empty—and it would make a splendid ballroom.

And the hall—well, there is nothing much in there now but that huge stone fireplace and a few oak boxes standing around, and a dreadful oak table all scarred and battered. But with some decent floor covering and a dozen or so deep armchairs and sofas, it would be ideal for house parties—a log fire in that tremendous hearth at tea time, can't you imagine it? For that is the thing nowadays—house parties—since the railways have made it so easy to get about, and one can invite guests from simply anywhere. Bedrooms should be no problem, for although, naturally, I haven't yet seen them, the upstairs passages are like a rabbit warren, and there must be accommodation to spare. The kitchens, I suppose, may be less than adequate, but something may easily be done about that—in fact it must be done since I am quite determined to entertain. What is the point, after all, of having a house that size unless one means to *use* it. Yes, I shall have to give some thought to the kitchens—and a really good chef who will bring his own kitchenmaids, since people will not come twice unless they are sure of enjoying their dinner. Well— the really good thing about it is that there is no Dowager Lady Chard to pull a long face when I set about making changes."

"And Matthew?"

"Oh, he will not care a scrap. He was not brought up at Listonby, you see. His real home is in Leicestershire, as you know, and he is not so attached to Listonby that he cannot bear a stone of it to be altered—not at all like the Floods and those dreadful Clevedons."

And so enchanted was she with her plans for Listonby Park that it was a long time before I could introduce, again, the name of Georgiana Clevedon, whose pointed face and sudden smile I had been unable to forget.

"Oh, they are connected to the Chards by marriage, I believe," she said carelessly, "and I cannot imagine why they think themselves so grand, for that abbey of theirs is the gloomiest place I ever saw. A quarter of the size of Listonby, and so old—beyond repair, I should think. It was a real abbey once, before whichever king it was knocked them down—Prudence will know—oh, King Henry VIII, was it?—well, the Clevedons bought it from him, or he gave it to them for services rendered, a million years ago by the look of it, and they built their house from the abbey stones. In fact part of it still looks like a nunnery—they even have a cloister which they seem to think quite splendid, although it is as cold as a tomb and just as foisty. They have no money, of course, and no hope of any that I can see, for Peregrine Clevedon is the most feckless young man I ever knew, and no woman in her right mind would marry him. And if Miss Georgiana imagines she can save the day by setting her cap at Blaize she will have a rude awakening. Blaize will not think of marriage for a long time yet, and when he does you can be sure he will make a brilliant match, something altogether exceptional. No—the best thing they can do is to sell off their land and their precious abbey with it—while they still have something to sell—for it would not surprise me to hear, any day, that it had fallen down."

We went to Albert Place to see in the New Year, my sister Celia, who had adamantly refused to risk herself outdoors, remaining throughout the entire evening on her sofa, so very much embarrassed by her swollen shape that even the presence of her kindly, down-to-earth father-in-law incommoded her.

"Are you comfortable, lass?" he asked her more than once, wanting, it seemed, to make a show of affection, to move her closer to the fire or farther away from it, some gesture expressive of concern, but she could only reply, "Quite comfortable, thank you," the sharpness of her tone implying, "Leave me alone. Don't draw attention to the sorry state I'm in. Don't stare at me."

We drank what I felt sure must be an excellent wine, served, in Celia's wedding crystal, on a silver tray.

"All the very best to you, lass," Mayor Agbrigg said, remembering, this time, not to look at her.

"I have told that girl a hundred times about these glasses," she answered. "Jonas, have I not told her that they must be rinsed—really rinsed clean—but no, she dries them with the soap still on them—Jonas, you will have to tell her again, for, in these circumstances, you must see that I cannot."

"Yes, Celia," he said quietly, not looking at her either, having no need, perhaps, of vision to know that her lower lip was trembling, her whole face quivering with the approach of fretful tears. "I'll speak to her in the morning. It can hardly be done now. Please do not cry over it. It is hardly worth so much agony."

"So you always say. You simply do not understand how these slovenly things upset me."

"You are quite mistaken, Celia. I understand exactly how much—and how often—you are upset. Are you tired now?"

"Of course I am. I suppose you are thinking I would be better off in bed."

"Only if that is what you would like."

But Mayor Agbrigg—the only other man in the room—was obliged to turn his back, making some excuse about mending the fire, before she would allow a completely expressionless Jonas to help her to her feet and lead her from the room.

"Your daughter is very fanciful," Aunt Hannah said. "One would imagine no other woman had ever been in her condition before."

But before my mother could answer, Mayor Agbrigg, putting down the fire tongs, said quietly, "She's hardly a woman, Hannah—just a little lass, scared out of her wits. I hope my lad understands that."

There was champagne at midnight—no one, now, to complain about the glasses since Celia, we had ascertained, was sound asleep—Mayor Agbrigg, gaunt in the flickering candlelight, raising his glass first to his wife, "Let's drink to your concert hall, Hannah—the grandest in the West Riding," and then to Prudence, his quiet smile conveying, "And we'll pave the streets as well, lass, while we're about it, and shift the sewage."

There was Jonas, his cool, narrow face giving no hint either of concern for Celia's condition, or of annoyance that she was managing it so badly, bestowing on me and Prudence the customary New Year's kiss, as correct and remote a brother as a husband, playing his role to perfection but with little feeling.

"Happy New Year, sir," he said to his father.

"Aye—let's hope so," the mayor replied, and we went home soon after, Mayor Agbrigg accompanying us to be the first foot across our threshold, Aunt Hannah waiting in the carriage while he carried inside the lump of coal for our hearth, the salt for our table, that would ensure our happiness and prosperity to come.

"Happy New Year," Prudence said to me, later, as we reached her bedroom door.

"Yes, darling—the same to you." But the radiance inside me had dimmed, leaving me cold, as scared, without exactly know-

ing why, as Celia, so that, like her, I needed the refuge, the bolt
hole, of my solitary bed, and the release of tears.

We attended the public meeting, called some days later, at the
Assembly Rooms, to put forward Aunt Hannah's plans—thinly
disguised as her husband's—for the erection of the concert hall.

"What have we got in Cullingford?" Mayor Agbrigg said
bluntly, in no way abashed by this gathering of millmasters who
could have bought and sold him ten times over. "We've got the
mills, and a few decent private houses. We've got the Mechanics
Institute and these Assembly Rooms, and the new station, and
that's about all. Folks that come here—and they're coming here
now from far and wide—are saying Cullingford's not a town at
all. They're saying it's not much better than a navvy camp. Now,
there's some as don't mind that, and some as do—there's some as
don't take offence when they hear tell that Leeds is growing
faster, and even Bradford's cleaner. But if we've got the muck,
friends, we've got the brass to go with it—enough brass, I
reckon, to set it all to rights."

And although it was not the speech Aunt Hannah would have
made herself, having had a great deal to say privately about the
need for cultural improvement—preferring her own quotation
"man does not live by bread alone" to Mr. Agbrigg's "Where
there's muck there's brass"—the haggard, rough-spoken man she
had married undoubtedly carried the day. A joint-stock company
was formed, finance to be raised by the taking-up of ten-pound
shares, any deficiency or any additional costs to be met, it was
discreetly understood, by that philanthropic gentleman Mr. Joel
Barforth. And henceforth my life was dominated by two issues,
the concert hall—Aunt Hannah's insistence on Corinthian pillars,
her flirtation with gas-lighting, her apparent disregard as to
which orchestras, in fact, would actually play there—and Caroline's wedding.

It was to be in June, not at Listonby as one might have supposed, but in our own parish church, since at this stage it was
Cullingford Caroline wished to impress, rather than the Chard
tenantry. And so, throughout the bleakest January I could
remember, I sat with her in the cosy back parlour at Tarn Edge,
toasting ourselves by the fire and talking of what was to be the
most splendid ceremony our town had ever seen.

"You understand clothes, Faith," she told me. "I've often noted it," and when the guest lists were put away, the pattern books would come out, samples of fabric, pencil, and paper for my sketches.

"I'll go to London. You could come with me, Faith. In fact we could go to Paris, to that couturier you're always telling me of. Why not? Father will arrange it."

But already, in January, there was a murmuring of unrest in France, hints that our own malcontents, the Chartists, were on the move again, threatening to carry their demands to Westminster and force them, if necessary, down the throats of any who were unwilling to listen.

"They'll get nowhere," Uncle Joel said, lighting one cigar from the embers of another. "These hotheads, Feargus O'Connor and the like—they've got the men, and now, with the trains, they've got the means to move them wherever they're needed to demonstrate. But what's a demonstration? They tried to stop the mills from working back in '42—went on the rampage both sides of the Pennines, taking the plugs out of the engines so the looms wouldn't turn. And what happened? It was the demonstrators who ran out of steam in the end, same as the engines, except that we soon started the engines up again, and all they really achieved for their 'brothers' was to lose them a few days' pay. The Chartists will be no different. They may have orators, who can tell them they should all have a vote, and that there should be a general election every year so they can practice using it—but they've got no organisers. There's no money behind them. We got the vote in '32 because men like me and Hobhouse and Battershaw and Oldroyd threatened to take our brass out of the Bank of England unless they gave it to us. What has Feargus O'Connor got to bargain with? He can call his mob out to break a few windows and throw a stone or two, but once they've rounded up the first half dozen and shipped them off to Australia, the rest will go home again. One man one vote indeed, and a secret ballot so the demon millmaster can't twist their tails on polling day. Well, I can't blame them for that. In their place I'd want the same—except I'm not in their place, and I've no mind to let my mill hands choose my government for me."

Yet it was rumoured that the London streets were beginning to be dangerous, that in Cullingford itself the hungry, the unemployed—the residents, one assumed, of Simon Street—were meeting in growing numbers to perform military exercises on the moors beyond Tarn Edge, a copy of the People's Charter in every pocket, a weapon of some kind in every hand, even hungrier men from Bradford, many of whom had been thrown out of work by the combing machines, coming to explain that the same thing was more than likely to happen to them. And, to my relief, it was decided that Caroline must do her shopping at home.

I could not have said that Nicholas neglected me. We met as often as before, talked, smiled, our relationship apparently unaltered. And perhaps it was the very lack of change that troubled me, for if it did not diminish it did not grow: and I knew there were times when he held back from me.

"Faith will know what I mean," he still muttered now and then, but increasingly, I could not understand him, was aware, simply, that something troubled him, my own senses, sharpened by panic, being quick to detect the slow building of a barrier between us; I could not always bring myself to name that barrier Georgiana Clevedon.

I knew him too well for that—or thought I did—for, unlike Blaize, he had never sought the exotic in women, had spoken, many times, of the need to settle with a partner of one's own kind. He may, from time to time, have enjoyed the convenience of a casual mistress—in fact I knew quite well he had—as exotic or as garish as our local music halls could provide, but in a wife, and Miss Clevedon, like myself, could only be available to him as a wife, such qualities must surely repel him. Nicholas was practical, shrewd, levelheaded enough to choose a woman who was right for him. And since Georgiana Clevedon, "rare bird of the wild wood" as Blaize had so aptly named her, was so very wrong, I was able, for most of the time, to convince myself that I was mistaken.

And in the moments when I couldn't—bare, solitary midnights that stripped me of hope and dignity—I concluded that if he wanted her, as he had wanted the actresses of the Theatre Royal, if it was passion, the reckless impulse of sensuality he had not managed to feel for me, then I would wait, closing my eyes and my mind to it, until it was over. I would say nothing, do nothing, I would be, as always, simply here when he needed me, making no demands, ready, like cool water, to heal him if she scorched him, ready to warm him if she proved cold, waiting, until the flame expired, to welcome him home, asking no questions, offering merely the strength of my love for him to lean on if she should weaken him.

But did he want her? Certainly no one but myself thought so, Caroline being too irritated by Miss Clevedon's open encouragement of Blaize, and Aunt Verity, who knew her eldest son rather better, too amused by it, for either of them to connect her in any way with Nicholas. Was it merely my overwrought imagination, my jealousy extending to every woman he met, because I had not, it seemed, succeeded in making him love me? Had he, in fact, given any real indication of regard for her? None. But I would have been easier, I knew, had he leaned forward to catch a glimpse of her ankle, on her second visit to Tarn Edge, when she had mismanaged her skirt at the carriage step—something he would have done automatically had it been any other woman —instead of staring, stony-faced, at the horse's legs, not hers. I would have been easier if, responding to her flighty, familiar manner, he had flirted with her, even treated her coarsely—anything. And I could not have explained, even to my mother, how his show of indifference where she was concerned, stabbed me to the heart.

Nor did she appear to want him. Blaize, beyond question, was her choice, and a visit to Galton Abbey, at the end of January, convinced me that, as Caroline had said, a choice of some kind was necessary, for, indeed, the estate was much encumbered, the brother deep-dyed in his extravagance, and Miss Clevedon, without doubt, would have to fend for herself in life.

We went first, of course, to Listonby Park, even my mother, unutterably bored now with Cullingford and eager to be off again, twittering with excitement as the house revealed its graceful lines to us through the mist.

"Caroline, my dear—how perfectly lovely." And so it was, the Great Hall sparse, as Caroline had warned, but noble, the carved oak staircase rising majestically from it, the dining room and drawing room—added a mere hundred years ago—of such frail beauty, the baroque plaster mouldings so mellowed from the original white to a delicate cream in places, in others a gentle grey, that I, too, was reminded of fragrant petals at the season's end, and wondered how anything so exquisite could endure.

And when we had taken tea by the crackling, smoking fire—"I must ask my father to advise me about that chimney"—had paced the long gallery up and down to admire the gilt-framed row of Chards, long dead, who would have turned over in agony in their weed-strewn graves had they suspected that any descendant of theirs could marry a tradesman's daughter, we were driven the three miles to the much smaller estate of Galton Abbey, to inspect a house of a very different order.

It stood at a bend of the River Law, which had somehow escaped the pollution of our mills, a hurrying, sparkling water still running free beneath a rickety bridge, swirling itself around a row of old stones which the nuns, perhaps, in Tudor times, had used to cross the stream. There was a steep, green hillside, ancient trees dipping their arms in the river, and the house, whose stones had heard the tolling of the convent bell, set in a slight fold of the land as if it had grown there, quite naturally, without the help of any man. And although I wanted to find it cold and dismal, like Caroline, I would have been enchanted, had I allowed it.

There was a hall here too, quite small, extremely dark, stone floors, stone walls, stone stairs leading to an open gallery, a feeling of age, a weight of memory and experience so strange, yet so haunting, so much in keeping with Miss Clevedon herself, that I was suddenly, fiercely grateful that only Blaize, not Nicholas, had found time to accompany us.

She received us alone, neither her brother nor her grandfather having returned from hunting, walking abruptly into the room in her inevitable dark green riding habit, its trailing skirt looped over her arm, two elderly gun dogs padding stiff-legged at her side, a pair of greyhounds, a frisk of terriers following behind.

"My word," my mother said, when the conventional greetings were done, "I hear you have a cloister—may we risk the encounter of a ghost or two?" And immediately, without ceremony, we were taken to see the cloister, a dim, empty tunnel leading to no tangible place at all but directly into the past.

"They pulled down the abbey church," she said, "my great, ever so great great-grandfathers. But they left part of the abbess' house, and this cloister, intact. I once spent the whole night here, as a child, quite alone, curled up in a blanket, just thinking about it. Don't you find it the most fascinating place in the world?"

"Absolutely," Blaize said, his eyes ignoring the intricate fan vaulting and resting directly on her vivid, eager face. And instantly her quite breathless admiration of the stone tracery, the hushed mystery of this ancient place gave way to a boyish, unabashed chuckle.

"Oh—nonsense—for you are teasing me. Pretending to admire the cloister, and looking at me instead—but I am not deceived."

"Miss Clevedon," he declared, his hand on his heart, a smile of pure mischief on his lips, "I am the most sincere of men—"

"He is the greatest flirt the world has ever known," Caroline said tartly. "And it is very cold in here—and the air not quite fresh. Matthew, I would like to go outside."

"So you shall, for I want to have a look at Perry's stable," Sir Matthew said, aware, one supposed, that quite soon he would have the purchase price of any horse in the county, despite the restrictions my uncle would endeavour to tie into the marriage contract. But Caroline was nervous of horses, Blaize not obsessive, Miss Clevedon remarkably agreeable to his suggestion that while his mother and mine returned to the house, we should take a stroll.

"Show me these famous abbey grounds," he invited her, and so we walked a while in the thin, sharp air, my feet and Caroline's uneasy on the stony pathways, Miss Clevedon striding out, her hips as narrow and flat as a boy's, no blood on her cheek today, but a certain translucence, a quick-rising vitality, her hair turning to pure copper at every uncertain shaft of winter sunlight.

She had spent all her life here, at the abbey, she told us, just a few miles distant from Tarn Edge, but as unaware of our existence as we had been of hers. The city, to her, meant London—and that to be avoided whenever possible—the rest mere collections of houses, a strange, restricted way of life she did not care to understand. She had been happy here—every day of her life she had been happy—gloriously content with the company of her brother and her grandfather, and their sporting friends.

And a mere half-hour of her company sufficed to make it clear that her brother, Peregrine Clevedon, who was reckless and spendthrift and would have fallen foul of the law more than once had it not been for his family connections, could do no wrong in her eyes, that her grandfather, Mr. Gervase Clevedon, was of a nobility and wisdom falling little short of the Deity, that her abbey was the master plan besides which the rest of the world's great buildings did not really signify. She was herself a passionate horsewoman, having ridden to hounds six days a week every season since she had turned five years old; and was no mean shot either, although she could not match her brother's record of killing ninety-six pheasants, one smoky autumn day, with ninety-six shots, eighty grouse with eighty shots, thirty-four partridges with thirty-four shots.

"I believe you pity those of us who have not lived as you have," Caroline acidly remarked, to which Miss Clevedon gave her sudden, almost startled peal of laughter, tossed her head, as restive and openhearted as a young colt, and declared that she believed she did.

"But you can hardly expect to live here forever? One assumes your grandfather is not immortal, and that your brother may marry . . . ?" But Miss Clevedon was not dismayed.

"Oh, but it is the abbey, and the estate that matter, you see," she explained to an increasingly distant Caroline. "When my grandfather dies it will all be Perry's, and then his children's, and theirs . . . We will still be here, life-tenants handing into the future what was given to us by the past. That's the great thing. That *is* immortality, don't you see?"

"How comforting," Caroline said, walking briskly forward, pausing as she reached the river bank, her eyes critically scanning the fragile bridge. "Can that be secure, do you think?"

"I daresay it is not," Miss Clevedon called out, "but I never use it." And catching up her skirt still higher, she sprang lightly on to the first steppingstone, and then the second, her boots up to their heels in water, swaying slightly, deliberately, as she flung down her challenge.

"Would someone care to race me to the other side?"

"I hardly think so," Caroline told her, Barforth fury visibly mounting, since it was clear to her that Matthew Chard, had she not been there to restrain him, would have plunged readily enough into the stream, good broadcloth jacket, best cambric shirt, and all.

But "I'll venture myself on the bridge," Blaize offered. "And rescue you at the other side."

"There'll be no need to rescue me, Mr. Blaize Barforth, I do assure you . . ." And they were off, Miss Clevedon leaping, splashing, from stone to stone, her hair coming down in a guinea-gold tangle, her feet kicking up a fine spray as she went, Blaize on the bridge, not hurrying but keeping pace with her, reaching out a hand, as they both came to the far bank, allowing her, for just a moment, to pull him forward towards the water.

"I'll give you a soaking yet, Mr. Barforth."

"I think you will not."

And then her quick, gurgling laughter as he tugged her sharply on to the grass and, for an instant, into his arms.

"Matthew, go after them," Caroline commanded. "They must not be alone together over there."

But to Matthew Chard, accustomed to the free and easy hunting society of Leicestershire, the sophistications of Oxford and London, these were the notions of Methodism, of the middle classes—shopkeepers' morality—and, lounging somewhat irritably against the bridge, he said, "Good Lord, Caroline—what harm are they doing?"

"None, if they come back at once. But if they go up the hill and out of sight, that young lady may well find herself compromised."

"Lord," he said again, half-amused, half-wishing, perhaps, that he had gone hunting, after all. "I have been up that hill alone with her a dozen times and thought nothing of it. These things don't signify, I reckon, in good—I mean, in the countryside."

But before she could give him her opinion of his countryside, knowing full well he had almost said "in good society," they were back again, Miss Clevedon breathless, almost beautiful, Blaize in no hurry to release her hand. And, smiling at him, fond of him as I was, wishing him well as I did, my treacherous thought still reached out to him. Fall in love with her, Blaize. Or make her love you—as you could, if you tried—if you wanted to.

We started for home soon after, Matthew Chard remaining at Galton to await the arrival of Miss Clevedon's brother, and the house was scarcely out of sight, the superb Barforth carriage horses making light of the distance, when Caroline, who had remained very cool, said to her mother, "I think you should know that Blaize has behaved very foolishly—in fact, very badly."

"I wonder," Aunt Verity said. "Have you, dear?"

"Yes and no," he told her, the understanding between mother and son quite complete. "Badly perhaps. Foolishly—I don't think so."

"I expect you have been flirting with Miss Clevedon?"

"I have."

"And enjoying it?"

"Immensely."

"And she may have enjoyed it too. But is it really wise, dear?"

"Of course it is not wise," Caroline cut in, "since the girl is angling for a husband, and he is too blinded to see why."

"My dear Caroline," he said, a perfect imitation of her own grand manner, "I am well aware of her reasons, believe me. Their property is in ruins, the brother is too wild for any woman to marry, and so Miss Clevedon has elected to make the supreme sacrifice. She doesn't like the idea of marrying a manufacturer— my word, she doesn't like it, and it is an indication of her devotion to her family that she is willing to undertake it at all. In fact I am flattered that, in my case, she feels it could be less horrific than she'd anticipated."

"Then you admit her to be an odious, unfeeling creature?"

"I admit nothing of the kind," he said, leaning sharply forward, "for she is every bit as enchanting as I have been telling her these past few weeks. And she is very far from being unfeeling—very far. I will tell you this, Caroline, she is exactly the kind of girl a man might come to love, quite foolishly, without at all wanting to, you may believe me. She could get inside a man's head, and his skin, and he could find himself quite unable to get rid of her, no matter how much he tried. It would take a warm-hearted man, of course, which puts me out of the running, you'll surely agree."

"So you have done with her?"

"Have I? Very likely. I am going to London at the end of the week in any case. And if it eases you, Caroline—since this will not shock Mother and Aunt Elinor, and Faith may stop her ears

—I have a friend in London who intrigues me, perhaps not quite so much as Miss Clevedon, but who is considerably easier of access. So—probably—you have nothing more to fear on her account, and mine."

"Well, I am glad of that, although you need not snap at me."

"What is it, Faith," my mother said, quietly for her. "Are you not well, dear?" And, forcing my mouth to smile, an effort made through a sudden weight of weariness, I said, "No—no—it's the cold, that's all, Mamma. Just the cold."

Chapter Ten

MY SISTER CELIA had her child at the beginning of February, a boy some weeks ahead of his time, who lived but a moment or two; and it chanced that when her pains started she and I were alone in the house together, Jonas in Leeds on business, my mother and Prudence on an excursion to Harrogate, Aunt Hannah so unacceptable to her that I sent at once for Dr. Ashburn, not daring to imagine the consequences to myself, and to Celia, if he could not be found.

"It is nothing," she said, plainly terrified. "Not at all what you are thinking, in any case." And seeing the beading of sweat on her thin, seventeen-year-old face, the utter panic in her eyes, my little sister trying hard, even now, to play the matron, I told her, "Nonsense. I may be unmarried, Celia, but I have learned that babies do not grow under a gooseberry bush—nor in the doctor's bag, either."

"Then you know more than I did—last year," she gasped, biting her lips, allowing me to take her upstairs and hold her hand, her fingers gripping hard, the sheer outrage in her face comic, had it not been so totally appalling.

"Darling—darling Celia—it's going to be all right."

"All right? It's disgusting," she cried out, teeth digging vixen-sharp into her lip, "disgusting—all of it—"

"Oh no, darling—it's natural."

"What do you know about it? You don't even know what I mean. It's horrible, I'm telling you. It's disgusting."

"Celia—I don't know—but I think you should calm yourself."

"Why? Why should I?"

"Because I think you should. And the doctor will soon be here."

"The doctor," she spat out. "The doctor—what's a doctor? Another man coming to maul me—dear God—don't leave me, Faith. I won't be left alone with him."

But Giles Ashburn, appearing blessedly, almost silently, would not have me stay, disengaging her frantic hand from mine with quiet authority.

"Mrs. Agbrigg, I am going to help you and you must help me to do so. Miss Aycliffe, if you will wait downstairs . . ."

"No," Celia screeched, thrashing her body wildly again.

"Yes," he replied, opening the door for me, leaving me with no option, although he had not even raised his voice, but to obey.

Jonas would be here before it was over, I thought, calculating the time of the last train, and my mother, who would come immediately on reading the note I had despatched to Blenheim Lane. But the afternoon had scarcely darkened, I had been but an hour or two, it seemed, staring into the fire, trying not to heed the muffled sounds overhead, not to dwell on my sister's frailty—my own helplessness—when Giles Ashburn was back again, telling me with his great quietness that although my sister was as well as one could hope her to be, her son, who had been born too quickly, too soon, had not survived.

"There was nothing that could be done," he said very carefully, uncertain as to how much, if anything, I knew of the process of human reproduction, and understanding the pains he was taking neither to shock nor offend me—since I might well have to endure it myself one day—I nodded, not wishing to increase his burden.

"May I go up to her?"

"It would be best if she could sleep now, for a while. My nurse is with her."

"Of course. Was she—much distressed?"

"Not yet. Later, perhaps."

And conscious suddenly, quite sickeningly, of the tiny, lifeless body which would have been my nephew—conscious of my sister's pain—I cried out, "It is such a waste."

"Yes," he said, still enveloped in his quietness. "I know. Miss Aycliffe, there is no reason now for you to stay. I shall be leaving shortly, since my nurse can do all that is necessary. May I take you home?"

"Oh no. She may wake, you see—and then there is Jonas. Someone must be here when he arrives—to tell him. He should not be allowed to hear it from a parlourmaid."

"That is good of you, Miss Aycliffe."

"Indeed it is not. But Dr. Ashburn, do sit down a moment, for you look quite done in. Will you take something—tea, or brandy?"

"A little brandy would be very welcome," he said, and fetching it myself to spare the harassed maids, I returned to find him leaning back heavily against the sofa cushions, a man who seemed younger, more vulnerable, than I had supposed.

"I beg your pardon," he said, half-rising, taking the glass from me and drinking, as I had seen him do before, almost with need.

"Are you quite well, Dr. Ashburn?"

"Why yes—quite well, thank you. I have been up all night, that is all. And, to tell you the truth, I am always distressed by death, which may seem strange, since I see so much of it. I had hoped to grow accustomed . . ."

"I am glad you cannot."

"Why do you say that?"

"Because to grow accustomed would be the same as growing hard, I suppose."

He leaned forward, drew a deep breath, of courage perhaps, and said rapidly, knowing the time ill-chosen but unable, it seemed, to prevent himself. "Sometimes you have been a great help to me."

"I? But what have I ever done?"

"You have—been there, in Blenheim Lane—where I knew I could find you. The theory that the sight of beauty—of what a man finds to be beautiful—refreshes the spirit, I have found to be most apt."

It's true, then, I thought. I am not beautiful at all, but he finds me so, which means he is in love with me. I wonder why? He is a clever man, sensitive and serious, distinguished in his way, and I have nothing in my head but fashion and small talk and Nicholas Barforth. Why should he fall in love with me? And I understood that the happy patchwork I had woven for all our lives was falling irrevocably apart. Giles Ashburn—who could have been so happy with Prudence, I was sure of it, and she with him —loved me and Nicholas did not: and wanting to spare him distress, hoping, that when it came to it, Nicholas would try to spare me, I began to murmur the remarks I had been taught to use on such occasions, and he to apologise for his familiarity, both of us talking quickly and saying nothing, when there was the sound of a horse, and Jonas came into the room.

He was, as always, immaculate, the sombre, neutral shades of the man of business, unruffled although he had ridden several miles from the station through a blustery evening, his face registering no surprise, no alarm.

"Dr. Ashburn?"

"Yes. Your son was born an hour ago, Mr. Agbrigg. Your wife has made a sufficient recovery, but not the child. I am truly sorry."

"Ah," Jonas said, his eyelids lowering very briefly, and then, "I see. I am sure you did your best."

"I believe so."

"Shall I go up to her?"

"Yes. She may need you."

I went into the hall, handed Giles Ashburn his hat and cloak since there seemed no one else to do it, assured him that my mother would soon be here, waited, in the open doorway, to watch him drive away. And when I returned to the drawing room Jonas was there before me, standing by the hearth, staring reflectively at the fire.

"You have not been long, Jonas. Is she sleeping?"

"No. She is not sleeping."

"What then?"

"She is awake."

"Jonas—if you are telling me to mind my own business, then I must tell you that she is my sister—"

"Yes," he said, taking the fire tongs and very deliberately selecting a piece of coal, breaking it neatly, without violence, into even segments and arranging them into a carefully contrived pyramid. "I will tell you then. She is awake. She has sent the nurse for a tray of tea. I went upstairs because I was told she needed me. I came downstairs again because she does not. Should she need me later, I will go up again. That is all."

"Jonas—please don't be impatient with her. I am impatient with her myself, often enough, but she is only seventeen, and it has been a—a shock."

His eyes still on the fire, watching his intricate building of the coal, he said, "I am never impatient. Quite the reverse. I have just been into the kitchen to make certain that her tray, when they take it to her, will be just to her liking. I have reminded them to use a white cloth and I have even held the cup to the light to make certain it is spotless and has no cracks. What more can I do for her, at this moment, than that?"

My sister's unnamed little child was buried some days later, Jonas standing chilled but unapproachable at the graveside, my mother and Jonas' father shedding a tear, Aunt Hannah looking stern, since she disliked any kind of failure and, although she was sorry for Celia, was beginning to have doubts about her fitness as a future cabinet minister's wife.

Celia greeted us on our return from the cemetery, her face like a stone, her body still full of that strange, rigid anger.

"Tea is just ready," she said. "I expect you will be glad of it, since the day has turned cold."

"Thank you," Jonas answered with scrupulous politeness, taking the cup she offered him, and then, excusing himself once more with great correctness, retiring to his study for the perusal of documents which would not wait.

"I believe it will snow before morning," Aunt Hannah said, to fill in the silence, to which we obediently chorused, "Yes, indeed."

"You are not looking well, Miss Aycliffe," Giles Ashburn murmured, having looked in for a moment because he had seen our carriage.

"Oh—I am quite all right, thank you," but, in fact, I was unable to shake off the chill of the winter graveyard, my bones aching, my chest tightening with the start of an influenza which kept me in my bed longer than it need have done had I been anxious to rise, thus causing offence to Caroline, who wished to consult me about the length of her wedding veil. And even before I ventured downstairs again, it was no secret to anyone that Georgiana Clevedon, having taken more accurately the measure of Blaize, had turned her green, woodland eyes and her sudden laughter on Nicholas.

He had danced with her the maximum permitted number of times—three, in fact—at an Assembly Rooms Ball, where Miss Clevedon, in an evening gown which Caroline declared managed somehow to look like a riding habit, had given further offence by her complete disregard of the etiquette Cullingford required of its young ladies.

"So these are the famous Assembly Rooms," she had said on arrival, speaking to Julian Flood, but her loud, flat squire's drawl audible to several others. "My word, I never saw the inside of a counting house, but this must be it."

While even the comfortable Mrs. Hobhouse, who had been brought up like the rest of us to consider poverty a sin which, like adultery and associated vices, must be concealed at all costs, had been shocked to hear Miss Clevedon declare herself as poor as a church mouse.

"Oh, I have but the one gown," she had said when Mrs. Hobhouse, trying to be kind, had admired it, "so I have no bother at all in deciding what to wear—it is simply this one, or, if it is not fit to be seen, I cannot go out at all."

"Lounging," Aunt Hannah told us, "at the buffet with the men —behaving, in fact, like a man herself. Thoroughly unbecoming, and I cannot believe any relative of mine could have thought otherwise."

And so, in fact, it seemed, for at a town meeting, some days later, called by Mayor Agbrigg to discuss the sorry state of Cullingford's sewers, Nicholas, as astonished as anyone else, perhaps, to see Miss Clevedon sitting there, had offered her no more than a curt nod, a cool word, and had left before the speeches ended, making it clear that he desired no private conversation with anyone. Yet Miss Clevedon had remained on her chair, managing at least to keep from yawning—a feat beyond the powers of many—while Mayor Agbrigg had attempted to curdle the assembled blood with tales of overflowing swill tubs in Simon Street, and Dr. Ashburn had put forward his much ridiculed theory that certain diseases, cholera not least among them, might be transferred not only by the touch or the breath of the sufferer, and by contact with rotting garbage heaps—all of which could be avoided—but by the drinking of contaminated water, which could not. Cholera, Dr. Ashburn had declared—quietly, but with immense firmness, Prudence told me—

had destroyed sixty thousand English souls only some sixteen years ago, confining itself largely but not exclusively to those areas where sanitation was haphazard, or where there was no sanitation at all. And unless something, in his view, was done about the open sewers of Simon Street, and the local habit of gathering water for domestic usage from any stagnant pool available when the standpipe ran out, then it was beyond question that the disease would strike again.

"He was most emphatic in his warning," Prudence told me, "and most courageous too, since I know how little he enjoys public speaking." And when Prudence refused, despite all my persuasion, to sink to the level of common gossip, I had to wait for Caroline to tell me that Miss Clevedon, having listened patiently to the end, had enquired, once more in that loud, flat drawl, "Now where is Simon Street? It sounds unlikely and most intriguing, and there is no doubt at all that one has a duty to help the poor. May one go and see it?"

"I suppose you will be wanting tea?" Caroline had replied, compelled to make the offer, she explained, since the girl, after all, was cousin to Matthew Chard, but feeling the coolness of her tone sufficient to ensure a refusal. But Miss Clevedon, with her quick smile, her coltish tossing of the head, had accepted with evident gladness, returning in the Barforth carriage to spend the rest of the day at Tarn Edge.

"I cannot think why Verity and Caroline encourage her," Aunt Hannah said, coming to sit with me the following afternoon, genuinely concerned, I think, at my slow recovery. Yet Georgiana Clevedon, despite her poverty, was the daughter and granddaughter of landed gentlemen who knew of no reason why she could not visit a manufacturer's household as freely as the cottages on the Galton estate, as freely as Aunt Hannah herself entered the millhouses at Lawcroft. She came and went as she pleased, appearing and disappearing to suit her fancy, not only in Cullingford but inside my head, so that I was never entirely without her, could never lose the impression of that pointed face, hovering somewhere behind my eyes, nor the sound of Blaize's voice telling us how easily even a stubborn man—and quite against his nature—could love her.

"If they would simply leave the matter alone," Prudence said when Aunt Hannah had gone, "then I believe it would be no more than a nine day's wonder. Blaize thinks so too. Men are prone to these fancies, and should be allowed, in their own good time, to grow tired of them. That is what Blaize says, at any rate, and since he has fancies enough for a dozen men, then I am inclined to think he is right."

But the sight of a gentleman's daughter displaying so marked a preference for the son of a manufacturer intrigued Cullingford. The suspicion that the young lady believed her social superiority too enormous to permit any embarrassment—that she was condescending rather than pursuing—gave much offence. And on the very day that I came feebly downstairs, having lost weight and colour, looking hollow, I thought, feeling as if I had dissolved, somehow, into a damp mist and could not take shape again, the drawing room was full of ladies, half of them well pleased to sympathise with poor, dear Verity Barforth in her troubles, all of them eager to pry from my mother the information Aunt Verity would not give.

"Faith dear, how very unwell you look," they said to me, reserving my plight, only half-guessed at, for later.

"I am very well, thank you," I went on repeating, my lips feeling stiff and cold, my smile an inward agony, for although my body was still limp, the congestion of my lungs not fully healed, my real sickness, I knew full well, was of despair.

The world had once been kind to me. It had placed me in a comfortable home far beyond the level of those who were obliged to labour. It had given me health and hope and an inclination to laughter; it had given me a nature which required to be loved, and now, without hope of the man I required to love me, I no longer knew what I was doing in the world at all.

"You must take care, dear," my mother's tea-time ladies told me, each one, on leaving.

"Yes, so I will, thank you, Mrs. Hobhouse—Mrs. Mandelbaum—" And then, half rising and finding my legs quite fluid, my whole body slipping, somehow, from its direction, I murmured, "I am not well enough, Mother, to go out just yet."

"No, darling," she said, shaking her head, smiling at me, her voice fainter than I had expected, her face too near to mine and then too far away. "Go back to bed. Miss Mayfield will sit with you."

"He has not sent her a note, or a flower," I heard Prudence

mutter angrily, and although I wanted to defend him, I lacked the strength to tell her I had neither expected nor wanted it. For what could he possibly write?

Blaize had sent me flowers in profusion. Giles Ashburn had visited every day. Jonas had called once or twice with cheerful news of Celia, who had been carried downstairs now to her sofa, and had even walked, with his assistance, to the window. Even Freddy Hobhouse, using any excuse to see Prudence, had brought me a jar of his mother's famous ginger marmalade to tempt my invalid appetite. But a few lines from Nicholas, saying "I am sorry to hear you are unwell," far from reassuring me, would have told me that he did not greatly care. His silence indicated that he was troubled on his own account, guilty on mine, and even in the weakness of my convalescence, the down-drooping of my spirit, I could not tolerate the thought that I might weigh heavily on his conscience. Whatever happened I would not be an uneasy memory, to him or to anyone.

Yet hope was not entirely at an end. Nicholas, I heard, had declined an invitation to dine at Galton Abbey, had excused himself from showing Miss Clevedon his father's mills, leaving Blaize to escort her around the sheds which, she freely avowed, had horrified and depressed her, the sight of so much close-confined humanity inspiring her to thoughts of revolution, the noise and the stench turning her stomach. He was behaving, in fact, like a man tempted, certainly—if the smouldering, brooding glances Amy Battershaw and Rebecca Mandelbaum described to me were anything to go by—but struggling to reassert his common sense. And knowing him to be sensible, I continued fitfully to hope, until the afternoon when Caroline burst in upon me to say that her father had forbidden him to see Miss Clevedon again, at which point I knew there could be little hope at all. "He has been sneaking off before the engines were shut down," she told me, flushed with indignation. "Riding halfway to Galton, and she halfway from there, to meet him. Really, the kind of assignation one may make with a housemaid. Well, my father has told him to put an end to it, and he, of course, has said he will not. And even my mother, who will never say a word against him, was unable to stay calm. Yes, we have all told him what we think to it—except Blaize, who was altogether impertinent, saying he should be allowed to get on with it and get rid of it in his own way. A point of view, I suppose, which may serve for a housemaid, but which in this case, is pure folly. Surely you must see that, Faith, for however much we may dislike her, she is a Miss Clevedon of Galton Abbey, cousin to the Chards and the Floods, and with the very highest connections in London, although you would not think it to look at her, and if Nicholas should compromise her and refuse to marry her, then all our reputations must suffer. Blaize may think such behaviour admissible, but the gentry would all band together—including Matthew—to say that one can expect nothing better of a manufacturer. And, quite frankly, although I stress that I detest the girl, I could not blame them. If she were a Hobhouse, we should have had her father already on our doorstep demanding that Nicholas name the wedding day—except that no Hobhouse, and no one else I have ever heard of, would dream of carrying on in this loose fashion. I said so, too, and I believe Nicholas would have slapped me for it, had not my father intervened. 'You cannot judge her,' Nicholas said, 'by your own narrow standards.' Yes, he said that, and I thought my father would have had a fit, and it was my mother who had to intervene then, or he would have given Nicholas a thrashing. My word, I have never heard such language as they threw at each other. Well, it is all misery with us just now, as you may imagine, for my father and Nicholas have not exchanged a word since yesterday and my mother is so afraid that Nicholas may walk out one morning and not return that she is wearing herself out, going from one to the other, endeavouring to make the peace. But, Faith—you really do look quite ill. I hope you may be fully recovered for my wedding. You look as if you need a trip to a warmer climate again—like your mother."

Yet even this escape, which I would have seized gladly, was denied me, for in that same month the French king, Louis Philippe, was driven from his throne by the Paris mob, escaping across the Tuileries Gardens with no time to put on his wig, haunted, no doubt, by the memory of another King Louis, not too long ago, who had lost not only his wig but his head. And as one by one the capital cities of Europe burst into flame and London itself began to simmer, when even in Cullingford, Mr. Hobhouse was jostled on his way to the Piece Hall, Mr. Oldroyd jeered by a ragged, street-corner mob, I understood escape to be impossible and composed myself, as best I could, strengthening myself daily, like an athlete, a soldier, to support this constant wounding, the certainty of greater injury to come.

At the beginning of March a stone was thrown at Aunt Hannah's carriage, not causing her horses to bolt, since they were too elderly for that in any case; but the intention had been plain, the missiles aimed not by unruly urchins but by hard and bitter men. And Aunt Hannah may have been displeased at her husband's simple comment, "They're hungry," for it had been a severe winter, following a poor harvest, the price of bread still high despite the removal of the Corn Laws, the advantage of repeal having gone as always, it seemed, to the masters rather than the servants, since wages—paid out to men who had no vote, no power but that of terror and disobedience—were still very low.

"They're hungry." And now, with the railways and the new penny post to facilitate communications, there were rumours once again of armed risings in the manner of the revolutionary French, the Chartists come to plague us afresh with their demands, which only Giles Ashburn, among all our acquaintances, did not consider to be excessive.

It was the result, he explained—talking to Prudence, making an uncomfortable effort not to look too often at me—of the reforms of '32, which had not gone far enough. Much had been promised in the great reform year, and much, indeed, received by the middle classes, which, for the first time, had won representation in a Parliament previously no more than a mouthpiece for the landed gentry. After the Bill of '32 any man in Cullingford who paid an annual property rent of 10 pounds or more could have his vote, to use or to sell as he thought fit, although the absence of a secret ballot somewhat restricted his choices, should he be in the employ of Mr. Joel Barforth, or a tenant of Sir Giles Flood. Yet these new voters, Dr. Ashburn calculated, had numbered no more than a mere thousand or so in a population of sixty thousand, a solid pressure group from the middle classes which had sent middle-class men like my father to Parliament to speak for them, in opposition to the gentry, and totally neglectful of the troublesome, if labouring, poor.

And having fought so hard for their own right to vote, their own freedom from the ground landlord, the titled farmer, they could hardly be astonished, Dr. Ashburn felt, at the Chartists, whose revolutionary demands for one man one vote would make the poor not necessarily rich but—since there were so many of them—very powerful.

"Their demands, in fact, are very logical," he said, so quietly that it was not easy to realise his opinions were treasonable and, if acted upon, could lead him to the gallows. "When your uncle, Mr. Barforth, fought hard to be represented in Parliament in '32, I am sure Sir Giles Flood thought him quite as much a revolutionary as he now thinks his operatives for making the same demands. There is no cause for astonishment, surely. In fact the Duke of Wellington himself has warned repeatedly that by extending the franchise even so far, his peers have done no more than open the floodgates, through which, sooner or later, the riffraff are bound to get through. And now, at least, he may have the satisfaction of seeing himself proved correct. The people have finally understood that they can rely on no one but themselves. The gentry will look after the gentry. The manufacturers will look after the manufacturers. Both these groups have made promises to the labouring classes which they have kept only in part, or not at all, or in such a way that no real benefit has been derived. The people, now, have chosen to look after their own interests, and they require the vote to do it. And to spare themselves yet another hollow triumph—the choice between voting for a millmaster or a squire—they require that members of Parliament should no longer, by law, be men of property. They wish to elect one of themselves, which also seems to be in no way astonishing. Sir Giles Flood may well have considered your uncle too ill-educated and too lacking in political experience to use the franchise correctly once he had obtained it—since he clearly meant to use it against Sir Giles. And, unfortunately, he may have been right, as your uncle is right now, when he says the same thing. But that, surely, is not a reason to deny the franchise. Would it not be better to educate those who are in need of it—which, I imagine, must be some 80 per cent of our nation —so that everyone may use his vote with responsibility, as seems best to him?"

"Precisely," my sister said, perfectly in tune with him, "for our system of education is deplorable. Our boys are taught Latin and Greek and little else, our girls are taught nothing at all, the labouring classes are taught—one supposes—to labour, which sometimes seems better to me than fine embroidery. How I would love to set up a school—do you know that? Yes, if they would let me have my money, I would open a school for girls which would be like no other school in the world—no watercolours, no samplers—real work, Giles. Only think how shocking. I imagine they would attempt to burn me at the stake."

"Do it, Prudence," I said. "Why not? Let's talk to Mamma. We could do it together—not even in Cullingford. We could travel together, until we found a place—get away . . ."

"Not you, Faith," she said, her voice almost hard. "You'll get married, you know you will—one day. You can send me your daughters."

And neither of us could miss the nervous tremor in Giles Ashburn's quiet face, nor how quickly he looked away.

I went out for the first time at the end of that week, braving the sooty March winds to call on Celia, who, cutting short my uneasy references to her child, talked solely of a new rosewood card table she had ordered, two months ago, and which now, being finally delivered, was not at all as desired. And returning home, ridiculously weakened by so brief an excursion, to be told that Mr. Barforth—Blaize, I assumed—was waiting to see me, I went alone into the drawing room, shocked beyond immediate recovery to find Nicholas there.

He was standing at the window, obscured by the half-dark which always prevailed in that room, a silhouette merely against the deep claret of the curtains, although I had no need of light to see his face. And knowing that this, surely, was the moment for which I had schooled myself, my first real encounter with pain, I took off my gloves and my bonnet, slowly, neatly, folded my hands, folded as much of myself as I could grasp and shut it away, before I asked, "Nicholas?" although the question was neither of his identity nor his intentions.

"Yes," he said, not moving forward. "There is something I have to say to you—and quickly I think."

"Then say it."

"I am come straight from Galton Abbey, where—in fact, I have just asked Georgiana Clevedon to be my wife."

"Yes, of course."

And as the words slipped from my tongue, my mind, too,

slipped a shade away from reality, leaving me with an odd sensation that this was not the first time he had said this to me, nor the first time I had so calmly answered. Like a recurring dream it had happened before, over and over again, in the part of my brain which controlled the source of anguish and fear, over and over, a wheel turning me slowly towards him and as slowly away again, so that I had grown accustomed to it, and would not break.

"Faith—"

"Yes."

"I had to tell you myself. You do see that I had to do that?"

"Yes I do. I hope you will be very happy, Nicholas."

"Oh," he said, striding forward, his face hard and strained, quite pale. "As to that—I hope so too. Many will think otherwise —but she is a rare person, Faith, truly—I know of no one like her. And I can only pray she may be happy with me."

"Yes, Nicholas."

And then, abruptly, his voice harsh, as if the words were forced from him through clenched teeth, he said, "They will say it is for my money on her part, and on mine because I am stubborn. It is more than that. I had to say that too."

"There was no need. I knew it."

"Aye," he said, a sigh of pure weariness escaping him. "You always know. You've known, these past weeks, haven't you?— known what was happening to me—why I couldn't even come and see you when you were ill. Well, I came, a dozen times, to the end of the street and then went away again—that's the truth —because I couldn't face you. I wasn't sure, until now, that I was even going to do it—it could all have been over, and there'd have been no need to say a word to you about it. You wouldn't have asked me any questions either, would you? No—I know damned well you wouldn't. You'd have made it easy for me— like you're doing now. Christ—I'd better go home."

But he didn't move and, unable to say more, I walked past him to stand with my face to the window, until the sound of the door slamming shut behind him, and the street door after it, released me from that terrible, fierce-clenched control and bent me double for a moment, winded and gasping, as Celia had been at the start of her travail.

"Faith," Prudence said sharply from the doorway, my mother

behind her, and straightening up, sitting down, my voice pronounced what was in my mind, so calmly that in some crazy recess of myself, I could have laughed at it.

"He is to marry Georgiana Clevedon. I do not think they can be happy, and I—really—do you know, I wish I could die of it. It would seem easier, except that of course I cannot—no one really dies of these things."

"How dare he come here," Prudence said, glaring at the window as if she would have liked to break through it and go after him, a sliver of glass in her hand. "It is an open acknowledgement that he recognises there has been something between you—that he has treated you badly. How dare he? He should have had the decency to keep away, and when I meet him again I shall tell him so."

"Oh no, dear," my mother murmured, her whole face, it seemed, brimming with tears. "I must ask you not to do so, for he will have trouble enough. He has Joel yet to face and—oh, Faith, my poor lamb, I should not tell you this, but it may help you to know how she has snared him. Verity was expecting it—oh yes, she was so despondent last night, for it seems he rode over to Galton on Monday and did not return until Tuesday, which did not alarm Verity until she learned that the grandfather had gone away to London, and the brother with him. My dear, they were alone all night together, in that isolated place—no, no, the maids cannot signify on such occasions— And what could he do but make her an offer after that?"

"Ah," Prudence said, "it does not surprise me."

But getting up and returning to the window, concentrating so hard on the last harsh tones of his voice that these other voices, seeking to comfort me, became a nuisance, a mere pestering of flies coming between me and the things I believed, had to believe, I said, "No. He loves her."

"Darling, surely not . . ."

And turning to my mother so fiercely that she retreated a hasty step backwards, I repeated his own words. "Yes, Mother. They will say it is for his money on her part, and on his because he is stubborn. It is more than that. He loves her, Mother. He believes it, and I believe it—and so must you."

And at least I had salvaged something. I had kept my faith with him.

Chapter Eleven

THERE WAS a most terrible, yet, in some ways merciful numbness inside me for a while after that, an absence of sensation which, although I knew it to be unnatural, did not manage to alarm me. I was suspended, it seemed, a little above and around myself, observing my own calm with a certain irony, knowing it could not last, praying only that it would last long enough for me to meet Nicholas again, as I would have to do, until I had seen him married, wished him well, waved his honeymoon train away, at which point, since I could not die and could not run away, I would at least be able to face myself—and Cullingford —again.

His news, of course, had created a predictable explosion at Tarn Edge. Aunt Verity, even, forsaking her tranquillity, pleaded with him most tearfully to reconsider, while Uncle Joel had been so moved by his wife's distress that even Caroline had been alarmed at the violence of his anger. Yet, in the end, when his threats of dismissal from the family business and from the family itself had been two or three times repeated, and Nicholas had declared himself perfectly ready to be cast adrift, it had become clear to them all that they did not really wish to part from one another, and so they sat down, more quietly, to discuss what must be done.

Aunt Verity, it seemed, while by no means unaware of Miss Clevedon's charm, simply did not consider her a suitable wife for Nicholas. Uncle Joel, when it came down to it, was still man enough to recognise a "rare bird" when he saw one, and could have been amused, even captivated by her, had he encountered her as the fiancée of a Flood or a Winterton, or of any man's son but his own. His main objection, after long deliberation, was that he failed to see the profit in such a marriage. In Caroline's case there was a title in the offing, his daughter—whose great-grandmother had spent her days in a weaving shed—elevated to Lady Chard of Listonby, her children in possession of hereditary lands and privileges which money alone could not buy. But, since it would be Peregrine Clevedon, not Georgiana, who would inherit the ancient domain of Galton Abbey, my uncle could not understand, in this instance, just what he was being asked to pay for.

"Wait a while, lad," he'd asked, almost patiently for him. "I know how these things can get in the blood, when you're young. And you're young, Nicky—by God, you're young. Give yourself a chance, lad."

But Nicholas was of full age, a man with the courage to face life on his own and the skill to succeed, and although, left to himself, my uncle may just have made good his threat of dismissal, seeing no real harm to it providing a door was left open should Nicholas wish to return, he knew the depth of Aunt Verity's feeling for her younger son, and would not run the risk of breaking her heart.

And I suppose it was a shock to him, and to the rest of the Barforths too, when they learned that Miss Clevedon's grandfather was as bitterly opposed to the match as they.

Mr. Gervase Clevedon, Squire of Galton, was descended, by junior line, from some of the greatest names in England, having himself married first a viscount's daughter and then the sister of a belted earl, both these ladies bringing little money but immense prestige to the abbey. Untitled and apparently penniless, he was, nevertheless, nobler than Matthew Chard, a man whose family creed was a simple one of service to Crown and country, whose own days were spent in the tireless, unpaid administration of local justice, a gentleman whose word had never been questioned because no promise of his had ever been broken, whose decisions, both as a magistrate and a landlord, were invariably in keeping with his own impeccable, personal code.

Clevedons, from the beginning of the line, had served. They had never sold themselves, never worked for wages. They had been rewarded by honours, never insulted by the payment of cash, which, even when there had been cash to spare, no Clevedon had ever carried about his person, like a grocer. They had served, freely and loyally, and expecting an equal loyalty from their own servants, had undertaken the care of them in sickness and old age, regarding all those in their employ, the tenants of their farms and their cottages, as members of their extended family.

The butler who served my uncle Joel at Tarn Edge, who had been imported from London, would be dismissed the very instant he gave less than perfect satisfaction, or would leave, without a backward glance, to take up a better offer. The manservant at Galton Abbey, who had inherited his father's position, and his grandfather's, would be supported, albeit meagrely, for the rest of his life, and would devote his last energies to anyone who bore the name of Clevedon.

"I work for money," Uncle Joel said. "And because I expect others to do the same, I pay good wages."

"I do my duty," Mr. Clevedon might have answered. "I am responsible for those born on my land in situations inferior to my own. I hold the land itself in trust for future generations, having received it from those of my name who held it in trust for me. I am true to myself and to all those with whom I have dealings. I offer loyalty and expect to receive it—a commodity which is far beyond price."

And so, although they were both decent, clever men, they baffled and offended each other, my uncle entirely convinced that all three Clevedons were conspiring to get their hands on his money, Mr. Clevedon every bit as certain that the Barforths would crawl on their knees—or ought to—for this alliance with his great name.

Like turns to like, they both said in their different ways. My son needs a sensible woman. My granddaughter needs a gentleman. My son is hard-working, shrewd, where any other man could make a penny he can usually find the way to make two. My granddaughter has been trained to accept the responsibilities of privilege, the duties of a manorial lady towards her estate and its people. She would give those two pennies away to anyone with a hereditary claim on the house of Clevedon, and leave herself starving. "There may yet be hope," Blaize told my sister. "They may argue the terms of the marriage contract too long, until the spark fades, and we shall have no marriage at all."

But Nicholas, having made up his mind, could not tolerate the delay, and at his threat—made with the calm of complete determination—to simplify matters by taking Miss Clevedon to Gretna Green to be married over the blacksmith's anvil, all opposition ceased.

"Well, at least now I can give some thought to my own wedding," Caroline told me. "Honiton lace, I wondered, Faith, for the veil—I believe the Queen had Honiton lace, did she not?"

And, still in that odd state of half-feeling, where a pin, sometimes, in my side would not have aroused even a cry, I replied, "Yes, and orange blossoms on her gown, which in your case would look splendid, Caroline, since you are taller and could have more of them."

But as the month reached its ill-natured, rain-swept close, my detachment seemed to be like a cloak that slipped, every now and then, from my shoulders, leaving me no protection from the cold. And since I would have frozen entirely had I remained in that torpid state, I awoke, first of all to panic, which, slicing through all my defences, warned me that I could not cope. How could I stand in the abbey church at Galton and see Nicholas married to another woman? I could not. It was as simple as that. And there were times when the dread of it caught me unawares, a vicious hammer blow battering away all vestiges of control, so that I had to lock myself away, upstairs, anywhere, to fight it. And if that hammer struck out at me on his wedding day, where could I run, with Amy Battershaw and Rebecca Mandelbaum, and my brother-in-law Jonas, watching me?

But I would attend that wedding. I would stand in that church, somehow, without a tremor, and smile. And afterwards, like everyone else, I would go up to Miss Clevedon—Mrs. Nicholas Barforth—and I would say all the things I would have said to any other bride.

"I hope you will be very happy," I forced my lips to speak in grim rehearsal. "May I say how much I admire your dress? May I call you Georgiana, since we are to be cousins now?"

I would do it. And I would do it well, not only for my own

pride's sake, but because it mattered fiercely that Nicholas—who had trouble enough and more trouble to come—should not feel troubled by me.

What, indeed, had he done to me? He had not asked me to fall in love with him in the first place. He had made me no promises. He had not compromised me, nor encouraged me to refuse another man for his sake. He had not jilted me, and I was quite wildly determined to give no one cause to think he had.

The truth of the matter was very simple. He had always liked me and had started to like me better. He had recognised me as the woman who would be good for him, but, unlike Jonas who had settled for the woman he could get, and had been glad, at the time, to get her, he had found the courage to stake everything on a woman he truly desired. If Matthew Chard had not brought Miss Clevedon to Tarn Edge, or had Blaize proved more susceptible, my patience may well have succeeded. But Matthew Chard had brought her. Blaize, as always, had been too intent on dazzling her to be dazzled himself. She existed. Nicholas did love her. If she was not in love with Nicholas now, I could not imagine it would take her very long to love him. It had happened, and if I was heartbroken and quite desperate at times, if I believed I had lost everything of value in my life, that the essential part of life itself was already over, then that was my concern, and I would be a poor, whining creature if I let it show.

And, growing more and more obsessed by my need to keep faith with him, the quality for which I had been named, it came about that only Blaize and myself had a good word to say for Miss Clevedon.

"Of course you must ask her to be your bridesmaid," I told Caroline. "It would look odd, otherwise—"

"Absolutely," Blaize added. "And I imagine we can make sure she does not come to church in her riding habit."

While to the assorted ladies of my mother's tea time, who had heard strange tales of the Clevedons but who, just the same, had a sneaking admiration for a real lord, a real lady, I said, "Her grandmother was a viscount's daughter," leaving Blaize to supply the details of a Clevedon who had graced the court of Queen Anne, another who had enjoyed the friendship of the Duchess of Kent, mother of our own, intensely respectable

Queen Victoria. And although these Cullingford matrons knew there was rarely any money in bosom friendships of that nature, they were impressed, nevertheless, and eager to hear more.

"We are doing rather well," Blaize told me. "They will all be falling over themselves presently to invite her to their tables."

"So I imagine."

"Of course they will not like her," he said, his eyes, which saw everything, knew everything, looking at me with a characteristic blend of curiosity and kindness. "But she is not so very dreadful, you know—just different."

But I had no intention of revealing my heartache to Blaize, whose own heart was too cool, too shallow perhaps for real understanding, consoling myself with the belief that if I had not managed to deceive him, then at least no one else suspected me. No one else. Yet my mother and Prudence were very kind to me, shielding me, in their different ways, from gossip, filling the gaps of my conversation when, every now and then, my throat was so tight that I could not speak, and Jonas, my brother-in-law, who had been wounded himself, not by love but certainly in his pride, watched me at times, remembering, perhaps, the night of Caroline's dance when I had seen his own composure stripped away.

"You will be the next one to be married, I expect, Faith."

"Do you think so, Jonas."

"Oh yes. I think so. I imagine you must see the necessity for it."

"Good heavens, Jonas. I am only nineteen—not quite on the shelf."

"By no means—but if you have suffered a disappointment there is really only one way to mend it."

"What disappointment?"

"Ah—my mother was wrong then? I am delighted to hear it."

"Jonas—exactly what do you mean?"

"Very little, it seems. My mother had formed the odd notion that you are attached . . ."

"I am not—absolutely not—it is positively untrue—"

"What is untrue, Faith?"

"What you said."

"I said nothing."

"Oh yes you did. You said that I was attached to . . ."

"Indeed? To whom?"

"To no one."

"Excellent. I will tell my mother she can be easy. But *had* you been attached to someone—who is to marry someone else—then the best course open to you would be to get married yourself. No one could then say—and there does appear to have been a whisper—that you might possibly be pining away for that unspecified someone . . ."

"Please don't play your lawyer's tricks on me, Jonas. I am not impressed."

But I wept a long time that night, wounded, as I believe he had intended to wound me, well aware that I had not convinced him: and, like all of life's ills, it was small consolation to me that I was not the only one, just then, who suffered.

It had been a hard winter in Simon Street, offering, as a Christmas gift, a hunger that by springtime had festered from hopelessness to rage, making the city dangerous again for those of us who drove out behind sleek carriage horses, who fed our pet dogs more regularly, more plentifully, than half of Cullingford could feed its children. There had been unkempt, haggard gatherings on Cullingford Green, Chartist banners held aloft in broad-tipped, big-knuckled hands, a mob, one morning, erupting into the Hobhouse mill yard when the gates were open at breakfast time, some of them willing to settle, then and there, for higher wages and ready to give a good week's work in exchange, some of them threatening that, with the vote in their hands, there'd be no need to ask for anything ever again, simply to take; others quite openly wanting to burn the mill down.

They had gone from Nethercoats to Market Square, their target undoubtedly the Piece Hall, which, being market day, was full of soberly dressed, serious-minded gentlemen of the middle classes, the younger of whom—not having been middle class for very long—not above using their fists, the elders having plenty to say about how they'd settled these matters in "their day." And in the ensuing hour of street-fighting, the scuffling and cursing, the stone-throwing and window-smashing, the violence had been put down, as always, by violence, by the staves and cutlasses of special constables, the hard-riding of a squadron of dragoons hired for the purpose, leaving a dozen men on the ground, another dozen dragging themselves away to heal or to die—as best they could—in some squalid bolt hole in Simon Street.

My sister Prudence went to the infirmary that day, against everybody's orders, to tend the wounded, helping Giles Ashburn to patch them up before they were taken to York to be imprisoned, or hanged, and by April, with the Chartist agitation at its height, the royal family—fearing, as so often before, a revolution in the bloodier, Continental manner—had been removed from London for safekeeping, the Whitehall area garrisoned and provisioned to withstand a state of seige, and 200,000 special constables sworn in to obey the Duke of Wellington's command.

"My word, how very stirring," my mother said, glad of anything to relieve her boredom.

"They're hungry," Mayor Agbrigg told us once again.

"They're greedy," Aunt Hannah replied.

"They're inefficient," said Uncle Joel, greeting with laughter the news that the Chartist leader, Feargus O'Connor, planned to assemble half a million desperate men and march to Westminster to present—or enforce—their petition for Parliamentary reform: to persuade, in fact, a reluctant government to grant the vote to every workingman or, if they refused, to turn them out and govern in their stead.

"Half a million men, indeed," my uncle repeated, his bulk firmly planted on my mother's hearthrug, the fragrance of his cigar smoke offending the very memory of my father. "Yes, half a million, which, to the naked eye would look like ten million. Excellent—for if he could get that half million to follow him, then he'd get everything he asked for, and more besides. But where are they to come from? Agreed—we have the railways now, but has Feargus O'Connor offered to pay the train fare for all those desperate men? Does he have the money? And, supposing they've all been told the name of the meeting place, has he remembered to tell them how to get there? And when the day dawns has it crossed his mind to wonder how many will manage to get out of bed on time, how many are likely to call at the alehouse on the way to the station, and stay there; or how many will have thought better of it? Half a million. He'll be lucky if he gets a thousand. And if it's a good summer, and a good harvest, and trade picks up, next year he'll get none at all."

And so it was. There were, in fact, more than my uncle's scornfully predicted thousand—twenty-three thousand, Giles Ashburn reported sadly, having received the news from my half brother, Crispin Aycliffe, who had been one among them—but so far short of the expected numbers that, with those special constables poised for the attack, with canon stationed at the ready on Westminster Bridge, and gamekeepers' rifles sprouting from the windows of the rich and famous, Mr. Feargus O'Connor, with true political flexibility, abandoned his march, and instead of leading an army to Westminster in triumph, drove there, alone and sedately, in a cab, his petition lying in forlorn bundles at his feet.

"I could have told him so," Uncle Joel announced.

"Aye—so could I," Mayor Agbrigg added, his meaning, I thought, not at all the same.

"I'm so sorry," I told Giles Ashburn, thinking of the men who had made that wild-goose chase to London, the men who had kept faith, as I tried to do, and who would be wandering now, footsore and disheartened, in an alien city; remembering the undernourished bodies he had himself stitched together, only a few weeks ago, and sent to York.

"It's always the way—people, quite simply, are like that," he said, and taking both my hands in his he bent his head and pressed not his lips but his forehead against them, a gesture of tenderness and weariness that held me quite still, a gesture of need which frightened and fascinated me, and from which I could not turn away.

The fight was over. Chartism, without doubt, was in ashes, its preposterous demands pigeon-holed away in some Whitehall archive, best forgotten. The Queen and all her special constables came home again, the English, after all, not being a people much given to wasteful, foreign ideas like revolution. And so there was nothing to mar Caroline's wedding day that June but a slight shower of rain as she left the church, and the indisposition of my sister Celia, who, being pregnant again, was unable to attend.

It was—as had been intended—the most sumptuous wedding Cullingford had ever seen, Caroline an imperial splendour in her satin and Honiton lace, her bridesmaids, myself and Georgiana Clevedon among them, wearing lesser copies of her gown which, as I had suggested, would make hers seem even more magnificent. And aware of Miss Clevedon standing directly behind me in the bridal procession, and of Nicholas not far away, I felt the stab of panic and saw, with disgust, that my bouquet was shaking in my hand.

I must not think of her now, should not think of her at all, yet I could think of nothing else, could not forget the fierce protest, followed almost at once by the weakness of pure anguish which had swamped me when her own wedding invitation had reached me some days ago. Just a plain, square card, gilt-edged, my name meaning no more to Miss Clevedon than the several dozen others Aunt Verity had listed for her, Barforth relatives and friends who would expect to see her married; my heartbreak meaning nothing to her since I was draining myself to my very dregs to conceal it. And as my mother handed the card to me, gingerly, pityingly, my senses, very briefly, had escaped their bondage and I had cried out, "I can't go, Mother."

"Yes, you can," Prudence had said quietly, barely raising her eyes from her own breakfast-time correspondence.

"I think you must, dear," my mother had murmured, looking away. And so I replied to the card in my own hand, instructed our coachman to deliver it, and on Caroline's wedding morning I began to smile and continued to do so throughout the day, as blankly and as brilliantly as a society hostess who knows none of her guests by name, and cares even less, but is quite determined to impress them all.

There were white roses heavily massed about the altar, baskets of white petals waiting to become a carpet for Caroline's satin-shod feet as she left the church, Lady Chard now, of Listonby Park, a Barforth no longer, although she would be a Barforth in spirit, I believed, until the end of her days. And I heard nothing of the service, remembered little but my uncle Joel, holding his daughter's hand for a moment with an unlikely tenderness before he gave it to Matthew Chard, and then, stepping aside, taking Aunt Verity's hand, for comfort perhaps, since emotion in this hard man was as rare and difficult as it had always been in Nicholas.

"Is this right for her?" his sudden frown seemed to be saying. "I've bought it and paid for it, but is it right?"

"Darling—she wants it," Aunt Verity may well have replied,

and as Caroline walked back down the aisle no one could have doubted her ability to fulfil her new role in life.

Celia had been lovely on her wedding day; Caroline, quite simply, was magnificent, and as the Wintertons and Floods swallowed their mortification and came to congratulate her, I found myself, for a moment in the confusion of the church porch, pressed close to Nicholas and understood that all my efforts had been in vain. I could not, after all, endure it—could not—it was as simple as that, and it was as well for me that, succumbing to the emotion appropriate to such a day, Mrs. Hobhouse and my mother, Miss Battershaw and Miss Mandelbaum and all the other bridesmaids except Prudence were crying too.

There was a pealing of church bells, and Caroline, her bridegroom looking very aristocratic but somewhat unnecessary beside her, was driven away in a carriage lined with white silk and drawn by high-stepping white horses, to a wedding breakfast specifically designed to overawe both the manufacturing and landed sections of our community. There was a marquee on the lawn at Tarn Edge, silver trays of champagne served by careful, professional hands, mountains of confectionery, a cake weighing —Aunt Verity had told my mother—a full two hundred pounds, decorated with sprays of white roses bound up with white satin ribbon, surrounding a figure of Caroline herself in gleaming satin, and Matthew bravely attired in hunting pink, an assortment of cupids cavorting at their feet.

There was Mrs. Hobhouse, telling each bridesmaid in turn, "You'll be the next one, love, it's always the way"; my mother in dainty, springtime yellow, holding out her hand for more wine, Jonas Agbrigg raising his glass to me, his eyes watchful, his mouth sarcastic. There was Prudence talking quietly to Mayor Agbrigg, a certain division of ranks as the landed interest installed themselves at one side of the marquee, the manufacturers at the other, the Floods and Wintertons gravitating naturally towards the Tempests, the manorial family of Bradford, the Ramsdens of Huddersfield, the sporting squires come down from the North Riding and up from Leicestershire, the willowy young dandies and languid ladies from London. While, facing them from the other side of that festive table, the millmasters and brewmasters and ironmasters, the master cutlers from Sheffield, the worsted spinners of the West Riding, and the cotton spinners from across the Pennines, stood their ground firmly, knowing they could buy out a Tempest or a Flood ten times over, pretending they did not care a fig for any man's pedigree. There was Giles Ashburn, finding his own level too, with Mr. Outhwaite, the architect, who was to design Aunt Hannah's concert hall, the vicar of the parish church, the headmaster of the grammar school, a knot of professional men coming between the commercial and aristocratic giants, Blaize moving freely from one group to the other, quite certain of his welcome anywhere, Nicholas not much in evidence, keeping Georgiana to himself.

There was Caroline—Lady Chard—a plain gold ring on one hand given by her husband, a diamond cluster on the other, which had come from her father, circling among her guests with a royal composure, and then dashing upstairs to change into another white gown embellished with swan's-down, which would take her on the first stage of her wedding journey to London.

And eventually, knowing that I must somehow release the iron grip I had again imposed upon myself, or be crushed by it, I walked off, as others were doing, a simple stroll, in their case, about the garden, in mine a taking-flight which led me beyond the formal rose beds, the lily pond, the lawns falling in smooth, terraced levels down the gently sloping hillside, to the summer house behind its screen of chestnut trees and willows. And since a young lady who wanders so far alone in the romantic setting of a summer bridal day may well be in search of other things than solitude, it was no matter for astonishment that Giles Ashburn chose to follow me.

He stood for a moment in the wide-arched entrance way, looking at me, seeing, perhaps, the image of me he had himself created, and I at him, seeing little—my eyes unaccustomed to the shade, and with the sun behind him—but the figure of a respectable, respectful man, medium of height and build, medium of colour, a face my memory retained only as pleasant, unremarkable, brown hair touched to auburn by the sunlight, brown eyes, I thought, with flecks of green in them, although for a moment I was not sure. A man who thought he loved me at a time when I was bruised and lonely and so desperately needed to be loved that his emotion seemed altogether miraculous, even though I knew full well that there could be no good reason for it, that I had done nothing to encourage it and, most likely, did not deserve it.

"You looked quite luminous in the church, Faith."

"Did I? I don't think I know what that means."

And, coming towards me, instead of saying, "Will you marry me?" although had that not been his intention I knew he would not have come here at all, he took both my hands once again and said simply, "I am so very much in love with you."

It was not the first time I had heard those words. There had been a young Frenchman, and an old Frenchman, a noble Roman who, having transferred his aspirations from my mother to myself, had made me the same declaration.

"How kind of you," I had replied to each of them, borrowing a whisper of my mother's sophistication, protected from the folly of believing them by my dream of Nicholas. But that dream was over. This man believed what he was saying, whether eventually he would find himself mistaken or not. And the simple, basic need to be warm again, to bask in the devotion he was offering, drew me towards him, the terrible rigidity of my spirit easing as his arms came around me, an almost childlike, entirely trustful nestling of myself against him, the relaxation of a tired body sinking into a healing sleep.

"My darling," he said, "I can't tell you—I can't tell you—" and closing my eyes, because his face, so close to mine, was still unfamiliar, I lifted my own face to be kissed, his closed mouth resting at first very carefully on mine and then, meeting no resistance, opening, his lips and his whole body still gentle, trembling with a need that thawed my own chilled senses not to passion but to gratitude.

Perhaps if he had made me a formal proposal, if he had listed for me his income and expectations, attempted to explain his feelings in words, I would have remembered a dozen reasons for refusing him, would have thought of my sister, and the sure fact that I—with Nicholas still engraved on my heart—could not be worth this outpouring, could neither match it nor merit it. But, instinctively, he had said only that he loved me, I had offered him my mouth to be kissed in reply, an unmistakeable gesture of consent in our narrow world, and as I continued to accept his kisses, to remain passively in his arms—the first man who had ever shown his need for me—I sensed, beneath his quiet dignity, his quiet endurance, something fragile in him to which both my mind and my body responded.

"I want you to be so happy," he said. "That is all I want, Faith —you, and our happiness together."

And even if I had wanted to reject him—which I did not—I had committed myself too far and could have found no way to do it.

Chapter Twelve

I ATTENDED Georgiana Clevedon's wedding three weeks later, an ordeal made bearable by the simple fact that my determination never to hurt Giles Ashburn had risen above all else. I had promised to marry him and whatever my motives had been it was a promise I would keep. And, far more than that, I would not only give him my hand in marriage, my dowry, and my most willing body, I would be the wife he wanted and deserved.

I didn't know why he loved me, but I wanted his love, that much was certain. I respected him, trusted him, admired him, recognised him both intellectually and morally as my superior. I was grateful for him. And as I watched Nicholas and Georgiana exchange their wedding vows, I closed my mind to them and made a personal, irrevocable vow that henceforth I would not only behave as if I loved Giles Ashburn, I *would* love him, as passionately and tenderly as he desired, in any way that he desired. And to do that it would be necessary not merely to conceal my feelings for Nicholas, nor to suppress them, it was essential that they should be destroyed.

It was no longer a matter of pride, no longer a need to spare Nicholas the embarrassment of feeling he had jilted me. What mattered now was that no one should ever say I had turned to Giles Ashburn as second-best. I must present myself as a girl radiantly in love, not only to him—astonishing and delighting him each evening in my mother's hall by my response to his kisses, the eager up-tilting of my face, my growing need to fold myself into him, to be warm again, and safe—not only that, of which only he could be aware, but a glow of joyful anticipation which would be apparent to everyone.

Nicholas must be my cousin again, no more and no less, since coolness would be regarded by some—by Jonas—as suspicious. And so I looked him directly in the eye as he came out of church with his bride, took his hand and kissed his cheek as a cousin should, and then kissed his wife, reminding her of our new relationship.

"I hope we may be friends, Georgiana, as well as cousins, now that you are to live in Cullingford."

And Blaize, standing between us, his smoky eyes seeing too much as always but not unkindly, advised her, "Accept the offer, Georgiana, for you may need a friend—in Cullingford."

There was no great gathering of prestige and power this time, a simple family ceremony in the chapel at Galton Abbey, slices of cold roast beef afterwards on a refectory table, a log fire barely warming the stone-clad hall, the aged Mr. Gervase Clevedon delivering up his granddaughter to the Barforths with as much reluctance as she was received. And once again the division of classes began to operate, Uncle Joel stationing himself before the hearth, Mayor Agbrigg beside him, dominating what warmth there was, since the July day had turned unseasonably cold, Aunt Verity and my mother attempting at first to entertain Lady Annabel Flood, who knew this house much better than they, and then drawing as near the fire as they could, to talk between themselves. Aunt Hannah did, indeed, make some attempt at conversation with Sir Giles Flood, who had installed himself in a high-backed oak chair of awesome, if uncomfortable proportions, but she was too mature, too regal for his taste, her position as mayoress reminding him too sharply of the changing times, while it was soon clear that his talk of horse racing, of which she did not approve, and of grouse shooting, which she did not understand, irritated and bored her.

Nicholas, quite clearly, was anxious to see the end of it, to have done with the drama and recriminations and take up his life again, standing in the scowling, lounging posture I recognised, talking to Blaize of mill matters, I thought, some crisis at Lawcroft he wished to be properly attended to in his absence, while Georgiana seemed occupied with her own brother, Pere-

grine Clevedon, the only person, perhaps, who really appreciated her marriage. Mr. Gervase Clevedon might never conde-
scend to accept Barforth assistance, no matter how great his
need; had, in fact, already gone deeper into debt so that Georgiana could have a dowry of sorts to take with her. But Mr. Gervase Clevedon was an old man, and when Master Peregrine
came to succeed him at Galton I did not think he would be slow
to see the uses of a brother-in-law with money to lend, nor
would he be timid in the asking.

But Nicholas' affairs were no longer my concern, and as the
awkward celebration came to its close and we went outside to
speed the bridal couple on their way, Georgiana having changed
her plain white gown for a going-away outfit of light green, a
dashing feather crowning her copper-coloured head, only then
did I falter for a moment, seeing the stern lines of Nicholas' face
soften as he handed her into the carriage, looking at her as his
father often looked at his mother—showing me the one thing I
had desired in life for myself—his mouth curving into its unwilling laughter as she whispered something into his ear; relief
in him, now, I thought, at leaving his father and the rest of us
behind, satisfaction at having finally got his way, a snap of excitement at the prospect of the night ahead.

"Good luck," Blaize called out.

"God bless you," Aunt Verity murmured.

"Well, that's it then," Uncle Joel said sourly. "I want you down
at Lawcroft, Blaize, first thing tomorrow morning, and every
morning until he gets home. Your uncle Agbrigg already has
enough to do."

And he was married and gone, his bird of the wild wood
caged, if not tamed, willing to feed from his hand; and none of
it had anything at all to do with me.

"I see you've taken my advice, Faith," Jonas said, appearing
beside me in the sudden, silent way he had, my enemy, I was
sure of it, not because I had once rejected him but perhaps because he needed an enemy, someone on whom to vent his long-
stored bitterness.

"Your advice, Jonas?"

"Why yes, Faith—about not staying single. I feel sure that
Nicholas will thank you for it."

"Dear Jonas," I told him, with my mother's voice, my mother's air-spun laughter. "Did you really advise me to marry Giles? If you did, then it is I who should be thanking you—believe me."

I had decided now what the whole course of my life must be. I could not devote myself to a cause, like Prudence, nor to bricks and mortar, upholstery and glassware like Celia, but I could devote myself, I believed, to a man who loved me. And I could see no reason for delay.

"Are you sure, dear," my mother had murmured on hearing my news. "Oh yes, I knew he meant to propose and he is altogether eligible—an excellent family and ample means, everything one could wish. It is just that I am surprised to find you so eager."

"You are providing yourself with a very peculiar son-in-law, Elinor," Aunt Hannah said tartly, for although Giles' income was more than adequate, he had no vast estates for Jonas to administer, no complicated business affairs for Jonas to entangle, no political connections which could serve Jonas' ambitions when the time came. But he could support me in sufficient comfort. He had a house ready to receive me at the top end—the decent end —of Millergate, where it joined Blenheim Lane. He loved me. How long could it take to apply a coat of paint to the dining room walls, acquire a trousseau and engage a personal maid, since he already had a cook-housekeeper, an outside man? Not long. And I was unwilling to remain in my father's sterile drawing room a moment longer than that.

There were to be no adult bridesmaids. My sister Celia, having miscarried her second child, was too frail in body and spirit, felt herself already too matronly, to oblige. I was uncertain of Prudence. Caroline was still honeymooning in the southern shires, Georgiana unthinkable. And I was grateful to my mother for the provision of some Aycliffe cousins, little girls all six of them under twelve, who, in pale blue gauze with dark blue velvet sashes, would serve me instead. But in my urge to give Giles Ashburn everything I thought he wanted, I designed myself a dozen wedding gowns and discarded every one, settling at last for a confection of lace and tulle, fifteen deep flounces from waist to hem caught up with silk ribbon, long flowing sleeves, a coronet of apricot-coloured roses securing my veil, the pretty anonymity which would make me simply "the bride."

I was sure of myself, very sure for most of the time, and when

I felt unable to ask Uncle Joel to give me away, refusing to admit to myself that I could not walk to the altar with a man who reminded me so strongly of Nicholas, and turned instead to my other uncle, Mayor Agbrigg, no one but Celia felt the need to question my judgement.

"Naturally you must suit yourself," she told me. "But I would not care to hurt Uncle Joel's feelings. He is not accustomed to being passed over, and people will wonder why."

"Nonsense," Prudence replied. "What a goose you are, Celia, for there is no cause at all for wonder. Mayor Agbrigg and Dr. Ashburn are close friends, that is the extent of it, and Faith will get her bride-gift from the Barforths just the same."

And when Celia had gone home, having too little trust in her new parlourmaid to remain long away, Prudence said with her habitual composure, "I had best set your mind at rest, Faith. I have never been in love with Giles, you know—at least, not in the way you understand it."

"Thank you, Prudence. I wasn't sure, and couldn't ask."

"Exactly. So now you may be easy. I have thought it over carefully, and to tell the truth I doubt if it is in my nature to feel an exclusive devotion to one person. I believe I resemble our cousin Blaize in that respect—which, of course, is considered delightfully wicked in a man and quite shocking in a woman. Blaize will never settle because the woman who may be waiting for him in the next room, or round the next corner, is always more enticing than the woman at his side. And with me—well, I am not light-minded like Blaize, but I am not ready yet to be restricted. Yes, I did think seriously of Giles once, I confess it, particularly when I knew Mother was coming home and I would have to play the dutiful daughter again. I was not at all looking forward to it, I can tell you, serving tea and conversation in the drawing room every afternoon and listening to that silly little clock ticking my life away. I thought Giles would free me from all that. I am fond of him, I respect him, in fact he is worth more than two of you, my dear, and possibly more than three of me, for that matter. But then he saw you, and was so thunderstruck by you, and I found I was not hurt by it, merely concerned that you would let him down. And I found, too, that I could easily manage Mother."

"I shall not let him down, Prudence."

"My goodness, I should hope not. Why should you? If what you want from life is to be adored then I know of no one who could do it better than Giles. You will find it so very pleasant that you will soon be adoring him back, make no mistake about it, and will have quite forgotten why you didn't adore him in the first place. And when you move into your house in Millergate, dear, you may invite me to stay with you should Freddy Hobhouse begin to pester me again, or should Mother try to take me to France. I am relying on you to be a most convenient chaperone."

We were married on a grey-gold October morning, the sun spread low across a hazy sky, my mind too occupied with cere- monial details to care that I had not entirely escaped the Bar- forths, Blaize having been asked to officiate as best man. And I was so grateful for the warmth and gentleness of Giles Ashburn, cushioning me from hurt, that the simple promise to honour him and obey him seemed inadequate when I would have cut off my hair and offered it as a sacrifice on that bridal altar had he required it.

But later, alone with him in the train going south to the flat Cheshire landscape of his childhood, the fact that I had given my life irrevocably into his keeping, losing my very identity in his, and that my sister was better acquainted with him than I, offered me a brief uncertainty. Yet he held my hand throughout the journey, assisted me from the train with the tender care my father had extended only to his Sèvres and Meissen, shielding me from a few scattered raindrops as if he thought me not only breakable but very likely to melt away, his every gesture a sepa- rate act of reassurance, an invitation to lean on him, to offer my- self not as a sacrifice but as an object of devotion and cherish- ing. And few women in the world—or, at least few that I have ever known—could have remained indifferent to that.

We spent the first few days in the pretty town of Knutsford, a bedroom and sitting room tastefully prepared for us at an inn where Giles was known, a log fire crackling in the hearth, a com- fortable woman offering us a wholesome dinner, hot chocolate at bedtime, her blessing for our future. And settling down in the vast, herb-scented bed, waiting for my husband, who had tact- fully allowed me to undress alone, my body, after the strain of the ceremony and the long journey, was too glad of the soft mattress and pillows, the flickering firelight, to be afraid. And I grew so drowsy that when the door did open I was startled and sat bolt upright, my heavy hair spilling forward to cover me like a curtain.

"I have never seen your hair loose before," he said, sitting down on the edge of the bed, a careful hand resting, just for an instant, on my head.

"I suppose not. I was almost asleep."

"Of course. You must be very tired."

And taking my face between his hands he kissed each corner of my mouth very lightly and murmured, "Sleep then, darling."

"Oh—should I?"

"I think so."

He got in beside me, again with the utmost care, so that no part of me was uncovered, and slid an arm beneath my shoulders, holding me not as I had expected but as if I had been a trustful, vulnerable child whose innocence must be protected, who must be rocked most lovingly and chastely to sleep.

"There is no reason to be in a hurry," he said into my hair. "We have all our lives, darling—every day of our lives— I don't want to rush you now, when you are tired and strained and worried, I suppose, about what is expected of you. Just go to sleep now, with your head on my shoulder. I shall be happy with that."

But I opened my eyes, far into the night, aware, in the confused moment of waking, that something was wrong, that the warmth which had enveloped me and lulled me to sleep was different now, no comforting arms around me but a taut presence, his back turned towards me with what could have been anger, until with the part of me I had inherited from my mother, I began slowly to understand.

"Giles? What is it?"

And receiving no answer: "Giles, I'm awake now. I won't go to sleep again."

I did not expect pleasure from this first encounter, knew, in fact, that this act, by which men set so great a store, was not designed to please women, simply to impregnate them and to make them submissive; but, turning to me with something like a groan, his hands were still gentle, his embrace retaining its wondering, almost apologetic quality as if it troubled him that, having been so moved by my body's innocence, he could no longer control his urge to despoil it. Yet I was not, in fact, so very innocent, had been virgin, perhaps, already somewhat too long, and his stroking, enquiring finger tips—ready to withdraw at my slightest movement of protest—released in me a strange, quite feline languor, a great stretching and purring in every limb which, very far from any proper ladylike disgust, was almost impatient with the carefully restrained quality of his desire.

And then it was over. No agony, a moment, merely, of discomfort and surprise. "Good heavens, so that's it after all." Just one brief instant when my body stiffened, drew back, and he, wishing to withdraw, feeling that he should withdraw, could not, taking final possession of me with a long, shuddering cry, of despair it seemed to me rather than triumph. No agony. Disappointment, perhaps, not in my heart, but in my puzzled limbs, which, having been stirred to warm anticipation by his caresses, had found this ultimate act quite inexplicable. After all, it *was* a purely male concern, as they had told me, for I failed entirely to see how the piercing of my body by that strange, masculine appendage could give me any pleasure. Yet I had not whined and whimpered as Celia may well have done on her wedding night, nor asked him how he dared, as I could easily imagine Caroline demanding of her Matthew, and feeling I had proved quite adequate, I smiled at him fondly through the dark, no thought in my mind of his own adequacy, his own satisfaction.

He got up suddenly and walked naked across the room, allowing me for the first time to see his fine-boned body, the odd fragility of shoulder blades almost piercing the skin, a fleeting impression of weightlessness that was not angular and awkward, not displeasing, before he covered himself quickly with his dressing robe and came back to me.

"I am sorry," he said brusquely.

"Why? Is something amiss?"

"No, no—except that you are only nineteen with no knowledge of life, and I am past thirty with enough experience to have done better than this. I should have allowed you at least a day or two of my company before submitting you to a desire you cannot share."

"Giles, darling," I told him, feeling a smile begin somewhere inside me, understanding his troubled frown, his anxiety, with the basic female knowledge my mother had bred in me. Yet perhaps because he wished me to be frail, had imagined me frail, he was not consoled, his need for self-punishment surprising me even more than the anguished climax of his sensuality.

"Well, it is done now," he said. "It will not always be so difficult, you can believe me. You may bleed presently. It is quite natural. Don't be alarmed."

"No, Doctor."

"Faith—please—" he said, and seeing that my flippancy had wounded him, I leaned forward feeling suddenly very strong and very sure of my ability to comfort him, although I did not altogether understand why he should be in need of comfort.

"Giles, I have not lived in an ivory tower all my life, you know. I have been to France and Italy where people are not so reticent as we are—and, in any case, my mother is much more outspoken than is usual in Cullingford. You have not hurt me, Giles—for, as a matter of fact, I am really very strong—and you have not shocked me."

"But I have given you no pleasure."

"How can you know that?"

"Dear girl, of course I can know it. I do know it. You bore it all very stoically and very sweetly, but you had no pleasure and expected none. I imagine you will have been told that women do not, and should not, enjoy these things. And in many cases that is quite correct. It is easier, you see, at such moments, for a man to think only of himself, to do only what pleases him, in the convenient belief that a woman has no sensuality. And I can perfectly understand that a woman who is always pregnant, either recovering from one birth or preparing for the next, must view her husband's demands with utter loathing. I have seen it, Faith, many times in my capacity as a physician—women who would do anything to escape what to them is simply their nightly servitude, women who fall ill expressly to avoid it. And having seen all that I have no excuses. I knew I must be patient, knew that I must take you gradually and carefully, little by little. Yet I could not. I have been every bit as self-seeking as the men I have despised, and if you should turn away from me in disgust I could not really blame you."

What a fuss, I thought, my word, what a fuss. Yet sitting up, strong and sure again, I tossed back my hair and, throwing aside the bedcovers with a steady hand, I offered the whole of my body to his eyes, without sensuality but without embarrassment, not desiring him yet but wanting him to desire me since that was what he wanted himself, and I required, most urgently, to fulfil his every need.

He spoke my name, a strangled sound, his face swimming for an instant before my eyes with an emotion so intense that my immediate instinct was to turn away from it, fearing I could not meet its demands. But I received his light, hesitant body without restraint, knowing that in this, at least, I would not fail him, holding him, learning to caress him—not too boldly since he did not wish me to be bold—until his honest, generous anxiety had faded away.

"I love you, Faith."

"Yes. Please love me, Giles."

And it no longer mattered that I didn't know why. Certainly he had not chosen me for anything I had ever said to him, for any similarities of intellect and outlook, for my wit or my ability to partner him in his labours. Perhaps, at the beginning, it had been no more than the colour of my hair, a trick of light and shade that had given my face the texture of some half-forgotten adolescent dream, so that I had assumed, in his mind, the identity of that dream. And what could it matter now? I had chosen to spend my life with him and as I watched our first morning come slowly peeping through the window, lying easily, contentedly in his arms, I believed I had chosen right. I could make him happy, I was every moment more sure of it. I could be the woman he wanted, whoever she was, whatever she was, even if she was not really me at all. Having lost what I had believed to be my life's purpose I had found another. Whatever else I might do, or might not do, I would not fail Giles Ashburn.

Chapter Thirteen

MY COUSIN, Blaize Barforth, took us to the theatre on the night of our return, some three weeks later, an evening which, in my eyes, seemed to mark my new status as a married woman. For although I had attended performances of Shakespeare in London, and of the opera and ballet in Paris, Cullingford's Theatre Royal had always been considered too raucous a place for a young lady. Yet, wishing to prove my sophistication to Blaize at any rate, I settled myself into the first of the dress boxes with no outward sign of curiosity, leaning forward to chat as nonchalantly as I could contrive to a young architect and his wife, to young Mr. Rawnsley of Rawnsley's bank and a lady who was not his wife, who were occupying the box next door.

And taking advantage of my new freedom, I found it entirely delightful to drink cold punch after the performance in the private supper room at the Old Swan, sitting between my husband and handsome, wicked Blaize who made no secret now of his tender relationship with a curly-haired, black-eyed comedienne, and his interest—uncertain yet, but promising—in another. It was delightful, too, to learn from Blaize's witty tongue the peccadilloes of so many of our town's founding fathers, that Mr. Hobhouse, with his fourteen fine children at Nethercoats, had two or three more, every bit as fine, scattered here and there about the county, while even the worsted spinner, Mr. Oldroyd of Fieldhead, had kept an actress of his own, long before his wife died, in a respectable—Blaize thought tedious—area of Leeds.

"But I thought Mr. Oldroyd wanted to marry my mother."

"So he does—which has nothing to do with actresses, Faith. And, while we are on the subject, I must give you a timely warning, for you should know that at least half your husband's female patients are madly in love with him."

"That does not surprise me, Blaize—not in the least. I merely wonder what is wrong with the other half? Are they blind?"

"Just sensible, I imagine," Giles said, taking my hand, his slightest touch causing me to sway towards him, lightheaded with offering, wanting him to take more than he already had, to be more demanding so that I could be more generous.

My new house in Millergate, not new at all but which had come to Giles with the practice, was not, in the estimation of any of my relatives, grand enough. It was, indeed, one of the last houses at the confused joining of the ways where steep, stony Millergate became Blenheim Lane, but by no stretch of the imagination could it be considered to stand in Blenheim Lane itself and Aunt Hannah insisted from the start that it would not suit me to live so near the town.

"Millergate is a shopping street," she said. "It is not residential. You are not acquainted with any of your neighbours, nor can you wish for their acquaintance."

Yet, as she well knew, Millergate, which, at its lower end directly entered Market Square by the Piece Hall and the Old Swan, was not so far distant from Simon Street that a frightened man could not reach us in the middle of the night, to beg Giles' attendance on a sick child or a confinement that, having lasted a day or two, was thought even by Simon Street standards to be going wrong. Nor was the doorway too imposing, the maid who answered the bell too dignified, the chair in the hall too daintily upholstered for an exhausted woman who had trudged from the canal bank with an infant strapped to her back, another straddling her hip, to take her rest.

We had a large parlour I could not really glorify by the name of drawing room, a red covered sofa and two deep armchairs around the hearth, a cheerful rug, a profusion of flowering plants in pottery bowls my father would have considered undignified. There was a stray cat brought home one night by Giles, a litter of kittens I had helped him to deliver the night after, my collection of wedding china and silver displayed, for the time being, in cabinets which were too small and did not exactly match each other. There was a dining room which also served Giles as a study, a large, half-tester bed in the front bedroom, three smaller rooms, a sinister room at the back of the house full of glass tubes and bottles with a small room off it, where Giles received patients, attics, a kitchen, which, since plain cooking had not formed part of my education, I could not feel to be my concern.

"I believe your Aunt Hannah is right," Giles told me at once. "It is indeed a poky place. I can't think why I never realised it before. Look around, darling, and when you find the house you want, then let me know. I really can't expect you to settle here."

But, like the kittens, I was warm in my deep, red armchair, unwilling, perhaps, to take on the management of a larger household so soon, since routine domestic matters, I found, did not interest me greatly, my tastes inclining to the decorative rather than the useful. And although, prompted by Celia, I glanced at a smart new villa in Albert Place, talked idly of buying an acre or two of land, even consulted a builder and an architect, I knew that Giles, who cared nothing for houses, wished to move only for my sake, and so I chose to remain in Millergate for his.

Nor did I feel the need to make any sweeping domestic changes. The old woman who had looked after Giles was more than willing to look after me, her chocolate cake being the lightest I had ever tasted, her good humour inexhaustible.

"Just sit you down, Mrs. Ashburn, and leave it to me. I know what the doctor likes for his dinner, and what you can do for him is make sure he sits down to eat it. Tell him to let them wait, when they come knocking on the door at dinnertime, because one thing you can be sure of, Mrs. Ashburn, is that they won't go away. He'll not lose his customers to Dr. Overdale and Dr. Blackstone, if that's what he's thinking, because Dr. Overdale takes his money in advance, and Dr. Blackstone sees none but the quality. Just you sit down, and have a big smile ready for him when he comes home."

And so I obeyed, hurrying into the hall at the sound of his gig, rushing downstairs to open the door for him myself, as obsessive in my care for him as Celia in her constant pursuit of domestic perfection.

It was naturally expected that Celia and I would see a great deal of each other now, for not only were we married ladies, empowered to share our knowledge of life's mysteries, but our husbands were both professional men, a doctor and a lawyer, who should have had much in common. Yet, although they were always very civil, very correct, there was little rapport between them, Jonas being too conscious that Giles, with his private income, had not been obliged to struggle for his education, nor to marry somewhat against his inclination in order to purchase his practice; Giles mistrusting Jonas' growing habit—prompted, one could not deny it, by Aunt Hannah—of offering his friendship only to those who had something to give him. There was no shrewder lawyer in Cullingford these days than Jonas Agbrigg, to which many others besides Aunt Hannah were ready to testify, a keen, cunning man who could be relied on to spot a loophole in any contract, the contracts he drew up himself being quite watertight, or, when that was impossible, offering a variety of escape routes, skilful, obscurely worded clauses and fine points of law which everyone but himself appeared to have forgotten.

Giles liked people. Jonas, very obviously, liked useful people, cultivating only the rich and influential who could be persuaded to help him, the rich and simple who would be likely to trust him, the rich and slightly sinister who had need of a clever man like himself, his social commitments throwing my sister into such panic that I would often go over to Albert Place and do the table decorations for the parties to which I was not important enough to be invited, or, if she was to dine out herself, would arrange her hair, choose her clothes, attempt to convince her that it was not unbecoming in a matron of eighteen to be just a little vain.

But, more often than not, she would reject the high-piled curls of my devising, would not allow me to spray her with the perfume I still ordered from the rue St-Honoré, insisting that a married woman should not embarrass her husband by making herself conspicuous, that a gentleman—according to our father's teachings—required his wife to be self-effacing in public, efficient at home, a model of propriety at all times of the day and, one assumed, of the night.

"You should take care," she told me. "Wearing such light colours as you do, and such low necks in the evenings, one could be forgiven for thinking you flighty. And how you ever find the time to do your hair so often, and in so many different fashions, I can't imagine. I have never a moment for such things. I am quite surprised at you, Faith, for those cats of yours are everywhere—and it would destroy me, really it would, thinking of those sharp claws anywhere near *my* furniture. You know quite well that Father would never have a cat in the house—not even in the kitchen."

Yet, however much she disapproved of my slovenly habits, the next time some gentleman of awesome importance was invited to dine, a client or a political connection and his sharp-eyed lady, I would heed her distress signals and spend a tedious afternoon draping her candlesticks in ivy, arranging small sprays of moss and roses at the corners of her table, giving her a centrepiece of brightly coloured blooms surrounded by drifts of pink gauze strewn with single rosebuds, any novel thing I could imagine while she, more often than not, having worn her nerves to shreds, would retire upstairs to be violently sick.

"What does it matter?" I asked her. "They're only people. Heavens—we've known Mr. Fieldhead for years. And what if he is a member of Parliament? So was Father."

But nothing could ease her torment, and knowing full well that her house contained not one single speck of dust—since she followed her housemaid upstairs and down every morning to make sure—that no guest of hers could have found anything, even in the most intimate recesses of her cupboards, but a most perfect order, she would, nevertheless, fret herself into a raging headache so that when those guests finally arrived she had nothing to say to them but a distraught "good evening," her mind dwelling in agony on the progress of the roast, the French sauce I had suggested and which she knew would never thicken.

"It's all right for you, Faith—you've never cared about such things. You just drift through life in your come-day-go-day fashion—and your husband doesn't seem to care either. A place for everything and everything in its place, that's what Father always said, and I agree—I can't bear to see things disarranged. I must have everything just as it should be. I can't help my nature—and I wouldn't expect *you* to understand."

Yet, in spite of my shabby hall carpet and my inadequate dining room, I entertained, in my haphazard fashion, far more, and I believed more successfully, than Celia.

Situated on the road most people took on their way out of town, my house was a convenient calling place, Mayor Agbrigg —Alderman Agbrigg now that his term of office had expired— stopping in almost daily for a cup of Mrs. Guthrie's strong tea, while Giles' bachelor friends, comprising the whole of our town's younger professional men, saw no reason to forego the comfort of his fireside, once they had ascertained that I, like Mrs. Guthrie and the easy, well-worn chairs, was perfectly agreeable.

Blaize came too, at unlikely hours sometimes, his high-stepping horses blocking the way, the hem of a satin skirt, the crown of a feathered hat just visible, often enough, inside his carriage, indicating the presence of a female who could not be presented to me. And now that I was married and allowed to know of such goings-on, he would occasionally involve me in his escapades, as he had done before, although now, instead of "If you should happen to see my father and he should happen to ask, do please say that you haven't seen me here at all," it was "Dear Faith— because you understand me so well—if you go to the Assembly Rooms tonight and you should meet Mrs. Woodley—yes, dear, *Mrs.* Woodley—do make it in your way to tell her I have been called away to Manchester."

"And how long do you expect to be away?"

"As long as I can contrive. Three days, I think—in fact we'll make it five, and tell her it is London. If it troubles you, you may say you simply think that is where I have gone—since who knows?"

"Should it trouble me?"

"I daresay it should. But you'll tell her, won't you, just the same?"

"I may."

"Oh, you will. You've always been a good girl, Faith."

"I daresay—but, Blaize—Mrs. Woodley, she's such an ancient creature."

"Thirty-five," he said, smiling. "And she has—enthusiasm. You'll know what I mean."

But quite often, he would come alone, spending lazy evenings by the fire, hot coffee and toasted muffins consumed at midnight;

Prudence, sometimes, having called at tea time and stayed to dinner, engaging him in verbal combat, demolishing the easy philosophies he invented expressly to tease her, deciding, more often than not, that she would not trouble to go home at all and calmly sending a note to Blenheim Lane, claiming her freedom of movement, of speech, of action, in a way which amused and delighted him.

"I believe your poor mother trembles before you."

"Nonsense. She never notices me, now that Mr. Oldroyd has started to call so often."

"So—clever Mr. Oldroyd. Does she mean to marry him?"

"She would be ill-advised to do so. And I would not consent to live with them."

"Ah—you are thinking of getting married yourself then, I take it?"

"Why should you say that?"

"Why, Prudence—my dear—if you will not live with your mother, then you must live with your husband, or with his mother. What else can a young lady do?"

"I will not always be a young lady. I am almost twenty-two. Eventually I shall be thirty, and forty—as you will be one day, Blaize dear—and capable, I imagine, of handling my own affairs."

"Now why on earth should you wish to do that?" he asked her, his smoky eyes brimming with mischief. "Why trouble your very charming head with the sordid details of everyday life, when you could easily find a husband to do it for you? I really can't understand your poor opinion of marriage. Believe me, Faith does not share it, and I—well—I will confess, hand on heart, that I envy Giles all this."

"Nonsense. If you wanted it, you could have it. You could be married tomorrow—except that you would probably fall in love with one of your wife's bridesmaids on your wedding day."

"Do you know," he said, as if the idea had just struck him, not at all unpleasantly. "I believe you may be right. And you have done me a great disservice, Prudence, by putting the idea into my head. It sounds so very apt that, now you have suggested it to me, I doubt if I could bring myself to resist it—should the occasion ever arise."

"Don't concern yourself. It never will. You will chase moonbeams all your life—looking for that one rare creature you are always talking about, who surely doesn't exist—or else you will marry a fifteen-year-old when you are ninety-three."

"Prudence," I told her, laughing, although what she had said was not impossible, "that is not kind."

"Oh," Blaize murmured. "I don't know—" And later, when Giles had been called out and Blaize, making light of it, had accompanied him, declaring he may as well hold Giles' horse in Simon Street than go home and explain his absence at the mills that day to his father, I asked her, "Prudence—do you think you could ever care for Blaize?"

"Fall in love with him, you mean? No, I could not and he wouldn't thank me for it should it be otherwise. A man like Blaize doesn't wish to be troubled by emotion."

"There is more to him than he likes to show."

"I'm well aware of it. He drove Giles over to Sunbury Dale this morning, didn't he, risking his beautiful sporting curricle on those moorland pathways so Giles could get there in time. Were you not afraid Giles would break his neck? Oh—they didn't tell you— Well, Giles was needed in a hurry, I don't know why—a mill chimney had collapsed and fallen into a shed, I'm not certain, and I suppose when Giles got the message it was already too late. Anyway, Blaize drove him there because Giles' horse would have surely foundered in this weather. And when they arrived he made himself useful too—I heard it from Mayor Agbrigg, so there is no call for you to look so put out—which is why Blaize was not at the mill today, and is in trouble with his father. Of course he will not tell Uncle Joel he was at Sunbury. He will let him think what he pleases. And I know it amused him, driving like a madman over the top moor, or he would not have done it. But he did go, he did help, which is more than his brother Nicholas would have done. Yes, Faith—Nicholas may have lent his carriage and paid someone to drive it, but he would not have gone himself. He wouldn't lose a day's business —not for anybody in Sunbury Dale at any rate. I expect you will be calling at Tarn Edge to deliver your bride-gift, now that they have been back from honeymoon for several weeks. We can go together."

Caroline, Lady Chard, was not expected back until the New Year, having married into a world where a wedding journey could last a twelvemonth or more, the happy couple returning, often enough, with their first child in tow. But the Barforth mills, unlike the tenant farmers of Listonby, could not be left to take care of themselves, and the new Mrs. Barforth had been installed at Tarn Edge for so long now that I knew my failure to visit her would cause comment, unless soon remedied. Aunt Verity had already called on me, bringing me a magnificent matching pair of Sèvres potpourri vases, a fortune casually bestowed and placed, just as casually, on my altogether unworthy mantelpiece. I had already purchased the dessert service I intended for Nicholas, a dainty, flowery, yet quite impersonal gift which had been standing for weeks now, ready wrapped, on the hall table, reminding me constantly of its need to be delivered. And when, a day or so later, I encountered Blaize coming out of the Piece Hall, and he, perfectly understanding my hesitation and the need to put an end to it, said quietly, "Faith, if you should have a moment to spare for my sister-in-law, it would be a kindness, since she is very much alone," I begged the carriage from Giles that very afternoon.

There had been no question of a separate establishment for Nicholas and Georgiana. Tarn Edge was plenty large enough to accommodate a second family, it was essential for Nicholas to be near the mills, while Georgiana herself, having been brought up to think of marriage as a transfer from one ancestral mansion to another, had neither expected nor wanted one of the smart new villas so dear to acquisitive, and possibly, in her view, vulgar middle-class hearts. She had simply taken up residence among the Barforths as she would have gone to the Chards or the Floods, as ready to leave everything to her mother-in-law as if Aunt Verity had been a duchess with three hundred years of domestic tradition behind her.

She was the wife not even of the heir, but of a younger son, a position which, in a noble family, would not have carried great weight. Had Uncle Joel been a Chard, Blaize would have inherited his title, his land, the house that stood upon it, in accordance with the rules of primogeniture, which ensured that ancient estates were not broken up, that ancient names remained tied to the land which, for centuries, had nurtured them. Blaize's wife would have taken precedence over Georgiana on every occasion, would have become mistress of Tarn Edge at the very moment of Uncle Joel's death, Aunt Verity retiring, just as im-

mediately, to some dower house or smaller dwelling, leaving little for Nicholas but a younger son's portion—not usually large—
and a career of sorts in the army or the church. And although
Georgiana must have known that in the world of commerce the
labours of both brothers would be equally rewarded, the profits
divided, that Nicholas could even be a far wealthier man than
Blaize one day, while Tarn Edge itself, for which neither of
them greatly cared, would probably be sold in due course, its
proceeds divided between themselves and Caroline, it seemed
very strange to her, her instinctive deference to the first-born
amusing no one but Blaize himself.

"She has the quaintest notions," my mother had told me. "She
talks to her horse more than she talks to Verity. You will find her
wildly entertaining." Yet there was something almost forlorn
about her that afternoon, as she received me in Aunt Verity's
small parlour—as large and considerably more luxurious than
the Great Hall at Galton—and although she could not at first
remember the exact nature of our relationship, I believe she was
relieved to see someone of her own age and sex.

"Of course," she told me, accepting my dessert service with
only token enthusiasm since, I supposed, in that superbly
equipped house, where the cupboards were bursting with
Wedgwood and Coalport, she could see little use for it. "I
remember now. You are an Aycliffe. Your mother and my father-
in-law are brother and sister."

"Yes, except that I am no longer an Aycliffe. I was married in
October, while you were still away."

"Good Lord. October. So you are newer to it even than I. And
your husband, does he have a place nearby?"

"A place? You mean an estate?"

"So I do, if that is what you call it. And I am sorry to be so
awkwardly spoken, for I suppose he must have a mill or—something of that nature?"

"No. He is a doctor."

"Really?" she said, honestly surprised, since I supposed the
possibility of marrying a doctor had never occurred to a Clevedon. "Do you know, I have never consulted a doctor in my life.
Not even when I took a tumble out hunting last season, and
dislocated my collarbone. My grandfather just tugged it back
again and told me if I wanted to be sick to get on with it and

then go home. Yet the ladies here who call on my mother-in-law seem always to be ailing. There was a Mrs. Agbrigg the other day, younger than I, I think, who seems altogether an invalid."

"Yes. Mrs. Agbrigg is my sister. She has always been frail."

"Oh—I do beg your pardon. I find these names and these relationships so confusing, and I know how important it is to get them right. It was so simple at home, you see. One knew exactly which Tempest had married which Chard, and who was related to the Floods and the Ramsdens and in which degree, because one had grown up knowing it. One had attended all the christenings and the weddings and listened to all the backstairs gossip. One knew not to mention Lady Winterton in Lady Bardsey's hearing, since Sir Morton Bardsey had mentioned her once too often—that sort of thing. Whereas here, with so many Hobhouses and Battershaws—such strange names—I have no idea what errors I may be committing. Really, sometimes I am quite lost—absolutely at sea—for I was taught never to mention money, never, never, never to ask how much anything cost or to tell what one had paid—never, never. Yet here they talk of pound notes quite openly, all the time. I was quite shocked when I heard a lady, just the other night, announce how many thousands she had spent on a seaside home, and I expected everyone else to be shocked too. But, in fact, I believe they were impressed. I suppose it is because they *earn* money, as we do not, which makes them so familiar with it."

Amused in spite of myself by her puzzled manner, her frowning, little-girl concentration, as if all Hobhouses looked alike to her and she despaired not only of learning their language but of ever distinguishing one from the other, I leaned slightly towards her and smiled, feeling older, although, in fact, I was slightly the younger, feeling that the task I had set myself might prove less difficult than I had feared. I had come here, certainly, to satisfy the conventions, to test the strength of my own resolution, but I had also come—as I did everything else these days—because of Giles. I was not certain how much he knew of my relationship with Nicholas, simply that he must know something, and what better way of easing his mind than to offer my friendship to Nicholas' wife?

"It was all so simple at home," she had said, quite touchingly, for although Galton was but a few miles distant I well knew that in spirit it was another world. And telling myself that she, at any rate, had not chosen to harm me, was apparently unaware that harm had been done, and must be kept in ignorance of it, I smiled again and said, "You will soon grow accustomed to us, Georgiana."

"Do you think so?"

"Oh yes, I am sure of it. If Aunt Verity's friends seem stiff it is only because they are minding their manners too hard, which surely won't last. And if you are bored at dinnertime when the Hobhouses and the Battershaws—and the Barforths—can talk of nothing but warp and weft, and their lustre cloths and shalloons, well, I have been hearing of such things all my life, and I can still neither understand them nor bring myself to care."

"Oh my word," she said, flashing me her sudden smile, her pointed face alive with a surge of vitality. "Can that be true? No, of course not, for I am quite certain you know exactly what constitutes a lustre cloth and are merely denying it to put me at ease. But it was kindly done, Mrs. Ashburn—Cousin Faith, I believe you are sent to me from heaven. Shall I ring for tea? At home we are obliged to go and shout down the passage, since we have not a bell in working order, and even then our old Honiman is so deaf, or does not choose to hear, that one can sit and play a guessing game—for money, if my brother Perry is about—as to whether or not tea will come."

But there were no such games of chance at Tarn Edge and when she had greeted the silver cake baskets, the trays of muffins and hot bread and butter with a slight shake of her head, as if with the best will in the world, she couldn't help finding such overabundance a trifle vulgar, she frowned suddenly and said, "Tell me, Cousin Faith, what do you do all day?"

"What do I do? I suppose—a hundred things."

"Then I wish you would tell me their names, for I imagine your husband must go out a great deal, and Nicky is never at home. I simply did not realise these mills were so greedy of a man's time. I have heard Nicky talk of his managers and I supposed they handled his affairs, as the land agent at Galton handles ours. But not a bit of it. Nicky must be at the mill every day, all day, and half the night sometimes. Even Mr. Barforth spends most of his time there, which my mother-in-law seems to find quite natural. Yet it is very strange to me. My grandfather attends Quarter Sessions, naturally, since he is chairman of the Bench, and holds Petty Sessions regularly enough in the back parlour at the abbey, and he is always out and about the estate. But he doesn't live his life by the clock, as they do. How can they bear to shut themselves up in this glorious weather? You do not ride, do you, Faith?"

And when I shook my head, she said sadly, "No. No one does. To the mill and back, to the train and back— Oh, dear. Nicky has given me the most magnificent chestnut mare, the loveliest lady you can imagine, and what am I to do with her? He will not allow me to ride out alone. He says it would not be understood. I could not bring a groom from Galton since we have but the one, and these fellows in the stables here simply cannot keep up with me. So there she stands all day in her stall, just a tame little canter every morning and home again. Well, he must take me to Galton at Christmas, for if I cannot hunt on Boxing Day I shall die of it—especially now that Matthew has succeeded his uncle as master, for Sir Richard was a dear man but so dreadfully old-fashioned. He *would* persist in setting off too early in the morning, before one could hope to unkennel a fox that was fit to run."

I left soon afterwards, having promised to come again, and to escort her to such entertainments as Cullingford could provide, and that evening Blaize called briefly to thank me for the care I had taken.

"It was good of you, Faith."

And, alone with him in the silent house, stung by his accurate knowledge of my situation, I said sharply, "Why?"

"You know why. I am sorry to see that it still hurts you."

"You see nothing of the kind."

"Good. I am delighted to be mistaken. You are married to the best man in the world, you know."

"I don't need you to tell me that, Blaize Barforth."

"No. I see. Good night, then."

"Good night. Blaize . . . ?"

"Yes?"

"Are they happy?"

"Possibly. She depends on him, since she feels everyone else to be against her, and he is still quite wildly attracted to her. She enjoys that, of course—why should she not?—and I think she appreciates him in other ways, and is rather grateful. You should understand that, Faith."

"Good night, Blaize."

"Quite so. And if that means 'don't call again,' I shall take no notice. You'll forgive me—you always do. And you need my light touch in this heavy world. Giles won't object to your gratitude. I shouldn't. One has to start somewhere, after all, and it's not a bad beginning. Without making the slightest effort I can think of a hundred ways in which a woman's gratitude could be really very agreeable. And you've got all the time in the world, you know, to fall in love with him. Let it come over you gently. It's bound to happen."

And, kissing my cheek, his mischief entirely without malice, he tipped his hat to me and strolled nonchalantly away.

Chapter Fourteen

THERE WAS A YEAR of peace and quiet content, a year that would serve as a model, I believed, for all the other years of my life, a deep, slow-moving river with no sudden, diamond-scattered cascades, no sharp, unexpected twistings and turnings, but with no stagnant, murky pools, no dried-up, stony places; a clean, deep water.

Caroline—who had been eight months away—came home at the end of a crisp, white January, requiring my immediate attendance at Listonby, so intent on her plans for improving the house and filling it with the grand acquaintances she had made on her travels, that when I enquired her husband's whereabouts, she said absently, "Matthew? Oh, I suppose he has gone out hunting. That is what he usually does, at any rate."

But Caroline, seated before the log fire burning brightly in the massive stone hearth, the stone-flagged pavement of the Great Hall covered with the first of her deep-pile rugs, was intensely happy, showing not the slightest trace of Georgiana's confusion and loneliness.

"That old housekeeper of Matthew's will have to go," she told me, before the upright little woman, whose breeding, perhaps, was a shade more genteel than our own, was barely out of earshot. "He can just pension her off with a cottage on the estate somewhere, which seems to be the custom, and will be a great kindness in her case, for she is far too frail to cope with the way I mean to go on. I interviewed one or two likely persons on my way through London, and I must have someone with style and experience and a great deal of endurance, for the people I mean to invite are accustomed to certain standards, and it won't be enough to merely give them what they are used to. Oh no—I mean to offer something better, something that will really make their journey worthwhile. My father has always operated that way, and I absolutely agree with him. I can do very little at the moment, of course, because it is going to be chaos until the alterations have been made—there is that huge upstairs chamber to turn into a ballroom, a new floor, certainly, and new plasterwork, and the long gallery to renovate before I can decently invite anyone to dance; and bedrooms and dressing rooms to see to—and it seems I am expecting a baby, by the way—but once all that is done with I know exactly what I mean to do. House parties, of course, throughout the hunting season, one after the other, since it is the surest way of keeping Matthew out of Leicestershire. He may think it the best hunting country in the world, but his house there is quite mediocre. I have no mind to sit in it half the year while he goes tallyhoing about the countryside, and so I shall bring all his friends to do their hunting here. We have stabling enough—carriages with champagne picnics in hampers for the ladies who do not care to ride—everything. I shall give a hunt ball, needless to say, which will attract absolutely everybody—not just provincials, but people from the Shires, and London. And a harvest ball too, I think, with a marquee on the lawn for the tenants. And my Christmases are going to be altogether spectacular. Naturally, I *want* to do all this, but quite frankly, I feel it would be expected of me in any case. I shall give a servants' dance too, which didn't seem such a good idea to me when I first heard of it, but I attended one in Shropshire and found it rather entertaining. It gives one's staff something to look forward to, at any rate—rather like the bonuses at Tarn Edge."

"And how did you find Matthew's friends?" I asked her, remembering Georgiana's bewilderment with manufacturing ways, supposing Caroline, in reverse, must have felt it too. But, unlike her sister-in-law, she seemed more inclined to mould her new environment to suit herself, and was apparently unaware that anyone could expect her to change.

"They were all extremely civil and glad to know me, which was very pleasant, and put themselves out to see that I was suitably entertained, although, strictly between ourselves, some of them are not nearly so grand as I had supposed. Matthew's aunt in Shropshire is, after all, an earl's daughter, her husband is Lord Macclesworth, which should count for something, and they are not short of money. Yet she has nothing in her wardrobe that you or I would care to put on, and leads a most quiet existence —my word, I was positively dull in her house. Acres of the most magnificent reception rooms and nothing in them but weaponry all over the walls, and empty floor space. And some of the others —well, Faith, this is very strictly between ourselves—but at one house I visited it was known, and apparently accepted, that one of Matthew's cousins had been—well—intimately involved for years with a man who was not her husband. My dear, absolutely everybody knew about it. The man was there, welcomed like any other guest, and arrangements had even been made to give them bedrooms on the same corridor, so they might have easy access. Yes, you may well look startled, for so was I when I discovered it, although Matthew laughed at me, and said it was nothing to make a fuss about—if the woman's husband didn't mind when why should he—or I? Goodness—can you imagine my mother tolerating such a thing at Tarn Edge—or anyone else we know? And I shall not have such goings-on here, I can tell you. Naturally I am not a schoolroom goose. I realise—now— that such things do happen in the world, but those who commit such indulgences should have the decency, at least, to conceal them. Matthew may call it hypocrisy, but if I gave them adjoining rooms in my house I would call it encouragement, and one has one's standards, after all. And some of the younger Chards, and the rest of them, are fearful gamblers—positively silly where money is concerned. I am not at all surprised so many of them are in difficulties. But, apart from that, I have no complaints to make. Well—I must have this baby first, and then we can start talking clothes again, Faith. No baby for you, that is very obvious, for you are really very smart, and so slender. I suppose you know that Georgiana is to have one too? Oh yes—and my mother is quite frantic because she will insist on taking that horse of hers over to Galton every Friday-to-Monday, tearing up the countryside and leaping her six-barred gates, which is very unwise. You should ask your husband to speak to her."

But Georgiana, intent on making her escape to Galton at every opportunity, had not endeared herself to Cullingford and I

—occupied almost totally with Giles—saw her very rarely. I sat a few places away from her on one or two occasions at Aunt Verity's table, large, formal dinners where she, having been warned, perhaps, that neither her hunting stories nor her tales of her brother's rash exploits both in and out of the saddle would be much appreciated, sat quite still, a little girl, I thought, dressed up in finery she found uncomfortable and which did not suit her, listening blank-eyed with boredom to this new language of profit margins, cash flows, the weaving of double-twills and silk warp alpacas, of paramatta cloth and mohair lustres, turning her head occasionally with the startled swiftness of a bird to look at Nicholas for a reassurance he seemed willing to give. But Aunt Verity caught a chill that winter and my uncle, obsessively anxious on her account, whisked her away to the south coast to await the better weather, returning himself only intermittently to clear up his sons' mistakes—as he put it—and to prevent them, in the flaring of their black Barforth tempers, from beating each other to death, Nicholas with his fists, Blaize with his needle-sharp tongue.

Blaize went to America in the spring, a trip which gave him so much personal satisfaction and filled the Barforth order books with so many remunerative demands for fancy worsteds that a return journey seemed beyond question and would prove, one felt, a standard feature of his life.

"I thought at the very least you would come back with an heiress in your luggage," Prudence told him.

"Next time," he promised. "Yes—it may well be, for some of those girls are quite extraordinary—they sparkle, just like a June morning—very wholesome, very nice— Unless, of course, I should encounter a red Indian princess. How about that, Prudence? That might even satisfy my craving for originality."

"I imagine it would kill your father. But you should not stay away too long, Blaize, for I understand your brother has stolen a march on you this time—"

"You understand that, do you?" he said, his grey eyes amused but unusually careful. "You mean the combing company, I suppose? Yes, I expect it could look rather sinister—as if he had taken advantage of my absence to convince my father. But he has been talking about combing machines for a long time, you know, and all it really means is that this time he has finally got his figures right, or my father would not have listened to a word. Well, it is a dirty business, wool combing, and I am not on fire to get into it."

"I understand he didn't ask you."

"Why, Prudence, how very understanding you are. And how sharp. No, as it happens, he didn't ask me. Law Valley Wool Combers is to belong to Nicholas—and my father, of course—which is a very sensible move, since all our wool needs combing and Nicholas will be obliged to give us priority over the Hobhouses and the rest. My word, my brother is going to be busy. A new wife, a new venture of his own to get off the ground, and our sheds at Lawcroft and Tarn Edge to manage, all by himself whenever I am away, which will be a great deal of the time. But, dear Prudence, if you imagine he is trying to push me out, you may be easy, for I shall have my share of the Barforth mills—oh yes—and keep my hands clean of engine grease while I'm about it. Nicky will probably make a fortune for himself, but he will also increase mine, you know. The new combing machines are speeding up the whole industry, the faster the wool can be combed the faster we can spin it and weave it, which means there will be more of it for me to sell—no more long faces among the shed managers, when I tell them the delivery dates I've agreed to. Don't worry about me, Prudence. I confess I like it. But there's really no need."

Nicholas' venture, of which he had spoken to me so eagerly, so long ago, soon became a reality, a low, scowling building not too far from Lawcroft Fold, dominated by a sign which proclaimed it "Law Valley Wool Combers," an enterprise, like all its predecessors, which brought prosperity to some, great hardship to the hand combers whose slow, laborious, none too healthy calling would soon be at an end. Some of them, of course—a few—would be employed by Nicholas, others would find work elsewhere, any work, but most of them, quite soon, were simply cast adrift, abandoned, unnecessary, their presence at every street corner becoming so menacing, so inconvenient, that something, it was felt, would have to be done.

"They're hungry," Mayor Agbrigg said, once again, knowing, from his own meagre past that, in work or out of work, the rent had still to be paid, body and soul held somehow—if only barely —together.

"They're impertinent," Aunt Hannah replied, having received her share of muttered threats and obscene gestures from men who, having witnessed the death of their trade and their hopes for the future, were not concerned with good manners.

"They're a damned nuisance," said many others, and so Mayor Agbrigg and my sister Prudence formed, almost singlehanded, the Wool Combers' Aid Association, with the object of placing these men in other situations or, when that proved impossible, of helping them to emigrate; Mayor Agbrigg persuading his colleagues to allocate 1,500 pounds from the rates for the purpose, Prudence, for many years after, continuing to receive letters from Australia and Canada, offering ill-spelled news—both good and bad—of the families she had befriended.

"I am collecting for the hand combers," she told Blaize at the start of the troubles. "Now then—I am curious to know what the size of your donation will be?"

"Oh—you may put me down for twice as much as my brother," he told her, those grey eyes wickedly twinkling, frankly admitting, that, in fact, he had offered her nothing at all.

But whatever strife there might, or might not be among the Barforths, I was not directly concerned in it. They were rich and would be richer, but I had riches too, a man who needed to see me and touch me, who hesitated, frowning, in the hallway if it seemed to him I was not there, his face warming instantly when he discovered himself mistaken. And if I was anxious about anything it was my conviction that I could not possibly give him enough, the inexplicable failure of my body, which so desired his caresses, to achieve the climax of pleasure he had described to me, and wished me to share.

"Giles, I am so sorry. Is something wrong with me, do you think?"

"No, no, darling—don't think about it. Don't try. Just let it happen—there's time—"

But always, turning to him eagerly in the night, my limbs would begin to glow expectantly beneath his hands, everything in me wanting this perfect unity he spoke of, a fluttering at the core of my body, the hopeful wing-beating of a caged bird I wanted to set free, struggled to set free, not for my own pleasure but to please him. Yet always, at the final moment, when I was sure that this time, finally, I would succeed, I could feel it begin to slip away, receding forlornly back to its source, unfulfilled, leaving me so desolate in the face of his disappointment that I could have wept.

"Giles, I'm so sorry."

"Darling, don't be."

"Does it make your pleasure less?"

"No—my pleasure comes in any case. And the real pleasure is that I love you."

"Oh yes—and I want to give you everything you want. You *have* to be happy, Giles. I must make you happy."

"You do make me happy. Don't distress yourself—that alone could make me miserable."

But the physical pleasure I could not attain became a symbol in my mind of the differences between us. I loved Giles. I was not in love with him in the piercing, consuming way I had been in love with Nicholas. And, in my desire to transfer that total feeling, all of a piece, from one man to the other, I came to believe this physical climax to be not only desirable but essential. If I could experience it, I would belong to him, and he would know that he possessed me. I must give him the satisfaction of seeing me completely enraptured, needing him, my body enslaved by his. I must. And my own determination, my fear of failure, created such tension inside me that, night after night, I did fail, my body defeating its own purposes.

"It doesn't mean I don't want you, Giles. I do—I do."

"I know. Just let it happen. Darling—I am asking too much, too soon."

"No! You're not. You could never ask enough. Why must you always try to take the blame? Don't be so *nice* to me, Giles, when I don't deserve it. If I'm inadequate, then tell me so."

And there were times when, my teeth clenched with frustration, I would have allowed him to beat me, to force out of me in any way he could the response I was so desperate to give.

But he was unfailingly gentle and in all other ways I knew we were happy. This was my life—and his—together, inseparable, my purpose, my reason for occupying my place in the world. I had recovered my pleasant pastures, and wanted no other.

Caroline was confined that June, a year after her marriage, bringing forth with characteristic flair not one child but two, a pair of healthy boys who came into the world with no apparent fuss, and were allowed to make none thereafter, lying quietly in their cradles at her bedside while she made out her lists of the furniture, the groceries, and the guests she desired to be delivered. Dominic Chard, who would be Sir Dominic one day, master of Listonby and all it contained, just a shock of dark hair, at present, on a lace pillow, a diminutive fist reaching out for the sunbeams as they came through her window, looking quite capable, I thought—like his mother—of grasping them. And his brother, his junior by just ten vital minutes, Master Noel St. John Chard, who, with no lands and titles for him to inherit, would have to look beyond Listonby for his livelihood. "I suppose the young one will be a soldier," she told me, having accepted my gifts and compliments. "Yes—a colonel of Hussars—I am not quite sure just what that is, but if it should be as grand as it sounds then that is what I shall make him. Colonel Noel St. John Chard—it sounds well, at any rate. We have already had a set-to about the christening, since Matthew has two cousins who are bishops, and my suggestion that we should settle the matter by having them baptise one infant each was not well received. They both expect to baptise the eldest, of course, and unless they come out of their sulks I shall ask the vicar of Cullingford to officiate, which would really put the cat among the pigeons. Well—I am ahead of Georgiana and she is not likely to catch up with me. In fact she is so flat still that one wonders if it is really more than her imagination. She will have the poor mite in a ditch, if she is not careful, with her horse for midwife. Well then, Faith, I shall expect you and your clever husband to the christening dinner."

Georgiana, however, gave birth a month later, luxuriously if not easily, in her bedroom at Tarn Edge, a process which, despite her athletic habits and stoical turn of mind, lasted for thirty-six agonising hours and required both the old-fashioned Dr. Overdale and the progressive Dr. Ashburn to bring about its conclusion.

She was still very weak when I called to see her, still confined to her bed, although I had allowed a full three weeks to pass by, but her face on the pillow looked so spent, her body so boyish and frail, somehow so vulnerable, something about her light

green eyes and the tumble-down mass of her coppery hair so
touching, that my lurking fear of Nicholas—for this was his bed,
his child, his woman—was evaporated by my sympathy.

"Georgiana, was it so very dreadful?"

"Oh yes," she said, smiling. "How nice of you to ask me that,
for now I can say that indeed it was—quite dreadful. Everybody
else has been telling me how well I look—when I know I look a
perfect fright—and how brave I was, when, in fact, I screamed
so loud that Nicky must surely have heard me above the racket
of his looms—or whatever. Yes—dreadful. I was quite angry, really, at being proved such a coward, which made me scream the
harder. Your husband was marvellous. Dr. Overdale told me to
'hush, hush little woman,' but your husband told me to scream if
I wanted to, and swear too, which I did, I can assure you. Well,
there he is—the cause of all the trouble—Master Gervase Clevedon Barforth. He is rather small, in fact one could lose him, almost, among all that muslin and lace they have draped over
him, but when he fills out a little I believe he may resemble my
brother. He has not much hair now, and not much of anything
else either, but you can see that what bit there is will quite
definitely be auburn, like Perry's. Would you like to hold him—
most people seem to think it obligatory—but if you shouldn't
care for it I will perfectly understand."

I picked him up awkwardly, having no experience of the
newborn, and feeling nothing beneath the elaborately swathed
shawls more substantial than a kitten, I put him hastily down
again, worrying, as I returned to her bedside, that I had somehow injured him.

"I wanted him to be born at the abbey," she said wistfully. "I
confess to you that I was quite wicked and went over there as
often as I could towards the end, hoping that my pains would
begin and I would have to stay. The walks I took—you can't
imagine—striding out up hill and down dale with Perry, who
even took me up in his curricle to give me a good shaking.
Heavens, we drove all the way to Patterswick, hell for leather, to
no avail. I did so want him to be born at Galton. I wanted to
call him Peregrine too, but Nicky says one Peregrine is enough,
although no one in the world could have objected to my naming
him Gervase, for my grandfather, and Clevedon for myself. It is

only right, after all, that he should have our family name, for if Perry does not marry then it will be this little Gervase, none other, who will inherit the abbey."

"Our cousin Nicholas may not care for that," Prudence said later when I had made my report. "I cannot think he has set himself to build an empire with the intention of seeing it squandered by the Clevedons. It is Caroline who wanted the land and the title. Nicholas merely wanted the woman, and Georgiana may as well make up her mind that Master Gervase Clevedon Barforth is destined for the mills."

The Clevedons too had relatives in high ecclesiastical places, but the christening of the infant Gervase was a very private affair in the abbey chapel, far removed in spirit from the ceremony at Listonby, which seemed more like a launching into society of the future baronet and the future colonel of Hussars than a baptism. The house, where alterations were still in progress, was crammed with Chards of all varieties, noble, religious, sporting, and military, who, having said all that was necessary on the subject of Master Dominic and Master Noel, attended a christening banquet in the eighteenth-century dining room, a triumph of truffled roast chickens and partridges in aspic, of lobster au gratin and spiced sirloin of beef; while outside, in the park, a whole ox was roasted for the Listonby tenants assembled at tables beneath the sycamores and the elm trees.

Caroline's new upstairs ballroom was still littered with carpentry and unfinished plasterwork but nevertheless there were two dances at Listonby that evening, the Great Hall cleared for family and friends, a marquee erected on the lawn and stocked with several barrels of ale to accommodate the farmers and villagers, the huntsman and his wife, the kennel huntsman and his exceedingly pretty daughter, who did not seem too alarmed by the attentions of Peregrine Clevedon.

There was a great deal of champagne, the party from the hall going outside at midnight to toast the sleeping infants yet again, tenants' daughters and gentlemen's daughters, officers and ploughboys, raising their glasses side by side, producing the exact degree of mingling, class with class, considered appropriate to the occasion, since the tenantry must be understandably eager to make the acquaintance of their new lady, understandably relieved that she had ensured the continuity of the estate, and of their leases, by producing this overabundance of heirs.

It was, in fact, an immense success, lavish yet so efficient that not even the most mercantile, nonconformist of hearts could have pronounced it wasteful, everyone enjoying themselves hugely but, at the same time, minding their manners, gaiety without impropriety—since impropriety would always find it hard to flourish beneath Caroline's eagle eye—a blueprint, one felt, of what she intended to make of her future.

"Well done," I told her.

"Yes," she said. "I believe it was. Not that I mean to rest on my laurels, I do assure you, for the moment one becomes satisfied one has set one's feet on the downward path. My father taught me that. He measures his success by his current trading figures—today's profit, not yesterday's—and I shall do the same. Just wait for my Christmas Eve ball, Faith dear. I think even my father will be impressed with that."

The foundation stone of Aunt Hannah's concert hall was finally laid that year to the hearty accompaniment of Cullingford's own brass band on the site she had herself chosen off Market Square. The ceremony was performed by a belted earl, an ancient gentleman who appeared uncertain as to the exact purpose of his visit. Yet he made himself pleasant enough afterwards at the reception organised in the Assembly Rooms by my aunt, who, although mayoress no longer, appeared to have retained the authority of the office, making light work of comfortable Mrs. Hobhouse, who had officially succeeded her. Mayor Hobhouse, indeed, looking portly and complacent despite the persistent rumours that trade at Nethercoats was not good, made no secret of his dependence upon Mr. Ira Agbrigg, being himself a man who preferred the afternoon comforts of the Old Swan to a spike-edged tussle with the Cullingford Waterworks.

"Here's my man Agbrigg," he kept on saying, much to the annoyance of Aunt Hannah and Uncle Joel, whose "man" Mr. Agbrigg undoubtedly was. "He's got the waterworks company by the tail at last, I can tell you. Neatly done, Agbrigg my lad, since if you're to be mayor again next time the purchase will come into your term of office, and you'll get all the credit."

"He did all the work," Prudence said in a whisper that was

meant to be heard, and indeed it was no secret that Mr. Agbrigg's efforts alone had persuaded the truculent directors of the waterworks company to part with their ailing giant for the sum of 165,000 pounds, and that he had not only calmed the fears of a startled corporation, unaccustomed as yet to handling such large sums of public money, but had obliged them to seek Parliamentary consent to the raising of a further 400,000 pounds, to be used for the construction of reservoirs.

"Such energy," Mrs. Hobhouse had once been heard to murmur, very spitefully for her. "Only think, Hannah, had it been put to commercial use, you might have been a millionairess, not just a mayoress, by now."

But Aunt Hannah, her own building projects fast becoming a reality, her husband's reputation as a popular hero providing her, at last, with ample compensation for his lack of social finesse, had replied merely with a smile and an inclination of her handsome Barforth head.

My mother was there too that day, allowing the outwardly respectable but—according to Blaize—inwardly lascivious worsted spinner, Mr. Oldroyd, to take her arm; she was flirtatious and ready, as always, to enjoy the conquest of any man, but bored, I knew, eager to be off on her travels again yet not certain, this time, just where she wished to go.

"You look nineteen, Mamma," I told her.

"My dear—I know, and it is very kind of you to say so. But what is the good of that when everyone else of my generation is looking so old? Darling, where have all the attractive men gone to—I was asking myself just this morning, for the world used to be full of them and now they have vanished entirely. Well, I have found the answer. They are here, of course, as they have always been, except that they are older—for Matthew Oldroyd was once quite handsome, before he became so dry and grey, and Bradley Hobhouse, my dear, when he weighed a mere sixteen stones instead of the ton of him you see today, was a man worth looking at. I confess I looked—once—and he at me— merely looked— But now, apart from my brother Joel, they are just a set of bloated or shrunken old gentlemen, and even Joel, you know, is taking on weight. Yes, I may look nineteen, Faith dear, but there are days when I do not feel it. Perhaps I should take to wearing purple satin like Hannah and Emma-Jane

Hobhouse, and compose myself for decay. I wonder, in fact, if it would have been better, after all, to have been born a matron, like Celia."

Celia had not attended the ceremony in the square, fearing to stand on her feet so long, fearing to be jostled in the crowd, and that the noise of the brass instruments would give her a headache, but Jonas had assisted her up the shallow steps to the Assembly Rooms, provided her with a chair and footstool, opened a window so that she could see something of the proceedings, and then closed it again when she declared she would take cold. And although there was no warmth in the care he took of her no one could have accused him of being other than coolly but unfailingly attentive to the whims of this frail little woman who had always felt the need of her frailty to make herself noticed.

"Jonas, this lemonade you have brought me is much too warm."

"I will fetch some ice."

"You know that ice gives me a headache."

"I beg your pardon. What shall I bring you then?"

"Oh—I don't know. Can't you think of something? There seems to be nothing but champagne, which is not good for me. I don't suppose they would trouble themselves to make me some tea?"

"I will go and enquire."

"Thank you—and not too strong, Jonas—for the last time I had tea here it was quite black and bitter and altogether horrid. Do hurry, Jonas."

He went off to do her bidding, and watching his cool, quite passionless retreat, Prudence murmured to me, "Our little sister seems to have the upper hand of her Jonas. Who would have thought it? I had expected to see things quite otherwise."

But I was less convinced. Celia, indeed, had always whined and complained, had always been a nuisance, but Prudence knew as well as I that it had stemmed from a combined sense of inadequacy and isolation. If Celia had grown up believing herself neglected—by an all-powerful father who had shown her neither interest nor affection, by her sisters who had openly preferred each other's company to hers—then she had been quite right. Only Miss Mayfield, at the cry of "My head aches. My back aches," had rushed to attend her, only a hurried summons to Dr. Overdale, a darkened room, "Be quiet, girls, your sister is ailing," had made her important. And now, the triumph of her early marriage fading, she was using those same ailments, the drama of her two miscarriages, to attract the notice, or to punish, the man who seemed determined to be a good husband—since it was a requirement of his prickly nature that everything he did should be done to perfection—but who did not love her.

"Well," I said to Prudence, speaking my thought out loud, "At least he's not in love with anyone else."

"Jonas?" she said. "Of course not. Good heavens, Faith, is that all you can think of? I never thought to see you so besotted with Giles. Well—I am sure he is very glad of it, even if it does make your conversation so limited."

We left the reception early, Giles having received a call of some urgency, and I drove with him to Simon Street, waiting in the gig while he went down a narrow court, a mere gap, man-wide, between two houses and entered the house behind them, which my father had built.

Simon Street, which had given its name to the entire area of alleys and back passages cobwebbing between itself and Saint Street, was not the worst place I had ever seen, it was simply larger, its tragedies, its brutalities, its degradations appearing worse because they were more numerous. Built long ago to accommodate the labour force of Low Cross Mills, it offered ample proof to the most casual eye of my father's boasted ability to squeeze in more humanity per acre than any other builder in the West Riding. Its damp, flimsy, two-roomed cottages sometimes housed thirty or more lacklustre persons, rarely less than eight or ten. The street itself was unpaved, an occasional heap of engine ashes thrown down to drink up the mud, the open sewage channels on either side of it seeping their liquid foulness into the uneven ground. But in the alleys beyond I knew there were no drains at all, no more facilities for the functioning of human bodies than was normally provided for stabled cattle, just dung heaps, rotting and poisonous, in any dark corner, a swill tub placed here and there overflowing with the festering vegetable garbage for which the pig men, when they troubled to collect it, would pay a penny or two.

I knew that the woman my husband had gone to visit was dirty, that all women who took up residence in these mean streets, no matter how careful their upbringing nor how precise their early ambitions, were dirty too, not necessarily from idleness or wickedness, but because the standpipe in Simon Street was turned on for scarcely more than half an hour a day. Few of these women possessed the pans and buckets in which to collect and store it, nor the strength to carry them even if they had. And I understood too, now that Giles had explained it to me, the impossibility, even for the fortunate owners of buckets and brushes, of scrubbing floorboards that were rotten, or walls that sprouted a continual mushroom mould of damp.

I knew that Giles' patient would, most likely, be drunk on his arrival, since gin, being cheap and easier to come by than water, was also much valued for its ability to dull the senses of smell, of hunger, of decency, to induce a state of contented apathy—much sought after in Simon Street—a shrug of thin shoulders which said, "What do I care?" I knew her children fouled the streets as casually as the packs of mongrel dogs I could see swarming everywhere, because my father had provided no privies, or so few that they were choked with ancient excrement, and the streets were sweeter.

I knew that in the hot weather—down those fearful alleyways —there were fly swarms, rat swarms, whores, and thieves, murder done for the sake of a shilling, or for its own sake alone; while on the strips of wasteland where my father had neglected to build, or his buildings had fallen down, I knew that women washed their infected bedclothes during the summer fevers, in the stagnant pools where others came to drink.

I knew, too, that the woman my husband had called on could not pay him, would take none of his advice, would continue to drink and breed and moulder her life away, failing, since no one else had ever valued her, to place any value on herself. And wondering what value the world would have accorded me had I been born in so irrevocable a trap, I was so fiercely thankful for my own life, that the sight of Giles coming back to the gig, smiling a little ruefully as he picked his way across the litter, caused my stomach to lurch with gladness, a glow beginning, small but very determined, at the core of me.

We drove off to higher ground, cleaner air, and sitting very close to him I said, "You are a marvellous man, Giles."

"By no means. I am an ordinary man. There is nothing at all remarkable about me that I can see."

"I say you are marvellous and don't wish to be contradicted."

He smiled, quiet and contained as he always was. "You may call me fortunate, if you like. I believe it would be a more accurate assessment. I have always had sufficient money for my needs, and so I can afford to be compassionate. Please don't admire me too much, Faith, for I shall never do great things in the world. I am moved by the misery around me but I am too content with my own life to be a true pioneer. I did not march to Westminster with the Chartists, as your brother Crispin did, although I believed strongly in every one of their aims. I do what I can in Simon Street, as much as I am asked to do, but I lead no crusades for reform. Basically I am just an ordinary man, concerned with my own affairs, with my home and my wife, and that she should continue to think me marvellous."

I got down from the gig in Millergate, opened my own front door, crossed my threshold, waiting as he saw the horse put away, my anxieties gone, my whole body dreaming and glowing —waiting for him.

"Giles."

"Yes, darling?"

And although I couldn't say, "Make love to me," since no woman educated by my father could ever bring herself to say that, it was there, unspoken, and more than that; no longer simply "Make love to me," but "Giles, let me make love to you."

Chapter Fifteen

WE SPENT our second Christmas together in quiet content, Giles' professional commitments obliging me to refuse Caroline's invitation to spend the entire festive season at Listonby.

"You can't miss my ball," she said, quite horrified, refusing to be diverted even by my discovery of a particularly fine silk brocade which would suit her to perfection, and the detailed sketches I passed on to her dressmaker. "If your husband can't come, then you must come without him. Goodness, he can't possibly want you to miss my ball either—the staircase is an absolute marvel and even my father has never assembled so many chandeliers together, one directly above my head when I receive at the top of the stairs, seven in the long gallery, the hall full of candles and Christmas trees, and I'm not even prepared to tell you what I've done with the ballroom. I want to *unveil* it, Faith, like a monument. You can't miss it, and you could be a tremendous help to me since I've never even met half the people who are coming. You don't have to dance with them if you'd rather not, but you could circulate—and chat. Naturally your husband wouldn't mind. He'd be glad to see you enjoying yourself—like Matthew."

And she was still puzzled, still half-offended when we met at Tarn Edge a few days before the event, the only afternoon, it seemed, when Aunt Verity could hope to gather her family together under her own roof, Caroline having only that much time to spare and Georgiana being quite determined, no matter what other claims her husband might have on his time, to go over to Galton for the hunting. But even when we were all assembled and had received our gifts, somewhat in advance, from the lavish Barforth tree, our menfolk were called away from us one by one, Giles to a human confinement, Matthew Chard to an equine complication, Nicholas to his combing sheds where a group of hand combers were showing every sign of ill-will towards his property. His father went off to assist him, Blaize to see the fun, leaving us with no male company but the infants Dominic and Noel Chard, installed in lonely state in what had been Caroline's nursery, and the infant Gervase Barforth, who, carried downstairs by his mother, was tickled and tossed about by her for a while as if he'd been a puppy and then carelessly abandoned on the edge of a sofa, to be rescued by Aunt Verity.

"Poor little soul," she said. "You may leave him at Listonby with me, Georgiana, when you go over to Galton, you know. I shall be staying with Caroline until the New Year and would enjoy having my three grandchildren all together."

But, glancing across at her son settled comfortably in his grandmother's arms—remembering his existence perhaps—Georgiana suddenly clapped her hands in delight and shook her head.

"Do look at the firelight on his hair—I told you, did I not, that it would be red, and so it is—red as a carrot at the moment, but it will darken, just like me and Perry. Oh yes, he is a wild, red Clevedon, that one, there is no mistaking it."

We saw in the New Year with my mother, who, still saddened by the premature decay of her admirers, talked of returning to France now that it was safe again, the new republic, in fact, being destined to fall an early victim to a second Bonaparte, a wily gentleman who, after spending some years of exile in London, would, before long, win election to the presidency and, like his uncle Napoleon before him, soon set about the business of making himself an emperor.

"I think this new France will suit me," she said, "for these political adventurers understand the value of gaiety."

But somehow her journey was never made, half-planned, half-prepared, abandoned a dozen times, so that she was with me on the May afternoon Giles came unexpectedly into the hall, letting the door slam shut behind him, and when I went out to meet him said quickly, "Don't touch me."

"Giles—?"

"Let me wash my hands first. I'll be with you presently."

And as he hurried up the stairs, he called out. "I have sent a message to Mayor Agbrigg, asking him to call. He should be here almost at once."

"There is trouble," my mother said. "One can always feel it. I shall leave you, Faith. I have little talent for trouble and would only be in the way."

Mayor Agbrigg came and spent an hour with Giles behind a locked study door.

"It is nothing," Giles said to me. "I must go out again."

"It is nothing," he said much later on his return. But when he had scrubbed himself and changed his linen—stowing his dirty linen away, I noticed, in his laboratory at the back of the house —I stood in front of him and demanded, "Tell me. I am not a child. I must know."

"There may be nothing to know," he said, walking away from me, making the brandy glass in his hand a barrier between us. "Dr. Overdale is sure I am mistaken, and Dr. Blackstone has called me a dramatic fool. I hope they may be right. I believe I have seen a case of cholera in Simon Street."

"But—Giles—there is always fever, surely, in Simon Street."

"Yes indeed. Typhus, typhoid, scarlet, any kind of fever you would care to name, and some that have no names at all. You may find them all in Simon Street, any day of the week. I said cholera, Faith, not fever."

"But you are not sure."

"I saw it, ten years ago, in a London hospital. This seems the same. But no, I am not sure, because I want to be wrong."

"And Dr. Overdale?"

"He has seen it too. He is an older man and he remembers the epidemic of '31. He wants me to be wrong so badly that he is insisting upon it. While Dr. Blackstone, who is even older, would like me confined to a madhouse. He takes the common view—as you did—that there is always something amiss in Simon Street."

"What can you do, Giles?"

"Go back there," he said, "in the morning, and see how far it has spread."

Mayor Agbrigg called again, late that night, and as they sat at my fireside drinking brandy, silence thick all about them, I said, "What is cholera?"

"I don't know," Giles answered, his eyes on his glass, his face in shadow. "Nobody knows."

"But we have had it before?"

"Oh yes. Our troops found it in India, thirty years ago. Then it appeared in Russia and spread like the plague, which is what they called it at first. So many peasants died in eastern Europe that for a time they believed the aristocrats were poisoning them, thinning them out so they'd be easier to govern, and there was nearly a revolution. It moved west, until every city of any size had it, and in '31 it came to London and killed eight thousand people there—sixty thousand, they say, in England as a whole. God knows how many really died. They didn't know what caused it, or how to treat it, and we still don't. Like everything else, it takes the very old and the very young to begin with, the undernourished and the weak—the easy pickings. It lives on dirt, breeds in rotting garbage heaps and open sewers, such as you can find so easily in better places than Simon Street. And when it gathers strength it seems to take anybody who gets in its way. I don't know, Faith. Some say it comes from the inhalation of bad air. Some say it comes from the drinking of water that has been fouled by excrement, and we've plenty of that in Cullingford. It involves massive vomiting, the bowels open, and the body can retain nothing. If it lasted long enough the patient would starve to death. But it's quick, and exceedingly filthy. We're at the beginning of May. If it is the cholera, then you should pray for a cool summer."

"Aye," Mayor Agbrigg said. "And what can I do for you, lad— if it is the cholera? I'll take the council by the scruff of its neck for you, not that I'll need to, for they're old enough to remember the last time, same as I am. What can we do?"

Giles shrugged, refilled the mayor's glass and his own.

"You can educate them to stop drinking cess water in Simon Street, and provide them with water they can drink."

"That I can. But tomorrow morning, lad—what then?"

"Chloride of lime," he said slowly, his eyes still on the warmly swirling brandy. "The houses in the stricken areas should be limewashed. You could get them to shift the dung heaps, though

God knows where they'll put them. They burned barrels of tar and vinegar, I believe, in the streets, the last time. I don't know if it helps, other than to make people feel that something is being done."

"I'll see to it, lad."

And when Mayor Agbrigg had gone, leaving Giles still sitting by the fireside, I slipped my hand in his and asked him, "Are you afraid?"

"Of course. If I could choose between going back to Simon Street tomorrow morning, or taking the London train tonight—with you—then I'd take the train."

"I'd come with you, Giles—gladly."

"I know," he said, smiling, that great air of quietness still about him. "What a pity there is no choice."

He left early the next morning, a beautiful pink and blue day, returning late in the afternoon, the distance he placed between us confirming my fears. In the same family in Simon Street one child had died, three others were ailing, the woman next door and two more across the street, six people in the same bed next door to that, so that even Dr. Blackstone was in doubt no longer.

"I am on my way to the infirmary," he said. "Every bed will be needed, and so I must send home—or turn out—as many as I can."

And Prudence, who had come to spend the evening with me, said quietly, "I'll come with you."

"My dear, you'll do no such thing."

"But I shall. Do be sensible, Giles. Not one of your nurses will remain when they know what is coming, or the ones who do will be too drunk to be of service. Gallantry is all very well, but you will need every pair of hands you can muster, and I shall oblige you to take mine."

"And mine," I added, with not the least expectation in the world of being refused, since he had never refused me anything before, until he said in a voice that was quite strange to me, "I think not. In fact I absolutely forbid it."

"My goodness," I told him, half laughing. "Then I shall just have to disobey."

"No—no. You will do just as I tell you."

"You must decide that between you," Prudence said calmly, beginning to fasten her bonnet. "But you have no authority to forbid *me*. Only Mamma may do that and I am well able to manage her. I may come and go as I please, unless she denies it, and there is every likelihood that she will bolt all the way to France, and leave me with Miss Mayfield, who is even easier to handle."

"I cannot take you to a source of danger, Prudence."

"You cannot stop me. You must make the best of it."

But in my case he was adamant.

"You are my wife," he said much later that night when I had reasoned and pleaded and threatened to no avail. "The law allows me absolute authority over you and I shall exercise it."

"Good heavens, Giles, I had no idea you could be so pompous. You can hardly lock me up. Not even my father ever threatened me with that."

Yet, when I persisted, finding it unthinkable that I should not be allowed to share his burden, he said simply, "Help me, Faith."

"But that is what I want to do."

"Then do it. I am no hero, Faith. I am uncertain and afraid and, in these next weeks or months or however long it may be, I shall very likely grow more afraid and extremely tired. I have to know that my wife is safe, or as safe as you can be in these circumstances. I cannot function otherwise. I have never asked you for anything before. I am asking you now for this. Help me."

And there was nothing more, for the moment, that I could say.

I remained at our fireside, fretting, through those early summer days, painful with anxiety, as frantic for escape—to get to his side—as a caged bird. Many times I had wanted to make a sacrifice on his behalf, to perform some huge act of courage for his sake, in proof of my devotion and gratitude, and now that it had come to me this tame cowering in the safety of my chimney corner was harder than any ordeal I had imagined.

"Dear God, there must be something I can do, Giles. I do believe, sometimes, that I am going mad."

And his answer was always the same.

"I need you now, just as you are. I have asked you to help me. Am I asking too much?"

Within days, it seemed, the infirmary was overflowing, the vagrants and whores, the lost children of the Simon Street district being picked up nightly in their dozens, drunk and terrified and vomiting their lives away, while in the alleys, the damp, be-fouled anthills my father had created, every house had its trag-edy, the stench of burning tar and vinegar heavy on the air, the stench of fear threaded evilly through it. From one of those back streets alone seventy-two carts of manure, animal and human, were removed by Mayor Agbrigg's volunteers, the half-rotted carcasses of dogs and cats were fished up from the streams and those festering waste-land pools where Simon Street commonly drew its water. Chloride of lime was issued free of charge by a terrified corporation, aware at last of the marriage between dirt and disease too late—for those who were to die—to effect its separation.

No one, now, could really cleanse those abominable hovels, where windows, pasted or boarded up to exclude winter draughts and summer flies, converted each overcrowded room into a stinking oven. No one could even persuade those who lived therein to give up their dead for burial before it suited them, the Simon Street custom of laying out adult corpses on what could be the family's only bed, infant corpses on the kitchen table, continuing to be observed, partly from the habitual delay in scraping together the funeral expenses, partly because under-takers and gravediggers were increasingly unable to cope.

The illness, as Giles had told us, struck swiftly and was just as swiftly over. A child could be playing in the streets one morning, splashing happily in the sewage channels, and could be dead the same evening. A man could walk briskly to his employment, whistling in the hazy summer dawn, and be on his knees in a retching, malodorous agony in the mill yard by breakfast time. Yet the Barforth men, the Hobhouse men, the spare, grey-faced Mr. Oldroyd of Fieldhead, continued to turn on their engines at five o'clock every morning, to stand at their gates, watch in hand, to admit the punctual and to lock out the late-comers, continued to patrol their weaving sheds and spinning sheds and combing sheds, admitting no reason why their production tar-gets should not be met. The Piece Hall continued to open its doors for the Thursday market day, the ladies of Cullingford, even, to continue with their tea parties, feeling this infection of the bowels—somewhat indelicate in itself even had it not been so lethal—to be largely a matter for Simon Street. But then a parlourmaid of the Battershaws collapsed with a horrific clattering of tea-time china and silver; a Hobhouse coachman and then a Hobhouse child began to vomit and excrete and shake without hope of control; at which moment Cullingford began to close its doors.

Prudence moved in with me, my mother (who could not prevent Prudence's attendance at the infirmary) refusing to expose her own person to the "miasmatic vapours" Prudence might well carry into her house. I received a firmly penned note from my sister Celia requesting me neither to call upon her nor to answer her letter until the danger of contamination should be over. "You are unable to avoid it," she wrote, "but I know you will have consideration for those of us who may." Caroline remained at Listonby. Uncle Joel and Aunt Verity were already in Bournemouth and wisely chose to stay there. But Aunt Hannah, who did not approve of hospitals, was among the first to march up the cobbled slope of Sheepgate to the rickety converted dwelling house we called the infirmary, and finding, as Prudence had warned, that such nurses as were available had either taken to the gin bottle or run away, promptly rolled up her sleeves, donned an apron, and set about the boiling of fouled bed linen, the preparation of turpentine compresses, the constant washing and even the consoling of the dying.

I stayed at home—as a married woman should—obeying my husband—as a married woman should—deciding a dozen times a day that it was impossible, that I was, after all, a woman capable of decision, not a child to be protected and controlled.

"I can't tolerate it, Giles."

"I can't tolerate it, Faith, unless you do."

"I am sure you can."

"I do not know. But what I do know is that I should not forgive you."

"Do as he asks," Prudence said sharply. "Can't you see how weary he is? Dr. Blackstone collapsed this morning—no, not the cholera, thank God, old age, I suppose, and the strain. They were obliged to take him home, and Dr. Overdale is not young either. The rest of them are too young, perhaps, and they rely on Giles. Don't trouble him. He has enough to bear, knowing that there's nothing he can really do—having to watch people die, with no real hope to offer them. Leave him alone."

And seeing, beneath the hard lines of her face, a reflection of the horror she had experienced that day—a horror which set her apart from all those who had not shared it—knowing that the foul odours of the sickness were still in her nostrils, the futility of human despair still clawing at her heart, I desisted, fed her—and Giles—when they came home and could bring themselves to eat, provided clean linen, cool beds in which I occasionally persuaded them to sleep, prayed a little, waited.

My uncle Joel sent instructions from Bournemouth that beer was to be issued to his operatives in any quantity they were able to consume, a gesture at once philanthropic and sensible, since if the disease was really carried by bad water, as Giles increasingly believed, it was as well to offer an alternative drink. But if the Barforth mill hands were grateful and a little more cheerful than some others, they continued to die just the same, and as that bright, blue and gold June began to merge into a hazy, slumberous July, it was known that seven hundred people had perished.

I was quite alone now, except for Mrs. Guthrie busying herself in my kitchen, with nothing to see from my window but an empty, sun-baked street which had once been the brash, bustling thoroughfare of Millergate, few carriages now, such as there were rushing by closed and furtive despite the heat, an occasional woman, head bowed, handkerchief to her mouth, hurrying on some essential errand, plainly terrified of the poison that must be rising from the very cobbles, seeping like slime down every wall, gathering itself for fresh onslaught in the heavy, yellow air. Long, terrible days, appalling nights when Giles, having slept an hour in his armchair, his stomach unable to cope with anything but brandy, would get carefully to his feet, put on his hat again, and go quietly away. Hours that stifled me, each one extending itself into an isolation without end, a walking through the empty corridors of an evil dream, so that I was startled one afternoon when my door opened and Georgiana walked into the room.

"Yes," she said without any explanation. "I was told you would be sad and sorry, and so you are. I am come to cheer you up, since it seems everyone else is terrified of setting foot across your threshold. Heavens, they do so like to imprison us, these husbands, do they not? Well, I have escaped mine today, but when I called in at the infirmary to see what I could do, I fell foul of yours, who at once ordered me away. Goodness, he was cross. No place for a lady, he said, which was unjust of him, since Prudence was there—so I can only conclude he meant no place for a married lady unless one carries written permission from one's lord. I cannot understand it. My grandfather would never have forbidden me to be of service if sickness had come to Galton. In fact he would have expected me to do my utmost, since it is one's duty, surely, to look after one's own people? He would have been positively ashamed of me, I can tell you, had I attempted to shirk. After all, if we do not set the example—I mean, if we accept the privilege, then we must also accept the responsibility— That is what I have been taught, in any case, and it sounds very right to me. Well, Nicky does not think so, of course. He has gone to his mill every day because business is business, he tells me, and it is not my business to nurse his operatives. Goodness, at Galton I have always gone into the cottages when there was fever, and so did my mamma and my grand-mamma. They are our people, after all—we knew their names and their faces. Yet I have heard Nicky call out, 'Hey, you there —you with the checked cap,' to a man who, it turns out, has been employed at Lawcroft for twenty years. I cannot understand it."

"Did Nicholas forbid you to come into town?"

"Oh yes," she said, accepting my offer of tea and settling herself comfortably on my sofa as if she meant to stay as long as she pleased. "So he did. But he is so cross with me today in any case that a little more will make no difference. I have been spending too much, you see—or at least, not spending, since I am allowed to buy whatever I choose, so long as it is gowns and fans and shawls and trinkets of any imaginable variety. But I am not allowed to give my money away. I have told him, either my allowance is mine, or it is not, and he says it is mine, but whenever I am penniless, which seems to be very often, he requires to know why. What have I to show for it, he asks, and, of course, if I have been over to Galton and bought new pinafores for the little girls at the village school, or have made a little loan to my brother, then I can show him nothing at all. And I wish he would not ask me, in that stern fashion, when I think Perry means to repay me, since he knows quite well that there is no chance of it. Is your husband so particular?"

"No. But I have no brother—at least, I have, but he is far away and has never asked me for money."

She refilled her cup, standing on no ceremony with me, her slender, abrupt body altogether relaxed, her pointed, kitten's face warming to its task—apparently not unpleasant—of cheering me.

"Then you are fortunate, for Perry is always in disgrace. My word, if my grandfather had but a suspicion of the half of it—but I am quite determined to keep it from him. When all this is over you must come again—come often, to Galton, for you would so like my grandfather. He is the very kindest of men, and I know of no one with such perfect integrity. But, of course, his standards are so very high, and Perry has always been a scamp. It is a part of his nature one accepts. It is simply Perry. My father was much the same, and since my grandfather has had a great deal to bear in the past—and takes Perry's escapades far more to heart than I—I do not wish him to be troubled again. I have dozens of new dresses, Faith. One cannot always be buying more of the same thing, and if I have money in my hands and Perry does not, then how can I refuse him? I could not, even if I wanted to. My grandfather will take nothing from me and so if I choose to help my brother, I cannot think why it should be thought unnatural."

We talked an hour longer of this and that, her horse, her child, her inability, after almost two years as a manufacturer's wife, to find the wherewithal to fill her days. And then, as my clock gave warning that the hour of four was upon us, she got to her feet, pulling on her gloves and her perky chip hat with its audacious green feather.

"Heavens—I must be on my way."

But hesitating, frowning, she held out her hand and then, pausing in the doorway, came back into the room again.

"Faith—tell me—you understand these things better than I, and may be able to advise me."

And, still frowning, she sat down again.

"Well, this is the way of it. Perry approached me a few days ago, in a great fix as usual. Not a great sum—one hundred pounds merely—not owing to a tradesman, unfortunately, since tradesmen can be asked to wait, but to Julian Flood, who has debts of his own and cannot. Oh dear, I did not wish to approach Nicky since he had scolded me just the day before about not throwing good money after bad, and so—because Julian can be very pressing and has right on his side after all, since it is a gambling debt, and gambling debts *must* be paid— Well—I went to Blaize, who was kind enough to oblige me, saying I may repay him when I can. Faith, if Nicky knew of it, would he be—very much put out?"

"Georgiana," I said, the whole of my middle-class, commercial mind aghast at her rashness. "He would be furious—and horrified. Georgiana, you must never, absolutely never go into debt."

She laughed, just a shade nervously.

"Goodness, you are as shocked as if I had confessed to adultery."

"Georgiana, in Cullingford adultery and debt amount to very much the same thing. In fact debt is probably worse."

"Yes, I suspected as much. But only a hundred pounds, Faith —from my brother-in-law, who seemed ready enough to spare it. And Nicky will never know. I can trust you not to tell him, and Perry will not."

"No. But Blaize may do so."

"Faith," she said, as shocked as I had been a moment before. "Whatever do you mean? Blaize would not betray a confidence of that nature. No gentleman would do so."

"Blaize would," I told her, suddenly very sure of it. "I am not saying he will, or that he intended it when he advanced you the money. But if it should suit his purposes tomorrow, or whenever —since you will be a long time in paying him back, if you ever do—then he would."

"But why? He does not dislike me—does he?"

"No. In fact I think he likes you very much. But Blaize is not a gentleman in the way you understand it, Georgiana. He may appear so, and he is certainly very charming and can be kindhearted—but his code is not the same as your grandfather's. He's a Barforth, and if he can get a return on his investment then he will."

"Then he dislikes Nicky—his own brother?"

"No, he doesn't. He may not have taken this affair of the combing company quite so calmly as he likes people to think, because it looks as if Nicholas is going to make a lot of money for himself, and Blaize can't really enjoy that. But it's not dislike. Listen,

Georgiana, we were brought up together, and always, if Blaize had something, then Nicholas had to have it too, no matter what it cost him, and if Nicholas had something, then Blaize either had to have it, or spoil it, or get something better to make whatever Nicholas had look small. Their father wanted them to be aggressive and competitive, and so they are. The difference is that Nicholas shows it and Blaize doesn't. But he's exactly the same. If he needs a weapon one day, he'll take whatever comes to hand. And, for heaven's sake, you may owe him a hundred pounds now but what happens the next time you need money quickly and can't ask Nicholas? You'll go to Blaize again, you know you will, and in the end it could be thousands. What would you do if Nicholas found out then?"

"Shoot myself," she said, half-ruefully, half-carelessly.

"I doubt it. Have you actually given the money to your brother?"

"No. I have it here in my reticule. I'm to meet him in half an hour, on the outskirts of town."

"Then give it back to Blaize. I don't believe he'd really allow you to borrow and borrow again until you were in a desperate plight, but no matter. A hundred pounds would be enough to infuriate Nicholas. I can't tell you how angry he'd be. And apart from that, if it became known that his wife had been obliged to borrow, then the whole of his commercial credibility would be damaged in Cullingford. Blaize wouldn't expect you to think of that, but he's certainly thought of it himself."

"Oh, dear," she said, looking down at the green velvet reticule in her hands, weighing it, considering, and then with that birdlike movement of her head, looking up at me with her sudden smile. "I do see. Well, never mind, Faith, at least I've provided you with something to think about besides the cholera, which means I have done you good. Good-bye then, I must dash, since my brother doesn't care to be kept waiting—even for money. I'll come and cheer you up again, and if I don't, then you'll know it's because we've gone to a debtor's prison, Perry and I, together."

And so it continued, time running slow, an airless July, the burnt-yellow skies of August, my fearful days made bearable only by the demands of Prudence, the occasional hour when Giles would allow me to approach him, a lightening visit, every now and then, from Georgiana, her raindrop chatter diverting me sometimes to sympathy, often to amusement and gratitude.

"I believe it will soon be over," Prudence said. "You will see— by September they will be haggling about the cost of a decent water supply again. There have been fewer cases this last week, and many of them seem likely to recover. It is abating . . ."

So it continued. Heat, fear, the lethargy of strained nerves that could strain no more and began to atrophy, an enforced idleness, that, an instant before it maddened me, engulfed me in a strange, torpid doze, the constant fatigue of doing too little, which was fast rendering me incapable of doing anything at all.

So it continued, until the evening, late, when Prudence came home, not alone, but without Giles.

Chapter Sixteen

SHE CAME INTO THE ROOM and stood by the empty hearth, Mayor Agbrigg beside her, their faces only half-visible since I had not troubled to light a lamp. And although I could not have said for certain—the next morning, the morning after—whether or not I had guessed their task, it seems to me now that I did.

We looked at each other for a while and then Prudence said in the crisp tone of everyday, which is perhaps the only manner in which one can bring oneself to say such things, "Faith—Giles was taken ill today while he was out visiting. He drove himself to the infirmary and wishes to remain there."

I don't remember what I answered, or if I answered anything at all. I simply remember moving to the door, assuming they would follow me, knowing the Agbrigg carriage must be in the street and that someone would drive me to Sheepgate.

"You cannot go to him," Prudence said, and I remember quite clearly how my incredulity, my inclination to scornful, nervous laughter gave way to anger as her hand descended on my arm, her arrow-straight body blocked my way.

"You cannot go, Faith. He asked us to keep you away. The infirmary is dangerous still, and he will not have you there."

Once again I don't know what I answered, merely that I went on walking towards the door, fighting her when she tried to stop me, dragging her with me, for I was taller and heavier and crazed, in any case, with my urgency. And I would have struck her, I think, and knocked her down had not Mayor Agbrigg

taken me by the shoulders, his hard, workman's hands biting
through the numbness of me, shaking me—since I was shouting
something now—to silence. But even then, shocked by this first
experience of male violence, I kicked out at him and hurt him, I
think, although he did not let me go.

"I'm going to him. I warn you—I'll walk . . ."

"Lass," he said, holding me in his thin, crook-shouldered embrace, the wiry strength of him greater than I had supposed.
"Lass—see the sense to it."

"There's no sense. He's my husband. You can't keep me away
from him."

"He doesn't want you," Prudence shouted, bursting painfully
into tears, and when I lashed out at her Mayor Agbrigg shook
me again.

"Lass—have your wits about you. You know what the cholera
is. It stinks, lass. He doesn't want you to see him like that.
There's nothing you can do for him. Let him fight it. And then
be here, to welcome him home."

"I can't. You must understand—I know you mean well, but I
can't. He needs me—he must need me—what good am I if he
doesn't need me now?"

"He wants you to be here, when he's well again. You'll weaken
him, love, if you worry him now—when he needs all his
strength."

"Write him something," Prudence said, and they brought me
pen and paper and sat me down before it. I began to write, docile, foolish words, and then, as they swam into meaningless hier-
oglyphics beneath my eyes, I clenched my hands into fists and
brought them crashing down on to the table.

"No. You may go to hell, Prudence Aycliffe, and you too, Mr.
Agbrigg. You will not treat me like a child any longer—none of
you, not even Giles. I will go to him and stay with him, and
when he is fit to be moved I will bring him home and nurse him
here, where he should be, not in that pesthole. You can't stop
me."

"I can," Mayor Agbrigg said, his big-knuckled hands biting
into my shoulders again. "Now listen to me. I love that lad as if
he was my own—I've wished he was my own. He pleaded with
me, not long since, to keep you away—begged me. I promised

him. And if I have to knock you out or tie you down, then I'll do it. And no matter what you may be suffering, lass, if I'd to choose I'd sooner be in your place than his. Think on that."

And when I had written my pathetic scrawl, "Giles, I love you. I love you," they took it from me and went away.

He died early the next morning with Prudence and Mayor Agbrigg beside him, and when they came to tell me I sat down and saw no reason to get up again. They told me they had given him my letter, that he had read it and understood it, but I didn't believe them. I had said to him so many times, "Giles, please love me." I had said, "I want you. I need you." But I had never told him that the gratitude, the desire to be warm and safe, the second-rate emotions he had settled for had started, slowly, to transform themselves into the total commitment I had longed to give him. And I believed he had died without being aware of it.

He had loved me, and I had not only lost him, I had failed him. I had held back from him. I had been too honest, refusing to say, "I am wildly in love with you," until it became the truth, not wishing to insult his integrity with even the whisper of a lie. Now I knew that I should have lied to him, since it would not have remained a lie for long, had already, for months, been very nearly true. And what I felt mainly was a hard anger, a bitter self-disgust. I was worthless. He had been important. There was no justice, nothing to believe in, just the blind, idiot-drooling of Chance, with which I did not care to associate.

A day passed—or so it seemed—and once again Mayor Agbrigg put his hard hands on me.

"I had a wife," he said, "a long time ago. We married young and we were poor and ignorant and content with each other. I never looked beyond her, and couldn't imagine a day when I'd be without her. We had eleven children, being young and ignorant, as I said—and lost ten of them, three in two days, something that happens often enough in Simon Street. But it was too much for my Ann. She turned inside herself, and died, of heartbreak, I reckon—leaving me with Jonas and a girl, Maria, who had a look of Ann, and died—you may remember—a year or two after I married your aunt Hannah."

"I don't care about that, Mayor Agbrigg. I know I should care, but I don't. I know that you're trying to help me. It doesn't help."

"No. Maybe it just helps *me* to talk about it. I've had more experience of losing than you have. But it still hurts me, lass, for all that. I was angry when my Ann died, like you are now, I reckon. By God, I was angry. I lived for her, you see, and she'd never harmed anybody. I hated the whole world the day I buried her. It passes, Faith, little by little."

"I don't care."

I didn't attend his funeral. I hadn't seen him die and I refused to watch them put that wooden box into the dry, summer ground, refused absolutely to contemplate what it contained. And when they came back from the churchyard to tell me who had been there and who had not, I wouldn't listen.

I sat in the dark, doing nothing. I put on the black dress Mrs. Guthrie got out for me and would have gone on wearing it until it hung in ribbons had she not taken it away from me and handed me another. I left the sheets on his bed and then, unable to sleep with his ghost—the nightmares that asked me was he really dead, since I had not seen him die—I moved my worthless, painful bones to the cold, narrow bedroom at the head of the stairs, a nun's cell, a place to do penance, and spoke sharply to Mrs. Guthrie when she tried to light the fire, to add a vase of flowers, an extra counterpane.

The cholera abated. For a day, a week, six weeks, there were no new cases. Three months passed and no one else died. And I didn't care about that either.

My mother went to France, Blaize to Germany to sell cloth, Georgiana miscarried a child whose conception she had not divulged, and was confined to her bed. Caroline began to issue invitations again. Mayor Agbrigg completed his purchase, on the town's behalf, of the waterworks company, and brought me his schemes and plans for the new reservoirs.

"Twenty-five miles of waterworks, lass," he told me, his craggy face warming as Jonas' never did. "Eleven reservoirs, when it's all done. A water area of over three hundred acres, with a cubic capacity of two thousand million gallons. Think of it, lass. They say I'm crazy, some of those colleagues of mine—plain crazy—but if I get what I want, and I shall, then there'll be no water shortage in Cullingford, no matter what. A tap in every house in Simon Street. I've said that often enough. The trouble is, they're all gentlemen on the council, lass, and they don't understand.

I'm the only one who's seen it from the inside, the only one who's lived in the muck, instead of just turning my nose up at it as I drove by. And my colleagues don't all see the point in spending all this money to provide something they're not short of themselves. But I'll get my way. I'll get my water. I spent the first forty years of my life dragging myself out of the gutter, and the next ten earning my place in the Piece Hall. Now I'll do something worth doing, lass—something *I* want, I reckon."

I didn't care.

Jonas called, when Celia had satisfied herself that my house was safe again, coming as a brother-in-law to offer his condolences and as Giles' lawyer to assure me that I was well provided for. It was of no interest to me.

My half brother, Crispin Aycliffe, wrote to me from London, expressing deep regret, suggesting he could come north to see me, or I south to him, if he could be of use. I didn't answer.

Aunt Verity, remaining in Bournemouth at the insistence of Uncle Joel, who had no intention of taking the slightest risk where she was concerned, wrote a long, warm letter, inviting me to stay with her. I didn't answer that either.

Mainly I sat in the dark, and would have remained there, perhaps, too long, passing the moment when it was still possible to open the door, to walk outside again, had not Prudence entered the room one afternoon, pulled back the curtains with a brisk hand, and said, "This is quite enough, Faith. He's dead. It was important to him to keep you alive, although if he could see you now he might wonder why. Look at you. Have you brushed your hair this week?"

"Leave me alone, Prudence."

"I have no intention of leaving you alone, make up your mind to it. You are coming upstairs now. You are going to make yourself respectable, and then we are going to Aunt Hannah's."

"Why Aunt Hannah's?"

"Because she has invited us, and it is necessary to make a start somewhere."

I got up because, knowing her stubborn nature, it was easier to obey than argue.

"You will have a mare's nest in your hair ere long," she said, taking a brush to it with a vengeance, hurting me deliberately, perhaps, in order to rouse me, although I was not aroused.

The late October sun was very bright as I went outside, very cruel with no tree foliage to shade it, dazzling me so that I was not obliged to look at anything as we drove up Millergate and Blenheim Lane, past my mother's house, and turned the steep corner which brought us to Lawcroft Fold.

The mill yard looked as it had always done, my aunt's house still there on the terraced slope above it, the sun glinting on the window where I had stood with Giles, at our first meeting, and watched the Chartists bringing their petition for the factory hands to sign. The Chartists were gone now, defeated, and I was defeated too. It didn't matter.

Aunt Hannah came into the hall to meet us, regal as always in her rustling purple, a handsome Barforth woman who had married a mill hand and made a mayor out of him, who had laboured at Prudence's side through the days of the cholera, and who must think me a poor, spineless creature, a nuisance. I believed her to be quite right.

"Sit down, dear," she said, and I sat.

"Will you take tea, dear?" And I took it, accepting milk and sugar, although I did not in fact care for sweet tea, because she had the sugar tongs in her hand, and I saw no point in asking her to put them down.

"Are you well, Faith?"

"Yes, quite well, thank you."

"Good. You are certainly very pale, but a little fresh air will put that right."

"I imagine so."

"You will have heard that Mayor Agbrigg's plans for the reservoirs are progressing well?"

"Yes. It is all very splendid."

"Your husband would have thought so."

"I believe he would."

"I am very sure of it. And, while we are on this obviously delicate subject—Mayor Agbrigg and I were both wondering, in view of Dr. Ashburn's undoubted services to the town . . . Well, dear, the fact is that old Miss Corey-Manning is to move to the coast to join her brother, which means, naturally, that her property is to come up for sale. The house is old and small and in a sorry state of disrepair but the gardens, as you may know, are extensive and extremely attractive. If my husband could persuade the town to purchase it, then it could be most easily converted into a park, the Giles Ashburn Memorial Gardens, we thought. Should you object to that?"

"Not in the least."

"You are very obliging, Faith," she said, putting down her cup and saucer rather sharply, allowing me to feel the snap of her impatience, her contempt for all silly females who engulfed themselves in melancholy when the world was so wide, when there was so much to do. "Yes, most obliging. I regret that your sister Celia is not so accommodating. I had hoped to persuade her to take tea with us today, but without success. You will have heard, I suppose, that she is in a delicate condition again? Well, she will insist on making herself into a recluse at such times, which cannot be good for her. I have told her repeatedly that we are all aware of the facts of life, that women do change their shape in pregnancy, but she has this morbid fear of being looked at—quite ridiculous. She should go about more and keep her spirits high. In fact—and I am sorry to have to say this—she should think of others, for a change, instead of dwelling so exclusively on herself. Jonas has his position to keep up, after all, and has as much right to her support as she to his. You did know she was expecting again?"

I did, but I failed to see how it concerned me. I had no child of my own, had been too preoccupied with loving, or not loving, Giles, to wonder why I had not conceived. Now it was too late.

Prudence made her excuses. She had another call to pay and would come back for me in an hour. I nodded, drank more tea, saw, quite clearly, that Aunt Hannah, who had never much cared for me, was trying to be kind and, somewhat vaguely—since it could not really matter—I wondered why.

"How is your mother, Faith?"

"Quite well, I believe. She writes that Paris is very gay again. She may be home, she says, by Christmastime."

"I am relieved to hear it. Her presence will be needed—and yours too—in the New Year. The concert hall is to be opened in April, and if it is to be dedicated to your father, then his widow and daughters must certainly be present. Naturally all building work has been delayed by the epidemic, a great many labourers were infected and the rest too drunk to be of service, but I have the most positive assurances that it will be ready in time. And so it should be. My word, it is a year now since the foundation stone was laid and I have heard nothing since then but excuses —architects and builders attempting to blind me with their expertise, telling me that construction is a slow process and that I must be patient. And now what do I hear? They are building a vast exhibition hall in London, of *glass*, my dear, to house this great international peep show in Hyde Park we are hearing so much about, and although it was only begun at the end of September—a week or two ago, in fact—they mean to have it ready for the grand opening in May. Seven months, my dear, no more, for something of quite colossal proportions, and all this eternity for one relatively modest provincial concert hall. However, one must only hope that Prince Albert and his committee are in possession of all the facts, for the man they have got to build it for them is quite extraordinary—a gardener, it seems, in the employ of the Duke of Devonshire. Yes, you may stare, a gardener. And although he attracted much notice by his construction of the conservatories on the duke's estate, one can only call him a brave man to undertake a project of this importance. Just think of it, Faith, a giant greenhouse to house exhibits from every corner of the world, and all the hundreds of thousands of men and women who will flock to examine them."

I thought of it, and found that I was not even mildly curious.

"My brother will be exhibiting something, I suppose," she went on, ignoring my polite but totally disinterested smile. "He scoffed at it to begin with, as did everyone else, but since there is to be a textile section and a prize to be won, I cannot imagine that my brother will let it go to someone else. I imagine we shall all be taking a trip to London next summer to congratulate him. That is something to look forward to at any rate."

"Yes, indeed it is."

She poured more tea, stirred her own cup reflectively, approaching, perhaps, the end of her patience.

"When you write to your mother again, Faith, you might mention that we have a slight problem with the concert hall. It has always been my intention that it should be dedicated to your father. His name was clearly stated when I sent out my original requests for subscriptions, and, until recently, I have considered the matter as being entirely settled. However, since the unfortunate accident to Sir Robert Peel—my dear, you cannot be unaware that he was killed, in July, by a fall from his horse? Really, Faith . . . Well—since then, it has been suggested to me that the hall should be dedicated to him. There is no denying the extent of his claims. He was a Prime Minister. He did abolish the Corn Laws, greatly to our advantage, while your father—as someone quite rudely pointed out—never served in anybody's cabinet. And recently, of course, even his building work, in some areas of Cullingford, has fallen into disrepute. But he was our member of Parliament for many years, he did contribute most generously towards local charities, and although it now appears that the quality of some of his lower-priced dwelling houses left much to be desired—in fact my husband means to use them as an example to persuade his colleagues to introduce building regulations— Well—times were different then. We were not so aware of sanitation, and one cannot doubt that had your father realised the consequences of poor drainage he would not have hesitated to put things right. But I see no point in involving myself, at this late stage, in arguments as to merit or lack of it. The project, from its very conception, was mine. The Aycliffe Hall it has always been, and I am quite determined to make a stand. I trust I may rely on your support?"

"Oh—absolutely." But she couldn't, and she knew she couldn't, for the Morgan Aycliffe Hall, the Robert Peel Hall, even the Giles Ashburn Hall, meant nothing to me.

"Very well," she said, straightening her back, smiling at me across the teacups, the smile I had seen her offer, sometimes, to Mrs. Hobhouse or Mrs. Mandelbaum, before the delivery of a telling blow. "And what is your news, Faith? Have you decided to wait until springtime to put your house up for sale?"

"I beg your pardon?"

"Springtime, dear. Much the best season for disposing of property, and that house of yours will not be easily disposed of. I always told you that Millergate was not a residential location and you will be lucky to get a decent price."

"Aunt Hannah, who on earth can have told you that I wish to sell my house?"

"Why, no one, dear," she said, giving me that cold smile again. "No one told me that it is Tuesday today either, but I am well aware of it. I am merely surprised that you have not already moved back to Blenheim Lane and left your Mrs. Guthrie to take care of the property until it is sold."

"Aunt Hannah, I have not the slightest intention of returning to live with my mother."

"Nonsense, dear," she said sweetly. "Of course you want to go home. And even if you did not, I cannot imagine any alternative. I have already asked Jonas to look about him for a possible buyer, and there is no reason at all why you should stay in Millergate and give yourself the trouble of entertaining strangers when they come to view. You may leave the management of your money entirely to Jonas, who will invest it most shrewdly and carefully, while the management of yourself must belong, once more, to your mother."

I put down my cup, feeling the need to keep my hands free, aware, beneath the fogbound ice in which my mind had been swimming, of a tiny, healthy spark that would—in a moment or two—be anger.

"I appreciate your concern, Aunt Hannah, but it is entirely misplaced. I shall be staying in Millergate."

"I think not."

"Then I am sorry to tell you that you are mistaken."

"Hardly, dear. You have always been scatterbrained, Faith, but even you could not be contemplating the possibility of living alone. You are far too young for that, and have far too little knowledge of the world. You may have been married, dear, but now your actual situation differs little from that of Prudence, except that you are somewhat the richer. No, no, you must return to Blenheim Lane at once. There is nowhere else for you to go, unless of course your mother should decide to marry again. Mr. Oldroyd, I understand, has been most pressing in that direction, and should she decide to take him—which would seem likely and not at all unsuitable—then you will be obliged to go with her to Fieldhead. I think you would find it a pleasant enough house in which to spend the time before you could decently consider a second marriage for yourself."

"Aunt Hannah," I said, hands clenched, a quite painful splintering inside my head as the ice gave way to let that spark of anger leap through. "How dare you say that to me?"

"I dare say anything I choose to you, dear," she told me,

remaining completely calm. "You were an excellent matrimonial catch in the first place, you know. But now that you have an additional income and are quite pleasant to look at, you will soon find yourself in demand again. Emma-Jane Hobhouse has already mentioned your name to me in connection with Freddy, since Prudence is so slow to make up her mind. And although I could not recommend him, the way things are going at Nethercoats, there will be plenty of others. No dear, we shall have no trouble at all in settling you."

"No," I told her, shaking with a most uncharacteristic fury. "You will have no trouble in settling me, because I will not be settled."

"Really? You mean to be defiant then—and rude?"

"Possibly, and I am sorry for that."

"And what *do* you mean to do with yourself, for I am bound to warn you that if you continue to sit in the dark and brood, then it is not only your aunt who will recommend your return to parental control—I believe that both Dr. Overdale and Dr. Blackstone would insist upon it."

"That will not be necessary."

"I wonder."

"Then please do not take the trouble. I am twenty-one years old, Aunt Hannah. I am no schoolroom chit, to be disposed of like a parcel—with no more sense than a parcel. I am a woman who has been married and I will decide what is to be done with me. I shall stay in Millergate, or I shall go elsewhere, but it will be my choice. I promised to obey my husband, and I did obey him, but I have never promised to obey anybody else. I am not sure what my rights are, but I am sure they exist and if Jonas will not explain them to me then I shall find someone who will. I don't believe that any of you—any longer—have the power to interfere."

"Good," she said, again with the utmost composure. "I cannot agree with you, of course. You may be of full age, but you are quite incapable of managing either your money or yourself. A widow of twenty-one years, my dear, must be a prey to every kind of malicious gossip, to every unscrupulous male—of which there are very many—and to every possible temptation, which you do not strike me as being strong-minded enough to resist. It is a most unsuitable arrangement, and I shall continue to 'interfere' with it as much as I please. If you persist in this folly, then I shall consider it my duty to keep a strict eye on you, and shall require Jonas to do the same. However, I shall pardon your rudeness, since even your display of ill-nature and poor judgement is preferable to the poor little drab who crept in to take tea with me an hour ago."

And she smiled at me again.

"Thank you," I said after a while, and looking round, imagining I had heard Prudence returning, I saw the sun, flooding through the window again, bringing me not only the memory of Giles, standing there so quietly, explaining to me the six points of the People's Charter, but Aunt Hannah herself walking down to the garden gate, and my mother telling us, "Poor Hannah. She is making a pilgrimage. She has gone down there so that we shall not see her cry."

And taking advantage of her unexpected compassion, which I knew would not last, I asked her, "Aunt Hannah, my mother told me once that you were to have married Aunt Verity's brother . . ."

"Edwin Barforth," she said, understanding why, and how much, I needed to know. "Yes. He was murdered down there in the mill yard, while I sat in the millhouse and made plans for our wedding day. The old millhouse has gone now. It was pulled down, some years ago, when Mr. Agbrigg and I felt the need for a larger garden to accommodate a carriage drive. Look —you may see from the window—it stood there, near the gate, just a small house, although it seemed ample to me then, and indeed, oddly enough, Mr. Agbrigg lived there, with Jonas, when he first became manager at Lawcroft. And I spent my first year there too, as his wife. Things turn out very strangely, do they not? I should have gone into that house as Mrs. Edwin Barforth. I eventually occupied it as Mrs. Ira Agbrigg. And now the house is not there at all. It was used for offices before we pulled it down."

"Did it trouble you?"

"Demolishing it? I don't think so. Aunt Verity seemed more moved than I, since she and Edwin were both born there. She was sixteen the night Edwin died, and I was twenty-three—Edwin a year older. We had been childhood sweethearts, I suppose one might call it, and I had grown up believing my future could

only be with him. It happened a little after suppertime. Verity
had gone outside and wandered down to the mill, shocked and
upset, of course, since she had seen her father killed by Luddite
rioters the night before. Edwin and I stayed at the millhouse,
telling each other we would soon be married, but I began to be
alarmed about Verity and sent him to fetch her. We believed
there was no danger. The Luddites had been rounded up, were
on their way to be hanged at York. But one had made his escape
and had come back to set fire to the mill— Foolish boy. He had
brought a kitchen knife with him, a common carving knife, and
when Edwin tried to arrest him there was a scuffle . . . My
brother Joel found them, ten minutes later, Verity screaming,
Edwin dying . . ."

"And that is why you went down to the gate when the
Chartists were here—to the place where the millhouse used to
be?"

"Did I? Yes, I suppose I may have done so. Quite stupid of
me. Is there anything else, of these matters which do not concern you at all, that you wish to know?"

"Do you think of him still?"

She smiled, Aunt Hannah who might not be kind to me tomorrow, who would certainly interfere with my life, would pry
and attempt to manipulate me every bit as much as she had
promised, but who was ready to help me now.

"I thought of him every day of my life—for a year or two—
and I believed it would always be so. And that was hard. But
then, I came to realise, quite gradually, that I could not exactly
recall the lines of his face—that he was slipping away. And that
was much harder. I tried, for a while, to bring him back but I
am an honest woman and I was forced to acknowledge that I
had lost him. That was not easy. Other matters intervened, you
see—not least a husband and an exceedingly brilliant son. No, I
rarely think of him any more. He was a young man of twenty-
four, I am a woman well into middle-life. What could we have
to say to each other now? I would recognise him—perhaps—but
he would certainly not recognise me. Come dear, I believe Prudence is returning—and you will not forget what I told you
about the concert hall?"

I shook my head, straightened myself, not strong precisely—
not yet—but stronger.

"Prudence," she called out, "I would like you now—since you seem to have possession of your mother's horses—to deliver a message to Celia. And since you are bound to pass the Mandelbaums' on your way you may step inside for a moment and tell them . . ."

And I knew I would not return to my sick hole again.

Chapter Seventeen

THE MORGAN AYCLIFFE HALL, which, in spite of all delays and anxieties as to rising costs, had not exceeded Aunt Hannah's original estimate of 20,000 pounds, opened, as promised, the following April with a musical festival Aunt Hannah declared should be an annual event.

The hall itself, a solid structure of Yorkshire stone, a soft, mellow shade of brown that April morning, although we knew it would soon be blackened, like everything else, by its share of Cullingford soot, was a fitting memorial for any man. The entrance, flanked by Corinthian columns, opened into a vestibule from which a much ornamented staircase extended two wide arms, giving access to stalls and galleries where three thousand persons could sit, some of them more comfortably than others, and improve their minds. And here, during that first week in April, I sat every evening, the widow of the deeply regretted Dr. Ashburn, the daughter of the now almost forgotten Morgan Aycliffe, imbibing a strong diet of Handel, Bach, Haydn, and Beethoven—selected largely by the Mandelbaums—while Aunt Hannah, who was tone-deaf, accepted her personal applause, drawing our attention—since the music defeated her—to the impressive proportions of the organ, the fact that the orchestra contained no less than eighty instruments, the choir more than a hundred singers.

My mother, attired in a different, pastel-tinted evening gown at every performance—since her mourning, for a son-in-law, had already ended—was presented with a bouquet of spring flowers at the conclusion of the proceedings and melted, most oblig-

ingly, into tears. Celia, who had miscarried early this time, and
was consequently well enough to attend, joined poignantly in
the weeping, although I doubted if her recollections of our late
parent were either particularly clear or particularly fond. Prudence, in dove-grey half-mourning with a stylish fall of white
lace at neck and sleeves, remained dry-eyed, while I, in black
beaded with evening jet, could see no reason for tears, preferring my mother's speedy return to laughter when Mr. Oldroyd of
Fieldhead began to ply her with champagne.

"You'll dine with me, all of you, at Fieldhead," he announced,
almost a declaration in itself since Fieldhead had seen no guests
since the day his thin, eternally ailing wife had been carried out
of it. And, seated at his table, I concluded that if my mother
chose to make herself mistress of this sombre but substantial
house and of the splendid mill just across the way, then it was
her concern, and Prudence's concern, not mine.

"If she marries him," I told my sister, "then I think we might
extract their permission for you to live with me."

"If she marries him," Prudence replied, "then she will regret
it, for he is as gloomy and pernickety a man as my father. If she
marries him, I will not be the only one obliged to ask his consent
every time I wish to cross the street. He will keep a tight hold
on her purse strings, and she will not enjoy it."

But Aunt Hannah, mistrusting the lightness of my mother's
character and anxious to see her settled before she disgraced us
all, was more concerned with Mr. Oldroyd's finances than with
his personality.

"It would be an excellent arrangement," she told us, having
quite made up her mind to it. "Matthew Oldroyd has no children and no close relatives. The Hobhouses may behave as if
they were his kith and kin, but in fact Mr. Hobhouse was only
his first wife's brother, which would count for nothing should he
marry again. Depend upon it, if your mother takes him, she will
inherit a second fortune and Fieldhead mill with it . . . My
word, I have never spoken to Jonas about the spinning trade,
but I do believe that if Elinor ever found herself with Fieldhead
on her hands, Jonas would know how to manage it most profitably . . . And since one third of it would be bound to pass, eventually, to Celia, it could be a very great thing for him—for them
both, for, between ourselves, I have given up all hope of Celia

ever making herself into a political wife. I believe the very idea of Westminster would throw her into a fit of the vapours. Yes—Fieldhead—my goodness, girls, I must consult most carefully with Jonas, for if a marriage is to take place, then the contract should be very precise . . ."

But, although Prudence bristled and retaliated in kind, I knew how much my aunt and her husband had done for me and was less susceptible now, in any case, to small irritations.

I was calm now. I brushed my hair again, night and morning, until it shone silver in anybody's candlelight, valuing it again as my only claim to beauty. I wore a black velvet ribbon around my neck at dinnertime, long drops of jet in my ears, scented my skin, listened with smiling attention to anyone who chose to talk to me. But I did it, as I did everything these days, not to please my family, not to please a man, but to please myself. My house was warm now and well polished, my cat purring amiably in her basket by the fender. I had wine for my guests, and conversation, my windows were open in the good weather, letting in air which many considered unhealthy, and light they thought imprudent, since it would damage my carpet and my complexion. I came and went as I pleased, although in fact I did not venture very far, an occasional visit to Listonby or to Tarn Edge, a weekly pilgrimage to Giles' grave, although I found very little of him there, a stroll in the Ashburn Gardens, which I had myself declared open by unveiling a statue supposedly of Giles, but which could have been any frock-coated, top-hatted gentleman. I was quietly, almost imperceptibly, free. Mrs. Guthrie, whose loyalty had been to Giles, had left me to the ministrations of a Mrs. Marworth, who was loyal to nothing but the twenty-five pounds a year I gave her. I was not happy. I did not even think about happiness. I was calm. And it was enough.

In June Caroline gave birth to a third son, exactly two years after her twins, a Master Gideon Chard, even bigger and darker than his brothers had been, so noisy and so imperious in his demands for attention that nurse was soon ordered to take him away.

"I suppose this one will go into the church," Caroline told me, receiving me in the lavish, deep-armchaired comfort of the Great Hall, having got out of bed a scandalous seven days after her confinement since, as always, she was expecting guests and had no time to play the invalid.

"Yes—that is the way it is done, Faith. The second son for the army, the third for the church, the fourth for the high seas—and if there is a fifth, one sends him out to the colonies, I believe, to make his fortune so that when he comes back one can pretend his money was not got from trade. Well, young Gideon can have the church here, at Listonby, to begin with since our vicar will be quite senile and happy to step down when the time comes. But I think he had best go to Oxford first to make some suitable acquaintances, especially when one considers that all the fashionable parishes seem to be in the south."

"In fact you mean to make a bishop of him?"

"Well—of course I do, Faith. Naturally I want to see him at the top of his tree, whatever it is. If one takes the trouble to do something, then one should do it right."

"Yes. I have heard your father say so many a time."

"And what is wrong with that?" she asked sharply, ready as always to do battle at the slightest hint that Barforth values could in any way be criticised—so ready, in fact, that I concluded they often were. "I will tell you this much, Faith. I am extremely fond of Matthew's family but if some of them would be ready to listen to my father, then they would not suffer for it. One has only to look at the Clevedons. My goodness, it is all very well to be charitable but Mr. Clevedon simply cannot afford it, and if one dared to suggest that Peregrine should give some thought to *earning* a living—well, I have learned not to make suggestions of that kind. Matthew merely smiled when I did so, but Georgiana was quite scandalised. 'He is the heir,' she said. 'There is the land.' And that was that. Well, my Dominic is the heir and he will not be required to earn a living either. But our land is not encumbered and if he shows an interest in politics I shall not discourage him—even though he is bound to be a protectionist and want the Corn Laws back again."

"You will have a Prime Minister, then, as well as a colonel and a bishop."

And although we laughed together we both knew that if Caroline made up her mind to it, it was not impossible.

"I do not see enough of you, Faith, these days," she said. "As soon as you are out of mourning, or into half-mourning, then I want you to come on a really long visit. In fact, since widow's weeds go on so long, I see no reason to delay longer than the autumn—and I would be glad of you then. The house will be full to bursting from September to March and you know how it is in the hunting season—so many women sitting around all day in need of entertaining. And although the men are out from dawn to dusk they enjoy a change of female company in the evenings. One would think so much fresh air might make them sleepy, but not a bit of it. In fact some of them tend to be quite giddy, and it would be a relief to have a woman in the house I can trust. You will be going to the Exhibition, of course? Yes, so I supposed. Well—I shall not, for Matthew and his friends have made up their minds to ignore it, which seems quite ridiculous since it has spread itself out all over Hyde Park. But there it is. They are all protectionists, you see, who do not care for Free Trade, and are telling each other that the Exhibition is strictly for the middle classes—an opinion I find hard to understand when Prince Albert virtually organised it singlehanded, and the Queen has been going there every day. In fact Matthew and I have had our very first quarrel over it. If I want to look at industrial machines, he tells me, then I may go and stand an hour in my father's weaving sheds. Naturally, he was sorry afterwards—extremely sorry, in fact—and I was sorry too. I could see how hurt he was when I declared I would go with my father. I rather expected him to forbid it, but he actually said, 'Please don't,' which touched me, I admit it. Anyway, I have decided not to go, so all is well again. Come to see me as soon as you return and tell me how easily my father has won all the prizes."

To begin with even Cullingford itself had not thought too highly of Prince Albert's Great International Exhibition, this scheme of displaying manufactured goods and the machines that made them beneath an extravagant glass house in Hyde Park; Cullingford being more concerned with getting its own manufactures out of the country at advantageous prices than with letting possible competitors so freely in. But, as Aunt Hannah had said, when it became known that there were prizes to be won, at the discretion of a jury half British and half foreign, Law Valley men concluded they might as well win them, and there was no doubt that Barforth fancy worsteds would be most prominently displayed.

The monster conservatory—Prince Albert's Crystal Palace—had been duly completed, its transparent walls covering an incredible nineteen acres of Hyde Park, enclosing within its structure the elm trees which no one had wished to cut down. It was more than three times larger than St. Paul's Cathedral, it was constructed in such a way that it could be dismantled and moved elsewhere at need, and had taken, in all, just seven months to build. It was magnificent, impossible, a brilliant conception, a madman's folly, according to one's point of view. It would not take the strain, it would fall down and shatter, killing thousands, it would be a breeding ground for the diseases, the vice, and corruption so many foreigners would be certain to bring with them. Something would surely go wrong with it, and when it was discovered that there were sparrows happily nesting in the branches beneath the glass roof, ready to foul exhibits and exhibitors alike with their droppings, and that shotguns, obviously, could not be used to dislodge them, one saw more than a few complacent smiles, a multitude who were very ready to say, "I told you so." But they, and the sparrows, had not reckoned on the Duke of Wellington, who, stamping irritably from his retirement at the Queen's request, had spat out the one deadly solution. "Sparrow hawks"; and within days the sparrows had fled.

The Exhibition opened on the first of May to a salute of guns, which did not—as had been predicted—shatter the glass walls. It remained open until October, Queen Victoria and her children coming regularly, drawing more stares herself, perhaps, than the acres of industrial and agricultural machinery, the triumphs of engineering and architecture, which had given such prosperity to her reign.

Aunt Verity and Uncle Joel, who had recently purchased a pleasant house near Bournemouth, went south in April, my uncle prepared, it seemed, if only temporarily, to leave his personal empire in the hands of Nicholas and Blaize. And since the railways were offering cheap rates—Cullingford to London and back for five shillings for the duration of the show—and London was sprouting with lodginghouses where respectable working-men could obtain bed and board for as little as threepence a day, a great many of our mechanics and artisans went south too, for the first time in their lives.

"London is teeming with them," my mother wrote from the house of an old political friend of my father's, "so quiet and well behaved you can't imagine, dressed up in their Sunday best. No drinking, no fighting, such as one sees in Cullingford. Incredible. And, of course, the foreigners, darling—quite sinister, some of them. One sees quite well that they are all revolutionaries come to lose themselves in the crowd, since they are welcome nowhere else. Do come, dear. The Exhibition itself is nothing but a vast bazaar, I must warn you, for one can have a surfeit, quite quickly I find, of gazing at machines, and there is little else to see that one could not pick up easily enough in Millergate. However—there are certainly acquaintances to be made, and naturally, if all goes well, there may even be knighthoods to be won. They tell me the Queen is in a mood to be very gracious to certain gentlemen who have offered her husband their support—who have backed his scheme, in fact, when the protectionist, fox-hunting set can do nothing but hope for hailstones, which would certainly tear his Crystal Palace down. Do come."

And once again I was aware of the division of ranks I had seen in operation all my life, the fox-hunting gentlemen of the Shires, for whom the whole concept of internationalism was repugnant, who saw this princely exhibition as no more than a vulgar display of trade-begotten wealth: and the cool, commercial men of the cities, who regarded no wealth as vulgar, and for whom the world, and its markets, could not be opened wide enough.

My sister Celia, disliking crowds, disliking heat and noise, disliking anything, it seemed, which would take her from the shelter of her own drawing room, had no inclination for the journey, but Aunt Hannah, having secured a fortnight's accommodation in the London house of Mr. Fielding, our member of Parliament, was ready to include both Prudence and myself in her party.

"Jonas will explain it all to you," she told us. "He will take excellent care of you." And we believed her, for although she had not gone so far as to regret the impossibility of his marrying all three of us, she was increasingly anxious that we should learn to depend on his judgement, to submit ourselves, in financial matters at least, to his authority.

Jonas, of course, was no longer a poor man, but both he and his step-mamma were aware that he had still a long, expensive way to travel before reaching that golden pinnacle of which his childhood brilliance had encouraged her to dream. And perhaps because, in Aunt Hannah's view, Celia had let him down, proving too timid, too nervous to suit his needs, she had come to regard it as logical and right that Prudence and I should make up the deficiency.

Should we remain unmarried we would be very likely to leave what we had to Jonas' children, in the event of Celia managing to carry one to full term, and, if not, to Celia herself. Should we remain unmarried, our social skills, which Celia sadly lacked, could, without any impropriety, be devoted to Jonas, since the world would have nothing but praise for a woman who graced her brother-in-law's table, entertained his guests, supported his ambitions, disciplined his children, in order to relieve the burdens of an ailing wife. Should we remain unmarried. And so, without meaning either of us the slightest harm—being quite convinced that we would be much better off, much safer with Jonas—she kept a watchful eye on Freddy Hobhouse whenever he approached Prudence, making short work of both Mrs. Hobhouse and Mrs. Mandelbaum when, in turn, they offered to take us to London.

"My nieces will be accompanying me," she told them in a voice that permitted no argument, but in the end only Prudence made the trip, returning to tell me that although Jonas had treated her as if she had been a schoolgirl, he had been quite informative on occasions, rather more human, she believed, on the days when the monumental splendours of the Machinery Court, the thrust and jostle of the galleries, had proved too much for Aunt Hannah and had obliged her to remain at home.

"It is really not to be missed, Faith, since it is not likely to happen again. You should go."

But I hesitated, decided against it, and then, as the anniversary of Giles' death approached, I took fright and was persuaded by Aunt Verity to go down to London and visit the Exhibition on the expensive, exclusive Friday and Saturday, and then to be her guest in Bournemouth for a week or two.

It was the hottest part of August, intense in all its colours, all its odours, the richness of grass and flowers pollen-heavy at the summer's end, the park swollen with its excited but orderly crowds, the crystal mansion itself an enormous, many-faceted diamond in the sun, every bit as miraculous as I had expected.

"We will take it in stages, my dear," Aunt Verity told me, lingering at the breakfast table of the very cosy little house she had taken for the season. "It is very vast and very fatiguing. There are pretty things and fearful things, and things which seem to have neither rhyme nor reason. And quite splendid things. My dear, in the civil engineering section they have a model of Liverpool docks with more than a thousand rigged ships—it is quite amazing. Gird yourself, darling, for at the risk of throwing you into a fit of the vapours I had best warn you that there are something in the region of fourteen thousand exhibitors. You will need a good pair of boots, and a smelling bottle."

Vast indeed and, for a while, exciting to be a part of that international throng, snatches of foreign speech, glances from liquid, foreign eyes returning me to the carefree journeyings I had made with my mother, her "special time," her butterfly days which she had known even then could not last. But, as my mother had said, once I had marvelled at the twenty-four-ton block of coal at the entrance, the crystal fountain refreshing the nave, the 1,500 feet of Cullingford exhibits, dominated, one was obliged to notice, by the Barforths; when I had spent an amusing half-hour watching the medal-making machine with its steady production of 50 medals a minute, the envelope-making machine with its even more impressive output of 2,700 envelopes an hour; when I had admired the texture of Aubusson tapestries, of Turkish silks and Indian pearls, the gleaming blades of Bowie knives, made in Sheffield for American Indian-fighters; when I had marvelled at household furnishings and fittings of every conceivable shape and size and ornamentation and my aunt and I had further amused ourselves by guessing the possible uses to which many of them could be applied, I discovered that machines have a tendency to look very much alike when one has seen several hundred of them, and I was not sorry to go outside.

Blaize, who had spent the winter abroad, escorted us about the Machinery Court on our second day, looking bronzed and handsome and very much in his natural habitat, having so many acquaintances now, both in London and overseas, that he could move through this cosmopolitan crowd with the ease of a man in his own drawing room. But I had seen little of him since Giles died, his light nature disliking too close a contact with life's harsher realities, and it was Uncle Joel himself who supplied us with lemonade, found us a seat in the shade, entertained us to a prolonged and lavish luncheon, and then—unwilling to leave his wife to the mercy of underlings—saw us on our way to Bournemouth.

Their new house, "Rosemount," which had been described to me as a "holiday cottage," was, of course, quite grand, a white-painted villa in a landscaped acre set high above the pleasant, hilly little town, its rooms a shade impersonal, being new and freshly decorated in apple-greens, mossy tints of lilac and rose, but spacious, airy, offering an undisturbed view of a green hillside scattered with poppies, scented with the freshness of blue air and a peaceful, sun-flecked summer sea.

"We shall be quiet for a day or so," Aunt Verity said, "and I confess I shall be glad of it."

But the Barforths were never quiet for long, the very next morning bringing a smart, highly polished landau to the door containing a dimpled, mischievous little lady—my mother—peering at us from the shade of an enormous ruched and frilled bonnet and an elaborate, ivory-handled parasol, accompanied by a gentleman I had never seen before, a curly-haired Irishman somewhere in middle-life but by no means in the state of decay of which she had been complaining. He was, in fact, well fleshed, square-cut, dark eyes that were never still, that noticed, I thought, even as he handed my mother down from the carriage, the graceful slenderness of Aunt Verity's figure, my own blond skin, a smile perpetually tilting the corners of his restless, possibly insolent, but certainly well-formed mouth.

"Good heavens," Aunt Verity said, scattering the rose petals she had been gathering for potpourri, "surely—it is Mr. Adair?"

"The very same, ma'am," he told her. "Absolutely at your service. You'll pardon the intrusion, I know, for I couldn't resist the temptation of making the acquaintance of Elinor's daughter."

And feeling that this was perhaps a man not much given to the resisting of temptation—a man, in fact, who liked to be tempted—I held out my hand, finding his grip firm and warm, if a trifle too much inclined to linger.

"Mrs. Ashburn," he said, his merry eyes concentrating totally on my face, inviting me to believe that for as long as his hand was in mine no other woman existed.

"Mr. Adair."

"She's beautiful," he said to my mother, still gazing at me, a man, it seemed, who appreciated his own charm and knew how to use it, who had relied on it, perhaps, more than once, to ensure his survival.

"Of course," my mother said. "Could any daughter of mine be otherwise? Faith, this is Mr. Daniel Adair, who was employed—a long time ago—by your father. You will give us tea, Verity, will you not? And then I am afraid we cannot stay. I simply thought you might care to renew your acquaintance with Mr. Adair, and would be interested to see that I had renewed mine. We are returning to London later in the day. Daniel, you may take my arm across the grass, for I declare the sun has weakened me—or something has at any rate."

And understanding from the sparkling quality of her laughter, the languorous, faintly wicked but completely joyful glances she had once bestowed on M. Fauret and Signor Marchetti, that she had taken another lover, I was amused at the thought of Mr. Oldroyd—who might still become her husband—and I was glad for her.

Georgiana arrived with her maid the following Friday, worn out, she said, and bored to distraction by London, her views on crystal palaces, on internationalism, on this pandering by royalty to the middle classes, exactly matching Matthew Chard's.

"Well, the city was always a poxy place," she said. "I must get it out of my system one way or another," and helping herself not to the suggested tea and cakes but to a bottle of red wine, she went out into the garden and remained there, sprawling gypsy-fashion on the grass, drinking and dozing, plaiting daisy chains with a listless hand, so that when Nicholas and his father appeared she was sufficiently mellowed to throw her arms around her husband's neck and bite him, quite hard I thought, on the ear.

"You've got grass in your hair," he told her.

"Yes. And I've been asleep with my face in the sun, which is going to make me as brown as a peg-hawker. I've had a glass of wine too, darling, which has made me feel—oh—very glad to see you."

They went off to their bedroom to change for dinner, my aunt and uncle to theirs, and spending a moment or two longer in the garden, since my own dressing, with no one to help or hinder me, would take less time, I eventually followed them. My black beaded evening dress and its half-dozen petticoats were laid ready on the bed, a cheerful, fresh-faced girl of the type Aunt Verity always had about her waiting to assist me. My silver-backed brushes, my black velvet ribbons, the perfume my sister Celia considered too exotic for a lady, scandalous for a widow, were all to hand. And as I brushed out my hair, peering at myself in the mirror with accustomed concentration, it could not matter to me that in the room next to mine Nicholas Barforth was very probably making love to his wife. It *did* not matter to me. I had not spoken a dozen words to him these past three years beyond the bounds of common politeness. I was better acquainted now with the unusual, annoying, facinating creature he had married than with Nicholas himself. But I had been obliged recently, by events totally beyond my control, to admit that my body, like my mother's, had acquired the need for a man's caresses and had proved far less docile, these past few months, than I liked.

Emotion did not trouble me. Emotionally I was cool and serene, indulging myself, as I had always done, with a little humour, a little vanity, remembering, even in these mourning garments, how to make my hair paler by running a black velvet ribbon through it, the effect of dark jet earrings against a fair skin, nothing to break the stark elegance of black and white but a pair of blue eyes, which, because they were shortsighted and weak, looked vague and cloudy and—one hoped—mysterious. And I took these pains, resorted to this artifice, not for the admiration of Nicholas or anyone else, but because beneath them I was still the plain, lanky girl my father had despised; and I would not let her show.

Cool, then, in the daylight, composed, even, with a branch of bedtime candles in my hand; less so when my disobedient body woke me in the night, or, worse than that, carried me in my sleep to the brink of an unfulfilled sensation and abandoned me there, the pit of my stomach burning, my limbs aching, straining to grasp that extra moment which would give me the relief I craved, and which was always denied. Relief, not love. Yet, as I well knew, the only relief available to me was in remarriage, and since that was still unthinkable I had no choice but to endure— as my father had taught me—with dignity.

I was the first to join my aunt and uncle in the drawing room that night, Nicholas and Georgiana lingering upstairs, Blaize not yet arrived, my uncle by no means pleased at the delay.

"He left London two days ago, and in a damned hurry at that. And now where the devil is he?"

But Blaize, who was fond of a good entrance, made one now, heralded by a mighty clattering of hooves and tearing-up of gravel, flinging his hat and cane to an eager parlourmaid and sauntering to greet us already in his evening clothes.

"I changed—*en route*," he said, the perfection of his attire proof enough that it had not been in a carriage. "And if I've kept you waiting I know you'll forgive me, Mamma, since I *am* your favourite son—which leads me to wonder where your other son has got to?"

"He's here," Nicholas said, coming into the room, Georgiana a step or two behind him, her green silk dress certainly expensive, its lace trim quite exquisite, but put on anyhow, shrugged on at the last moment with laughter and whispering, her body still languorous with pleasure, her bright hair ready, at the first of her abrupt movements, to come swishing and tumbling down.

"I presume we may eat now?" Uncle Joel said, and so we ate, a delicious meal, as Aunt Verity's meals always were, Nicholas eating to satisfy his appetite, Blaize with a shade more appreciation than that, Georgiana pecking sparrow-like at this and the other, drinking, "to drown the memory of London," she said, raising her glass, and then, "To the memory of green meadows and pastures."

"To ploughed fields and muddy ditches," Blaize answered her, refilling her glass, leaning across the table to tuck a loose strand of her hair back into its uncertain, copper-tinted coil, his eyes straying, perhaps only from force of habit, to the low neck of her dress.

"To wet moorland mornings," she toasted him.

"To wind and foul weather," he replied.

"Don't you hate London, Faith?" she asked me.

"No. I like it. I like cities altogether."

"Yes," she said, considering me, her head on one side, her glass, I noticed, empty again. "I suppose they suit you—you're so polished and sculptured and poised. I can't even imagine you in a flutter. Oh, Faith—Faith—why is it you always do things right, whereas I—? It's not fair. Why do you look like a swan, when I'm such a bedraggled duck . . . ? Doesn't she look like a swan, Nicky? Blaize, doesn't she?"

"She does," Blaize said, raising his glass to me. "A very gracious, clever swan, my Faith."

"*Your* Faith," Nicholas said, looking up sharply, scowling through the candlelight.

"Oh my," Georgiana chuckled, her tipsy face alive with delighted mischief. "Goodness gracious—wishful thinking, eh, Blaize? My brother Perry took a fancy to her too—oh yes he did —he saw her at that dreadful concert hall and very nearly had a fit. Who is she? *How* is she?—possible, likely, not one chance in a million? Get her to Galton, little sister, and . . ."

"That," Nicholas said through his teeth, "is enough. Georgiana, I warn you . . ."

"Oh lovely, he's angry with me," she said, bathing us all in her smiles. And then, just as abruptly, her flaunting recklessness changed to a quite touching remorse.

"Oh, dear. Faith, I do apologise. I like you so much, and I wouldn't upset you for the world."

"I'm not upset."

"You must be."

"Only if you insist on it. I think I'd rather feel flattered instead —although I can't agree that you look like a duck, Georgiana."

"Nor I," Blaize murmured, smiling at me. "A little bird of the wild wood, perhaps, swimming all bewildered and amazed in a duck pond. How's that?"

We went back into the drawing room, disposing ourselves suitably, Aunt Verity's eyes watching both her sons with care, ready, as she had always been, to step between them.

"Shall we go for a walk in the moonlight, Nicky?" Georgiana said, offering a reconciliation.

"Presently. Blaize, I met a friend of yours from New York yesterday morning. A Mr. Grassmann."

"Oh yes. A pleasant fellow."

"So he seems. But before you make promises about delivery dates you could check with me that they're possible."

"Ah well," Blaize shrugged. "It's just that I have such confidence in you, Nicky—never so much as crossed my mind that you wouldn't be able to manage."

"It should always be possible," Uncle Joel cut in from the luxurious ease of his armchair. "I don't want to hear excuses about deliveries that can't be met. I always met mine."

"Well, you're damn well going to hear them, Father," Nicholas snapped, "unless you can make him understand that when the looms are working to capacity he ought at least to know about it and make his arrangements to suit. I'm not complaining about the orders he brings in. He looks after his side of the business all right, and I look after mine. But we've got to keep each other informed. And you've got to follow things through, Blaize. This Mr. Grassmann was looking for you, the other morning, not me. And where the hell were you? And what am I supposed to say to him when he tells me what you've promised him, and I know there's no chance of it—unless we expand again."

"Which is what you want, Nick," Blaize murmured.

"Do I?"

"I reckon so—unless you're finding it too much, with the wool combers on your hands—"

"And what would you know about it?"

"It's so warm in here," Aunt Verity informed us, intending to be believed. "Joel, come out into the garden—if we're to expand again there's no need to do it tonight, and I have a most interesting word to say to you about Elinor. Nicholas, do take your wife for that walk in the moonlight. Faith will go with you—and Blaize, one supposes, will do—well—exactly what Blaize supposes."

"Mother dear," he told her, laughing. "You couldn't possibly be cross with me, could you? No—of course you couldn't."

"Sometimes I think I could make the effort, dear—really." But they were smiling at each other, even my uncle—although he muttered that in his case it was no effort at all—looking good-humoured enough as he took his wife's arm and led her outside.

It was an intense blue midnight, velvet-textured, quite beautiful, the grass fragrant with sleeping poppies, the sea moving in a gentle, lullaby-rocking some way below us; a time, it seemed, for steady pathways, for breathing deeply, quietly, for listening. But after a moment or two of strolling, Georgiana, abandoning her little-girl air of decorum, became a restive colt again, impatient of all restraint.

"Let's go down to the sea, Nicky."

"You said a walk in the moonlight. This is a walk in the moonlight."

"Oh, I suppose it may be thought so in Cullingford. But when there is sand down there, and sea water and rocks, how can you bear to stay so tamely on the grass?"

"I can bear it."

"I can't," she said, and taking up her skirts, she was off, flinging down a challenge as I had once seen her do at Galton Abbey, except that this time nobody followed her.

"It's wonderful," she called up to us. "Oh—do come down— it's not living, up there, on the path, it's just doing the right thing. And who really cares about that. Do come down here— we could fetch some wine and fruit and stay up all night to watch the sun rise. Why shouldn't we? It's something to *do*, something we can remember—not the night we slept in our comfortable beds at Rosemount, but the night we spent on the beach—the night we did something different, that we—well, I won't say it, Nicky, because you'll kill me—but you know what I mean. We'd never forget that. Do come."

But Nicholas, who may have been excited by her earlier in the day, was moved now to do no more than shrug his shoulders and turn his head away, the better to light his cigar against the wind.

She disappeared, hidden by a curve of rock and, as we paused, Blaize glanced at his brother and said, "I can see you don't mean to go after her."

"No."

"Well, it's none of my business, of course, but she's had more than a glass or two, and she could fall—"

"I doubt it."

"Or she could wander off and get lost."

"She'll not do that."

"Ah well. I don't want to get my feet wet either, but really, Nicholas—I suppose the answer is that if it worries me I should go and fetch her myself?"

"That's about it. My guess is you won't find her, and she'll be back here before you are. You'll ruin your shoes for nothing—but, as you say, if it worries you—"

Blaize shrugged and walked off gingerly towards the beach, not liking his task at all since he was a man who cared about his shoes and appreciated their value, leaving us quite alone and, for a moment completely silent.

"She will be all right, you know," he said.

"Yes, of course."

"Are you cold?"

"No. I'm perfectly all right."

"Faith—?"

"Yes?"

"I'm sorry—about your husband, I mean. I didn't know him very well but he seemed a decent man. How have you been—since he died?"

"I can cope with it, Nicholas. Georgiana was extremely good to me, during the epidemic."

"Yes. She can be very kind."

Silence again, waiting and listening to the night, wishing that Blaize would return, feeling, not awkwardness exactly, not emotion, but something akin to sorrow that even now, when so much time and pain and joy, so much living, had flowed between us, I was still not at peace with him.

"You *are* like a swan," he said suddenly, making the words into an accusation, and because it was the only possible thing to do, I laughed—my mother's laugh—airy, without substance.

"You mean I have a long nose, and large feet? Thank you, Nicholas."

"I have never really seen your feet, and your nose looks well enough to me."

Silence again, heavier this time, no possible thought now of laughter, no thought either of making any of the dozen pretty excuses that would have obliged him to take me back to the house, to his mother, who would know, as well as I, that he was unhappy, dissatisfied, angry, that in such a humour he could be dangerous.

He lit a cigar irritably, not asking my permission, inhaling deeply like his father, scowling at the sea.

"Faith," he rapped out at me sharply. "I don't have to warn you about Perry Clevedon, do I?"

"Heavens—you certainly don't."

"Good. I think I have never met a more worthless man. Stay clear of him."

"Goodness," Georgiana said, appearing in the unlit dark behind us, the hem of her dress soaked in sea water, her hair coming down with all the abandon that suited her so well, "are you quarrelling with Faith now? I could hear you growling at her as I came back on to the path. What on earth can she have done to make you angry?"

"Nothing," he answered, and then, tossing his cigar away in the direction of the sea, he said quietly, "Faith knows what I mean."

Chapter Eighteen

THE NEW YEAR at once offered us two events of considerable importance. My uncle, in recognition of his services to industry, his charity, his willingness, no doubt, to support Prince Albert's Exhibition, which had meant so much to our Queen, received a baronetcy, becoming Sir Joel Barforth of Tarn Edge, while my mother, taking advantage of the general mood of celebration, announced her forthcoming marriage not to the decaying Mr. Oldroyd but to the unknown, excellently preserved Mr. Daniel Adair.

He was by no means, it seemed, a stranger to us all.

"Have you lost your senses, Elinor?" Aunt Hannah demanded, striding into my mother's house as if she meant to burn it down, infuriated by the loss of the Oldroyd money, certainly, already mourning the death of her hopes of seeing Jonas at Fieldhead, but considerably shaken at a more personal level too. "I have never been so shocked in my life, and I must give you notice that if you go through with this preposterous marriage then I shall disown you."

"I shall be sorry for that, Hannah."

"But it will not stop you? No, I feared not. Then I can only hope that Joel may find the means to restrain you. It is an insult to your husband's memory, and to his daughters— You are allowing the man to make a fool of you—again—and, worse than that, you are very likely to ruin yourself. If no other way can be found, then I think that Joel and myself and your children would do well to join together in having you declared—well— unfit to manage your affairs—insane."

"Oh, dear," my mother said, smiling at me a little mistily when Aunt Hannah had gone. "I did not expect them to be pleased, and Hannah had such high hopes of Mr. Oldroyd, of seeing Jonas master of Fieldhead. But they cannot stop me, you know, and Hannah will not disown me, whatever she says. She is too fond of me for one thing, and for another there may still be some money left when I have done. Daniel will certainly be expensive but your father was always a careful man, and his will does not allow me to spend it all. Well, Faith, I had better tell you since you are the very dearest of my daughters, and neither Prudence nor Celia are speaking to me in any case. Yes, as you will have guessed, I knew Mr. Daniel Adair very well, a long time ago, ten years before your father died, in fact. Your father was much occupied with politics in those days and appointed Mr. Adair to manage his business affairs. While your father was in London, I was here, in this house, a young woman still, and I can only think it unwise, you know, of any man to neglect a young woman of my sort—or of your sort, Faith, for that matter. My word, I fell in love with Daniel quite wildly, and was determined to run away with him—well, he ran away, I confess it, but not with me. Your uncle Joel persuaded him, with pound notes, of course, to leave me, and then persuaded me to return to your father, who did not at all want me but who feared he might lose the next election should there be a scandal. A sorry tale, and perhaps, all those years ago, I might have wished Daniel had been more courageous and willing to starve with me in a cottage. But he was not, and I would not really have cared for it in any case. Your uncle told me to return to my husband, to serve out my sentence, in fact, since he felt I had earned my share of your father's fortune. And he was quite right. I endured ten years longer, and no one can accuse me of being other than a most dutiful, most submissive wife."

"And you remained in love with Mr. Adair all that time?"

"Oh, dear, no," she said, "life is not like that. And when your father died I was too enchanted by my freedom to be in love with anybody but myself. It was my special time, I told you, and I also told you that I knew it would be quickly over. Depend upon it, if I had not encountered Daniel again I might well have married Matthew Oldroyd and made myself nearly as rich as Verity. But I did encounter him, not at all by chance, since he has from time to time been associated in business with your uncle Joel. He had informed himself of my circumstances and knew that I would be visiting the Exhibition. He has no money to speak of, of course, since he has just returned from the West Indies where his ventures have not prospered. Poor Daniel. You must be well able to understand that he needs me."

"Indeed. But, Mother, that is hardly a reason for marriage."

"No, dear. Then I will give you one. He deserted me, I suppose, and I should have detested him. I did not. I understood that having known great poverty he could not risk it again, and I was forced to admit that the few months I spent as his mistress were the most luminous of my life. I had been a sad little woman with an old, grey husband, and Daniel transformed me. He can certainly be a scoundrel, but that has never been unattractive—Joel has been a scoundrel in his day—and Daniel has a great capacity for laughter. You tell me I look nineteen, Faith dear. When Daniel Adair touches me I am nineteen. And I can afford him now. You need have no fear of the consequences. He is not so young as he was, darling, and a time comes when even the most seasoned wanderer is grateful for a comfortable home. And can you think of any reason—really—why he should not be fond of me?"

I couldn't, and when I dined with them some days later—Celia having refused the invitation, Prudence, who had no choice, sitting throughout the meal in spike-edged silence—I concluded that, whatever his faults, and they might well be numerous, his easy, good-humoured charm was beyond denial. He was a man, I thought, who could cheat but who would do it very pleasantly, a man whose roguish smile and all too apparent virility might be compensation enough to a woman like my mother—like myself—for any lie.

Yet Prudence, who was far more intimately concerned in the matter than I, would not be reconciled, could in no way contemplate the sharing of a home not only with Mr. Adair but with his son—whose existence had been kept secret from us until now—a young gentleman of six or seven years old, whose black eyes and amber-tinted countenance betrayed a hint of something warmer than Irish in his blood.

"If my mother imagines," she told me, "that I shall submit myself to daily contact with that dressed-up navvy and his offspring then she is much mistaken. I shall demand control of my money and I shall come to live with you, or if you will not have me I shall make other arrangements—I shall set up a school as I have always wanted, and earn my own living, free from encumbrance! In fact I shall go to Jonas Agbrigg at once to ascertain the exact nature of my rights—you had best accompany me."

But Jonas, when applied to, was quick to point out that Prudence had no rights at all. Naturally he was just as disgusted at our mother's lack of judgement as we were, had as much to lose from it as we had—more, in fact, since the administration of the Oldroyd estate alone, much less its possession, would have made him a decent profit—but he had re-examined our father's will most minutely and could only describe it as unbreakable. The half of his fortune that was held in trust was safe from the assault of even the most skilful fortune-hunter, but could not be paid out to us during our mother's lifetime. The other half was hers—and Mr. Adair's—absolutely, while Prudence's dowry could only be made available on her marriage, or failing that, at the joint discretion of my mother and Uncle Joel. And we could none of us imagine that Mr. Daniel Adair would allow his wife to consent to any such dissipation of funds.

"Had there been a way through it," Jonas told us, without the slightest change of tone or expression, "then I would have found it. Had there been a way to twist the meaning to suit our purposes then I would have twisted it. We are talking of Celia's money too, after all, and my expenses—Prudence dear—are probably a great deal heavier than your own."

"There's the porcelain," she said. "I'll sell it, before that little monster of a Liam Adair sets about the job of breaking it, for I never encountered a more unruly child in my life. Will you handle the sale for me, Jonas?"

But once again my father, with his innate distrust of female judgement, had imposed conditions. The porcelain could be sold as an entire collection or in separate pieces, but only with the consent of Prudence and her husband. Should she attempt to offer it for sale before her marriage or—horror of horrors—without the permission of her spouse, then its possession would revert to that other weak-minded female, her mother.

"I will never forgive him," Prudence said bitterly.

"I doubt if that will trouble him unduly," Jonas told her, fold-

ing the documents neatly away and slipping them into a drawer
of his massive, masculine desk. "Your father did not mean you to
be independent, Prudence. He intended you to be married, and
I can see no alternative for you but to obey—unless, of course,
you are prepared to wait until your mother dies, which is unlikely to be soon. You had best take Freddy Hobhouse, who will
make no objection to your selling the shirt from your back, much
less your porcelain, since every penny he can muster is needed
at Nethercoats."

"And is that the best you can do for me, Jonas—with all your
cleverness?"

"It is," he said coldly, getting to his feet as an indication that
the consultation was at an end, that his time—being male and
free—was of value in Cullingford. "The absolute best, Prudence,
as matters have turned out."

And they stared at each other, steel-eyed adversaries, detest-
ing each other since it was in neither of their natures to admit
that she would have made him a better wife than Celia, that his
intellect and his perseverance could have proved more congenial
to her than Freddy.

"Oh yes," Blaize told me that afternoon, calling in to see me
on his way back from town. "There are no deadlier enemies than
those who could have been friends. If Aunt Hannah had not
made him so greedy, and your father had not made her so awkward—who knows? But poor Prudence, this is the end of her
liberty it seems, for I imagine Dan Adair will keep her very
close to home."

"I don't see why he should concern himself with her at all."

"No—but then you don't know very much about disreputable
men, do you, Faith. He has been a rogue all his life, I imagine,
and now, having made up his mind to be respectable, he will be
very, very respectable indeed—you may take my word for it.
Family prayers every morning, I shouldn't wonder, and no unmarried young ladies of *his* household running unchaperoned
about the streets. As I said—poor Prudence."

"I hadn't thought of that. Why don't you marry her yourself,
Blaize. One supposes you must eventually marry *somebody*—?"

"Ah—one supposes. Not yet, dear."

"You are still looking for that rare and special creature Prudence used to tease you about, are you? The one who is always in the next room?"

"It does rather seem so. But in the meantime—it occurs to me —you wouldn't care to dine with me one evening, next week perhaps, would you, Faith? I have a rather pleasant little apartment in Leeds—nothing grand, but worth looking at, and I have very passable dinners sent in from the restaurant across the street."

"Heavens," I said, thoroughly delighted, knowing that although it was not a serious request, merely an exploratory one, he would not have asked at all had he not been tempted. "What an idea. And you're not even very ardent, are you—asking for next week instead of this week—or tonight . . ."

"Well, at least you didn't take a fit of the vapours, and with a little rearranging of my commitments I could manage, shall we say, Wednesday?"

"I really think we'd better not."

"Yes, now that is just what I expected you to say, but I know you won't blame me for making the attempt. You are looking very well lately, Faith—quite precious, like something cut out of cameo glass."

"Goodness—first I'm a swan, then a cameo. Whatever next?"

"My very good friend, I think," he said, moving towards me, his intention to kiss me so obvious that had I not desired it I could easily have turned away. But I remained motionless as his mouth came to rest, butterfly-light, on the corner of mine and then slowly took possession of it, a leisurely, accomplished embrace which stirred nothing inside me but appreciation of his expertise, a certain pleasing blend of amusement and affection.

"Now why on earth did you do that, Blaize Barforth?"

"One takes one's opportunities—and it wouldn't be a hardship to do it again, believe me."

"No, but think of the inconvenience to yourself. I know that young widows who live alone are supposed to go in for this kind of thing, but in our case, with Aunt Hannah to watch over us . . ."

"Exactly," he said. "How clever of you to think of that." And knowing that he had certainly thought of it himself, I wondered. It could be no secret to him that, since the Exhibition, Nicholas had called once or twice to see me exactly as he did himself. And why should it surprise anyone that Nicholas—or Blaize—should stop a moment, every now and then, in Millergate to pass the time of day with their widowed cousin? What comment could it cause? Yet I knew, and perhaps Blaize knew, that there was cause for comment, cause for concern.

"Faith, I've been shouting myself hoarse all morning and the Old Swan is like an oven. Will you give me tea?"

And I gave him tea, sitting a yard away from him, listening, smiling, "understanding what he meant" and pretending, sometimes, both of us, that I did not, sharing the strain, easing the tension, making no move towards him, refusing to face the possibility that he could approach me, telling myself, when he had gone, that it was entirely innocent and believing it, because it was what I wanted to believe. He never mentioned Georgiana. I never mentioned Giles. We talked, as we had done years ago, of ourselves in isolation, as if our lives were in no way connected with other lives, certainly not with each other.

"What have you done today, Faith?"

"Oh, mad adventures from morning to evening—my cat on the rooftop wailing to get down, and I think my chimney needs sweeping. And you, Nicholas?"

"Bought myself some new combing machines, although God knows where I'm to put them."

"Isn't the mill next to yours for sale—the old Barraclough place?"

"Aye—and I've had a look at it."

"And you could use it?"

"I reckon I could—if I can get the money."

"Oh, you'll do that all right. Will it take a great deal to put it right?"

And listening while he offered me his facts and figures I must have known that I was re-creating for him the atmosphere he had once found attractive, that by fulfilling his need I was increasing it.

Uncle Joel, aware no doubt of the contribution his operatives had made to his Exhibition medals, his baronetcy, his general, altogether stupendous success, entertained them that summer to a grand banquet held under canvas on the lawns at Tarn Edge. He had, it was true, deprived many of their fathers of a liveli-

hood by his introduction of power looms twenty years ago, but
the new machines themselves had given rise in this younger generation to a new class of mechanics, skilled men who, with a
trade in their hands, were moving out of Simon Street to cleaner
pastures and who, with the aid of the Mechanics Institute my
uncle had sponsored, were no longer illiterate labourers, but
men who could increasingly lift up their heads and pay their
way. He had always been known as a hard master but there was
no job in his factories, however dirty or dangerous, that he could
not and had not done himself. He demanded punctuality and
self-discipline, both of which he practiced himself, but for a
good day's work he had always been willing to pay rather more
than Nethercoats or Fieldhead, and had been the first man in
the Law Valley, long before the law compelled him, to introduce
a ten-hour working day.

And now, having proved to the Hobhouses and to the miserly
Mr. Oldroyd that even without exceeding the legal ten hours his
factories could make higher profits than theirs, he had invited
his employees to dine, spreading before them a gargantuan feast
which, Aunt Hannah had informed me, included no less than
five hindquarters of beef, one hundred and fifty legs of mutton,
forty hams and tongues, chickens and ducks and pigeon pies
without number, three hundred and twenty plum puddings, a
mountain of fruit and nuts, sponge cakes, tarts of every variety
and description, washed down with as much wine and ale as
every man, and every woman, could decently carry.

There was, of course, a certain segregation, natural or otherwise—family and friends, shed managers, engineers, designers,
skilled men and their families, all in self-conscious Sunday best,
keeping themselves a trifle apart from the lower echelons, even
the burlers and menders, sedate, matronly looking women for
the most part who spent their days repairing faults in the
unfinished pieces, letting it be known they felt themselves a cut
above the mass of common weavers. But Sir Joel Barforth
strolled leisurely that day among them all, shaking any hand
that was held out to him, a word and a smile for everyone, a
cigar for every man, a trinket in the napkin of every woman,
sharing a joke here, a reminiscence there, putting himself and
his possessions on display to satisfy their curiosity and to whet
their appetites, to increase the ambition of some, the envy of

others, although all of them—the ambitious and the envious, the ones who wanted this magnificence for themselves, and the ones who wanted no one to have it—were all willing to drink his health that day.

I put aside my widow's weeds for the occasion, not eagerly but knowing it must be done. I was twenty-three years old. I had worn unrelieved black for two years. It was enough, and so I chose a gentle dove grey, a wide, tiered skirt edged with white lace, slit sleeves showing lace beneath, a grey satin bonnet with a white plume curling behind, a cameo at my throat, a frivolous, lacy parasol, gloves, and dashing, high-heeled boots of white kid.

"My word, how smart," my mother said, coming to collect me with Mr. Adair, since Prudence, who would still barely speak to her, had chosen to accompany the Agbriggs. But after so long in mourning even these neutral colours seemed excessively bright and, as I entered the gardens of Tarn Edge, if Aunt Hannah had rounded on me with a "Good heavens, girl, you are improperly dressed. Go home and change," I would not have been astonished.

The family table, of course, surrounded by flowering plants and hothouse blooms in copper bowls, was a sight to behold, Aunt Verity—Lady Barforth now—sitting beside her daughter, Lady Chard, and amiable, healthy Sir Matthew. My mother was beautiful as always, Aunt Hannah undoubtedly majestic, Mr. Agbrigg a famous man in his own right now that he had brought water, if not to Simon Street, to very nearly everywhere else. Prudence, dressed with her usual quiet elegance, while not precisely willing to speak to Mr. Adair, was at least taking pains that it should not be obvious. Even Celia, looking older than either of us, I thought, seemed ready to enter into the general spirit of enjoyment, finding no more than a few, very trivial errands for the impeccable Jonas.

Blaize, as much in his element as Caroline, had clearly been set the task of making himself pleasant and was performing it admirably, far better, in fact, than Nicholas, who seemed morose and preoccupied. While Georgiana, splendidly attired in honey-coloured silk, her earrings of gold and topaz looking too heavy for her tiny, pointed ears, sat in complete silence, not sullenly but rather, it seemed, because there was nothing she wished to say.

"They have been having a terrible set-to, Georgiana and Nicholas," Caroline whispered to me. "So you will oblige me by keeping an eye on her. He was growling at her when I arrived and she was wringing her hands and wailing, 'Oh what have I done now,' in that way she has, half-laughing, half-crying—I can perfectly understand why she provokes him. You will have noticed that neither her grandfather nor her brother are here, which may have something to do with it—certainly Perry is head over heels in debt again, which is always a bad sign. Well, they must sort it out later, for nothing must be allowed to spoil my father's great day. I told you, did I not, that he would win all the medals, and so he has. Even Matthew couldn't bring himself to ignore that and I must say that he has backed down most graciously. If there should ever be another exhibition I shall have no trouble at all in attending it."

Sir Joel having returned from the grand tour of his property and his personnel, the meal began, and ended, most jovially, my uncle, who had received his share of loyal toasts, standing now to raise his own glass to his wife.

"I have this to say," he announced, "and you can all hear it. Without Verity I'd have nothing and I'd be nothing. And if I had to choose between all this and her, then I'd throw the lot away. I may be embarrassing her now—and by the look on her face I am—but the only real treasure I have is in her. There'll be men here today who'll look at this house and the mills, and say, 'He's been lucky.' They're wrong. Hard work made the mills, because I was ready to get myself out of bed every morning when others weren't, and ready to labour, often enough, into the night when the rest had gone home. That, and guts I reckon, and a knack of understanding what was needed and how to supply it. There's no luck in that. But if any man looks at my wife and says, 'He's been lucky,' then that man is absolutely right. He could even go further and tell me I've got more than I deserve. So we'll drink now to Lady Barforth—my wife."

He put down his glass, took both her hands in his, and kissed them, not raising them to his lips but bending his head, a most gallant salutation. Nicholas and Blaize pushed back their chairs and going to her side kissed her in their turn and, in a rare moment of brotherhood, hugged each other hard. Caroline, forgetting to be Lady Chard, threw two fierce arms around her father's neck, her hand clasping her mother's behind his back. The brothers kissed their sister, husband and wife embraced again. "Hannah," my uncle said, reaching out for the sister who was, often enough, a nuisance to us all but who had helped him through his early, leaner years. And both she and my mother kissed him and each other.

It was a moment of great emotion, of great beauty, this family united by pride of achievement, and my eyes swimming with tears, I loved each and every one of them, my soaring, splendid uncle, his graceful wife, my annoying, resourceful aunt, my frivolous little mother, artful Blaize and ambitious Caroline— Nicholas. They were my people.

But they were not, it seemed, and never could be Georgiana's, for lounging in her chair, tapping a fork against her glass with an irritable hand, she was not merely bored, like Matthew Chard, but thoroughly oppressed. The very colour of her hair faded, it seemed, by the completeness of her misery. And on such a day, when the Barforth ladies themselves were there to be looked at, when every shed manager's wife would want to count their jewels and the flounces on their dresses, would feel entitled, quite rightly, to a word and a smile, her attitude—whatever its cause—could only give offence.

Yet her attitude itself puzzled me, for although I had seen her capricious and reckless, I had never before seen her hard, the scornful curve of her lip as she muttered something to Matthew Chard being quite new to me.

"One would have thought a title might have pleased her," my mother murmured, seeing the direction of my eyes, but clearly my uncle's baronetcy was no more to her than an extension of the exhibition she had so despised, a hollow sham as tainted by trade as everything else about him, an insult, perhaps, to the "real gentry" whose titles had been won on the field of battle or on the tortuous pathways of diplomacy, granted for services freely given, not bought and paid for.

But none of this surprised me. I had expected Georgiana to feel this way and was worried, rather, that she—basically so warmhearted and who meant so well—should let it show, concluding that some affront must surely have been offered to her own family, that she had been forced once too often into the position of choosing sides: and had chosen.

"Come, girls," Aunt Verity said, moving towards us, "I think we should circulate a little and make ourselves known. Faith dear, there will be a great many, I imagine, who have grateful memories of your husband, and would be glad of a word with you. And, Georgiana—I believe Nicholas will be wanting to present his employees to you."

But as we began to disperse Georgiana continued to sit at the empty table, not sulking, but totally and quite alarmingly separate, her solitude made more conspicuous by the fact that she herself seemed unaware of it.

But others were not.

"Mrs. Nicholas Barforth," Aunt Hannah enquired, "are you not well today?"

"Georgiana," Caroline called out as she took her father's arm, "you had better come with me."

"Leave her," Blaize said to me.

"Georgiana," Nicholas ordered, "get up." And staring at him for a moment quite balefully, she suddenly leaped to her feet and raising her hand allowed the fork with which she had been toying to fall with a careless, destructive clatter on to the table.

"Good heavens," she said. "Such a commotion. One wonders how you would all behave at a Coronation."

And pushing back her chair she gathered her expensive, embroidered skirts together and set off down the garden at a spanking pace, bestowing an ardent, almost hysterical greeting on everyone she passed, leaving a trail of astonishment—and embarrassment—behind her.

"Dear God," Nicholas said very low, no anger in him now, a strange, sorrowing note in his voice, the nearest approach to defeat I had ever seen in the sudden droop of his shoulders: and if there had been a decision to make I must surely have made it then.

I stayed late at Tarn Edge that day, later in Blenheim Lane, so late in fact that Prudence, who had planned to return home with me, elected to spend the remainder of the night in her own bed. And so, quite by chance, even my housemaid having gone upstairs, there was only my housekeeper, Mrs. Marworth, to exchange a startled glance with me when we heard the gate open and a knock on the door, even that good lady, having some experience, it seemed, of the ways of young widows, melting discreetly away when, in answer to my enquiry, we were told, "Nicholas Barforth."

"Nicholas. What is it? I didn't hear your horse?"

"No. I left her in the Old Swan yard. I'd better warn you I've had a glass or two. You're not obliged to ask me to come in."

But, without answering, I walked away from him into the parlour, spending a long moment in lighting a lamp, adjusting the candles on either end of the mantelshelf, so that when I had finished he was sitting on my sofa, allowing me to choose the safety of a separate chair.

"Would you like a drink, Nicholas? I think I have some brandy."

He smiled—the unwilling, rueful grin breaking through the cloud of him in a way that had always seemed to me like a reward.

"No—no, thanks. How is it you always make everything seem so smooth for me, Faith? I'm here, in what amounts to the middle of the night—when I shouldn't be here at all—and you haven't even asked me why. And if I got up now and went away without saying anything you wouldn't make a fuss, would you? I could even come back tomorrow and be sure of my welcome."

"Yes, you could. But I'd be concerned, Nicholas. I might not ask what was wrong because if you didn't tell me of your own free will I'd assume you didn't want me to know. But I'd wonder —and worry. There's no doubt about that."

He swallowed hard, painfully, the slump of his shoulders heavy once again with defeat as he leaned forward, staring at the empty summer hearth, his hands clasped loosely together, his dark face, without its shielding anger, vulnerable to hurt.

"I want to talk to you, Faith."

"Yes, of course."

"I mean really talk to you—not about combing machines and tea parties. Can I do that? I'll leave the instant you tell me."

"I know."

"All right—so what do I say? God knows—I'm at the end of myself tonight, I reckon."

"Yes. I think I know that too."

"And I'm a selfish swine to come here and pester you with it—which hasn't stopped me from coming. I never really supposed it would. I went down to the Swan to get drunk, which may seem pointless to you—except that getting drunk *would* have kept me away from you. But it hasn't happened. I'm not drunk. Remember—I'll go at once, when you tell me."

"Talk to me then."

"About, Georgiana?"

"Yes. What happened between you today."

"Nothing that hasn't happened before. Nothing that should even matter all that much—nothing I didn't expect, right from the start."

And throwing himself backwards suddenly against the sofa he stretched his whole body and gave a long, deep-draining sigh.

"Money, Faith—that's all. And I've got plenty of that. Bills—dressmakers' bills, milliners' bills, that she'd had the money to pay and told me she had paid. Apologetic little women coming to see me and saying they know it must have slipped her mind, and they don't like bothering me with trifles, but it's been six months now, eight months now— It shouldn't even bother me that she gives every penny she can beg or borrow to her brother—since I must have known she would—or that she can't see what all the fuss is about, since tradesmen are just tradesmen and she's gentry, and nobody called Clevedon or Flood or Winterton, or Chard, I reckon, has ever been in a hurry to pay his tailor. It shouldn't bother me that the money I work for—and scheme for—buys her brother his place at the Flood's whist table, since a gentleman is in honour bound to settle his gambling debts. I can afford it. I was ready to afford it, when it was worth it to me. So I'm to blame. I know it. Shall I go now, Faith?"

"Do you want to?"

"Oh no. I know exactly what *I* want. I won't leave until I'm told."

"In fact you want me to make the decision. You're ready to accept the blame for your situation with Georgiana, but not for—whatever should come of this."

"That makes me sound very low, Faith."

"So it does."

He got up, one hand on the mantelpiece, one foot tapping

against the fender, not irritably, merely to release some particle of his tension, and, had I permitted myself, I could have gone to him then and there—guilty as he was, full of wine and self-pity, hurt and hunger—and put my arms around him, making everything smooth for him yet again, telling him that he had no need to coax nor to plead in order to reach me; telling him, quite simply, that I was here.

"Let me say just this," he muttered, "and then I will go away. You may not believe me, but I mean it when I say I'm to blame. Georgiana is now exactly as she has always been. She didn't deceive me by pretending to be otherwise, and she never promised to change. I'm the one who has changed. She fascinated me. Christ—she burned me so badly I couldn't see beyond her. And the only difference between that and being in love must be that it doesn't last. And when it goes it leaves nothing but amazement that it could ever have existed at all. And so I've ruined my life and hers too, because she knows I can't put up with her any more. And how can I expect her to understand why? She has a right to believe that I've cheated her, since I once told her that all these things I find so bloody impossible could make no difference between us. She has the right to feel ill-used when the rest of them criticise her and I don't defend her—as I promised —or when I criticise her myself—as I vowed I'd never do. I swear it—whatever she may do to me, I make her so miserable sometimes—so damned miserable—I can see the colour go out of her and because it upsets me it makes me worse. And I believe I understood today that there isn't any cure—that things will always be like this. My father doesn't often stir much emotion in me, but I was proud of him today. I recognised myself in him today, and I recognised what he feels for my mother. I could have had that too—couldn't I, Faith? And so I went down to the Swan because I couldn't stand thinking about it. I couldn't face up to the fact that I was in a trap—of my own making—and that I couldn't smash my way out of it, couldn't talk my way out of it, couldn't even buy my way out of it. Christ . . ."

"Nicholas," I said slowly, very carefully, "a moment ago you said you knew exactly what you wanted. You had better tell me what it is."

He sat down again heavily, a man who had been brought up to believe he could get anything he wanted if he worked for it, fought for it, who had been very sure of himself and who now could not tolerate frustration, a man who could understand the reasons for his captivity but would not accept them. Yet, no matter what fears I entertained, nor how many feeble attempts I made to be resolute, to listen not only to the warnings of shock and shame but to the simple, straightforward urgings of common sense, my body knew—had known from the moment he arrived—that he had only to touch me, a hand, merely, on mine, or not even that much, a hand reaching out for me, and I would answer.

It was completely wrong. There was not even a whisper of right, not the slightest breath of justification, no good, to anyone, could possibly come of it. He was here in a moment of weakness, knowing—as I knew—that however much he desired me, however much he might come to love me, he could, in the final instance, only do me harm. And because he was not cruel, and no more self-seeking in love than most men—than most women —by harming me he would most likely harm himself. He knew quite well he should not have come here at all. I knew I should not have let him in. Yet if we were no more self-seeking than the average we were no more self-sacrificing either. We were human, imperfect, and I, at least, had stood apart from life for too long. And more than that, perhaps I was still young enough to believe that what I would have instantly recognised as madness in any other woman could, in my case, be otherwise; that I was stronger, possessed the capacity to love more completely, for I was in no doubt that I did love him.

"I want a great many things," he said quietly. "And I know it's all impossible. I want to turn the clock back, I suppose—a long way back, years back. It can't be done. I'm sorry, Faith. I'll go now."

But I had allowed him to leave me too many times in this manner, in those slow, peaceful days when it had seemed right to wait for him to fall in love with me, days when I had remained motionless, believing time to be my ally, and had lost him. Perhaps I had needed only to hold out my hand and push him with the very tips of my fingers in order to pass from one level of feeling to another, from the friendship we had always shared to desire. And perhaps, too, we would all be dust and ashes, mouldering in eternal decay, tomorrow.

"I'll go now." But he didn't move, and when I didn't answer he said sharply, "Yes, I'll go—for if I don't— I hurt you once, Faith, didn't I? I can't do it again."

"That's nonsense, Nicholas."

"What—?"

"It's nonsense—that's all. It just proves that we know the right answers, that we know what we ought to say and do. And it's nonsense. Why don't you say what you mean? You don't intend to leave and you don't think I'll make you. *Say* it, Nicholas. Let's be honest, at least with each other."

"Faith—" he said blankly, taken off guard, for the first time in his life very nearly, and very briefly, shy. And then, his hard, brown fingers plunging for a moment into his hair as if he required to clear his head, shake it, perform some positive, simple action that was entire and straightforward in itself, he leaned forward and whispered, "Come and sit beside me."

"Presently."

"Now, Faith—please."

I got up, walked across the room to him, and sat down carefully on the edge of the sofa, arranging my voluminous skirts so that no part of them touched him, although his breath was already in my nostrils, filling me with the devastating awareness of a hard, tough-fibred chest behind his shirt-frill, good red blood beneath, a powerful, beautiful male body wanting mine.

"All right," he said. "I'll be honest. It suits me that way, in any case. I could have been happy with you, Faith—couldn't I? I know it. It's what I should have had—would have had. I cheated myself of it. And that's not the whole of it. I reckon I could live with that. I did live with it, until that night in Bournemouth, last year. I wanted you that night, but I thought it would pass. It hasn't. I want you, Faith—in every way a man could want you—badly. And I've got one life, that's all, and so have you."

"And do you expect to get me?"

"Yes," he said, a sudden flash of excitement, of victory in his face. "I think so—I think I do. Faith, you're shaking—"

"Yes—delirium, I expect—hold me—"

And although I couldn't really believe I had spoken that last command—hold me—I heard it, he heard it, obeyed it, his arms instantly around me, his mouth and his hands possessing as much of me as my cumbersome garments permitted.

"Not here, Nicholas."

"Upstairs, then? I have to take you now, before you change your mind."

"Darling—that's not romantic."

"No, I daresay. But once it's done it's done and there's no going back. Once I've got you—when I *know* I've got you—then I'll be romantic."

He carried me up the narrow stairs, no tender gesture of gallantry but a rough lifting from the ground because it was quicker that way and I was as conscious as he was of the need for haste. He was not gentle, nor did I require it, for it was urgency alone in those first moments that nailed us together, the need for possession, the need even to punish one another, my whole body burning, wanting him quickly, quickly, so that my petticoats were an irritation to be torn away, his shirt an encumbrance that his hands and mine disposed of together. And it seemed right that his hard, heavy body, emerging from its elegant, social wrappings, should crush me and hurt me, too intent on the conclusion of his desire, the simple act of claiming me—since that was what we were about—to think of giving me pleasure. We were as adversaries, bent on taking and devouring the whole of one another, grasping and clutching and biting, a fierce penetration that I answered just as fiercely, until whatever it was inside me that had obscured the source of rapture was invaded, split asunder, and it poured over me, wave upon wave of it, terrifying me and thrilling me at the same time, leaving me docile and bemused and irrevocably possessed.

We lay for a while in silence, recovering, easing ourselves apart, and when it seemed to me that his breathing had slowed and deepened into sleep, I got up and went to the window, needing, I think, to be a yard or so away from him to experiment with the sensation of shame. Yet, taking a deep breath, waiting for it to start, nothing happened to me with which I could not cope.

I knew, in this cooler moment, the enormity of the social and moral crime I had committed, for which I, as a woman, would be required to pay a far higher price than Nicholas. Discovery, for him, would mean no more, perhaps, than a personal explanation with his wife and with his father, a certain winking and sniggering among the crowd when he entered the Piece Hall. "The young devil, he got the Ashburn woman, did he? Good luck to him," since it was well known that a man took his pleasures where he could find them, and a woman who surrendered was no better than a whore in any case.

But for me the retribution would be terrible and complete, a total casting-out which would oblige even my mother and Prudence to treat me as a stranger, if they wished to retain their own reputations. But—although I did not wish to lose them, had no idea how to face life without them—I had done nothing I could find it in my own heart to regret, had done nothing, certainly, that I would not be prepared to do again. And having decided that much, I could see no purpose in self-torment.

I am no longer sure if I thought of Giles in that solitary quarter of an hour, it simply seems to me now that I must have done so, for I could hardly have been so calm had I not realised that my feelings for him had been so different that they could still exist, quite independently, alongside my love for Nicholas, which had always been there. I sought no excuses, no justifications. That was simply the way of it. And if there was a price to pay then—because I was a Law Valley woman who understood about the settlement of debts—I would pay it.

"Are you awake?" I murmured, and he crossed the room in two strides, his arms coming tight around me.

"Aye—awake and watching you. You'll be thinking about your husband, I expect, and maybe I've been thinking about my wife. And I've got this to say to you, Faith Aycliffe. I reckon you must love me a fair amount or you'd not have let me near you in the first place, and whatever it costs me—whatever it costs you— I've no mind to let you go. Don't whine to me now, and say you didn't mean it to go this far, for I won't take it. It's happened. I've got you, and I'll keep you—one way or another—that's one thing you can be sure of."

"And when did you ever see me whining, Nicholas Barforth?"

"Never," he said, one hand going gently now into my hair, finding my cheek and the nape of my neck. "I never did."

"No—just as I've never seen you romantic."

He pressed his mouth against my forehead and I felt his lips curve into their slow smile. "Yes—well I did promise that, didn't I. Come back to bed then, Faith. What we did just then was need—I expect you know that. So we'll go back to bed now, I reckon, and make love."

Chapter Nineteen

IT WAS ENOUGH, at least for Nicholas, in those early days, to know that his physical possession of me was beyond dispute, to rejoice in his complete mastery of my body's needs and if he did not precisely wish to see me in a state of abject slavery—and I am not altogether certain of that—he desired, most assuredly, to increase those needs, *did* increase them, so that my body, quite separately from my heart, was famished and painful without him.

I lived through fevered days that should have terrified me and did not, content to take what I could, as if I stood, somehow, at the very rim of the world, some outer threshold where I must clutch each moment as it came and live it intensely, to the limits of myself.

And having no experience of the stage management of adultery, I was surprised how often we could be together.

His horse in the Old Swan yard would cause no comment, and should anyone look for him in the bar room and not find him there, there was the Piece Hall across the way, Mr. Rawnsley's bank, the offices of Jonas Agbrigg, who handled the legal complexities of the Barforths, no reason at all to suppose he had taken the brisk, ten-minute stroll to my kitchen door, conveniently screened by a high-walled yard, with no neighbours to bother us. And if he should be seen in Millergate, coming to me or leaving me, what of it? It was a busy, commercial thoroughfare, containing not only the millinery and the bakery he would hardly patronise, but the premises of the architect, Mr. Outhwaite, who dealt with all repairs and extensions at Lawcroft and Tarn Edge, the saddlery, the importer of cigars and fine wines where no one would be astonished to see him.

I could not be certain we were safe. I rather thought that we were not. But that first breathless August, that first mellowing of the year into September, my eyes were too dazzled for caution, my mind lulled not by recklessness, but by the perilous, languorous philosophy of the opium-eater, who, knowing perfectly well that he may die of his addiction, does not even want to resist it.

To begin with he came only in the evening, having purchased the discretion of my Mrs. Marworth, who, being too afraid of him to betray us in any case, and worldly enough to rather enjoy this kind of thing, would admit him through her kitchen and then prepare herself to tell anyone else who called that I was not at home. But he required, I think, some further commitment, some act of rashness on my part, and was soon urging me to folly.

"We have a house in Scarborough, Faith. My parents never go there now and I will confess to you that Blaize has used it, and that I have used it— I'm being honest, you see, like you said. I've done this before, except that I haven't, because it's different now—if you see what I mean? We could stay the whole night together, Faith—two whole nights. I've never made love to you in the morning. Of course you can get away. Yes, yes, you can— you can if you want to—"

"But I can't go to Scarborough, Nicholas. I've never travelled alone."

"You can. You've travelled all over Europe with your mother, who is the most feather-headed female imaginable. If you got her from here to Naples and back again then you can find your way to Scarborough. Mrs. Marworth can go as far as Leeds with you, which will take care of chance meetings on the platform in Cullingford, and I'll have someone meet you at the other end. *Do* it, Faith. The couple who keep the house open for us won't even remember your face—I'll pay them to forget it. *Do* it. It's October now. Nobody we know goes to Scarborough at this season. You've got a friend, somewhere, haven't you, that you can say you're visiting?"

And so I went to Scarborough, arriving in a state of extreme nervous exhaustion, convinced that every tree I had passed en route concealed a prying Cullingford face, that the spare Mr.

Collins who had been sent to meet me in a closed carriage, and his comfortable wife, waiting to give me tea, were spies in Georgiana's, or Aunt Hannah's, pay. But the house, set high on the cliff-top, was surrounded by trees in full burnished, autumn leaf, its garden offering a view of the little grey town climbing downwards to the bay, the castle a stern sentinel above it, the streets empty, it seemed, of anything but the fresh October wind, the stirring of salt-dried foliage, the tang of sea spray.

"This is the first property my father bought outside Cullingford," Nicholas told me. "His first attempt at being alone with my mother." And for three miraculous days, we were alone together, three rain-washed days; grey-tinted mornings which found us still in the same bed, no hurry, no sudden, chilly departures, a slow and lovely reaching out for one another in the moment of waking, free to enjoy this new-found luxury of making love in the uncertain, marine daylight which revealed to me, more exactly than any candle flame, the complex pattern of bone and muscle beneath his skin, the tight-clenching of his jaw in the moment of pleasure, the harsh hands and limbs of conquest, allowing me no quarter, and then the warmth of him afterwards, the cherishing.

"Dear God, Faith—it gets better every time. Doesn't it?"

"Yes, it does."

"Then tell me—tell me what it does to you."

"It consumes me—and then it makes me dream about the next time."

"Now that's what I like to hear. Give me half an hour, will you, and then we'll see about that dream—"

There were three, blustery afternoons, my hair tangled with sea-wind, walking together through a mist beaded with raindrops, losing ourselves in the grey sweep of sea and sky, laughing as we took shelter from the suddenly slanting rain, running back along the cliff path, giddy with freedom and laughter, to doze on the sofa before a busy tea-time fire.

There were three evenings that could go on forever, until we chose to end them, and which led us warmly, gently, to love and sleep and the new morning. It was the best time, the special time, so good that there was bitterness at its ending, for those three perfect days had shown us too clearly how all the days of our lives could have been, and we were no longer satisfied.

He startled me badly a few days later by striding into my house in the middle of the afternoon.

"Nicholas—Good heavens—anyone could have been here."

"Mrs. Marworth said not, and I've told her to say you're not at home to anybody else. I was thinking of you. I was there, in Millergate, at the saddler's, and I thought why the devil shouldn't I see you? Why the devil shouldn't I? Give me a kiss, Faith—I've got all of five minutes."

And so it continued.

"Faith—are you there? I'm just up from the Piece Hall, and I was thinking of you. Come here—closer than that—ten minutes, that's all."

Until one day, at the perilous hour of tea time, he strode into my drawing room, his arms lifting me roughly from the ground.

"I was thinking of you—badly. And why the devil not? I've got half an hour, Faith. Come to bed."

"Nicholas!"

"Yes, in the afternoon. Scandalous—your Mrs. Marworth thinks so too, I expect, but she's ready to stand in your door-way and say you're gone to Leeds, should anyone want to know."

And I went upstairs, laughing, and locked my door, undressed myself slowly as he lay on my bed, allowing him time to see how the late autumn sunshine, slanting through the chinks in my curtains, dappled my bare skin. I was, I think, half shocked, half excited—since no decent woman made love in the daytime except in Scarborough—and perhaps that, in itself, was exciting, for leaning over him, pouring myself against him, I was full of a wicked, tantalising playfulness that became, at its conclusion, the purring content of a slumberously stretching cat.

I watched him dress, loving him, adoring the hardness, the darkness of him, a body that would take on weight, perhaps, in middle-life, as his father's was beginning to do, but which now was wide at the shoulder, narrow in the hips, his stomach taut and flat, beautiful. And sitting down at the bedside, his hands finding me beneath the covers, he said, "Why don't you stay here, in bed, until I come back tonight?"

"My word, what a sultan you are. You'd like that, wouldn't you, thinking of me lying here all day, ready and waiting for you . . . ?"

"I would," he said, his eyes narrowing, his hands touching me again, awakening so easily the tremor, the faintly expanding glow that was the beginning of wanting him. "Yes, I'd like that, Faith. By God, I would."

And although it was a joke—or so I imagined—I was obliged to take him seriously enough on the afternoon when, having accompanied my mother on a shopping expedition to Leeds, I returned, parcel laden, to be told by a smug Mrs. Marworth that "the gentleman" had called.

"Oh dear," I said, no more than that, disappointed but not seriously alarmed until he strode in, late that night, his jaw tight, his whole body crackling with the anger everybody at Lawcroft Mills had learned to dread.

"Nicholas—darling—?"

"Don't make excuses," he snarled, throwing his hat viciously onto a chair back, although I had made no attempt to do so, having done nothing, I believed, which required it. "You could at least be here, couldn't you, when I call? That's all I ask. I don't ask you to come to me, do I? I don't ask you to walk up that damned rutted back road, night after night, from the Swan —no, I do that little job myself. I don't ask you to get out of a warm bed in the middle of the night and ride five miles in the rain—well, do I? I don't ask you to snatch every chance you can to get to Millergate and then be obliged to go away again, like as not, because your sister, or some other damned interfering female has got here before me. I just ask you to be here. Can't you do that much for me? Aren't I worth that much? And what else have you to do? Where the hell were you, in any case? In Leeds with your mother. Splendid, Faith—just splendid. All right—I won't trouble you again in the daytime. I'll make a bloody appointment if you like—or I won't come at all."

And after that my days became, each one, a small earth tremor of anxiety, shooing callers away from my tea table before they wished to go, hovering always within sound of the window and the door, refusing, adamantly, nervously sometimes, to go out unless I had first made Nicholas aware of it.

"Oh no, Mamma. I don't want to go into town today. No, I am not as bad as Celia—it is simply that I am not inclined . . ."

"Good heavens, Prudence, if you need a new bonnet I imagine you may choose it without me."

"Celia—I never expected you to come today, in this weather. I imagine you will not be staying long? Oh—Jonas is to collect you on his way from the office. Well, you had best have your bonnet on ready, for he is always in a great rush."

And if it was Thursday, market day at the Piece Hall, and the likelihood of Nicholas in town, I would be on tenterhooks until she had gone away. I saw no one else. Blaize, who represented my greatest danger, was abroad that autumn, Aunt Verity in Bournemouth, my uncle joining her whenever he could, which, in Nicholas' view, could not be often enough. Caroline was occupied with the building of a new servants' wing at Listonby, Georgiana—although I quite deliberately did not think of Georgiana—was rarely in Cullingford during the hunting season. Prudence, blessedly, was busying herself with the progress of Mayor Agbrigg's reservoirs, her attention being diverted from me by such considerations as the transporting of so tricky a substance as water the twenty-five mountainous miles from its sadly porous resting place at Cracknell Bridge to Simon Street. My mother was making ready to embark on her new life as Mrs. Daniel Adair, Aunt Hannah intent on preventing it, if she could, and if not, of devising some other way in which Oldroyd wealth—anybody's wealth—might be channelled to Jonas.

Yet there were other dangers besides discovery, not least among them being Nicholas' inability to tolerate frustration, the headstrong, possibly ruthless side of his nature, which was fast making him a force to be reckoned with in the textile trade, but which caused him to howl with the rage of a maddened bull sometimes, when it became too clear to him that he could never organise his personal life so logically and conveniently as his weaving sheds. In the world of commerce Nicholas did not walk around obstacles, he smashed them, flattened them, got rid of them one way or another, and if he hurt his own iron fist in the process, then he would have allowed for it in advance, made sure that the price would be right. But in the world of personal relationships, the complex tangle of feelings and demands and recriminations, the conventions which governed us, the decencies we were forced to observe, irritated him, goaded him often to recklessness.

"I don't want to leave you tonight, Faith. Why should I? I

could stay until morning—couldn't I?—and go to the mill from here."

"No you couldn't—not in your evening clothes."

"Christ—it won't do, Faith. It's not enough—is it? Well—is it?"

But always—because I was not ready to talk of his wife and his son, because it was too soon and I was afraid, in any case, of how I would feel when I faced the reality of it, afraid of the questions I would ask and of his replies—I would hush him, smooth the moment away, pour the length of my body against the length of his to distract him from the future, filling his mind only with me, as I was at that one, irreplaceable, fleeting moment.

And when I had pushed the forbidden images of his domesticity away, I was left to consider the appalling possibility that I might conceive a child I would be able to explain to no one.

Yet, on the first occasion I was obliged to make Nicholas aware that I was not *enceinte*, his immediate reaction puzzled me. He would be relieved, surely, I had thought, but I had forgotten the solid Law Valley belief that a pregnant woman is a docile woman, who will cling to the father of her child forever—or for as long as he finds convenient—and I was surprised when he pressed the palm of his hand against my stomach, and said, "If it should happen, you know, it wouldn't be the end of the world."

"It would be the end of mine."

"Thank you, Faith."

"Heavens, Nicholas—for what?"

"For telling me you don't want to have my child."

I took his wrist in the tips of my fingers and moved his hand away, got up, angry and very hurt, striving to push away from my memory the image of Georgiana's spent face, her thin, exhausted body after her son—Nicholas' son—was born, my own terrible hesitation before I had taken Gervase in my arms, my fear, on returning him to his cradle, that I had injured him.

"I wish you hadn't said that to me, Nicholas."

"Yes, so do I."

And then, standing behind me, his arms around me, his mouth against my ear: "I'm sorry. You're quite right to be put out. I am unjust. I am ill-tempered. Anything you like. I love you, you see. I want all of you, and it sours me, sometimes . . . You'll have to put up with it. But if it happened, Faith—and it's only sense to admit that it could—yes, I know, by rights, we'd have to call it a disaster. But don't be afraid of it. You can trust me, I reckon, to look after you. Can't you?"

"Of course."

"I'd take you away from here," he said decidedly. "Your mother would have to know, but I could fix her. She could go abroad with you until it was over—not that I'd care who knew about it, but I know you couldn't take the scandal and I wouldn't expose you to it. I'd get you a house somewhere and set you up in style. I know you've got money of your own, but I wouldn't want you to use it. To tell you the truth, I sometimes think it would suit me better if you had no money at all. Don't worry, love, I'd look after you."

But what he really meant was, "You'd belong to me then. You'd *have* to belong to me, for nobody else would want you," and although it was what the purely female part of me craved for, I had a cooler, more rational side to my nature which was unwilling to be so close confined. He would get me a house, a splendid one I had no doubt, but where? Far enough, certainly, from a suspicious, hostile Cullingford, too far for his lightning, afternoon visits, too far to leave his horse at the Swan and walk to me those three or four nights a week that now formed the basis of my existence. A secret house where I would bring up a secret child in luxurious solitude, nourishing myself on his visits, with nothing else to do but wait for him, dreading, as I grew older, that eventually he would not come. And although I loved him enough for that, and did nothing, indeed, but wait for him in any case, I was still, to some extent, in control of my life. I may never avail myself of it, but I still had the possibility of choice, and change.

"Am I completely selfish, Faith?"

"Oh yes—but so am I. I expect I would make a prisoner of you too, if I could."

"Is that what you feel—that I want to imprison you?"

"Yes—I feel that."

"Christ," he said. "You'll have to forgive me, but I believe you're right. All I can promise is that I'll try not to torment you with it—I'll try."

But the promise, as I suppose we both knew, was in vain, his jealousy proving so acute, so all-consuming, that it often passed beyond reassurance, beyond reason, to a point where nothing less than my actual imprisonment could have given him ease.

"Nicholas—it can only mean you don't trust me?"

"God knows what it means. All I know is I can't help it and I can't stand it. A moment comes, in the day—or in the night— when I feel—Christ—I feel bereft. And when that happens I have to see you and, more often than not, I have to make you suffer for it— I know, believe me, how much I hurt you. And what eats into me then is wondering how long you'll put up with it. Please—Faith?"

And knowing what he wanted me to say I said it quickly, lovingly, and went on saying it until his need—for that day at least —was over.

"I love you, Nicholas. I understand. It doesn't matter."

We returned to Scarborough in November, four days, this time, shortened from the week he had intended by the exigencies of his combing machines.

"I'm making money," he told me as we sat by the happily crackling fire, my head on his shoulder. "My own money, Faith. And I can't tell you what that means to me. I could live easy, for the rest of my life, on what comes out of Lawcroft and Tarn Edge and Low Cross. My father has fixed them up so well that I wouldn't have to change a thing. I could just saunter down there two or three times a week—when he's gone—to interview my managers, which is as much as I reckon Blaize means to do, and the boost they've had from my father would see me through. Well, Blaize may be content to live like that, with nothing to show for himself but another man's money in his pocket. But not me. I said I could do it, and I'm doing it. The Wool Combers is mine, and it's growing, and I've got plans for Lawcroft and Tarn Edge as well, if my father could just bring himself to trust me, or take himself off to Bournemouth and leave me alone."

"But he's in Bournemouth now, surely, most of the time?"

"Oh yes. But he keeps coming back again. One morning my door opens, or I walk into a shed or into the countinghouse, and there he is, going through the ledgers, checking up on me. And I've got to admit that the questions he asks are the very ones I'd rather not answer. Eyes in the back of his head, my father—

unless, of course, he's had a word or two with Blaize the night before."

"Does Blaize really know what goes on?"

"Aye," Nicholas said, chuckling into my hair. "Blaize knows. It's his money, love, same as mine—the Tarn Edge part of it at any rate—and he doesn't mind getting his hands dirty when it comes to counting it."

Perfect days, once again, soon over—too precious to waste by talking of an impossible future—and on my return I was embroiled at once in the fierce opposition to my mother's marriage, which would take place, she declared, at Christmastime.

Celia invited Prudence and myself to dine, a council of war which would have been uncomfortable enough without the tensions of Celia's table. And after a perfectly served but none too ample meal, Celia's anxieties as a hostess being for the spotlessness of her silver, the perfect arrangement of her plates and dishes rather than the food, we returned to her drawing room to discuss what might be done.

My sister, need it be said, allowed no tobacco anywhere in her house, obliging Jonas to step outside if he wished to smoke an afterdinner cigar, complaining fretfully on his return that the noxious fumes, still clinging to his coat, were more than her carpet, her damask wall covering, and her stomach could be expected to tolerate.

"Well," she said, quickly inspecting the coffee tray from which I knew we would be foolish to expect more than one cup. "So here you are, Jonas."

"Yes, Celia."

"Good—since we are all awaiting your wisdom, and the coffee has gone quite cold while we were about it."

But Jonas, aware that her habit of measuring out exactly so many coffee beans and no more from her store cupboards disallowed the ordering of a fresh pot, merely accepted his lukewarm cup and drank it quite slowly, disinclined, it seemed, for wisdom.

"And what have you to tell us, Jonas?"

"Not a great deal."

"Then I have something to tell all of you. It strikes me you are taking this matter very calmly—so calmly, in fact, that I wonder if my mother is even aware of the repugnancy everyone—absolutely everyone—must feel. She has always been inclined to make herself conspicuous, ever since my father died—and this marriage! Well, she can only have one reason for it—you must know what I mean— Yes, of course you do—and although I don't like to speak of such matters, especially in the hearing of a single woman . . . Goodness, it is disgusting at her age—at any age—"

"You mean she is in love with him?"

"If that is what you like to call it. No doubt she calls it by that name. I believe there is another—"

"Passion," Prudence said tartly, irritated as always by Celia's assumption that at twenty-five she must, by virtue of her single status, be as blindly and totally innocent as Celia herself had been at sixteen.

"Really, Prudence."

"Really, Celia. I may be without direct experience, but my eyesight is keen enough. I washed and changed dozens of cholera victims during the epidemic and it did not escape my notice that not a few of the girls brought in from the streets—all of them unmarried, some of them too young to be married—were in various stages of pregnancy. I am also aware that in certain areas of our town one may obtain the sexual services of an eight-year-old child, should one be so inclined. Such a child was brought to Faith's door one night, while her husband was alive, somewhat in need of repair . . . If you don't wish to believe me, Faith will confirm the truth of it."

"No she will not," Celia said, her face frozen, as my father's had often been, into a mask of complete composure, her whole manner suppressing not only the brutality but the sheer untidiness of back-street lust, of any kind of lust. "If such things exist, then I have no reason to know about them, and neither have you. There is nothing like that in Albert Place, nor in Blenheim Lane. And we have met tonight because we have a real problem to discuss. Jonas—what are we to do about my mother?"

He smiled very slightly, amusement in him being always faint, a little obscure, since one could never be quite certain of just what, or who, had amused him.

"I have already told you, Celia," he said, his long, pale eyes occupied with the immaculate, empty cup in his hand. "Not a great deal. Your mother is a mature woman in indisputable possession of her fortune. And since there is nothing in our legal system to prevent a widow from remarrying, nor to restrict her choice of husband within the correct degree of kinship, there is nothing to be done on that score. You may not approve of passion, Celia, but it is not yet a criminal offence in our society, nor does it provide just cause for the detention of its victims in an asylum. Admittedly, in certain cases, one may regret that it does not—but it does not. You cannot *forbid* your mother. It did occur to me, however, that it might be possible to *frighten* her by providing evidence that Mr. Adair is not a proper person—"

"Which assuredly he is not."

"Not in your view, Celia, nor in mine. But my investigations revealed nothing which would be likely to alarm your mother. His background, of course, is very humble, which, once again, is hardly a criminal matter—even though he is brazen enough to let it show—and, in fact, his very vulgarity has saved him from certain situations, certain legal ties, which would otherwise have delivered him into our hands. He was married for the first time in Ireland as a young man but the union was in common law only—which means, in effect, that they announced their intention of living together and did so—and the woman is dead now in any case, the children adult and dispersed. He has a few debts but his creditors, very sensibly, have agreed to wait until he is married for settlement, and no one is dunning him. He has no criminal convictions for fraud or theft or anything else—by which I mean he has never been caught. There is a woman in the West Indies, certainly—we have young Liam Adair to show for that—but she is too far away to make a fuss, or attempt to claim her rights. Their marriage will not have been legal in any case and at least he has relieved her of the expense of bringing up the child—a rather gallant action, one could almost say, for a common man. There was an entanglement, some years ago, with a married woman—almost on our doorstep it seems—but it was quickly hushed up. And I believe your mother may already know about that."

I knew about it too and remembering my mother's vivid face as she made her confession—"those few months I spent as his mistress were the most luminous of my life"—I found myself unable to meet Jonas' cool gaze, wondering, most uncomfortably, *how* he knew, what else he knew, convincing myself, with a surge of panic, that nothing would be likely to escape him for long.

"You have been very busy, Jonas," Prudence said, and smiling again with that faintly malicious amusement, he told her, "Yes, indeed. Where money is concerned I think you may trust me to do everything one can."

"So I have always believed."

"Quite so. And in this case it has also been done in your best interests as well as the interests of my wife. I am as sorry as anyone else that I could find neither a useful scandal nor the prospect of exposure as a criminal to use against him. The only other method left open to us would be to offer to buy him off, which, in view of the healthy state of your mother's finances, could hardly succeed. And there is always the risk, in such negotiations, that he would take our money and marry her just the same."

"Then what is to be done?"

"I have already given my opinion. What do you think, Faith?"

And with Nicholas' face filling my mind I said incautiously, "I think—since she cares for him and we cannot prevent it—that we should leave her in peace."

"Oh yes," Celia burst out, "of course you would take that view, Faith, for I have never known you when your head was not in the clouds. And it is all very well for you to talk so, when you have a house and an income of your own, and no children to consider. Well, I have no children either, not yet, but Dr. Blackstone assures me that there is every likelihood—in fact, since Prudence is so well informed on these matters I may as well tell you I am expecting again, or so it seems, which gives me every good reason for disliking the idea of that man setting himself up in Blenheim Lane. Oh yes, you may depend upon it, he will take advantage of my mother's foolish generosity. He will spend every penny she has on himself and that ill-mannered child, and any other children he may have hidden away somewhere. And if that does not alarm you—since you are so comfortable already—then you should give some thought to Prudence, who will be obliged to live with him."

"Not for one moment longer than she must," Prudence said tersely, and Jonas, looking at her from beneath his heavy, crafty eyelids, gave her a deliberate and very sarcastic smile.

"Indeed," he said. "Then I take it we are soon to congratulate you on your forthcoming marriage?"

"I see no reason for that."

"I see every reason."

"Well, I hope you do not," Celia cut in, growing petulant, having tired herself out with her emotions and the fatigue of preparing even this small family dinner party. "For if you are thinking of marrying Freddy Hobhouse merely for the sake of convenience, then I must tell you it would not be convenient at all. Aunt Hannah was here yesterday, and the day before, warning me that you might do that very thing—as if she imagined I could do anything to prevent you—and I am bound to admit she is quite right. Nethercoats would eat up your money in a trice, and if Freddy has encouraged you to believe he stands to inherit from his uncle, Mr. Oldroyd, then Aunt Hannah says you must bear in mind that he has nine brothers and four sisters. Freddy's portion would not be so splendid, and the inheritance is by no means certain. My word, when I think that my mother could have had it all."

"You are quite mistaken Celia," Prudence informed her coolly. "I have no intention of marrying Freddy Hobhouse, either for his convenience or mine. I would not insult him, nor any other man, in that way."

"Then you will never escape from Blenheim Lane," Jonas said, a certain bleakness, I thought, in his eyes, an indication that he, too, had not forgotten the loss of Fieldhead Mills, and would be unlikely to forgive my mother for it.

"I cannot agree, Jonas."

"Eventually you will be forced to agree. You are a financial prisoner, my dear, which is the most complete captivity there is. I am in agreement with my wife when she says Mr. Adair's cash requirements are likely to be heavy. I think you may safely assume that your mother will not allow you a penny—nothing, at least, beyond the strict necessities of ribbons and toilet waters and the clothing suitable for a 'daughter-at-home.' And without money, dear Prudence—believe me, yes believe me—there is no freedom and no dignity either."

"Jonas—" I said, glancing at Celia, fearing that he would expose himself too far for her comfort, that his bitterness might wound her. But she was gazing down at her hands, barely listening to him, and getting up he walked irritably across the room and stood, one narrow hand on the mantelshelf, looking down at the meagre fire.

"You may talk splendidly of independence, Prudence," he said. "But ask yourself—how are you to afford it? Do you have in your possession at this moment even the train fare to Leeds? And if you had, what could you do there? There is no employment you could possibly take. Employment, for ladies of your station, does not exist. And if it did, you have no training, nor are there any establishments for females in which training could be obtained. Dear Prudence—you have told me all this yourself many a time. If you have a choice in life at all, then it is simply this—you must either marry a young man like Freddy Hobhouse, who would be easy enough for a clever woman like you to handle, or you must marry an old one, like his uncle, Mr. Oldroyd, in which case you would be a widow—and a comfortable one—that much the sooner."

"Must I?" she said through her teeth. "Must I really . . ." And it was Celia, oblivious to the undertones of her husband's voice, hearing nothing but the surface, who broke through what might have been an all too revealing altercation.

"Well," she said, "I am not so clever, but I can think of another solution. You could come and live here with us, Prudence, for if I am to start a family at last both my mother and Mr. Adair would be bound to see that I could make use of you. And since you are always talking about education and how none of us have any idea of bringing up children you would enjoy busying yourself with mine."

I returned home, the matter by no means resolved, bringing Prudence with me, Nicholas having left that afternoon for Liverpool. And as she settled herself in front of my cosily blazing fire —since I had not acquired Celia's habits of economy—she said, her eyes as bleak as Jonas' "I cannot tell you how much Celia's house, and Celia's life, oppresses me."

"Yes—but I don't think she is unhappy. Jonas is not satisfied—which may be very clear to you, and to me—but Celia seems unaware of it. She appears to have what *she* wants from her marriage, at any rate."

"So she does—which may be because she has no more conception of what marriage should really be than he has—except that she is a hopeless case, and perhaps if Aunt Hannah had let him alone he could have been different."

"And what should marriage really be like, in your opinion, Prudence?"

She smiled. "Yes, of course, you are about to tell me that I know nothing about it, and you are quite right. I merely base my judgement on the marriages I see around me, and none of them fills me with envy. Perhaps I have been single too long. If Father had lived, I would have had little to say in the matter. He would have chosen some worthy man for me, before I had left my teens, and I would now be making the best of it, like everybody else. But I have been free for some years now, Faith, and nothing tempts me to change."

"You mean *no one* tempts you to change. There are happy marriages, Pru."

"Where? Show me. I can think of happy individuals, some of whom are married, but it strikes me that in every marriage there is one partner who dominates, one who submits, and I should not like to do either. I can't think it necessary, or right, to do either. Our mother and father lived in peace because she submitted in every way to his will and to his opinions. Mayor Agbrigg lives in peace with Aunt Hannah by stealth—oh yes he does—by allowing her to have her way so often that when, just occasionally, he does something his way she hardly notices. She dominates and uses and despises him. Jonas tolerates and despises Celia. I don't wish to run the risk of that."

"Yes, but both Mayor Agbrigg and Jonas married for money. Celia married because she wanted to be married. Aunt Hannah—I don't know—because she thought she could make something of Mayor Agbrigg, and knew she could make something of Jonas."

"Exactly—because she wanted to do something with her life and, being a woman, could only do it through a man. That is what Aunt Hannah settled for—secondhand glory. I'm not ready to do that. It wouldn't be enough for me to push a man into building an empire. It wouldn't satisfy me to have a clever son and to feed myself on his triumphs. I'm willing to do the work and accept the responsibility—like Aunt Hannah does—but I want the credit as well. I'm not prepared to stand in any man's shadow—at least, not simply by virtue of the fact that he's a man and I'm a woman who shouldn't make herself conspicuous."

"Not even if you loved him?"

"Faith—I thought we were talking about marriage. I'm not sure about love either. Uncle Joel and Aunt Verity are in love, I suppose. He demands every instant of her time and attention, which she gives him very willingly, as you did with Giles. It seems to make her very happy—and you were not miserable—but I'm not sure I could cope with such total devotion. It occurs to me that I might come to see it as just another kind of captivity. Giles loved you, I know, but he didn't *share* the realities of his life with you, Faith."

And suddenly, sickeningly aware of the coffin I had refused to look at, the grave I still tended so carefully, knowing it to be empty, I cried out, "He didn't even share his death with me."

"Oh—darling—I'm so sorry. I shouldn't have said that—I didn't mean—"

"I know what you meant. He shielded me from life, as if I'd been a child. I know it. That was what he wanted, Prudence—and I would have given him anything he'd asked for."

"I know," she murmured, looking away from me. "And I used to wonder how long you could continue to take the strain. It would have stifled me, I know it, very soon . . ."

"No. I loved it. I needed it. I was safe with him . . ."

"Good," she said, her crisp tone instantly drying up the source of my approaching tears. "Obviously I am not looking for safety. Perhaps I had better find myself a missionary, since at least they have no objection to working their wives, very often to death . . . Perhaps that would suit me better than sitting at my embroidery in the drawing room at Nethercoats listening to Freddy telling me not to worry that the mill is collapsing because he will always take care of me—or sitting at Fieldhead waiting for Mr. Oldroyd to die."

And swayed by this mood of confidence, and because the need had been growing in me for weeks—because Prudence had shared everything else with me and I couldn't bear to be alone with this any longer—I fixed my eyes on the fire and said very quietly, "Prudence—for the past six months I have been Nicholas Barforth's mistress."

"Have you," she said, no more than that, her voice blending quite naturally with the stirring of the logs, the ticking of the clock; and as I turned sharply to look at her, she shook her head and smiled, amused by my astonishment.

"Well, and what did you expect me to say? What do you want me to say? I am hardly likely to encourage you. And you surely don't need to be told you are the biggest fool in Creation."

"No. You can safely assume I know that."

"And you couldn't imagine—or expect—that I would assist you, or allow myself to be used as an alibi?"

"No. I don't expect it, and wouldn't ask."

"Well then—am I to urge you to break off with him?"

"No. I won't do that."

"I imagine you will be obliged to, eventually—but we won't go into that. Are you feeling guilty on account of Giles and Georgiana, and want me to scourge your conscience?"

"Not even that. I manage very well for myself on that score."

"Yes, I can well believe you might. What do you want, then? You realise, of course, that if you are caught you will have to leave the district in disgrace—whereas he will not. And if you are not caught—well, dear, I wouldn't care to grow old, sitting at this window, waiting for him to come a-calling whenever he can spare a moment or two away from his combing machines, and his wife. Why have you told me, Faith? You must know my character well enough to realise that I wouldn't be prepared to sit here and listen to the tale of how marvellous he is, repeated over and over, to ease your conscience, and your loneliness? Faith—what are you hoping for?"

"Nothing," I told her, knowing she would believe me, knowing, very fully now, that it was true. "I love him, that's all. That is what I am—a woman who loves Nicholas Barforth. That is all there is to me."

"How gratifying that must be," she said, "for him, at any rate. Poor Nicholas, it must be so very difficult for him now, being obliged to continue his married life—and, of course, he does continue it, for if he had stopped sharing a bed with Georgiana the maids at Tarn Edge would have been quick to spread the word."

And as I gasped at the blow, she went on smiling at me as Aunt Hannah had once done, ruthless in the administration of what she hoped might be a cure.

"But you will have thought about that many a time, I imagine, on the nights he cannot be with you. Certainly it would prey very much on my mind—in your place. But don't worry, darling, for it may not be such a bad thing after all. There is always the possibility that she might conceive another child, and die of it."

"Prudence," I cried out, aghast, terrified now in case a time would ever come when I could hope for Georgiana's death—or admit to myself that I could—and, slapping one hand decisively against the other, a schoolmistress calling me to order, she said, "Let us look at things as they are. He married her. No one expected that the marriage would succeed—or could succeed. But he loved her enough, not so long ago, to break your heart on her account. He could very easily do so again. And if he does not abandon you—either because he has had his fill or because someone forces him to do so, or even because his conscience stirs him to admit that he is doing you immense harm—then what else have you to hope for but her death?"

I bent forward, my head touching my knees, and after a moment, she came to sit beside me and slid her cool hand in mine.

"Poor Faith. You are the last person in the world I would wish to hurt."

"I know. Don't worry about me, Pru, for I am neither stupid nor helpless. He is what I choose to make of my life for as long as I can, and you mustn't blame him for that. It seems very unlikely to me that I could love anyone else—not now. It seems to be a requirement of my nature that I should love him, and I will just have to cope with it. If hard things are said of me—later—I would not expect you to defend me."

"That, my dear," she said, her fingers tightening around mine, "would hardly be for you to decide. I would defend you, or not, as I chose—just as you are now choosing to put yourself in a position which could require it. Faith—all our lives someone has been telling us what to do, what to say, what to think, and even if it had been done from a sincere desire to protect us, which I doubt, it was always intolerable to me. And I wonder, truly, what credit there is in doing right if one has never been allowed the opportunity to do wrong? I am sick of petty tyranny, Faith. I want freedom for myself—the freedom to make my own mistakes, to make a stand and declare that what is right for you, or anyone else, need not be right for me—and so how can I deny the same thing to you? I have never greatly cared for Nicholas Barforth, but what right have I to say you are wrong to love him? I could not live as you do, nor feel as you feel, but what right have I to forbid you to feel it? I think you are bound to suffer for this and harm others with you, but if you are prepared for that suffering, what right have I to say you must not? If this is what you choose to do, and can accept the consequences, then do it. I believe you are wrong, but you will not forfeit my affection. I merely hope that you will survive, and be given the opportunity to choose better, next time."

But there could be no next time. There could be Nicholas, and I could not see beyond him. Nor did I make the attempt, for he had possessed the whole of me and I wanted no part of myself back from him. Yet I could not sleep that night, irritated by the thin whimpering of an early December wind, and by morning I knew that I must reserve some small measure of independence, that I must, against the urgings of my own nature, retain an area of my life that belonged only to myself, a foundation, however slight, on which to build—whatever I had left in me to build—when it was over.

Chapter Twenty

MY MOTHER was married on a white winter morning, a swan's-down sky streaked faintly with pink, the crackle of new snow underfoot, the parish church dusty and cool in its emptiness, since only Prudence and myself and Jonas sat on the bride's side of the aisle, a quartet of Adairs, fresh from Ireland, occupying the other.

She wore blue velvet, carried a huge white fur muff; there was a white feather in her hat, a rapturous satisfaction in her cloudy blue eyes. She was marrying the man with whom she was perhaps no longer quite so romantically in love, but whom she most ardently desired. And I could see no reason why he, with his roguish Irish eyes, and his rogue's charm, should not desire her too.

"I am going to be so very happy," she told us, tripping out into the churchyard. "My word, what a lovely day—every day is going to be lovely from now on. I will tell you something, Faith dear—it is going to be strawberries and champagne every moment—yes, as a girl I did so long for my strawberries and champagne. And now—you will know what I mean. Perfect content."

But only our aging governess, Miss Mayfield, who, with young Liam Adair tugging at her hand could count on many years of employment yet, seemed wholeheartedly to agree.

They were to go to London, making no promises to return until the New Year, and, waving them off at the station, I think I was more than ever aware of approaching change, that this

Christmastime—this season of sentiment and good will, this family festival—would be difficult, and dangerous.

Aunt Verity, just back from Bournemouth, called to take tea and to enquire about my mother's wedding, her smile as sweet as it had ever been, sensing no treachery, no awareness that she was face to face with adultery, the mistress of her much-loved son.

"You will come to us, dearest, on Christmas Day afternoon," she said. "Caroline has promised me an hour, which is very generous, and Georgiana does not go to Galton until Boxing Day. We are not going to Listonby until the New Year, for your uncle has not been well and I think we had best be rather quiet. But we shall look forward to seeing you, Faith—it has been much too long."

And because I could not hide from them forever, because sooner or later I would have to take Georgiana's hand and smile, with Nicholas looking on—because only Aunt Verity's absence had enabled me to delay this long—I chose not to fall ill that Christmas morning, as I might have intended, and sent Prudence a note that I would share her carriage.

There was the usual splendid pine tree in the hall at Tarn Edge, the lamps already lit in the drawing room, a mountain of logs blazing and singing in the hearth, their tangy odour blending with the tea-time muffins, the drift of Barforth cigars that had scented all the Christmases of my childhood. Aunt Verity's home, warm and easy, when mine had been cold and difficult, Nicholas, even then, being the hope I brought with me, the memory I took away. And pausing a moment in the doorway, watching them, my uncle at ease in his armchair, his legs stretched out to the fire, Caroline opposite him in the matching chair, enthroned as became her station, Georgiana sprawled on the sofa, looking out of the window, wishing herself already at the abbey, I wondered who suspected me, knew, with a surge of blessed relief, that no one did, until a head turned, a pair of smoke grey eyes flickered over me, and Blaize came across the room to kiss my hand.

"Blaize, how lovely to see you. Caroline—it's been an age. *Georgiana*, how are you?"

And these, I knew, were the bones of adultery, my treacherous handclasp, the false smile I gave her as she sighed and stirred herself listlessly to greet me, the criminal ease with which I nodded, through the firelight, to her husband—my lover—and enquired, "How are you, Nicholas?" as if I had forgotten his dark head, on my pillow, just a few hours ago. And worse than that—far worse—was the pleasure it gave me to see that she was not looking her best, that boredom, as always, had taken her colour away, that her pointed face, without its vivacity, was quite plain.

"I make her so miserable," he had told me, and seeing that she was indeed miserable—whether on his account or for lack of the open moorland of Galton—I was obliged to struggle with myself, fiercely, to strangle the beginnings of delight—of a most evil-hearted gratitude. There was a toddling, black-eyed Dominic Chard now to swell the family circle, and his not quite identical brother Noel; a slightly smaller but exceedingly determined Gideon Chard, needing frequently to be restrained. There was an agile little demon called Gervase Barforth, climbing on every chair back, attempting to mount the fender until his father —my lover—removed him by the scruff of his neck, called out, "Georgiana," and, when she took no notice, strode across the room and dropped the protesting little boy into her lap.

"Can't you do something with that child, Georgiana?"

"Oh," she said, her green eyes only half open. "What is there to do? I could drown him, I suppose—although it would seem rather a waste of my initial effort . . ."

"One rings for nanny, surely, at such times?" Blaize murmured, stepping easily—as he so often did—to her rescue. "Even a poor bachelor like myself knows that much . . ."

"Faith," Caroline called out, visibly shuddering at the piercing quality of her nephew's howls as he was carried away, "come and sit over here with me. You have been playing the recluse lately and I have started to wonder why. There is no admirer, I suppose, that we have not yet heard about?"

"Why no, Caroline—what an idea."

"That is exactly what I said to Matthew, when Aunt Hannah enquired. Faith would have told *me*, I said—didn't I, Matthew? Well, you will come to us for three weeks in February—I am quite set on it. My new servants' wing is quite finished and I should enjoy your opinion."

And, anchored to Caroline's side, her interest in her own

affairs claiming the whole of mine, I was spared the necessity of talking to anyone else.

She had been down to London in November to watch the funeral of the Duke of Wellington, a gentleman who would not be much mourned in Cullingford, since like Sir Giles Flood and probably Sir Matthew Chard, he had not wished to extend the vote to commercial men. But Caroline had been impressed by the ceremony of his departure, the muffled drums, the military bands playing their dirges, the magnificent black and gold funeral car bearing the coffin draped in crimson velvet, the hero's sword and marshal's baton, his white-plumed hat, set out upon it. She had been touched by the sight of the duke's poor old horse following on behind, his empty boots hanging, reversed, from an empty saddle, but, rather more to the point, she had made the acquaintance of a certain Lady Henrietta Stone, a woman of decided fashion with a house in Belgravia, who was bringing a party to Listonby at the beginning of March.

"You had best stay on with me for that too," she said. "For Hetty Stone is really very smart—city smart, not county smart—and I shall be obliged to put myself out for her a little. And you could cast a glance at my wardrobe, Faith, if you wouldn't mind, for I have brought some new evening gowns back with me from London and there is something not quite right about them. I told Matthew you would be able to spot it instantly."

Tea was served quite magnificently; we ate, drank, smiled, made Christmas promises of companionship, solidarity—"We must see more of one another—my word, how time slips away—do you remember, when was it? Five years ago? Impossible"—and as Aunt Hannah and Caroline began to stir themselves and cast meaningful glances at their husbands, both ladies having numerous other demands on their time, the ordeal seemed almost at an end.

"Well, all the best to you," Aunt Hannah said, getting to her feet.

"Aye," Sir Joel answered her. "We'll take a glass of wine, before you go, Hannah, and drink to what we've had, and what's to come. Well then, here's health and happiness to all of you, may you all prosper . . . Here's to old friends and absent friends and new beginnings—not forgetting our little Elinor . . ."

And as we toasted each other, warmed by the easy emotions

of the season, Georgiana, who had taken a brooding glass or two already, got up from the sofa and swayed forward towards Nicholas, stumbling against him as the trailing hem of her gown caught against the fender, her hair a burnished, beautiful copper in the firelight.

"Oh, dear," she said. "Oh yes—we must drink to that—new beginnings—and forgiving each other our trespasses. Dear Nicky, do forgive me my trespasses, although I expect I shall trespass again . . ."

And because I couldn't look at Nicholas, I turned my head away and found Blaize's smoky, quizzical eyes watching me.

My mother returned home in February, "a cat" Prudence called her, "sitting in a cream pot," and immediately the resentments that had been so far held in check came bubbling to the surface when it was seen that Mr. Adair had every intention not only of playing the devoted husband but the fond, somewhat overzealous step-papa.

"Family life," he said, beaming at us as we gathered around my mother's dinner table—his dinner table now. "I never realised, Elinor, in my wandering days, how much I was missing. And here it all is—my little boy and your lovely girls, you and me—there's nothing to beat it, and nothing to beat us, so long as we stick together."

And in his urgent desire to be respectable, to be accepted, Prudence was forced to play a most unwilling part.

Gone now were the days when she could eat a solitary breakfast in her own room, spending as long as she liked in perusing the letters and papers brought up on her breakfast tray. Now she was required to eat every meal *en famille*, sharing her news and her correspondence with a jovial but very determined Mr. Adair, an easygoing rascal transformed overnight, it seemed, into a patriarch who considered it his duty to watch over his womenfolk, to know, at all times, their exact whereabouts and their intentions, what they were doing and with whom.

Gone now the days when my mother's carriage, more often than not, was at Prudence's disposal, when she had merely to say, "I'm off now, Mamma. I'll be back presently."

For the horses, these days, were in Mr. Adair's gift, and he was not generous in their bestowal.

"And just where is it you're off to, m'darling?"

"I have visits to pay."

But young ladies, in Mr. Adair's scheme of things, paid no visits that did not include the chaperonage of a mother, did not —most decidedly—concern themselves with reservoirs and the resettlement of unemployed wool combers. Young ladies were young ladies, motionless and sweet as lilies, proving by their constant presence at their mother's side that they were the products of a happy home, content to share that home with a new, enthusiastic father.

And since "sticking-together" was very much in Mr. Adair's best interests, I soon found my own freedom invaded in a way I had not expected, my time eaten away by "family teas," "family dinners," "family Sundays," in which, at my mother's urgent request, I was invariably included.

"Just do this for me, darling," she would implore. "Just let me get settled—I'm so happy." And since her personal happiness was beyond question, an effervescent fountain of it sparkling in her eyes, her laughter, the eagerness of her whole dainty body— because there was something achingly young and vulnerable in her face, which could not fail to move me—I submitted, afresh, to the captivity of that drawing room, my father's black basalt urns still on the mantel shelf, his fragile china figurines still there, in their glass-fronted seclusion, but the whole house fragrant now with Daniel Adair's almost continual cigar, loud with the hearty male presence no Aycliffe had ever possessed, cluttered—as we had never dared to clutter it—by the playthings and the playmates of an untidy, seven-year-old child. And when Prudence, appalled by the discovery of scratches on the panelling, fearful for her porcelain, enquired of my mother how she could tolerate the antics of young Liam Adair, the answer, with a blissful, languorous smile was, "Ah—you see, dear, he reminds me of his father."

I did not believe that Mr. Adair intended us any harm, at least not if it could be avoided, for he was a man who took pleasure in women and would have preferred, if possible, to be fond of us and have us fond of him in our turn. But self-interest had long been not only a habit with him but a necessity and like any other aging, yet still powerful stallion, he was unwilling to see two well-dowered mares depart from his herd, to squander themselves elsewere.

Like Jonas, he could not marry us himself—would not have wished to marry us since my mother sufficed him gloriously as a wife—but our possessions tantalised him, challenged him, and before long, or so it seemed to us, the Irish Sea was thronging with hopeful Adairs, coming, at the summons of their clan chieftain, to the marriage market.

"Oh, dear," my mother told me, bursting in on me unannounced, to my immense consternation, "I am afraid Prudence is very vexed, for the house is full again and she declares she is about to take herself off to Aunt Hannah's until they have all gone away, since Daniel has made it very clear he does not approve of her staying here alone with you. Do talk to her, Faith, for they are Daniel's relations, after all—my relations now—and I wish she would not be so sharp. I am sure there was no reason for her to slap Liam, this morning—at least, not so hard—when he picked up that Meissen bowl from the hall table— My goodness, the poor child was just curious to see what was written underneath, for which she was entirely to blame since she had been telling him everything was marked on the underside with the maker's name . . . Yes, I know the porcelain is hers, but she cannot take it away until she is married, and to box the child's ears so violently was certainly extreme. After all, nothing had been broken, and now she is talking of packing the whole collection away in boxes and storing it in the attic, which I feel sure Daniel will not allow. Indeed, he is the master of the house now. It is *his* attic and if he tells her she may not use it I am sure one must consider him to be in the right. And since the porcelain attracts so much notice and everybody knows how much it is worth, what would people think should it not be on display? It would cause nothing but gossip and spite—do talk to her, Faith, for I live in dread of a confrontation between them. I am not quite ready for it yet. Do explain to her that I am really so very happy . . ."

But my mother's happiness in no way consoled Prudence for the loss of her own freedom.

"The porcelain is mine," she told me hotly. "My father spent fifty years of his life collecting it, and if Mr. Adair wishes to display it to his friends then he had best keep that little monster under control. Miss Mayfield can do nothing with him, but I am not so delicate, and if I find him just once again playing near the cabinets he will have cause to remember it. So—we have another cousin from Kildare, just arrived this morning. A fine young gentleman, something of a scholar, we are told, and so he may be, except that he has not yet pronounced a word in my hearing that I could understand. Delightful, don't you think? I am to be denied the company of my own friends and forced into his. When Freddy Hobhouse called this morning no one informed me of it. He was told I was not at home, and sent away. And I am by no means certain that all of my letters are delivered. How dare he, Faith? Truly—how dare he? Well, they are bringing the Kildare cousin to meet you later this afternoon, so you had best beware. Perhaps he is to be offered the choice between us, and he will certainly pick you, since you are better-looking and richer."

And, inwardly trembling, I rushed to Mrs. Marworth and begged her to be on the lookout for Nicholas, to warn him, explain to him, to tell me, at once, if he had seemed put-out, if there was any hope of seeing him again that day.

I could not avoid Caroline's invitation to Listonby, enduring three weeks of gruelling activity, gnawing anxiety, since Nicholas had first asked me to cancel, then ordered it, then tried to coax me out of it, and, failing that, had spent a terrible and totally unreasonable hour declaring me flighty and unfeeling, a giddy butterfly like my mother, incapable of denying myself a moment's entertainment.

"If you can do without me for three weeks, then I reckon you can do without me altogether. Of course you must go to Listonby, darling. I perfectly understand it. There's no telling who you might meet there. By God, there isn't. You could even come back with a Matthew Chard of your own. And who am I to stand in the way of that? He might not marry you, of course, but then, neither can I. And they say a change does everybody good."

I should have defended myself, of course, should have grown angry, told him to leave and take his poor opinion of me, and his injustice, away with him; but I threw my arms around him instead and held him, the whole of my body pleading with his, until the rage of his jealousy had subsided.

"I'm sorry."

"I know."

"I say things in temper—do things in temper—"

"Yes, I know that too—like the day you wouldn't get on Cullingford's first train . . ."

"Christ—I'd forgotten about that."

"I've never forgotten anything you've ever done—at least, the things I know about."

"She'll have her house full of young sparks from London, Faith, who'll see you as fair game—who'll think that's what she's invited you for. And it maddens me that I have to let that happen. It wouldn't happen if they knew you belonged to me . . ."

"It won't happen in any case. I love you, Nicholas."

"I'll ride over when I can. It's a big house and, knowing the gentry, they'll all be doing the same thing."

"Not if Caroline catches them, Nicholas—would it be safe?"

"You don't want me? If that's it, then say so . . ."

"That's not it, Nicholas—you know it couldn't be. It's Caroline. You know she never misses a thing and—and Georgiana is almost certain to ride over."

"I know," he said, his jaw set and strained. "And shall I tell you something—I don't care. I mean it, Faith—I don't care. Oh yes—I *should* care. I know I'm in the wrong. I'm the criminal—not you, not Georgiana— I'm the adulterer. I'm the fool. It was my mistake that brought us to this—not yours, not hers. I know. Well—it makes no bloody difference because I won't accept it. I might get hurt, and so might you. It's the chance I'm taking, and you'll have to take it with me."

And after this explosion perhaps Caroline's hectic house was, for the first day or two, almost a refuge.

I had no reason to believe her other than perfectly happy—for she would have said so otherwise—her relationship with her husband having a definite physical aspect, despite her streak of prudishness, both of them enjoying, I thought, a hard day's work, a hard day's sport, followed by an uncomplicated, energetic bedding about which no one could ever have induced her to say a word. Sir Matthew rose, invariably, at first light, breakfasting, every hunting morning, on slices of red beef and raw eggs beaten up in brandy, which would see him through the excitements of the day. The gentlemen would then set off, not too early—since a fox, being a night-feeder, is sluggish at daybreak and provides no sport—returning triumphant, ardent, sometimes very frisky but rarely before dinnertime. And preoccupied with what she considered as her side of their bargain, her guests, her children, the domestic details and dramas of her tenants, the new servants' wing her father's generosity had enabled her to build, I doubt if Caroline gave him a thought before then.

Like all the Barforths it was her belief that if one took the trouble to do anything at all one should do it splendidly, and her new wing—which she showed me the very hour of my arrival—was built in two sections, allowing not only a most efficient grouping of related employments, but a segregation of the sexes. The original servants' hall had been much extended, a giant buffer now between the butler's domain on the left, the housekeeper's on the right, the butler's pantry being surrounded by all the requisite offices where menservants were likely to be found, capacious wine cellars and beer cellars, the plate scullery, the room for the polishing of boots, the room for the polishing of knives, the room where lamps were cleaned and filled, the strong room, the gun room, the door—in full view of the butler's eagle eye—which led to the single bedrooms where the footmen and valets and assorted, or visiting, menservants slept.

The housekeeper's room was similarly surrounded, by stillroom and linen room, the room where the Listonby china was carefully catalogued and stored, a narrow passage leading to the vast kitchen area where the head chef, whose artistic temperament required a certain degree of privacy, had a small sitting room for his own use, giving him easy access to the pastry room, the game larder, the fish larder, the meat larder, the bakehouse where Listonby's daily bread gave a permanent, spicy fragrance to the air.

There was another passage, narrow and dark this time, leading to the steamier fragrances of the laundry room and ironing room, where cheerful, sturdy girls worked—rather more barearmed and bare-bosomed than Caroline liked—at their washtubs and mangles, singing to attract the attention of the stable boys—or so Caroline thought—as they carried their baskets of linen outside to dry.

And in this complicated, busy household—where Caroline, I felt certain, knew the contents of every cupboard, was as precisely aware of the cost of anything and everything from a fullscale banquet to the replacing of a chipped cup—I was able to

lose, temporarily, the keen edge of my anxieties, living from the
ceremony of breakfast, the savoury-laden sideboard, the somno-
lence of newspapers and gossip in the Great Hall afterwards, to
the more elaborate ceremonies of luncheon and five o'clock tea,
the ultimate complexity that was dinner. I busied myself in
changing my clothes as the occasion and the weather required,
flirted mildly with a visiting, nonhunting gentleman or two,
talked personalities, dress fabrics, fashionable philosophies with
visiting ladies, walked to church with Caroline on Sunday mornings, watching with affectionate amusement as she acknowledged the salutations of her tenantry, the deference of her parson, the slap she administered with her gloves to her children,
and to her husband, when the sermon inclined Sir Matthew to
doze, the future Sir Dominic, the future colonel of Hussars, and
little Gideon, the future bishop, to misbehave.

Nicholas did not come, but, quite soon, Georgiana appeared,
riding over from Galton to join the hunt, vivid and outrageous as
she always was in the company of her own people, astonishing
those young sparks Nicholas had feared on my account, by her
daring and endurance in the saddle, her sudden flights of fancy
that ended, to Caroline's intense disgust, in a midnight steeple-
chase, from Listonby church tower to Galton church tower, no
holds barred, no quarter given, no farmyards and no fences
spared, with champagne in the abbey cloister for the survivors, a
great deal of splashing in the abbey stream, and Peregrine
Clevedon discovered in such flagrantly promiscuous circumstances with one of Caroline's married, decidedly tipsy female
guests, that my cousin could not be persuaded to overlook it.

"But it's just Perry," Georgiana explained. "He's like that,
Caroline. He won the race, after all, and you must admit the
woman was willing. Matthew—do make her understand."

But Sir Matthew had taken the measure of his Caroline by
now and shrugging his heavy, lazy shoulders rather apologetically, not only submitted to her judgement but saw that it
was carried out. The lady was asked to take her departure. Mr.
Peregrine Clevedon, who had, in fact, committed his mis-
demeanour on his own property, not Caroline's, was severely
reprimanded, and for the next day or two, she patrolled her
guests with the air of a good governess who has every intention

of keeping her class in order, a procedure which, rather than giving offence, appeared to provide considerable amusement.

I returned to Millergate exhausted, aching for Nicholas, yet it was Mr. Adair, my mother's lover, not my own, who came first to welcome me home, his bright black eyes roving merrily around me, shrewd eyes and a shrewd brain behind them, a man experienced in the ways of the world who, I was quick to realise, could be another threat to me.

"So you're home again, my lovely girl—that's good, since home is where you belong—except that I know how your mother is breaking her heart to have you back in her own nest again. It's not safe, she thinks, for a bonny young thing like yourself to be living here all alone. Fretting she is, which I don't like to see—but there now, what was it I came for? Yes indeed, you're expected at dinner tonight—and she said, now what was it?—yes—Sunday, some little trip she's planning. We'll collect you mid-morning."

I went to Scarborough again in May, but this time, because Mr. Adair had raised a quizzical eyebrow at my explanations of visiting an old acquaintance in York—a friend, it had pained me to add, of my late husband—I was tense throughout the journey, exhausted on arrival, almost sick with nerves when Nicholas, who should have been there to greet me, arrived late. And instead of the magical days of escape we had planned we found ourselves compelled—at last—to admit that there could be no escape, and that one of us, or both of us, would be required to make a sacrifice.

He had a wife and child who might mean little to him just then, but he had a thriving business which mattered a great deal and anchored him firmly to Cullingford. Could he sacrifice that, and possibly his share of the Barforth mills with it for my sake, and start again somewhere else? I had a family who would not easily let me go. I felt love for one sister, a growing feeling of responsibility for my mother and Celia. I had a reputation for which I cared only spasmodically but the loss of which would be damaging to others. Could I leave them all behind and creep away somewhere, to the cloistered existence of a kept woman, a cherished prisoner? Yes, Nicholas, told me, I could. If I loved him, I couldn't hesitate.

But could I forget how Georgiana had flung herself against him that Christmas Day, offering reconciliation, or how wretched she often appeared lately, her spirits and her colour fading, as his temper grew shorter. Yes, he told me. She was his responsibility, not mine. He was the adulterer. His was the guilt and the blame, and his shoulders were broad enough.

Could I ignore the simple, honest truth that so long as I remained in his life there was no hope of peace for any of us? And I knew better than to ask him that.

But spring is a cruel time for the making of such decisions, an impossible time, and Nicholas refused to be thwarted in any case.

"If Dan Adair suspects you, then he suspects you," he said bluntly. "And if he comes sniffing around Lawcroft asking me to buy his silence, or around Millergate trying to blackmail you into going back to your mother, then I'll flatten him, and I reckon he ought to know that. I can't see what he'd have to gain by going to my wife, or to my father, but if he did, I'm not even sure I'd give a damn. My father can throw me out of Lawcroft and Tarn Edge but he can't shift me from the Wool Combers, and if Perry Clevedon took it into his head to shoot me I could change his mind with pound notes. It would suit Blaize, at any rate."

And although the greater part of his nature would have gloried in announcing his possession of me to our narrow world —"This is my woman and be damned to the lot of you"—I knew, beyond the slightest shadow of doubt, that if he lost his share of the Barforth mills to Blaize, a day would surely dawn when he would most bitterly regret it.

The summer drained me that year, shredded my nerves and evaporated my spirit, for, my own anxieties apart, I seemed the constant prey of all those who had cause to complain of my mother, so that I felt besieged, day in day out, by Aunt Hannah, who required to know when we could expect my mother's jew-ellery to go up for auction and then her petticoats, by Pru-dence, who, in her own intense frustration, had no thought for mine, by the Irish cousins, by Daniel Adair, whose plans for me were every bit as specific as for my sister, and, not least of all, by Celia, whose fast developing pregnancy, she felt, was not at-tracting its share of notice.

"Faith—you will never believe what Jonas has done to me. He has invited the Battershaws to dine. Yes, I know they are among his best clients and we have dined twice with them since Christmas, but how am I to manage? Oh yes—I can order the meal and see that everything is spotless and perfectly tidy, but Jonas should understand that I cannot be *looked at* in my condition—"

"Celia, there is nothing yet to show."

"No, but I get so fatigued, Faith, by dinnertime, and when the maids are quite likely to bring out smeared glasses and chipped plates unless I make sure of it, and cook is so unreliable about timing, I don't see how I can be expected to sit there with a smile on my face and chat. You must come and do it for me."

I did, Jonas taking advantage of my presence, I thought, to include our member of Parliament, Mr. Fielding, and his political agent in the party, gentlemen whose good offices would be needed should he decide to embark on a parliamentary career of his own. And so it happened that when Celia, who had quite genuinely worn herself out by a day-long flurry of cleaning and polishing, retired to bed soon after the meal, I remained in Albert Place very late, chatting pleasantly to two gentlemen I had no wish to impress—and so impressed rather easily—and to Jonas himself, who relaxed almost to humanity without the presence of his wife and his mother.

He escorted me home afterwards, a quite natural courtesy, stepped into my hall a moment to thank me, since I had put myself out for his sake, and although the house was perfectly silent, Mrs. Marworth's smile quite bland—and although Nicholas had been warned well in advance of my plans—no one could have failed to identify the odour of tobacco betraying a male presence behind my drawing room door.

"Mrs. Marworth—" I gasped, desperately seeking help from anyone, but having no help to give me, she had already disappeared down the corridor, leaving me with my horrified guilt and my brother-in-law.

"Jonas . . ." I said, just his name, bowing my head, I think, as if for execution, since he would be well within his rights to demand the identity of my caller, and when I raised it again I couldn't read the expression—my sentence—in his clever, lawyer's face, had no idea at all what his faint smile might mean.

"Yes, Faith. Thank you for your help this evening. I will leave you, now that I have seen you safely bestowed. Good night."

"Oh, Jonas—my goodness . . ."

And incredibly he shrugged his narrow shoulders and touched me, very lightly, with a cool finger tip.

"Good night. There is nothing for you to be concerned about —except that I believe one of your chimneys may be smoking, and you should attend to it. Celia will be very glad to see you, I expect, should you care to call tomorrow."

Yet, although he did not betray me, gave no indication when I saw him again that he had observed anything amiss, exerted no pressure on my movements or my activities, the mere fact of his knowledge weighed upon me, burdened me.

An endless summer, hot days, a yellow sky hanging low over Millergate, heavy days spiced with a whisper of faraway excitements, since in exotic lands I could scarcely imagine, the Tsar of Russia had invaded the territory of his brother monarch, the Sultan of an ailing Turkey, an event in which—for reasons I was slow to understand—we seemed likely to become involved.

We could not, of course—or so a dozen people told me— tolerate the presence of Russian aggressors so near to India, but the truth was that we, the greatest military nation in the world, the conquerors of Napoleon, had been at peace for almost forty years now, and even in Cullingford a great many men were eager to hear the beat of martial drums, to show the Russian giant, the Austrian giant, any giant at all, that we had lost none of our vigour. And I found it easier, at tea time, at dinnertime, at the concert hall and the Assembly Rooms, to ponder the fate of such unlikely places as Constantinople, Sebastopol, the Crimea, than my own.

"There's nothing else for it. We've got to fight them," Sir Matthew Chard declared, with no more idea than I as to where the Crimea might be found.

"Aye," Sir Joel Barforth answered him. "Fight them, and I'll sell you the uniform cloth to do it in."

"Will it make any difference, Nicholas?" I asked, and he told me, "No. I almost wish it would."

I went to Scarborough, most dangerously in June and August, not daring to step out of the garden for fear of the summer crowds, twice in September, a hunted animal at my arrival and my departure, a few feverish days in between, immense fatigue at my homecoming, a dry-mouthed panic until my first encounter with Daniel Adair, with Aunt Hannah, with Jonas, reassured me that I had not been caught. I became dangerously, uncharacteristically emotional, prone to unexplained tears and sudden bursts of laughter. Loud noises startled me, flickering evening shadows loomed out at me, distorted into fearsome shapes that caused my stomach to lurch, my heart to beat in the wild palpitations to which my robust body was not accustomed. When my sister Celia, who had spent at least half of her pregnancy in bed, gave birth to a daughter that July—Miss Grace Cecilia Agbrigg, a silken little creature with a curl or two of dark hair and enormous liquid eyes—I wept unrestrainedly at my first sight of her, wept when I was asked to be her godmother, stood throughout her christening with tears seeping from my eye corners, ruining the lace ribbons of my bonnet. There were long nights when sleep would not come at all, other nights of fitful dozing threaded by terrible dreams of myself hurrying through mean streets, a glimpse of Giles Ashburn in a doorway, nothing but an empty room when I ran frantically inside, his figure in the distance, the beloved quietness of him shredding away to mist the instant before I reached his side. A sick tortuous wandering in the dark, a sudden jolting to wakefulness and the certain knowledge that although my love for Nicholas was deeper and more intense than ever, a change of some kind would have to be made.

A change. Yet, having told myself that I must make it, that it *must* be done, having rehearsed the reasons until they became welded to my brain and gave me no rest, I was unprepared both for the nature and the manner of it, when it came.

He arrived very late, the second night of October, restless, ill-tempered, I thought at first, disinclined for conversation, barely listening to the few remarks I made. And then, blunt as he always was in moments of emotion, he snapped out, "I had better tell you, before you hear it from someone else. Georgiana is pregnant again."

"I see."

"No," he said, taking me by the elbows, squeezing hard. "You don't see."

But I would have none of that, pulling away from him, hurting myself, putting as much distance between us as my tiny drawing room allowed.

"There is no reason to make excuses to me, Nicholas, because you have—because you have made love to your wife."

"You knew it," he said. "If you were married, you'd have had to do the same. You knew that I was obliged . . ."

"No. I know no such thing. Be honest with me, Nicholas—that's about all there is left now. When it happened—whenever, how often—you wanted it. Don't insult me, and—just don't insult any of us by pretending otherwise. And don't tell me your reasons—don't—they have nothing to do with me. I'm not angry, Nicholas. I have no right to be angry. Just allow me—a moment or two . . ."

I stood with my back towards him, willing him to keep his distance, knowing—whatever I really felt, whether I had it in me to endure this, to weather it, or not—that I must not endure it, that I must use it as a wedge to force us apart. And even in that first moment of shock I remembered Prudence, telling me, "She may conceive another child and die of it," and I knew that that alone was sufficient reason for our separation. I did not want her to die. I must continue not to want it, for if it should happen and I had the slightest cause to suspect myself, I knew I could not live with it, could certainly never live with Nicholas.

"Nicholas . . ." I said, and crossing the room he took me by the shoulders, carefully, as if he feared to damage the remnant that was left to us; and even that, I knew, was slipping fast away.

"Don't say it, Faith. You don't want to cause her pain, and neither do I— God dammit, I don't hate her. The child is mine and I'll look after it, as I'll look after the other one—and her. For the rest of my life I'll support her, in style, so she can go on supporting her brother. I'll patch up her abbey and pay out whatever it costs to keep her land in good order, and her brother out of jail. But I won't lose you, Faith. I'll be patient with her now. I'll keep my temper and indulge her whims and fancies until this is safely over. But I won't lose you. I won't throw you away for the sake of the Clevedons. Believe me."

But it was over. I mourned him all night, dry-eyed, my whole body aching, despairing. I mourned him the next day, my real self locked away weeping and desperate, while the cool shell of my Aycliffe self-control served tea to Aunt Hannah and Prudence, listened and smiled as my mother told me of yet another Irish cousin, and that she was very happy. I mourned him the night that followed and the one after, came downstairs before dawn to wander in sheer desolation from room to room, a burden to myself, which I could not lay down.

It was over, and when he came the fifth night and rapped a stubborn hand on my window, it was still over. I opened the door to him because it did not occur to me to do otherwise and when he came into my parlour I made some anxious comment about the state of him, since he had walked up from the Swan in the rain. But it was still over.

"You can ask me to leave," he said. "I didn't go the first time and I won't go now."

"Yes, you will."

"Do you really mean to turn me out in the rain."

"Yes, I do." And I believed it.

"Then do it, for I've got nothing to offer you but trouble—I know it. I know all the answers. I'd tell any other man in my position to pull himself together and get over it. I can't."

He stayed in my bed until morning, a risk we had never taken before, and as I let him out through the kitchen before Mrs. Marworth was awake, he held both my hands and kissed them, kissed my ears and my chin and the nape of my neck, unfastened my nightgown and kissed my bare shoulders, reckless and heedless, pressing my body hard against the cold, tiled wall.

"I love you, Faith. Do you believe me?"

And I believed him.

"We're all right again now, Faith." But I could not believe that.

Chapter Twenty-one

I WOULD NEVER GO to Scarborough again, at least, not until Georgiana's condition was resolved one way or the other, for she had miscarried before, might miscarry again, and false and treacherous as I was, I wanted him to be with her if she did so.

But by November he had quarrelled with Blaize and with his father, had narrowly averted a strike at Lawcroft, for which his own intolerance, his own autocratic temper—Blaize insisted—had been to blame. He was tense and miserable, dreading, as I was, the approaching Christmas season when family festivities would draw us all too close together. We had much to discuss, having parted already a second time, being well aware that we were teetering on the brink of a third, and although our reconciliations seemed powerful enough to propel us from one crisis to the next, we must surely, one day, reach our limits.

And so I risked myself once again on that solitary journey, Mrs. Marworth accompanying me to Leeds, well content with the steady supply of Barforth guineas in her pocket, my happy excitement of earlier times transformed now into a kind of sad determination, since this visit could well be—*should* be—my last.

It was a grey afternoon, a high wind churning the sea, the steep little town quite empty as I was driven through it, the house empty too, only the housekeeper standing discreetly in the doorway, telling me, as always, that there was a fire in the parlour, a fire in Mr. Barforth's bedroom, muffins for tea. But of Mr. Barforth himself she couldn't say, for she was paid merely to make his mistress comfortable, not keep her informed of his comings and goings.

"Muffins?" she said, clearly having reached her own limits, and so I took off my gloves and my fur-lined, hooded cloak, and ate muffins and indifferent gingerbread, poured tea for the sake of giving myself an occupation, and left it on the tray to go cold.

"Dinner," she told me, "in an hour, madam, if it's convenient." And since it was convenient for her, I went up to the bedroom that contained the most poignant of my memories, allowed the fisherman's daughter they were training as a maid to get out the new gown I always brought with me, a light aquamarine, this time, cut low to display the strands of gold filigree Nicholas had given me and which I could only wear here without need for explanations. I brushed and dressed my hair, put his pearl and diamond drops in my ears, his heavily coiling gold snake with its topaz eye around my arm, perfumed my shoulders, threw a lace-edged cashmere shawl around them, and went down to dine, realising that while I had been dressing, the moment had come and gone when he could possibly reach me tonight.

"Crab, madam—fresh-caught this morning," the placid, disinterested woman told me, meaning perhaps, "He has jilted you, madam—well, isn't it always the way," for she had been with the Barforths a long time, and had seen their women come and go.

But there could be a dozen explanations. Simple things, like the destruction of Lawcroft Mills by fire, things I could live with, like strikes and floods and damaged machinery, which had nothing to do with Georgiana. And whatever had happened there would be no way to send me word.

I slept alone, bitter cold all night, listening to the wind—listening for Nicholas—breakfasted alone before a roaring fire, eating heartily of the smoked haddock and creamed eggs because the woman was mildly curious now as to whether or not I might be brokenhearted. And afterwards I went out into the raw November wind, walking as far as I dared—taking the chance we always took that there would be no one here at this season—until I felt as grey and chilled as the weather, could have whined as dolefully as the grey air irritating the surface of the sea.

It was an omen. Nothing had ever kept him away before. I

had drifted, as always, allowed my emotions, not my reason, to make my decisions, had, in fact, made no decisions at all, and now—having known for a long time exactly what I had to do—I had left it too long. Events, other people's decisions, had overtaken me. And even now, although I knew very definitely that he would not come and that I should return home at once to discover the reason, I doubted if I would do it. I would most likely stay here, waiting for him, as I had waited these past eighteen months, as I had waited all my life, straining my ears for the sound of his arrival, telling myself, "Just a little longer. Surely a little longer can do no harm?"

But as I walked back to the house something quickened my step, some impression of activity as I opened the door that caused my stomach to lurch hopefully, eagerly, the unmistakeable fragrance of cigar smoke reaching me as I entered the hall, offering me yet another reprieve.

"Is Mr. Barforth here?" I called out.

"Yes, madam, in the drawing room," the woman replied, and my joyful, giddy feet took me through the door and halfway across the room before I stopped, comic, I suppose, with shock, and realised it was Blaize.

"I *am* Mr. Barforth, after all," he said. "My word, Faith, if you mean to faint, then do it gracefully—here, on the sofa, for I have had an abominable journey and hardly feel up to lifting you if you should fall on the floor."

"Blaize—what on earth—"

"We'll come to that presently. Yes—yes, I knew you were here. I have come on my brother's business, not my own, and he is neither dead nor dying, merely in the very foulest of tempers because events have conspired against him . . . Really, Faith, you had better sit down."

I obeyed, arranging myself very carefully, composing my body and my mind, allowing a moment to pass until I could ask, just as carefully, "Did he—send you?"

The smoky eyes twinkled, his face, which had been quite expressionless, coming alive with the brilliance and mischief of his smile.

"Hardly that. Even Nicholas does not imagine himself to be in a position to *send* me anywhere. But he was in such a blind fury when he realised he couldn't get away that I—well, it wasn't difficult to understand that he had a most pressing engagement. I concluded it could only be you."

"Have you known for long?"

"About you and Nicholas? Well, yes, as it happens, so I have. But you needn't worry about that. I'm fairly certain no one else can have access to my source of information. I use this house too, sometimes, and Nicholas was obliged to check his dates with me. I do apologise, Faith, these practical details may sound sordid to you, but there was no other way it could be done. I knew simply that he was meeting someone here, not necessarily the same person every time, but I like to know what goes on around me, and I intercepted a glance or two—of agony, I might add, on at least one occasion—between you."

"That's guessing, it's not the same as knowing."

"No. And so I enquired. Mrs. Collins, our housekeeper here, is a good soul and I asked her to describe you. Naturally she shouldn't have done it, since Nicky pays for her discretion just the same as I do, and his money is as good as mine—it can only be that I have a winning way with housekeepers."

"I daresay. Does Nicholas know you are here?"

"Ah well—I didn't exactly make the offer, nor admit to knowing of any reason why I should. And since it was not made he neither accepted nor refused. But I think you may safely assume that he knows."

"And there is no chance that he may get away after all?"

"I am sure there is not. There was some crisis at the Wool Combers and in the middle of it my father descended on him in that quiet way of his—like a bolt from the blue—having made the journey from Bournemouth especially to see him, with a list of complaints and suggestions as long as both his arms. He is staying three days, and Nicky would need a cast-iron alibi to get away from him. Fortunately for me I was in Bournemouth a week ago, to endure my own inquisition, and my presence was not required. In fact I rather imagine I might have been in the way."

I looked at the fire for a while, then at the window, the garden, cowering at the approach of winter, noticed, without knowing why I cared, that a light, persistent rain was starting, washed ashore by the changing tide.

"It was very good of you, Blaize, to come so far."

"Yes, I think so too. You may take it that when I saw him hurl a spanner at one of his own machines, with my father looking on, I grew alarmed. And it would have worried me, I believe, to think of you sitting here, listening for carriage wheels, until Monday."

"Luncheon, sir, in half an hour," the industrious Mrs. Collins announced, her dour face crinkling with smiles as he said, "Excellent. Crab, Mrs. Collins?—it's what I came for."

And so, once again, I ate crab, drank a dry, well-chilled wine, smiled, with the perfect attention of Morgan Aycliffe's daughter, as Blaize talked of this and that and nothing at all, merely filling the spaces between us until it should please him to tell me at least a portion of the truth. For I did not believe he had made this tedious, inconvenient journey merely to deliver a message from Nicholas; he knew I did not believe it, and, understanding something of the subtle byways of his nature, I knew too that whatever it was it would not be simple, and that I would have to take care.

We took coffee and brandy in the drawing room companionably enough and when we had exhausted the gossip of our mutual acquaintances—the clock telling me already that I could not leave today even if I chose—he said, "Forgive me, Faith, I don't mean to pry, but since we are here and the subject is bound to be on our minds—it has been something over a year now, with you and Nicholas, hasn't it?"

"A year and a half, or very nearly."

And rather than an embarrassment it was almost a relief to me that he knew, for although I did not always trust him, he was clever and worldly-wise, a man whose vision was unclouded by convention and whose opinions, in matters perhaps not of the heart but of the senses, might be shrewder, certainly better-informed, than my sister's.

"I find that rather long," he said, warming the brandy glass in his hand. "Three months might have been delightful. Eighteen months—well, that strikes me as rather extreme. After that kind of eternity it has either become a habit, or one is very much in love. And remembering Nicky's temper yesterday morning, and knowing you as I do—well, I suppose it has to be love."

"Of course I love him. Good heavens, Blaize, what are you thinking of? Would I put myself in this position if I didn't love him? I may be behaving like a light woman—or seem to be—but I can assure you that I am not . . ."

He smiled, raised his glass to me.

"I know, my dear. That is one of the reasons I came."

"And the others?"

"Presently. Give me your reasons first, Faith—for instance, just what are you hoping for?"

"Nothing—as you well know."

"Well then—I have no right to say this, of course—but isn't it time you broke off with him?"

"Of course it is."

"And do you mean to do it?"

"Yes—yes, of course I do. I know I have to do it. I've done it twice already. I intended to do it again last night—tonight—although I may not have managed it. I may have opened my mouth, determined to tell him, and other words would have come out. It's happened often enough before."

"Even when you know it would be for his own good?"

"Do I know that? He doesn't think so."

"Of course he doesn't. He wants you. That's more than enough for him. I believe it would have been enough for my father too, in his day. And you must know that a gentleman's code doesn't allow him to break off with a lady, even in these circumstances. I freely admit that such a consideration would carry very little weight with me, but Nicky is rather more honourable than he seems. The break will have to come from you, Faith."

"I know—I know—I know all the reasons. I know. It's just that when it comes to it none of them seem quite strong enough . . ."

"I see. Then we shall have to find you another reason, shall we not? Something you'd feel quite unable to justify."

He got up, poured out more coffee, another brandy for himself, stirred the fire, as attentive to his own comforts as a cat, a light, luxurious man who played life's games so exquisitely that I wondered if he could really be of any help to me after all, since to him it may well be the game itself that counted, and the quality of the playing.

"Can you give me such a reason, Blaize?"

"I can try. I can tell you what I see, from my vantage point on the outside, which is often a very good place to be. I know my brother rather well, Faith, and he is not really the man for adultery, you know. It may not trouble his conscience unduly—at least, not more than he can cope with—but he finds it exceedingly irksome just the same. And adultery, if it is to be successful—if it is to be worth the trouble—must be enjoyed. There are men who can be more excited by the challenge and the danger of clandestine meetings than by the woman herself. There are certain, undomesticated men—one of them not a million miles away from you—who find the very lightness of it well suited to their natures. For it should be light, and it should be brief. Nicholas is not that kind of man. I might enjoy slipping in through your back door, Faith, but Nicholas doesn't care for it, and unless you put an end to this the day will dawn when he'll surely come striding in through the front, and be damned. If he did that, I believe several people would have cause to regret it."

I had no answer to give him. What answer could there be? And, allowing me a moment's reflection, he said quietly, "He should have married you in the first place, I think we must all be agreed on that. But he did not. He married that strange little creature, whose caprices no longer enchant him—or very rarely, since he is certainly the father of her child. She is difficult, I grant you. But she has an enormous need for affection—something you should be able to understand—and does very badly without it. I realise how badly he wants you, Faith, but I've yet to be convinced that he couldn't do well enough with Georgiana —if there was nothing to prevent it. Yes—yes, I know. You are going to tell me he doesn't love her, and that she doesn't love him, and you could be right. But if he took it into his head to *behave* as if he loved her, she would certainly respond to it. She is as miserable and down-drooping sometimes as a stray dog, and for the same reasons. If he held out his hand, she'd gladly come to heel now, I believe. She'd soon begin to effervesce and sparkle again, which would be an encouragement to him, since happiness makes her very enticing . . . And he may well find it in himself to forgive her her trespasses."

I swallowed, quite painfully, and leaned forward to the fire, a chill striking me abruptly across the shoulders.

"You really are Georgiana's friend after all, aren't you, Blaize?"

"I believe so. I realise you doubted it. She told me, a long time ago, that you had warned her against borrowing my money. There was really no need, you know. I can't think of any circumstances in which I'd be prepared to call the debt in. And, for once in my life, my intentions were of the very best. I thought it might help her to live, not in peace exactly with Nick, since peace is not really in her nature, and it's a dull little thing, in any case, but in the kind of harmony that would suit them both. I'm truly sorry to say this to you, Faith, but there have been times, even this past year, when they *could* have approached one another. You saw her yourself on Christmas Day, offering him far more than a reconciliation. And can you be certain that he would not have taken it—and made the best of it—had you not been standing there? I can't be certain. Now then—there's the reason I'm offering. Is it strong enough?"

I got up, walked across the room and back again, making my skirts swirl around me, full of bitterness, suddenly, and a desire to hurt him—because he was absolutely right—but with no idea at all how I might punish someone so elusive, so self-sufficient, as Blaize.

"It could be strong enough. But then again, you may have made a terrible mistake. A woman will usually sacrifice herself for the man she loves. She might be less willing to sacrifice herself for another woman—even his wife. You have convinced me that she needs him. Can you convince me that he needs her?"

"Oh—as to that," he said, getting up too and leaning a lazy arm along the mantel shelf, "Nicky can find other satisfactions. The keynote of his character is ambition, you must know that very well. He will build himself another Barforth empire and be well content with it. Certainly he wants you, but he wants other things too. His options are many and various. Georgiana has no option at all but to be his wife."

"Can you see no wrong in her, Blaize?"

"My dear—of course I can. The whole of Cullingford knows her as a most unsatisfactory woman. She can do nothing right for Cullingford. And if I happen to find some of her faults extremely charming, I'm ready to admit that she can be perverse and wrong-headed, that her judgement of character, particularly the Clevedon character is unsound and will continually lead her into trouble. But she was looking very frail yesterday morning, cowering away from his anger, although he was not angry with her and didn't pretend to be—very frail . . ."

And he had given me the most powerful reason of all.

We walked in the garden for a while then, and afterwards took tea and muffins and a certain apricot preserve for which Blaize declared Mrs. Collins was famous, although it had not been offered to me before. I dressed calmly for dinner, the turquoise dress again, the gold chains, the perfume, smiled with frank amusement at the flower-decked table, the scented candlelight, the richness of the sauces; although I was not delighted to see crab again.

"You are quite right, Blaize. You must have a way with housekeepers. Mrs. Collins can hardly be making these attempts at haute cuisine on my account."

"No—she is rather fond of me. But I have to admit that I might have done better not to have praised her crab so highly. We may see it tomorrow morning at breakfast time, I warn you, and I haven't the heart to complain. But the champagne is very nicely chilled, and not too sweet . . ." And I could have been enchanted—was, on the surface of my mind, enchanted—by the easy flow of his conversation, his accurate assessment that even a women with a broken heart retains her vanity and can find pleasure in talking about herself.

In the drawing room there was a branch of candles on a low table, the leaping firelight answering the candle flame, the lamps remaining unlit in deep pools of shadow, and as I agreed, against all the rules of Cullingford society, to take brandy with him, he warmed my glass in his hands, gave it to me very carefully, and said, "You are an incredibly beautiful woman, Faith, you know."

"I know no such thing. I take a little trouble with my appearance, that's all."

"Yes, I believe that is what I mean. I think at some time of your life you must have made a deliberate study of yourself, and I admire that enormously. It was Georgiana who called you a swan, wasn't it—and she was so right. That long neck with an elegant head at the end of it, turning so slowly and staring, sometimes quite arrogantly, just like swans do. Yes, I happen to know it is because you are shortsighted and that when you look through people in that rather distant way of yours it is because you actually don't see them—but the effect can be quite devastating. And when the light is too strong for you, instead of blinking and squinting like an owl, as most shortsighted people do, you very languorously close your eyes—I have often noticed it. And if, once upon a time, you had to sit and practice it in front of your mirror until you got it right, then I salute you for it. And your perfume is very exotic—really—very nice   ."

"In fact I am an enchanting creature altogether."

"So you are. You are your own creation You were quite plain once, but no one would notice it now."

"Thank you, Blaize. You have just told me that I am still plain, and that you have found me out."

"Which is the greatest compliment I can pay, since I am not nearly so handsome myself as I pretend to be."

We laughed, easy with wine and firelight, well satisfied with our own artistry, colleagues almost, so that when he left his chair and came to perch on the sofa beside me—my wide satin skirts requiring him to keep a certain distance—I was not at all worried by him. He had kissed me before, he might well kiss me again, and like the last time, it would be no more than an exchange of expertise.

"Yes," he said, those shrewd grey eyes examining me from the high-piled crown of my head to my décolletage, and lingering there, at the separation of my breasts, quite openly, the corners of his mouth tilting into a wry smile. "You understand your own body perfectly in one sense. You know how to adorn it and how to display it to glorious advantage. You are not even coy with it. You know I am looking and you allow me to look, quite calmly . . . You knew, in advance, that I would be bound to look and would not have uncovered your shoulders had you not felt, even secretly, that you deserve it. I like that attitude too. I am only sorry you haven't yet understood another facet of your nature which seems very clear to me. What would you do if I touched you, Faith?"

"Well, I wouldn't scream for Mrs. Collins, who certainly wouldn't help me in any case But what is this facet of my nature I haven't understood?"

His eyes brushed over me once again, very much amused this time.

"Not yet. Tell me something first. How do you see yourself, Faith—no, not the swan's-down and the velvet ribbons of you—yourself?"

"I don't," I told him, stretching myself a little on the sofa, my posture far too relaxed for good manners, seeing all this as no more than one of his sophisticated, complex games. "I don't see myself at all. I don't do anything so positive as that. I drift, Blaize. I just float on a lake—like a swan, I suppose, if there is a muddle-headed variety. When the sun shines I fluff out my feathers, and when it doesn't, I try to weather the storms. I don't know where I'm going any more than a swan does—except that a swan, I believe, takes a mate for life, and I seem unlikely to do that—the way things are turning out . . ."

He smiled. "It will surprise you then to be told that, in my view, you could be a very sensual woman—which must make you unique in Cullingford."

"Blaize—good heavens—I don't even know what that means. You are calling me wanton, I suppose."

"Certainly not. I have encountered wantons in plenty, and it is not at all the same. Wantons will give themselves for a variety of reasons, but rarely for the pleasure of the giving, and the taking. I'm suggesting to you, Faith dear, that you have—or might have —a capacity for that particular kind of giving and taking for its own sake. And that is rare in women—or, at any rate, I have met it very seldom. But—and I am forced to heave a sigh over it— you are a lady. And because sensuality, as we all know, is not lady-like, you have confused it with romance. You must be madly, wildly in love—or think that you are—in order to give yourself, and you are gaining nothing by it, Faith—nothing at all—in fact you are refusing to acknowledge what could be the most satisfying part of your nature."

"Blaize—really . . ."

"Faith—definitely. You love Nicholas and so you may give yourself to him. You lose Nicholas and so your life as a woman is at an end. You believe that no one else could ever rouse you to passion or to pleasure, because you could love no one else. I wonder if the swan believes the same when it loses its mate and sits all forlorn on the riverbank for the rest of its life? It would sadden me if you were to do that, Faith."

I sat up, straight-backed, angry, uneasy with him for the first time in my life.

"I don't wish to continue this conversation, Blaize."

"Of course you don't. It's not a proper conversation at all. But the fact that we are here alone together is not proper either. You may relax again, Faith, you know, for I didn't come here intending to seduce you. Not that I wouldn't enjoy it—my word, I'd take you south, I think, some secret little Italian garden, so you could uncover those splendid shoulders for me all day long in the sunshine. And afterwards we'd still be friends."

"Blaize . . ."

"Yes—so we would. But then, you couldn't be stirred by me, or any other man, could you, because we are not Nicholas. And if, in fact, you *could* be stirred a little, you'd have to fight it, wouldn't you—just as hard as ever you could—because then you'd have to wonder whether you'd loved him quite so desperately after all."

"Blaize, I shall be angry with you in a minute."

"You'd do far better to come to bed with me. Now that would be a strong reason—you'd never bring yourself to face Nicholas again after that, you know."

And because it was preposterous and shocking—and because it was true—I leaned my head on the back of the sofa and laughed weakly, a shade tearfully, considerably astonished—beginning to wonder—about the part of myself that could understand his sophisticated logic, that could mould itself so easily into his atmosphere. And I wondered too what had happened to the part of me that should have been scandalised, should have had a fit of the vapours and demanded to be taken home.

"You wouldn't care for it, Blaize—I'd be far too horrified at myself to be a satisfactory companion."

"Yes," he said. "I know. What a pity." And leaning towards me he touched the side of my head and my ear, the gesture of smoothing out a stray ringlet I had seen him make to Georgiana, although I knew that not so much as a single hair of *my* chignon could be out of place.

"Yes—truly—what a pity, Faith. You'd feel obliged to hate yourself, and me, afterwards. I know that very well, darling, and I won't tease you any longer. It's just that—well, you may call me a frivolous man if you like, but surely these grand passions don't remain at fever-heat forever? Not unless one nurtures them. And I wonder, my dear, if you might feel obliged to do that too. The same thing applies to what I told you about taking another lover. If one recovers from a grand passion, then was it really so very grand in the first place? Perhaps one could have resisted it—should have resisted it. Might it be more convenient not to recover at all. Believe me, I can perfectly understand how a middle-class lady may feel compelled to cling to her illusions. And now—since you are beginning to dislike me and those lovely shoulders of yours are starting to prey on my mind— perhaps we should say good night."

I got up very calmly and moved towards the door, feeling that I was walking through water, forcing my way through slow but irresistible currents, a seaweed tangle of impressions and emotions I would need time to unravel. But he reached the door before me, opened it, handed me the branch of bedtime candles on the hall table, bowed very slightly, his smile in no way unkind.

"Dear Faith," he said. "You have not had quite so desperate a day as you expected. You could even have enjoyed my company if you had put your mind to it. And that should be an encouragement to you, since we are agreed that I am not unique and irreplaceable, like Nicholas. Perhaps I would admit it to no one else, but there are hundreds of men like me."

Chapter Twenty-two

I SET OFF for Cullingford the next morning, at some risk to myself since I had no real explanation for so early a return, but no accusations awaited me, merely a hastily scrawled note from Nicholas saying he had been despatched to London by his father on urgent business and would be perhaps a week away. And I sat with the letter in my hands for a long time, cradling it, since it was the first I had ever received from him, and then, again with that strange sensation of walking through slow-rippling water, I went to the fire and burned it, not for reasons of safety but as a test of my own courage.

I had a week then, in which to permit myself the luxury of remaining, if only in spirit, his mistress, a week before I would stand here and dismiss him. And this time I could not say, "I love you, but it is for your good," since I had said that before and neither of us had believed it. This time I would have to say, "It is for my good. I'm weary of it, I don't wish to continue," and although I didn't believe that either, I must contrive, somehow or other, to convince him.

I no longer chose to dwell on it. I wished simply to *do* it, freeing my mind for the torment that would come after. There could be no more swan-drifting, and if, after all, I found myself marooned in some desolate marshland of the spirit, I would take myself and my grieving elsewhere, so that he, at least, could get on with his life. I would go abroad, perhaps, and take Prudence with me, whatever anyone had to say, for if I was strong enough to separate myself willingly from the man I loved, whose possessive, autocratic nature would neither accept my reasons, nor forgive me, then I could make short work of a dozen Daniel Adairs.

Yet, as often before, I had waited too long, and when Aunt Hannah walked through my door, the third day after my return, perhaps, before she had even taken off her bonnet, I knew it.

"No," she said. "Do not trouble yourself to offer me tea. You have troubles enough without that, my girl, and what I have to say to you will not accord with teacups and bread and butter. In fact it may well take your appetite clean away—and I confess to you that I have none."

"Aunt Hannah—what on earth is the matter . . . ?"

"You may well ask," she said, her back so straight that she could have had a poker inside her bodice, her expression confusing me since, beneath the self-righteous anger which I was accustomed to see in her, lay something else which could, just possibly, be satisfaction, a certain smugness that some opinion, some guess of hers had proved correct, presenting her with yet another opportunity of getting her way.

"Is it—my mother?"

"No dear," she said, arranging her skirts very deliberately, smiling the blank, bright smile of social occasions, the one she used before demolishing the clamour of some rebellious committee, the smile, indeed, which she had offered me long ago, before forcing me from my damp fog of mourning for Giles. "Your mother is as well as one could expect her to be. She is in love, you see, which seems endemic at certain seasons. As her daughter you should understand it. In fact you have been so bright-eyed and blooming at times, and so jumpy and droopy at others lately, that I could be forgiven for imagining you to be in love yourself. Can you tell me that I am mistaken?"

And as often seems to happen when one faces the impossible, when one knows oneself overtaken by the ultimate disaster, I experienced no shock, no desperation, only a strange acceptance that may properly belong to the dying, and said quite calmly, "What do you want from me, Aunt Hannah?"

"Nothing, dear. I am not even sure I shall wish to know you for very much longer. Well, Faith, you were always a feather-brain. Your character has always contained too much of your mother and too little of your father, and I wonder why it should surprise me to find you in this atrocious situation. You may know that your mother once attempted to ruin herself by just such a criminal attachment. I prevented that. I shall endeavour to prevent your disgrace in the same manner. What have you to say to me about that?"

But I could say nothing and smiling again, as if my silence seemed quite natural to her—my reaction exactly as she had intended—she continued, not with the accusations and reproaches I had expected, but in another manner entirely.

"At least, Faith, you must be ready to admit the soundness of my judgement? I told you, some time ago, that you were not fit to live alone, and so it has proved. However, since your mother lacked the authority to compel you to return home, and was too busy about her own affairs to keep anything like a proper watch over yours, I felt it—right, shall we say—to do what I could, in her place. I am an exceedingly busy woman, Faith, and may not have been so vigilant as I would have liked. But my niece, Lady Chard, confirmed my suspicions on your account as long ago as last Christmas, when she remarked you had been playing the recluse, and wondered if there was an admirer you had not told us about. You denied it. Lady Chard believed you. I did not. And my observations—dear me, Faith—the state of your nerves sometimes when I have called here unexpectedly, supposedly to complain of your mother—your little heart pounding and your ears straining for that caller at the back door who must be warned in time and sent away. My goodness—and these visits of yours to York, to this acquaintance who never visits you in return . . . Heavens, my dear, not even your mother would have believed you had she troubled to think about it, and I feel sure her husband does not. Tell me, was the weather fine in Scarborough last Friday-to-Monday?"

"Cold," I said incredibly. "And rather blustery."

"Good. I am glad you do not feel the need to whine to me, or insult me with pleas for my forgiveness. I shall not forgive you. Nor shall I trouble you with a description of how deeply your behaviour has disgusted me, since I imagine all that disgusts you is that you have been found out. I shall occupy myself instead by attempting to remedy the situation, as I once did with your mother, not out of any consideration for you, but because your disgrace must touch us all. You are not just 'anybody,' Faith. You are a member of a well-respected family, the niece of Sir

Joel Barforth and of Mayor Agbrigg, who are both revered, and rightly so, in this town. You are the daughter of Morgan Aycliffe, to whom the most splendid building this town possesses has been dedicated. You are the widow of Dr. Giles Ashburn, whose memory is held in high regard by all of us. You are the sister-in-law of Jonas Agbrigg, who is about to take his place on our town council and whose standing in the legal profession demands unblemished respectability. Jonas, in fact, will be deeply shocked when I inform him of this, since he has appreciated your assistance to Celia as a hostess, and had hoped to call on it again—something which now must be out of the question. I have no intention, my girl, of allowing you to damage these worthy men, you can be very sure of that. And I shall not rest until you are decently married."

I opened my mouth to speak, my whole body leaning towards her in protest, thinking of Irish cousins, Mr. Oldroyd of Field-head, some husband, any husband willing to take a blemished bride.

"Aunt Hannah," I said, refusing it, but she held out her hand, palm upwards, in a gesture commanding enough to have silenced a meeting in the Assembly Rooms itself, and said, "Yes, Faith. There is no other solution. I believe my sources of information to be discreet—certainly they are reliable—but I am not the only interested party capable of making enquiries. There is no time to lose. I have delayed so long only because I was unable to ascertain the gentleman's identity. In the final instance, of course, I would have come to you and forced his name out of you, but that will not be necessary. I believe, my dear, that when you have recovered from your emotions, you will have cause to thank me, for I have already been very busy on your behalf. I have just spent a most uncomfortable hour with that rascal of a nephew of mine—uncomfortable for him, I hasten to add—and whether he likes it or not, I shall force him to put everything right.

And seeing my total astonishment—for Nicholas was in London and could put nothing right in any case—her lips parted once again in a smile of the most complete satisfaction I had ever seen, revealing her cleverness and her superiority to me as a cat must reveal itself to a mouse.

"Yes, you may well stare, Faith, for he is the most complete

rogue of my acquaintance and I did not expect him to be reasonable. But he could not deny that he went to Scarborough last
Saturday and did not return until Sunday. Nor can he deny that
you were with him, since you were seen by a certain Mrs.
Guthrie, who was once in your service, and who is now, in a
manner of speaking, in mine. He cannot deny that you were
alone in that house together, especially since he knows that the
housekeeper would be obliged to answer truthfully should her
real employer, my brother, Sir Joel, put her to the question. She
has her place to consider, my dear, and would not risk losing it
on your account. Yes, Faith, I believe I have done very well for
you. A great many females have attempted to trap my nephew
into matrimony, but in this case he overlooked the fact that he
would have *me* to deal with. Good heavens, girl, what ails you?
Most assuredly I cannot condone your wanton behaviour, but so
long as it remains between the three of us it may be brought to
a rapid—and highly profitable—conclusion. He has faults in
plenty, no one doubts it, but he is a Barforth, and I have always
believed that family money should remain, whenever possible, in
the family, and it has long concerned me that he would encounter some impossible, grasping woman on his travels—someone
who would be no good to us at all. Well—it is a great thing for
you, my girl, for do not forget that he will be Sir Blaize one day,
since he is the eldest son. Joel and Verity may not quite like it,
for although you are not a poor match, you are not the best he
could have made. But faced with the alternative scandal there is
nothing else to be done. You have made your bed, my dear—
both of you—and now you must lie on it."

I had never lost consciousness before, and did not precisely do
so now. I was quite simply and horrifyingly unable to speak, but
Aunt Hannah, being well used to reducing her fellow creatures
to speechlessness, did not appear surprised at that. She may, in
fact, have considered it most appropriate, lingering no more
than a quarter of an hour longer, advising me, when inbred politeness tried to force me to my feet at her leave-taking, to
remain seated, to go to bed, in fact, and stay there, since I
looked ill, most gratifyingly chastised.

"I have warned Blaize," she said, "that I shall require his answer by tomorrow morning. Verity should be here by then, since
my brother finds he must remain in Cullingford for some days

yet and appears unable to live without her. If my nephew chooses to be stubborn, then she and his father will be informed of it, and Joel will find a way to make him honour his obligation. However—I do not anticipate that things will come to that. I shall call tomorrow then—and if Blaize should come today I must ask you not to receive him. Contact between you at this point would be unwise. If he is looking for a way out, then he may persuade you into fresh folly, and it seems to me that you are all too persuadable. Remember—you are not at home to him."

But I could not get to Blaize quickly enough, would have sent messages to Tarn Edge and then gone myself had he not appeared, a half-hour later, judging his time shrewdly, I thought, since Aunt Hannah would not be likely to return so soon.

"My word," he said, throwing down his hat and gloves with great nonchalance. "I am a trapped man. I have been avoiding this very thing for years, and now . . ."

But then, seeing my face, the huddled posture of my body in the chimney corner, he crossed the room quickly and would have taken me in his arms had I not backed away.

"Heavens, Faith—you will not die of it."

"Blaize, is there anything you can do to stop her from telling your father?"

"Nothing. She wants me to marry you. It has worried her for a long time that I might dissipate my inheritance, or bestow it unsuitably. Like Prudence, she fears I may take a child bride when I am ninety-three, and there would be no hope then of any Barforth money finding its way to Jonas. She disapproves wholeheartedly of what she thinks we have done, but it is manna from heaven to her just the same. I could leave you an even richer widow than you are already, and who would you have to turn to then but Jonas?"

"It is as bad as it could be, then?"

"It is. She will tell my father, and when she does Nicholas will not keep silent. Mrs. Collins will not keep silent either, I'm afraid, so there will be ample confirmation—quite the most explosive scandal Cullingford has ever known, by the look of it."

"Yes. Then really—do you know—I think I had better die of it. I'm not being in the least dramatic. I can think of no other solution—that's all."

He smiled, took my hand, and leading me to the sofa sat down beside me.

"Yes, it had crossed my mind you would feel like that. What weapon would you use? You have no gas in this house, and poison is unreliable. You could jump from an upper window, of course, but it is by no means certain, and before you throw yourself under someone's carriage horses you should take into account that you might kill the driver and a few passing children as well."

"There's the railway," I said, and was almost startled when he shuddered quite violently.

"You are quite serious about it, then. But no, not the railway —please don't think about it again, Faith. It would solve the problem for you, perhaps, but not for the rest of us. Aunt Hannah is really very honest and very courageous, you know. In the event of your suicide she would feel herself very much to blame. She'd say it was because I had refused to make an honest woman of you, and then Nicholas would knock me down and spend the rest of his life believing he had killed you. Really— you had better marry me, you know."

"I shall have to go away, then, as far as I can, and at once— before your mother gets here. Dear God, she's expected in the morning. I must leave tonight. It doesn't matter where. You can help me to do that, can't you, Blaize."

And as panic surged over me again I couldn't sit still, couldn't stay in this room a moment longer, must go immediately and pack my bags and if there was no train, no coach, no donkey cart to escape in, then I must run.

"Yes," he said. "I could do that, I suppose. I could buy you a ticket for the London train and drive you to the station. But what then? I couldn't explain your disappearance to Aunt Hannah, nor to your mother, and the whole sad story would come out just the same. Nicholas would come after you, Faith. He couldn't leave you to fend for yourself. Even I couldn't accept such a sacrifice from a woman."

I saw my hands clench into fists and come crashing down, impotently, on my knees again and again, my whole body rocked backwards and forwards by the enormity of my frustration and my fear. I heard my voice moaning, "Dear God—what can I do then?—whatever can I do?" and the sound irritated me so that my mind said, "Stupid, hysterical woman—be still. Can't someone make her be silent?" I saw Blaize put his hands over mine, unclench my fingers, smooth them out, and hold them steady.

"Oh, dear," he said. "I wonder if you realise what a blow you have just struck me? I have just asked you to marry me, a request I have never made before. And all you replied was, 'I shall have to go away—at once—' And that, my dear, is hardly flattering—hardly at all."

"Blaize, for heaven's sake—stop playing games. You can get out of this the moment you want to. I don't think I can get out of it at all. Just don't bother me with nonsense—just don't—when I'm trying to find a serious solution."

"It is a serious solution," he said, and releasing my hands, he leaned back a little, apparently at ease, his eyes quizzical and careful, but not without concern.

"It depends on what you really want, Faith. And you have almost no time at all to make up your mind. Aunt Hannah has made a somewhat natural mistake. She knew you were meeting somebody in Scarborough. She sent one of her minions to find out, and the person in question saw me. Well, I have been avoiding traps of that kind for years and when I had got over the shock, I could hardly ignore the poetic justice of it. However, we are discussing your feelings now, not mine. Faith, there are several things you could do. You can wait here and allow the storm to break over you, or you could go to London and warn Nicky of it. I have the address where he may be found and you could easily reach him there, or I could even take you there. Either way, my father would be waiting for him on his return. There is absolutely nothing I can do to silence Aunt Hannah, short of telling her the truth, and there's no guarantee she'd believe me. The chances are she'd see it as a trick to get myself out of trouble and land Nicky in it instead—which you must admit I've done often enough in the past—and I'm not sure what would happen if she asked him for confirmation. Obviously the truth *would* come out, because Mrs. Collins knows about you and Nicky, but by that time everybody else would know about it too, and the result would be exactly the same. Nicky and my father are not on good terms at the moment, you know, in any case, and the explosion would be quite devastating. My father is not precisely fond of Georgiana, but she is his daughter-in-law, she is expecting his grandchild. She's not in good health, and neither, I think, is he, which makes his temper shorter. He wouldn't want to throw Nicky out, and Nicky wouldn't want to go. But that is what would most likely happen. It would cause immense distress to both of them, in the long run, and worse than that to my mother."

"I know—I know—you don't have to punish me all over again with it."

"I think I do. I think it essential that you should see things very clearly. Nicky and I have no legal claim on the mills, Faith. They belong to my father, and can be disposed of as he sees fit. The deeds of partnership are already drawn up, I know. They've been lying in Jonas Agbrigg's desk drawer for some time now, waiting until my father feels the urge to sign them. It's the golden carrot he's been using to good purpose, but as matters stand we're just employees, and he could disinherit either one of us, or both. So you see, if you allow Nicky to quarrel with him, you will be doing me a great service. What you must ask yourself is whether Nicky, in a year or two, would begin to wonder about the disservice you had done to him. He has the Wool Combers, of course, but he's short of capital and when it was known he had broken with my father, the bank might not continue to support him."

"Blaize—I know . . ."

"And there is Georgiana, and young Gervase, and the new baby. I imagine you must have intended being very discreet until after her confinement. You'll know more than I do about the dangers of shock and distress in pregnancy and I'm sure you wouldn't want to put her at risk—more than she is already. I'm not sure what would happen to Georgiana, if all this came out into the open and you and Nicky went away together. Obviously he'd continue to support her and the children. And even if he lost the Wool Combers for lack of financial assistance—because all businesses need that kind of help in their early days, you know—then my father would support them anyway. So there'd be no physical hardship. She could go back to Galton, I suppose, although I'm not sure she could, or would divorce him. An Act of Parliament is required for the dissolving of marriages, you know, Faith—which costs a lot of money and takes a great deal of time—and since divorced persons don't remarry in any case, it would make no real difference to your situation. No one could ever speak to you again—no one you'd want to speak to, that is —and if you had children, I can't imagine that anyone in Cullingford would speak to them either. The discrimination against bastards is really immense, and strikes me as very unjust —but there it is. And there is always the possibility that Nicholas, eventually, would redeem himself by going back to his wife. The world is very unfairly balanced for a woman. Georgiana would only have to forgive him, and everyone else would be glad to do the same. He could come back to Tarn Edge, take his place in the mills, they would even kill the fatted calf for him. But no one would ever forgive you. I suppose he would make you a very adequate allowance—and I might call to see you now and then . . ."

I got up and began to pace around the room, backwards and forwards, up and down, a great release of energy that took me nowhere, losing myself, at every step more thoroughly, in the maze of my female situation, a dark dream-walking where every door that beckoned cheated me and was no door at all. And in the end—like Prudence, like every other woman—there was no choice but to submit, in this masculine world, to the requirements, the decisions, the mercy of the nearest, most sympathetic male.

"Are you trying to drive me mad?"

"I would prefer not to. Do you want me to take you to London, to find Nicholas?"

"What else can I do?"

"Can you really live with the scandal, Faith—for the rest of your life?"

"What else can I do?"

"Can you cope with the constant strain of pleasing him, which is not the same as loving him, since he will be all you have in the world. And he's not easily pleased. He'll growl and complain sometimes, and even if he doesn't mean it, you'll die every time it happens, because you'll think you're losing him."

"What else? Dear God—what else is there now?"

"And supposing you *did* lose him? You could, Faith—so easily. He's had money all his life—lots of money—and so have you. Can you cope with poverty? The Wool Combers could eat up your money sooner than you'd imagine, because Nicky has grand ideas. If he lost it, he'd be tempted to come home for more. And what then? Every man you met would know about you—men always know these things—and I wonder if you have any idea just how coarse men can be once a woman has lost her reputation?"

"Blaize, for pity's sake . . . You can extricate yourself. I can't. He can't."

"Yes," he said, very casually. "You can. You can marry me."

I fell down onto a chair, my head in my knees, and began to sob, an ugly, gulping sound that hurt my chest and my ears and such self-esteem as remained to me, and he waited, offering me no comfort, until my body staggered painfully towards composure and I raised my head again, wiping my face with my sleeves, feeling drained and sick and furious because my hysteria had weakened me further and had solved nothing.

"I'm sorry. It's over now."

But he made no immediate answer, obliging me, by his very silence, to admit my need of him, to realise fully and finally how alone I would be now, how totally abandoned, without him.

"Good," he said at last and very quietly. "Well then—since it's over—may we pass on to more constructive matters than tears? Dear Faith, my proposal startles you I imagine because you can see no reason for it. Well—how can I make you understand? A man marries for a variety of reasons, you know that as well as I do. And you must also know that, in our little world, it is very rarely for passion. Faith, I am turning thirty and I have had my share of amorous escapades. In fact, lately, I find that I am tending to repeat myself—it is all very pleasant, of course, and the wandering life I lead presents me with ample opportunities. But no man wanders forever—your mother's husband would offer you confirmation of that—and when I do come home, quite frankly, I am no longer comfortable at Tarn Edge. The house is big enough, and the service is excellent, but my nephew is extremely noisy, a new baby is unlikely to add anything to the atmosphere that I shall care for. And, if possible, Georgiana and Nicholas should be left alone. My mother is of the same opinion, and when she is not there, I feel somewhat *de trop*. I could take a house of my own, of course, but that would involve me in a mountain of domestic trivia and apart from that I am a little tired of being so very eligible. It strikes me that every woman in the Law Valley with a daughter to marry has come running after me at one time or another, and I'm sorry to say that my taste doesn't run to young, innocent girls. I show my face in Cullingford, and there they are, put out on display, all tremulous and eager and ready for anything that might succeed in making them 'Lady Barforth' one day. They besiege me with invitations to dine with them, to dance with them, anything I like with them. I have to listen to their music, look at their watercolours and their embroidery, and anything else they can show me—within reason—that might tempt me. And it doesn't tempt me at all! There are men who very much like virginity but—frankly—I have had no experience of it and even if all these fifteen-year-old dimples and curls succeeded in moving me, how could I ask a mere child to manage my affairs when I am abroad, or to manage me when I am at home? I would be at the mercy of my wife's mother, and that wouldn't suit me at all. The alternative would be to look outside our charmed circle, as Nicky did, but we both know all about his problems and I may not do any better. I know several attractive women, in London and elsewhere, who might be ready to marry me, but Cullingford is not kind to strangers. I would rather marry you, Faith. We are at ease with one another. You are intelligent and kind-hearted. You have excellent taste. You would be a good hostess and a good friend. You have a lovely body and a more sophisticated mind than is usual in a Law Valley woman. Yet you are a Law Valley woman. You understand the way in which I conduct my business, and the men with whom it is conducted. And several times I've done more than glance in your direction—I've looked hard and I haven't been indifferent. These seem very adequate reasons for marriage to me. And as for that rare and special creature I've talked so much about—the one who is always in the next room—well, I think I am quite content, you know, to let her remain there. If I ever opened the door, the chances are that I'd be sadly disappointed. She'd most likely turn out to be quite commonplace."

I walked another step or two and then stood quite still, my head bowed in a brooding silence, wondering what time it was, what day it was, why everything he said to me sounded so logical, so easy, until the moment his voice stopped speaking.

"And you would accept me, knowing that my only motive could be the need to escape from Nicholas?"

"My dear," he said. "You married my very good friend Giles Ashburn for exactly that reason, and he had no cause to complain of you. If you decided to devote yourself to me in the same fashion, I wouldn't complain either."

I sat down beside him, not intentionally, but because my legs had simply released my weight, and he slid his hand into mine, a light, undemanding touch, telling me I could take him, or not, and we would still be friends, warning me, perhaps, that he was no rock to lean on, as Giles had been, that he would never seek to possess me nor allow me to possess him—but that we would be friends.

"It's not possible," I said. "Blaize, how can you even think of it? You know that I'm in love with Nicholas. And he's your brother—you even *look* like him."

"No," he told me, not the slightest tremor in him anywhere. "You're quite wrong. I don't look like him at all. He looks like me. And the resemblance isn't really very great. He's blacker and bolder and heavier by at least a stone. And you know quite well I was born believing that, sooner or later, everybody is bound to like me best. What else have you to tell me?"

"That even if I—and I couldn't—that Nicholas wouldn't let it happen."

"My dear, I'm not planning to ask him. Faith, you spoke of going to London. My bags are already packed. I have to go and see as many of my Continental customers as I can in case this damnable war with Russia, which seems almost certain now, should make travel difficult. I intended to leave at the end of the month, but there's no reason why we can't set off together—tonight. We'd be creating a small scandal, darling, to cover a greater one. Elope with me, in fact. A few weeks in France and Germany, consternation in Cullingford, and we can be married somewhere en route. You can trust me, I think, to work out the details. They'd hardly be beyond my organising capacity. You'd meet with some coolness, of course, when you came home, but my mother will help us with that. If Lady Barforth of Tarn Edge is willing to receive you—and Mrs. Agbrigg of Lawcroft Fold—then everybody else will do the same. So—I have brought you to the point of realising it is not impossible after all. What is troubling you now?"

"Nicholas is troubling me now."

"Yes, I rather thought he might. But Nicholas makes the elopement necessary, surely you can see that? If he comes back from London to learn we are to be married, he'd be bound to ask the reason why. And I can't see myself explaining it. He wouldn't give you up to me, darling, just to avoid a scandal he thinks he can cope with, and to keep a wife he thinks he doesn't want. And even if by some miracle he could be persuaded to see reason, could you stand the strain of a family wedding? Could he? He'd be far more likely to shoot me at the altar than act as my best man."

"And if we go away together, then he'll think we became lovers in Scarborough, won't he, Blaize? He'll think I fell out of love with him for your sake . . ."

"Exactly. What else could he think? Aunt Hannah will tell no tales once we're gone. She'd have nothing to gain by it and my father might accuse her of having pushed us too far, and she wouldn't risk that. As you say, Nicky will certainly think you have jilted him, in a particularly heartless manner at that. And he'll be hurt, there's no doubt about it—badly hurt even, for a while. He'll be foul-tempered and foul-mouthed and he'll kick his machines, and his operatives, all around Lawcroft mill yard until he's worked it out of his system. I speak flippantly, because that seems to be my fashion when something troubles me. But really, Faith—really—the more it hurts him the better, because when he's feeling thoroughly wretched who else is he likely to turn to but Georgiana? He would be miserable. She would be miserable. It would be very natural—wouldn't it?—if they should be drawn together. And that, surely, is one of the things we are aiming for. Very well, I have demolished that objection—give me the next."

I leaned forward, struggling against the current of his logic that brought me constantly back to him, the warm tones of his voice filling my mind, hushing my panic, easing me, convincing me that this outrageous thing was not only possible but obvious —desirable—that it was right, and could be pleasant, because he said so.

"Blaize, take care. Don't confuse me and persuade me. You are not selling me a thousand yards of Barforth worsted, you know."

"No, darling—it would have taken me all of ten minutes to do that."

"I can't even believe this is happening to me. You make it sound so simple—and so right—and perhaps it could be . . . But—Blaize—"

"Yes, what is it now? I suppose it must be Nicholas again?"

"Of course it is. He's your brother, and he'll probably be your business partner. I could avoid him, but you couldn't. You'd have to see him every day—work with him . . ."

But my mood was quieter now, my objections more hesitant, his hand on mine much firmer.

"There's that to it, of course. But that's my problem, surely, darling, and there is little love lost between me and Nicky in any case. We don't work together, Faith. We're involved in the same business and we put up with each other. The whole of Culling-ford knows it and no one would be surprised to see our rela-tionship take a turn for the worse. People would only think we were bickering over the money, and most of the time they'd be right. And it may not always be so. People mellow. If he finds enough to content him in Georgiana, he may find it easier to tol-erate me. And if he doesn't—well—we shall be equal partners in the Barforth mills when my father dies, but partnerships can be dissolved. He could take Lawcroft and Low Cross, and I could take Tarn Edge, and we could go our separate ways. And if my relationship with Nicky is the only thing to be sacrificed, then I believe we might come out of this well enough."

I sat for a long time after that, leaning my head on the back of the sofa, conscious of a gradual draining away of energy, try-ing, for a while, to halt the dissolving of my will into his, the slow drifting of my whole self towards the refuge he offered, the submission he had presented to me as inevitable. And then, very slowly, as one flow of quiet water enters another, resistance ebbed away.

"You are going to marry me then?"

"Yes."

"Good. Then there is one promise you must make me."

"Only one? I think you are entitled to ask for more than that."

"Ah well—most of the things I could ask for, you will give me in any case. This one promise will suffice. Nicholas must never know the true circumstances of our marriage. And since neither

Aunt Hannah nor I will tell him, you must not do so either. He must go on believing that you willingly abandoned him, either because you liked me better—which has happened before in his life—or from motives of self-interest, because you knew I had more to offer. You saw the chance of an advantageous marriage and you took it. If he's to think well of Georgiana, he must begin by thinking ill of you. And I'm bound to admit I wouldn't be altogether comfortable otherwise. Will you promise me that?"

"Blaize—that is one promise I would have performed in any case."

"Of course. So—let's think of you, now—and me. I told you my bags are packed, but I may not have mentioned they are already at the station. We have only your affairs to put in order, darling, and I'm here, at your disposal, until train time. There's a note to be written to your mother, and a line to Aunt Hannah too, I think, which we'll have delivered in the morning—simply that you have gone away with me and expect to be married when they see you again. You may go upstairs presently to arrange your boxes, and while you're about it I'll have a word with your housekeeper, and make it worth her while to be on our side. But I think we might have a moment together now—come here, darling, for if I am to be blamed for seducing you, I might as well take advantage of it . . ."

But with his mouth once more on mine, his hands beginning a gentle, stroking exploration of my shoulders, the curve of my breasts, the outline of waist and thigh, the cool, fresh scent of him invading my nostrils, I felt a new panic.

"Blaize—I can't go from one bed to another—just like that—so quickly—"

"Oh, but you can," he said, his mouth against my neck, his hands delicately parting the folds of my collar. "Not here, of course—not now—but tonight, darling, wherever we find ourselves, I shall manage to provide you with champagne and a good dinner, and a good bed, and I am not at all the kind of gallant gentleman who would allow you to sleep in it alone. You will have to make your full commitment, darling, make no mistake about it. I may not look the part, Faith, but I am a Law Valley man. I expect a return on my investments, just as much, and just as soon as I can."

And being a Law Valley woman I could not quarrel with that.

Chapter Twenty-three

IT WAS, of course, a preposterous relationship, which should soon have foundered. It did not. Our first night together should have ended in tears on my part, bitter reproaches on his, a mutual embarrassment neither of us could overcome. Incredibly it ended in laughter, inspired partly, I must confess, by the endlessly flowing champagne Blaize considered an essential part of seduction, but largely by the split in my own nature, the practical Law Valley part of me which understood the reason for this immediate commitment—for once it was done it was done and there could be no returning—the part which said, "You have made your bed so now it is only common sense to lie on it as comfortably as you can"; and the other part, the submerged part, released by Blaize's persuasive hands, the woman in me who could enjoy, if only briefly, the languorous, sensual life of a pampered courtesan.

I should have been abominably burdened throughout those early months by the memory of Nicholas and of what he must believe I had done to him. I did not forget it. But I was a woman who, if I had not precisely made a decision, had made a promise which my self-respect would force me to keep, had entered into an arrangement the terms of which I perfectly understood and which I was determined to fulfil. I knew exactly what Blaize required in a wife and I saw no point at all—even before we were married—in holding anything back from him.

A good hostess, he had said, and a good friend, but Blaize Barforth's "good friend" would need to be resourceful, independent, good-humored, sensual, unfailingly patient, and from the start I became all those things, partly because this was my final opportunity to make something of my life and I couldn't fail it, but also because Blaize himself, who demanded constant attention, expected at all times to be pleased, was well worth the pleasing, a challenge to any woman's ingenuity.

I should not have found pleasure in his arms—not so quickly—and when I did I should have felt soiled by it, betrayed by my own sighing, demanding body. Perhaps if he had been sympathetic and allowed me to be sentimental, I would have done exactly that, but the sexual act to Blaize was not so much a matter of need as of skill, a slow appreciation that could occupy the whole of a balmy Mediterranean afternoon —if he had one available—an experience which took on the shades and character of its constantly changing situation, a cosily bolstered French bed, a moonlit terrace overlooking the sea, my back supported by silk-embroidered cushions, a couch in a southern garden, as he had once promised, the spray of a nearby fountain feather-light against my bare skin, a dappled moonlight coming down to us through the chestnut trees. And from the start his expertise defeated me.

"No—no," he told me that first night when I turned to him too quickly, knowing it had to be done and wanting it over. "There's no rush. I have to find out what pleases you, darling. And you have to discover what pleases me. I won't tell you—and I won't ask—because it's in the finding out that we'll have the fun."

And in full lamplight he explored my body from the crown of my head to the soles of my feet, returning unerringly to the tender places, his hands and his mouth inviting me, persuading me, to pleasure, coaxing it from me and nurturing it into the most acute physical joy of my life, leaving me exhausted but clear-headed, since emotion had scarcely been used at all.

From those first, difficult days when only the iron discipline of my father's teaching enabled me to conceal how desperately I was grieving for Nicholas, Blaize intrigued and satiated my senses, filled my nights with pleasure, not infrequently with amazement, my days with a constant flurry of occupations, little errands to run on his behalf, people to meet, dinners to be eaten in gay company or romantically alone, race meetings and theatres, elegant concert halls and wicked, fascinating pavement cafés, shopping, spending, railway stations, sinister foreign taverns, luxurious hotels. He kept me busy, laughed at me, pampered me sometimes, abandoned me, at other times, for days on end in unfamiliar places while he made lightning trips alone, presumably back to Cullingford. He indulged me, amused me, entertained me, kept me waiting in strange restaurants without ever making explanations, expected me, at a moment's notice, to be ready to take a train, or a coach, to be as fresh at the end of a journey as I had been at its beginning, expected me, at all times —since I had declared myself to be a woman and not a child— to cope alone, to stand firmly on the two adult feet of which I was possessed. And if it was exhausting, sometimes exasperating, it was exciting, leaving me no time to brood on anything else, and I did not dislike it.

We were married eventually in Bournemouth, but it was clear to anyone with the slightest knowledge of mathematics—and there were few in Cullingford who could not do their sums— that we had travelled together on the wicked Continent for several months before he took me to his mother at Rosemount Lodge, and Cullingford, quite rightly, knew just what that meant.

"My mother will help us to put everything right," Blaize had said, yet, oddly enough, it was not Aunt Verity who came to our assistance after all, but the irascible Sir Joel himself.

"I don't understand this at all," Aunt Verity told Blaize on our arrival at Rosemount, having offered me no more than a cool hand in welcome. "If you wished to get married, you had only to say so. Obviously there is rather more to it than that. Are you going to tell me what it is?"

"I shouldn't think so, Mamma," Blaize cheerfully replied, and instead of the explosion I had anticipated, Uncle Joel, from the depths of his armchair, gave a grim but decidedly humorous chuckle and got to his feet, his face still showing the strain of the chest infection he had endured that winter, but his eyes very keen.

"It strikes me you'll have to be content with that, Verity," he said. "There'll have to be a wedding now, no matter who likes it and who doesn't. And I'm not sure I dislike it. To tell the truth I've had about enough of fancy marriages, and if he's gone about it in a peculiar way, then your eldest son has always been like that, Lady Barforth—wouldn't you say? I reckon he's fancy enough, our Blaize, without taking himself a fancy wife. And a Cullingford girl was good enough for me. So we'll get you married now, Faith Aycliffe, just as quick as we can, and as soon as the weather's warmer and I'm feeling up to breathing some bad Cullingford air again, *I'll* take you home and get you settled where you belong."

My mother, Prudence, Aunt Hannah, and Jonas came down for my wedding, my mother melting into easy tears of forgiveness, Aunt Hannah, her eyes as shrewd as her brother's, telling me that only her sense of loyalty to her family and her Christian duty inclined her to welcome me back to the fold.

"How very enterprising of you," Jonas told me. "Obviously there has been no time to draw up a marriage contract but I trust your husband will see no objection to leaving your personal affairs in my hands?" And smiling at him, I didn't believe he had betrayed me, for if Jonas had decided to ferret out the identity of my lover, I felt certain that he, unlike Aunt Hannah, would have got it right.

I took Prudence on a brisk stroll along the cliff top and, before she had time to question me, said, "I can't tell you why. I promised not to tell anyone."

"Ah—you had a reason, then? I imagined it to be just the whim of a moment." And then, her voice still angry but no longer with me, she said, "There is no need to tell me. They are calling you a sly minx in Cullingford. Everybody's mamma is pretending to be scandalised, when half of them would have put their daughters willingly on that London train in your place— and Celia is so torn between delight at having you so rich and shame at knowing you so wanton that it has quite made her ill. Well—I believe it has made me ill too. They have used you, haven't they—one of them or both of them, Nicholas or Blaize— what does it matter? You were manipulated and bewildered, weren't you, and convinced that you had no choice? No—no, don't say anything. I don't know the details, and don't wish to know."

"Prudence—please—I can ask no one else. Have you seen Nicholas?"

"Yes," she said, and that was all she would say.

Caroline, who was paying a visit to Lady Henrietta Stone in Belgravia and could easily have come to Rosemount to see me married, declined, expressing herself much shocked at the manner in which I had snared her favourite brother. She was fond of me, in fact she had been very fond of me, but an earl's daughter, she felt, would not have been too good for Blaize, and when he dined with her in London, she did not scruple to tell him so.

Georgiana, who could not attend, being very near her time, scrawled me a hasty message of good will. "What wickedness. What a lark. What fun. One can always rely on Blaize to do things in style. My brother Perry could not have done it better."

And although I asked Prudence again, and then again, I could persuade her to tell me nothing of Nicholas.

There was a high, very fragile blue sky on my wedding morning, shreds of cloud blown this way and that by a cool wind which, as I was driven to church, obligingly uncovered a glimmer of sun for me. White satin, of course, even had I not been a widow, would have been inappropriate on this occasion, but Blaize, as Georgiana had said, required things to be done with style, and my dress, ordered in Paris from M. Albertini, was perhaps the most elegant I had ever owned, its cream-coloured skirt filling the carriage, the sleeves a cascade of cream lace, enormous cream silk roses on the waist and the bodice, a silk and lace flower garden on my hat. Blaize kissed my hand at the altar as tenderly as if he had loved me all his life, I smiled up at him just as mistily, and afterwards, since we had already had our honeymoon, Aunt Verity moved our belongings from the two small spare bedrooms we had been chastely occupying at Rosemount Lodge into the large, double-bedded one, and we were married.

"Will it be different tonight, I wonder?" Blaize said, stretching himself out beside me.

"Yes—you have made an honest woman out of me and so I shall behave like one. I am a wife now, not a mistress, so I shall keep on my nightgown and turn down the lights."

"Well—that would be something new in my experience, at any rate. But, in fact, my married darling, you will do exactly as I say, for I am your husband now and my authority over you is very nearly life and death . . ."

"So it is—does that please you?"

He shrugged. "I've not really considered it. I don't think it matters to me either way, for if I should need the authority of the law to possess you, I'd feel myself to be something of a failure, and something of a fool as well, I reckon. And whatever the law may have to say, you'll only give me what you want to give me, or what you can—and I shall do the same. I think we shall manage well enough with that."

He went to Cullingford a few days later, leaving me with my aunt—my mother-in-law—who, although she was kind to me again, alarmed me sometimes by the questions she did not ask. And when he returned he had sold my house in Millergate and had brought sketches of another to show me, which, while asking most courteously for my opinion, I suspected he had purchased already.

It was at a spot called Elderleigh Hill, a few miles out of Cullingford on the road to Listonby, not rural precisely since the low, neatly folded hills were no barrier to those belching chimney stacks, the lightest of breezes coming smoke-laden across them, but it was still green in patches, still fragrant with blossom in springtime, the house itself, built almost fifty years ago in the prince regent's day, being an elegant, classical box, a Grecian temple against the medieval cathedral that was Tarn Edge.

"I am sure it will suit you," he told me, and realising he had actually said, "It suits me," and because, most of all, I desired to be settled, I had few complaints to make.

"You will have a long drive to the mill every day."

"Darling—I don't go to the mill every day."

"Well, it seems very nice and quite large—can we afford it?"

"Oh, as to that, I imagine my father will buy it for us. He keeps Nicholas in luxury at Tarn Edge and is always buying Caroline the odd farm or two. He's bound to do something on similar lines for me. If you're agreeable, I will send Jonas Agbrigg word to complete the transaction, for I want to get you settled before I leave for New York."

"Blaize—you didn't tell me you were going to America."

"My dear—I'm telling you now."

"And I can't come with you, I suppose."

"No, darling. These intensive selling trips are not suitable for ladies, believe me. I would have no time to spare to be with you, and some of the places I visit are not ones in which I could very well leave you alone. Nicholas may call it self-indulgence, if he pleases, but in fact what I do is extremely hard work. You couldn't possibly enjoy it."

"You saw Nicholas—when you were in Cullingford?"

"I could hardly go to Cullingford without seeing him. He was more or less as I'd expected him to be. I am to buy the house, then? Good. There are some alterations I know you'll be bound to make. The wallpaper is quite appalling throughout, so you will need to be nearby, darling. I shall take you to Listonby before I leave and I expect you'll be so busy that you'll hardly miss me."

"Blaize," I said, quite horrified. "Caroline will not have me."

"Of course she will. I have already spoken to her and it is all arranged. She may scold you for ten minutes, but she likes to be at the centre of things, and is really quite lonely sometimes, you know. She will find you a pleasant change from Hetty Stone, and Listonby is very convenient for Elderleigh—"

"Dear God . . ." I said, and then, seeing the quizzical arch of his eyebrow, reminding me of our arrangement, that he had warned me from the start that I could not lean on him, I took a deep breath and then another, and smiled.

"Yes, of course. The house will keep me fully occupied. I shall try to have it ready by the time you come back again."

"Good."

And having made his point, won his day, he crossed the room and kissed me.

"I have no choice in the matter, Faith. I plan these journeys well in advance. My customers are expecting to see me, and if I don't arrive they will make it their business to see someone else. And I'm not asking you to face Cullingford alone. I shall be back in plenty of time for that. We will tackle the Assembly Rooms together, and Aunt Hannah's drawing room, and anywhere else you fancy—that I promise you—but Listonby is hardly Cullingford, after all. Your presence there will be very well advertised. No one will call who doesn't wish to see you. And there will be no reason for you to go into town."

And that was as much as he would say to me of Nicholas.

I embarked then on a period of my life, lasting almost a year, in which I was continually called upon to do the impossible and, somehow or other, did it. Listonby was easy enough, for although Caroline herself was stiff with me for a day or so, Lady Hetty Stone, an almost permanent guest, was a worldly woman, half-amused, half-bored by the middle-class notions of Lady Chard, and more than ready to make friends with any woman who had a husband as charming as mine.

"You will like Hetty Stone," Caroline told me, a command not a recommendation, and although her thin, languid body did not please me, her die-away airs and graces were frankly irritating, her intelligence was shrewd enough, her pedigree of the very highest, representing for Caroline, who had so easily conquered the squirearchy, a new challenge. For Lady Hetty was the offspring of no fox-hunting Tory squire living on his rents of one pound per acre, his acreage rarely surpassing the thousand, his influence powerful, perhaps, if strictly local, but of the Duke of South Erin, a Whig grandee of awesome, international dignity, whose acquaintance could open new worlds for Caroline. And although Lady Hetty herself had married unwisely, a younger son who had first dissipated his inheritance and then died of his dissipations, she possessed nevertheless the entrée to those glittering Mayfair staircases where the high nobility received their guests, had been received at Court, could drop famous names so casually, yet so thick and fast that her board and lodging at Listonby were amply justified.

"I have stopped using place cards at dinner," Caroline told me. "Hetty Stone says in London no one does. It is up to the butler to recognise one's guests and remember where they are to be seated. Well—Charlesworth is not very pleased about it, and I am forced to agree it must be easier to identify Lord Palmerston and Mr. Disraeli than a collection of hunting gentlemen, or commercial gentlemen, who tend to look very much alike, but he will have to do the best he can. You could keep your eyes open tonight, Faith, and give him a little nod in the right direction—since you will be sure to remember everyone."

Yet she invited no one who could embarrass me, or, if she did, they did not appear, and once again I encountered the impossible and performed it, knowing Nicholas to be but a few miles away and living, in surface calm, with the dread of turning a corner one day and meeting his anger, his hurt, suffering his reproaches, the temptation of going myself to find him and telling him the truth. It was impossible now not to think of him.

Impossible. I had no way of preventing it, but by then I knew I was expecting Blaize's child, the most binding commitment I had ever made to any man, the ultimate possession, and it was a blessed relief to turn my mind inwards, to the new individual inside me, constantly marvelling at the functioning of my own body, which knew so exactly how to nourish this new life about which my mind, and my inexperienced hands, had no knowledge at all.

I had believed it impossible to drive over to Elderleigh every morning in Caroline's landau, with Hetty Stone, who found my company less exacting than Caroline's, more often than not at my side. Impossible to survey those well-proportioned yet ill-decorated rooms, to strip them, in my mind, of some other woman's poor taste and do them up again in a fashion I hoped would be pleasing to Blaize. Impossible to convey my requirements—Blaize's requirements—to a daily procession of craftsmen, and tradesmen, impossible to make such sharp enquiries to various establishments in London when the furniture, the glass, and the china we had ordered together were not delivered on time. Impossible—when I had not the slightest knowledge of such things—to install new stoves and boilers, give orders for the cleaning and repairing of chimneys so that my husband could be warm and adequately fed.

Yet gradually the ceilings were relieved of their ugly, lumpy mouldings and acquired a delicate tracery of acanthus leaves picked out in gold, the cloudy colour of the plasterwork echoed by the flowery pastels of the Aubusson rugs we had shipped over from France. The drawing room walls lost their busy brown flowers and were covered in honey-gold watered silk, the dining room in wild rose. The windows, quite suddenly, were clean and intricately draped in muslin and velvet, the marble fireplaces polished, the mantel shelves ready to receive my bridal offerings, a French clock set in the midst of porcelain flowers, potpourri vases painted with the pastoral landscapes of Watteau, embellished by the china roses and carnations of Meissen, the classical figures of white biscuit porcelain which my father had so loved. Furniture began to arrive, a rococo sofa inlaid with mother-of-pearl, a vast, honey-coloured velvet one, gold-striped brocade chairs, a capacious half-tester bed with curtains and valances in pale lemon silk.

"Impractical," said Caroline.

"Beautiful," said Hetty Stone. "Your husband demands a great deal of you, Mrs. Barforth."

"My husband is that kind of man, Lady Henrietta."

And, before very long, there was a cook in my kitchen, a parlourmaid to serve my tea, lay my dinner table, keep my fine linen in order, housemaids to clean and polish and carry water, a little girl to scour my pots and pans and devote herself bravely to the black-leading of my new, monster stove with its several hot plates and ovens, to the feeding of its viciously crackling fire and the replenishing of its cavernous, constantly steaming boiler. I had a butler, considerably less grand than Caroline's, to answer my door, take care of my silver, watch over my wine cellar, wait at my table. I had a footman to clean the boots and polish my cutlery, to deliver my messages and go out with me in my carriage, to mend my fires and light my lamps. I was well housed, well served, too busy for the self-indulgence of brooding. I had proved not only my ability but my good faith so that when Blaize came home he had no more to do than see to the accommodation of his horses.

I had no idea if he had missed me or was glad to see me again, certainly he did not tell me so, but his appreciation of my domestic arrangements was generous, his home-coming accompanied by flowers and champagne and a great many presents, a lace fan on ivory sticks, a lace shawl, an extravagant parasol that could have been a swirl of sea foam on an ivory handle, exquisite, impersonal things, luxury goods which could have been given by any man to any woman.

But later. "Oh yes—you may care for this," he said, and tossed into my lap a cameo heavily framed in gold, the glass cut into the shape of a full-breasted swan, a unique token, the only one, I imagined, in the world, since he must have ordered it to be made specially for me.

"Yes," he said. "I thought it might move you—so drift towards me, darling. I may appear dainty in my appetites but I get hungry—like any other man—when I have been away from home."

It was to be the pattern of our life together, rapid, casual departures, abandonments almost.

"Blaize—you didn't tell me you were going to London—Germany—New York—the Great Wall of China."

"Darling—I'm telling you now."

And always some impossible task to be completed in his absence.

"See to this for me—that for me—why don't you turn the back parlour into a library for me while I'm away?"

And on his return the wine, the gifts, the costly bric-a-brac, and occasionally something to touch my heart, something to amaze me, from a spray of the year's first snowdrops bought for a penny at the roadside, to something as rare and precious as my cameo swan.

But that first home-coming, in its way, was also the end of a reprieve, for now I had not only to face the reality of living with Blaize as his wife, in his home—a far different matter from the nomad existence of hotels, rented villas, other people's houses we had experienced until now—but I would be forced to take my place in Cullingford again. And that, clearly, was impossible.

I *could* not enter the Morgan Aycliffe Hall on Sir Joel Barforth's arm—my pregnancy, thankfully, as yet not showing—and listen, seated between him and Blaize, to an organ recital given by the willowy young Austrian Rebecca Mandelbaum was determined to marry. But it happened.

"There's no cause for alarm," Sir Joel said, his smile telling me that he, at any rate, was planning to enjoy himself. "Anybody who wants to speak to me will have to speak to you, Faith. And I reckon there's not many here tonight who can afford not to speak to me."

And so it proved.

There was, perhaps, a hushed moment of malice and curiosity, a certain drawing aside of skirts in the vestibule to avoid contamination as I passed. But then: "Good evening, Faith dear," said Mrs. Mandelbaum, who, having a disobedient daughter of her own, did not wish, perhaps, to throw stones.

"Good evening," said Mrs. Hobhouse stiffly, not really liking it—since none of *her* girls would ever behave in this manner—but too much aware of financial difficulties at Nethercoats to offer a downright snub to any Barforth.

"Mrs. Blaize Barforth, how very nice to see you," said Mr.

Fieldhead, our member of Parliament, sensing the approach of a general election and knowing where a large proportion of his campaign funds came from.

"Ah—here is my niece," said Aunt Hannah loudly. "Faith, I believe you are not acquainted with Mrs. Birkett, who is new to our area?" And there was no doubt that Mrs. Birkett, whose husband was attempting to establish himself as a shipping and forwarding agent in Sheepgate, had no objection to being acquainted.

It was done, and I found, once again, as had been clear to me on my return from France long ago, that everyone considered their own affairs to be far more pressing and interesting than mine. My sister Celia was pregnant again, determined to have a boy this time since she had been brought up to believe so firmly in the superiority of the male, and when I called in Albert Place, she was far more concerned with the insubordination of her nurserymaid, the sloveliness she *knew* went on in her kitchen, than any misdemeanours of mine.

"So you are in the family way at last yourself, are you," she said. "Well, I can tell you here and now that you will not like it—just wait until your ankles begin to swell and your head to ache and until you are too stout and breathless to get up from your chair. Not that you will suffer all that much, I suppose. No, you will just sail through it as you do with everything and will probably get a boy first time. Indeed I hope you do, for your husband is to inherit a title, after all, and will want a son of his own to pass it on to. You had best get it right now, and then you may not be obliged to go through it again."

My mother, having secrets of her own, asked no questions and, in any case, was fully occupied with her Daniel, who merely winked a merry eye at me and whispered, "Clever puss." Aunt Hannah, now that her husband had been persuaded to accept a third term of office, was engrossed with new building schemes, a town hall, no less, which could not possibly be completed under her husband's aegis but in which Jonas, who had already taken his place on the council, could surely officiate.

And, in any case, there were soon other topics worthy of general discussion, the arrival, for instance, of a certain Mrs. Tessa Delaney, a lady no longer in her first bloom of youth but of a most luscious appearance, who had taken up residence in Al-

bion Terrace, and was known, by some mysterious bush tele-
graph, to be no lady at all but the kept mistress of the widower
Mr. Oldroyd of Fieldhead.

Could one receive Mrs. Delaney or not? Most definitely not,
declared Aunt Hannah. Perhaps one should not be too unkind,
suggested Mrs. Hobhouse, who had a vested interest in keeping
Mr. Oldroyd single, and was relying on Mrs. Delaney to do it for
her.

"She gives excellent cream teas," Prudence said innocently,
replying to Aunt Hannah's startled exclamation with a casual,
"so Freddy Hobhouse tells me. And Jonas should be able to give
you confirmation, since I believe he advises her on her investments."

"Jonas," Aunt Hannah announced with dignity, "has a great
many clients, who rely implicitly on his judgement. But they are
not all persons with whom one could wish to take tea."

And when the burning question of Mrs. Delaney became
exhausted there was the even more ferociously disputed question
of the war with Russia, the appalling, incredible story that far
away in the Crimea thousands of our soldiers were being murdered, not gloriously on the field of battle but vomiting their
lives away as Giles had done, of cholera, dysentery, filth, and
neglect.

I did not really understand why we had joined the Turks in
their fight against the Russians. Perhaps no one really knew. It
merely seemed to my weak female intelligence that peace, having lasted so long, had begun to appear stale so that any war
would have been welcome, and we had chosen the first that
came to hand. We had grown too fat and too prosperous, it
seemed, too bored, ashamed, almost, of our prosperity, and a
testing ground was needed, an opportunity for our young men to
show us their valour, to replenish the glory of Waterloo, which,
being forty years distant, was growing middle-aged and dim.

"We must fight them," Matthew Chard had declared more
than a year ago, and when our troops finally sailed eastwards
they had gone as conquerors, avenging angels, confident of
glory. And since Cullingford had its share of reckless, half-
starved young lads who had run off to be soldiers, finding an occasional flogging at the hands of a sergeant no harder to bear
than an overlooker's strap in the mill yard, our streets were full

of proudly weeping mothers and sweethearts getting ready to welcome the heroes home.

The Chards and the Clevedons were both amply provided with military connections, gallant young captains and high-ranking officers of the stamp of Lord Cardigan, who spent 10,000 pounds a year of his own money to smarten up his Hussars, and they set off eagerly, these gentlemen, some of them taking their private yachts, their wives and their mistresses with them. And because it would all be very soon over, because the men who had beaten Napoleon would have to do little more than display their red coats and their medals to put these insolent Cossacks to flight, a great many civilians went out too, equally encumbered by mistresses and hampers of champagne, worried in case they should arrive too late and miss the fun.

Matthew Chard would have gone himself had Caroline allowed it, Peregrine Clevedon and Julian Flood went off together, returning unshocked and unscathed with gifts of Crimean hyacinth bulbs for Georgiana and Caroline. And I suppose they were all slow to believe, like the rest of us, that courage alone—and there was plenty of courage—was not enough, that the Duke of Wellington, lulled by his own fond memories of Waterloo, had left us an army without reserves, that these glorious men, being immune neither to sabre thrusts nor bullets, had no one to replace them when they fell but raw recruits, illiterate most of them, desperate and juvenile, rushed into battle after a mere sixty days' drill.

But there was far worse than that, for when our army, already riddled with disease, made the final leg of its journey across the Black Sea, there were transports enough provided for the men themselves but too few to include their bedding and cooking utensils and tents, such trifling items as bandages, splints, chloroform, stretchers, which were all left behind. And when the battle was won our wounded—the victors—lay on the ground, unattended, in some cases, until they died.

The ones who were sent back to the military hospital at Scutari lay on the ground too, we heard—a relative of Matthew Chard's among them—since for some unaccountable reason there were no beds; unwashed since there were no buckets in which to carry water—if there was water; unfed since there appeared to be no kitchens in working order; unbandaged, naturally, since no one had remembered about bandages. And so they died too, connections of the Chards and the Floods and connections of our mill hands from Simon Street all together, a fair proportion of wives and mistresses dying with them, since there was still the cholera.

A Simon Street lad limped home from Scutari, having had his leg amputated without even the anaesthetic of a bottle of rum, having lain on the bare deck of a troopship for fifteen days waiting to come home with nothing to shield his mutilated body from the sun, leaving his youth behind him and with nothing in front of him but a bleak apprenticeship to the beggar's trade.

I joined the committee formed by Aunt Hannah to assist him and the girl who had borne his child, and the others who came after him, talking of gangrene and starvation and a woman called Florence Nightingale, who had promised to see that their mates were fed. And with the stench of that in my mind, the remembered horror of Giles Ashburn's ending, my present anger and pity, my personal dilemma seemed much reduced indeed.

The day after the organ recital my uncle paid a visit, with both Nicholas and Blaize, to the business premises of Jonas Agbrigg in Croppers Court, where the deeds of partnership were finally signed, converting the private empire of Sir Joel Barforth into the firm of Sir Joel Barforth & Sons, an event which would have been celebrated by a family dinner at Tarn Edge, another impossibility, cancelled only because Georgiana, who had suffered a severe attack of milk fever after the birth of her daughter, was not yet well enough to come downstairs.

Nicholas was not at home when I called to pay my respects to his daughter, Miss Venetia Barforth, named, one supposed, for some ancestress of the Clevedons. Aunt Verity, for reasons I did not care to examine too closely, told me at once that he was not expected back for some time, while Georgiana herself was still too much the invalid either to enquire, or to care, why I had neglected her. The child, lost in her lacy cradle, was the smallest I had ever seen, the merest whisper of a human life, her helplessness touching a certain helplessness in me so that it was a relief to be told I could not stay.

"Poor Georgiana. She almost lost her life," Aunt Verity told me as we walked together down the wide staircase, the wide velvet sofa where I had gossiped with Caroline still there on the landing, warmed by the jewelled reflections from the great window. "In fact at one point Dr. Blackstone told us that there was no hope—that it was merely a matter of time."

"How terrible."

"Yes," she said, pausing as we reached the hall, her clear eyes reminding me suddenly of Blaize. "Terrible indeed. I have never seen Nicholas so frantic. Naturally one would have expected him to be deeply moved, but I really thought—for a while—that he would lose his mind. I found him leaning against the wall outside her bedroom door, not crying precisely but groaning, telling me—or himself—that he didn't want her to die—which, of course, he didn't. No, I have never seen him in such agony, nor so drunk afterwards, I might add, when we knew she would recover. Faith—I do beg your pardon. You carry your own condition so well that I had quite forgotten—I have had three children, dear, quite easily, and your mother had no trouble to speak of. There is every reason to suppose you will be the same."

There remained, after that, the final impossibility of meeting Nicholas again, the unthinkable moment when I would hold out my hand to him and he would either take it, or refuse it. But it was widely known in Cullingford that the Barforth brothers were not good friends, that neither appreciated the contribution the other made to the business, that Nicholas, his looms working to capacity and to order, saw his brother's constant journeyings as self-indulgence, while Blaize insisted that without his self-indulgences there would be no orders to fill. And no one expected to meet them drinking together at the Old Swan, nor in the same box at the theatre with their wives.

I had seen him in the distance often enough those first few months after my return to Cullingford, had turned sick and fled. Aunt Verity, perhaps quite knowingly, had described to me his torment at Georgiana's confinement, having recognised guilt in him as clearly as I had. And if he had been aware of his own guilt, and of mine—if he had understood that it would have been too much for either of us to bear—then would it suffice to clear his pathway to forgiveness and a new beginning? I prayed that it would, selflessly for his sake, selfishly for my own, since I knew my peace of mind depended upon it. And if, at times, I knew it could be no more than a fairy tale, that life could never arrange itself so neatly as that, there were other times when I believed all might come right because I wanted to believe it, and because Blaize had said so.

But when the time of our meeting finally came, it was not at all as I had imagined it, rehearsed it, for by then my pregnancy was so far advanced that I was heavy not only in body but in the senses, my emotions lulled, half-dormant, pulse beat and heartbeat sluggish and expectant, my identity as a woman submerged in my role of breeding female, too placid and patient to arouse or experience any kind of passion. And my condition alone gave him a socially impeccable reason for not looking at me too closely, since Celia was not the only woman in the world to avoid male eyes at such a moment.

I had called for the first time at Blaize's office at Tarn Edge, and interested in this room where he spent so much of his time, intrigued by this aspect of him as a man of business, by his elaborately furnished desk top, the huge table where samples of Barforth cloth were set out, the window which gave him so perfect a view of the mill yard where he endeavoured as little as possible to set foot, I barely moved, barely drew a breath when Nicholas came into the room, more samples in his hands.

"Ah—Faith," he said. "Are you well?"

"Yes, Nicholas. Are you?"

"Fine, thanks. Look here, Blaize, is this what you want for Grassmann?"

And he handed the samples of cloth to Blaize, who took them to the window, where they examined them together in the daylight.

"It's not what *I* want for Grassmann," Blaize said. "It's what Grassmann wants for himself. What about that piece for Remburger?"

"Christ—it's still on the loom."

"But you'll have enough ready for me to show? Remburger arrives in London on the twentieth."

"Aye—you'd better come downstairs and have a look. It's still got a boardy feel to it, to me."

"Well—it's not my place to put that right. I thought Mayor Agbrigg was supposed to see to it?"

"So did I. And where the hell is he? I should have been at

Lawcroft an hour ago. Every time I show my face in these damned sheds it's the same story. If you're coming down, you'll have to come now."

They walked to the door, warp and weft, delivery dates, profit and loss on their minds, and holding myself very still, I said, "Nicholas—is Georgiana feeling better?"

"Yes—she's mending. Kind of you to enquire."

And, as in most moments of intense crisis, it was over before it had begun. He had neither taken my hand, after all, nor refused to take it. He had spoken to me. I had answered. The next time we met we would speak again. "How are you?" "I am very well." It had happened. It was possible after all.

But as I drove home, my mind once again inexplicably linked with his, it seemed to me—who had always known what he meant—that he would rather have seen me dead than married to Blaize, that he would forgive neither one of us, would make no effort to understand, would not wish to understand, and that Blaize, who knew everything that went on around him, must, from the start, have known that very well.

Chapter Twenty-four

BLAIZE, with his usual skill in avoiding times of domestic crisis, was not at home when our daughter was born, returning some days after the event when she had lost that first crinkled petulance of the newborn and I was reclining comfortably—even elegantly—among my lace pillows, my wrists and shoulders scented with lavender water, my hair well brushed, my humour tolerant, since I had not, in fact, suffered a great deal and could not have imagined him holding my fevered hands and sharing my groans in any case.

"You will have to forgive me," he said. "And you must admit you were a little ahead of yourself—"

"So I was. I thought it best to hurry, since there is Caroline's hunt ball to consider, you know. She is expecting me to be up and about in plenty of time for that. She's over there—your daughter—behind that frilly canopy."

"My daughter," he said. "Good heavens—" his enthusiasm for parenthood being only lukewarm, having thoroughly disliked Georgiana's haphazard nursery arrangements at Tarn Edge. But as he glanced down into the cradle, expecting nothing but red-faced, peevish anonymity, I saw his glance sharpen, momentarily, with interest, his eyes narrowing as he took a longer look.

"Well—I must say she's not quite the ill-tempered little frog other babies seem to be. In fact she's really rather nice . . ."

"Of course. But then, you always do things better than other men, don't you."

"So I do," he said, coming back to my bedside. "But not too often, darling, in this case . . . Faith—are you really as well as you look? I *did* come back as soon as I could, you know, and I really thought there'd be a week or more yet."

"Good heavens—Blaize Barforth, can it be that you are feeling guilty?"

"I wonder."

"Then there is no need. I did quite well without you. In fact I did so well that I am beginning to wonder what all the fuss is about. And Celia is most upset with me for being so cheerful. She thinks it positively improper."

"Yes—but then, you see, you don't have to work hard to attract your husband's notice, do you—like Celia?"

My daughter, her birth so physically easy but so emotionally overwhelming, the first unconditional love to enter my life, since no matter what kind of woman she might become—and I had no way even of guessing—we would remain bound together. It would not be necessary for me to approve of her. I would not even need to like her. I would always love her. And the certainty of it gave me peace and purpose, transforming me from a decorative object to a useful one. I had done something of note in the world. I had taken on the kind of total commitment my nature craved, and even though the nurse and the nurserymaid were of more practical use to my daughter in those early days, I knew that her health, her appetite, the bloom in her cheeks, the growing flesh and fibre of her had come to her through me.

We called her Blanche in compliment to her pale, quite exquisite colouring, the fair hair and almost transparent blue eyes, the ivory and silver of her.

"She's beautiful," everyone said.

"She's like her mother," Blaize replied.

She *was* beautiful. I was deeply content. So long as I remained in my lacy, flowery bedroom, within the four walls of my elegant house, the limits of my garden bordered by its hedge of lilacs and rhododendrons, I was happy. But I was married to a man for whom the world was very wide, who had chosen me not for my breeding qualities but as a partner in the gracious style of living he required, as a mistress, an entertainer, a good friend, and my new role of mother was simply added to these, in no way supplanting them.

"Should you really get up so soon, dear?" my mother asked

me, holding my three-week-old Blanche carefully on her satin lap.

"Oh yes, I think so. There are some German customers coming north in a week or two—and then some Americans—and they will have to be entertained."

"Dearest, I never thought to see you so busy. It suits you."

Remembering the sparse, cheerless nursery of my childhood, I decorated a fairy-tale, upstairs world for Blanche: pastel walls enlivened with sprays of vivid dream flowers, bright rugs which Caroline thought gaudy and would collect dust, window boxes crammed with daffodils that first springtime, and china bowls of the Crimean hyacinths Julian Flood had given to me and which my nurse—believing the flowers would use up the air and suffocate my daughter—never failed to remove at night time. I dressed her like a princess—better than a princess, since it was my experience that the aristocracy did not spend lavishly on childhood—I pampered her, played with her, placed incredibly costly, incredibly fragile ornaments on her mantel shelf so that she might grow up accustomed to beauty.

"You will make her very soft, and very vain," Caroline told me, but knowing rather more of the world, I thought, than Caroline, I believed that every female was entitled to her share of vanity, that it was, in fact, a most useful weapon, a great comfort.

I was the first woman in Cullingford to wear a cage crinoline, delighting in the freedom of movement this light, metal structure gave me, for it had taken a dozen horsehair-stuffed petticoats to puff out a skirt even half so far, and if some of my acquaintances—Caroline among them—were uncomfortably aware that this vast, gracefully swaying skirt had nothing beneath it but lace pantaloons, fresh air, and legs—"My dear, how can you manage to sit down? And what on earth is to happen in a high wind?"—it suited me, and it was not long before others followed my lead.

My clothes became much talked about, not only in Cullingford but in the neighbouring, more cosmopolitan Bradford and Leeds, where Blaize had many friends. And I did not dislike it. I had plain, pastel-tinted afternoon gowns, delicate creams, near whites, with the exotic contrast of a richly patterned crimson shawl draped loosely around them. I had a walking dress—much copied the first year I wore it—of coffee-coloured foulard des Indes trimmed with black velvet, a brown bonnet trimmed with black satin and black feathers, a sable muff Blaize had brought back from some unspecified journey. I had light summer dresses with sleeves of puffed muslin and tulle, wristbands of ribbon, pearl, and coral, an evening gown—worn for the Listonby hunt ball and greatly appreciated by not a few fox-hunting men—in a deep, grape purple cut scandalously low and worn with no jewellery, contriving to give the impression of a nude body emerging from a dark, gauzy cloud. I was the first of my acquaintance to wear my hair in a net made of strands of pearl, a net of gold chains, the first to order black, military-style boots from my husband's bootmaker, to wear Spanish mantillas of black and white lace. And when I persuaded Caroline and Prudence into their first crinolines I had already mastered the little gliding steps necessary to make those capricious cages dip and sway, how to get myself through a doorway and into a carriage without disaster, how to walk across a room without leaving a trail of broken china to mark one's passage, how to judge correctly one's distance from the drawing room fire, the bedtime candles, for even I was obliged to admit that once these colossal skirts were set alight there would be little for even the most agile of women to do but burn with them.

Blaize gave me a victoria to drive in, far preferable to the more conventional landau, since the victoria, which had no doors, allowed for a better arrangement of my skirts. He abandoned his own curricle for the newer, light-shafted, far more vicious cabriolet, which, when he was in residence, carried him from Elderleigh to Tarn Edge at a killing speed. And we became a fashionable couple, as Blaize had intended, giving easy, quite informal dinner parties when he was at home, the house at all times ready for his return and the reception of anyone he might bring with him.

"Faith darling—this is Mr. Remburger from New York."

And I no longer said, "Blaize—you didn't *tell* me he was coming," but "Mr. Remburger—I have so looked forward to meeting you," knowing that if it happened to be winter there would be a fire in the best spare bedroom, if it happened to be spring, there would be bowls of lilacs and forsythia, roses in the summer,

profuse enough to please the most exacting guest. I knew—
because I made it my business to know—that my pantry shelves,
although minute in comparison with Caroline's, contained at all
times their share of delicacies and dainties, that the wine which
should be chilled would be chilled, the wine which should be allowed to breathe would already be breathing, for if my staff was
small and my own temperament not exacting, we were all aware
that in domestic matters Blaize was very exacting indeed, and
my household functioned around a general desire to please him.

When he was at home I existed in a state of pleasant anticipation, of surprise blended sometimes with a mild annoyance,
sometimes with an honest delight, a certain stretching of my intellect and my powers of invention, for although he was never
morose, never ill-tempered, suffered no jealous rages as Nicholas
had done, no urge to punish me in order to test the depth of my
love—since he did not ask me to love him and was not in love
with me—he did require to be entertained.

He was not, in any conventional sense, a domestic man. He
wanted comfort, certainly, luxury whenever possible, and although he knew the cost of it and was ready to pay most
generously, he did not wish to know the details of how his
candlelit dinners, his scented pillows, his immaculately laundered linen, were contrived. Nor did he expect to find me
harassed or gloomy—since he was never so himself, expecting no
passionate welcome on his home-coming, no questions, no complaints, no demands—since he made none himself—but requiring, instead, the same affectionate companionship he gave to me.

And he was a witty, easy, charming friend, an imaginative
lover.

"You might care to wear this for me, Faith," and he would toss
me a peignoir of scandalous transparency, or an evening gown
that appeared to commence at the waist. And when it transpired
that Mr. Remburger of New York was also an admirer of bare,
blond shoulders, Blaize was immensely amused, by no means
displeased to see that other men desired his wife.

It was, perhaps, not a marriage in the way the Law Valley understood it, since Law Valley men did not encourage sensuality
in their wives, being more inclined to fall sound asleep after domestic love-making than to lie easily entwined together in the
lamplight, drinking champagne and telling each other how very

pleasant it had all been. And most Law Valley wives, far from encouraging such nonsense, would have been acutely embarrassed, if not downright horrified by it.

But within the privacy of our bedroom Blaize treated me neither as a sexual convenience nor as a matron who could be asked to do no more than her duty, but as a high-priced courtesan, showing no signs of burning passion and expecting none, quite simply enjoying me, an essential ingredient of his pleasure being that I should enjoy him. And if the Law Valley would not have understood the black lace peignoir, the velvet ribbon I sometimes left around my neck when all else had been discarded, the leisurely arousal that could begin as he leaned through the candlelight towards me at dinnertime to touch my hand, or brush his mouth against my ear, and might not reach its conclusion until after midnight, then I understood it very well.

"Now then, darling—are you longing for me now?"

"I believe so."

"Then I think you may long a moment more, Faith, and appreciate me better—don't you?"

"Yes—since you do so like to be appreciated."

"That's right, darling—drift over me, just melt— You know, I think we do this very well."

"You mean you think you do it very well."

"Mmmmm—but you're coming along nicely, Faith."

He made no enquiries into the state of my emotions. He saw Nicholas daily when he was at the mills and talked of him quite easily when the occasion required it, displaying a lack of curiosity about the past—even as to what my feelings might have been for Giles Ashburn—which I at first mistook for consideration, until I realised that he was, quite simply, not curious.

"Blaize," I asked him, just once. "Why is everything so easy for you?" and laughing, understanding my meaning exactly, he had replied, "Because I am shallow, darling, and superficial and immensely self-centred. And it is my firm intention to remain so . . ."

But it was, of course, less simple than that. He felt no anxiety with regard to me, or to Nicholas, because, never having been in love himself, he did not really believe in it. He enjoyed what he had, he had everything he enjoyed, and had not spoken in jest of his childhood belief that everyone, sooner or later, must prefer him to Nicholas. We had made an arrangement which was clearly congenial to us both, had sealed it with the birth of our daughter, Blanche. What more was there to be said?

The war with Russia ended, largely, it seemed to me, because everyone had grown tired of it rather than because anybody had actually won, and we celebrated the peace with fireworks in the park at Listonby where Blaize and I were frequent guests, especially now that Caroline, in hot pursuit of the Duke of South Erin, needed to show his sister and his sister's friends that not all the Barforths were unsophisticated. I continued to sit on the committee, chaired by Aunt Hannah, for the relief of the mauled remnants still dragging their way back from the Crimea, remembering Giles acutely every time I visited one of them in Simon Street, a fine, charitable lady I wondered if he would recognise. I found employment for the wives of men who were now unemployable, gave money to those who had no women to support them, took arrowroot and soup and blankets to sick children, to soldiers' women—beggars' women—who, despite my aunt's instructions to the contrary, became pregnant again—and again.

Yet when a gentleman who reminded me strongly of Giles as he would have been had he lived to be a little older gave a lecture in what had once been a church hall at the lower end of Sheepgate, on the use of contraceptive sponges which, if soaked in vinegar and washed occasionally, might be of help, there was a *frisson* of horror among the respectable middle classes. My sister Celia, who had miscarried now for the sixth time, found it too disgusting to contemplate; others, for vocal if somewhat vague reasons, considered it contrary to the law of God, while Aunt Hannah condemned Prudence soundly for her support of this charlatan, and me for inviting him to dinner.

"There is such a thing as self-restraint," Aunt Hannah said.

"I have never noticed it," Prudence told her.

"Not the most romantic suggestion I've ever heard," Blaize murmured, wrinkling a fastidious nostril when I mentioned the matter to him. "But, of course, if it could be contrived by a clever woman so that there might be no distinctive odour—so that the gentleman concerned might be quite unaware of it— then I can't really think the gentleman would mind."

Prudence spent as much time as she could in my house, escaping whenever possible from the restrictions of Blenheim Lane, the Irish cousins, the affectionate but eagle-eyed Mr. Adair. She was twenty-eight now—approaching twenty-nine—a desperate age for a single woman, and although her unmarried status did not disturb her—since Freddy Hobhouse was still willing to put an end to that—she was frequently in despair at the slow frittering away of her time, the bonds with which my father, even from the grave, continued to bind her, and which Daniel Adair had no intention of letting go. She had longed to go out to the Crimea and offer her services to Miss Florence Nightingale and had been prevented not by the general outcry but by a simple withdrawal of funds which had made her journey impossible. She longed to set up a school where girls of the new generation could be taught—as she put it—to raise themselves above the level of pet animals, but Mr. Adair, being fond of pet animals, would not hear of that. Young ladies belonged in their mother's drawing rooms. Young ladies did not go out unchaperoned—as Prudence had been accustomed to do. Young ladies did not read newspapers, nor hold political discussions, nor express their opinions on the subject of back to back houses, which Mayor Agbrigg's new building regulations were striving to prohibit. Young ladies, on all topics of importance, shared the views of their senior male relative, and the only alternative open to them was to take a husband, who would be selected by that senior male himself. And although Daniel Adair did not really believe a word of all this, and, far from disliking Prudence, was rather fond of her, he was a man who enjoyed a good fight, finding it a pleasant change from a surfeit of conjugal bliss, and could never resist his part in the running battle between them.

"I'm rich," she said. "Men want to marry me for my money. I own a fortune in porcelain, and I can't raise a penny."

And it was Blaize who suggested, "No, you can't sell your porcelain, of course, but I wonder if there is anything in your father's will which forbids you to give it away?"

"Why should I do that?"

"Oh—generosity, I imagine. There are a pair of Wedgwood urns I have often admired which would look very well on my study mantelpiece, and a porcelain nymph that rather reminds me of Faith. If you should choose to give them to me—or to

Faith—I'm not sure anyone could complain. And should it occur to anyone that I might have paid you for them—well, I cannot think Jonas Agbrigg would be willing to take a mere supposition to court."

"I will check the will again with Jonas," she said, and when she had gone I told him, "That was very clever of you, Blaize."

"Yes—but then, we know I am a clever man."

"It was also very good-natured. Those urns can't be cheap, you know."

"I do know. But bear in mind that I actually want them—which makes me just a shade less generous. And if she is suffering from too many Irish cousins, you might care to suggest to her that an engagement is not a marriage, but carries a fair amount of protection . . . I have it on good authority that Aunt Hannah, in similar circumstances, once engaged herself to a parson with small intention of marrying him."

"That hardly seems fair."

"No, but it would give Freddy Hobhouse the boost he needs. I also have it on good authority that my brother is thinking of making an offer for Nethercoats, and if old Mr. Hobhouse sells out there will be nothing for Freddy. He is not a partner, and Nicky's offer is unlikely to be generous. There might be enough to keep the old couple in a house on the coast, and to make some provision for the girls, but Freddy and the boys will have to fend for themselves. If he got engaged to Prudence, it might be no more than a stay of execution—but the promise of her money might make Mr. Hobhouse less ready to sell, and even if it didn't, he'd be bound to put up his asking price. You see, I'm being good-natured again."

"Yes, I do see. You want to make Nicholas pay more for Nethercoats."

"Ah—but if it would help Prudence and Freddy—and I'm sure Nicky could find the money. They think the world of him at Mr. Rawnsley's bank."

"It's not a game, Blaize—not to them. Prudence couldn't jilt Freddy if he lost his business. She'd feel obliged to stand by him."

"I know," he said, his smoky eyes brimming with amusement and self-knowledge. "But Freddy is a gentleman, don't you see. He'd release her."

Yet, whether or not she was inclined to take advice of this nature, I noticed that quite soon a whole series of familiar objects began to appear, the Wedgwood urns, the white biscuit nymph, a pair of Grecian dancers in Meissen porcelain, a biscuit Venus by Sèvres, a bare-shouldered, female figure from Vincennes mounted on a jungle of ormolu foliage.

"How generous you are, Blaize. I believe Prudence is saving hard."

And, remembering that he had also been generous to Georgiana—that he had a *penchant* perhaps, for ladies in distress—I wondered if he had once included me among them.

I went to Listonby that autumn on a prolonged visit—Blaize having left for some exotic destination—my presence being required since Caroline, now that her sons were out of the nursery—no longer found the start of the hunting season altogether congenial, fretting a great deal in private that her seven-year-old twins could now take their fences like little men—or so their father assured her—and by no means pleased to see them come home to her in so indescribable a state of filth and exhaustion.

But Georgiana, who had taken her own son up on her saddle from his babyhood, determined that, like all the Clevedons, he should ride before he could walk, had no such qualms, and scant patience with Caroline's heart-searchings.

"Good heavens, if either of them breaks a leg it will mend. It's the horses' legs we have to be careful of, darling—one has to shoot them, you know, after a bad fall. And if there are times when one would quite like to shoot one's children, I'm sure there's no fear of it. I'll keep an eye on your boys for you—and they're both quite careful in any case, they just jog along with the grooms when they're tired—not at all like my Gervase . . ."

But Caroline well knew that Georgiana, once her blood was up, would keep an eye on no one, would leave her own Gervase in a ditch if he happened to take a tumble; while Hetty Stone, who was no equestrienne but who regularly drove herself out to the covert-side, would have no time either for little boys, being more inclined to keep her eyes on their fathers. And each hunting day contained its share of misery, no leisurely tea tray in her bed these days, until the meet had departed, but a strained presence, hovering in the hall, her whole nature torn between Lady Chard, who must, both by rank and inclination, have a fine appreciation of such things, and Caroline Barforth, frankly revolted by such recklessness, such waste.

"It's quite ridiculous," she would tell me as we watched them set out, all dash and clatter in the stable yard as they tasted the air of the fresh morning, the occasional cursing and the laughter as some nervous animal went skittering out of control shredding Caroline's nerves to agony as, with outward calm, she ordered the serving of stirrup cups.

"Quite ridiculous—taking children of that age—it can't be good for them. And the language they are exposed to—and the manners— Did you hear Perry Clevedon just now, yelling like a madman? And Julian Flood is every bit as bad. They will go through a dozen horses between them this season, ruin them—whatever Georgiana may have to say—and I would like to know who pays the bills? Well, in fact, I do know it, for Georgiana is keeping an entire stable over at Galton, for Perry's convenience, and she could only have the money from Nicholas. It doesn't occur to her, one supposes, that he might need his spare cash for something else—that it would suit him better to put it back into the business, or to get another business off the ground. And that animal she has bought for Gervase is enormous—my goodness, I told Matthew at once that if he had any thought of getting such a monster for Dominic or Noel then he and I would certainly quarrel. And now he has taken Gideon out as well—to ride with the grooms, he says, since that is what he did himself at that age."

And, of course, that was the root of her dilemma. She did not really want her children to hunt—did not, in fact, much care for hunting men apart from Matthew—but the Chards, the Floods, the Clevedons, certainly the South Erins, had always hunted from childhood, and she was determined to fit her sons for their inheritance. She did not really want to send them to Matthew's old school where they would be required to wash in cold water at a standpipe in an open yard, like the lads from Simon Street, and would be flogged when they misbehaved as soundly as factory boys were strapped by their overlooker—as no schoolmaster had ever dared to flog her middle-class brothers—but young squires had always been treated so, and were sent to school, after all, not to be educated but to be toughened into men who could lead a Light Brigade, armed only with sabres, into the mouths of Russian cannon, who could acquire the passionless hauteur of privilege which had so attracted her to her husband. She did not really want her sons to sally forth, gun in hand, and slaughter with their own not always accurate shot the pheasant and grouse which would replenish her larder, would have much preferred to purchase her game clandestinely but safely at her back door, as they did at Tarn Edge. But every young gentleman must know how to handle himself at a *"grande battue,"* must be worthy of his place in a walking line of guns, must know how to shoot flying and how to shoot well. And if armed gamekeepers and mantraps were really necessary for the discouragement of poachers, then she, as the wife of a justice of the peace who also happened to own the game being poached, could hardly disagree.

"I know they must enjoy country pursuits," she moaned. "I know, and they are all so brave. But it seems so wasteful sometimes—wherever the fox goes they go, regardless of whose crops they are riding down, and I feel sure the tenants don't like it—except, of course, that since we own the land I suppose they can't complain. Do you know, Faith, really, sometimes I think some feckless lad from Simon Street could understand Perry Clevedon and Julian Flood better than I do. They take every day as it comes, no thought for tomorrow, not the faintest notion of saving anything or planning anything. They don't pay their debts in Simon Street either. And as for the other thing—my word, I have been hearing all my life about immorality in the weaving sheds, but if you had the faintest notion of what goes on in that abbey cloister night after night— Hetty Stone may smile at Matthew when I complain about it, and imagine I don't see her—and he might smile back since I know he thinks I am a prude—but it is not *right*, Faith. It is not responsible. Hetty Stone may be a duke's daughter and think it a great lark that her brothers were all sent down from Eton and Oxford, and that one of them is keeping a quite famous actress somewhere off Bedford Square—although I must confess he was a hero in the Crimea . . ."

"Caroline, your own brothers have not been angels."

"I wouldn't know about that," she said, instantly bristling. "And whatever they may have done, the business has not suffered by it. They get out of bed every morning and go to the mills, and they pay their bills on time too—right on time or no one in Cullingford would trade with them. Yes—yes—I know old Mr. Clevedon wears himself out looking after his tenants, and that they are all ready to go out and fight for Queen and country at a moment's notice, and will govern the country, without getting paid a penny for doing it, because they think it is their duty. But they don't happen every day, do they—wars and cabinet appointments—it's not 365 days a year, every year, like the mills. Oh, dear, I do hope Matthew remembers about Dominic and Noel—and I am certain he will forget about Gideon."

But it was young Gervase Barforth who went over his horse's head that morning, landing on his head on a stony patch of ground from which his uncle Perry eventually retrieved him and tossed him by the scruff of his neck to his mother, the kind of treatment both Peregrine and Georgiana had received often enough themselves at that age. Georgiana rode back to Listonby with him across her saddle, his face quite grey, his posture, when she allowed him to slide to the ground, decidedly unsteady.

"Just put him to bed," she said. "He'll be all right. No bones broken, and he'll know better next time."

And when, having ascertained, as she put it, that he would live, she rode off again, it was perhaps unfortunate that Caroline, alarmed by the child's persistent stupor, took it upon herself to send for Nicholas, certainly unfortunate that he arrived late that afternoon in a black fury, half an hour in advance of his wife.

I had no wish to be present but could not avoid it when she came striding into the hall, her habit looped up around her arm, mud-spattered and glowing and beautiful as she'd been the first time I had seen her, her boots as careless now of Caroline's carpets as they had been that day of Sir Joel's, that rare bird of the wild wood who had, very briefly, submitted to her captor's hand but who was flying free again, a lovely lark-soaring of the spirit that halted, in mid-air, as she saw her husband.

"Good heavens," she said. "What brings you here? Are the mills on fire? Has Cullingford burned to the ground?"

"No," he told her curtly. "But there could be other reasons just as drastic. Your son, for instance. He had a riding accident earlier in the day, as you are well aware. He might have died—

an hour ago—or be on his deathbed at the very least. And since his mother could not be found, it would seem fairly natural that they should send for me."

I saw the colour drain away from her face, her eyes, against that sudden blanching, a startling, terrified green. I saw her body sway forward a little and then right itself, one hand pressed hard against her stomach, and then, her eyes fluttering from me to Caroline, she said, "No—no, Nicky—he's not dead—and he's not dying. Faith would be crying, and Caroline would be wanting to murder me . . . It couldn't be true."

"I think it could."

She advanced into the room, swishing her crop against her skirt, nervously flexing her free hand, her colour very high now, her temper rising with it, her courage the greater because I could see she was a little afraid of him.

"He took a tumble—it happens, Nicky. It's happened often enough to me. And I brought him home at once."

"Now that *was* good of you."

She stood for a moment looking down at her hands, her crop still nervously slicing the air, and then, throwing back her head in an abrupt movement, her light lashes beaded with tears, she said, "Nicky, don't be hard—please—don't be sarcastic . . . I can't talk to you when you're like this. There's no harm done. If you think I should have stayed with him, then perhaps you're right . . ."

"No—no—it couldn't be right to deprive you of a day's sport."

"Nicky," she moaned, the note of despair in her voice so piercing that I wanted to cover my ears. "It wasn't like that. I only did what it seemed—natural—for me to do. He didn't need me. Caroline was here. Nanny was here. If I'd stayed, they'd have shooed me away. I've been carried home myself like that—worse than that—time and time again and taken no harm—it builds character, don't you see—that's what Grandfather always says."

"I daresay. But you're a Clevedon. He's not."

"He's my son . . ."

"So he is. And you have a daughter, I seem to remember, back in Cullingford, who'll be lucky to see you again before Christmas—who won't see much of you at all until she's big enough to sit a horse, I reckon."

"Oh, dear," she said. "Oh, dear—oh, dear . . ." And she began to pace up and down the room, hands clasped around her elbows, hugging herself, rocking herself almost, in her agony. "You won't understand me, Nicky—you just won't— I *do* care for the children. Yes—more than you care—yes I do—and you won't see it. You won't let me care in my own way. You want me to be somebody else all the time, and I can't do it, Nicky—I've tried and I'll never do it. You want to think I neglect them—yes, I know it. Nicky, you've hurt me now—it's done—it's enough—don't be hard . . ."

"Damnation," he said, swinging abruptly round to the fireplace, his back to us, his hand tight-clenched on the corner of the mantel shelf, and seeing the opportunity of escape, I fled outside into the fresh air as far away as I could, hoping Caroline would have the sense to leave them too. And, unaware of the direction I took, feeling his anger as if it had been directed against myself, feeling her misery just as acutely, I was startled by the sound of sobbing, astonished, as I turned the corner of the house, to see Julian Flood slumped against his horse's neck, his shoulders heaving with an uncontrollable anguish, and Matthew Chard standing beside him, white-faced and sick, his own balance unsteady.

"Matthew—good heavens . . ."

And instantly, because they were gentlemen who did not exhibit their grief before a lady, who had endured their share of floggings in youth to enable them to withstand pain, Julian Flood stopped crying, almost straightened himself, and Matthew Chard came hurrying to meet me.

"Faith—we've had a bit of bad luck, I'm afraid. Perry Clevedon has taken a bad fall—happened just after Georgiana left us —wanted to get back home, she said, to see to her boy . . ."

"How bad?"

"Oh—bad—his horse reared up, went clean over and fell on him. It's the worst fall there is."

"And he's—dead?"

"Oh yes—dead when we picked him up. I can't think he knew much about it. Well—I doubt if knowing that will help Georgiana, but I'd better tell her . . ."

"No. Nicholas is here. Let him tell her."

"Thank God," he said. "Oh—thank God for that. I don't know how she'll go on without Perry—in fact I don't think she'll go on at all." And squeezing my hand, his whole body brimming with gratitude, he left me and hurried off to Caroline, and to Nicholas.

Blaize, by some miracle, came home for the Clevedon funeral and perhaps I surprised him—certainly myself—by the extent of my relief.

"I couldn't face it without you."

"Darling—you flatter me, but I've never seen myself as a rock to lean on. And what is there for you to face? It's Georgiana, surely, who will need a rock. Let us hope she has one."

But she was most amazingly composed, standing erect and quite still beside her grandfather, her eyes dry, her face chalk-white against her black veil, a fragile figure, supporting an even more fragile, almost visibly aging man, for Perry had left no sons, at least none that could be acknowledged, and they were burying not only his recklessly broken, carelessly wasted body, but the end of their ancient line. And once more, as at all momentous occasions, there was that deep division of ranks, Aunt Verity and Caroline and even myself, representatives of the manufacturing classes, being ready to shed a tear, the gentry standing like soldiers around the graveside, even Julian Flood, who had been drunk ever since the accident, having sobered himself up that day, his wild, handsome face as expressionless as granite.

The Clevedon tenants, the pensioned-off retainers, the household servants, the village schoolmistress were all there, knowing far better than I what this death signified, and there was complete silence as he was laid to rest in his own ground, silence as we walked back from the abbey church to the house, only the October wind stirring the leaves, the crackling of logs in the stone-flagged hall, old Mr. Clevedon taking us each one by the hand with perfect courtesy, his whole body quite hollow, his hopes in ashes, but his mouth pronouncing the words he believed it right and proper for him to speak.

We took a glass of wine, arranged ourselves in awkward groupings, Nicholas with his mother and Caroline, Hetty Stone attaching herself to me because Blaize was there, Julian Flood going off suddenly to get drunk again, one supposed, Matthew and those other country gentlemen engaging Mr. Clevedon in painstaking conversation. But Georgiana, who had stood so very still—who had surely never been so still in her whole life before—was nowhere to be seen, did not appear, and after an agonising hour, when everybody wished to leave and no one liked to be the first to go, Blaize put his head close to mine and murmured, "Where is she?"

"I don't know—upstairs perhaps?"

"No. She didn't come back to the house. Try the cloister, Faith."

And when I raised my eyebrows in surprise and didn't move he said, "Yes, Faith—*do* it. Someone should look for her. I can't —not without causing comment—and clearly Nicky doesn't mean to."

I went outside, unhappy with myself because I didn't want this mission, unhappy with him for asking—uneasy in my heart, in my bones, ready to weep myself for a man I hadn't really known and hadn't liked because the tears were there, inside me, and needed to be shed—apprehensive, and irritable, because if I found her, I had no idea what Blaize expected me to do for her, no idea of what I would have it in me to offer.

But my first sight of her was enough to cancel out any other feeling but compassion.

She was in the cloister as Blaize had foreseen, sitting on the ground, her back pressed against the wall, the arched, fan-vaulted ceiling reducing her to the proportions of a weeping doll. And I had never seen such tears, for they seemed to come not from her eyes alone but from the pores of her skin, a wild fountain of grief more terrible somehow because it was still quite silent, no shuddering, no crying out, just that drowning of her face and her spirit in water.

"Oh, Georgiana," I said, and sat down on the uneven, stony ground beside her, feeling that words would be of no avail, that I could merely offer her the comfort of another human presence, as one comforts the newborn, or some stricken animal.

But she was a Clevedon too—above all she was that—and after a moment she nodded, shook herself slightly, and gave me a rueful, tremulous smile.

"I loved him so much, you see."

"Yes, I know."

"Did my grandfather ask you to look for me? No? I'm so glad. I wouldn't let Grandfather see me cry. I came over to Galton at once—after it happened—to be with him, and if I'd broken down and cried I'd have been no use to him. So I didn't cry. I couldn't let Grandfather down. I'll go back in a minute."

And as she began to dry her face with her hands and her sleeves, I gave her my handkerchief and watched, with great respect, as she restored herself to composure.

"There—am I decent now?"

"Yes—quite decent. But give yourself a little longer."

"Yes—can you understand me, Faith? I loved him, but it was more than that. I've been sitting here thinking about it, and it seems to me that I've never been alone before. So long as there was Perry I couldn't be alone. He was here, you see—every day of my life. He was older than I and so he was here, waiting for me, when I was born. My father died and my mother went off somewhere and I never saw her again. I don't remember either of them. Just Perry, and Grandfather, and the abbey. I think I was the happiest child in the world. It's here, in these stones, all that fun, all that joy—I left it here for Perry's children, like it was all left here for me."

She stood up and suddenly pressed her whole body hard against the wall, her hands caressing the uneven surface, making contact with her past, finding and holding the two hopeful, eager children who had played here, their minds so perfectly in harmony that reaching out for it again, remembering, her face lost its taut agony, and she was beautiful.

"Georgiana . . ."

"Yes—don't worry. I'm still here. I'm not mad. I know I can't really hear his voice, Faith, but in this place it just seems to me that I can. And that's lovely, you know. Don't look so alarmed, darling. I know what I have to do. It's the abbey, you see—so long as there's a Clevedon here it doesn't matter which one. We change our faces, but it's always the same person, really, underneath the skin. Grandfather thinks it's over—that's why he's grieving—but the abbey will come to me now, when he's gone, and I'll look after it for my Gervase. I was never certain that Perry would marry, and I knew I'd better have a son—just in case. I was right, wasn't I?"

"No," I said, and although she had not really asked me a question, she turned to look at me, startled but still, in her fey humour, smiling.

"Why, Faith, whatever can you mean?"

I knew it was not the time to speak to her of such things, but there might never be another moment when she would be ready to hear me, another moment when it would be possible for me to speak, and I had let too many of my life's opportunities pass by. I had given Nicholas up for many reasons but not least among them had been the hope that he would turn to her. He had not yet done so. But now, in her grief for her brother, for the man who had really dominated her emotions, claimed her loyalties, surely, at last, she could turn to Nicholas? Surely something could be salvaged, so that the fairy tale Blaize had convinced me was a reality might finally come true.

"Faith—you are looking at me very strangely."

"Am I? Then it is because—because you must take care. Georgiana, this was your world, but it can't be your world now because it's not your husband's. And it may never be Gervase's. He's just a little boy, and you were quite right when you said he would grow to look like Perry—he does—but you married away from here. Georgiana—his name is Barforth."

She sat down again, with one of her abrupt movements, on the old stone, and because I could not tower above her, nor appear to dominate her, I sat down too, this hushed, airless place seeming more than ever like a tunnel into the past.

"You are telling me, I suppose, that Nicky will expect Gervase to go into the mills?"

"You must know he will."

"He has never said so."

"I believe it must seem so obvious to him that he might not have thought it worth mentioning."

"And it seems obvious to you?"

"Yes, it does."

"Just as it seems obvious to me that he should not."

And for a while she sat perfectly still again, another moment of communion with everything that had a meaning for her, before she startled me with the familiar, birdlike movement of her head, the abruptness of her smile.

"No. It will not happen, you know. If Perry had inherited, and married, even then it would not have happened. I have been feeling very weak, lately, Faith—oh, I told myself it was because I had not recovered from Venetia, but it was not that. I felt overwhelmed, somehow—as if I had failed at everything I had endeavoured. And so I had. I felt that I had nothing to give anyone, and that is a very desperate feeling—so hard to accept that there was nothing in me that anyone could want. You do see, don't you, that now—when I have this great gift—not just the abbey, but all that goes with it—when I know that Gervase feels as I feel—that he knows it is the land that nourishes us—then I can't hold it back from him. All the rest is just money, Faith—and there's so much of it."

She stood up, held out her hand to me, and her touch was hot and excited, her face as vivid as I had ever seen it.

"It's the cloister," she said. "It does me good. I thought I'd come here to die, an hour ago. I thought if I went on sitting here, very quietly, that I'd just fade away and no one would miss me. But it helped me, like it always does, and now I must go and take care of my grandfather. I'm strong now."

Chapter Twenty-five

SIR JOEL AND LADY BARFORTH did not come north for Christmas that year, my uncle having suffered a recurrence of his chest complaint, which could only be aggravated by our damp, sooty air, and so they contented themselves by inviting my mother and Mr. Adair, Aunt Hannah and Mayor Agbrigg, to join them at Rosemount Lodge, dividing the generations, not unpleasantly, for the first time.

I spent the greater part of the festive season at Listonby, watching with admiration as Caroline organised her massive household with the same skill and energy her father and Nicholas devoted to their weaving sheds, her unerring eye for detail, her iron discipline ensuring that one celebration merged into the other as threads are drawn together into some complex pattern on the loom, her guests being presented only with the finished product, a task which, because she performed it superbly, appeared almost effortless.

There was a dinner of seventy covers on Christmas Eve, ending at midnight with carol singers at the door, lanterns and largesse and even a scattering of snowflakes it seemed quite possible she had arranged herself. There was the manorial progress to church on Christmas morning, the delivery of Christmas hampers to the Listonby poor, an afternoon of children's games in the Great Hall, festooned with holly and mistletoe, everybody's nanny very much in attendance while the gentlemen took their port and madeira and cigars in the library, the ladies gossiped around the tea-time fire.

There was a new pony apiece, in the stable yard, for Dominic and Noel and Gideon Chard; young Liam Adair, who had been left in my charge until my mother came home, amusing himself by bullying Georgiana's highly strung Gervase, until Dominic settled the matter by knocking Liam down. There was little Venetia Barforth, an auburn-haired Christmas-tree fairy, taking her first excited steps, my pansy-eyed niece, Grace, patiently allowing herself to be kissed by any sentimental lady, her curls to be ruffled by any gentleman, although Celia, who had been invited to dine, found after all that she was not quite well and could not stay. There was my ivory and silver Blanche, lovely and still as a figure carved in biscuit porcelain, aware, it seemed to me, from her infancy that she had no need to make a noise in order to be looked at.

There was dinner itself, another vast spread of geese and turkeys, port jelly and brandied plum pudding, a ceremony crowned by the carrying in of a boar's head, stuffed—I happened to know since Caroline had attended the procedure herself—with fillets of its own flesh, crowned with a forcemeat of rabbit and partridge, tongue, and truffles. There was the Boxing Day meet, a ball to follow when Julian Flood, finding no one else to take his fancy, pursued me with an ardour that amused my husband, but which caused Caroline, when she became aware of it, to give him firm warning that unless he mended his manners he would be sent home.

"Dearest Caroline," he told her, collapsing in a fit of his wild laughter, "that is one of the reasons I come here, don't you know, to run the risk of being sent home again."

But he remained for the full twelve days, was sober enough, every evening at dinner, to raise his glass and drink most loyally to his Queen, for whom no less than five of his cousins had fought and died in the Crimea. And remembering that the Floods had always sacrificed themselves in this way, that their family motto was "loyalty is its own reward," Lady Chard forgave him.

No one at Listonby was ever aware of work being done. No one ever met a flustered housemaid on the stairs, nor encountered a servant anywhere but in the place he ought to be, correctly attired, impassive, almost leisurely. Yet for those twelve days of Christmas no fewer than thirty guests ever sat down to dine, and every morning, as if by magic, fires were burning

brightly in those thirty bedrooms reserved for their accommodation, cans of hot water, warm towels, an array of personal
requisites, stood ready on thirty washstands, thirty sets of garments were laid out, freshly laundered and pressed, thirty more
an hour before luncheon and before tea, thirty more at dinnertime. No matter how early one descended, the logs in the Great
Hall blazed out their welcome, the dining room sideboards
groaned with dishes of gammon and kidneys, sausages and eggs,
smoked haddock and woodcock, hot bread and cold bread, fruit
in and out of season. Newspapers were always to hand, their
pages well ironed and clean, writing paper always available and
a liveried footman waiting, unobtrusive but alert, to deliver one's
notes. Likes and dislikes were remembered and attended to—
written down, I happened to know, most assiduously by Caroline—so that a guest with a preference for turbot found turbot
awaiting him, a lady with a passion for whist found a whist
table and a steady supply of partners at her beck and call. And
every night, no matter how late, an apparently unruffled Caroline, well versed in the ways of the gentry by now, saw to it that
those thirty persons were safely tucked into their *own* warm
beds—or cool beds if that was their fancy—assuming, because
she expected her wishes to be obeyed, that they would stay
there until morning.

Yet the very perfection of it all was a little wearing, and I was
not sorry to be home again, nor entirely cast-down when my
mother returned to claim young Liam Adair whose talkative
presence at my table was not always pleasing to Blaize. But the
Adairs visit to Bournemouth had given Prudence a fresh taste of
freedom, a refusal to relinquish it which ended in the direct confrontation between her and Daniel Adair my mother had always
dreaded. There was some rapid, verbal cross fire, centring eventually on the porcelain, Mr. Adair having seen rather too much
of it in my hands for his comfort. And when Prudence defended
herself by declaring there were pieces missing that *she* could not
account for, they went through the whole collection item by
item and, at Prudence's insistence, stored it away in the attic.

"That suits me fine," he told her, whereupon she went through
it all again the following morning, having realised, somewhat too
late, that porcelain stored in packing cases would not be so easily missed as porcelain on display.

"Yes, that suits me fine," Mr. Adair said again with a roguish twinkle, making it his business to be seen, on several occasions thereafter, leaving the house with a hastily wrapped bundle under his arm which could so easily have been a costly vase, the whole of the Wedgwood dinner service, piece by piece.

"He could take it, little by little, and sell it and I'd never know," she said and appalled not only by the possible loss of her property but by the increasing triviality of her mind, she took the most daring, most positive step of her life.

"I feel that I'm drowning," she said. "I'm becoming hysterical —that damnable man is turning me into a proper old maid. Unless I do something about it soon I won't be fit to do anything at all." And telling my mother that she was staying with me she went instead to Bournemouth to request my uncle's intervention in the release of her money.

Naturally—having recovered from the shock of having his eldest niece appear, alone and unannounced, on his doorstep—he would not hear of it. Nothing in the world would induce him to put 20,000 pounds of Morgan Aycliffe's money into the hands of his unmarried daughter, even if he had the power to do so, which he had not.

"Get married," he told her. "That's what women do. If you want to teach children their letters, then have some of your own. That's the other thing women do."

But Prudence, knowing this to be her final opportunity, had her facts and figures, and her objections, ready.

She wished to open a school for girls. There was no proper education of any kind available for females. She was herself ill-educated and consequently unable to teach others, but she could employ those who could, and see to it that the teaching was efficiently carried out. She knew the size of the house she required, its exact cost, the staff she would need to run it, the salaries she would have to pay her teachers. She had already drawn up a list of the subjects she considered appropriate, the fees she would charge for day girls and boarders, what extras she would include, the hours to be devoted to study and to more recreational activities, the quality of the food she intended to serve.

"Nonsense," he said. "Daydreams—or delirium. Go to bed

now. You'll feel better in the morning. And then you may go back to your mother, young lady, where you belong."

But the next day he asked her, "And what's the point to this education? I can see no call for it. Girls exist to get married and I'm not sure I'd like a clever wife."

"You *have* a clever wife."

"Aye, so I have—or I might not be listening to you at all. So where are your pupils to come from? I can think of no man in Cullingford who'd pay you to fill his girl's head with fancy notions—and it's always the man who pays."

But again she was ready. She would offer not only a rare opportunity for academic achievement but a degree of polish as well. Her girls would study literature and mathematics, science and philosophy, but there would be music and dancing too, the art of receiving guests and presiding at a correctly arranged dinner table, the art of gracious living which Cullingford was beginning to appreciate: none of that would be neglected. Her girls would be cultured but they would also be polished, and would make excellent wives for this new generation of manufacturers whose horizons were broader, their expectations greater. The world was changing. There was a demand for the type of establishment she was proposing. She could fill that demand.

"Aye. That's your day girls. What about your boarders? They like to keep their daughters safe at home in Cullingford."

Indeed. But she had been out in the world long enough to know that there were plenty of girls who were an inconvenience to their parents, girls, in fact, who could not be acknowledged by their parents, but for whose accommodation and care money could be found.

"Little indiscretions of the aristocracy, in fact," my uncle asked her, to which she replied, "Exactly. I believe Caroline's friend, Lady Hetty Stone, could be of assistance to me there, since her brother—who will be a duke one day—knows of just such a child."

"Does he, by God. And you reckon Mrs. Hobhouse and Mrs. Rawnsley might like their girls to get to know a duke's daughter?"

"It's a start," she told him firmly. "I have to make myself known. I have to make a reputation."

"Do you reckon you can make any money?" he asked. "I'll say good night now, Prudence. You'd best be off in the morning."

But she stayed another day, spent an hour or so walking with him on the sea front, another hour in his study attempting to get her figures right, and came away with the satisfaction of knowing she had provided him with a great deal of amusement and some food for thought. She had also informed him that since, in her view, it was unbusinesslike to make any kind of proposition unless one had more than expertise to offer, she was prepared to hazard her own savings in the venture, representing all she possessed. And she had been honestly delighted at his reaction to the figure she named.

"You didn't save that out of your pin money, my girl."

"No, Uncle Joel. But it is mine just the same."

She announced her engagement to Freddy Hobhouse a few weeks later, making his mother very happy, her own mother somewhat less so until Daniel Adair, being a gambling man who knew how to cut his losses with style, shrugged his generous, Irish shoulders, and wished her well.

"He's not the one I'd have chosen for you, my girl, but if he's what you want—if you *do* want him . . . ?"

And he appeared far less surprised than most of us when it became known that she had taken a lease on a substantial house at Elderleigh Hill, half a mile away from me, not, as was first thought, as a home for herself and Freddy, but as a school.

"Oh, dear," my mother said, floating into my house at an unusually early hour. "You must talk to her, Faith, for I cannot understand it. Her dowry has not been touched, and the porcelain is all there, for Daniel has had it out of the boxes again, and checked it over . . . My goodness, he is not at all angry, he seems to think it a huge joke—it is simply that people are asking me, and I must have something to say . . . Does she mean to marry Freddy, or does she not? For if she does and he has agreed to allow her to use her money for any purpose other than Nethercoats, then Emma-Jane Hobhouse will do her best to put a stop to it. Between ourselves I believe they were on the point of selling out and one cannot blame them for wanting to know where they stand. If they should lose their buyer and then Prudence should change her mind, I really don't see how we could be held responsible. But Emma-Jane Hobhouse is one of my

oldest friends—and has quite the wickedest tongue of anyone I
ever encountered when she is aroused. Do talk to her, Faith. Or
ask Blaize. He will know."

But Prudence was not forthcoming. Blaize, beyond a passing
remark that Nicholas might not get Nethercoats so cheaply now,
if at all, had nothing to say, and like everyone else, I was
obliged to wait a few weeks longer until Aunt Verity, paying a
surprise visit to Cullingford, announced that she, having wished
for some time to make a personal contribution to the town in
which she had been born, had finally decided what that contribution should be.

"It came to me," she said, "quite suddenly, as if I could hear a
voice positively begging me to do it. I had been thinking about
it for an age, considering this and that, and then, all at once,
there it was. Yes, I thought, we have our grammar school, which
did so well for my boys, but when Caroline became too much
for nanny there was absolutely nowhere to send her—nothing to
do but fill the house with music teachers and dancing teachers
and someone else for French and for drawing, which was such a
bother. We had a French governess, I recall, who was quite tem-
peramental and another I would not have cared to inflict on my
worst enemy—and another who could hardly take her eyes off
Blaize, if you'll forgive me for mentioning it, Faith dear. So—
Elinor—I have decided to open a school for girls, and I am relying on you and Mr. Adair to allow it. Yes, Elinor—your permission is certainly required—for I have set my heart on having
Prudence to take charge of it, and if you refuse then, of course, I
shall not proceed—which will be such a pity. Joel thinks it an
excellent idea, and although I am to use my own money I think
we can rely on him to be generous."

And when Lady Barforth made a request, which Sir Joel
clearly expected to be granted, it would have been unwise on
the part of any Adair—of anyone at all—to refuse.

"Obviously he has lent her the money," Blaize said, very much
amused. "Good for her, although he will make her earn it. If she
went to him with her tale of wanting some useful work to do
then work is exactly what she will get, for he will expect to be
repaid. I can't imagine what private agreement they have made,
and clearly she has my mother's blessing, which is more than
half the battle with my father, but he will see to it that she

keeps her side of the bargain. Well, he must be getting bored in his little paradise—it may do them both some good."

"And Freddy—was Freddy your idea, Blaize?"

"Now why should you think that?"

"Because her engagement to Freddy could annoy Nicholas—could keep him out of Nethercoats."

"Really?" he said, his grey eyes completely innocent. "Do you know, you are not the first person who has suggested that to me. Brother Nick was in my office just this morning, and even he—well, he didn't put it quite that way—he simply dropped into the pool of conversation the remark that Prudence's money could hardly be enough, and unless the Hobhouses stopped shilly-shallying around they might find themselves without a buyer—or with nothing to sell. He may have expected me to pass the message on."

"So Freddy *was* your idea."

"Faith—he offers excellent protection for Prudence. If she is engaged to marry him, then she'll have no cause to waste her time fending off anybody else—an end to the Irish cousins. And rather more than that, for if Freddy—her affianced husband, her future lord and master—doesn't object to her playing schoolmistress then no one else can have anything to say against it. Naturally, if she went ahead and married him it would be a different story since he'd be in honour bound to use every penny she has to try and stop the rot at Nethercoats. But then—will she marry him, or won't she? My bet is she won't."

But Freddy Hobhouse was a good-natured, hard-working man, his own sound common sense hampered, from boyhood, by his easy-natured father. He had shouldered as many family responsibilities as he could, made personal sacrifices for his brothers and sisters, had waited a long time for Prudence, and the thought of him troubled me.

"I believe you are using him, Pru," I told her. "Is it fair?" But Prudence, these days, was no longer the frustrated woman who had frittered her time away in bickering with her stepfather, and fussily, almost neurotically, counting her porcelain. Nor was she the girl who had devoted herself with such unflagging energy to the affairs of Giles Ashburn and Mayor Agbrigg. Now she had work of her own to do, her own decisions to make, being no longer obliged to content herself with carrying out the decisions of others, and having demolished the objections of Sir Joel Barforth, was certain to make short work of mine.

"Is it fair? Very likely not. But then, you can't be certain what my intentions are with regard to Freddy," she said crisply. "If I should seem to be using him, then you must admit he has shown himself quite ready to use me. He may have been patient, but he has not been celibate, you know, all these years. He has made his little excursions to the Theatre Royal, when he could afford it, as they all do. And if he had encountered some other woman with a few thousand a year who had been willing to marry him then I cannot believe he would have let her pass him by."

"I suppose not. So you have got everything you want, Prudence?"

"Perhaps I have. I have got my independence at any rate, and even if you are beginning to think me hard, the truth is that I am sorry to have been obliged to get it by stealth. It would suit me far better to come out into the open and say, 'This is what I have done. This is what I intend. This is what I am'—far better if I had been able to claim the money that is mine, instead of selling my vases clandestinely to your husband, and using his father, and Aunt Verity, as a screen—pretending it is theirs, when really it is mine. Well—that is the way of it. And as to Freddy, you will have to wait and see, my dear—and so will his mother."

Opinion, of course, in private was sharply divided, the Hobhouses themselves frankly suspicious but, as matters stood, unwilling to do anything which could further jeopardise their position. It was not that Mr. Hobhouse had mismanaged Nethercoats, but rather that he had not managed it enough, for the business, founded by his grandfather, improved by his energetic father, had seemed so secure when it came to him that his naturally easygoing disposition had not received the stimulus it required. Mr. Bradley Hobhouse, quite simply, had not been a hungry fighter, not really a fighter at all, a comfortable man of hearty appetites who had married a comfortable wife, both of them so accustomed to live in conditions of prosperity that they could imagine no other. Joel Barforth, until his sons were of an age to do it for him, had continued to descend on his mill every morning, to ensure that his orders were carried out to the letter. Mr. Hobhouse, when trade was good, had lingered at home, taken an afternoon stroll to the Piece Hall to enjoy the respect his name commanded, had spent a great deal of his time discussing the wool trade over the punch bowl at the Swan. Mr. Joel Barforth had known, at all times, exactly what his managers, and his sons, were doing. Mr. Hobhouse knew what they said they were doing. Mr. Joel Barforth had been the first man in the valley to mechanise, had ruthlessly abandoned his handlooms for power-driven machines, had been the first man to stop producing the plain, well-nigh indestructible cloth for which the valley was famous and to develop the lighter, fancier materials which a changing society required. Mr. Hobhouse, a heavy man who liked heavy worsteds, had clung to the belief that his customers liked them too. And by the time it became clear to him that, with so many newcomers to the industry, the world was no longer clamouring for Hobhouse goods, no longer so ready to take whatever he supplied because it was obtainable nowhere else, it was too late.

Freddy alone, of course, could not halt the decline, nor, indeed, would Prudence's fortune be enough to restore his credibility at Rawnsley's bank. But a connection with the Barforths could only be seen as a step in the direction all at Nethercoats wished to take—it *might* suffice to tide them over until the miracle they had all been praying for made its mind up to take place —and it was hoped, moreover, that it might soften the heart and loosen the purse strings of the great worsted-spinner, Mr. Oldroyd, whose late wife had been Mr. Hobhouse's sister, Freddy's aunt Lucy.

Mr. Oldroyd, admittedly, was not a lonely man, for having failed to marry my mother, he continued to find ample consolation in the scandalous Mrs. Delaney, whose charms and whose excellent cream teas were still readily available to him in Albion Terrace. But—although provision would no doubt be made for her at his decease, as provision would be made for a young lady in Leeds one assumed to be his daughter—the Oldroyd fortune was one of the most important in the Law Valley, and if he approved the marriage of Freddy and Prudence there was no reason why a sizeable portion of it should not find its way to them, instead of to certain Oldroyd cousins who were officiously staking their claim. There was no reason, in fact, why Mr. Oldroyd—if suitably softened and impressed—should not take

Freddy into his business, should not make him a partner, the beneficiary not merely of a portion, but of the whole.

And so Mrs. Hobhouse was all love and kisses to Prudence, the desperate quality of her affection moving me to sympathy, and my sister to laughter.

"Poor woman. She will do anything to get me, and if she manages it she will have the surprise of her life. If I ever do go to Nethercoats, then she will first have to move out of it, I do assure you, and take her sons and daughters with her, for I have no mind to play nursemaid and governess free of charge."

"Prudence, you *are* growing hard."

"I do hope so—for it is a hard world."

Yet, with Freddy himself, she was exacting but, occasionally, quite tender, commandeering his services most ruthlessly at the schoolhouse—"Freddy, if you would just fetch me this, carry me that, lend me your carpenter, your glazier, your wagon"—but, since he had his share of the warm Hobhouse temperament, she would allow him to hold her hand under my dinner table, would go with him, quite happily, for moonlit strolls in my garden, returning with the air of a woman who had been heartily kissed and had not found the experience unpleasant.

She would be thirty that year, a fine-boned, elegant woman, crackling with energy, compelling in her excitement, her new zest for life. He was thirty-five, heavy and easy, a man, as she said, who had not been celibate, who knew what he wanted from a woman in the moonlight and was clever enough, perhaps, to realise that her brain was keener than his, not too proud to accept it. Would she take him, after all? Would she use him, as men had been trying all her life to use her—to use me—and then discard him? Would she dominate him, instead, and bully him into some compromise that did not include his troublesome family? I couldn't tell.

"She's a joy to watch," Blaize told me. "Do what you can to help her, Faith. I won't count the cost." And I had no need to be told.

Help came to her from many sides.

"Dear Prudence," Georgiana told her. "I cannot think why you are doing this, for I believe if you were to shut me up in a house with several dozen children I would end by murdering them all

—but do take my Venetia when she is older. Take her now if you like. She is only a girl, after all, and so I suppose I can have my way where she is concerned. They have sent Gervase to the grammar school, didn't you know? Yes, he goes there every morning with the younger Hobhouse boys to do his sums, so that he can work out his profit and loss, I imagine, when the time comes—except that it will not come, for he will not learn. Naturally I wanted to send him to Kent, where Perry and Julian Flood went to school, but I am not breaking my heart over it. In fact I am very much inclined to smile, or would be, if Gervase didn't hate the grammar school so much. Well, he will not have to dirty himself in a countinghouse, for he cannot add two and two, poor mite, and it is quite useless for Nicky to stand over him and growl that he is not trying when it is plain to everyone that it is simply not in his nature. He has only to look at a column of figures and his mind becomes quite blank, which I perfectly understand, since I am just the same. Well, you will not plague my daughter, will you, Prudence, with such things. If she is happy and has good friends, then I shall be content. I have had a word with Hetty Stone and I imagine you may have her relative whenever you like, since no one else wants her in the very least. And Caroline knows such masses of people—she is sure to help."

Indeed she did, help coming too, rather surprisingly, from Jonas, who, although by no means prepared to fetch and carry like Freddy, had his own academic experience to draw on, and, his own Latin being perfect, his Greek flawless, his knowledge of French, mathematics, history, geography, the literature of several countries, enormous, he was not to be deceived by the pretensions of others. And, moreover, for the first time he seemed willing to suggest, rather than tell Prudence what she should do, steering her quite gently away from one very glib teacher of mathematics and directing her attention to another, working out a most ingenious timetable which he submitted not for her admiration, but her approval.

"Why, Jonas—that is quite brilliant. Why didn't I think of it?"

"Well, it is similar to the one used by an acquaintance of mine from Cambridge. I cannot take all the credit for it."

And we wondered, Prudence and I—had Aunt Hannah not

insisted of making a lawyer, a lord mayor, a cabinet minister out
of him—whether he would have been happy as a schoolmaster.

My aunt and uncle came up from Bournemouth at the start of
the good weather, my uncle still showing the strain of the winter, although, as usual, his descent on the mills was immediate
and dynamic, the sharpness of his eye and his opinions quite un-
dimmed. And for a day or so even Blaize was less inclined for
laughter, arriving at his office a little earlier, leaving considerably later, while it was widely known that Mr. Nicholas Barforth, now that his personal enterprises were prospering, was
exhibiting a marked reluctance to do things any way but his
own.

Caroline was to leave for London at the beginning of July, to
spend the summer season with Hetty Stone, her aim very clearly
to make the acquaintance of Lady Hetty's brother, now the
sixth, or possibly even the seventh Duke of South Erin, and to
bring him back to Listonby in triumph, as her guest. But she
had the time to arrange a dance in her father's honour, knowing
how much it pleased him to see her receive the county at the
head of her brilliantly illuminated staircase, a duke's sister
standing a step or two behind her, making sure she did everything in the correct Mayfair manner but somewhat in her
shadow, just the same. And because it also pleased him, from
time to time, to see his family gathered together—and there was
nothing Caroline would not do to please her father—she summoned, rather than invited, us to dine that same evening in the
exquisitely frail, century-old saloon she reserved for intimate occasions.

Caroline had changed nothing in this room, leaving the baroque plasterwork, which had once reminded Aunt Verity of
gently decaying petals, to continue its mellowing from the original white to a blend of musk rose and honey, retaining the fragile chairs with their tapestry covers in the same misty shades, a
table polished by generations to the appearance of ebony glass,
nothing else in the room at all but hushed space and memory.
Yet, despite all her efforts, it was from the start an uneasy gathering, an evening when nothing seemed altogether right.

I had dressed as always, most carefully, knowing that it was
expected of me, that I had a small local reputation by now to

consider as well as my husband and my vanity. And since Listonby was not really Cullingford I took out a dress I had ordered from M. Albertini in Paris—which I had been reserving for our next trip to London—a tremendous skirt stitched over its wire cage in tiny white frills that had the appearance of feathers, a neck so low that Caroline would certainly raise pained eyebrows over it, my swan cameo pinned on what little there was of the bodice, a pearl scattered velvet ribbon around my neck. Clever, I had thought, checking the finer details in my mirror, something Blaize would appreciate, but when I came downstairs, trailing my shawl behind me, to receive his applause, he merely said, "Very nice—in fact, *very* nice," quite automatically, and all through the journey from Elderleigh, barely said a word.

"Did something happen at the mill today?"

"Dear me, no," he said, stifling a yawn. "Does anything ever happen at the mill—anything worth mentioning, that is?"

"Well—you are certainly out of humour."

"I beg your pardon. It is my footloose nature, I imagine, telling me I have been in Cullingford rather too long. I am in the mood to be off again, I think—and really, one should take advantage of it, for we are in constant need of new markets. Nicky, of course, can't bring himself to agree . . ."

"He doesn't want you to go?"

"Possibly not. Perhaps it would suit him better if I stayed and took what he calls my share of the responsibility at Lawcroft and Tarn Edge—especially now that Mayor Agbrigg is mayor again and too busy with his building regulations to be much use for anything else. Which sounds quite reasonable, of course, until one realises that what he really wants is for me to take the weight off his shoulders so that he can do some private empire-building of his own. If I'm in Russia—which is where I'd dearly love to be—Nicky can hardly spend all day at the Wool Combers, can he, nor at Nethercoats, for that matter, if he manages to get his hands on it after all. He'll have to spend his time concentrating on Joel Barforth & Sons, as I do—and we really need those new markets, you know."

Georgiana and Nicholas did not arrive together, Nicholas coming from Tarn Edge, Georgiana from Galton, where she had been staying with her grandfather, having taken Gervase with her, I'd heard, to enable him to avoid school.

"Good evening," Nicholas said to me, giving Blaize no more than a nod by way of greeting.

"Georgiana," Blaize replied, "you're looking very beautiful," but she wasn't, for her extremely expensive ballgown, the kind of overembroidered creation she bought because she imagined that was how a manufacturer must want his wife to look, did not suit her, the complicated arrangements of ringlets in which she had imprisoned her coppery hair were too heavy for her head, and she herself too much aware of it, holding her neck too stiffly in case it should all come tumbling down. She had emeralds in her ears, bracelets on both arms, a gold and emerald necklace, jewellery she was at the same time too hardy and too air-spun to carry, a woman dressed up against her nature, and more uncomfortable every minute with this false image of herself.

And throughout the meal which Caroline had planned as a joyful family reunion, Nicholas and Blaize addressed not one word to each other; Freddy Hobhouse, unaccustomed to Listonby, talked only to Prudence; my sister Celia, for some reason, seemed unwilling to speak to anybody, which was clearly displeasing to Jonas, creating so tense an atmosphere that everyone around her seemed inclined to whisper, leaving us with the brittle, social chatter of Hetty Stone and my mother, Aunt Hannah's well meant but heavy-handed determination to "bring us all out of ourselves," Sir Matthew's vague geniality, Mayor Agbrigg's clear intention of leaving well—or ill—alone. While even Sir Joel, for whom the celebration was intended, would have preferred, I thought, to have been placed a little nearer to his wife, finding even a yard of mahogany and cut crystal an unacceptable barrier, these days, between him and his Verity.

"I can't think what ails them, Faith," Caroline muttered as we left the table. "One puts oneself out, and is it too much to expect that they should do the same—especially with Hetty Stone looking on, thinking that everything she has ever heard about manufacturers must be true. After all, it is for Father. And if Nicholas and Blaize have had a set-to at the mill then they should have left it there. And Faith—really—what *is* the matter with Celia? She was most odd at Christmas and I declare she is odder tonight. Mark my words, she will start feeling unwell in half an hour and will make Jonas take her home, and if she does then I shall not invite her again. I suppose you know that certain people are beginning to feel sorry for Jonas. I was talking to Mr. Fielding and to several of his political associates just the other day—one of them by no means without influence in the party— and they were all saying the only fault they could find with Jonas Agbrigg as a future candidate was his wife. I couldn't bear to hear that said of me. My goodness—I'd hide my head in shame. You'd better talk to her, Faith. Well—I can't feel that this is going to be one of my most successful nights."

But, positioned at the head of her staircase between Sir Matthew and Sir Joel, waiting to receive her ball guests, Caroline's spirits began to revive, finding the same healing quality in the glittering ballroom behind her, the long gallery beyond it, as Georgiana found in the cloister at Galton. And as those august names, one by one, were announced: "Sir Giles Flood and Mr. Julian Flood. Sir Francis and Lady Winterton. Lord and Lady de Grey. The Honourable Mrs. Tatterton-Cole. Colonel and Mrs. Vetchley-Ryce," I knew her mind was already exploring next season's triumphs when, surely, if she made herself pleasant enough and useful enough to Hetty Stone, the Duke of South Erin himself would be advancing up her painted, panelled staircase to greet her.

I danced a great deal as I always did at Listonby, responding easily to the enchanted world Caroline had created, her lovely, high-ceilinged ballroom panelled at one side in glass so that every drop of cut crystal in her chandeliers was doubled, every swirling, satin skirt had its partner, every soaring violin an echo, everything—as Caroline had always intended—being at least twice as large as life. I went down to supper with Julian Flood, who kissed my shoulders on the stairs and asked me, with a composure that was almost offhanded, if I would care to meet him one Friday-to-Monday in London. But I was a fashionable woman who knew how to deal with that, a woman who invited attention and could not complain when she received it. I was Blaize Barforth's wife, too sophisticated by far to dance with her husband, merely smiling, making an amused gesture with my fan, which certainly, in his opinion, signified, "Good luck, darling," when I saw him strolling downstairs with Hetty Stone.

Prudence sat in the long gallery with Freddy, surrounded by portraits of ancestral Chards, no severe schoolmistress that night but allowing him rather more liberties, I thought, than holding her hand. Celia, who had been invited with the rest of us to stay the night, went home, a certain friction arising between Jonas and his father when Jonas—involved in serious, possibly lucrative political conversation—had, at first, insisted that she should remain. And in the ebbing and flowing of the crowd I did not miss Georgiana until Caroline took me sharply by the elbow and hissed, "Come downstairs—at once. Come and talk some sense to her."

But it was too late. All I saw, through the wide-open doorway, were the horses on the carriage drive, two men in evening dress already mounted, another waiting for Georgiana as she flew down the steps, cupping his hands to receive her foot and throwing her up into the saddle, her expensive satin skirts bunched wildly around her, the lovely, quite fragile line of her profile, her throat, her breasts, fine-etched against the dark as she threw back her head, laughing and crying together.

"Georgiana," Caroline called out, and looking down Georgiana raised an arm in a military salute and they were off—Julian Flood, Francis Winterton, Rupert Tatterton-Cole, the reckless, hard-drinking young men who had ridden with Perry Clevedon —and Perry Clevedon's sister—riding off now on some mad escapade, Caroline clapping both hands to her ears as they started their hunter's yelling, their horses tearing past her lodge gates as if the whole world was burning.

"She was bare-legged," Caroline said, aghast. "Didn't you see? My goodness—the whole of Listonby is going to see, for she is riding astride. I have never been so shocked—so mortified—in my life."

"She has gone to look for Perry, I suppose," Blaize casually offered, when I found him. "I imagine Perry might seem more real to her than some others she has seen here tonight."

"She's an original, that one," Hetty Stone murmured, her hand still on Blaize's arm, her fingers flexing themselves with a feline movement of satisfaction that told him he was original too.

"She'll kill herself," Caroline insisted, too furious to copy Lady Hetty's Mayfair nonchalance. "And just where is Nicholas? Obviously he will have to be told."

It was past three o'clock of a beautiful June morning before the last carriages had rolled away, and although Caroline had declared she would not go to bed until Georgiana returned, having some slight concern for her safety and a great deal for her reputation, Sir Matthew, who could, on occasion, be firm, eventually led her away, allowing the rest of us to follow.

I slept perhaps an hour, it seemed no longer, waking to an odd sensation of being quite alone, and raising myself on one elbow, saw Blaize standing against the window, looking down at the carriage drive.

"Darling—is she back?"

"Hush," he said, and as my head cleared itself of sleep, I could hear in the distance the sound of hoofbeats, one horse, I thought, coming slowly, a hesitant clip-clop that did not convey the speed and dash of anything Georgiana would be likely to ride.

"Hush," he said again, and as I got up and joined him at his vigil, realising now that he had not slept at all, I felt once again that careful, feline probing in him, the curiosity but also the concern.

"Now," he said. "Here she comes. And I imagine you are about to see a species of destruction. Yes, I knew he'd be there to meet her. Even good old Matthew knew that and had the sense to take Caroline away."

And, far below me, I saw the back of a head, the broad, dark shape that was Nicholas, saw the glow of his cigar as he dragged the tobacco deep into his lungs, the taut anger in him as he tossed the butt away.

"I don't think I want to see this, Blaize."

"You might as well. I intend to."

She took a long time to reach him, coming as reluctantly as if she were struggling against a tide of air, and even when the driveway ended and he stood directly in her path, she rode up and down in front of him for a moment, unwilling to dismount.

Her complicated chignon was gone, her hair hanging loose to her waist, lifted from underneath by the early breeze so that it billowed a little and blew forward across her face. And it was clear to me, no doubt clear to us all, that a moment ago, with the sun on her bare shoulders, that delicious breeze under her hair, she had been intensely happy, intensely sad, and that now it was over.

"Did you think I had run away?" she called out, her horse continuing its fretful little promenade on the gravel.

"No. I didn't think that."

"Well then—what shall I do now?"

"Take your horse round to the stables, I imagine."

And as he turned to go she pressed the whole of one arm against her eyes and cried out, "Nicky . . . Damnation, never mind. You will have to help me down."

He walked forward, stood without raising his arms at her stirrup, and, putting her hands on his shoulders, she kicked her skirts free and somehow or other slid to the ground, stumbling against him, righting herself with obvious difficulty as he moved away.

"Oh, dear—I have lost my shoes."

"You will have to go barefoot then."

"Nicky . . ."

"Yes?"

"Don't you want to know why?"

"No. I can't say that I do."

She dug her fingers hard into her hair, pushing it away from her forehead, fighting it almost like seaweed, her body brittle, high-strung with desperation.

"Nicky . . ." And her voice was desperate too. "Don't walk away. Be angry—knock me down and kick me if you want to— anything . . . Just don't walk away."

But he had left her and a few moments later I heard his step in the corridor as he passed our door, the click of his door opening and closing.

"Very clever, little brother," Blaize said, speaking in the direction Nicholas' steps had taken. "Yes—I said it would be destruction, but that was starvation. I didn't know he could be so subtle."

"Blaize—any man would have been angry."

"True. And 'any man' would have said so. Any man would have dragged her down from that horse and shaken her to her senses. Any man would have lost his temper and let her feel the sharp edge of it—especially a man like my brother Nick, who's known to be well endowed when it comes to temper. I told you —very clever. She was brought up on strong emotions, you see. He could love her, or hate her, and I believe she'd thrive on either. Since he obviously knows that, it would appear he doesn't want her to thrive."

"Things are—very bad then—between them."

"As you see. He can be very stubborn, and very foolish."

"Why? Because he won't always play out your schemes—like the Cullingford train . . ."

"Yes," he said, "the Cullingford train—but bear in mind, before you accuse me of meddling, that he *wanted* to take that train. There was nothing else, that day, he wanted more. Like I said—stubborn and foolish."

I got back into bed, unbearably chilled, although I do not think the room was cold, and lay there shivering, silent, for there was no part I could take in this conflict, and I did not want Blaize to take part in it either.

"You must be tired, Faith," he said. "Go back to sleep."

But I was not tired. I needed him, not to love me, perhaps, certainly not to hate me, but to make some move towards me, to offer me more than his wit and his charm, his skills as an entertainer and a lover, to ask more of me than that. And because he was not a man who wished to be needed it seemed, for the half-hour it took to calm myself, that he too, albeit unknowingly, was starving me.

Chapter Twenty-six

THERE WAS MUTINY in India that year, a screaming, murderous fury against British rule provoked, it seemed, not entirely by the Enfield rifle, the heavily greased cartridges on which no Hindu, no Muslim, could bring himself to bite, but by a simple fear of an alien religion, a dread, encouraged by dispossessed yet decently Hindu princes, that forcible conversion to the Christian church was just a matter of time.

The princes, quite clearly, were thinking of their principates, which had been annexed by Christian governors, the sepoys were thinking of their souls, the British may not have been thinking too keenly at all, so shocked and surprised were they when a small flame of disobedience—just a handful of rebellious sepoys not far from Delhi, a local matter which should have remained so—became, overnight, a holocaust.

And because there were Chards and Clevedons and Floods serving their Queen in India as they served her everywhere else, there was tension at Listonby and at Galton, a certain well-controlled anger, an even more firmly suppressed sadness.

There was a Chard in Delhi when the hysterical sepoys first flooded into it, leaving a trail of dead Europeans—regardless of age, regardless of sex, regardless of anything but light skin and light eyes—in their path. A very young Chard, in fact, just eighteen years old, who, when the Indian garrison joined the mutineers, took his stand at the arsenal with the few British fighting men who remained, defended it until defence became an impossibility, blew it up to prevent the guns from falling into mutinous hands, and then died from a sabre thrust—Matthew told us —in the groin.

There was an aunt of Georgiana's among the four hundred women and children at Cawnpore who were rounded up by an enterprising princeling and quite literally butchered, their dismembered bodies thrown down a well.

There were distant relatives of the Floods and the Clevedons, high-minded, cool-headed ladies, wives of career officers— younger sons earmarked for military greatness like Caroline's Noel—who found themselves trapped in the beseiged Residency at Lucknow, keeping themselves not only alive but in good spirits throughout five months of continuous shelling, the continuous threat not only of murderous sepoys but of smallpox, cholera, rats, and starvation, stilling their hunger, when the food supply was failing, on a banquet of curried sparrows.

There were English ladies, products of the fox-hunting shires, who gave birth on the hard ground, in ditches, in bullock carts, and were murdered moments later when the wail of the newborn betrayed their hiding place. There was the vengeance afterwards, the sepoys who may or may not have been responsible —since to men who had seen such atrocious female slaughter *any* sepoy would do—tied to the mouths of guns and splattered to eternity.

There was heroism and savagery on both sides, treachery and self-sacrifice. At Listonby and at Galton it was present, vital, real. To the Barforths it was very far away.

In Cullingford trade was good, Barforth looms were working to capacity and to order, our own streets quieter than they had ever been, and cleaner too, since the water from Mayor Agbrigg's reservoirs at Cracknell Bridge had started to flow. The handloom weavers who had once staged a mutiny of their own had disappeared, absorbed by our weaving sheds, our workhouses, or the gold fields of Australia from which no Law Valley millionaires, to my knowledge, ever returned. And every morning the stroke of five o'clock released that patient flow of women, shawl-covered heads bowed in submission to the cold and to their labouring condition, a faceless, plodding multitude going to their ten hours of captivity at the loom, returning to the captivity of fetching and carrying, of bearing child after child in Simon Street.

My sister's school was opened in the autumn by Lady Barforth, who expressed immense pleasure at the brightness of the rooms devoted to study, the good cheer prevailing in the sleeping rooms, the spacious if somewhat Spartan dining hall, the pleasant outside acre where the girls could cultivate their own plants and flowers and could take healthy, easily supervised walks.

"Why should we trust our girls to Prudence Aycliffe?" had been the immediate reaction but her day girls, comprising the daughters of all those in Cullingford who could pay Prudence's fees and wished to stand in well with the Barforths, were numerous, her most interesting boarder being a ten-year-old Miss Amy Chesterton, who may not have been aware that she was the daughter of the new Duke of South Erin, although everyone else knew it. And for the first month Jonas Agbrigg himself gave instruction to the senior pupils in mathematics, the lady engaged for the purpose having fallen ill, bringing, quite often, his own four-year-old Grace to leave in my care, since Celia was again unwell, requiring not merely rest and quiet, it seemed, but total silence.

I would not—before Blanche was born—have described myself as being fond of children, was not, even now, fond of all children, but, having gone through the dangerous agonies of childbirth, I saw no point in leaving the result of it entirely to nanny, contenting myself by playing the mother for ten minutes at tea time as my own mother had done. I had been Blaize's wife for almost four years now. Within the limits he had set for us I was by no means unhappy. But in restless moments—when I knew I could not fill my life with lace and ribbons and table talk—moments when I asked myself uncomfortably, "What next? What else?" I believed I could find the answer in Blanche.

I had no wish for more children. This one silvery little elf sufficed me, but from the start my sister's daughter, Grace, had always moved me, her dark curls, her solemn heart-shaped face, her wild-rose prettiness offering such startling contrast to Blanche, her response to my attentions sometimes hesitant, sometimes eager, since her mother was too tense these days for caresses, too concerned with grass stains on her daughter's skirt, mud on her shoes, to take her romping on the lawn, too prone to her sick headaches to endure anything so harrowing as childish laughter.

And so I spent the fine weather, when Blaize was not at home, tying ribbons in my niece's black curls, my daughter's blond ones, letting them preen themselves in my earrings and bracelets, shawls and bonnets, taking them to pick rose petals for potpourri, to find wild blackberries and stray kittens, against Celia's instructions, since roses have diseased thorns, blackberry juice cannot be removed from a dress, kittens have claws to disfigure a child for life, and fur to give a child fleas.

We had picnics on the lawn at Elderleigh, braving the earthworms, the moles, the bird droppings, the general nastiness with which Celia believed it to be infested. We walked in the woods beyond my garden—Blanche astride my shoulders more often than not—trailing our feet through the fragrant October leaves, ignoring the squirrel, that most vicious of beasts, which might descend from its tree to savage us, the quagmire into which we might tumble, the gypsy who, with blandishments and chloroform, could overpower a lone woman and steal two little girls away.

A lovely child—Miss Blanche Barforth—taking her world for granted, knowing herself to be at its centre, the reason for its existence, taking me for granted too, finding me commonplace, I think, in comparison with her far more interesting but frequently absent father. A sedate child—Miss Grace Agbrigg— and a careful child, sensing the atmosphere around her before plunging into it with the caution of a wary kitten, accustomed to being told, "Hush—Mamma is poorly. Hush—you will make her worse," so that she was puzzled, sometimes, because I did not suffer from the headaches which, in her slight experience, were the normal condition of women, even more puzzled that such things as gloves carelessly left on a chair, forgotten newspapers in the drawing room, a cigar butt in an ashtray, did not produce in me the spasms they invariably brought on in Celia.

"Is she really no trouble to you?" Jonas invariably asked me.

"No—no. Please don't stop bringing her, Jonas. I really want her." I did not want Liam Adair. I could think of no one, in those early years of our acquaintance, who could possibly have wanted Liam Adair, but increasingly I found him abandoned on my doorstep and, meeting his insolent twelve-year-old eyes with foreboding, was obliged to let him come in.

"Darling—if you could just have him for an hour," my mother would call out, not even getting down from her carriage. "I am obliged to run over to the Mandelbaums and, really, they have so many things one can see at a glance are valuable—and breakable. Those harps and violins—you know what I mean— and since he has been sent home from school again in absolute disgrace, and poor Miss Mayfield is having the vapours— Just an hour, darling."

But the hour would prolong itself to luncheon, to tea time, to breaking point, to violence on one memorable occasion when Blaize, who had raised a hand to no one in years, took a riding crop to him in atonement for a stray dog let loose in the stables, which had caused considerable turmoil, and a horse to bolt.

"If I were never to see that young man again it wouldn't break my heart," Blaize said, considerably irritated not only because he had torn a shirt cuff in the scuffle but because Liam, who was big for his age, had taken not a little holding down. "In fact, Faith, you could arrange matters so that I don't see him."

But Blaize was so often away, and on the fine afternoon that Liam tossed a half-dozen live frogs into my kitchen, occasioning so great a flapping and clucking of housemaids that I at first thought my house was on fire, I raised a fist in retribution and then, seeing those pompous, portly little creatures at their hopping, entirely unaware of the havoc they were creating, I suddenly found myself obliged to bite back my laughter. And then, catching the merry Adair sparkle in his eyes, did not bite it back but laughed out loud, forfeiting my cook's good opinion as I helped him to retrieve the invaders and carry them back to their pond.

"Don't do it again, Liam Adair."

"Oh no—there'd be no fun in doing it again."

"Then don't do anything else. Why are you such a nuisance, Liam?"

"I don't know. It's just what I am, that's all—a nuisance— everybody says so."

And so he was, a nuisance to my mother, to his father, to his schoolmasters, who sent him home at least twice a week for fighting, so that often, instead of going to Blenheim Lane, he would arrive at my house with a torn jacket, a cut lip, blood pouring from his nose, a grin invariably on his lips.

"Liam—good heavens—by the look of it you didn't win."

"Course I did—and there were three of them, two Hobhouses and a Rawnsley, that's why I look so beat. But I smashed them, all right—headmaster wouldn't have sent me home otherwise."

"And what do the Hobhouses look like?"

"Not pretty. But they weren't pretty before."

"Neither are you."

But, in a way, he was, a big-boned, lanky boy as black as any woodland gypsy, a heavy, overcrowded face lightened by the Adair smile, the whip of Adair insolence and humour that would make him, one day, a man as attractive and possibly as reckless as his father.

"Liam—your coat's in ribbons. Did you get a thrashing today?"

"Course I did. The big Hobhouses came looking for me, after I'd smashed their brothers, so I smashed them too—or very nearly— Well, not *very* nearly, but it wasn't as easy as they thought it would be. And then when Mr. Blamires came to stop it, and I wouldn't stop—because whatever he says they weren't killing me—he gave me a flogging for good measure. So what I want to know is can I stay for tea, because my dad's at home this afternoon, and if he catches me he'll give me another."

And understanding that three floggings in one day were more than enough for any man, I fed him, darned his coat, and when he believed the coast would be clear, sent him home.

"Liam—why do you fight so much?"

"I don't know. It's what I do, that's all."

"I won't have him across my threshold," Celia told me. "And my mother knows it. I'm sorry, but there are limits to what one can endure. I have enough with my own child to look after, and my own home to run. I hope you had them scour your kitchen floor with lime after he brought those frogs in—and how you can laugh about it, Faith, I'll never know. It would have made me ill."

But so many things made Celia ill—so many things had always done so—that I paid little attention until my mother pointed out that she was, indeed, taking a turn for the worse.

"My dear, she never goes out. She sits in that house and watches them polish it, and it can't be right. If I've invited her once I've invited her a hundred times, not just to Blenheim Lane but to teas and concerts and trips to Leeds, and there's always a reason, at the last moment, why it can't be done. She's not well, or Grace is not well, or her housemaid has just given notice—she's had eight girls this year, Faith, and not one of them lasted a month. I declare, I go into her house feeling something a little less than my age and come out feeling a hundred. And Hannah, of course, is far from pleased about it, which is only to be expected since it is bound to affect Jonas, although she does no good at all by lecturing Celia so often and telling her she is letting him down. Of course she is letting him down—one is obliged to admit it—but there is no need to say so quite so often, and so strongly. If it did any good I might not object, but, in fact, it makes her worse. Well, I never expected to say it, but sometimes I feel sorry for Jonas. There are to be no more children, you know. Strictly between ourselves Jonas consulted Dr. Blackstone and then told Celia that he could not risk her life again, so that is the end of it. Not that Celia will care about that, although I cannot answer for Jonas, since, after all, he is a man . . ."

But Celia, when I finally persuaded her to refer to the matter, *did* care, not for the end of her physical relationship with Jonas, which she had always found somewhat inexplicable in any case, but because any kind of domestic failure troubled her, reminding her too closely, perhaps, of a childhood where she had never been placed higher than third. Not only the sex act, it seemed, was difficult for Celia to understand, but life itself, the injustice of a world in which she had obeyed all the rules, and yet had not succeeded in making herself valued. She was the only one of my father's children who had not only obeyed his teaching but had believed in it, had pinned her faith and her heart's hope on the security it had offered. He had told her that if she did certain things and avoided others she would be happy. She had done these things—had made herself a model housekeeper, a domestic angel, devoted herself entirely to hearth and home, had safeguarded her reputation, had never made herself conspicuous, had been innocent, dependent, respectable—yet somehow the formula had not worked. She was not happy, was listless, confused, uneasy. She had done nothing wrong. My father, should he return from the grave, could only approve of her, could only shudder at his frivolous daughter Faith—who had even been scandalous, and got away with it, for a month or two—his strong-minded daughter Prudence, who had flaunted every one of his decrees, laughed in the face of his known intentions. Yet we were well and strong and she was not. It was not fair.

"Do spend a little more time with her, Faith dear," my mother asked, and listening to her through those dreary afternoons when I, setting out to cheer her, came away with my own spirits depressed, I understood clearly that after the solitary triumph of her marriage—of beating every one of us, even Caroline, down the aisle—nothing else had lived up to her expectations.

"It's this house that makes me ill," she said. "It is far too small and dark—I can hardly see into the corners. If we could move to Cullingford Green, or right away to Patterswick . . ."

But when Jonas suggested a number of houses she might like to view, her objections were enormous, the difficulties immense —the staff, the furniture, the problems of selling the house they already had—and although Jonas promised to see to everything himself the project was shelved.

"If I could go to Scarborough for the summer, it would put me right."

But to exist in lodgings was unthinkable, a rented house full of hazards, for what would she do if nanny gave notice, what would she do in any case in a town where she had no friends, since she could never bring herself to speak to strangers?

"If Jonas would not always be accepting invitations without asking me, and then looking so put out when I cannot manage it. I am not at all fond of eating in other people's houses as he very well knows, especially since one is obliged to ask them to dine here afterwards—and it worries me to owe hospitality all around."

But when the invitations ceased she complained that her friends, and her husband, were neglecting her.

"Oh, so you have come to see me, have you, Faith. Well, no one else has been near me for a week or more, and Jonas can think of nothing to do but spend his time playing schools with Prudence."

"She's not interested in anything, that's all," Prudence said, her own interests legion, her vitality a blazing beacon. "She hasn't enough to do and doesn't want to do anything, anyway. Why worry about it? We know dozens of women like Celia."

And because it was true, and because she was indeed so very gloomy, I found myself easily distracted on the days I had intended to see her, very ready to drive on, past her house, and go somewhere else; and when I did pay a visit, I managed not to linger too long.

I went, now and then, to Galton with Georgiana, for she knew of no reason why she and I should not be friends, and saw nothing to concern either of us in the growing tensions between Nicholas and Blaize.

"I did not think it possible for anyone to quarrel with Blaize but I see Nicky has managed it," was her sole comment, showing no curiosity as to the nature of their conflict, assuming, as most people did, that it was financial rather than personal, Cullingford being very ready to understand why they should watch each other—and their own backs—so keenly, since no Law Valley man is averse to stealing a march on another.

"Never mind them, Faith," she said. "It's a lovely day. Let's go and see my grandfather," and bundling her amber-haired Venetia into the carriage—my dainty Blanche usually managing to get more than her share of carriage space, being careful, at a tender age, not to crumple her skirts—we would set off at the spanking, nervous pace with which Georgiana did everything. And more often than not Gervase would accompany us—far too often—since she would seize any opportunity she could to keep him away from school.

"He hates it. He's not good at it. If Nicky had been willing to send him to a decent school, then it would have been different. What could Cullingford Grammar School possibly have to teach him in any case? Heavens—a *grammar* school. He'll profit far more from half an hour's conversation with Grandfather."

And there was no doubt that the Squire of Galton's example could do a child no harm, for when I had accustomed myself to the extreme formality of his manners, I found that his company had a soothing quality, as if the very nobility of his spirit had somehow extended itself to form a barrier between Galton and a rude, money-grubbing world. He was, I felt, a man who may have been all his life autocratic and narrow of outlook but never mean, a man who, with the barbarians at his gate, would have changed his coat for dinner, who would, even if his heart was breaking, offend no one by a display of unmannerly emotion. A fine and gallant gentleman, assisting his granddaughter from her carriage as if she were a duchess, shaking his great-grandson by the hand with the courtesy due to the heir apparent of a nation, rather than a few hundred acres of moorland.

"How do you do, Master Gervase?"

"How do you do, sir?" So that even young Gervase, who was tense and excitable, an odd child in many ways, who could chatter with the shrill persistence of a starling or sit, for hours on end, in an unnatural silence, relaxed in his atmosphere, obeying this august great-grandparent with a readiness he did not display elsewhere.

Yet who, indeed, would not have obeyed Mr. Gervase Clevedon?

"Come," he would say very quietly, and everyone within earshot immediately came.

"We will go now," and everyone would stand up and follow him.

"We can't have this sort of thing, I'm afraid," and whatever it was, from village youths brawling in the market place to the practice of diluting ale in the Galton taverns, one felt the evil would instantly cease.

He had no money, existing entirely on his rents, no coal deposits, no mineral deposits having been found on his land. It was well known that, many of his tenants being elderly, he had not increased his rents for some considerable time. He would take no money from Georgiana—since a gentleman did not impose upon a lady and he was genuinely concerned at the state of her marriage in any case—yet at his advanced age he continued to fulfil all the responsibilities to which his station had called him, sitting in Petty Sessions in his own home, a back, downstairs room being reserved for the purpose, to dispense justice in matters of drunkenness, common assault, falsifying of weights and measures, poaching, and paternity. He rode considerable distances, in all weathers, to take his place on the Bench at Quarter Sessions, where more serious offenders would be committed to prison, to Australia, or to the gallows. He spent long, tedious hours in the saddle busying himself about the affairs of his tenants—his people—making improvements he could not afford, because he believed it his duty to do so. He was, at all times, available to defend the interests of anyone who resided on his land, anyone who had ever eaten his bread and his salt, or whose father had eaten the bread of his father.

"I love him," Georgiana said, breathing deeply. "My Gervase will be just like him—don't you think so, Faith?"

Yet young Gervase had another grandparent, the shrewd, indestructible Sir Joel Barforth, a head taller, a stone or two heavier than Mr. Clevedon, who had set his own sons to work at an early age in his weaving sheds and his countinghouses, teaching them that although the gentry might consider service to be its own reward it was the business of a Law Valley man to buy when prices were cheap and sell when they were dear.

"Aye," he would say, looking down from a height which his grandson clearly found awe-inspiring. "His manners may be very pretty, I grant you, but can he do his sums?"

And Gervase, wild-eyed and unsteady as a colt, would turn for protection to his mother, who could not do her sums either, the pair of them, more often than not, ending in a fit of the giggles under Sir Joel's grim eye.

My uncle was ill again that winter—nothing, he said, that he couldn't cope with—but he came north unexpectedly in the spring, several days ahead of Aunt Verity, and immediately there was trouble.

"What the hell's this? What the devil's that?" was heard throughout every corner of Tarn Edge, Lawcroft, and Low Cross, while his visit to the Law Valley Wool Combers, in which his financial interest was small, produced such a flare-up between him and Nicholas that the building itself seemed threatened by the blast.

"And what's this I hear about you sniffing around Nethercoats again? You'll overstretch yourself, my lad. Aye—and a little bird whispered to me the other day that you'd been over to Horton End a time or two, going over Sam Barker's dyeworks as if you meant business. And whatever you have to say to me about it, I'll say this to you. I don't want his bloody dyeworks, and you can't afford it."

He cancelled, out of hand, a trip Blaize had been planning to Russia, refusing to listen to Blaize's explanation that since war between the northern and southern states of America seemed quite likely there was a growing need to explore new markets.

"Bloody rubbish. War's good for the wool trade—always has been. You just fancy staking yourself to a night or two with a ballerina," a remark repeated to me by Blaize himself, who found it amusing, although he made no comment as to its accuracy.

On the domestic front, too, nothing could please him. His house at Tarn Edge—the house he had built for Aunt Verity—was going to ruin in Georgiana's hands. The servants, with no one to care what they did, were doing nothing. His bedroom was cold, so was the food, the horses were better cared for than he. Where *was* the damn girl, riding around all day like a lunatic? Why did that boy of hers have to keep on staring at him like a scared rabbit? Why was his granddaughter allowed to make that caterwauling day in, day out? Why was no one there to check her?

"Get that lad to school," he bellowed at Georgiana. "And then get yourself back here and do something useful—look after your home and your husband, and see he has something fit to eat when he gets back from the mill— Yes, just you do that, my girl, since it's the mill that pays for your fancy thoroughbreds and your Arab stallion. And look pleasant about it—God dammit!"

"I am not an employee in your weaving sheds, sir," she told him coolly, and the veins swelling in his forehead, his answer was immediate and damning.

"That you're not, lass, for you'd not have lasted so long in my sheds. I get value for money from my weavers and you'd have been told, long since, that you didn't suit me."

And whether or not this was an opinion which Nicholas might privately share, he could hardly allow anyone else to express it, his defence of his wife resulting in the most uncomfortable dinnertime the maids at Tarn Edge—who talked to my maids—could remember, Georgiana drinking glass for glass with her warring menfolk and retiring to bed in a state which even her greatest well-wishers could only have described as drunk.

"It can't last much longer," Blaize said, having by no means abandoned his Russian trip, whether ballerinas and balalaika players were included in it or not. "I don't precisely think of him as an ill-wind, but he'll blow himself out eventually, at least as far as Bournemouth. And by the time he realises I've gone to

Moscow I shall be on my way back. I may be late tonight, darling—I promised to call in and pay my respects to the punch bowl at the Swan."

But he was back in the middle of the afternoon, his cabriolet coming up the drive so fast that I met him in the hall, his distress alarming me the more profoundly because I had never seen it before.

"Faith—get your hat. It's my father. He had some kind of an attack in the yard at Tarn Edge— We took him up to the house and the doctors are still with him. It must have been—two or three hours ago. Faith—I think he's dying. I don't believe it. It's not a thing I ever expected him to do. I was furious with him this morning, Faith—ten minutes before it happened—I couldn't wait to see the back of him—and now . . ."

Aunt Verity was believed to be already on her way to Cullingford, having arranged to join her husband and have a look at her school, but messages had been sent off in case she had delayed, train times had been checked, a carriage already waiting to fetch her from the station. But Caroline was somewhere in the home counties visiting with the South Erins, and there could be little hope of reaching her. Nicholas and Georgiana were already at Tarn Edge when we reached it, Georgiana in her dark green habit, having just come in from riding, Nicholas leaning against the mantelpiece, scowling at the fire, remembering his own explosive desire to see the back of his father, perhaps, and regretting it, knowing that it couldn't now be mended. And a great deal of the afternoon went by, straining towards a cool, spring evening, a great deal of clipped, meaningless conversation mainly between Georgiana and myself, before Dr. Overdale appeared and invited us upstairs.

Sir Joel Barforth was in the centre of his vast, canopied bed, supported by pillows into a sitting position, the scraping sound of air struggling to enter his diseased lungs dominating the room, dying, there could be no doubt of it, of the same engine fumes, the same factory smoke, the same five o'clock trek to the mill yard, which killed so many of his operatives. And because he knew it, and, having believed all his life that time was valuable, was not prepared to waste it now, he gestured to Blaize and Nicholas to stand one on either side of him, refusing—apart from a brief pressing together of the eyelids which may have been the chasing away of tears—to permit himself the luxury of emotion, since his spending power was coming to an end and he had need, in this extremity, to be thrifty of what remained.

"Listen," he said. "And pay heed—since it's for the last time."

And because it was no more than a hoarse whisper rising up to them through layers of pain, they leaned towards him so that, raising one hand and then the other with enormous labour, he took each of them by the arm and held them fast.

"*Listen*—stick together, lads. You need each other. Just listen. You, Blaize—you don't understand those machines and never wanted to—don't underestimate the man who does. Nicky—it's not like it used to be. You could have built that business up from scratch like I did—I know it—you're like me, lad, and you could have stood on your own, in my day. There was just me and Hobhouse in the valley with anything worth selling, and the world was our market. There's hundreds now, Nick, producing the same, wanting their share of the market. And the world's not getting any bigger. It's getting smaller. Somebody has to go out there now and sell. They won't come knocking on our door, like they used to. They had no choice before. Now somebody has to go and tell them we're the best."

His voice, quite suddenly, disappeared, a terrible moment when, for a split second, there was panic in his face because he hadn't said enough and thought he could never speak again. But, if death had actually touched him, he snarled at it, shook it away, his knuckles showing white as he clung to Nicholas' arm.

"Stick together. And if you can't, then remember this—you'll need a good man in your sheds, Blaize. You'll need a salesman, Nicky. *Find* one, both of you, before you split the business. Christ—do you understand me?"

"Yes, Father," Blaize said. "It's all right—we understand."

"Nicky?"

"Yes," he said. "Oh, God—yes." And having fought each other, exasperated each other, loved each other so well, I don't know why it surprised me that they were crying.

"Look after your mother," he said. "Whatever you do to one another, and to anybody else, keep her out of it. See to it that she's all right. Georgiana—you'll not be sorry to see the back of me, I reckon, but do the best you can. Now then—they tell me I've got to rest, so leave me to get on with it. Faith—you can stay. The rest of you go downstairs. I'll see you again, I reckon—presently . . ."

"Faith?" Nicholas said sharply, but Blaize simply nodded. "Of course," and went out, taking Georgiana's arm, Nicholas following, leaving us alone.

"Come here," he said, and I moved to his bedside, not knowing what he wanted of me, aware only that his power, his glorious fighting spirit was dying far more slowly than his body, and whatever it was I would perform it.

"I'll need you closer than that," he said, reaching out a hand that, from weakness and failing vision, missed mine by several inches. "No—I've no mind to pry out your secrets, if that's what you're thinking. Just come here, and hold my hand—"

And I was amazed by the strength of his grip, the cruel effort of will that fastened his hands to mine and kept them fastened, a man raising himself by agonising inches from a quicksand, knowing exactly what must befall him should he let go.

"Hold on to me, lass," he said, "for I can't go before my wife comes . . . And I'll have to work at it—concentrate—and by God I'll do it— I reckon you know something about loving, Faith —so hold me fast—rouse me if it seems I'm slipping away, for I'll not go before I've seen her again. And keep the damned doctors away from me, lass. They'll be in here in a minute, earning their fees, fretting me and giving me something to make me sleep, I reckon—which won't do, because I might never wake up again. Can you do that for me, Faith Aycliffe . . ."

"Oh yes. Yes I can."

And for those next hours I sat and held him—as I had not been allowed to hold Giles—joining my spirit to his as death, very slowly, began to lay claim to his body, paring him down, stripping away one layer of life after another, until there was little left but the fierce whispering of his will, forcing those exhausted lungs to take another breath, and another, that failing heart to take another beat, dragging enough of himself away from extinction each time it threatened to engulf him so that there would be something left of the man who had loved her when his wife came.

"How long now?"

"Not long."

"I can't feel your hands, Faith. Are you still holding me?"

And I dug my nails into his flesh, pinched him, strained every muscle I had to jolt him just a moment or two nearer to train time.

"How long now?"

"Just half an hour. They've gone down to the station. *Now,* listen, there's the train—she's on the platform—*now,* Joel Barforth —she's in the carriage. *Now*—she's coming."

But I had heard no train, the carriage had left but not returned, the doctor had leaned over me, pursed his lips a dozen times. "I think, Mrs. Barforth, that the rest of the family should be called. His sons will expect to be with him at the end."

And when the man persisted and would not obey me when I ordered him to leave us alone and that the responsibility would be mine, it was the remnant of Joel Barforth himself that raised a head, somehow, from those pillows and spat out a last obscenity which chased the doctor away.

"I'll make it, lass—by God, I will—and if I don't—if the train should be late—tell her . . ."

"I'll tell her nothing. You'll do so yourself."

But I had believed him dead twice already, had shaken him and screamed at him, had grown hysterical with his need, her loss, the strength and beauty of their combined passion, had exhausted bone and muscle, ached, sweated, bitten my lips until they bled, before I heard the carriage and she came running across the room to him, his wife of thirty-five years, to throw herself into his arms with the passion and despair of a girl of seventeen. And there was nothing for me to do but close the door very quietly and walk away.

They were, as before, in the small drawing room, Georgiana in the big armchair, Nicholas leaning against one corner of the fireplace, Blaize at the other, both of them smoking, empty teacups and brandy glasses on a tray, Georgiana's riding crop carelessly abandoned on the hearth rug, and it seemed a hundred years since I had last met them, another place, their taut, untidy lives having no bearing on mine since they had not witnessed the suffering I had just shared, had not been privileged to see that outpouring of devotion.

They had moved, in one sense, a little ahead of me, in another had fallen far behind, for they had had time now to come to terms with bereavement and were already making room for other things. They had shed their tears, had their tea, to them their father was already dead, and whatever they might privately feel about his loss—and I think they each felt a great deal —they were faced now with the task of living without him, and with one another.

Nicholas threw his cigar into the fire and immediately lit another, his face full of the scowling anger he always used to screen emotion, his voice curt, aiming itself at Blaize rather than addressing him. And because I had entered the room in the middle of their conversation, with no idea of what had gone before, it seemed doubly strange to me.

"So—you'll be Sir Blaize Barforth, second baronet, tomorrow, by the look of it. How does that suit you?"

"I imagine I can handle it."

"You'll have seen the will, I reckon?"

"Yes. I had my half-hour with Jonas Agbrigg. I expect you did the same."

"So I did. And you understand the implications?"

"Do I?"

"I reckon so. Fifty per cent of the business to you and fifty per cent to me."

"Which seems reasonable enough, brother."

"I'd say so—provided we're both ready to earn it."

I walked past them, ignoring them, feeling their unspoken questions in the air behind me—What did he ask you—tell you —give you? Is he dead?—ignoring them, and I stood at the window looking out—away from them—aware mainly of my own hands clasped tight together, the knuckles as white as my uncle's had been when he had clung to me a moment ago, his voice, still in my ears, infinitely more real to me than the voices behind me which were no more than the shrill twittering of birds, incomprehensible, irritating.

"In certain circumstances," Georgiana said, "Blaize would have everything, since he's the eldest son."

"Ah yes," Nicholas told her, "the good old rule of primogeniture. But that's in good society, darling. This is Cullingford, and we all know a title doesn't pay the rent."

"But just the same," Blaize drawled, "you think he could have left you a little something extra in compensation, do you?"

"Maybe he did. He left me the sense to know that unless we

pull together—now that he's not here to stand between us—we're going to waste a lot of time, and a lot of money, getting nowhere."

"Ah—I take it then that I'm to pull in *your* direction. Is that what you're saying to me?"

"I might be—and then again I might just be telling you not to pull against me for the sake of it, because it tickles your sense of humour . . ."

"*Telling* me?"

And their bird-twittering got inside my head, senseless little noises cheapening the real words I had heard upstairs, my aunt throwing herself across that room, her whole body saying, "I love you, Joel," knowing that she had fulfilled his whole life's purpose, and he hers; and I couldn't bear it.

"Stop it," I said. "Stop it—now!" And my hands became fists crashing down on the window sill before I swung round and shouted at them again. "Stop it!"

I saw Nicholas' brows come scowling together, Blaize make a movement of surprise, and backing away from them, although neither had attempted to touch me, my legs gave way and I fell down on the window seat, appalled not so much by the violence of my tears as by the knowledge that I could not control them. I was a grown woman who knew that no grief lasts forever, yet, huddled there, I was a child sobbing and howling in the dark, beyond the reach of my adult logic, alone and terrified until Georgiana flung herself down beside me and took me in a thin, nervous embrace, her slight body shielding me as best it could from those keen Barforth eyes. And even then I continued to weep, releasing the pain of my entire lifetime against her narrow shoulder, the inner chamber in which I had stored it wide open, the floodgates broken.

"Poor Faith," she said, her small, hard hands accustomed to the handling of mettlesome horses holding me fast. "You are breaking your heart, and it is not for Sir Joel either—oh no, it is for something else, someone else . . . Oh, dear, I am so sorry—I didn't know—I thought you so happy with your lovely clothes and your cool, elegant life—I thought it suited you. How sad to be so mistaken, for you are miserable, aren't you—as miserable as I am . . ."

I heard the door slam as Nicholas left the room, heard his step behind me on the gravel as he walked past the window, and then other sounds, other voices which would make it easier for me to raise my head, as I would have to do, and look at Blaize.

But when I did look up all I saw of him was the back of his head, through the open doorway, as he bent to kiss my mother's cheek, and then Aunt Hannah's, his courteous, quite graceful shepherding of them upstairs to the wide landing where the doctor was waiting to greet and console them. I was gracious and graceful as always, and quite alone.

Chapter Twenty-seven

AUNT VERITY shut up her house in Bournemouth and moved back to Tarn Edge, mainly because this house, of all others, contained her most cherished memories of her husband, partly because the state of her younger son's marriage was causing her serious alarm. But if Georgiana had neglected her domestic obligations in the past, Aunt Verity's return enabled her to abandon them completely, for the house was Aunt Verity's personal property in any case, and Georgiana had never concealed how much she disliked it.

"An absolutely, first-rate hotel," I heard her tell Julian Flood one evening as they sat in the hall at Galton, a pair of retrievers scuffling companionably under the table, Georgiana's greyhound bitch curled daintily in her lap, the level of the brandy bottle much reduced.

"Yes—that's Tarn Edge. My word, now that my mother-in-law has come home one can see how it is that Caroline does so well at Listonby—if one cares, that is, for first-class hotels."

But Georgiana's barb seemed always to wound herself, would turn almost immediately to a laughing, flaunting self-reproach.

"Well, thank goodness for my mother-in-law, since I can do nothing right, and at least now the fires are lit when they should be, and there are muffins at tea time. How is it that I could never manage muffins? She simply orders them and they appear, but she remembers to interview cook every morning, you see, and tells her what will be required—whereas I—well—I can never remember tea time, let alone muffins. I am a sorry creature, Julian—come and drown me in the stream. It's all I'm fit for."

And, as that sad year merged into the next, she was rarely seen in Cullingford, riding off very early in the morning before Aunt Verity—or anyone else—had time to pack Gervase off to school, or, failing that, going herself, sometimes, to snatch him from his academic prison under the startled eye of a headmaster who could refuse nothing to a Barforth.

"Why not?" she told me. "He learns nothing in any case. He just sits there wishing himself at Galton, so I may as well make his dream come true, just as long as ever I can."

Yet, although he showed no aptitude for the manufacturing life, I was by no means certain that Gervase's enthusiasm for country pursuits matched his mother's. He could, indeed, ride the tall, spirited roan she had bought him, looking, with his auburn hair, his sharp-etched profile, for all the world like a miniature Perry Clevedon, but I wondered if the excitement in his face was perhaps occasioned not so much by a dash of his late uncle's recklessness as by the overstraining of his nerves, a spice of something that could be akin to terror? He could trudge out with Georgiana across the dry August fields, a gun across his arm, to attend the annual slaughter of grouse on Galton Moor, but I—a frequent guest at Galton in those days—couldn't help noticing that he was often sick the same evening, feverish and chilled the morning after, apologetic when he was told to stay behind but happy enough, I thought, to allow Liam Adair to go in his stead.

Gervase Barforth, in fact, was a child who belonged nowhere, a boy who, wishing to please his mother because he loved her and to please his father because he was afraid of him, seemed unlikely to please either, torn by a conflict which did not exist at Listonby where the young Chards were being raised in the belief that it was their duty to please only themselves.

"He's soft," said Liam Adair, a boy no longer but a young man approaching his fourteenth year with all the insolent swagger of a guardsman. "He never hits anything when he comes. Georgiana hits everything, and I don't do so bad—we got a 120 brace last time we were out. But Gervase just dithers and shuts his eyes. And I'll tell you this, he don't much like the dogs."

But when a pair of hound puppies ran off, one of them to a mangled death in a mantrap in Galton woods, the other only barely surviving an encounter with some sharp-toothed wood-land predator, it was Gervase who resisted Georgiana's immediate intention of putting the bleeding, whimpering little creature down.

"Darling—it's merciful."

"But it might get better, Mamma."

"Oh no, darling. And even if it did it could never chase foxes, which is what hounds are made for. It would not be fair to it, Gervase."

"I think it should be given its chance."

"Well," she told him, her face very serious, "if that's what you want to do—if you think it's best—then I think you should do it. But if you take the decision, darling, then you must take the responsibility as well—all on your own. That's what people in command, or in office, have to do, and if it goes wrong they have to take the blame."

"Yes, Mamma."

I sat up with him half the night on a bale of straw, sharing the vigil which Georgiana felt—perhaps rightly—he should have endured alone because I could see no empire-builder in him, rather a glimpse of Giles Ashburn, who, as a boy, might well have done the same.

Georgiana came once, lantern in hand.

"Are you sure, Gervase—quite sure?"

"Yes, Mamma."

"He's going to die, you know, darling . . ."

"You can't really know for certain. I understand about taking the blame."

And nodding her head, courteous and friendly as her grandfather, she went away.

"You don't have to sit up with me, Aunt Faith—unless you want to."

"Well—I'll stay a little longer."

And having done what we could for the ailing pup we buried it at two o'clock of a cool, damp morning, Georgiana's child ashamed that he had lacked the good sense, the guts, to shoot it in the first place, Nicholas' child scowling, telling himself it was a dog, that was all—a damned dog—and refusing to cry.

"He'll know what to do next time, at any rate, the poor lamb," Georgiana said. "Don't think me hard, Faith. He had to *choose*, you see. He knows now that he chose wrong and made the poor dog suffer longer than it need have done. He made that decision —a gentleman's decision—and he's faced up to it like a gentleman. He'd never have learned that lesson, you know, at the grammar school."

Caroline had taken her father's death very badly. She had set off on her visit to the South Erins, believing him safe and well in Bournemouth, had been called from the ducal breakfast table to be told he was dead, in Cullingford. And she was haunted by the confusion, the shock, the terrible disorientation she had suffered. Caroline had always known where she was, what she was doing there, what she intended to do next, but his loss had disturbed her sense of direction, set her askew, and she could not entirely right herself. He had left her enormously well provided for. She could continue to dazzle the county with her receptions, could extend her house and improve her estate as much as she desired, but, without her father there to see, without the deep satisfaction it had always given her to please and impress him, that desire was considerably diminished, arousing in her a melancholy which not even gifts of venison from the Duke of South Erin's deer park, nor Lady Hetty Stone's firm promises of luring her brother to Listonby, had the power to dissipate.

Sir Joel, not Sir Matthew, had been the audience before which she had played out her life, his applause, not Matthew's, her chosen reward, and she was bewildered at its loss.

"He liked it here, at Listonby, Faith. He didn't want it himself, but he liked to see me have it, doing it all so much better than Hetty Stone could manage in a thousand years, even if she was born to it. And do you remember, the last time we were all here together, how sulky everybody was—how nobody would speak at dinner, and how Georgiana went tearing off in her ball gown . . . I'll never forgive her for that. I'd planned it all for him, and I wanted him to be proud. I wanted him to see what I was doing with his money—because it *was* his money—and that night before he went to bed he walked me down the long gallery and kissed me, and he said, 'I'll say this for you, lass, you've always been a good investment, one of the best I ever made.' And he was telling me he loved me. Oh, Faith, I didn't know how ill he was. I wouldn't have gone near South Erins if I'd known. I'd have gone straight to Bournemouth. I'd have stopped him from coming up here, tiring himself out for those brothers of mine, who could do nothing but plague him. Look—you remember the portrait I had done of him last year? I've moved it from the dining room and put it in the gallery, I don't care what the Chards may say."

And when the future Sir Dominic Chard, home from his exclusive public school for the holidays, was heard explaining to a friend, "Oh no, that is not a Chard, that is my manufacturing grandfather," he was no doubt amazed at the violence with which his mother fell on him and boxed his ears.

"Don't ever let me hear you say that again."

"What have I said wrong? He wasn't a Chard, was he? He wasn't born at Listonby?"

"No, he wasn't," she shrieked, raining haphazard blows on him with every word, an assault, I might add, which his public school training enabled him to withstand like a rock. "And if it hadn't been for him there wouldn't have been a Listonby. Just you remember that, young man—just you remember it . . ."

"Dearest—" Hetty Stone murmured, as always slightly amused if a little pained by her friend's occasional breaches of good conduct. "The servants, dear—one really doesn't give them cause to gossip . . ." But Lady Chard—Caroline Barforth now in full fury—pushed her astonished mentor away—ruining, perhaps, all hopes of that ducal visit—and aiming a final, most accurate blow at her son, screeched contemptuously, "The servants. They eat my bread and they'll do as they're told. And so will you."

I had never been very close to Aunt Verity. She had been kind to me, in my girlhood, as she had been kind to most people, but she had been too radiantly happy in her own life, perhaps, to require any affection from outside, and I knew she had been suspicious of my marriage, worried, quite naturally, on her son's account rather than mine. Yet, in those first months of her widowhood I was increasingly drawn to her, finding, even in her bereavement, that she was the most complete woman I knew, knowing very definitely that her marriage was the only one I had ever envied. I knew that everything I had ever desired for myself had been shown to me, very plainly, during those hours I had spent at my uncle's bedside. I had witnessed the kind of love of which I believed myself to be capable, the intense, exclusive emotion which I had glimpsed between them in my girlhood, had wanted then, wanted now. But I had failed to give it to Giles, had been prevented from giving it to Nicholas—largely by Nicholas himself. Blaize did not much care for intensity, and there were times that year when I suffered a great hollowness of the spirit, when I looked at myself and saw a graceful, beautifully adorned, empty shell.

Had I been born a citizen of Simon Street my anxieties could not have extended beyond rent money, porridge money, the stark necessities of shelter, a blanket, a cold water tap, a few pennies desperately hoarded to pay a doctor for a sick child. Had I lived in Simon Street I would have been too exhausted to care. But life had given me the leisure and the luxury to contemplate the condition of my heart and soul, and to understand that, once again, the pleasant pastures of my existence were not enough.

In the eyes of Cullingford I had everything any right-minded woman could possibly desire, a place in society and the income to maintain it, a fascinating if somewhat foot-loose husband who had even given me a title, his father's death, which had made him Sir Blaize, having created me the second Lady Barforth of Tarn Edge. But I could not recognise myself in that title, could hardly remember myself as Faith Aycliffe, had failed to live up to the expectations of Faith Ashburn. What was I? The wife of a man who shared less than half his life with me. The mother of a girl who would become a woman entitled to a life of her own which might hardly include me at all. And, increasingly aware that the silk and champagne atmosphere of my marriage no longer sufficed me, I took the false solution many women find in similar circumstances. I gave more dinner parties, ordered more clothes, dressing Blanche—as she became five and six—in miniature copies of my gowns, a child with her father's cool stare, her mother's vanity, accepting quite naturally that a father was someone who took the train and came back with presents. I tended my garden, made vast indoor arrangements of daffodils and forsythia, white and purple lilacs, roses and ferns, polished beech leaves and dried grasses in season. I joined this committee and that committee, all of them chaired by Aunt Hannah, for the improvement of this or that evil. I took care of Liam Adair, of Grace Agbrigg, of Venetia and Gervase Barforth when no one else was inclined to do it, my house—when Blaize was away—being a depository for inconvenient children, harassed women, occasionally of a hopeful gentleman whose advances I resisted, since Blaize allowed me to be flirtatious only when he was there to see. I did what I could for Celia, removing from her shoulders the burden of Jonas' ambitions by inviting them both to dine as often as possible with me, always including in the party those people who could be of most use to Jonas. I visited the Lady Barforth Academy for Young Ladies whenever Prudence would have me, even my services being appreciated during an outbreak of measles, an occasional bout of homesickness among her boarders. I went to Leeds with my mother, to London now and then with Blaize, occasionally to Paris. I should have been happy.

Perhaps I could have been. Blaize had not slept the night his father died nor even tried to, remaining alone downstairs, smoking, brooding, refusing both my comfort and my company.

"Darling, do go back to bed," he had told me. "I'm restless and wide awake, and—really—I can manage very well." And I supposed that Nicholas might have said much the same, if more bluntly, to Georgiana: "Leave me alone. I don't need you."

They had stood at their father's funeral as granite-faced as any Flood, any Chard, and had gone, both of them, to the mill that same day, Blaize returning very late, his face unusually strained and grim. Yet which particular thing had worried him, angered him, hurt him the most, he would not say.

"Brother Nick is preparing to be unreasonable, it seems."

"And will you be unreasonable too?"

"I imagine he will think so."

I was still very careful of Nicholas, a relationship resting entirely on "Good evening, are you well?" not even listening to the answer, a dryness in my throat even now when I encountered him a chair or two away from me at the Mandelbaums' dinner table, a refusal to discuss him at those gossipy, feminine tea times, which—in view of the known hostility between him and Blaize, and of Georgiana's supposedly scandalous conduct—won me an undeserved reputation for family loyalty.

"Faith will not say a word against any of her relations," they said of me in the better areas of Cullingford, but I was obliged, often enough, to hear others speak those words for me, to learn —from Mrs. Mandelbaum, Mrs. Hobhouse, Mrs. Rawnsley—that the Nicholas Barforths, far from living in peace, were scarcely living together at all.

"My dear, there's no point in inviting them to anything since she's always at Galton and he's always at the mill. If she bothers even to come, the chances are she'll come abominably late and unsuitably dressed. And if he comes without her he never has a word for the cat—just scowls and makes cutting remarks, and drinks. Well—she drinks too, there's no doubt about it, for the maids at Tarn Edge make no secret of it. She can match him glass for glass, I hear tell, which is more than my poor husband —Mr. Rawnsley, Mr. Hobhouse, or Mr. Mandelbaum—has ever been able to do. Poor Verity—my heart goes out to her. It can't be easy, when she's brought up a family of her own, to be saddled with those grandchildren while their mother goes a-gallivanting. And they're not *easy* children. That little Venetia is a handful, anyone can see it, and I wouldn't want a boy of mine to look so peaky and so overstrung as that Gervase—which is not at all to be wondered at since when she has him at Galton, instead of sending him to school, he's allowed to sit up until all hours of the night, playing cards and drinking her brandy too, if the truth be known."

I heard—in Blenheim Lane, at Nethercoats, at Albert Place— of the terrible evenings at Tarn Edge when husband and wife would not exchange a word. I heard of the glass that a frantic, probably tipsy Georgiana had hurled at her husband's head, the fork she had hurled after it, both missiles striking the back of his chair. "Speak to me, dammit," she had shrieked at him. "Curse me to hell if you like, but say something."

"I'll say good night, I reckon," he had told her, calmly brushing the splintered glass and the drops of brandy from his sleeve. "I'm expected at the Swan and I ought to change my jacket. Sleep well." And he had left her.

I heard about her screaming rages, the slap he had once been seen to administer not passionately but merely to silence her, the night he had dragged her upstairs, pushed her through her bedroom door and locked it, remaining himself on the outside, his motive once again no passionate revenge—no passion at all—but simply to prevent her, at a late hour of the night, from taking Gervase to Galton.

I heard of the night she had returned from Galton, wet through, having driven herself in her brother's old curricle.

"Nicky, I came—it occurred to me—in fact, I've come to say I'm sorry."

"And you've driven ten miles in the rain to tell me that?"

"Yes."

"And you've left Gervase behind you at the abbey?"

"Oh—yes."

"Then how is he to get to school tomorrow? Isn't that the very thing you should be sorry about?"

I heard it all and all of it, every word that was spoken, every word that was implied, hurt me. I had cared for Nicholas all my life. He had been my hero in childhood, the tremulous dream of my adolescence; as a woman I had loved him. I had committed myself to another man and would fulfil that commitment to the letter. But there was no magic ingredient in my marital fidelity, my maternity, to obliterate that caring. Most of the time I cared for him only at a submerged level. I did not burn for him, no longer thought of him in that way—managed, for periods of varying lengths, not to think of him at all. But I continued to care, to be concerned, to suffer acutely, at unguarded moments, from a surge of guilt against which I had no defence. I wanted to ask, "Am I entirely to blame for his bitterness, his stubbornness? And if so what can I do to mend it?" But since Blaize was the only person I could have asked, and I was not certain I could cope with his answers, I kept silence.

Yet, in other ways, Blaize talked of Nicholas quite freely, enjoying the fast-accumulating tensions which he, from time to time, quite deliberately set himself to aggravate.

Nicholas had always been ambitious but now, with no one to restrict his management of the mills, his appetite for expansion became keener, his requirements more exacting. With Blaize so often away he was the Barforth that Cullingford knew best, the man who commanded instant attention when he entered the Piece Hall, the man his operatives looked out for in the mill yard since he was known to be a hard master—as autocratic and shrewd as his father had been, not always quite so fair—and nothing went on at Lawcroft, or Tarn Edge, at Low Cross or the Law Valley Wool Combers, or at Sam Barker's dyeworks either, now that it was his own, that he wasn't aware of. He worked long days, long nights, taking the escape, perhaps, of many men who are not content at home, and the feats of endurance he performed himself he expected in others.

Joel Barforth, to ensure punctuality, had locked his factory gates at five-thirty every morning, obliging the late-comers to stand outside, patiently or otherwise, until breakfast time, considering this loss of three hours' earnings to be punishment enough. Nicholas Barforth continued to lock his operatives out but, finding that the loss of three hours' pay did not compensate him for his loss of production, fined them as well, a practice which improved the time-keeping in his sheds but won him no popularity. Joel Barforth, to some extent, had been approachable, capable of exchanging a word or two with a familiar face, in a loom gate, capable, if reminded in advance, of offering congratulations and an appropriate ribaldry to an overlooker who was to be married. Nicholas Barforth was not concerned with personalities, only with efficiency, did not wish to be acquainted with the private lives of his operatives nor to recognise their faces. He came to his sheds for the sole purpose of work. He paid others to do the same. That was the extent of the relationship between them and he would tolerate no other. He understood the machines. He knew exactly what they could produce and exactly the time needed to produce it. And if his targets were not met, his reputation was such that shed managers were reduced to a state of abject terror by the mere threat of it. Yet, for those who could survive his demands, his tempers, his sarcasm, his refusal to accept any excuses, his apparent conviction that everybody enjoyed hard labour as much as he did, although he gave no praise, no thanks, his financial rewards were good. He wanted value for money, but when value was given he would pay, and it was a constant thorn in his side that the man he valued least was the only one he could not dismiss, and who made sure of paying himself most handsomely.

"Brother Nick was in good form today—do you know, he's a year younger than I and I believe he looks ten years older. My poor mother. She'll have a miserable dinnertime with him tonight, for he'll plague her half to death about my Russian trip."

"Are you going to Russia, Blaize?"

"Of course I'm going to Russia, darling—a week on Tuesday as it happens—and he'll growl, I imagine, until I'm back again. Poor Mother, and poor Nicky too, because he tried so hard to stop me, and couldn't manage it. We had the whole gala performance—my word, he could have been Father, except that Father *would* have stopped me, I suppose. And since we both knew that, and I said so in any case, it hardly improved his temper."

"Must you provoke him, Blaize?"

"Yes, I think I must. It makes him that much more anxious to get rid of me."

"Can he get rid of you?"

"He's not sure. He could buy me out, of course, but the cash for one half of Joel Barforth & Sons is too steep for any man I ever heard of. And if he did find it, or came up with some scheme to pay me off over a number of years—to give me a good living, in fact, and nothing to do for it—there's no guarantee I'd accept. The only thing he can do is to split the business—give me my share and send me on my way, if I'd agree to go. And he's tempted to ask me. Not that he likes the idea of parting with a fraction of the business, but then, if I'm really such an incompetent fool as he likes to think, I'll make a mess of it, won't I, and might be glad to sell it back to him at a price he can afford. But—and it's quite a substantial but—he may be well known in Cullingford but the only face the Remburgers and the Grassmanns know is mine, and it must have crossed his mind that if I leave I'll be likely to take my customers with me."

"Wouldn't it make your life a little harder, Blaize—if you split?"

"You mean wouldn't I have to go down to the sheds rather more, and stay at home a bit more often? So I would—but, darling, don't join with my brother in underestimating me. I may not understand the machines but I do understand commerce. I can add and subtract and work out my percentages every bit as fast as Nicky."

"Then why don't you try to get on with him?"

"Ah," he said. "Yes. Why indeed? If you can give me a reason, darling, I'd be grateful, for I'm running out of mine."

He left for Russia even earlier than he'd planned, giving me no exact idea of when I might expect to see him again. I knew I would hear no word from him unless there should be a little task he wished me to perform, or should take it into his head to have me meet him in London or in Paris, where, on arrival, I might discover, from some casual comment, that he had already spent a week in Berlin, or in Rome, with no explanation as to why he had gone there. But, far more likely, I would be taking tea with Aunt Hannah one afternoon and she would say, "I understand from Mr. Agbrigg that the Russian trip was worth while after all." And it would transpire that Blaize had arrived in Culling-ford that very day, on the morning train, gone straight to the mill, eaten his luncheon with Mayor Agbrigg at the Old Swan or at Tarn Edge with his mother, and that when I unpacked his treasure chests that night there would be something among the trinkets, the luxuries, the costly little toys for Blanche that could not possibly be Russian.

"Good heavens—I didn't realise they had such exquisite glass in Moscow."

"No, darling, they don't. It's Venetian."

"And how was Venice?"

"Perfectly lovely. Gondolas floating in the moonlight just as one imagines it."

And I couldn't suppose for a moment that he had floated in a moonlit gondola alone.

I took tea with Aunt Verity the day he left, finding some slight suggestion of tears about her, an unusual frailty that prompted me to ask her if she was not well.

"No, dear. Merely tired. To tell you the truth I have been in-dulging myself. My husband wrote me very few letters since we were rarely apart but, naturally, the ones I did receive I have kept—quite curt little notes, some of them, reminding me to do this and that—not love letters at all. But reading them just now, I could see him scribbling away with not a moment to spare, probably growling out instructions to somebody or other while he was doing it— And—well—I allowed myself to realise that I shall never stop missing him and that there is nothing I can do about it. I began to dwell on the finality, and to frighten myself with the idea that I couldn't cope—which is nonsense, of course, since one can cope with anything . . . But I was rescued from my misery—before it had gone on *too* long—by Nicholas. He came up from the mill to make sure Gervase had gone to school —which, unfortunately, he had not—and he spent an hour with me."

"Is he well?"

"No," she said gently. "I am sure he is not. Oh—his health is good, of course. But I would not say he was well."

"I'm sorry."

"Yes. I believe he is in danger of becoming a very hard man and I shall regret that. People say my husband was hard, and so he was in many ways. But he had areas of great warmth. He loved me, and Caroline, and he loved the boys too—and would have made great sacrifices for any one of us. Nicholas is growing hard in quite another way—a very cold way, and I am afraid that quite soon all that will matter to him is the accumulation not so much of money, as of the power it conveys. He tells me he will own the town and then the valley, and I am ready to believe him. I can even understand it. I have lived all my life surrounded by ambitious men, and I have seen ruthlessness often enough before. I have even appreciated it on occasions when there was a purpose to be served. But lately Nicholas has shown himself to be ruthless without cause, as if he took pleasure in it for its own sake—and he can do himself no lasting good."

She paused, looked at me for a moment very reflectively, and then, shaking her head, she sighed.

"I may as well tell you, Faith, since you will eventually hear it, and in fact it must be of great concern to Prudence. We all know that the Hobhouses have been struggling for a long time to keep their heads above water. Just as we all know that Nicholas has offered several times to buy them out—and has not increased his offer, I might add, after each refusal but quite the reverse. Well—he has now done something which must surely sink them at last. Oh, dear—I don't know if it is commercial practice or downright bullying or calculated fraud, but whatever one may call it I seem to be caught in the cross-fire and don't much like it. Some time ago Mr. Hobhouse was—as Mr. Hobhouse often is—quite desperately short of cash. His borrowing from Mr. Rawnsley's bank had reached its limits. Mr. Oldroyd of Fieldhead—his brother-in-law—is not famous for generosity and, in any case, it has always been Hobhouse policy not to upset him, because of his will. Mr. Hobhouse looked around him

and saw Nicholas, or Nicholas put himself in Mr. Hobhouse's
way—I don't know—but what I do know is that when Nicholas
advanced him the money he must have been well aware that it
could never be repaid. Yes—yes—Mr. Hobhouse is very rash
and much too hopeful, I know it. The tide, in his view, is always
on the turn—that is his way—we all understand him. I suppose
he was relying too much on your sister's dowry, and since he is
kindhearted himself he felt that Mr. Oldroyd, deep down, must
be the same and wouldn't really abandon him with his back to
the wall. Well—my son Nicholas is demanding his money. Mr.
Hobhouse cannot pay. Mr. Oldroyd will not oblige. Mrs. Hobhouse came to me in tears, for she has a large family and is a
woman I have known all my life. I spoke to Nicholas and I
could not reach him. The law is on his side. He wants Nethercoats. He has found not only the way to get it, but the way to
get it cheap. He didn't ask me to admire his cleverness. He simply shrugged his shoulders. It was not easy for me to hear
Emma-Jane Hobhouse describe him as heartless and greedy—
especially when there was no defence I could make. Yes—I
could lend Mrs. Hobhouse the money to repay him. I could easily afford it, as she wasn't slow to point out. But to do that
would be to damage my own relationship with Nicholas—and
whether he values that or not it is about the only thing he has
left."

"Aunt Verity . . . ?"

"Yes, Faith. You know as well as I do that he has no relationship with Georgiana, which is not entirely her fault. I have
told him so and he agrees with me. I have told him that if he
made the first move she would probably be ready to make the
second—glad to make it. He agrees with that too. Nicholas was
very close to me, Faith. All his life he has done things in temper,
in stubborn pride, and then regretted it. You have cause to know
that, I imagine. Even his temper is different now. It burst out of
him, once, quite spontaneously—a true, snarling, red-blooded
rage, a true emotion. Now he uses it when he needs it, manufactures it almost to order, which is not at all the same. And gradually, this past year or so, I have felt him moving away even from
me. It has been like entering a familiar house and finding, one
by one, that all the doors are closing. Well—I am sorry for that,
and even sorrier that he has felt the need to shut out his children

in the same fashion. Yes—they have a great deal of Georgiana in them, Venetia even more than Gervase. But nevertheless, they are his children—my grandchildren, like Blanche and Caroline's boys. And I think I would like to tell you, Faith, that if I seem to give more of my time and attention to Venetia than I give to Blanche it is because—well, who else is here to do it?"

"Aunt Verity, please don't worry about Blanche."

"Oh, but I don't worry about her, Faith dear. She has you, and if Blaize is something of an absentee father I imagine he gives her good measure when he is at home. And besides, she has enough of Blaize in her to be able to cope with life very well on her own, when the time comes. Venetia is very different—the wildest little girl I have ever known—not wilful and headstrong like Caroline or like Nicholas himself—no—altogether Georgiana's child. It is Venetia, believe me, who most resembles Peregrine Clevedon, not Gervase, and because she is enchanting and openhearted at the same time, so eager and hopeful, my heart bleeds for her. Nicholas will always take care of them, of course. He will pay their bills, and very handsomely. They will have the best of everything money can buy, there's no doubt of that. Quite simply he doesn't wish to be personally involved with them. He doesn't want to know them and he doesn't want them to know him. It worries me dreadfully."

The calling-in of the Hobhouse loan became common knowledge soon enough, causing all the resentment my aunt had feared, for although Mr. Hobhouse had been foolish and there was usually little sympathy in Cullingford for a man who could not hang on to his money, he was popular, had been with us for a very long time, while Nicholas Barforth, a much younger man, had shown himself too devious, was not much liked in the Piece Hall in any case, where it was felt that he already had too much and had got it both too easily and too soon.

Cullingford, with the exception of Mr. Rawnsley of Rawnsley's bank and the astute Mr. Oldroyd, believed that Mr. Hobhouse should be given time to pay. Nicholas Barforth would not make that time available. Mr. Oldroyd was applied to again, Mr. and Mrs. Hobhouse, Freddy, Adolphus, and James spending the best part of an afternoon at Fieldhead, reminding him, perhaps, of his wife, their dear aunt Lucy, who had come to him from Nethercoats with a considerable dowry in her hands.

Mr. Oldroyd was seen in Lawcroft mill yard the following day, in conversation with Nicholas, and dined with him at the Old Swan that night. The next morning Mr. Oldroyd conveyed his regrets to Nethercoats, declining to throw good money after bad, a decision for which Nicholas Barforth was blamed, since his purchases of Oldroyd-spun yarn were considerable enough to allow him to exercise a little persuasion.

And it was largely to escape the gossip, in which Prudence was inevitably involved, that I packed Blanche's boxes and mine and went to Galton with Georgiana, looking for quietness and finding instead that I was soon infected by her restlessness, the impulses which drove her on her wild, midnight riding, that caused her suddenly in mid-sentence to take flight, splashing across the abbey stream, scrambling up any stony hillside which seemed steep enough, dangerous enough to challenge her reckless spirit, moving so as not to stand still, shouting so as not to listen, running without direction, unless it was towards Julian Flood's equally restless arms.

I was not sure of it. "Julian, darling, I have stones in my shoes," and flopping down on to the grass she would stretch herself full length while he undid her shoe, pulled off her boot, his fingers curving far too easily around her ankle, as if he had done it all too many times before for any outward show of passion. It was not flirtation. They simply touched each other a great deal, jostling and back-slapping in the stable yard. "Help me over this fence, Julian." "Lift me down from this gate," and she would lean against him as frank and affectionate as she had been with her brother.

"*You* love me at any rate, don't you, Julian?"

"Of course."

"That's good—we're alike, aren't we, you and I?" And although she had talked in exactly the same fashion to Perry, Julian Flood was not her brother and in his case the barrier of comradeship, which had been fragile enough with Perry, could easily be crossed.

"Faith, darling, I'm going off with Julian this morning—over the hills and faraway—God knows where. You don't mind seeing to Venetia until I get back, since my nanny is half-witted and yours so supercilious that I daren't for the life in me ask her myself."

And while she roamed the hillsides, the highways and byways of her beloved outdoors and of her own nature, I found myself for the first time involved with a girl-child who had no time for my stories and my games of make-believe, a tiny, red-haired imp who found nothing to amuse her in my trinket boxes, an agile little creature who did exactly as she pleased and was impossible to catch. One moment she was there, passive, her face, like her mother's, growing plain with the ebb of her vitality. The next moment she had vanished from the face of the earth, no one had seen her go, no one could find her. Consternation while my pulses fluttered, my mind full of that perilous abbey stream, the quarry a mile away, the shaft of some ancient, worked-out mine, my sympathy going out to my sister Celia, who experienced this terrible anxiety needlessly, perhaps, but every day. No trace of her anywhere and then, in the very place one had looked a moment ago, she was there, her woodland green eyes blinking in amazement at the fuss, the sorry spectacle of Aunt Faith on the brink of nervous tears.

"I went outside," she would tell me. "Just out . . ." And no more than that could I ever discover.

Gervase was with us too, playing truant again from the grammar school, his presence another bond between Georgiana and Julian Flood, for failing Perry, what better example than the future lord of the manor of Cullingford could she find for the future squire of Galton to follow?

"Julian, do show him how to load that gun. No—no, darling, you have to really make your horse *work* to get him over that gate—watch Julian. There, you see, he did it with a yard to spare. No, darling, you're too stiff in the hips and the knees, sit *easy* in the saddle, like Julian. And Gervase, look at Julian's feet —straight forward, darling, not sticking out like yours. Do look, Faith. Isn't he coming along splendidly?"

One morning, as they were all three riding up and down the stream to accustom Gervase's nervous animal to the fast-flowing water and I was leaning on the bridge, taking a final breath of Galton air since I was going on to Listonby that day, I looked up and saw Nicholas walking towards us from the house.

"Georgiana," I called out, conveying, against my will, a warning, and seeing him too, she said, "Damnation," and, turning her horse's head, sent it careering out of the water and up the hillside, turf and stones flying, and was off across the open fields, Julian Flood behind her. I waited until Gervase got his horse up the bank and, taking his bridle, walked him back along the path where Nicholas was waiting.

"Father," he said, very pale, that wild look in his eyes again, clearly expecting to be blamed. But Nicholas merely nodded and told him, "Take your horse to the stables and then tell them to clean you up and get your things together. It seems to me you should be at your lessons."

"Yes, Father." And he rode away, his toes turned sadly outwards, slouching in his saddle, smaller than he had been a moment ago.

We were quite alone, the whole of the Galton estate spreading around us, the bare hillsides, the empty fields, a vast, smoky autumn sky, Mr. Gervase Clevedon away somewhere at his Quarter Sessions, two little girls—his daughter and mine—safely indoors in the care of a few indifferent maids, six years separating us from the last time we had been together and he had persuaded me, against my own judgement, to go and wait for him in Scarborough.

I didn't know him now. He had been the boy who had defied his father and refused to ride on Cullingford's first train, who had said so often, "Faith will know what I mean." He had been the young bridegroom who had told me, "They will say it is for my money on her part, and because I am stubborn. It is more than that." And later he had said to me, "Faith, I won't let you go." He was a stranger now, the man who was about to ruin the Hobhouses, who had shut the doors of his nature to his mother, his wife, and his children. The man who would ruin his own brother—my husband—if he could. I didn't know him.

"Good morning, Lady Barforth," he said, and I laughed quite easily.

"Heavens, don't call me that. Every time I hear it I look over my shoulder expecting to see your mother."

"I daresay. She's at Listonby. I've just come from there. I understand you're to join her."

"Yes—with Blanche and with Venetia too, if you don't mind. Are you taking Gervase back to Tarn Edge? Nicholas—I don't know how long Georgiana will be . . ."

"Don't you? She'll be back as soon as she sees me leave, I

imagine. I just came to pick up the boy. She knows that and knows she can't prevent it—so what point is there in starting a battle she can't win?"

And we walked in silence up the narrow little track and into the cloister that would lead us to the abbey house.

"And how are you Faith? Well?"

"Yes—very well."

"I'm glad to hear it. How long have you been here—five days? Six days? And how long has Julian Flood been with you—?"

"Nicholas, I don't think you should—"

"What? Ask you to betray a confidence? Darling, you don't have to tell me. He's been here night and day, I imagine. And why not? What else has he got to do? These things happen."

I walked a step or two ahead of him, stung by his familiarity, which had been intended to sting me, embarrassed by his mention of Julian Flood, which had been intended to embarrass, the word "darling" having come as coarsely from his tongue as if I had been a music-hall dancer. And I was aware again of the silence around us, nothing but my angry footsteps to break it, that vaulted roof arching away into a timeless, treacherous distance.

"Come, Faith. You're a sophisticated woman. You understand how it is."

"Yes," I said, turning to face him, meeting the granite wall that was his anger. "I understand. As you say, he's been here all the time, and so have I. I've seen nothing to suggest that there is anything between them but friendship."

"Then he's a fool," he said bluntly. "And so is she. So far as I'm concerned it couldn't matter less. You have my permission to tell her so."

"I don't want to know about it, Nicholas."

He stopped and lit a cigar, the fragrant trail of tobacco in the air somehow very wrong in this place, a quite deliberate desecration. "No. I imagine you don't. I merely mention it in case you should feel uncomfortable—adultery does have that effect on its spectators . . ."

"*Nicholas!* There is no adultery."

"So you tell me, in which case I'll tell you again—he's a fool. I took him for a man who could recognise his opportunities."

I walked on again, and then came to a halt somehow facing the fluted, crumbling stone of the old wall, my hands clasped tight together, my whole mind remembering him, knowing he was still there, unwilling perhaps but painfully present behind the hardness, the coarseness, the grim-textured façade.

I could neither hear him nor see him. I could simply feel him there, know him there, one part of me finding it ridiculous that I could not turn around and touch him, the rest of me anguished, terrified that I might do it. And already there was a whisper inside me, a warning that said, "Be very careful," for his will had vanquished mine often enough, easily enough in the past, and I had no greater resolution than before.

"My dear sister-in-law," he said, a certain harsh amusement in his voice. "You seem very agitated. I do apologise if I have given you cause . . ."

"There's no need to apologise."

"Good. But nevertheless, you are upset—?"

"Yes."

"And is there anything I can do?"

"You could believe me about Georgiana and Julian Flood."

"Could I? I'm not so sure of that. Belief, you see, implies a measure of trust and I really don't think it would be wise . . . I imagine you know what I mean."

"Yes. I know. And you're quite wrong."

"Really? I should need to be convinced of that. Could you convince me?"

"No," I told him, sighing out the words, despairing over them. "Because there are things I can't tell you . . ."

"And have I asked any questions?"

"No. I almost wish you had . . ."

He came to stand beside me, heavier than my body remembered him, his nearness creating an imbalance in my reasoning so that at the same time he was the man I knew best in the world, and a total stranger.

"In fact you'd like me to shake the truth out of you to ease your conscience, so that afterwards—like most women—you could say, 'He made me do it.'"

"I would not—"

"I'm glad to hear it, because I couldn't oblige you. And is there even a mystery? You saw the chance of a good marriage. You took it."

"No . . ."

"You mean it's not a good marriage?"

"No, I don't mean that. But it didn't happen—as you suggested —from self-interest . . . You must know that. You do know it."

"I know nothing about it, Faith. I was away at the time, if you remember, and when I eventually got to know about it your motives seemed plain enough. If I'm wrong, then tell me so. But I shouldn't ask that of you, should I? Let's forget I did, because I expect you've promised to keep quiet and it doesn't pay to break your word every time. We'll say no more about it."

Yet I knew, very clearly, that he intended me to say a great deal, that every word he spoke was pushing me harder against that stone wall, driving me into a corner the better to search out the source of my caring, the source of my guilt. And if he needed to know the truth there was no doubt at all that I needed to tell him.

"We'll say no more," he repeated softly, firmly, and, weak with relief, I took a step away from the ancient stone, imagining myself free, until I understood from the glimpse of satisfaction in his face that he had done no more than loosen my reins and had found a sure way to bind me again.

"That brooch on your shoulder," he said with false indifference. "You wear it a great deal, I notice."

"Yes—yes I do."

"And so you should, for it's a pretty complement—a cameo swan. A present from Blaize, I reckon."

I nodded, dry-mouthed, afraid again, wondering what he could find in a brooch to use against me, knowing, in his present mood, that there must be something; and he smiled.

"Of course it is. It's got his stamp all over it. And he'd put himself to a lot of trouble to get it."

"I believe he may have done."

"There's no doubt about it. He'd go a few hundred miles out of his way to find a jeweller who could design it and cut it, time and money no object. That's Blaize."

"Yes."

"Whereas I'd never think of such a thing. I'm not ungenerous. My wife has a diamond or two and some good emeralds, but there's no particular finesse about that. Any man with a decent bank account could manage it."

"Does it matter?" I asked, meaning, "Where are you leading me?" and it was to the unspoken question he replied.

"It doesn't matter to me because I'm not a man for personal relationships. Oh yes, one tries a little of this and a little of the other as a young man, but in the end a man with any sense at all finds out what he's good at and where he can best make his profit. And the truth is that close relationships don't suit me. My mother sometimes gets upset about it, but if I am hard, as she says, then I find it quite natural."

"I don't."

"I daresay. But then, you knew me best in my younger days, when I was still trying out a few sentimental notions."

"Such as marriage—and love?"

"Well, marriage at any rate. And adultery, I suppose, from which I must exonerate you since you were not married at the time and betrayed no one—well, not a husband—"

Self-pity perhaps, and bruised conceit, the Barforth inability to accept that he could not have everything his way. And forcing myself to remember the weight of his jealousy, his temper, his injustice, I tried to take refuge in anger. He's selfish, a part of my mind insisted. He's hurt, another replied. Both were true. It was the hurt that mattered.

"Nicholas—you may find this hard to believe—you may not even want to believe it—but I never deceived you. Blaize didn't deceive you either. He came to Scarborough that weekend for no other reason than to tell me you couldn't be there. He didn't touch me. He didn't try to touch me. I don't think he particularly wanted to. Certainly I didn't want it."

And even these few words scorched me, took my breath away, hurt my throat and my tongue in the speaking, caused my will to flicker into its last feeble resistance, pleading with his will, "Please, Nicholas, let that be enough. Don't make me say any more."

But having waited so long he was not disposed to be merciful.

"Faith—dearest Faith—I have four mills to run. How much time do you imagine I spend wondering just when, and how, you got into bed with my brother?"

But he had wondered, had tormented himself with it, and pressing my back to the wall, turning my face away from him, the cold stone easing my burning cheeks, I knew I was about to give him the answer. I had been wrong about everything else, very likely I was wrong again, but I had contributed more than my share to his load of bitterness and this much, at least, was owing. It was the only promise Blaize had ever asked of me. I didn't want to break it. It was against my nature to break it. I understood why it should not be broken. It made no difference.

"Listen," I said, closing my eyes, pressing my face harder against the stone, each word leaving me with great effort, great labour. "We were seen together in Scarborough, Blaize and I, by someone who informed Aunt Hannah. She assumed that we were lovers. She was going to tell your father. You were in London. Georgiana was expecting Venetia and you were as worried and confused as I was about how you'd feel if she should die. I was terrified. I'm terrified now."

And it had been waiting for me a long time, this cloister, where nuns had walked barefoot in penitence, a right and proper place for the scourging my spirit required. I felt his hand clench on the wall above my head, a feeling of unbearable strain communicating itself from his body to mine, tightening the air around us until I could scarcely breathe, and then, suddenly, he threw back his head and gave, no groan of pain, no string of curses or reproaches, but a short, quite savage peal of laughter, showing me at last the true meaning of punishment, since nothing could have wounded me so much as this.

"Christ," he said. "So that's how he did it. The clever bastard. He convinced you that you were saving me, did he? Yes—I could have worked it out, I reckon. It's like him. It's like you."

And he laughed again, the sharp, ugly sound of it stripping me bare and flaying me.

"Stop it, Nicholas. You've hurt me—it's enough."

"When I'm ready," he said. "When I'm good and ready."

And then, the mirth vanishing, whipping out of him and leaving his face granite hard again, he took me by the shoulders, his face very close to mine.

"But it didn't work, darling, did it? He played God once too often, didn't he? And don't you ever ask yourself why? Oh yes, he gave you his reasons, plenty of them, and they'd seem good to you at the time, because he can talk the birds from the trees, we all know that. But what was he really after? It wasn't done for my sake, Faith, and it wasn't done for yours, you can rely on that. It's the Cullingford train all over again. I wouldn't play then, and I won't play now. He should have known that."

I got away from him, ran down the cloister into the house, and he drove off a half-hour later with his son, leaving me to face Georgiana, who appeared as if she had been awaiting the signal, just as his carriage went out of sight.

"He's gone then?"

"As you see."

And she stood for a moment staring in the direction he had taken, too deep in her own thoughts to notice that I had been crying, that I was very near to tears again.

"He thinks I'm having an affair with Julian," she said. "It's not true—of course it's not true. Heavens, if he really thought about it—wanted to think about it—he'd know it couldn't be true."

And then, her voice very low this time. "Ah well—he has a mistress in Leeds and another in London—did you know that? No, of course you didn't, and I shouldn't know either, except that one always knows. Yes—one knows and one should be able to accept it with resignation—and dignity. One should make no more of it than a simple 'My dear, men are like that,' which I've heard so many women say. I can't say it."

She turned away as if she meant to go inside and then turned slowly round again, drawn against her will to the empty road he had just travelled.

"If it hurts me, then you'd think I'd be able to tell him so— wouldn't you? Just go to him and tell him? I can't. He wouldn't answer, you see. And when he won't talk to me it hurts me so much that I can't risk making it happen. So I just go on pretending there's nothing I want to say to him."

She turned away again, her narrow hand making a gesture of finality.

"Well, so much for that," she said. "There's always the abbey —always my blessed cloister— At least nobody can take that away from me."

Chapter Twenty-eight

THE CALLING-IN of the Hobhouse debt was still the subject of every tea time, every dinner table, when I returned, my sister Prudence walking up from Elderleigh schoolhouse the moment she became aware of my carriage on the drive, for now she must either marry Freddy or break off with him, and the decision was harder than she had anticipated.

Freddy had waited more than ten years for her—not, as she continued to insist, very patiently and certainly not without diversions. He had gone regularly to Bradford every Tuesday and Friday for years to treat himself to the supposedly medium-priced charms of a lady who kept a tobacconist's shop in Darley Street, had paid brief court to Rebecca Mandelbaum before her Austrian musician won her heart. But, at this crisis in his family's fortunes, circumstances had placed him in Prudence's hands and, in the prevailing mood of sympathy, Cullingford would expect Prudence to do her duty by the Hobhouses, or would condemn her as a heartless jilt.

"Not that I care for that," she said. "Why should I care what anyone thinks of me?"

But she was fonder of Freddy than she had intended, attracted, in spite of herself, by his weighty, lazy charm, his constant good humour in adversity, the sheer hard labour he had given to Nethercoats, his lack of rancour when all his efforts had been defeated, one by one, by his father. And she could no longer deny that she had used him.

"Of course I did. And why not? No one thinks ill of a man for using a woman. It is what men are supposed to do, and women are supposed to put up with it. If I had lost *my* money, it would have been taken for granted that he would break off with me, and they would have called him a sentimental fool if he hadn't. But it is not the same for me. I am a woman and so I am expected to sacrifice myself and everything I have for the sake of his incompetent father. And if I don't, I run the risk of losing my reputation and my school—for no Law Valley man will allow his daughter to be educated by the heartless woman who jilted Freddy Hobhouse, in case my pupils should follow my example —in case I should take it into my head to teach them that a woman has as much right to be considered as a man. I've laboured hard for my independence, you know that. Dear God, how I've laboured—and it didn't please me that I had to lie and scheme for it, and hide behind Sir Joel Barforth in order to maintain it. But I'm succeeding, Faith. I'm gaining the reputation I set out to gain. I'm being taken seriously, not as the daughter of Morgan Aycliffe with 20,000 pounds and expectations, but as myself—for what I've made of myself. And I can't lose it. I might share it, but I won't lose it. I won't sink my money and my identity in Nethercoats. If Freddy wants me, he'll have to break off with his family first. He'll have to choose my business instead of his own."

But such an idea would have been considered preposterous, downright criminal, in Cullingford, and Freddy, who was no revolutionary, who was kindhearted and easygoing and extremely attached to his even easier-natured father, would not listen to it in any case. He would marry Prudence if he could. He would plough every penny she brought with her and every penny he could raise elsewhere into his ailing Nethercoats. And if he failed, then he would take any man's wages and work himself to death to provide for her. He would give her the shirt from his back, the last crust from his table, and go cold and hungry himself, but nothing would induce him to see what in her opinion was reason, in his opinion treachery, nothing—absolutely nothing—would persuade him to allow her to provide for him.

A woman's dowry and her inheritance belonged by right and custom to her husband since wealth of this kind had been earned and accumulated by a fellow male—her father—but there was an ugly name for a man who lived on the fruits of a woman's labour, and Freddy Hobhouse would not be called by that name.

"Good heavens," my mother said. "What a diverting notion. He would have to do exactly as she told him—can you imagine it? No more 'Darling, may I have a new bonnet?' but 'Unless you mend your manners I shall not buy you a new coat.' Really—one can see the advantages to it. Daniel has explained to me that by law even a woman's earnings belong to her husband, but I can see that it is not at all the same. A man knows in advance the size of the dowry he is getting and once he sets his hands upon it no one can have it back again. But earnings—well—all she needs to do is threaten to stop earning, and if he depends upon her income he will be obliged to let her have her way— Yes, so he will, just as we are obliged to let our husbands have their way, for the same reason. My dear, it is revolution, and although I am perfectly happy with my Daniel—indeed I am—I think the idea of such power could quite turn my head, were I a younger woman. Earnings. Good heavens—your father would turn in his grave. Quite suddenly I am able to understand why he was so careful to teach you nothing. What a dangerous, tantalising notion—to earn a living of one's own."

But others were less tantalised, and perhaps it suited me to rush to my sister's aid, doing my very best to defend her actions and her name, since I could no longer defend my own.

I had made my confession to Nicholas in good faith. Like his mother I had felt that bitter shell hardening around him and had wanted to pierce it, however slightly, to reach the part of him that could still find joy in life, not necessarily with Georgiana, certainly not with me, but somehow, with someone. But once again I had blundered. I had not reached him. Possibly there was nothing left to reach, and I had done no more than lay myself, and Blaize, open to his malice. I had dredged deep into my store of courage, drained it and myself with it to make that revelation, and he had laughed at me. What would he do now? Would he keep it to himself, or, appreciating its worth, would he toss it casually at Blaize the next time they quarrelled. And how would Blaize react to it? I had rarely seen him angry, never with me, but how could he live in peace with a woman who had put such a weapon into his brother's hands, a woman who understood full well how lethal that weapon could be, and that Nicholas would not hesitate to use it.

I had no defence. I had wounded Nicholas long ago before the granite had encased him and he was still vulnerable to pain. The wound remained, if only in his pride, and he would hurt me now if he could, not in anger but in calculation, as a lever to dislodge Blaize from Tarn Edge. He would use me as he had used the Hobhouse debt, a few thousand pounds well spent to bring Nethercoats to its knees, a cheating woman to do the same with his brother, and waking suddenly in the middle of one tormented night it seemed to me that I had nothing more to lose, that I might as well go to him and beg, as abjectly as he liked, for mercy. I was in his power, as I had been all my life in the power of one man after another. I was a female, one of nature's penitents. I would accept the role assigned me and plead. But by morning I knew that by doing so I could only drag myself further into the mire, for knowing him as I still did, the dark side of him as well as the light, I knew he would take my pleading and anything else it pleased him to extract from me, would play cat and mouse with me for as long as it suited him, and would still betray me.

I would not wait then, and delving inside myself once more for my feeble content of courage, decided that I would tell Blaize myself as soon as he came home. I would prepare him so that he could have his defence ready, and I would accept whatever retribution he chose to inflict, aware that the punishment itself could hardly be worse than my dry-mouthed dread of it. But when he arrived with the fur cloak, the Russian boots, the gorgeous oriental robe, the icons, the samovar, his cool quizzical gaiety, it was easy to convince myself that, after all, he would not take it hard, that he would shrug this off as lightly as everything else.

"My word," he said when we had dined and made love, when he was lounging easily among the pillows and I, the encrusted Eastern robe draped around my satiated body, fear again in my heart, had told him about the Hobhouse debt, as a means of introducing Nicholas' name. "Yes—I quite see your sister's dilemma. Shall I solve it for her? Nothing prevents me from lending Hobhouse the money to pay Nicky, and I doubt I'd require any better interest rate than the look on my brother's face."

"No. Blaize—don't do that—please don't . . ."

"Darling . . . ?" And leaning forward, supporting himself on one elbow, he turned his cool, grey eyes full on my face. "Is there any particular reason why I shouldn't?"

"Yes. Yes, of course. There'd be another great explosion, you know it, and—well, I think your mother has had enough to bear. She was telling me just the other day how concerned she is about the pair of you."

"Yes, I believe she is. Well then, I shall try not to aggravate her fears—although she could lend Hobhouse the money herself, of course. I doubt if even Nicky would do too much snarling at *her*."

"Blaize, for goodness sake, can't you leave things alone—just for once?"

"Darling," he said, with his unique smile. "Are you accusing me of meddling?"

I didn't know what I was accusing him of, didn't know what he was thinking or feeling, what he wanted, cared about, if, indeed, he cared for anything. I had lived pleasantly, sometimes very happily, with the surface of him and had no idea what lay beneath it. I had worn my lovely clothes for his entertainment, had given him my body in every mood and manner his imagination could devise. I had laughed with him, enjoyed with him, preened myself with him, had not precisely trusted him but had believed he could trust me. I spent five days of silent agony, an earthquake stirring beneath my feet each evening when I heard his carriage, the qualms subsiding only when his smile told me that all was well. I went to Aunt Verity, determined to make my confession and ask her help, and could not. I made up my mind to lie, when the blow fell, to brazen it out by declaring that Aunt Hannah herself—or Jonas—had said something to make Nicholas suspect the truth, and I had merely confirmed it. I doubt if I could have done either.

"My brother has been making himself very pleasant," Blaize said on the sixth evening as we were dining alone, a bowl of late roses on the table between us, the curtains drawn against the chill of the November night. "I wonder why? I agree, the orders I brought back from Moscow are altogether supendous, but why, I ask myself, is he so pleased about that? It merely proves

I was right to go in the first place, and gives me an excellent reason to go again."

And throwing down my napkin, my eyes fixed on the candle flame, I said harshly, "I'll tell you why. He knows about Aunt Hannah and Scarborough."

A long time went by. The candle flame got into my eyes, filled them, and when they had regained their focus I saw his hand lifting the wine bottle from its ice, filling my glass and his own, his face so entirely without expression that for a sickening moment I wondered if I had actually spoken at all.

"Blaize, did you hear what I said?"

"Oh yes," he said, raising his glass and sipping reflectively, his face telling me nothing. "I heard. Thank you, Faith. That was splendid—absolutely splendid."

I got up, impeded for the first time by my crinoline, walked to the window and to the fire and back again, alone, it seemed, in the room, although he still sat there at the table, drinking his well-chilled wine, enjoying, for all I knew, the excellence of its bouquet, the effect of the candlelight on his silver and his crystal, these things adequately consoling him, perhaps, for the betrayal of his silly, sentimental wife.

"Blaize—say something to me." And perhaps my voice reminded me of Georgiana's. "You must want to know how—and why—at least that much . . ."

"Darling, if he knows it can only be because you told him."

"Yes—yes I did. And, if you want to know, I have bitterly regretted it."

"Well—that's something, at any rate."

"He came to Galton while I was there, to fetch Gervase away. He was upset . . ."

"And you consoled him."

"I broke the only promise you ever asked of me . . ."

And once again a Barforth male, from his height, or his depth, had it in him to laugh at me, although this time there was no cruel explosion of mirth, merely a chuckle that had a wry sound to it, his amusement directed at us both.

"Ah well—as to promises and their making and breaking, perhaps I am not the man who should complain. Faith—do sit down. Now that you've just stabbed me in the back don't add to my discomfort by all that nervous pacing."

"Blaize, don't you care at all?"

"Yes, as it happens, I do. I think I'll just step outside and smoke my cigar in the garden, if you don't mind. I'll join you for coffee presently."

I had them clear the table, ordered coffee to be served in the drawing room, sat by the crackling autumn fire and drank one cup, then two, aware, I think, of the beauty of the room, the light green silk walls, the creamy Aubusson rugs, the discreet elegance which had marked our lives together, which had contented my nature almost completely, as Blaize himself had almost contented me. And although I was no longer afraid I was inexpressibly saddened, the misty, quite gentle sorrow one feels sometimes at the summer's end, the first glimpse of age in the face of a woman who has lived by her beauty.

"I am sorry," he said, coming in through the long windows. "I've kept you waiting rather a long time, haven't I, for the pronouncing of your sentence."

And, knowing the qualities he most admired in a woman, I answered calmly, "Shall I send for more coffee?"

The tray was removed, another brought in its place, I filled his cup, adding sugar, no cream, in the way he liked it. He drank, replaced the fragile Wedgwood cup on the tray and, since we were alone, lit another cigar.

"I find," he said, "that we have evolved a very agreeable way of life together. Am I right in assuming that you value it too?"

"Yes. I value it."

"Well then—what more is there to say? I'm very loathe to lose anything I find pleasant, Faith, you must know that. I was inclined to be rather put-out, half an hour ago, but then, thinking it over, I'm bound to admit that had you been my mistress in the first place and then eloped with him, I'd soon have found a way of persuading you to tell me why. So I can hardly be surprised that Nick has done the same."

"And you're not—disappointed?"

"In you?"

"Of course, in me."

"I shall get over it. And at least I'll be ready to defend myself when Nicky mentions it—if he ever does. Really—it makes very little difference."

"I'm glad you think so."

"Faith," he said, leaning as near to me as my skirts allowed. "Did you expect me to throw the soup tureen at your head or brain you with the candelabra? That's not quite my style, you know. I'm altogether the wrong Barforth for that sort of thing. And, in any event, that's not the way of it—is it, my love?—between us? If you want to make amends you can treat me with very obvious affection the next time we are all together—it won't hurt to let him think you like me best—it won't hurt me, that is . . ."

And although it was not forgotten, although from time to time I saw, or imagined I saw, a certain coolness, a certain watchfulness, we did not speak of it again.

Mr. Oldroyd of Fieldhead died very suddenly that November, his demise occasioning an inevitable, if discreet, rejoicing at Nethercoats, where it was assumed that Freddy at least, who had been a favourite nephew, must surely benefit if not in entirety at least substantially enough to settle the Barforth debt.

"Only think," my mother breathed, quite ecstatically, "if Freddy should get it all, for I cannot think what else Matthew Oldroyd can have done with it. Prudence could then be mistress of Fieldhead, which even she would find most agreeable. And just think, too, darling, that it could all have been mine. Well—I would have given it up twice over for my Daniel, but, I confess, I would be well pleased for my daughter to have it in my place. Do give her a little push, Faith. Earning a living is all very well, but Matthew Oldroyd was very rich, you know, and if it all comes to Freddy, there will be a hundred young ladies ready to share it with him. Tell Prudence that."

But Prudence had no need to be told for although Freddy himself was still her devoted slave, his mother, in the interval before the will was read, made it plain that, with the Oldroyd millions at his disposal, Freddy would have no need to settle for a self-willed schoolmistress no longer in her first youth, whose opinions were, to say the least, peculiar.

"She thinks he may help himself to a biddable little chit of fifteen," Prudence said. "One of my pupils, in fact, rather than myself. Well, I do not at all blame her for disliking me. I merely hope that if Freddy is to be so rich he will have the sense to keep it away from her, and from his father—for if he does not we shall see Nicholas Barforth at Fieldhead as well, five years from now. Poor Freddy, he will allow them all to impose upon him, you know. He will give his father the means to ruin Nethercoats all over again, and provide so handsomely for all his brothers and sisters that they will be too busy spending it even to thank him. Poor Mr. Oldroyd too. They say he was very mean, very careful with his money, and it must have saddened him to know how recklessly the Hobhouses would throw it away."

A prophetic utterance, certainly, on my sister's part, for it had clearly saddened him so much that he had, in the end, found himself unable to give them the opportunity, the Oldroyd will providing a scandal which contented Cullingford for many a long day, acting as a stone flung into murky waters, its ripples spreading wide and, to some of us, most painfully.

As expected, provision had been made for a certain Miss Jamison in Leeds, a few trifling bequests to household staff, an insulting 500 pounds apiece to his brother-in-law, Mr. Bradley Hobhouse, and to Emma-Jane Hobhouse, his wife. To his favourite nephew, Mr. Bradley Frederick Hobhouse, he left the sum of 10,000 pounds, with the suggestion that it be used for the setting up of some personal enterprise. But the bulk of his estate, his spinning mill at Fieldhead and Fieldhead millhouse, his railway shares, his brewery shares, his substantial bank deposits, were to become the property of one Mrs. Tessa Delaney, who, it appeared, was not Mrs. Delaney at all but, for the past year, had been the second Mrs. Matthew Oldroyd of Fieldhead.

"Oh, dear," my mother said. "I fear there will be trouble. My poor Celia."

And although it was not immediately clear to me why my sister Celia should be involved I was soon elightened by the visit of a distraught Mrs. Hobhouse, who, with nothing more to hope for, nothing more to lose, would have been glad, I think, to see the whole of Cullingford consumed in flames. She was not herself to blame for her family's ruin. She would not blame her husband. Who then? A conspiracy, no less, the greedy, evilhearted Barforths standing solidly behind Nicholas to rob her of her home, to put her and her children out in the street. She was no fool. She could recognise criminal practice when she saw it, and what had it been but that? Who had persuaded Mr. Oldroyd to change his will? Nicholas Barforth. Who had drawn

up that new will? Jonas Agbrigg, who happened to be married
to Nicholas Barforth's cousin, whose father, Mayor Agbrigg, was
a Barforth employee, whose mother was Nicholas Barforth's
aunt. And who had suggested that Mr. Oldroyd should marry
his disgusting hussy in the first place, who would have thought
of such a thing but the lawyer Jonas Agbrigg, since he would
know how easily they could otherwise have overset the will?
Who had attended that abominable ceremony of marriage?
Jonas Agbrigg, she announced, her soft bulk quivering with
fury, for she had enquired, had been informed, had found him
out in all his perfidy. Who had dined at her table, looked her in
the eye, and smiled, knowing all the while of the dagger he had
helped to thrust in her back? Jonas Agbrigg. Who, in his capacity as the Hobhouse family lawyer, had advised her husband
time and time again to sell out? Jonas Agbrigg. Who was
brother-in-law to Prudence Aycliffe? And what had he told her
that had prevented her from marrying Freddy years ago? And
how much had Jonas Agbrigg been paid for his treachery? What
bribes had he taken from Nicholas Barforth and from the whore
Delaney? And what had happened to the first Mrs. Oldroyd's
jewels? Could we expect to see her diamonds in that trollop's
ears, and her pearls around the scrawny neck of Mrs. Jonas
Agbrigg, who had been Celia Aycliffe, another cousin to Nicholas Barforth?

"Yes, you have carved me up, all of you, carved me up nicely,
and I hope you are satisfied. But I still have my tongue, Lady
Barforth—Faith Aycliffe that you were—and I shall let it be
known what you have all done to me."

"Mrs. Hobhouse, you must not say these things. You will only
hurt yourself."

"No," she said, her mighty chest heaving, her breath as laboured as my uncle's had been in the hour before he died. "I
shall hurt *you*. And don't imagine you can get your tame lawyer
Agbrigg to buy my silence for I will not be silent. I know what I
know, Faith Aycliffe, about your aunts and your sisters and your
cousins, and your precious mother, who is no better than she
should be, and never has been. I know what I know, and I shall
say it."

And so she did, at every tea table to which she was invited—
and who could fail to invite her now?—and at her own tea table

at which every lady who kept her own carriage, whose husband was well placed enough to have an interest in such matters, eagerly attended, offering the stricken Mrs. Hobhouse the utmost in sympathy and understanding, patting her hand quite tearfully as they made their escape to my mother's equally busy drawing room in Blenheim Lane, or to the court Aunt Hannah had long established at Lawcroft Fold.

"I will silence her," Aunt Hannah said grimly. "I will sue her."

But Jonas, maintaining his habitual cool distance, would consider no legal action. The woman was hysterical. Women, in his experience, often were. Certainly he was well acquainted with Mrs. Delaney since, for several years, he had taken care of her investments, and had negotiated the purchase of her house in Albion Terrace. Certainly he had known of the marriage since he had attended it, and of the will, since he had drawn it up, but no sane person could have expected him to divulge such information to anyone. To do so would have been a serious breach of professional conduct, of which he had never—neither in this case nor in any other—been guilty. In view of her obvious afflictions one should extend to Mrs. Hobhouse the leniency due to all those of an unbalanced mind.

But, as my mother had foreseen, the effect on my sister Celia's already ailing nerves was of a very different order. Mrs. Hobhouse, even at the height of her dementia, had not quite dared tackle Georgiana, but Mrs. Jonas Agbrigg—little Celia Aycliffe—had seemed a natural and easy target. She had spent twenty raging minutes in Albert Place, reducing Celia to such a state of palpitating, choking hysteria that even Mrs. Hobhouse had been terrified by it and had rushed away, leaving her shawl and gloves behind. They had put Celia to bed, heavily dosed with laudanum. Jonas, at last compelled to action, had written a cold letter to Mr. Hobhouse, warning him of the consequences should he permit his wife to molest Celia again. Aunt Hannah, without Jonas' knowledge, had gone to Nethercoats herself to return the shawl and gloves, but had been denied an interview with Mrs. Hobhouse, who had also taken to her bed.

"You may tell her I shall call again," she informed the interested parlourmaid, who, uncertain as to her next month's wages, could be relied on to let Mrs. Hobhouse know how angry, and how very determined, Mrs. Ira Agbrigg had seemed.

But Celia, who had been unwilling to venture out a great deal before, would no longer go out at all, maintaining herself behind drawn curtains in a state of siege that reminded me strongly of my own behaviour after Giles died. I too had sat like this in the half dark doing nothing, staring at empty shadows on a black wall, but whereas I had been angry, Celia was deeply, most distressingly afraid, displaying as much alarm at the sound of her own doorbell as if she believed an avenging army had made its camp outside her door.

And indeed, in a way, she did, for was not the whole of Cullingford talking about her, would they not whisper about her behind her back the moment she showed her face? Well then, she would not show it. She would stay in her own home, lock her door, keep her curtains tight closed, and unless they chose to stand and scream abuse at her through the window, or climb on her rooftop and hurl it down her chimney, then she was safe.

But was she? What of the servants? What of that parlourmaid with the shifty eyes, and cook, who had never liked her? What were they saying about her in the kitchen? Oh yes, she knew, muttering that her husband had taken money from Nicholas Barforth to persuade Mr. Oldroyd to change his will, that he had taken money from Mr. Oldroyd himself, suggesting that there was even something between Jonas and Mrs. Delaney—oh yes, she knew—making up these vile stories because Jonas had attended Mrs. Delaney at her home once or twice with documents to sign. And because cook knew, and the maids knew, that she and Jonas were obliged now—because of Celia's health— to sleep apart. Yes, they had assumed the worst, believed the worst, and were spreading it, whispering it at the garden gate to the maids next door.

And what of Grace, who was at school now with the two younger Hobhouse girls? What was she being made to suffer, what were they saying to her about her mother? Grace had better stay at home and be safe too.

"No," Jonas said. "No—darling." And although it was the first time I had ever heard him use such an endearment to Celia, it produced nothing but a storm of tears. Had he no consideration for his own child? Did he want them to poison her mind against her own parents? After all, he had exposed them both to this and Grace was delicate too. Yet, oddly enough, in spite of

Grace's still dainty appearance, the wistfulness of her pointed face and her huge, dark eyes, she had a surprising resilience, a tendency to spread her wings in fresh air and sunshine that I recognised from my own too-sheltered childhood, and I was glad of Jonas' insistence that she continue her lessons with Prudence.

"Then she will have to come to you, Faith, after her class and wait until Jonas can fetch her," Celia told me. "For if it is seen that I can afford to send the carriage for her every day, they will think Jonas keeps his own and will wonder where the money is coming from. Except that they will not wonder—they will say it is from Nicholas Barforth, or Mrs. Delaney."

Mrs. Hobhouse's venom, it seemed, had no power to make itself felt at Tarn Edge, where Georgiana and Aunt Verity, and Nicholas, continued to live their separate lives, Nicholas calmly continuing his negotiations for the purchase of Nethercoats, his offer considerably reduced, it was believed, now that the Hobhouse resources were at an end. And shortly before Christmas it became his property, to be used for the weaving of silks and velvets, the existing orders for worsteds to be transferred to Lawcroft.

The Hobhouses departed with a sufficient income, one hoped, to support their younger children in a small house in Bridlington, leaving the older boys to fend for themselves, and since there is always a tendency in a commercial town to forgive a rich and powerful man, it was considered generous of Nicholas to employ Freddy and James at Lawcroft, even finding a niche of sorts for Adolphus at Low Cross. But I was frankly astonished to be told by Liam Adair, who still called regularly to show me his black eyes and to boast of his prowess with a shotgun, that my mother's beloved Daniel had also taken service with Nicholas.

"Oh no—no surprise at all," Blaize murmured, looking amused no matter what his exact feelings may have been. "He needs someone to sell his silks and velvets, after all, and since he can hardly do it himself and I'm not likely to do it for him, Daniel Adair is just the man. Not exactly my calibre, need it be said, but he'll do well enough, and Nicky is only following my father's advice. He's preparing for the day when he can buy me out, or throw me out—if it ever comes—and from Dan Adair's point of view, it's no more than common sense. Your mother won't live forever, and if she goes before him, the Aycliffe money comes to you and Prudence and Celia, not to him. He needs something to fall back on. Well, good old Nick, he's got the Wool Combers, and the dyeworks, and Nethercoats to call his own. If he goes on working his eighteen hours a day he'll be able to pay my price before too long."

"Will you sell?"

"I wonder," he said. "Let's keep him wondering too."

And I knew his light, cynical eyes were saying to me, "Yes, darling, just wonder, for what you don't know you can't tell."

Chapter Twenty-nine

FREDDY HOBHOUSE had been too occupied by his family's tragedy—in consoling his mother, moving her to Bridlington, finding places for his brothers, settling his own 10,000 pounds on his four sisters so that they could get themselves decently married, by the collapse of his father into total, often drunken helplessness—to have time to consider his personal affairs. But once the sale of Nethercoats was completed, his parents safely installed in their new home—waiting, as Mrs. Hobhouse put it, to die—he came to see my sister and released her from their engagement. He had nothing now to offer her. He was a shed manager in the employment of her cousin, and no one in Cullingford would expect a Miss Aycliffe to descend to so lowly a station. Cullingford, in fact, was now entirely on her side and would think her a fool if she did. But, knowing her contrary nature, her sneaking fondness for Freddy himself, I was less certain.

She walked the half mile from her house to mine immediately after the interview, her eyes red, she told me at once, because of the cold east wind.

"Well," she said, sitting down very straight-backed, sniffing slightly as if the wind had affected her nostrils too. "I have been properly punished for my independence of mind. I have asked a man to marry me and have been refused. I am probably the only female of our acquaintance to whom such a thing has happened, and it is not at all pleasant, I can assure you."

"You asked Freddy to marry you?"

"I did. I could see nothing against it. That octopus of a Nethercoats is gone now. We are in no danger of being strangled by it. I am doing extremely well, especially now that my financial arrangement is with Aunt Verity, rather than Uncle Joel, and although she accepts my repayments she usually manages to find a way of giving me the money back again. With what I earn, and with what Freddy can earn, we would be well above the level of starvation. I have a good house—a very good house—and marriage would release my dowry and all my lovely porcelain, which would enable me to pay off my debt to Aunt Verity, and to extend my premises."

"And Freddy . . . ?"

"He wouldn't have me. He is being manly, you see, and gentlemanly too. He would really have liked to put his head on my shoulder and have a good cry, I could tell. And I wouldn't have minded a bit. But no—it's not manly to cry, so he just rode off to those terrible lodgings in Gower Street he thinks I don't know about. And I expect he'll send just about every penny he earns to his mother. His shirt was not quite clean either, and I can't tell you how much that distressed me. He's never had to think about getting his laundry done before."

"You had better stop feeling sorry for him, Pru. You may begin to enjoy it, and then we shall see you doing his laundry yourself."

"And why not?" she declared, her back straightening even further. "If I decide to ask my laundry maid to put his linen in my tub, which stands in my scullery, in my house, I know of no one who could prevent me."

But we both knew that Freddy himself would prevent her, and I, at least, assumed there was no more to be said.

With the departure of Mrs. Hobhouse, interest in Nethercoats began to wane, the most pressing problem that winter being whether or not one could acknowledge and eventually receive the second Mrs. Oldroyd, now established very cosily, one supposed, at Fieldhead. And on the whole, since it was assumed that the Oldroyd mill would now be offered for sale and the lady would soon remove herself and her ill-gotten, or hard-earned, gains elsewhere, it seemed hardly worth the trouble.

I saw her, very occasionally, driving out in her silk-upholstered landau, once in the parish churchyard when I made my weekly pilgrimage to Giles' grave, and she, presumably, was performing the same office for Mr. Oldroyd, a tall woman with the kind of timeless profile I had seen among Italian peasants walking like barefoot queens to the grape harvest, erect and commanding, yet, like all women who have lived in life's shadows, instinctively discreet, taking an opposite pathway so I would not be obliged to greet her.

But she had done me no harm and waiting until our paths crossed, as was inevitable in that small space, I said, "How do you do, Mrs. Oldroyd?"

"How do you do, Lady Barforth?" she replied, her voice a rich contralto, her self-possession absolute, no surprise in her, no gratitude, no satisfaction, at my willingness to acknowledge her, a faint suggestion that she had chosen, not rushed, to acknowledge me.

Yet, during those early months of her widowhood—presumably her first since no one believed there had ever been a *Mr.* Delaney—she made no attempt to thrust herself upon our sensibilities, making no changes at Fieldhead and restricting her hospitality to the few who had been accustomed to her famous teas in Albion Terrace.

"A clever woman," Blaize said. "If Freddy Hobhouse had the sense to make himself pleasant in her direction he might end as master of Fieldhead after all. She can't be much on the wrong side of forty, and it strikes me she's in no hurry to pack her bags and leave. She has the money, Freddy could give her the respectability, which is about the only thing it can't buy. And I understand that when someone, who may have been Nicholas Barforth, enquired the asking price for Fieldhead, not even Jonas Agbrigg could explain the lady's intentions. Unless, of course, he knew and wasn't telling, which one could bring oneself to believe of Jonas. Why don't you ask your sister?"

But Celia, at the very mention of the new Mrs. Oldroyd, was apt to stiffen, like an animal at bay, to lower her voice and glance swiftly around her, so terrified of being overheard that it was an effort to catch her muttered opinions at all. Mr. Oldroyd, quite naturally, had seen the necessity of appointing someone to look after his widow's concerns, to see to his investments, to keep the business going until it could be sold, and then to wind the estate up profitably, in exactly the same way as my father had appointed Uncle Joel. In the Oldroyd case, since the lady had no relations, or none she cared to speak of, the obvious person had been Jonas, a choice which would have caused no comment at all had he not been named, by Mrs. Hobhouse, as an arch conspirator. And I was totally unable to convince my sister that the gossip had abated, that every visit Jonas made to Fieldhead—since no one expected a lady to attend her lawyer in his chambers—was not noted down and conveyed to Mrs. Hobhouse by some evil-wisher, that Celia's household expenditure was not checked by servants and shopkeepers and tradesmen for the telltale increase that would proclaim Mrs. Hobhouse to have been right.

She would not, that winter, purchase so much as a new bonnet for Grace and was thrown into a state of intense anxiety when, among my several Christmas presents, I gave the child a fur-lined, velvet cloak.

"Heavens, Faith, must you be so extravagant? I can't let her wear a garment like that. Everybody would want to know where it came from—how I could possibly afford it."

"Tell them Blaize brought it back from Russia, since Blanche has one just like it."

"But I can't tell anybody anything, don't you see. They won't ask *me*. They'll just tittle-tattle and make up their minds it came from Fieldhead. And if they get the idea that Mrs. Delaney is giving presents to Grace, they'll all think they know the reason why."

"Really, Celia—such a fuss."

"Oh, it's easy for you—you just sail through your life. Nobody has ever accused your husband of malpractice, nobody is going to ask you to receive that woman . . ."

"Celia, surely Jonas has not asked you to invite Mrs. Oldroyd?"

"No," she said, her hands clutching at one another, holding on to one another as if every part of her body was independently afraid. "He has not. Not yet. But he will. She wants to stay in Cullingford, I know she does. The mill is not sold, is it? The house is not sold, certainly, and is not going to be sold, for she has ordered new curtains. I know because Jonas' clerk came here with some documents the other day and said something about Fieldhead looking more comfortable, as if he imagined that I *knew* what Fieldhead looked like—that I had actually been there . . . which is what they must all be saying. And when I asked Jonas he just said, 'Good Lord—new curtains, no more—' which I think is quite sufficient. And if she is to stay then she intends to be received, and someone must be the first to do it. I lay awake all night thinking about it, for if he forces me to have her then who am I to ask to dine with her? How am I to manage it? In fact I cannot manage it, and I told him so. He doesn't realise the implications. If we are seen to be living in that woman's pocket then it won't be long before somebody starts saying he forged that will."

"Celia—Celia—nobody could think that. Not even Mrs. Hobhouse could think that."

And stiffening again, glancing furtively around, she muttered, "Oh yes, they could. You just don't know how wicked people are, Faith—how very wicked. And that woman—Mrs. Hobhouse—sitting there in Bridlington, waiting—like a spider—just waiting. And that other woman at Fieldhead, who doesn't care—who'll just swallow us up to get her way . . . They could say anything."

Yet, although her misery touched me very deeply, my own life had its claims. I could, more often than not, think of many things I would rather do than sit in the dark with my sister, an opinion shared by the majority of our acquaintance, so that she was left increasingly alone.

"She saddens me," my mother sighed, her own life, now that her Daniel had found something interesting and profitable to do, being sunnier and easier than ever.

"She makes me feel inclined to give her a good shaking," Aunt Hannah declared, her fingers clearly itching to make a start. "I am sorry to say this to you, Elinor, but she should not have put my son in this difficult position. He will be mayor of this town, ere long—would, indeed, have accepted office already had he not been so overburdened at home—and a lady mayoress cannot sit in her parlour and hide, you know. I shall allow her until after Christmas and then, if she has not righted herself, I shall tell her so."

We spent Christmas once again at Listonby, returning to find an official letter from Nicholas informing Blaize that, in view of the difficulties they experienced in working together it would seem advisable that their partnership be dissolved. He was prepared to purchase Blaize's half of the business at a stated figure, a sizeable down payment and the balance to be taken as a percentage of his profits over a number of years, an arrangement which would provide Blaize with an easy living.

"My word, he's richer than I thought," Blaize said, and leaving the communication unanswered, calmly proceeded to make plans for a second Russian visit in the spring, which the profitability of the first, and the war clouds menacing the unity of the northern and southern states of America, amply justified.

"You must answer him, Blaize."

"Yes, I imagine he must think so too."

And sitting down at my writing desk he penned a casual note of thanks for the letter which, he declared, he had safely received.

"You could leave this at Tarn Edge, Faith, some time when you happen to be passing. Just put it with the calling cards on the hall table. He'll find it."

Nicholas called at Elderleigh for the first time a few days later, his height and breadth filling the doorway as he came into the drawing room, an invader in my house, too big and abrupt for the dainty, cabriole-legged chairs on which he declined, in any case, to sit, preferring to plant himself on the hearthrug as his father used to do, his anger well under control but too fierce, just the same, for the pale silk on my walls, the muted atmosphere of my life.

"You could give your husband this," he said, handing me a long, brown envelope. "I imagine you know what it contains. It's a good offer. He won't get a better, and he may not get another. Tell him that."

"Shouldn't you tell him yourself, Nicholas?"

"No. I can't talk to him, and he won't talk to me. Until now I've used my mother as a go-between, but it's not fair to her—the poor woman happens to be fond of us both—and I reckon we've caused her enough distress. You'll have to serve instead."

"I see. Are there any other messages you'd like me to deliver?"

"Not at the moment. Does he discuss his affairs with you?"

"Is that any of your business?"

And it surprised me how much easier it was to meet him at this level of cool hostility, to speak only to that granite shell, forgetting the man it had once contained.

"Very likely not. But if he should ask your opinion, then think carefully about your own position before you advise him. There are two ways of doing this. He can sell out, or we can split the business. Lawcroft and Low Cross together have about the same asset value and profitability as Tarn Edge. I can take one and he can take the other. I might be persuaded to it. But he'd have a mill to run then, wouldn't he? All of it, not just the bits and pieces he fancies, and if he ran it into the ground you might just find yourself living in Bridlington next door to the Hobhouses. He doesn't like work, Faith. He never did. You could be Sir Blaize and Lady Barforth very comfortably—in London for instance—on what I'm offering."

"Oh—so we're to be banished to London, are we?"

"Not necessarily. There are other places. If you persuade him to sell and move away from here, I can only feel it would be to your advantage."

I picked up a small object from the table in front of me, a paperweight, a fan, a posy of porcelain flowers—I was never certain, afterwards—replaced it, moved it an inch or two on the polished surface, and then, looking up at him, smiled.

"Heavens—we are talking of *my* advantage, are we? I do beg your pardon, Nicholas, for I have been very dull-witted. I thought it was your advantage we were discussing."

"Indeed," he said, biting off the word at its final letter, his jaw muscles clenched tight. "So we are. I wouldn't be here at all unless I had something to gain, for I am not much given to social calls these days. However, in this case, the advantage could be mutual."

And once again, speaking only to that hard shell, I looked him full in the face, and smiled.

"Are you playing the squire with me, Nicholas—ordering me off your land? Will you set your dogs on me if I disobey?"

There was a brief silence, the familiar tightening in the air.

"You seem intent on quarrelling with me, Faith. I really wouldn't advise it."

"No—but then, I'm not sure that I consider your advice to be very sound, Nicholas. I can't know what your financial resources are but I imagine this offer must stretch them quite considerably —if it is accepted."

"My word," he said. "Lady Barforth has a commercial mind after all. Yes, I would be somewhat overspent, which you may take as a measure of my determination. I have had enough of carrying passengers. Blaize is a passenger. The more I think of it the more it strikes me that London would be the ideal destination for him."

The afternoon was drawing in, winter shadows filling the garden, entering the room to stand thickly around us, a bird somewhere, far away, winging homeward across the thin, grey air of this sad season, a great void inside me, a sense, suddenly, of futility, for what would it all matter next year, or tomorrow, a deep regret that so much inside me had been wasted.

"Would you like some tea, Nicholas?"

"Of course not."

"No. Then will you tell me why you cannot work with Blaize? He's not a passenger, and you know it. Your father told you not to undervalue him and I don't believe you do, since you've been careful to get Daniel Adair to take his place. I thought for a while it was because of me. But it's not that, is it?"

And turning my face towards the window, the expanse of dead garden, the grey, nervous wind, I closed my eyes to await the answer I knew would come.

"No, Faith. It has little or nothing to do with you."

"Well—?"

He crossed the room and stood beside me at the window, looking out for a moment in silence at the dark trees, sketched in February charcoal in the distance, the wind rising now, scattering the remaining corpses of last year's leaves across the sleeping lawn, tossing against the windowpane a peevish handful of rain.

"I don't deal in personalities," he said quietly. "I told you that once before. I gave up personalities—people—a fair while ago. A sensible man stops playing the games he can't seem to win, and goes in for something more suited to his nature. I want the Barforth mills, Faith, simply because I want them. I shall most probably do anything to get them. Blaize is just a hurdle in the course I've set myself, an extra dash of spice to the challenge if you like, no more than that. And when I can call Tarn Edge and Low Cross and Lawcroft mine I know damned well I won't be satisfied. It won't be long before I'll find something else—need something else—to go after, another hurdle to cross, and when I cross it, all that is likely to matter to me is the next. Some men feel like that about women. Blaize feels like that about women, as you must know. Frankly, I prefer my satisfactions to his. Take him to London, Faith, and go on looking pretty for him as long as you can. If he stays here and tries to force my agreement to a split, then something may happen to sour his temper, which would make your life no easier."

"My life is not difficult, Nicholas."

"Of course it isn't. And I'm sure we're all anxious that it should continue to be just as pleasant. Give him my letter. Try to convince him that his marriage to you is no thorn in my side. You could even let him know that his support of my own wife against me is something I can tolerate without much trouble. He's always been meddlesome, and I'm quite accustomed to it. Georgiana can always visit him in London when she feels the need of his advice, or when she's run through her allowance by the second of the month and doesn't feel she can tell me. She may find it marginally less convenient than running to his office at Tarn Edge, but I'm not disposed to worry about that. You should take care, Faith, for knowing his whimsical turn of mind he must find her dependence on his judgement—and on his generosity—very appealing."

I walked away from him, moving very slowly through the darkened room to the table where I had put down his letter and, picking it up, I passed it from one hand to the other, studying it carefully, no anger in me at all, nothing but a deep, calm sadness.

"May I go through the points you have raised with me, Nicholas?"

"By all means."

"Yes—first of all, then, you are telling me that Blaize is incapable of running a business and that unless I prevent him from making the attempt I could find myself destitute?"

"I reckon there's a fair chance of it."

"Yes. That is what I thought you meant. And then, in case that should not frighten me enough, you dropped a little hint about Blaize's past reputation with women—a slight suggestion that it may not really be past at all."

"Did I really go so far as to suggest that?"

"Oh yes—indeed you did. Is it against the law, Nicholas, to destroy a letter addressed to another person?"

"I believe it may be."

"Ah well—I cannot imagine you will see any profit in bringing me to justice." And holding the letter with the tips of my fingers I dropped it quite daintily into the fire and stood very still, blocking the hearth with my wide skirts until it shrivelled at its edges, spurted with a brief flame, blackened to a heap of ash and then to nothingness.

Behind me Nicholas made no movement, no sound, and when the small murder was done I turned, still calm enough, to meet his eyes.

"You have declared war on me, have you, Faith?"

"Oh no. Whatever was in your letter you may write again. If you send it here I will make sure Blaize receives it. He is no more likely to ask my opinion than you would ask Georgiana's, but if he should ask then I will answer in the best way I can. I don't really know how I would advise him. I haven't decided yet. But when I do, it will be for my reasons, Nicholas, not for yours."

He walked towards me, his face, with the light behind him, almost invisible so that he was very close to me before I could see the familiar tight-clenching of his jaw, which seemed, for just a moment, to be painful rather than angry, the fine lines around his eyes, the deeper ones from nose to chin etched by a weight not of temper but of disillusion that made him a harder, older, wearier man than he should have been.

"So be it," he said very low. "I'll have it on his desk when he gets back from London."

"Oh—he's going to London, is he?"

"Yes, on the evening train."

And, incredibly, he smiled at me.

There was a storm later that day, a cloudburst, it seemed, directly overhead, releasing a slashing torrent of rain that soaked my hapless laundrymaid to the skin in the two or three minutes it took her to empty her washing line. And within half an hour the garden was waterlogged, each pathway a separate rivulet rushing to its mainstream, which was the Cullingford road. I went to bed early, cold, besieged by the weather, threatened all night by the growling of thunder, the spikes of lightning on the other side of my curtains, waking to an awareness of rain still falling, an uneasy sky.

And I was instantly embroiled in the kind of domestic drama which, that day, was not unwelcome. The fires would not light, the stove would do nothing but lower and sulk. Blanche, who had slept soundly all night oblivious of the tempest, was demanding her breakfast and there was no breakfast to be had. There was no hot water, no milk had been delivered, and when a stable lad was finally despatched to the farm to enquire, his returning tale was one of pure disaster. The countryside had been reduced overnight to a bog, Cullingford itself was drowning, it was useless, the farmer's wife had said, to milk her cows when the end of the world was clearly nigh. Far better, it seemed, to spend the time remaining in prayer and so, while the lightning continued to flash across the sky and the rain to fall, they abandoned, in my kitchen, all attempts to boil water and draw fires, and went down on their knees, remembering that the wise woman of Knaresborough, Mother Shipton, had long ago predicted this.

"Nonsense," I told them, not altogether certain of it myself. "She said the world was destroyed by water last time—which everybody knows—and that it would end by fire this time. I don't see any fire. I only wish I did."

But the moaning and the sobbing, the "Our Fathers" from my Protestant cook and the "Hail Marys" from my two Irish housemaids continued, and in the end, abandoning my crinoline for an old woollen gown and a few petticoats, I managed the drawing room fire myself, having seen it done often enough in happier conditions, and huddled over it, reading stories to an indignant Blanche, until Prudence came.

Not one of her day girls had arrived at school that morning. Her boarders were in varying states of disarray. Her competent teacher of mathematics had locked herself in the broom cupboard and, in view of the panic she had been spreading, could remain there indefinitely so far as Prudence was concerned, telling her beads and muttering of sins which, in other circumstances, would have been most entertaining. Prudence herself had come only to check on my safety, at some risk to her own, and, with a houseful of girls in her charge, could not stay. And I suppose we were both aware that every stream in the hills with which Cullingford was surrounded must by now have transformed itself into a fast-flowing cascade, pouring into the city streets, that by now, in the low-lying districts, every cellar, every warehouse, would be awash, that the level of the canal, encircling one half of the town with its murky waters, would be insidiously rising.

I put on the Cossack boots Blaize had brought me from Moscow and walked with Prudence to the end of the garden, determined that my courage should match hers, and returned, soaked and soiled and exceedingly apprehensive, to find a drowned apparition on my doorstep that was Liam Adair.

"Well, I am your brother," he said cheerfully, amazed at my concern since I should have had the good sense to know that no lightning in the world could ever have the nerve to strike him, no thunderbolt could be strong enough to block his way. "I thought I'd best come and rescue you since Blaize is snug and warm in London."

And even the fact that I had managed, so far, to rescue myself, occasioned him no dismay. He had been up before dawn, except that really there had been no dawn, and had had a fine time. Sheer panic, he told me, and what fun it had been to watch people splashing ankle-deep, knee-deep, in flood water, cursing and struggling and yelling about their carpets and their cats and their grandmothers, what fun to see packets of raw wool come floating out of the Mandelbaum warehouse, the milliner, at the bottom of the river that was Sheepgate, baling out her shop like a boat, water, hat moulds, feathers, and all. He had rescued a litter of puppies from a cellar and almost been drowned for his pains. He had tried to right a brewer's cart in Market Square and had held any number of screaming horses. He had gone down to Low Cross Mill, the only low-lying Barforth property, where his father and Nicholas were salvaging what they could from the sheds, and then, growing bored, had fought his way through falling tree branches, a tidal wave of nameless dangers, to Elderleigh.

"Your mother said I was to go to Celia, but I thought I'd rather come to you. Celia's got Jonas, after all."

But had she? Jonas, I knew, had gone to Manchester some days ago and I had not heard of his return, nor could I ignore the fact that Albert Place was not on high ground, was, indeed, constructed in a marshy hollow where water could collect. And there was not only Celia, there was Grace.

My coachman refused, rudely, explicitly, to get out the horses. He valued his job but had no mind to commit suicide for it, since there was no man alive who could control horses in this weather. And even when the lightning had abated, leaving only the perils of rutted tracks turned into bog and slime, branches and boulders and the incessant rain, he continued adamantly to disobey.

"Do you think we can get there on foot, Liam?"

"Well, I can. I don't know about you."

But we set off together, my skirts a sodden encumbrance, my cloak so heavy that quite soon it served no purpose but to delay me and I took it off, finding a strange exhilaration in this exposure to the tormented sky, the slashing yet somehow cleansing attack of the rain. I had never been outdoors without a bonnet before but now, striding bareheaded towards real issues, towards real danger, a lifetime of convention was discarded as easily as my cloak, tossed aside into the nearest puddle, leaving me clear-sighted and resolute.

Yet Celia, if we succeeded in reaching Albert Place, would not be so resolute. And although I had never felt stronger in my life I knew I was driven mainly by determination, that my pampered body would not enable me to get back to Elderleigh with Grace in my arms. Nor could I put my sister and her child in a cart and pull them to safety as others were doing, women frailer in build then I, who, having laboured at the loom, were using that strength now, that gritty endurance, to make their escape.

A moment came when my chest seemed torn apart, my breath deserted me, whipped out of my body by the wind, and for an instant of sheer panic, I knew my ability to breathe again was shattered. I was choking in cold air and rain water, dying in some alien place since nothing in these terrible streets was familiar to me, and had it not been for Georgiana I would have had no choice but to turn and struggle home again.

No man, my coachman had said, could control horses in this weather, but he had reckoned without a woman, for suddenly there she was, driving the Barforth landau, her drenched hair hanging like seaweed about her shoulders, her familiar green riding habit black with rain, a trio of children clutched together on the silk cushions, three more like a tangle of kittens on the carriage floor.

"Georgiana," Liam called out, his face blazing with excitement and with pride. "Good old Georgie. I knew you'd do it." And, setting her passengers down, dispersing them with instructions to run to the nearest house, she leaned her whole body against the wind and laughed down at him, her face beautiful as always with animation.

"My God, there's no lack of water in Simon Street today. I've made a dozen trips already and on the last one a woman almost gave birth right behind me. Come on, Faith, if you'd care to risk it, for these brutes are likely to bolt at any moment. They'll do one more journey, I think, before they're finished."

"But you're not finished," Liam said, scrambling up beside her.

"Oh no," she told him, one rope of her seaweed hair blowing across her face, her hard, narrow hands firmly managing the reins. "Come on, Faith, they're rescuing wool down at Low Cross, which is all very fine, but I come from Galton and I reckon we're more inclined to rescue the sheep before the shorn fleece. Celia? Lord yes, we'll do something about her, and then let's have an adventure, shall we, or break our necks—either way it leaves them with something original to put on our tombstones."

We took Celia and Grace back to Elderleigh—Celia cowering and silent in the landau, her eyes tight shut—deposited them with Prudence and then, Georgiana having exchanged her spent animals for mine, we set off again for the dips and hollows of Cullingford, where people well accustomed to living without water were now dying of its surfeit. Georgiana, at considerable peril to herself, somehow controlled Blaize's fractious horses, while I waded into the mean, porous dwellings my father had constructed—where Giles Ashburn had met the seeds of his death—and brought out those who were too young or too old to walk away. And when we were threatened by men and boys and strong, desperate women who saw no reason to walk when they could ride, Georgiana used her driving whip as the best argument.

My arms may have ached, and my back. I was not aware of it. Nor would Georgiana permit me to be aware of it.

"Come on, Faith, we've got room for that little ragamuffin over there—we'd best have a look at the next street—Faith, that poor woman looks likely to jump out of her bedroom window if you don't restrain her. Come on, Faith—*noblesse oblige*, you know. I might not be good at paying my debts, but I do understand that I have to pay for my privileges."

And so I half-struggled, half-swam through heaps of liquid foulness, up rickety staircases and down again, a child on my back, another straddling my hip, and then, with an unlikely assortment of humanity crammed all around me, closed my eyes as Georgiana flourished her driving whip and somehow forced those quivering beasts to move sensibly forward to the upper reaches of Blenheim Lane and Horton End where Cullingford's more public-spirited ladies had opened their doors, their blanket boxes, and their soup tureens.

"Come on, Faith. One more journey. When you reach the point where you know you can't endure it really means you can endure just a little longer—that's what Grandfather says."

But the very moment she judged the horses were approaching their limits she shook her head, shrugged her narrow shoulders. "That's it then. They're not people. One can't ask them to make sacrifices," and drove carefully home.

And I was at once too exhausted and too exhilarated, too indescribably filthy, too much aglow with kinship for Georgiana, to have any time to spare for Celia.

Chapter Thirty

THE SKY CLEARED, the waters receded, exposing an atrocious litter of splintered wood and broken glass, dead dogs and cats and rats, the dray horses which had fallen and been shot where they lay, the old man who sold matches and drank gin at the bottom of Sheepgate, a young man who had been struck on the head, it was thought, by a falling beam and had drowned in an inch or two of rain.

Damage to property had been immense. The old warehouses on the canal bank behind Market Square had sagged, in some cases, like damp paper, while even the more substantial property of the Mandelbaums, in the same area, although it had kept its roof intact, had received its share of flood and cess water in the cellar, occasioning a total loss of the bales stored.

Everybody, in fact, lost something. Not a few lost all they had and overnight the workhouse and the infirmary were bursting at their seams, every available church hall overflowing with the homeless. Aunt Hannah occupied herself completely with the collection and distribution of food and clothing and medical supplies, her husband devoted himself with equal efficiency to the question of where these unfortunates were eventually to be housed when the churches reclaimed their halls for parochial purposes. Jonas, in pursuit of his civic ambitions, assisted him. Prudence and myself and even my mother had similar work to do. We were busy. Too busy even to glance at Celia.

Her house had not suffered irreparable harm. A half inch of water had entered her front door, ruining her carpet and making a certain amount of redecorating advisable, but her furniture, her china, her personal bits and pieces had escaped damage, her upper floors were altogether unblemished, neither she nor Grace nor any member of her household had been hurt or even taken cold. And in the midst of such appalling destruction, she found no one, including myself, with the patience to understand why she was so reluctant to return to Albert Place, remaining at Elderleigh long after the new paint was dry at her home, the walls repapered, a cheerful, busily patterned carpet laid in place, insisting that beneath it, the floorboards still retained the foul, floodwater smell, while in her cellar strange things, brought in by the deluge, still lingered.

The cellar was swept clean, limewashed, swept clean again. She would not venture inside it. She could smell something, she insisted. Jonas, for all his thoroughness, had missed something.

"Will you keep her another week or two?" he asked me, and the cellar was limewashed once more to no avail.

"It smells," she said flatly. "And this carpet is the colour of slime. I cannot think what possessed you to choose it, Jonas."

"Largely because you would make no choice yourself, Celia. I will have it taken up and replaced."

"Yes—yes—do that. Two new carpets in two months, so that everyone will wonder where the money is coming from—except that they will not wonder, they will imagine they know."

"Celia," he said sharply, "this is all nonsense. You have a home and a child, and you cannot trespass on Faith's hospitality forever."

"Oh there is no trespass, Jonas." I told him, "She may stay as long as she pleases."

"Naturally she inconveniences you," he said as I walked with him to his carriage. "Naturally—but if you could keep her awhile longer—well—quite frankly I cannot feel I am the best person to be with her when she is in this humour. I believe I once told you that my mother suffered from an affliction of the nerves. Poor woman. I could understand her sufferings, I could even suffer for her—but I couldn't cope with it. I feel that I am coping badly now. I try to be patient—in fact I am patient—but she senses the effort it costs me and I believe it adds to her strain. You have an easier nature, Faith, which might be of more help to her."

"Don't worry about it Jonas. She's my sister, after all. She may stay as long as she pleases."

But, although Blaize was unfailingly polite, her continued presence could only be irksome to him, her stilted dinnertime conversations depriving us both of the opportunity for any real discussion at a time when it was badly needed, and although he never asked me to hurry her departure, I felt that he expected me to do it, knew that he had intentionally delayed his return from a recent trip to London in the hope of finding me alone. And so I was inclined to agree with Aunt Hannah when, walking unannounced into my breakfast parlour one morning, she declared, "Now look here, Celia, this simply will not do. You have had a shock but so has everyone, and if you remain here much longer people will begin to ask the reason why. And no one is likely to believe it is because of an imaginary odour in your cellar. They will say you have quarrelled with your husband because of Fieldhead, my dear, and will rake up all this nonsense about a conspiracy to defraud the Hobhouses. It amazes me that you, who are so afraid of gossip, cannot see that."

"There *is* an odour in my cellar, Aunt Hannah."

March became April, Celia remaining like a little mouse in my chimney corner, asking nothing, in this world of large tabby cats, but to be left alone, and eventually it was Blaize himself who dislodged her by the simple announcement that he was taking me to Paris.

"I expect you will want me to go away then, Faith?"

"Darling—you can hardly stay here alone. How could you do that?"

"No," she said, "I couldn't." And getting up she left the room, walking like a young girl in disgrace who, fearful of adult anger, has been sent to bed.

I accompanied her the next day to Albert Place where Jonas, deserting his clients and his commitments, was waiting. The house, very obviously, had been spring-cleaned, an odour not of slime nor of any other foulness, but of beeswax greeting us as we went inside. A large bowl of daffodils stood on the hall table, late hyacinths perfuming the drawing room, the tea table covered in immaculate white damask, freshly baked scones and gingerbread daintily arranged on white, gold-rimmed china. The brass fender gleamed, the ornaments on the mantel shelf were arranged so perfectly that even my father could not have faulted them, a matching pair of flowery Coalport vases, the ormolu clock with its fat cupids spaced precisely between them, a tapestry fire screen at each corner of the hearth, her favourite chair and footstool ready to receive her, her embroidery frame to hand.

"How beautiful," I said.

"Yes," she replied.

"Are you quite comfortable?" Jonas asked.

"Yes," was her answer.

And when we had taken tea together I, with packing to do, was obliged to hurry away; Jonas, with a business to attend to, could not linger; Prudence, who had taken temporary charge of Grace, would have no time to call; my mother would be too occupied with the culinary and amorous demands of her Daniel to look in for more than a moment; Aunt Hannah too concerned with the still unsolved plight of the town's homeless to worry overmuch about a woman who could sit all day in idleness by her own fireside, drinking her tea from fine china.

She remained, perhaps, for some hours quite cosily installed in her chair, stirred far enough to ring her bell and give orders for Jonas' dinner, lamb cutlets in onion sauce, curd tarts, and then, changing her mind, rang again to say that apple tarts would do better and that cook should remember to add an egg white to the accompanying whipped cream. She made some enquiries into the state of her linen cupboards, some slight complaints about the starching of Jonas' shirts and Grace's petticoats, appearing, to both her cook and her parlourmaid, a little tired, a little dazed, which was, in fact, very much as usual.

But when Jonas returned that evening, she was, quite simply, not there, had not been heard or seen to leave the house, to go upstairs, or even to move at all, but was not there. And it was only after Aunt Hannah and Mayor Agbrigg had been called and much frantic searching had taken place that a maid, sent to bring up more coal, drew their attention to the cellar door, jammed, it seemed, by its new coat of paint; and, levering it open, they found her huddled at the bottom of the stone steps, dead from the fall, or from fright.

I could in no way accept it. "There *is* an odour in my cellar," her voice whispered to me all through those first unspeakable nights, and she had gone down, candle in hand, not to investigate, I was sure of it, but because she had been compelled to it, drawn by the very things which so repelled her. And there, in the half-dark, she had finally encountered them, no slimy debris of the floodwaters, but her own fears and futilities lurking in the shadows. She had seen her own face, perhaps, on the freshly limewashed cellar wall and, running from it, finding herself shut in with her own sad image, a woman who could find nothing to replace the values of her childhood which had failed her, what had she done then? Surely, she had needed only to call out and someone would have heard her? Had she panicked, stumbled over the hem of her gown and fallen? It was possible. But a panic-stricken woman might have been expected to make some sound, to beat frantic hands on that unyielding, new-painted door, would not—perhaps—have placed her candle, still burning, on a shelf at the cellar head as Celia had done. A hysterical woman would not have been so neat, so thoughtful. What then? Had she turned at the cellar head, looked down into the perilous shadows, and thrown herself into them, choosing not to come out again? And all the time, while she had been staring at that blank wall, I had been filling my boxes with armfuls of lace, my windows wide open to the April day, planning what I would wear and what I would buy in Paris.

And together with Prudence, I could find no comfort, no escape from the stark knowledge that we had never taken her seriously.

I had not credited my mother with the strength to attend the funeral but she was there, hiding behind thick mourning veils supported by an honestly grieving Daniel Adair and by Aunt Verity, who, like my mother herself, looked old that day, and very weary. Caroline, puzzled but defiant, privately thinking Celia a madwoman but ready to challenge anyone else who dared say so, had brought Dominic and Noel and Hetty Stone, thus demonstrating to Cullingford that if the Chards and the South Erins believed the tale that Celia had accidentally stumbled then everyone else would be well advised to do the same. Freddy Hobhouse arrived late, having begged an hour's leave of absence from Nicholas, and stood with a self-conscious arm around Prudence, while, at the very last moment, as the coffin was being lowered into the eager spring ground I saw Nicholas himself on the fringe of the crowd and knew with what unease my sister would have viewed his presence.

"Go away, Nicholas Barforth," her memory pleaded, its eyes furtive, terrified. "If you show sympathy to my husband they will say it is because he helped you to get the Hobhouses out of Nethercoats and Mrs. Delaney into Fieldhead."

And perhaps Jonas, standing in chalk-white, painful rigidity at her graveside, heard her dead voice too, a thin whisper in his mind teasing him as she had never done in life with her dreadful riddle. "Did I fall by accident, Jonas—playing the good house- wife, checking the soundness of my cellar? Did I do that? Or was my life—our life together—so burdensome to me that I was glad to throw it down? Did you kill me? Or did my father, and your mother, and Mrs. Delaney, do it for you? Guess, Jonas. For- ever go on guessing."

We returned to Albert Place in silence and sat, equally silent, in that immaculate drawing room, my eyes checking the tea tray as Celia's would have done, for smeared silver, a less than per- fectly laundered napkin, my heart somehow swollen inside my chest, straining against the inner wall of my body as if it would burst. Joel Barforth's death had moved me, but he had been a man of another generation who had lived, not long enough, per- haps, but fully. Giles Ashburn's death had deeply grieved me, but he had seemed too admirable, too complete, to be compared with myself. But with Celia the comparison was all too dreadful and too easy. Celia—my younger sister—could have been my- self, a woman who had lost her life before she had started to live it, who had achieved no more than I, and beneath my shock and my sorrow I felt an appalling restlessness, the stirring of needs, of hopes I did not wish to recognise, a sense of time rushing away from me and myself reaching out for it, my body and spirit aching to fly forwards and upwards, my feet anchored firmly in muddy ground.

My mother and Daniel Adair drank their tea and went away.

"Dear Jonas," Aunt Verity said, her mind full of her own loss. "Will you really be all right, staying here—alone?"

"Perfectly, Aunt Verity, thank you."

And she went away too.

"You're welcome to come back with us, lad," Mayor Agbrigg

said gruffly. "Since we're keeping Grace a night or two we may as well all be together."

"No thank you, sir. I'm better in my own home."

And perhaps it surprised me that Aunt Hannah did not insist.

"I'm sorry Sir Blaize could not be with us," she said to me in passing, her voice dwelling, heavy with sarcasm, on his title.

"Yes. I'm sorry too." But I saw no reason to explain that Blaize, who had gone urgently to Leeds that morning, had promised to be back in time for the funeral, should have been back, and that his absence did not in the least surprise me.

Aunt Hannah and her husband took their leave, only Prudence and myself remaining in what seemed to be an empty house, Jonas so remote in spirit that, my mind sliding over the edge of reality, I had a brief, nightmare impression that he was not there at all, a shadow merely, standing with one foot on the fender, one hand on the mantel shelf, staring unblinkingly at the fire.

"We had better go now," Prudence said, but grief had taken her angrily and before I could intervene she muttered, "Yes— what is there to stay for? What else can we say about what must surely have been the most completely wasted life . . ."

"Thank you, Prudence," Jonas said without stirring.

"Please don't thank me. I'm not in the mood for social niceties."

"You're feeling guilty are you, Prudence?" he said, his head turning very slightly, his long, pale eyes opening and then closing again rapidly to shut the living man away.

"Yes. I'm feeling guilty. Aren't you?"

"Jonas . . . ?" I murmured enquiringly as Prudence went into the hall to get her bonnet, my hand moving forward instinctively to touch his shoulder and then, somehow, retreating.

"Yes?"

"I'm not sure. I know you're suffering. I don't ask your reasons. How can I help you?"

"Take your sister home."

"Jonas—she doesn't really blame you. If she blames anyone then it must be my father, I think, more than you—"

"Really? It was your father, then, was it, who loosened the hem of Celia's gown so that she caught her heel and tumbled down the steps? You amaze me."

And catching a fleeting glimpse of the anger, the horror, the pain of that cruel riddle inside him, I turned and fled.

I returned Prudence to her school, myself to my shrouded house, the windows deeply curtained in mourning, nothing to greet me but my butler's professional sympathy, the curiosity of my parlourmaid, who, believing tea to be a certain cure for all ills, brought me a full pot accompanied by the even surer comforts of hot scones and gingerbread.

"You'll feel better with that inside you, madam."

"Yes, I expect so."

And I made no enquiries as to the possible whereabouts of Sir Blaize.

He arrived an hour later, bringing an impression of cool air and spring rain with him, ruefully smiling an apology he did not expect to be denied.

"Darling—you'll have to forgive me . . ."

"Yes. I expect I shall."

"Faith, I'm really sorry. I tried to get here on time . . ."

"Of course."

"Faith—it was hardly my fault that a goods train came off the rails at Hardenbrigg Cross, half an hour ahead of me . . ."

"Really? How terrible. You had better change your clothes for you are quite wet through."

We ate a solitary meal, no guests since we were in mourning, no visitors from abroad since we should have been ourselves abroad, in Paris, no word spoken beyond the strict limits of civility—"May I refill your glass? Please and thank you. This sauce is excellent. I will tell cook," for although I believed every word of his ride from Hardenbrigg, that for once he had not tried to evade an irksome duty but had considerably inconvenienced himself to perform it, his absence at my sister's graveside seemed a symbol of the inadequacy of our relationship, and I could not forgive him for it.

My mother had collapsed with perfect trust and confidence against her Daniel's shoulder and been almost carried from the cemetery in his arms. Aunt Verity had been supported by the ever-present awareness of her husband, a memory in many ways more real and vital than the living presence of her eldest son. Aunt Hannah, iron-faced, iron-willed as she was, had nevertheless put a grateful hand on Mayor Agbrigg's arm while he, looking more deeply shaken than anyone, had placed his gnarled, unsteady fingers over hers and squeezed hard, each one drawing strength and stamina from the other. Even Prudence had rested her head briefly against Freddy's shoulder and, stumbling on the stony pathway from the churchyard, had found his hand instantly on her elbow, steadying and guiding her. Only I—and Jonas—had stood alone, not merely for the half-hour it had taken to bury my sister, but for a long time before, and a long time after, bearable, perhaps, to Jonas, who had always been alone, whose very nature was steeped in solitude, but unbearable to me.

"Faith," Blaize said as we drank our coffee, sipped our brandy in the muted light and warmth of our drawing room. "Are you not being a shade unreasonable?"

"I daresay."

"But you don't mean to forgive me?"

"Lord—what is there to forgive? The train was late. It happens often enough. It's not as if I'd been relying on you . . ."

"No—you'd hardly have been doing that."

"Shall I give you some more coffee?"

"Please. Was my mother much distressed? If you can't believe I meant to come for your sake, then at least you must see I was concerned for her. The last funeral she attended was my father's and it must have reminded her . . ."

"I don't suppose she wants to forget. She looked very sad but she wasn't alone. Nicholas was there for part of the time—and even if he hadn't come she wouldn't have been alone. I don't think she ever is."

He blinked, not shutting away tears, of course, since Blaize did not cry, but perhaps a possibility, a memory, of tears.

"Quite so. And what did you make of Agbrigg? He was wearing his usual dead-pan lawyer's face when I called."

"Yes. But what does that signify? Jonas never shows his feelings in any case, and he certainly wouldn't show them to you, Blaize. Not after the beatings you've given him."

He blinked again, this time with frank surprise.

"Faith, I do assure you, I've never laid a hand on him."

"Oh yes you have—all of you. He was the only boy at the grammar school—surely—who'd come out of a weaving shed, the only one whose mother wore clogs and a shawl, and whose father had a cloth cap he had to doff to your father. And you all let him know it. If he'd been tough and strong I suppose he could have thrashed you all. But since he was puny, as well as being poor, the only thing he could do was pretend he didn't care. I think he's been pretending ever since. I think he's been pretending so long that most of the time he convinces himself."

He leaned forward, took a cigar from the intricately embossed silver box I had given him several Christmases ago, raised his eyebrows in automatic enquiry as to whether or not he might smoke—yet another request he did not expect to be denied—although when I nodded he kept the cigar unlit in his hand.

"How is it you know so much about him, Faith?"

"Oh—heavens—because I think he was fond of me once. For about half a minute he let me see it and then it disappeared, but so quickly that I could never be sure. What I am sure of is that he's suffering now. I felt it today and if I can help him—"

"Can you help him?"

"Probably not. I can look after Grace sometimes, since she gets on well with Blanche, and I can show him sympathy, at least—can't I?"

"Darling—are you asking my permission?" he said, his voice light, one eyebrow raising in faint sarcasm, definite amusement. "I wouldn't dream of interfering with your sympathy. At the very most I might advise you not to be too liberal with it. If he was fond of you before there's always the danger that he could grow fond of you again, especially now that he's lonely and nobody else seems to care much about him."

"And would you object?"

"My dear," he said, leaning back against the sofa cushions, his subtle face mischievous and relaxed, his intention, I thought, to fend off my mood of introspection with laughter. "Why should I mind? I have the most perfect confidence in you, and if you chose to bask in his adoration for a while—well, that's natural enough and I'd see no cause for alarm."

I should have laughed. The mere idea of Jonas openly adoring me—or anyone—and of myself basking in its glow should have provided ample cause for mirth, as Blaize had expected. But instead of the unwilling smile, the pathway to easy reconciliation —because I couldn't bring myself to tell him, "I needed you, Blaize. I'm afraid and uncertain. I need you now"—I looked at him for a moment, quite coldly, and astonished myself considerably by asking, "And you, Blaize? You do your share of that particular kind of basking, I know. Do you do more than that?"

"I beg your pardon?"

And although I heard an inner voice very clearly urge me, "Stop this. Change this dangerous, foolish topic now, while you still can. You have nothing to gain by it," I could not obey.

"I said, do you do more than just bask."

"I wonder."

But even then, aware of his cool cynicism, which would make him a formidable opponent for any woman, I was compelled to continue.

"You wonder? Well—that is a very clever answer, Blaize, and I am sure you can think of a dozen just as clever. Obviously I am not so subtle, because I don't know what you mean."

"Perhaps I don't know what you are asking."

"This—are you unfaithful to me?"

"Oh, dear—I—really—I do wish you hadn't said that, Faith."

"Yes—so I imagine."

He got up and stood for a moment half-turned away from me, one long, beautifully preserved hand—not the hand of a Law Valley man at all—resting on the mantel shelf, his face extremely careful.

"Shall we say—no, I am not."

"I don't believe you."

"Faith—perhaps you should."

"I don't."

He sighed, his fingers flexing themselves against the polished marble before he turned to face me.

"Then shall we say—occasionally, briefly, and never in Cullingford—in fact a long way from here. Faith—this is all nonsense, you know. It can't be a shock to you."

"Did I say it was? I didn't say I cared, either."

"No—you didn't. I hardly expected you to. But I didn't begin this conversation, Faith, and I'm not eager to go on with it. You've had a very difficult day . . ."

"So I have. Shall I go to bed with a headache, like Celia used to do—so as not to be a nuisance . . . ?"

"*Faith*," he rapped out, the first threat I had ever received from him. "I think that is more than enough. Is there a point to any of this? I have never pretended to be other than I am. I accepted you as you were. I don't believe it would help you—and it would considerably annoy me—to go over that old and painful ground again. I *am* sorry, Faith. If you are having an emotional crisis, then I may be able to understand it, but I'm not ready to share it. In fact it will be far better for us both if I go down to the Swan until it's over."

He looked down at the cigar still unlit in his hand, replaced it carefully in its silver box, straightened the sleeve of his jacket.

"I don't want to hurt you, Faith. I refuse to be hurt by you. We have had a pleasant life together so far. Do you deny that?"

I shook my head, still obstinate and miserable, a danger to myself and to the very fabric of that pleasant but artificial life—that sham—more willing, in that moment, to have endured a beating at his hands than the cool logic of his mind, the sharp wit of his tongue.

"Good. I'll leave you then."

But he paused an instant in the doorway, and looking at me as I sat, hands clenched in my lap, said quietly, "I give you everything I can, you know—as much as it is in my nature to give. Which is rather more—in fact a great deal more, Faith Aycliffe —than you give to me."

Chapter Thirty-one

WE MADE OUR TRIP to Paris as soon as circumstances allowed, a delightful round of gaieties during which our relationship appeared, on its surface, to be unaltered, except that he was much more considerate than usual, a shade less affectionate, and that he went out alone two evenings and one afternoon without the flimsiest of explanations. I bought dresses from M. Albertini, went to theatres and to amusing little suppers afterwards, drank a great deal of champagne, conducted lighthearted, very temporary flirtations because, in this sparkling Paris of the third Napoleon and his Empress Eugénie, who had brought the first crinoline to England as I had introduced it to Cullingford, flirtation was an acceptable means of passing the time. I drove out in the Bois de Boulogne as I used to do with my mother, acknowledging masculine admiration with a sidelong glance, a half-smile, as she had. I allowed a gentleman—on the afternoon Blaize so mysteriously disappeared—to kiss the palms of my hands and the nape of my neck, a pastime of which I soon tired. I was pleasant, talkative, brittle, uneasy. I was a woman turned thirty who, beneath her carefully acquired poise, was no longer certain of her direction. While Blaize, beneath his witticisms, his teasing, his social chatter, would not talk to me.

The American war, as Blaize had foreseen, was now raging, a circumstance which provided ample justification for his expensive exploration of new markets, and would send him off to Russia again before long. But on our return to Cullingford he was subjected, at once, to pressure from Nicholas, who considered he had been kept in ignorance of his brother's intentions quite long enough.

During our absence there had been trouble at Low Cross, the smallest and oldest of the Barforth mills, Mayor Agbrigg—who was famous for his caution—having noticed a series of fine cracks in the soot-blackened, weather-beaten walls. Nicholas—at once—had emptied the mill, absorbing as much of the work force as possible elsewhere, even paying compensation to others, while the old wooden beams, never intended to take the weight of power-driven machinery, were replaced with cast iron, winning himself a certain amount of grudging respect since everybody knew of masters who had ignored such warnings until shattered floorboards, falling machinery, and crushed bodies had proved their architects right. But "shoring up and making do" not being in Nicholas' nature, he would have much preferred to knock the old building down and start again on a far grander scale, an operation which—since it required Blaize's agreement—brought the question of their partnership to the forefront again.

A long brown envelope made its appearance on my hall table, delivered this time by the coachman from Tarn Edge, followed, a few days later, by another.

"I'm glad to see Brother Nick keeping himself so busy," Blaize murmured, and I learned, not from my husband but from an irate Caroline that although he would not agree to sell he was prepared—if properly persuaded—to split.

"Either way would considerably upset me," Caroline announced, having driven over very early from Listonby, her intention to recruit me to her service being very plain. "They have the best business in the valley, they are both clever men—or so they would have us believe—yet they are worse than Dominic and Noel used to be at five years old, ready to murder each other for the biggest slice of apple tart. Well—they have been squabbling all their lives, those brothers of mine, and it is high time now that they grew up and learned to get on together. You should tell Blaize so, Faith, and keep on telling him until he believes you. Georgiana is hopeless of course, and doesn't care what happens, but I am relying on you. I should certainly never allow Matthew to be so foolish. My father devoted his life to those mills and I refuse to see his efforts wasted. Goodness—if he had left the mills to me there would have been none of this futile wrangling. Remember, Faith—talk sense to him and let him see you won't take 'no' for an answer."

Yet, in reply to my cautious enquiry, "Caroline says you want to split the business?" Blaize merely lifted a nonchalant shoulder. "Ah well, if Caroline says so—but, of course, there is always the chance I may change my mind tomorrow."

And it was hard to face the truth that my husband did not trust me.

"Blaize, is it decided yet? Which way is it to be done?"

"Darling, why do you keep on asking? Is Caroline pressing you for an answer?"

Even Georgiana was better informed than I.

"Are you not sick to death of it?" she demanded, walking into my breakfast parlour and helping herself to toast and coffee. "I declare it is the most vexing thing I ever heard—especially since I hear nothing else. Blaize will not sell and Nicky will not split. Caroline, I believe, has lost her wits since she seems to think there is something I can do about it. Even my mother-in-law spoke sharply to me the other day. Well—they may do as they please. And while they are making up their minds I shall do as I please and go over to Galton to stay with my grandfather."

The Duke of South Erin was finally enticed to Listonby that winter, happy to escape a London made gloomy by the death of the prematurely aged Prince Albert.

"You'll adore him," Caroline told us, a command rather than an opinion, and indeed he proved amiable enough, an older, slightly more sophisticated version of Matthew himself, requiring no more complex pleasures than a spot of good hunting and shooting and a handsome woman to laugh at his jokes at dinnertime.

I attended the ball Caroline gave in his honour wearing a vast confection of black chiffon that entirely filled the carriage, a diamond on my hand which Blaize had tossed into my lap that morning because he thought Caroline would expect us to look our best. Georgiana had a new diamond too, Caroline wore the whole of her not inconsiderable collection, Aunt Verity not very far behind.

"Very civil of you to take so much trouble," the duke told Caroline at the end of the sumptuous celebration.

"It is something of a family tradition," Caroline replied, blinking hard, her firm chin for just a moment quivering so that I knew she had actually said, "I haven't done this for you at all. I've done it for my father."

The Lady Barforth Academy for Young Ladies was also honoured by a ducal visit, the noble gentleman wishing to check the progress of his natural daughter, although his paternal impulse was soon replaced by another impulse, of amusement this time, of curiosity and a definite if grudging admiration for Prudence.

"Never met a governess like her," he said. "Clever women always did make me uncomfortable and that one terrifies me."

Yet, from then on, the school was a regular recipient of game from the ducal deer parks, pineapples from the ducal pine pits, hampers of strawberries and other exotic fruits from the greenhouses the designer of the Crystal Palace had built, and a steady stream of enquiries from titled gentlemen—or their legal advisers—to whom my sister's school had been most highly recommended.

My daughter Blanche became a pupil there on her seventh birthday, an arrangement, it must be said at once, from which she obtained no academic distinction, having decided even then that her silver curls and cloudy turquoise eyes, a dash of her father's elusive charm, would be more than enough to win the prizes *she* desired from life.

"She's not stupid," Prudence told me. "And she's not lazy. In fact—in her way—she's rather clever and quite determined. It's just that—well—she doesn't see the point to education. After all, whenever we have a distinguished visitor he may have a dutiful look at Grace Agbrigg's mathematics or Amy Chesterton's handwriting but then he'll take a very long look at Blanche. So why should she take the trouble to work at her copperplate, or do her sums?" And I understood that my beautiful Blanche was of far less interest to Prudence than her other niece, the intellectually promising Grace Agbrigg, or Georgiana's impish Venetia, who, when she could be restrained from making her escape through the nearest window, had an entertaining, if totally undisciplined, mind.

"Blanche will marry well," Prudence said. "There's no doubt about that. Venetia could marry a prince or could elope with a chimney-sweep. Grace—I don't know—I think I love Grace. I would like Grace to do something quite extraordinary."

Jonas, too, maintained his interest in the school, coping admirably at the same time with his depleted household and his daughter, their relationship being in no way demonstrative yet certainly of great importance to them both, based, it seemed, on mutual respect, the interest and sympathy of a clever man for a clever child.

"They manage so very well together," my mother enthused, but there was no doubt that Aunt Hannah, although she had felt sincere grief for Celia, had no intention of allowing her son to be alone for long. His marriage to Celia had been the very best, at the time, he could have possibly hoped for, but his circumstances had vastly altered since then. He was a man of substance and distinction these days, whose opinions carried weight with our town council and were not disregarded by our local politicians of the Whig persuasion. He was the master of a fine house in Albert Place, kept his own carriage and a smart suite of offices in Croppers Court, and although Celia's share of the Aycliffe money would pass now, when my mother died, to Grace, this—although initially disappointing—was not altogether a bad thing since it would prevent the child of his first marriage from becoming a financial burden to his second.

The world of matrimonial opportunity was suddenly wide open again for Jonas, and as his period of mourning—so much shorter for a man than for a woman—reached halfway to its close Aunt Hannah began to give serious thought as to who this second wife should be. Naturally he would marry again. A woman—certainly our own widowed Queen—might be allowed to bury her heart in the grave of her departed husband, in fact it was considered right and proper that she should, but a man, especially a man with a child to raise and his way to make in the world, had no choice but to be practical. And in Jonas' case, according to Aunt Hannah, perhaps the time had come to be magnificent.

Most men in his position, of course, would have been thinking along the lines of some sober, sensible woman of mature years, a lady, certainly, of some gentility and a little money but selected mainly for her skills as a housekeeper, her patience with motherless children. But Aunt Hannah, who had been obliged to take what she could get for him last time, acquired, quite suddenly, what seemed to be a new lease of life, all her old ambitions rekindling to such a fever heat that his frequent visits to Prudence's school, where several ladies of the mature and sensible type were employed, caused her immense alarm.

"I do not care to see him hobnobbing quite so much with those schoolmistresses," she told me. "And I am relying on you, Faith, to keep your eyes open. You are a woman of experience, as I am, and it can be no secret to you that men have certain requirements which often lead them into great foolishness. I have no intention of allowing Jonas to be trapped by one of Prudence's spinster ladies, I do assure you, since there is no doubt that each and every one of them would give their eyeteeth—and very likely their virtue—to have him."

Prudence herself, of course, had she not been placed within the forbidden degree of kinship, would have been an ideal choice, being richer than Celia, infinitely more energetic, her very independence of mind a quality which would have been of great use to a man embarking on the political life. But, failing Prudence, there was Rebecca Mandelbaum who, having been deceived by her Austrian musician, was still languishing at home, a virgin of thirty-three summers and large financial expectations, who could find consolation for her own loss, perhaps, in a man who had also suffered. And if she could not, then there was the youngest Battershaw girl, not yet in her twenties but old, it was felt, for her age, and—perhaps best of all—the daughter of Mr. Fielding, our member of Parliament, an alliance in the grand, Whig manner which rejoiced Aunt Hannah's heart.

At her suggestion I invited these ladies, suitably chaperoned, to dine with me in their turns, seating Jonas beside them at table, letting it be seen, in accordance with my aunt's specific instructions, that any arrangement with the Agbriggs would include the Barforths too. But Angelica Battershaw, I felt, was too giddy, the twenty-five-year-old Miss Fielding too plain, Rebecca, although sweet-natured enough, handsome enough, still dwelling on her departed musician, and—quite fiercely and irrationally—I wanted Jonas to have some warmth in life, some joy, a little gaiety.

"It could well be Rebecca," I ventured when my aunt pressed

me, having learned that Jonas had spent a comfortable evening at the academy, thrashing out some knotty philosophical problem in the staff sitting room over red wine and ratafia biscuits.

"He seems to enjoy her company, Aunt Hannah."

"Good," she said. "I confess I would have preferred Maria Fielding, but the Mandelbaums are well placed and I shall not complain. I shall leave Rebecca to you, Faith. Flatter her and coddle her a little, show her some new way of doing her hair and lend her one of your lace shawls—that sort of thing. And while you are about it I shall get to work on the parents. Naomi Mandelbaum is a good soul who has always been easy enough to manage and George is a sensible man. His daughter may be rich but she is no longer young and after that unfortunate attachment if he can get her decently settled he'll be glad of it. You could introduce her to Grace and work on her sympathies, and then, if Jonas makes his intentions clear around Christmastime, they could be married as soon as his full year is up. After all, she'll be thirty-four by then and no one would expect her to delay. Really—it will be very suitable."

So it was. A sizeable dowry, a sedate, healthy woman who would do her duty and cause no trouble, who was not brilliant yet perfectly able to entertain his guests without strain, and be kind to his daughter. Yet I too had been present that evening in Prudence's sitting room when Jonas had entertained us with wine and philosophy, had seen him relax easily into the academic atmosphere of his youth, and, having taken more than a glass or two myself—enough to remind me of lost loves and opportunities—I flung my arms around him at parting and told him, "When you marry again, Jonas, I want her to be beautiful and generous and madly in love with you. I want you to adore her . . ."

"How kind," he said smiling, steadying me since it must have been apparent to everyone that the second Lady Barforth was well in her cups. "But I think I may have passed the season for such things, you know."

"Oh, dear—is it winter already? Then I'd best invite Becky Mandelbaum to dinner again, I suppose—"

"Yes," he said very quietly, a man, I thought, who had never allowed himself to neglect his opportunities, however burdensome he had known they would prove. "I believe you should."

In the spring Mayor Agbrigg's final term of office came to its close, an event deemed worthy of some expression of gratitude and respect since he and Aunt Hannah between them had been responsible for the concert hall, the reservoirs, the Giles Ashburn Memorial Gardens, the passing of an Improvement Act which had resulted in the lighting and paving and, in some cases, the widening of streets, the knocking down of old, dangerous buildings, and a set of building regulations—at which my father would have shuddered—to oversee the more solid, more hygienic construction of new ones.

The Agbriggs had brought both water and culture to Cullingford, had concerned themselves with both public health and public buildings, had worked hard and often successfully to transform what had been little more than a mass of humanity huddled together in one place into a community with a sense of civic pride. A debt, clearly, was owing, and since we paid our debts in Cullingford, a banquet was held in honour of our mayor and his lady at the Assembly Rooms, followed by speeches and praises, the presentation of a silver salver that would not have disgraced a baronial hall and of a gold mayoral chain, twenty-eight ounces in weight, worth a lordly 240 pounds, which Mayor Agbrigg wore for the first, if the last, time that night.

Every gentleman who had held civic office since the date of our incorporation was present, with the exception of Mr. Hobhouse, who had rather tactfully declined; every industrialist, members of all the professions, several politicians of several parties, Jonas, who would soon have that chain of office around his own neck, sitting beside Rebecca Mandelbaum, who would soon be his wife, Aunt Hannah, showing, at the only public banquet in Cullingford for years which she had not arranged herself, the face of a woman who is seeing not all, perhaps, but a sufficiency of her dreams come true.

There was still the town hall to build, with its banqueting hall and mayor's parlour where she herself would be unlikely to hold court, her husband having firmly announced himself unwilling to stand for re-election. There was the art gallery and museum to be completed in the Ashburn park, the growing need for a library now that so many people were learning to read. But Jonas and his placid Rebecca could do all that for her—because she had made it possible for it to be done at all—and I had never seen my aunt so gloriously, almost girlishly happy as on that night.

I took Blaize to the station in my victoria some five days later, presented my cheek to be kissed as he boarded the train, smiled, pronounced my calm good-byes—asking no questions so as not to be reminded that he would give no answers—and walking out, chilled suddenly, into the station yard, I found myself unwilling to go home, could see no reason, no use in being there, and drove instead to Lawcroft Fold.

It was a calm, commonplace day, nothing, as I drove in at the top gate—wishing to avoid the mill yard and the possibility of Nicholas—to disturb me, nothing to surprise me at the sight of the equipage I believed to be Jonas' standing outside the door, until Jonas himself appeared and drove off without greeting me, his wheels almost shaving mine on the carriage way, the glimpse of his face telling me something was awry.

Mayor Agbrigg was in the drawing room when they announced me, standing at the window looking down into the mill yard, his hunched shoulders frailer than I had realised, the lines of his face deeper, dustier somehow, like crevices in old stone.

"Faith, lass—" he said.

"Uncle Agbrigg—what is it?"

And in reply he gestured towards the old lady scarcely recognisable as my aunt, a grey face with two raw streaks of crimson beneath the cheekbones, grey hair—why had I never noticed her hair was so grey?—escaping in impossible disorder from its pins as if she had tugged at it in fury or despair, shaken her head and screamed out some total protest. "Never. I will not have it." And Jonas—for it could only be he—had walked away from her, leaving her to grapple with her first defeat.

Had he refused to marry Rebecca Mandelbaum after all, since I well knew nothing had been settled, much less announced? Had he decided to sell his practice and go into some rash academic venture, some scheme that would relax and humanise him even if it made him poor? I hoped so. Fervently I hoped so. Yet Aunt Hannah and her husband had helped me once, and I too had a debt to repay.

"Aunt Hannah," I said, kneeling on the floor by her chair, "let me help if I can—or if you would like me to go away again—?"

"No," she said, the movement of her lips hard and painful as if she feared they would crack. "Stay awhile. You will have cause to avoid me soon enough. Tell her—Mr. Agbrigg—what has been done to me."

"Not I. I'll have nothing to do with it."

"He's your son, Ira Agbrigg."

"No," he said, turning to face her, the bitterness in him shocking me, amazing her. "Your son, Hannah. You had the moulding of him. That was the condition you made when we married and I accepted it. Your son—not mine and not his mother's—yours."

She got up slowly, her body aching, I thought, from some inner violence, some grievous wound that, because she was Hannah Barforth, she chose to ignore, and *would* ignore even if it killed her.

"Quite so, Mr. Agbrigg. I feel sure that my niece, Lady Barforth, cannot wish to be bothered with that."

And turning to me, her face a mask of false, quite painful cordiality, she said brightly, "You will be interested to learn, Faith, that Jonas is to be married."

"Yes, of course—but we supposed, surely—in the spring—?"

"Ah yes. Then let us suppose no longer. He is to be married the very minute he is out of black arm bands—an eager young bridegroom of something over forty, a blushing bride of forty-five, or fifty, or sixty beneath her paint, for all one knows. Yes—he is to marry the second Mrs. Oldroyd, the luscious Mrs. Delaney, the widow of a dozen husbands and not a single wedding ring to show for it, if the truth be known. And I warn you, Faith, if you ever allow her across your threshold then I shall not have you across mine."

She sat down again. Mayor Agbrigg returned to his silent scrutiny of the mill yard. I stood between them, uncertain as to what consolation I could offer, what they would be willing to receive, seeing, with Aunt Hannah's eyes, the tarnishing of that gold mayoral chain, that princely salver, feeling her bleak conviction that she would be remembered now not as the woman who had built the Morgan Aycliffe Hall but as the mother of a man who had made himself master of Fieldhead by marrying a whore.

"Your sister Celia was not such a goose after all," she said, her voice harsh, her face very cold. "The mill was not sold, the house was not sold. Celia knew why and none of us would believe her. She said the servants were whispering about Jonas and Mrs. Delaney—yes, so she did—and perhaps they had good cause."

"Aunt Hannah, I don't believe that."

"Why not? He called on her often enough, didn't he? And when Celia complained we said it was natural for a lawyer to call on his client. But now you may as well believe the worst of him, Faith, since everybody else will. He used to call on her before Matthew Oldroyd died—before Matthew Oldroyd married her—to advise on her investments, or so he said. But can you prove to me that they were not lovers even then? They could have worked together to persuade Matthew Oldroyd into that scandalous marriage, for which I was the first to condemn him, and still condemn him. Why not? Emma-Jane Hobhouse said there was a conspiracy and we ignored her just as we ignored Celia. Well—I must write to Emma-Jane and give her the good news, and if it crosses her mind that Jonas may have pushed your sister down those cellar steps, I wouldn't be the one to blame her . . ."

"Aunt Hannah—no—I won't listen to that—"

"Then you'll be the only one who won't listen to it, and gloat over it. It fits—it's a good story—and who asks—who cares—for the truth of it?"

"Aunt Hannah, you can't believe such things of Jonas."

But getting up again, her fists clenched, those raw, red spots once more mottling her cheeks, she took a quick stride to her work table and back again, and staring straight at me hissed through clenched teeth, "Yes I can."

"No, Aunt Hannah."

"Oh yes, Faith Aycliffe. Yes. You don't know what he is capable of. He would sell you, or me, or his own daughter to the highest bidder, and now he has sold himself to a brothel-keeper. He is going to live on the earnings of a whore, for what else is Fieldhead now but that? He is going to marry a woman I cannot receive, that no decent female could ever be asked to receive, and when I pleaded with him, reminding him of all I have done for him—of all I still could do for him—he answered me—he said, 'Such a fuss, Mamma, for when all is said and done I am only following your teaching.' Yes, he said that to me—"

And after a moment of anguished silence, her breast heaving with her poisoned emotions, she said hoarsely, "I used to love him—just an hour ago," and sat down again.

There was nothing I could say to her. There would have been no point at all in telling her she would eventually forgive him since, most probably, she would not; no point in suggesting that the rumours and the gossip would soon die away since even in commercially minded Cullingford there was a dividing line between good money and bad, and Jonas' reputation would never recover. Men would do business with him, of course, would even dine with him, eventually and privately, at the Swan. But that gold chain of office, that splendid town hall with its stained-glass windows and Doric columns would pass now to others; and what would happen to Grace?

An hour ago my aunt's life had been full, her intentions plain. There had been Jonas' wedding to arrange and then his election. There had been his term of office, during which the town hall would have been completed, the grand opening banquet with herself beside him encouraging his taste for public life so that he might at last make that momentous journey to Westminster. There had been the possibility of more grandchildren, and, failing that, there had been Grace's debut into West Riding society, another marriage contract, in due course, to negotiate. And now, at one stroke, he had taken away everything she cared for, had tarnished her respectability by tarnishing his own, had robbed her of her committees, her functions, her grandchild, had broken her heart.

"What am I to do?" she said, not with Jonas, I thought, but with herself, for her days, now, would be long and empty, shrinking, one after the other, to the dimensions of a "woman at home" who was not much needed anywhere else.

"I'm not well," she said, pressing her hands to her head, the first time I had heard her speak those words, or seen her make that gesture—my mother's gesture—of feminine frailty. And rushing for the door, the strongest woman I knew and the stateliest collapsing before my eyes, she disappeared, going upstairs to hide as my mother, and Celia, used to do.

"Shall I go up to her, Uncle Agbrigg?"

"Nay, lass, it's not you she wants. And Jonas won't be going up those stairs again."

"Someone should."

"Aye. I'll go myself presently. There's nobody left but me now, I reckon—whether she likes it or not—"

"Uncle Agbrigg—you don't mean to forgive him either, do you?"

"Nay, lass," he said, his craggy face relaxing into a brief smile. "And that surprises you, does it, since all he's doing is marrying for money, same as he did before, same as I did myself. No—no —I'll not hold that against him. I could even admire him for it because even when a man recognises himself as a callous, scheming devil it takes guts to say so. And as to the woman, yes, she's a whore all right, but I take a different view of that to your Aunt Hannah. I reckon poverty can make a whore out of any lass—when it comes down to whoring or starving there's not much choice at all—and we don't know what Mrs. Delaney was like at her beginnings. A lass from Simon Street, maybe—or somewhere like it—abused by her mother's husband one night when he was drunk and pushed out of the door the morning after. And when that happens to a lass she'll be sure to find the brothel-keeper waiting. Nay—it's not Mrs. Delaney who troubles me. Maybe I got to thinking just now of another lass from Simon Street and wondering what she'd make of her Jonas now. Maybe it crossed my mind she'd tell me it was all my fault."

He crossed the room and sat down heavily, closing his eyes in pure weariness. "I reckon you don't know how I came to be acquainted with your aunt Hannah, Faith. It might ease me now to talk about it, and you're a good lass. I clawed my way up from the very bottom of the muck-heap, Faith—a muck-heap neither you nor your aunt can even imagine. And by the time I met Hannah I'd got as far as Low Cross, from mill hand to overlooker to shed manager to manager of the whole lot, doing Joel Barforth's dirty work for him when he had any—and there were times when he had. Sickness came. I lost three bairns— nearly lost my wife—I *did* lose her, I reckon, because she couldn't bring herself together. And Miss Hannah Barforth helped—found me a woman to clean the house, saw to it that Ann—my wife—was fed, had a look at Jonas and made up her mind he was wasted on me, and on my Ann. And it was Hannah who put the shame into him—shame of his beginnings and his mother. I saw it happen and I let it happen because even if I didn't like it, I thought it would spur him on, make him fight that much harder—and I knew how hard he'd have to fight. You don't mind if I smoke, lass?"

"No. What happened to your wife, Uncle Agbrigg?"

"She died. I once told you how, and what it did to me. But men don't grieve for long, they can't afford it. Well—this was the way of it. Hannah was turned thirty by then. She'd lost the man she'd wanted and she'd been let down by another. She was sick of living in other women's houses and the choice was between a fancy parson she reckoned would never make a bishop, and me. The parson had his 100 pounds a year and his gentility, I had Jonas and she picked me. Her brother didn't like it, but when Hannah wants something there's no stopping her. What she says she'll do, she'll do, and so we got married—Hannah and me and Jonas. And that was always the way of it. She could run the town through me, she reckoned, but she could run the world through Jonas. Well, I let her have her way and I saw him grow into a man I didn't like—which has nothing to do with loving. He's my lad, Ann's lad, and I don't have to like Ann's lad to love him. She wouldn't much like him herself, I reckon, although she'd fret herself into her grave all over again in case the woman should make him unhappy."

"And it doesn't worry you?"

"No," he said, quite decidedly. "That it doesn't. He knows what he's going into. He's made a mathematical calculation of it and he finds that the embarrassment is outweighed by the gain. In fact she's worth it to him, and there's no more to be said. It's Hannah who worries me now."

"What will you do, Uncle Agbrigg?"

"With Hannah? Well, first of all, lass, I'd best get myself upstairs and convince her I'll not be mayor again, because that's what she'll be wanting now. No—I'm getting on in years, Faith, and so is she. She'll take the loss of Jonas hard—I can understand that—but he's gone, and maybe that could suit us now, Hannah and me. Maybe it's time—well, my Ann's dead, there's no denying it, and the man Hannah fancied has been long gone too. And if there hasn't been love between us we've grown accustomed to each other—we respect each other, I reckon. Maybe we even like each other."

"I like you, Uncle Agbrigg."

"Well, that's a feather in my cap and no mistake. So you'll come and see us in Scarborough, will you, when I've convinced her that Scarborough's where she wants to go—a little house on the cliff, away from the smoke, on account of my bad chest, which I'd never noticed until she pointed out to me how bad my breathing was—"

"Oh yes, Uncle Agbrigg, I'll come."

"Good," he said, getting up and rather awkwardly patting my cheek. "Good. I was nobody when she met me, Faith. Just a man who wanted to better himself and didn't much care how. But now—well, I built those reservoirs, I reckon—I got the water in. She's got no reason to be ashamed of me now. And, do you know, Faith, I think we could even be happy."

Chapter Thirty-two

I DROVE FOR A WHILE quite aimlessly about the streets, knowing that I should go home yet absolutely unable to turn myself in the direction of Elderleigh. Already it was late afternoon; Blanche would have returned from school by now, and I had left no clear instructions about dinner. Yet, despite the urgings of common sense and duty, "home," whatever it might mean to me, whatever it consisted of, was the one place in the world I could not—at that moment—tolerate.

I drifted an hour longer, half-thinking, dream-thinking, letting the familiar streets go by with nothing, in any one of them, to detain me, nothing to distress me or to please me—just space and time with myself caught up in the crowded void of it, making the best I could of every quiet water, every ebb tide, every stony wasteland in which it stranded me. Space, and time, and a slow-dropping, soft-penetrating sadness.

And then I went to Albert Place and asked for Jonas.

He was dressed to go out, to Mrs. Delaney I was forced to imagine, but when I began to apologise for my intrusion, insisting I had looked in only for a moment, since I didn't really know why I had come at all, he told me, "Do sit down. I am in no hurry, Faith—and not greatly surprised to see you. Have you come straight from Lawcroft Fold?"

"Yes—in fact, no, since I have been driving around a little—going nowhere—"

"Composing yourself to face up to my villainy?"

"Is that what it is? I don't think I care about that."

"But you must be—shocked?"

"Yes. Indeed I am. And sad—so terribly sad that I don't know how to explain it. Jonas—is this right for you?"

He sat down in the chair facing mine, his face, in shadow, looking tired, not creased and dusty like his father's, but somehow quite hollow.

"Well," he said, "thank you at least for that, Faith."

"For what? Because it worries me that you could be miserable? I suppose it worries Aunt Hannah too, although she wouldn't say it. She will miss you cruelly, Jonas. And she will never be reconciled."

"I know," he said, giving me once again the impression of hollowness, as if the living impulses that had filled him had all been carefully reduced and put away. "Had she calmed herself by the time you left?"

"Oh no. I don't think she knows how to calm herself, but I believe your father might do it for her. He wants to retire and take her to Scarborough, or allow her to take him there."

He smiled, his long eyes still hooded by their heavy, shielding lids.

"Well, there would have been no chance of that had I married suitably and taken office as mayor. So I may have done him a service with my perfidy."

"I can't think you perfidious."

"Why ever not? Miss Mandelbaum will surely not agree with you. Celia would not agree with you either."

"I don't know that I want to talk about Celia."

"I don't see how it can be avoided. You tried to comfort me when she died. I realise you would like to defend me now, and in that case you should know the truth. Faith—whatever you may have glimpsed in me these past months—a little more humanity than you had supposed, perhaps—then don't deceive yourself. Yes, the capacity exists. I have even toyed with the idea of developing it. I would like to be happy. I would like to care for a woman who cares for me. It has never happened. It never will happen."

"Jonas—it could happen. You haven't looked—you haven't tried—"

"Nonsense," he said flatly, a lawyer once again, demolishing my immature logic, my foolishness. "We are talking of marriage —an exceedingly tight contract which requires obedience from one party and supportiveness from the other, happiness, so far as I am aware, from neither."

"Jonas, that is legal jargon and you are hiding behind it."

"Faith, it is the truth. I married your sister for a down payment of 20,000 pounds because I was desperate to buy out old Corey-Manning. On the very day I buried her I *knew* the way to Fieldhead Mills was open to me if I chose to take it. Walking back from the cemetery, I knew I *would* take it. I have no excuses, Faith. I am no longer a poor man. I could live comfortably on my present income, here, in my pleasant house with my very charming daughter. We have a great deal in common, Grace and I. We could read together, travel abroad together. We could talk together. I could become very scholarly and possibly very content. The thought of it, even now, gives me a whisper of pleasure. And, failing that, I could marry Rebecca Mandelbaum, who would suit me well enough, and buy myself a seat in the House of Commons with her dowry. Political power interests me. For many years I wanted it rather badly. I believe I could have it now. So—there you see my choices. Contentment, power, or cash. It took me moments, Faith—no more—to decide. Do you still want to defend me?"

"Yes."

"Knowing how miserable your sister was with me?"

"Yes. Celia carried her misery inside her. You were not to blame."

"Once again, she would not agree with you. I'm not sure I agree with you myself."

"Then you should. My father crushed her, Jonas. You should know that. He took everything that was real and special out of her and filled her up again with the trivial little bits and pieces he thought proper in a woman. And so she was never a woman at all. I don't know why Prudence and I escaped without too much damage. Perhaps it was because we never really believed in him. And in that case—if that is true—then Celia must have loved him. Poor Celia—that was her misery—not anything that happened to her afterwards—not you— You wanted more than she knew how to give, that's all. Any man would have wanted more . . ."

He turned his head sharply, a moment of emotion to be concealed instinctively, as he had always concealed such things, an act of self-preservation in a world which did not encourage the finer feelings in a lad from Simon Street.

"Yes, Faith. I wanted more. Six months before I married her a house in Albert Place, an income, a decent working capital—all that—seemed beyond my wildest dreams. Six months later and it was—well—inadequate."

"And now, Jonas?"

"What, now?"

"Will Fieldhead suffice you any better?"

"Probably not. But I could never live at peace with myself if I let it pass me by. It will make me almost as rich as Nicholas Barforth—certainly as rich as Sir Blaize. Now ask yourself, Faith, how a man of my origins could turn his back on that?"

"And Mrs. Delaney?"

"Yes—Mrs. Delaney?"

"Is she—agreeable to you?"

He smiled at me again, wryly. "You mean do I desire her? Not particularly."

"Then how can you commit yourself—Jonas, you can't force yourself—surely—not all the time—not forever—?"

"I could," he said. "If I had to. Fortunately it is not quite so bad as that. Mrs. Delaney is experienced enough in that direction to know how to please any man—she does please me, in fact, since we have already consummated our intentions, at her suggestion, not mine. I believe her motive was kindness. She could see I had been somewhat deprived—frustrated would have been my description, famished was hers, and no doubt she was right. She satisfies my appetites most thoroughly—and pleasantly—and I am grateful. It is not the same as desire."

"You mean it is not the same as love."

"Yes, I suppose that is exactly what I mean. I hesitate even to use the word."

"Is Mrs. Delaney in love with you?"

"My dear—hardly that. She has a weakness for intellectual men and a hankering, not for respectability since she recognises it to be beyond her, but for stability perhaps. She has led a wandering life and, like Rebecca Mandelbaum, she feels the need to be settled. Oh yes, I have been obliged to serve my apprenticeship to her cause. She has allowed me to manage Fieldhead since Mr. Oldroyd died and has kept an eagle eye on my methods. She required very definite proof of my commercial acumen, I do assure you, before expressing herself willing to place her fortune in my hands. She is a sensible woman, who accepts my limitations, and her own. Naturally she realises I can no longer make her a mayoress, since the city fathers will have none of me now. She understands that my mother, and your mother, and a great many other ladies will never receive her. But in her own eyes and in the eyes of her past acquaintances she will be a married woman. She trusts me in so far as it is in her to trust any man. And my presence beside her spares her the attentions of other fortune hunters. Small matters to you, perhaps, but then you have never been much exposed to the coarser side of the great world."

"And Grace?"

He sighed.

"Yes. Grace. She may, I imagine, entertain some doubts as to my rightful place in her estimation but at the same time she will be one of the greatest heiresses in the Law Valley. She will have Celia's money, Matthew Oldroyd's money, Tessa Delaney's money, my money, all in due course—and I shall make a great deal of money now, Faith, in addition to all the rest. Fieldhead will be her official home, of course, but I think I may leave her with Prudence for a while—Monday to Friday. Remember, Faith, I *am* a lawyer. My new will is already drawn up and waiting to be signed after my marriage. In the event of my death the guardianship of my daughter will pass to you and Blaize, if you will accept it. You may be sure that where Grace is concerned I have left nothing to chance."

The maid came in to light the lamps and check the fire, glanced enquiringly at us and went out again, her interruption conveying to me the lateness of the hour but no inclination whatsoever to take my leave.

"You may lose her, Jonas."

"I know. But I would lose her in any case. She will marry, sooner or later, and at least now I can give her the freedom of choice I lacked myself. With Fieldhead behind her she can afford to marry where she pleases. She can even afford not to marry at all."

"It is all decided, then?"

"Yes, quite decided."

"What can I do for you, Jonas?"

And for just a moment, caught unawares by my offer of help when he had anticipated condemnation, there was pain in his face.

"Should Grace turn away from me you could offer—such consolation as occurred to you and which she might be ready to accept. You could express the opinion, at Cullingford's tea tables, that my daughter's reputation cannot suffer from exposure to such a stepmother."

"Jonas, I would do that in any case."

"Of course you would. I have simply allowed myself the pleasure of asking, since there is no one else I would wish to ask."

"Prudence—?"

"Of course. There is Prudence, who may never forgive me but who will help me just the same. Nevertheless, it is you I wish to ask. That is the place you hold in my life. You must know why. It seems pointless to deny it, just as it would seem equally pointless, at this late stage, to put it into words."

He got up and moved away from me, quite deliberately putting distance between us—allowing me a moment to realise that he had almost said he loved me, that, in other circumstances, I could almost have welcomed it—and then he resumed his seat, composed, neutral as always, his face serious but gentler, I thought, than before.

"You should not worry about me, Faith. You should think of your own affairs, which may need thought."

"Why do you say that, Jonas?"

"Because I am a devious man, an expert in the deciphering of motives and meanings, and the drawing of conclusions. And it is no secret that the Barforth pot is about to boil over. I see you in the midst of it and it troubles me. Faith, I have no right to ask and you are not obliged to answer, but there is something amiss with your life, is there not? It gave me pleasure just now to ask for your help. It would mean a great deal to me if you would allow me to help you."

And having accepted for so long his own personal judgement, that he was indeed devious and calculating and self-seeking, it amazed me that I could now turn to him with the perfect trust I had previously extended only to Giles. All my life I had seen him through other people's eyes, through Prudence's hostility for the brother-in-law who could cheat her of her inheritance, through Aunt Hannah's driving ambitions, her almost pathetic desire to fulfil herself in him, through Celia's fretful complainings, through Caroline's frank contempt for "the Agbrigg boy." I had believed him to be cold and crafty and so, on occasion, he was. Only recently had I come to realise that in gentler circumstances, like those which had moulded Giles Ashburn's character, he would have grown differently. Only now did I realise it fully and my heart ached for the waste of him.

"I don't know what is wrong with me, Jonas—only that something is."

"Blaize?"

"I don't know anything about Blaize. I thought him my dearest friend, but I seem to have rather lost him, now. We are beginning to lead our own lives, except that I am not physically unfaithful . . ."

"There are other kinds of infidelity."

"Yes. I believe he may think so. But I don't know how to defend myself. I don't really know what I am guilty of. Our marriage was bound to be difficult. Blaize himself is difficult. But it isn't that. Something, at some point, came between us, something large and definite and quite invisible. There's nothing to grapple with. And if Blaize knows what it is then he won't tell me. He won't tell me anything at all."

"And have you asked him?"

"No. I can't ask him."

"In fact you have allowed the silence to fall and now you can't find your way through it."

I shuddered. "Well, I shall just have to go on as best I can."

The maid appeared again, hovered, her agitation reminding him that he had ordered his carriage an hour ago, reminding me of the woman whose claims on him were far more valid than mine.

"Heavens, it must be getting late."

"Yes, I fear so."

I got up shakily, against my will. "I don't want to go home, Jonas."

"My dear, where else is there for you to go?"

"I know—I know."

"Faith—listen to me. I understand the art of being alone. I

have always lived separately, and inward—and I shall simply continue so to do. You are not made that way. When the conflict in your family comes to a head, and if you are forced into a position of choice, you will have to choose Blaize. You must know that. My hope for you is that you will want to choose him."

I could find no member of my family willing to accompany me to the wedding of Jonas and Tessa Delaney. My mother and Aunt Verity, at Aunt Hannah's urgent request, declined, feeling that their loyalty was to her rather than to her adopted son. Prudence, fearing the effect of the marriage on Grace and bitterly disappointed in Jonas himself, declared that wild horses would not drag her to see the foul deed done. Blaize was out of town. "I'll come with you," Georgiana offered. "I don't care a scrap for Mr. Agbrigg or Mrs. Delaney, but if you want my company then you shall have it." But her grandfather, who had been ailing for several months, took a sudden turn for the worse so that instead of a wedding she was called to a deathbed; and I went to the parish church alone.

It was a heavy morning of late August, a yellow sky pressing down upon the city, a tight, dusty quality in the air that promised heat, and even as I got down from my victoria and walked across that familiar churchyard, I hoped to see Aunt Hannah, grim and resolute, hostile and bitter, but present, in the church porch. I even waited a moment, not seeing her carriage, hoping for the sound of her unsteady nags, or at least the heavy footsteps which might bring Mayor Agbrigg, coming alone to offer a measure of reconciliation. But the church was almost empty, just the law clerks from Croppers Court, the managers from Fieldhead who knew which side their bread was buttered, and Nicholas Barforth, come, one supposed, to pay his respects to a new power in the valley.

"Good morning, Lady Barforth."

"Good morning, Nicholas."

And I stepped into the pew beside him, knowing how conspicuous I would seem should I sit elsewhere, the entrance of the stately, timeless bride preventing further conversation between us, bringing me an unwilling image of Celia coming down this very aisle to this very bridegroom, beautiful—for the first and only time in her life—a breathless, delicate bloom that had soon

perished. And behind her came Giles Ashburn's bride, on fire
with gratitude, running—although she didn't know it then—
from Nicholas Barforth to Nicholas Barforth, determined to keep
faith with him yet losing it, keeping faith in the end not even
with myself. "I give you everything I can," Blaize had told me,
"which is rather more—in fact a great deal more, Faith Aycliffe
—than you give to me." Yet was he asking for my love or simply
telling me to be satisfied? "I give you everything I can—everything it is in my nature to give." Surely that could only be a re-
minder of our agreement, a warning that I should content myself
within the limits he had set and to which I had consented? Certainly I had overstepped those limitations by questioning him
about his infidelity, and had lost his trust long before that by
breaking the one promise he had asked of me. "I give you
everything I can, which is rather more than you give to me."
Did he want more? Could I give it? Assuredly I could, for I had
indeed thought of him as my dearest friend—as Nicholas and I,
in spite of all the love, the pain, the need, the rich complexity
between us, had never been friends—and I had missed Blaize
acutely since he had withdrawn from me. Did he want more? It
was the hope with which I tried to nourish my bleaker moments,
a pale, hesitant little hope which soon failed. For Blaize, above
all, was an opportunist, who had never, to my knowledge,
practised self-denial. If he wanted something from me, from
anyone, he would ask. And there was no denying that since
Celia died, and my own needs had somehow sharpened, whenever I tried to approach him I encountered nothing but cool air
and my own sadness.

We came out of the church into full sunshine, the second Mrs.
Agbrigg taking her husband's arm with authority, her handsome
head, beneath its relatively modest bonnet, held high, a smile of
composure only faintly tinged with satisfaction on her full, dark
red lips.

"Lady Barforth, how kind of you to come," she said, by no
means overwhelmed at my generosity, understanding it had
been done for Jonas, and considering herself a match for Lady
Barforth any day of the week. "And Mr. Barforth, too—how
kind. You *will* come back with us now, to Fieldhead, I know,
and take a glass of champagne."

"So we will," Nicholas said, kissing her hand, amused, I

thought, at meeting someone whose presence was as commanding as his own, and who took it for granted she would be
obeyed. "That is—I'll come if my sister-in-law will give me a
ride in her carriage since I left mine at the Swan."

"But of course—" murmured Mrs. Delaney-Oldroyd-Agbrigg,
and although a visit to Fieldhead was the last thing in the world
I intended, the memory of Nicholas' horse left in the Swan yard
the last thing I could bear on such a day, we drove off together
to be greeted on arrival by the new master of Fieldhead himself,
alighting from his own carriage to escort us into the house I had
last entered in the days when Mr. Oldroyd had wanted to marry
my mother.

The new mistress of that house had, as yet, made few changes
beyond the crimson velvet curtains which had so grieved my
sister, but her casual offer of a "glass of champagne" was, of
course, more elaborate than that, a well-garnished spread of
galantines and pâtés, the angel cakes and chocolate cakes for
which she had become famous, a sure indication that I would be
obliged to stay far longer than the quarter of an hour I had allowed.

"Dear Lady Barforth—do take a little of this—and that—
another glass," and because I was tearful again, thinking of
Celia, wishing Jonas well with all my heart yet not certain that
he would be well—that Grace would be well—I meekly accepted her food, her wine, strolled into her garden to admire her
plants, a glass of champagne in my hand, too many, already, in
my head, so that when I found myself alone with Nicholas, in
view of the others but separated from them by low box hedges,
several yards of roses, I was not sure if she—with her harlot's
knowledge and complicity—had arranged it.

He had a glass in his hand too, a cigar in the other, his skin
and his hair darker, it seemed, each time I stood close to him
than the time before, the resemblance between him and Blaize
growing smaller with the years as he became heavier, more dom-
inant, Blaize lighter, more elusive.

"You'll be glad to see your brother-in-law doing so well for
himself," he said, not asking me but telling me in the grand
manner of Jonas' new wife.

"I shall be very glad, if she can make him happy."

"Oh, there's not much doubt of that, surely."

"I do hope not."

"I'm sure not. She keeps a good house and a good table. She's given him the best business in the valley after mine—and I imagine she's accommodating in other directions. She knows what she wants, our Tessa Delaney, and since it happens to be Jonas I reckon he's set for life. I just hope she'll give him time off to handle one or two little matters of concern to me, since he's still my lawyer . . ."

And the fact that he had mentioned these matters which were of concern to him was a clear indication that they must also be of concern to me.

"I'm sure she will."

"Yes. Well, I'd best finish my drink and take my leave, for by rights I shouldn't be here at all. I've had word from Galton that Mr. Clevedon died in the night, so I should get over there, shouldn't I?"

"Nicholas—you should have gone at once."

"I do know that, Faith. But I was already on my way here when Georgiana's messenger caught me and I thought—well—since Mr. Clevedon was beyond any help of mine, I might as well carry on and give my support to the living. And, in fact, since I *am* here, I may as well remind Jonas that the estate can now be properly valued, and that he should start looking around him for a buyer—if he hasn't found me one already."

It was, perhaps, the strong sunlight, the wine which, curdled by shock, dazzled me, causing the rich colours of the garden to rush away from me into a pale obscurity and then back again, their impact crushing my stomach to nausea. But it was essential to right myself, for I knew he had followed me into the garden on purpose to tell me this, that my knowing it had some significance that I must be calm enough to understand.

"Nicholas, you can't sell Georgiana's abbey."

He took the glass from my hand and set it down on a low wall, his own beside it, the sun making diamonds of what had probably been the first Mrs. Oldroyd's—Miss Lucy Hobhouse's —wedding crystal.

"As it happens," he said quietly, "you are quite mistaken. It is not even Georgiana's abbey. The Galton estate is not held under entail nor under any kind of settlement whatsoever. The reigning Clevedon has always been able to dispose of it as he thought fit

—which, admittedly, has always been to the next male Clevedon in line. My wife's grandfather has decided differently. He could have left the property in trust for my son, but in fact, and very sensibly, he has left it to Georgiana. And since, as you well know, anything a married woman inherits belongs automatically to her husband, then we can safely say that Galton is mine."

"Are you trying to kill her, Nicholas?"

"Are you not being a trifle melodramatic, Faith? I am disposing of a few hundred barren acres and a house that would take thousands I can't spare to put right. I am disposing of what could be a future millstone around my son's neck, and a present distraction from what he ought to be doing in life."

"Does Georgiana know?"

"No. Until we find a buyer—which may not be easy—there's no need for her to know. She may as well enjoy the grouse moor as long as she can. You could mention it to Blaize, if you like. He knows so many people, and, as I said, a customer could be hard to find. The bare market value would satisfy me, and it can't be high—"

"You want me to tell Blaize, and you don't want me to tell Georgiana. Is that it?"

"I'm not aware that I want you to do anything."

But what his voice spoke to me was not of market values and purchasers, but of destruction, not only the ruin of Georgiana's bright childhood, the very essence of herself, but a doing to death of the last shred of our remembered emotion, a final hardening of his nature for which I was probably partly to blame, and couldn't bear.

"Good-bye then, Faith—I'll just have a word with our bridegroom and kiss the bride, and be on my way."

But I had to say more, he expected more, for the slight intake of my breath before speaking halted him, caused him to turn and face me.

"Nicholas . . ." And it was the ultimate opportunity. There would be no other.

"Nicholas, I've already lost you twice . . ."

"What are you talking about now?"

"You know very well. If you do this cruel thing . . ."

"I fully intend to—"

"Then it will be like losing you again."

"There's nothing in me for you to lose."

"Nicholas—I don't want to go through it a third time . . ."

"You survived before—"

"Yes, of course I did. I had to, and meant to. But you owe me something for that survival, Nicholas. Oh yes—you came to me, knowing I was in love with you, and told me you were in love with Georgiana, and I wished you joy. I didn't cling to your coattails and embarrass you with my silly broken heart. I wished you joy. I tried to mean it, and I certainly behaved as if I meant it. Don't you remember that?"

He glanced quickly across the box hedges, where the new Mrs. Agbrigg was still plying her guests with cake and champagne, and taking my arm, his hand hot but very hard, very steady, he drew me even further down the garden, to the deep spreading cover of a chestnut tree.

"I remember it, Faith. I hurt you. You crucified me. If there was a debt, I paid it."

And it was more urgent than ever now, more vital, for the time allowed us was running out.

"I paid it too, Nicholas. Listen to me—please, please—and just hear what I'm saying to you, not what I've said before, or what you think I might have said. I could have tolerated the scandal, Nicholas. I could have tolerated the isolation. I could have tolerated the risk. I loved you so much and I'd loved you for so long. I was ready to grow old waiting for you—or so I thought—and it was then that I discovered the one thing I couldn't tolerate. When Georgiana was ill with Venetia I had to wonder how I might feel if she died, and I knew I couldn't live with myself if what I actually did feel turned out to be gladness. Nicholas—I was ready to spend the rest of my life waiting for you. I *couldn't* spend the rest of my life waiting for her to die, wanting her to die—and if we'd stayed together, openly or secretly, I couldn't have avoided wanting it. I know what it would have turned me into—and you. There'd have been nothing but bitterness left between us in the end—which is all there seems to be now. But at least she's alive, and intact—something was salvaged. Nicholas—don't waste that . . ."

I could see the tender green of the chestnut leaves waving above me, dappling the sunshine, an intense blue sky, the richly overburdened earth of high summer. I could see my own hand offering itself to him with the shaky, groping movement of an old woman, although my skin, amazingly, was still smooth, my flesh still firm, only my spirit, it seemed, having aged a hundred, difficult years. I saw his hand, the square, workmanlike palm, the long, brown fingers, a heavy gold ring on one of them catching the sunlight as they closed very briefly, very painfully, around mine.

"Harden yourself against me, Faith. When they say I'm a callous devil, agree with them. The evidence is plain to see."

"I know. I see it, and know it to be true. Somehow I can't believe it."

"I'm sorry," he said, releasing my hand. "Really, Faith—if I could change it—but I know myself too well. I knew how you felt, and I shared it. I didn't want her to die either. But in the end I reckon something in me got twisted instead, or something you obviously don't much care for took root—I don't know. Either way, I'm not likely to change now. I don't dislike the way I am. It's easier, Faith—easier for me, at any rate. You'll understand what I mean. And don't forget to ask Blaize if he can find me a customer. He'll understand me as well."

Chapter Thirty-three

BLAIZE RETURNED HOME in time for Mr. Clevedon's funeral, accompanying me to Galton and then to Listonby, where we stayed for a subdued Friday-to-Monday, respectful of the dead and marvelling that Georgiana should be so calm. And although I opened my mouth a hundred times to tell him of Nicholas' plans for the abbey, a clamp descended on my tongue, a paralysis took hold of my throat, releasing me only when my brain had consented to speak of something else. Why? I couldn't be certain. Was it my great and growing reluctance to speak of Nicholas to Blaize, to speak of Nicholas to anyone, an inexplicable difficulty in so much as pronouncing his name, which caused me, when it could not be avoided, to refer to him as "my brother-in-law," "my cousin," "him." Or was it merely suspicion, a notion that Nicholas' motives had been other than they seemed. He had wanted me to tell Blaize. And in that case perhaps it would do Blaize no good to know. Yet whatever the rights and wrongs of it, the motives and manoeuvrings, I could not bring myself to tell him and as that tense August turned amber with September, the days quickening into the smoky pulse beat of autumn, I felt treacherous without understanding the nature of my treachery, uneasy and overburdened with a guilt which surely was not mine.

I saw a great deal of Georgiana. I stood beside her in the churchyard as Mr. Clevedon was laid to rest, walked with her afterwards in the cloister, meeting Nicholas' eyes as we went into that timeless passage, and meeting them again when we came out, unable to recognise either satisfaction or disappointment in him when her strange serenity made it clear I had divulged no secrets.

"It doesn't matter so much about Grandfather," she told me. "It was different with Perry, because he hadn't even started to live his life. Grandfather had nothing else he wished to do, and it's only our faces that change, after all. We're still here. You must have heard me say that before, since it's the creed I live by."

And crushed by pity and anxiety, remembering the Georgiana who had comforted me on the night Joel Barforth died, the Georgiana who had driven her horses through the flood, the vivid, loveable, laughable Georgiana of her better days, I went straight to Blaize and announced, "There's something I must tell you."

"Well, darling—if you must—" And that first quizzical lift of his eyebrow froze me, forced me, after a moment, to produce a trill of light laughter, a careless, "Oh, never mind. It doesn't signify."

Yet every time I heard her step I clenched my nerves in agonised expectation of disaster until her face told me she was still, in her own mind, the possessor of her ancestral acres, their rightful guardian for future generations as her grandfather had been, her unusual calm arising—I well knew—from the deep satisfaction of believing she was now empowered to pass them on intact to her son.

I lay in bed one night deluding myself with the nursery tale that Nicholas had changed his mind, that he could not, after all, perform this act of extreme cruelty. I awoke, far into the night, cold and horrified, recognising my delusion, my mind refusing any other function but to repeat over and over, "How will she bear it? How will she survive it?" And I knew, of course, that she would not.

It was a very fragile morning towards the end of September, a thin, pale sky, a light haze slanting across thirsty grasses and flowers blanched by the long, summer heat. My daughter was at school, my household quiet after the bustle of rising and breakfasting, the lull before anyone need think of luncheon. Blaize, who had travelled overnight from London, was somewhere in the house, having made no appointments until the afternoon. My windows were open, a scent of full-blown roses drifting through them, the scent of potpourri within, a huge, overburdened bee expiring on my window sill, birdsong in the elm trees at the edge of the garden, nothing to distract me from the sound of a sporting carriage driven at speed, nor the sight of Georgiana's face as she brought it to a perilous, shuddering stop, and came running indoors.

She looked very much as I had anticipated. I was prepared for it. And I had seen grief before. I had seen women from Simon Street who had lost eight out of ten children. I had myself lost a husband. I had seen the agonised collapse of Mr. Hobhouse as he had handed over the keys of Nethercoats, and of his children's futures. I had never seen a woman facing the loss of everything she possessed, everything in which she believed, her creed, her immortality, and the sheer savagery of it, the sheer nakedness, was overwhelming.

"Blaize?" she said as I ran to meet her, his name jerking itself out of her with the unco-ordinated movement of a marionette, and understanding that she needed to conserve every drop of her self-command I nodded and made a gesture of assent. But Blaize too had heard the approach of that aged curricle which had once belonged to Perry Clevedon, had recognised the wild, rake-hellish driving, and came quickly into the hall, sensing alarm with the fine, farsighted sensitivity of a cat.

"Georgiana?"

And as she began to speak, her face, once again, was the face of a tormented doll, the terrible effort of wooden features forcing themselves to emit human sounds when the only sound, perhaps, in her mind was a scream of raw hate and vengeance.

"I met a man on the road to Galton—a tenant of ours—how ridiculous—"

"Yes, Georgiana?"

"A man—as I said—who asked me if there was nothing I could do to stop the new master from—"

"What is it, Georgiana?"

"Nothing."

"Yes—what is it you can't say?"

"—to stop the new master from selling the estate."

"Dear God—" Blaize said.

"And so I told him what nonsense, and he said everyone in the village was talking of it—which couldn't signify because people do talk so in country places—so I went to the village—yes, I went to the village—"

"Georgiana, will you sit down?"

"Not yet. Blaize, if it should be true, you do know that I couldn't bear it."

"I know. Have you seen Nicholas?"

"No. I knew that's what I had to do. So I got the curricle and came back here as fast as I could. I drove right into the mill yard at Lawcroft and right out again. Blaize—I *couldn't*. My hands burned on to the reins and I couldn't let go—couldn't get down. Blaize—I have to know."

"Yes. I'll go and see him right away."

"Thank God for you, Blaize," and swaying forward, as if, like a soldier dying of wounds, she had endured only until her message had been delivered, she collapsed against him, allowing me to see this man who had warned me he would never be a rock for me to lean on, standing firm as a rock now for Georgiana, his body supporting hers to my drawing room sofa and then holding her, rocking her like a child, the caressing note of his voice whispering comfort against the dishevelled head she pressed against his shoulder, so that abruptly, painfully, my mind was flooded by sharp-etched memories of all the other times he had helped and protected her. Blaize stepping in adroitly to shield her from malice and back-biting in the early days of her marriage. Blaize going to fetch her from the sands at Bournemouth, worrying for her safety when Nicholas had remained on the path with me. Blaize waiting up the whole of one summer night at Listonby, watching from the window until she had ridden home. Blaize making the journey to Scarborough that fateful day to persuade me, harass me, frighten me into giving Nicholas up, not for my sake, but for hers, seeing me, perhaps, as no more than a threat to Georgiana's peace of mind. Blaize—so many years ago—leaning forward in his mother's carriage, saying to Caroline, "She is exactly the kind of girl a man might come to love quite foolishly, without at all wanting to." Blaize *then*, his voice continuing, cool, unforgotten. "She could get inside a man's head and his skin and he could find himself quite unable to get rid of her, no matter how much he tried." Blaize *now*, offering her the strong shoulder for her tears, the warm, protecting arms for her reassurance as he had never offered them to me. And through the layers of my pity, my remorse, my toleration, something stirred, heaved, made its long-subdued protest so that the only clear thought in my head was, Take your hands off that woman.

I left the room quickly, gave instructions that my husband was not to be disturbed, mentioned the word "discretion" to my butler, who interpreted it correctly as keeping as many people as possible out of the way. I walked back to the drawing room door, stretched out a hand towards it, and could not move any further, caught painfully and perhaps ridiculously in a nightmare panic. I had stood in dreams, many times, exactly like this, in a familiar house, nothing to threaten me but the knowledge that somewhere, on an upper floor, was a room I must not enter. And so I would not enter it. There were other rooms in my dream, pleasant rooms, no reason at all for my feet to mount the stairs—although they mounted them—no reason at all to find myself standing at that one forbidden door, hypnotised by the nameless terror behind it.

I stood at that door now, waiting, as the fear took shape. I went inside and there it was, my own blindness, my own inadequacies, the futile knowledge that I had entered far too late. And as I crossed the threshold Blaize did not even raise his head to look at me.

Georgiana was sitting alone, a brandy glass in her hand, Blaize leaning on the arm of the sofa, not touching her but alert, intuitive, *there*, to anticipate her need.

"Promise me," he was saying, "that you will stay here while I'm away—no running off in that crazy curricle, Georgiana, no wild schemes. I don't know how long I'll be, since Nick could have gone to any one of the mills, or the Piece Hall, anywhere. And when I do find him it could be over in ten minutes or it could last all day. I must know that you'll be here when I return."

She drank off her brandy, set down the glass, and sat for a moment staring down at her own narrow hands, the tension in her slight body so piercing that it got into my own nerves and sinews, drawing them out in subtle anguish.

"I'll stay," she said, her voice no more than a hoarse whisper, her eyes still fixed on her hands, which now had coiled themselves into fists. "And, Blaize—he must want something—surely? —something more than it seems—?"

"Oh yes—I do believe so."

"Then tell him, please, that I'll do anything. Yes—it's not businesslike, I know, to make offers before one knows the asking price. I've learned that much from being so long a manufacturer's wife. But, you see, when something is beyond price, nothing one offered could be too much. You have *carte blanche*—"

"I know," he said quietly, and pressing his hand lightly against her shoulder he got up and went out into the hall, asking me with a glance to follow him.

We stood in the open doorway waiting for his carriage to be brought round, my arms folded as if against the cold although the sun was shining, the air still and heavy with the fragrances of summer's end.

"You don't seem much surprised about this, Faith."

"No. I'm not surprised," and I was smiling, in the way sacrificial victims are supposed to smile on their way to the altar, as my voice continued. "I already knew."

"I beg your pardon?"

"I already knew. Nicholas told me on Jonas' wedding day."

"You will have a reason, of course—and I do hope it is a good one—for not telling me?"

"No. No reason at all."

"And is that all you can say?"

He walked down the shallow steps to the carriage drive, leaving me in the doorway, my arms still folded, taking with him the first flare of his annoyance, so that when he returned his voice was curt, his eyes not angry, I thought, but disappointed, disdainful.

"Faith—there's no time now to have this out. But let me explain this—if you'd told me the estate was to be sold—as you should have done, as any woman without a personal axe to grind would have done—then all this unpleasantness could have been avoided. I don't know what Nicky's up to. Possibly he does want to get rid of his wife. Possibly he does see the abbey as a bad influence on his son. Those may, or may not, be his reasons I don't imagine for one moment he'd sell the estate to me, but if I'd known in advance I could have used an agent and no one the wiser— However—since there's no chance of that now—I shall just have to find another way."

The carriage was driven smartly round from the back of the

house and I went with him to the step, hugging myself tighter, the cold which seemed to be attacking me from within, making me shiver.

"Faith," he said, wanting, I think, to give me a second chance. "Her roots are so deep in that soil that if they were taken up she might just wither—not necessarily die, although one can't be certain—but just wither. If I can prevent it—however I can prevent it—then I will. You must understand that."

"Yes, of course."

"And you'll help? You'll look after her now?"

"Of course."

"Thank you," he said, and because his eyes were still careful, asking me, "Can I trust you?" I gave him such reassurance as I could, not being myself quite certain of it.

He stepped up into the carriage, drove off, and I went back inside to help him, as I had promised, smoothing out the tangle of detail he had neglected. I sent a note to Prudence asking her to keep Blanche and Venetia until they were sent for, another, infinitely more cautious message to Aunt Verity explaining that Georgiana was with me, and that all was well. I conferred somewhat apologetically with my cook about the luncheon we had not eaten, making no firm promises about dinner. And when it was done I went back into the drawing room and sat down in a thick silence, waiting for the blast which must alter the course of both our lives, which had already shaken mine.

For a long time we had nothing to say to each other, Georgiana being not really present in the room at all but far away in the meadows and moorlands of her childhood, the long summertime of her adolescence, reliving those eager days with Perry drop by drop—Perry, who could never be lost because Galton could never be lost—and although I struggled hard to pity her as I should, to love her as I believed I did, I couldn't rid my memory of her trusting head on Blaize's shoulder, nor my own anguished cry, Take your hands off that woman, although I knew he had never really touched her.

Yet what did touching matter? He had touched other women, beautiful women, I supposed, made anonymous by distance and by his own nonchalance. I had accepted it as an essential part of his nature. But tenderness, concern, the ingredients, surely, of love for Georgiana, all that was, quite simply, beyond acceptance. I could neither tolerate it nor even contemplate it with anything approaching reason. Yet I had seen it. I forced myself to look at it again and as I did so, jealousy assaulted me, left me gasping and sick, left me foolish and astonished and bitterly cold.

"Blaize must have found him by now," she whispered at last.

"Yes. I imagine so." And there was coldness in my voice because coldness was all I had.

She got up, paced a moment, sat down again, her hands on her knees.

"I didn't know he hated me so much."

"Didn't you?" And I had spoken harshly to punish myself, for all the things I hadn't known.

"Faith—?" she said, her start of surprise clearing my head enough for me to realise my own strangeness, and that she was not to blame.

"Georgiana—do forgive me. I can't think why I said that, since it can't be true."

"Don't you think so?" she said, and as she leaned towards me her pointed face was almost eager.

"I wouldn't mind hate, Faith. I understand it. If Nicky had been with me this morning when I heard about the abbey I could have turned on him so easily with my driving whip and killed him, I believe—really—if I'd managed to hit him hard enough in the ten minutes before my head cooled. It's not a pleasant feeling, perhaps, but at least it's alive. At least it's not silent. And if he wants to punish me like this then he must hate me—surely? What else could it be? There's no profit to be made from selling my land; the money I'd need to keep it going would be nothing to him. It has to be for my chastisement."

"You sound as if you want him to hate you."

"Oh, dear," she said, pressing the palms of her hands against her eyes. "I believe I do. How terrible—except that if he can still feel so strongly— I don't know. Perhaps we could just *talk* again. A little thing like that would be a great deal."

"And the abbey? Could you forgive him if he sold it?"

"No," she said, suddenly on her feet in one, knife-edged movement, her body so rigid with terror, reminding me so strongly of myself face to face with that nightmare door, that I threw my arms around her and held her fast, not with the comforting as-

laize but as one drowning woman might cling to an-
of us separately floundering.
—what is it?"

othing. Pay no attention to me. Don't worry. Blaize will be
ack soon. He means to buy the abbey and give it back to you,
somehow or other, and he'll find a way—truly he will . . ."

"And you wouldn't mind that?"

"Of course not. Why should I? Why *should* I?"

"I wouldn't claim it for myself," she whispered, her lips very
pale. "If he could keep it for Gervase that would be enough—
and it might satisfy Nicky. I'd agree never to set foot on Galton
land again if I could be sure it was still there, for Gervase. I
hope Blaize has thought to tell him that."

But Blaize returned by mid-afternoon having achieved nothing, having made the mistake, in fact, of going first to Lawcroft
so that by the time Nicholas' whereabouts had been ascertained
he had already boarded the Leeds train.

"I left a message with the stationmaster asking him to come
here," Blaize told me, still watchful. "We can do nothing now
but wait, which gives him an advantage I don't like. Faith—
when he arrives take Georgiana upstairs and stay there."

And I was not to blame—although perhaps Blaize did not immediately agree—when my butler, either from a surfeit of curiosity or an attack of nerves, blundered, showing Nicholas
directly into the drawing room and allowing Georgiana no time
to escape.

She shot to her feet, alert and desperate, her breath catching
on a low moan, but Nicholas merely glanced at her, her attitude
of defence telling him all he needed to know, and turned instead
to Blaize.

"I understand you were looking for me."

"Yes. I expect you know why."

"I expect I do."

And already the conflict was between the two of them, as it
had always been, the Barforth males who could submit to no authority but their own, who had fought each other since their
nursery days for anything and nothing, and who were closing in
now, on the battleground of my drawing room carpet, to put an
end to it. And I started to shiver again.

"You took your time," Nicholas said. "If you'd come to me sooner, I reckon we could have spared the ladies . . ."

"I didn't know about it sooner."

"You mean she didn't tell you?"

"She didn't tell me."

"Didn't she, by God," he said, his mouth twisting into a smile that was deliberately sardonic and unkind. "Now that does surprise me, and it's a pity. But never mind. I didn't want this to happen so publicly, but there's no help for it . . ."

And sliding a hand inside his coat he took out a familiar brown envelope and set it down with a brisk slap on the table.

"That's my new offer for your share of the mills, Blaize. I've had to slightly reduce the down payment, I'm afraid, since times are getting so hard. But I'll tell you what I'm ready to do. I'll throw in the abbey to make up the difference. How does that suit you? Otherwise, of course, the estate goes under the hammer."

I heard a strangled sound beside me which must have been Georgiana and then, for a dreadful moment, could hear nothing but my own pulse beat, my own protest, for I had suspected it could be something like this and had wanted, most acutely, to be wrong. Hate and punishment would have been a beginning. Reconciliation a possibility. But, as always—and I *should* have known—it was hard cash, ambition, the limits he had chosen for himself, the limits within which he felt powerful, and safe, and which he had no desire to cross. "Personal relationships don't suit me," he had once told me and I had not believed him. But he had wanted it to be true, had forced it to be true, and I believed him now.

"You clever bastard," Blaize said, sitting down, I think, because his legs, in that moment of shocked revelation, failed to support him, looking, for the first time, older than Nicholas, his frame leaner, more brittle, too light in substance to combat the bold, tough-fibred bulk of the younger, far more ruthless man.

"Yes—you clever bastard. You used Oldroyd's whore to get Nethercoats, and Galton to get me." And as his words ended, heralding a deep silence as chilling and insidious as sudden drifts of snow, I continued to shiver. If Blaize accepted this offer, if whatever it was he felt for Georgiana proved strong enough for him to make this sacrifice, then I knew our marriage would be over. Yet if he refused it, and harm came to her as a result, then we could have no real future together either. Guilt, I thought, or solitude. Which is it to be?

I saw Blaize only from my eye corner, Nicholas not at all. Georgiana standing chalk-white, arrow-straight, her hands clenched, the taut concentration of her face telling me she was well aware of the sacrifice which had been demanded, the implications of its acceptance. And already, for me, it was over. This morning I had been aware of a few vague sorrows. This fine, early evening I knew I had been my own sorrow, my own disaster. All I wanted now was to go back to the evening Blaize had given me my cameo swan, to relive that home-coming and the next, to make sure there would be another; and I could see no real chance of it.

"I reckon you can give me your answer straightaway," Nicholas said, obviously in no doubt of it, and as I made a half turn, intending to leave the room—since I could not doubt it either—Georgiana suddenly lifted her head, her cheeks flooded with colour, and crossing to Blaize's side, looked directly at Nicholas and said, "It won't be necessary for him to give an answer at all."

He began, I think, to tell her to be silent, but she made a gesture of quiet command that I had seen before, a gesture the squires of Galton, perhaps, had made from time immemorial so that now it was bred into their heirs. And although she was young and slender and very certainly a woman, it could have been her grandfather standing there, or his grandfather, a line of upright, honourable men whose code it was to sacrifice themselves, at need, for the good of others rather than allow others to be sacrificed: a line of men—and women—who could be narrow and overbearing, but could also be very true and very strong.

"Please don't say anything, Blaize. There is absolutely no need. For even if you could be persuaded to agree to this monstrous coercion, I would not allow it."

"Georgiana," he said. "You shouldn't—" but she silenced him too, with that same movement of calm authority, a woman I had not seen before, who had been badly hurt, assuredly, but who seemed able to meet and to overcome this new pain as bravely as the madcap girl in her could gallop home from the hunt with a broken bone or pick herself up bruised and laughing from a stony ditch.

And the whole room was completely full of her.

"Oh, Nicholas, how very like you," she said. "I have been sitting here all the day trying to decide just why you hated me so much, whether you wanted me dead so that you could marry again, or merely wished to drive me insane so that I might be locked up out of your way, or whether, perhaps, there could still be a spark of a quite different insanity left between us—such romantic notions. I thought you were doing it all for passion, when really—oh my goodness—I see now it couldn't possibly be that. It's just a matter of business, isn't it? What else? And really, Nicky, it won't do, you know. Don't you think we've embarrassed your brother, and poor Faith, long enough—and to no good purpose? I think we should leave them in peace."

"Be careful," he said, "be very careful, Georgiana—" but although the threat was there, the anger of a man who had forgotten how to be thwarted, it was less than I had supposed, an indication that even he was aware of the change in her, the sudden deepening of her nature, a moment of growth and self-knowledge leading her to a threshold it should be our privilege to watch her cross.

"You must think very poorly of me, Nicky, if you imagine I would lay claim even to my rightful inheritance at such a price."

"I'd think you a fool if you didn't," he told her, recovering from his initial shock with the speed of a seasoned campaigner, his body alert now with the stalking caution of a predator circling her defences, certain of breeching them since he no longer believed in the existence of a woman—or a man—who could not be bought or bullied or otherwise persuaded.

"Georgiana," Blaize said, with quiet pleading. "Indeed, you must be careful. This is no game."

"Oh—I think it is. What else can one call it? Nicky wants your share of the mills. He has the money to buy but no weapon to make you sell. But then my grandfather dies and, gambling on his belief that I cannot live without the abbey and that you will not allow me to be destroyed, he decides to use me as that weapon. A very simple game—and very effective—except that I will not be so used. Good heavens, Nicky, you have not the slightest chance of success. I have only to say I do not want the abbey and all your cards fall down."

"Then say it, Georgiana," he told her, menacing her quietly, almost casually, since he still believed her to be incapable of any such thing. "Say it and mean it—"

"I . . ."

"Yes, Georgiana—"

"I don't want the abbey—not on your terms."

He swung away from her, his back briefly turned, and when I saw his face again he was actually smiling.

"Ah yes—I see you qualify your statement. You don't want the abbey on my terms—which doesn't convince me that you're ready to give it up."

"I believe I am."

"I doubt it. What you really believe is that I won't go through with the sale. And if that's the hope you're clinging to, then you couldn't be more mistaken. I'll do it, Georgiana. Ask Blaize."

"He'll do it," Blaize said, still strangely brittle, very pale.

"Ask Faith."

"He'll do it," I answered, my mouth stiff and awkward to manage. "He'll really do it, Georgiana . . ."

"I know," she told me almost kindly. "He'd have to, I realise that, to save his pride and ease his temper. I know—strangers walking in the cloister, riding in the stream—I'll say it for you, Nicky, to save you the trouble of taunting me. I know."

She made a small gesture with her hands, pushing some unseen object away, and smiled, shakily but with resolution.

"Nicky, I would like to make you understand. This morning I believed no price could be too high. I was wrong. The Clevedon land nourishes the Clevedons—you've heard me say that often enough, too often I suppose—but only if we deserve it. No, no— I'm not talking fairy tales. If I accepted your quite shameful terms, then the crops wouldn't fail and the cows wouldn't abort, I know that very well. But if I lost my self-esteem I could hardly consider myself a Clevedon, and I'd have no right to the abbey then. I'd be the stranger in my own cloister, and I would prefer not to be there at all. There's no need to take the abbey away from me, Nicky, I'll give it to you freely, even if the law says it's not mine to give—for it seems to me that, in this case, the law is showing very little common sense."

She paused, her hands clasping themselves jerkily together, the great strain in her face sharpening every feature to a heart-rending clarity, her eyes a darker green than I remembered, her eyebrows a deep copper, a dusting of freckles across her resolute, patrician nose, a beading of sweat above her lip, the merest suggestion of tears blinked fiercely away whenever she felt them threaten. And she had not yet done.

"Yes, Nicky—I'll give it away, and let me tell you what it is I'm giving—since you see everything in terms of what it could fetch in the market place. I don't understand such things but I can tell you what my gift is worth to me. Every happy day of my life is in that house. My father and my grandfather are in the churchyard, and my brother, who was not a good man—but I loved him. To you it is a heap of stone. To me every stone has a voice. But it doesn't matter. Take it all, Nicky, and sell it, because if it has become an instrument of harm—a weapon—then I can't wish to keep it. My grandfather would not have kept it himself on those terms. My son, if he grows to be the man I am hoping for, would not wish to receive it from me at such a cost to others."

Nicholas said, "How noble. Perhaps you'd care to visit your tenants tomorrow and explain why they're to be dispossessed." And I could have slapped him, hurt him.

"You can't turn them off—surely?"

"Some of them, yes, I can. The choice is yours."

"Then do it, Nicky."

Once again he turned away, allowing the silence to fall, Blaize and myself remaining on the edge of it, Georgiana standing with her hands neatly folded now, her head high, waiting with at least a surface calm for the next blow.

"What now, Nicky?"

"Just this. Don't stand in my way, Georgiana. You'll surely regret it."

And this conventional threat surprised me, caused me to glance at him keenly, half-afraid of seeing defeat in his face, although I wanted him to be defeated. But there was not even a spark of anger in him now, nothing so warm nor so weak as that, nor even any great coldness. Calculation, certainly, and shrewdness, a perfect readiness to manipulate his wife's finest feelings, as if they had been figures on a balance sheet, not from greed, or jealousy, or any kind of passion, but for the sake of the manipulation itself. And for a moment Georgiana allowed him to look at her in silence, her body relaxing now beyond calm to a strange and moving serenity.

"I believe you are right," she told him. "I will regret it. But not for the reasons you suppose. I have been so afraid of you sometimes, Nicky, and now, quite suddenly, I can see no cause. What can you really do to me? The law allows you full control of my body, and my spirit, we all know that—but I have already told you that the law, in these matters, is sadly lacking in sense. All I need to do is refuse—and go on refusing— And if that is a very alarming step to take, at least the first time—and it *is* very alarming—I would get used to it. Eventually I would be bound to prevail. The abbey is the only real cord you had to bind me, and now it's gone I do believe I'm free. How very astonishing, but really, Nicky, what else can you take away from me?"

"I wonder," he said smoothly, almost as if this unexpected resistance, this stretching of his ingenuity, was giving him enjoyment. "Let's see. There are the children—"

But even this—which I had anticipated with dread—did not dismay her.

"Yes, indeed. The children. In law you are their guardian and I am nothing—I realise that—just the brood mare that gave them birth. And who ever heard a brood mare complain of ill usage when one takes her foals away? Yes, Nicky, the law allows you to treat me in just that fashion, for I have made enquiries as to my exact rights and have been correctly informed that I have no rights at all. But, for all that, I am not sure you can do it. My children are no longer babies who can be locked away in a nursery with a nanny to bar the door. You could keep me out of Tarn Edge, but you can hardly keep Gervase and Venetia in— not all the time. And your mother would not help you to do it in any case. If they love me and want to be with me, then they will come to me, whatever I have done, wherever I may be. It may not be in accordance with the law but it accords well with reality. I am not afraid of it."

"I take it you are thinking of leaving me, then?"

"Yes," she said without hesitation, but without hurry, as if it was the most natural thing in the world. "I have been thinking of leaving you for some time."

And when I made a flustered movement of escape, a muttered plea that they must wish to be alone, Blaize silenced me with a gesture, while neither Nicholas nor Georgiana appeared to notice my interruption at all.

"It can hardly surprise you, Nicky."

"It doesn't. I suppose you had planned to live at the abbey."

"Yes. I had planned to be discreet, as a woman should. I thought if I went over there for a month, three months, six months together, then there would be no gossip when it became a year—forever."

"You could still do that, Georgiana." But even before she shook her head I doubt if he expected to be taken seriously. For the abbey, as a weapon, had lost its cutting edge. Whether in the end it would be relinquished or not, she had shown Nicholas that she could live without it and I understood, with a mixture of respect and sorrow, a touch of grudging amusement, that he had put it out of his mind. The abbey had been a possibility. It was so no longer. And his acute, deliberately narrowed brain would soon be leaping forward—if it had not already begun—to explore other possibilities, some other way of settling his differences with Blaize. I had been reluctant to witness his defeat. He was not defeated. He had simply put the matter in abeyance.

"No, Nicky. I wouldn't like to do that now."

"What would you like, then?"

And lowering her eyes, she said, almost in a whisper, overcome even in her new-found strength, by the enormity of the request she was making, "I think—in fact—is it possible for us to be divorced? There have been some new laws, have there not?"

"Yes."

"Then what must I do?"

"Please—not here," I said in anguish, for divorce, although possible now in law, and in London, was unknown in Cullingford, was as shameful, as unforgiveable, as great a casting-out as it had ever been, and I didn't want that for her. But turning to me, half-smiling, she said, "Oh, Faith, I am so sorry, but please don't stop me now, for if you do I may never find my voice again. And it must be said. I can't live with you again, Nicky, and it is for your sake as much as mine. We have not been good for each other. No—*that* we have not. To begin with I was foolish and inexperienced and easily hurt and you were never altogether sure you loved me. Sometimes it was to distraction—although that was long ago—sometimes hardly at all, even from the start. You confused me, Nicky, and by the time I gained some understanding of the things you needed in a woman I rather imagine you had discovered them elsewhere—and I was very lonely. I was not self-sufficient, you see, when we married. I had never needed to be. I had grown up among people who loved me and who told me so. We lived *together,* not separately each one in his private eggshell. And silence terrifies me. Sometimes I had to get to Galton just to convince myself that I wasn't dying . . . I could feel the blood turning sluggish in my veins and I had to keep it flowing. Well, I am a little more in command of myself now, and a good deal older. I have learned, really, that what I must do is the best I can, and our remaining together would not be for the best . . . It would not be honest. We have damaged each other enough. And I think we have failed each other enough. I have seen your father, sometimes, as hard as you. But what he felt for your mother always came through it. I have never been able to do that for you, Nicky. And you have never learned to accept me as I am. You have wanted me to be myself and different from myself all together, and it has been too much to ask. I have soured you and you have stifled me. And why should we continue to spread the misery of it through our lives, and our children's lives, so that the Cullingford tea tables might not be shocked? I suppose they will call me a whore when I leave you but I shall not feel like one, and you will know I am not. Will it be very difficult?"

For a moment I thought he couldn't answer, but then he spoke gruffly, gratingly almost, as if the words had been forced through some blockage in his throat.

"To leave me? No—no difficulty except that you have no money and I would not be obliged to support you. Divorce? Relatively simple nowadays—if you are ready to supply me with proof of your adultery."

"I have not committed adultery, Nicky."

"No. I never thought you had. But if you wish to obtain a divorce there is no other way."

"You could not . . ."

"No. Adultery on the part of a husband is not a ground for divorce unless it is accompanied by other offences of which I am not—and couldn't be—guilty. I'm sorry. I don't make the law. In this instance I simply benefit from it. I would have to track you down like a criminal—which is how the world would see you, and treat you. I would have to catch you with your lover, like a thief caught with his loot. And then I would have to take action against you. If I succeeded then, it could only be because the charge of adultery had been proved, which would allow the Cullingford ladies to call you whatever names they liked. I am not sqeamish, Georgiana, but I wouldn't enjoy doing that to you. And even then you would not save the abbey. Should our marriage be dissolved you could take nothing away with you. Your abbey, your children, the few hundred pounds your grandfather left you, would still legally belong to me—unless I chose to be generous."

"And would you?"

"I don't know."

"We'll talk about it, shall we?"

And when he, quite clearly, had no answer, she made it for him. "Yes, I believe we will. My goodness, how strangely our prayers are sometimes answered. What I hoped for—even a day ago—was that we could somehow begin to talk to each other. And now— Ah well, I am no schoolroom goose. I won't live with you again, Nicky. Oh no— I haven't altogether displeased you tonight, have I? I may have spoiled your scheme but you don't really mind that. You'll soon concoct another. And I've been bold, at least, and interesting. I've struck back at you, which you can't quite help liking . . . I know. And I know it wouldn't last. There'd be silence again very soon, and it's far better for us to live apart and learn to talk— Oh, dear—I think—yes, really, Nicky—I would like to go back to Tarn Edge now. Faith, if I may use your mirror a moment?"

And as I made a move towards her I had no need of Blaize's restraining glance to tell me she needed to be alone.

Chapter Thirty-four

I DIDN'T BELIEVE that anything more could be said, certainly I could not have spoken. But after a moment Blaize got to his feet, and looking at Nicholas, nodded and smiled wryly, almost wonderingly, his face plainly showing the stress of the day.

"It occurs to me that the lady may have won herself an abbey all on her own," he said.

"It could well be—or not. Who knows?" And picking up the long, brown envelope, Nicholas looked at it for a moment and then tore it neatly into two even pieces.

"All right, Blaize. So much for that. I don't see the point in suggesting we could work together again. Do you still want that split?"

"I'm not sure I want it but I'll take it. I think it's the best we can do."

"We'll see Agbrigg in the morning and get the figures right. And then you can set yourself up as a manufacturing man. I'm not usually free with advice but I'll tell you this much—you'll need somebody reliable to look after your sheds."

"Yes, I know. Are you starting to worry about me, Nick? I thought I might take Freddy Hobhouse off your hands. He's reliable enough, and he might feel easier about taking my money than yours."

"He might at that. I wouldn't stand in his way—since I don't need him. And if you should happen to sell the sheds back to me in a year or two it would help to know they'd been properly managed."

Blaize smiled, nodded again, a swordsman, I thought, accepting a challenge.

"I'll have a word with him then. Who knows—it might even boost his confidence so high that he'd marry my wife's sister and make himself a rich man again—rich enough to buy his own sheds back, I reckon. And Nick—since we're exchanging advice —don't rely too much on Dan Adair. He's good but he's not young, and it's hard out there on the road—harder than it used to be."

"I know. I've got a lad or two coming up. I wouldn't waste your time worrying about me, Blaize. There's no reason for it."

"No reason at all. I notice you can't say the same for me."

And this time it was Nicholas who smiled.

"I reckon not—but we'll see how it goes. And if it goes downhill, Blaize, then I expect you'll have the sense to pull out before it's gone too far. Because even for Tarn Edge, I'm not the man to throw good money after bad."

"That's what you're hoping for, is it, Nick?—that I'll pull out at the first slump in trade, or that I'll get bored . . . ?"

"No. I don't deal much in hope. It's what I'm expecting."

"I'll see you in Croppers Court then, first thing tomorrow—if Agbrigg's wife allows him to practice law so early in the day."

"Aye. And after that we'll meet in the Piece Hall—if you can remember where to find it."

"Oh yes—and if I should happen to miss the right turning, I'll find somebody to direct me."

Georgiana came back, not entering the room but hovering in the hall wanting urgently to be gone, an air about her of a woman who has been very ill, resolute in spirit but still bodily frail.

"Is the carriage coming, Blaize? I need a breath of air."

And as they went outside to await the arrival of Nicholas' horse and the ancient sporting curricle which had been Perry Clevedon's, I stood at the window and looked out at them, no longer shivering with that inner cold but far distant, yet, from any certainty of warmth and ease.

I saw Georgiana lean down a moment as she drew on her driving gloves to say a word to Blaize and then drive off, steadily, skilfully, her destination apparently clear. I didn't know if she would succeed, or could succeed. I was proud of her. I loved her. I saw Nicholas lift himself briskly into his saddle, a powerful silhouette in the twilight, quite certain of his own success, as I was certain of it too. And as I watched him ride away I knew, with the relief one feels at the ending of physical pain, that he had no need of my anxiety, my remorse, no need, in fact, of me at all. I had seen him change and had believed myself responsible for it. I realised now that he had not changed but simply progressed, quite normally, to the man his nature and his ancestry had always intended him to be.

Had Georgiana never come his way, had he married me instead, I would not have contented him. He would still have required Nethercoats from the Hobhouses, Tarn Edge from Blaize, anything and everything that challenged his ingenuity, any woman, perhaps, who—like the widowed Faith Ashburn—had said "we must not." And although, had I understood all this a dozen years ago, I would still have married him, I had not done so. I had taken other directions, opened other doors, so that now I could look back at him, from their various thresholds, and understand that neither of us had been to blame.

I had sat, long ago, by my fireside and told my sister, "I am a woman who loves Nicholas Barforth. That is all there is to me."

That woman had meant what she said. For her it had been true. But that woman, very gradually, had become a chrysalis for someone else who, for a long time, had been painfully, sometimes eagerly emerging. It was no longer in me to love with that overwhelming, self-destructive intensity. I was no longer capable of submerging myself in another person, nor did I wish to do so. I had indeed loved Nicholas Barforth but there was far more to me now than that. What I wanted now was to love, with clear eyes, a man who saw me clearly, who would allow me air to breathe and space to grow, who would not need to prove his manhood by reducing me to a state of slavish adoration or childlike dependence, a man, in fact, who was strong enough, and sure enough, to value me as a woman. And there was only one man who had ever offered me the enormous gift of freedom.

"Faith," Blaize said, somewhere in the room behind me, my first awareness of him being the warm odour of his cigar, the fresh citrus of the toilet water he wore.

"Yes."

"I was sharp with you earlier. I'm sorry."

And for a few moments we talked around ourselves, of other people, other aspirations, approaching each other slowly, and with care.

"Will Freddy Hobhouse come to you, Blaize?"

"Oh yes—not that Nick will worry about that, since whatever Freddy can do he can do it better. He'd be hard-pressed, perhaps, if I took Dan Adair . . ."

"But you won't?"

"I can't. I've asked him already and he'll use me, I imagine, to push up his value with Nick. But he has the sense to stay where he's needed—which is hardly with me. Even Freddy knows that much, or if he doesn't then Prudence will soon explain. If she marries him, she'll learn how to drop me a hint occasionally that he's thinking of starting up on his own with her capital—knowing I'll be inclined to change his mind with pound notes."

"Prudence wouldn't . . ." I began, and then, meeting his quizzical eyes, "Yes—so she would." And although he was smiling at me, the time had gone when I could have leaned towards him, surrendering into laughter. It would not suffice.

"And Georgiana . . . ?"

"Yes?" he said, cautious now and very intent, and sensing the change in him, remembering acutely the comforting arch of his arm around her, I shivered, feeling a sharp stab of pain, a swift upsurging of hope—of excitement almost—when I saw he understood the reason why. And I knew I could say anything to him. Here was the man who knew me best, the friend, the lover, who expected me to be neither better nor worse, nor anything other than myself. Here was the man who required to maintain his own individuality but would allow me to keep mine, and I was at ease with him, warm with him, stimulated by him; I was adult with him.

"What shall I tell you about Georgiana, Faith?" And I knew he would tell me anything I asked, even if it hurt me, since I was no household angel to be protected and petted but a woman capable of judging the amount of hurt she could withstand.

"She was the rare and special person you used to talk about, wasn't she? The one who was always in the next room. You said you'd stopped looking but, of course, since it was Georgiana all the time— It was Georgiana, wasn't it?"

"Yes," he said, quite gently, not out of kindness for me but because it was a gentle matter. "So it was. And you must see that she remained rare and special precisely because I left her in that other room."

"Yes—but then, would you have parted with your half of the mills for me?"

"I can't believe," he said, looking at me very steadily, "that you would ever have placed me in the position of having to do so."

"No, I suppose not, which would be a compliment . . ."

"It is a compliment."

"I daresay—except that it makes me sound so very boring . . ."

And once again we were close to that easy, pleasant laughter, that companionable surrender, until he took my hand, pressed it, and said, quite ardently for him, "I have never—absolutely never—found you boring."

"Then tell me . . ."

"Yes. Faith, I was twenty-three or thereabouts when I first met Georgiana, and it was too soon for me. If I'd been ten years older —perhaps—but I really don't think so. I wanted her as she was that first Christmas—do you remember?—with mud on her skirt and blood on her cheek, trampling her dirty boots on my father's carpet—because to a frank, free spirit like hers what could carpets matter? There was a skylark inside her sometimes, and I didn't want to see it crushed and caged. Nicky tried to do that as perhaps any man would have done who really loved her—since what man could feel safe with a skylark? It escaped today and took flight. I'm glad—very glad for her, and for myself too because it was a lovely thing to watch."

"And will it last?"

"Possibly not. She's not Prudence, who can stand alone. She may come to earth and find herself tied to Julian Flood, for I believe he loves her—certainly he needs her—and if she goes off with him to provide grounds for her divorce Julian will be unwilling to release her. He'll marry her if he can, which will make her our lady of the manor. . . . I doubt if Nick will put any obstacles in her way. He'd rather see her settled, I imagine, with Julian Flood than wandering alone, a prey to any man. But on the other hand she may fly very high and very far. I wouldn't wish to follow her. I find myself somewhat firmly attached to the ground and—all that apart—I have lived with you now, Faith, for a long and valuable time. I couldn't welcome anything which might spoil that."

"Why?"

"My word—" he said, but whatever easy, witty remark had risen to the surface of his mind was immediately suppressed as he saw the necessity for my question. Why indeed? And it must be stated, not masked by humour, but stated very clearly. The old limits we had set ourselves, which had long been crumbling, were now almost broken down, the old restraints abandoned. We were almost at liberty, had almost disentangled ourselves from the past. And there was no doubt it was a big step we were taking.

He got up and crossed, characteristically, to the fireplace, leaning one arm along the mantel shelf, looking reflectively, ruefully, at the arrangement of tulle roses I had placed in the empty hearth.

"I think I can tell you why. But I would like you to tell me something first. When you heard about the plan to sell the abbey why didn't you come to me?"

And although it would not be easy it was certainly fair, for if I had needed to know about Georgiana I could not refuse to talk to him of Nicholas.

"I think—really—it was because I knew he wanted me to tell you. And I concluded, in that case, that it would do you no good to know."

"You didn't trust him, in fact?"

"No," and it had to be the truth, or else he would know it. And indeed it was the truth. "No, Blaize. Perhaps I never have trusted him—I thought otherwise but now it seems to me that I never really did. I don't mean it unkindly. I think I mean, not that I didn't trust *him* but that I never trusted his judgement. There is a difference."

"Yes indeed. You mean that his judgement would always be heavily weighted to his own advantage?"

"I suppose I do."

He looked down at the flowers a moment longer and then, raising his head, gave me his brilliant, quizzical smile. "Faith, I must warn you that my own judgement is invariably weighted in the same direction."

"I know that. Perhaps I feel that your advantage is bound to be mine . . ."

"Thank you," he said, and coming to sit on the sofa beside me took my hand. "I'll answer your question now. You asked me why I didn't want to spoil our life together. I should be able to make you a lengthy and beautiful reply. I can't. I find, in this one instance, that my salesmanship deserts me. I had occasion to wonder, some time ago, how I would feel if you left me. I found myself unable to contemplate it. I have never been able to contemplate it."

"Blaize—I have never thought of leaving you."

"Of course not. I realised that, which indicates—surely—? Now what does it indicate? That I suspected your reasons for remaining beside me were not so strong as I would like? That I wanted to make them stronger? Good heavens, must I make a declaration? You know perfectly well what I mean—perfectly well—but if it pleases you to see me stumble . . ."

But he was very far from stumbling, was treading, in fact, as surely as he had ever done, and squeezing my hand once again, he got up and crossed to the window, making a great and totally false display of impatience.

"Dammit, Faith, I have had a very difficult day, you know. I hardly slept a wink in the train last night. I am greeted this morning by my sister-in-law swooning in my arms, and when I pick her up my wife can do nothing but glare at me, claws out, like an angry cat. I am then obliged to dash off on a wild goose chase into town in search of my brother, who was in none of the places he should have been, and then home again to find my wife in no mood to care that I had a raging headache and had missed both my luncheon and my tea. Tomorrow morning I have to get up early to go and sign my freedom away, and I have just had the devil of a job to persuade my wife that it is her duty—and ought to be her pleasure—to honour and obey me—and should she care to cherish me as well I'd hardly complain—and would be well pleased, exceedingly well pleased, to cherish her in return . . ."

I crossed the room to him, my throat tight with tears, and put an arm around his shoulder, one hand under his chin to turn his subtle, mischievous face into the light.

"Blaize—such a declaration . . ."

"Indeed—such as I have never made before, and sincerely meant."

And then, as his weight seemed greater than I had expected, "Darling—you really are tired, aren't you?"

"I really am. My head really does ache. On such basic issues you have no reason to doubt me. I think it is high time you sent me to bed."

He went upstairs while I, lingering a moment in the hall, gave instructions for his early breakfast, named the hour he would require to see his carriage waiting on the drive, and then walked slowly, one step at a time, delighting in my body's every movement as it took me not in the direction which had been chosen for me, or which I had accepted as a compromise, but in which I truly desired to go.

I reached the landing, turned down the hushed, deep-carpeted corridor, remembering my past desires without regret, with the affectionate amusement that can only arise from self-knowledge. I had wanted to be adored, and Blaize would not adore me since adoration is given to idols, the passive objects of men's imaginings. And a man cannot share his warm, imperfect humanity with an idol. I had wanted to be needed, but Blaize, self-contained and elusive as he was, would never need me as Giles and perhaps even Nicholas had once done, refusing to weaken either of us by dependence. I had wanted a rock to lean on, but he had paid me the compliment of allowing me to stand alone; and, when circumstances required it, we would lean on one another.

I had wanted to trust him. I did trust him. I had wanted a home-coming. I stood already at the door.

He was waiting in a room that was darker than usual, a single lamp, well shaded, on my toilet table, showing me a mere outline of his head and shoulders, very little of his face.

"I thought," he said, "that—perhaps—you might have something to tell me."

"Yes. I love you Blaize."

And although he smiled—wishing to make a show of lightness, of accepting it merely as homage due—I couldn't miss the tremor in his face, the flicker of relief as his arms came around me, holding me with all the warm assurance I had required and then passing through trust and cherishing to an intensity I had never shared with him, no familiar ease now but an emotion new-born, uncertain as yet but ready to grow.

"Thank God," he said, the words whispered so lightly against my ear that I could have missed them, although I seized them and held them fast, knowing he could not sustain himself much longer at this high key.

"How very pleasant," he said, "to be so consistently in the right."

"Yes, darling . . . ?"

"Well—you can do no more than agree. I have been saying all my life, have I not, that sooner or later the Barforth one prefers is bound to be me? And if you have taken a great deal of convincing, then at least . . . ?"

"You have surely convinced me now."

And it was all I had ever needed to say.

W
—